HOW FAR?

A Tale of Determination, DNA, & Drama

BY BOB WILBER

outskirts
press

Outskirts Press, Inc.
http://www.outskirtspress.com

ISBN: 978-1-9772-5039-1

Cover Image by Todd Myers and Bob Wilber

Outskirts Press and the "OP" logo are trademarks belonging to Outskirts Press, Inc.

PRINTED IN THE UNITED STATES OF AMERICA

To my incredible wife Barbara,
who puts up with me and motivates me every day.
Your love and support are absolutely priceless

To my mother, who all through her life
instilled in me a love for the written word

To Greg Halling, who has now guided and mentored
me through two books. He has made me a better writer
and has become an invaluable friend

To all my family and friends who have pushed me,
supported me, and cheered me on throughout this process.

Thank you!

FOREWORD

I used to see Bob Wilber a lot in press boxes at NHRA drag races.

Topeka. St. Louis. Chicago. Sonoma. Indianapolis. He was always there.

He'd glide in, grab a stat sheet, mix it up with the other PR reps and slip out the door.

Everybody seemed to like the guy. I wanted to like him, too.

But we didn't speak for years. Not really.

I was a Kansas journalist. When I was managing editor at The Leavenworth Times, the NHRA invited me to Topeka to see a race. Suddenly, I remembered how much I'd loved drag racing as a kid.

My mind exploded in a burst of header flames, and from that day in 1992, I covered every NHRA event at Heartland Park Topeka. It didn't matter if I lived in Leavenworth, Hays or Hutchinson. I made the drive.

Along the way, I also made lifelong friends. Publicists like the late Joe Sherk, Rick Voegelin and Dave Densmore patiently endured my questions, arranged interviews with their drivers and trusted me to cover the sport with respect it deserved.

Then there was Bob. Always there, but only briefly, on his way back to the pits. We'd nod at each other and say hello, but that was it.

Until one day, I said something too loudly in the press box about people who never seem to learn from their mistakes. For a guy who only showed up at races a couple times a year, I was always saying things too loudly in the press box.

As I headed down to the track, Bob sauntered up beside me.

"You know, in minor league ball, I had this teammate," he said. "Same sort of thing. We'd just look at the guy and say, 'Can't be taught.'"

"You played minor league baseball?"

"Yeah, Detroit Tigers and Oakland A's systems. Dad played for the St. Louis Cardinals and then managed or coached until he retired."

As it turned out, the guy had led a fascinating life, which you can read about in his autobiography, "Bats, Balls and Burnouts."

We started making it a point to talk whenever I showed up at a race. Our conversations were never especially profound; we simply enjoyed each other's company.

Honestly, after The Elkhart Truth was sold and I moved to Ogden, Utah, to run the newsroom at the Standard-Examiner in 2015, I didn't expect to hear from Bob again. I hadn't been to a race since the 2013 U.S. Nationals.

But out of the blue, he emailed me in Ogden and asked if I'd edit the book that became "Bats, Balls and Burnouts." I immediately agreed.

It was a journey I wouldn't trade for anything.

Bob could write. He could always write. His blogs and news releases were sharp, witty and perceptive.

At first, his book read like a string of news releases. Then he got it. He became a storyteller — a sharp, witty and perceptive storyteller.

Over the course of a year, as he wrote his autobiography, we became brothers. It's hard to believe there was ever a time when all we did was nod at each other across the press box in Topeka.

That was two books ago.

— Greg Halling
Yakima, Washington
July 2021

Greg Halling is executive editor of the Yakima Herald-Republic in Yakima, Wash. He started his career as sports editor of the Emporia Gazette, then went on to run newsrooms in Leavenworth, Hays and Hutchinson. His staff at the Elkhart Truth in Elkhart, Indiana, won a National Press Club Award for The Elkhart Project, a year-long collaboration with msnbc.com on the city's recovery from the Great Recession. He also spent nearly three years as editor of the Standard-Examiner in Ogden, Utah. He has a tattoo on each forearm — one honoring Steve Earle, the other Warren Zevon. Which probably tells you everything you need to know about him.

CHAPTER 1

Brooks Bennett

My name is Brooks Bennett. I've had an interesting life, and I've met a lot of very cool people along the way. One of them, a longtime friend of mine, is Eric Olson. Yeah, that Eric Olson. The hockey player. We've known each other since the fall of 1987 when we met on our first day of college. We've pushed each other, tested each other, challenged each other, infuriated each other and loved each other. It's life. It's like that.

We're writing this book together, but we're doing it separately. We're not even talking about the details, so you might find some things we remember differently, or don't remember at all. But that's the fun part. We did discuss an outline, so that our stories would be on something close to the same pace, but we're leaving the details and the feelings for the writing.

My strange life started in Huntington Beach, California. That was basically what you'd call good fortune, too, because my mom and dad, Carol and Rick, moved to Southern California from Erie, Pennsylvania just a few years before I was born.

Why they did that probably will tell you a lot about me and my upbringing. They both wanted to be hippies (maybe more like pseudo-hippies) and California was the place to be if that's what you were after. I think you can say they didn't quite fit in back in Erie, and Dad often told me he never really felt like he was at home there. Whenever he'd say that, my reaction would be to roll my eyes and say, "That's deep, dude!"

For as long as he could remember, Dad said he felt like Erie was a place he had to get away from. Finishing high school had to come first, but he never lost the feeling that he didn't just want to leave, he had to leave. It was his dream to live in sunny California and surf whenever he wanted. For him, California was heaven.

How did a dude from Erie get so totally into surfing? My dad was a wanderer from the day he got his driver's license. I think they call it "wanderlust," right? When he watched surfing competitions on TV the sport blew his mind and, to him, it seemed like the sandy beaches and rolling waves (and the bikinis) were on another planet. At 18,

1

he drove all the way to L.A. to spend the summer there, staying with a total stranger, a friend of a friend of another friend who got out on his board every day.

My dad learned to surf the first day he was there and he was totally shredding by the time he went back home three months later. When he got in his Volkswagen bus to make the long drive back to Erie, he made up his mind that as soon as he got home he was packing up and moving. That didn't happen, because as soon as he got home he met my mom and she was the one thing more attractive to him than the beach. The longing for the beach never left him, but within a year they were planning a wedding. Within another year, they were husband and wife and on the move. He picked Huntington Beach because of the surf.

It didn't take much to convince my mom. She was an artist (oils and watercolors), a yoga expert, and the kind of person who was never afraid to take a total leap of faith and then rely on the goodness of others. She was also a heck of an athlete in high school, running distance events on the track team and playing volleyball.

My dad fancied himself as an artist, too. He had messed around with mixed media stuff since his early teens, whether it was parts and pieces glued to canvas or sculptures made of whatever he could find lying around. My folks were made for each other, because neither one ever saw any sort of career in their futures. They'd do whatever it took to keep a roof over their heads, but neither was going to spend 40 hours a week working in banking or insurance. The art, and in my dad's case the surfing, came first. Living a rich life was way more important than getting rich doing something they didn't feel any affinity for.

My dad was an incredible athlete, just like my mom. He was good at everything he tried, even the first time he ever played golf when a friend dragged him to a course and he shot a legit 89 the first time out. As far as I know, he never played again until I was an adult and got him back out there. Yeah, he was that good.

He was an avid bicyclist, a runner, and a baseball player right up through high school. The way he always explained his baseball approach included lines like, "I saw it as a thinking man's game, rather than an athletic deal. I studied pitchers like Jim Palmer because his mechanics weren't just perfect, they were beautiful. Seriously, on the mound he was elegant. That's exactly the right word. Elegant.

"My coaches mostly just thought I was nuts with all the talk about arm slots and mechanics. They just wanted me to throw hard, and I'd tell them right back that it wasn't about throwing hard. It was about missing bats. That didn't exactly make me real popular with the coaches I had, because I was never afraid to speak my mind. They wanted me to be a bulldog. I wanted to be an artist with the ball. I wanted to be a pitcher, but by 13 they wanted me to be a thrower. It didn't work out very well."

And then at the end of high school the whole "flower power" thing seemed like the perfect escape for him. He was also an incredible guitarist, and he never took a single lesson. He just taught himself to play and he rocked it.

Mom was the same way, but they weren't really classic hippies. They never lived on a commune or anything, and as far as I know my dad never did anything more hardcore than smoking some weed and drinking beer. My mom has never gone crazy with anything other than Cabernet or Merlot, and that was mostly later in life. They both loved what they did so much they never wanted to try anything harder or more dangerous than weed or wine.

After they got married, they sold what they could, gathered up every penny they could find and headed west. My dad said they had enough cash for the gas and that once they arrived they'd have enough money left to live on for three or four months, which would give them time to get settled and put a life together. That was the summer of 1966. I was born June 29, 1969.

I don't remember for sure the first time I surfed, because my dad was out there any time there were waves, and I was on his board with him by the time I was three. Obviously we were never rich, with my dad working in board shops, or tending bar, or other odd jobs that gave him the flexibility he craved. My mom created artwork that she sold at flea markets and art fairs while she also taught yoga for a bit of a steady living. They made just enough to get by in rental properties in a couple of different beach towns or suburban cities in Southern California. We moved a few times, which meant I never had a lot of friends. But about the time I turned 10, I found a remedy for that — baseball.

Baseball was life, and I was good at it. Like, really good at it. Everywhere we went, and every time I had to change schools again, baseball was what got me through it. In baseball, every new team is an instant set of new friends.

Surfing was fun (I still call it rad) and I got on the water as often as I could, but it's a loner sport. It's good for the soul to be out there, one with the waves, and I dug it like a love affair. But baseball … baseball was life.

As I said, Eric and I are writing this book together. These are our stories, on the diamond, on the rink, at home, and on the road. Some of it came easy. A lot of it was horribly difficult. But here we are, two friends who were as different as the dirt and the ice we found to be home, who probably never should've been more than buddies while in school, but who have a lifetime of stories to tell.

I hope we tell them well.

CHAPTER 2

Eric Olson

I'm Eric Olson. If you're a hockey fan, you might have heard of me. If not, I'm here to tell the story of my life in general, and specifically the story of my friendship with Brooks Bennett. I'll try my best not to get too technical on the hockey things.

If you're from Minnesota, you may know about my hometown, especially if you're a hockey fan. But otherwise, probably not. I'm from Roseau, Minnesota. That's basically pronounced "RO-zo." With a population of around 2,600 it's hard to find on a map. If you try to find it, here's a hint: Go all the way to the top of the state.

A lot of people have heard of International Falls, which claims to be the "Icebox of the Nation." That's a bold claim, but Roseau is north and west of International Falls, so we had to "go down there" to play them in hockey. Basically, the towns of Roseau and Warroad (about 20 miles away with about 1,600 residents) are located just south of Canada and mostly in the middle of nowhere. The nearest big city is actually Winnipeg, Manitoba. It's only about 115 miles north and when I was young you could cross the border without a passport, so that's where we went for big department stores. Duluth is more like 280 miles to our southeast. Minneapolis is a hike. The Twin Cities are 385 miles south, and we know the route well. Many of us would get down to "The Cities" on a regular basis.

So, what exactly is so remarkable about Roseau - Warroad and their rivalry, which could sometimes be intense but almost always respectful? The two schools produce hockey players. Very good hockey players. I can't say why, and no one seems to really understand it, but if you're from here you play. And you play a lot. And you get better. Some of us even got better than just about anyone.

Between Roseau and Warroad, the boys high school teams have won 11 Minnesota state hockey championships, and they've been runner-up 11 times on top of that. Think about that for a second. You can't get to a state championship game without beating a whole bunch of bigger schools from much bigger towns. It's almost impossible to win one without getting past at least one or two huge schools from the Twin Cities. Schools like Edina and Burnsville are so much bigger they might actually have more students than Roseau has residents.

So, that's how I grew up. I learned about the legends at a young age and I began to skate just about the same time I began to walk. Most of the guys I've ever played with don't remember the first time they skated. Once you can walk, they put skates on you.

Is it cold in the winter? You bet it is, but it wasn't something we thought much about when growing up. We do get all four seasons, and we make the most of the warmer ones, but it's not like 20 below zero surprises us. We deal with it. And we skate and play hockey. Walking to school in subzero temperatures was something we were all pretty used to.

My dad and mom, David and Cindy, were pretty much just regular folks from Roseau. By the time I was growing up, my dad owned the family hardware store he took over from his dad, and he ran it himself. Before I was born he also played hockey, at Roseau, then at St. Cloud State, and then in the minors as a pro. He also married my mom. When his pro career was over, they returned to Roseau like so many of us do.

Once they were back in Roseau for good, my mom was busy raising us kids but she also worked part time as an administrative assistant (or secretary as they called it back then) at Polaris Industries, the largest employer in town. If you've ever ridden a snowmobile, there's a decent chance it came from Roseau.

Dad met my mom in school and their romance blossomed in 11th and 12th grades. They got married a couple of years after graduation. Of course, my dad left Roseau when he was recruited by St. Cloud State so my mom went with him, getting a series of jobs in restaurants, retail stores, or wherever she could find work that allowed her to get to all of his home games. They got married while he was still in school, but they did that back up at home. From what I've heard, it was quite a big affair.

When Dad went off to play in the minors, in places like Seattle, Portland and Spokane in the Western Hockey League, my mom went there too, even after my oldest brother was born. It couldn't have been easy, but it didn't make them a rarity in terms of hockey marriages. Lots of guys chased the dream and lots of great women went with them, helped support them, and raised their children.

Within seven years Mom and Dad had five kids. I'm the youngest, born June 5, 1966. My three older brothers (David Jr., and identical twins Brent and Jon) all played hockey, and my big sister (Elizabeth but known to everyone as Betsy) played in a lot of pick-up games, even with the boys. Being the runt of the litter, I was not only younger than all of them but smaller too. They took turns beating the crap out of me on the ice, but it was never dirty. They just wanted to toughen me up.

Hockey became central to my life, but it was always a battle. Not much came naturally or easily to me, but I loved the game by the time I was playing at the Mites level as a little kid. By the time I was in Squirts, as a nine-year-old, all I wanted to be was a hockey player. The challenge to get better was something I grew up with. I was a good student, and serious about school, but hockey was my passion. I didn't just play it. I studied it and worked at it. It took me to a lot of places and introduced me to a lot of people.

Brooks Bennett is one of those people. We both have a lot of stories to tell. These are those stories.

CHAPTER 3

Brooks Bennett

After their romantic courtship and marriage, my mom and dad really did pile everything they owned (or at least everything they valued) in Dad's VW bus, and they headed west pulling a small U-Haul trailer.

They found a place in Huntington Beach the second day they were there. It was an apartment above a detached garage, about three blocks off the beach and maybe a half-mile north of the famous pier at Huntington, where all the daredevil surfers came ultra-close to the pilings to get the best waves. The garage belonged to the Louviers, a couple in their 40s who lived in the house in front of it.

The home was probably built in the late 30s or early 40s, and was similar to most of the homes in middle class beach towns like Huntington. These wood frame bungalows, with a peaked roof over the front porch, started a block or two off the Pacific Coast Highway and extended inland for a few miles on quiet tree-lined streets. People not from California often picture upscale places like Malibu or Newport when they think of beach towns, but most were actually like Huntington back then, and even now the little bungalows are still around in many areas. They just cost a lot more these days.

The owners of the house and garage were kindred spirits with my folks. They were artists. They charged my mom and dad $150 a month for the studio apartment, which featured one bed, a bathroom, a couch, a radio and a small kitchen. To my folks, it seemed like paradise.

The biggest bonus, though, was that the owners had transformed the main part of the garage into an art studio and they offered my mom space down there. It didn't just seem like paradise; it really was paradise.

Within a few days, my dad found a job at a board shop and a few months later he added a bartending gig to his duties. By far, it was the most simultaneous work my dad had ever done, but both jobs left him time to hit the waves almost every day, at least when the surf was up.

My dad always told me, "The whole thing was just meant to be, man. We drove out there not knowing where we were going to live or how we were going to do it. On the second day, we found the apartment, and it was owned by two artists who had a studio right below it. Then I walked in the board shop and said, 'I'm looking for a job' and the owner said, 'When can you start?' It was crazy, man. It was meant to be."

At first, my mom volunteered at a yoga studio, then landed a job there when the owner realized Mom was a far better instructor than she was. They were gainfully employed in their new hometown. Dad was right. It was meant to be.

It didn't take much time for my dad to turn the bus into his own customized VW surf machine. It already had a roof rack, so no problem strapping a board to that if he wanted to venture anywhere other than the pier. He took the bench seat out of the back of the bus, to make it one big space, and then followed the trend among other surfers by pinning colorful beach towels up on all the windows to act as curtains. Decals on the windows were not frowned upon, either.

I once asked him if the bus ever had actual flower decals on it, and all I remember him saying was, "That may or may not have happened." I'm putting my money on the "may" option.

He'd had the bus since he could drive, after finding it parked behind an apartment complex back in Erie. He put a note on the windshield, with the phone number for the house, and a couple of days later a guy called and asked him if he wanted it. The guy said, "It runs, but you'll be working on it a lot to keep it that way. Ever worked on cars before?" My dad had not, and had never owned one before either, but the guy said, "It's a Vee Dub. They're really easy to work on. You can find books at any bookstore that will show you just about everything. You can put new brakes on it, replace the exhaust, change the oil and fix just about anything else. It'll be good for you! I'll sell it to you for $200." My dad had a car, and a cool one it was. Red body, white roof, with the white extending down the nose of the bus, coming to a point behind the front bumper. It was a 1962 and it had the small rectangular windows on the sides of the roof, above the regular windows. If refurbished to its original glory, it would be worth a small fortune today.

He said he did get one of those books. I'm not sure if the series of books "For Dummies" was out at the time, but that's what it was. Step-by-step instructions, with diagrams, for doing basically anything you'd ever need to do to a Volkswagen, whether it was a Beetle or a bus. The rear-mounted engine was air-cooled, so no coolant system to worry about. That's one of the reasons VWs were so popular in California. They didn't like it super hot and they definitely didn't like high altitudes where there was less air to cool the motor.

He drove the bus to SoCal right after his senior year of high school, vowing to move back permanently as soon as he got home and broke the news to his folks. Then, right after he returned home and was still working up the nerve to tell his parents what he planned to do, he was browsing through an antiques store looking for some fun pieces he could make some mixed media art with. When the clerk in the store looked at him with her dark brown eyes and auburn hair that fell in soft curls, he melted. She was the most beautiful girl he'd ever seen.

It took him three straight days of going back to the store to actually ask her out, and when he did she started laughing. At first, he thought she was mocking him but she said, "I was beginning to wonder if you could put a sentence together, much less have the nerve to ask me out. Of course I will."

At that point, moving to Huntington Beach as soon as he could save up some money became nothing more than a backup plan. It was love at first sight for him. He had no idea if she felt the same, but he wasn't going to rush into it anyway. It was too important.

The counterpoint, or what he called the "truly bad news," was that he was drafted into the Army and was facing a one-year stint in Vietnam, after going through basic training.

He was scared to death and thought about going to Canada, but he couldn't bear the thought of leaving behind the woman he was so desperately in love with. Then a very cruel fate intervened. He was out running one day and didn't see a curb, or the fact there was a pothole just beyond it. It was like falling off a small cliff. He went down in a heap, hyperextending his left knee and tearing his anterior cruciate ligament. If you're a football fan and your favorite running back goes down with a full tear of the ACL, you know it's the kind of injury that can end a football career, especially back then. What it also ended was any chance of going to Vietnam, because he failed his Army physical. He also knew that almost all the sports he loved were going to be out of the question, starting with running. Eventually, he'd go through enough rehab to be able to surf again, but even jogging was out, at least at anything beyond a slow "old man" pace, as he called it. Orthopedic surgery, back then, was nothing like it is now.

He said he would've gone to Vietnam if he hadn't gotten hurt, but there probably couldn't have been a worse fit for Dad than the military. My father was movie star handsome and he'd grown his hair out by then, basically down to his shoulders with bushy bangs right down to his eyebrows. He looked like he should be on a stage playing guitar, but I can't even fathom him in fatigues with a buzzcut. And if it wasn't for that trip and fall on the sidewalk, I might never have been born. I don't like to even think about that.

I've seen enough photos from back then to see how soulful he looked at that young age. Like a man totally wise beyond his age. He had that long brown hair and deep-set eyes that still make me think of James Taylor. In the old photos, the facial hair comes and goes but it was always neatly trimmed, and he never had a big unruly beard. His clothing choices centered around denim work shirts and blue jeans, usually tight hip-huggers with bell bottoms. He looked like one very cool dude. And he was one very cool dude.

I think he definitely had his priorities right, looking for enrichment and happiness as his main mantra. He just needed enough money to do the things he loved. He worked odd jobs, he served drinks in Erie dive bars, and he even worked for the city once, doing an inventory of bridges and overpasses. He got paid to drive his VW around the city to document every bridge and overpass, and then he'd spray paint a date of its inspection next to the date of its construction. He made $1.80 an hour. The tips at the bar were better and more fun to earn. He genuinely liked people, so the bar was way better than driving around by himself.

He also played his guitar in a local band, whenever they could get gigs. They started performing for actual people in high school, but mostly just at parties. They needed a name after they began playing bars when they all turned 18, and he swears they were pretty good. I believe him, because he still is an amazing guitarist and I don't think he would've gotten much out of it if he was on stage with a bunch of guys who were terrible. They picked the name The Dandelions. Seriously. Like, I've seen photos and everything.

He told me they made a flat rate of $60 per gig, which they'd attempt to split four ways after they paid for gas. Their biggest break was at a bar in Youngstown, Ohio, about 100 miles away. The bar was pretty big, and they weren't a Youngstown band, but they played well and the songs they played seem to really impress the local kids, including some early Beatles and Rolling Stones tunes they covered, in addition to a lot of other "British Invasion" songs other bands weren't even attempting to do. In Erie, my dad figured, they were seen as just a bunch of local kids playing kind of weird music. In Youngstown, they were a hit!

That Youngstown venue had a pretty large capacity, like maybe 500 people, Dad figured. After a few huge gigs there, they went to the owner and said, "We'll come back once a week if you want us to, but from now on we split the cover charge." The owner went for it, and those gigs would net the guys about 250 bucks total. That was huge money and I'm sure the whole band felt like they were not only rich, but also on their way to stardom.

After he met my mom, the band thing kept going for a while, and she liked to go to their gigs, but the weekly Youngstown trips were a grind, his knee was still very painful and he had bigger priorities by then. He said it was one of the hardest decisions he ever made. He quit the band and put the guitar away. He was in love with a beautiful girl who looked like Connie Francis (but even prettier) and he wanted to marry her, though he was petrified of asking.

My mom had kept working at the antique store, after my dad had worked up the courage to ask her out. It didn't pay much, but she loved being around old things that you needed a special eye to appreciate. As she would say, "One person's junk is another person's miracle. You have to imagine the history to see the value."

She was painting a lot then, mostly with oils, but she dabbled in watercolors and even pencils every now and then. She loved it so much she used to tell me she had a hard time selling anything because it meant letting her creations go. But, she parted with enough to make some cash, and combined with her pay at the store there was enough to have "walking-around money." Both of them were fortunate to still be living at home, because they certainly didn't make enough to pay much rent, but it meant a lot to them to never have to ask their parents for a handout or a loan. I think DNA is a wonderful thing. My grandparents weren't hippie wannabes in any way, but they were open-minded enough to let the kids have the freedom to chase their dreams.

My mom used to tell me about the heavy philosophical discussions she and Dad would get into, usually late at night. They were both deep thinkers, at a time when so much was changing in America and those changes often came at a steep or violent price.

9

They shared so many of their visions and dreams, and took things they talked about to "some very deep levels, man" as my dad would say, when he described those same conversations. He said they could peel away their thoughts "like an onion, dude. You just keep peeling and peeling and you get to places you never knew you could get to, much less understand. We were made for each other. I swear we could read each other's minds."

Once it became obvious to my dad that the two of them were so bonded, at such a very intense level, that getting married or at least committing to one another was the only option, he finally dialed up his courage and asked her. No, he did not have the ring already bought and in his pocket. He was still thinking there was a 50/50 chance of the answer being something like, "I love you dearly, and so deeply, but marriage is just a legal thing. I need to be free and so do you."

She said yes, and they both cried. Then he had to explain the ring thing and his lack of confidence. That turned her tears into laughs.

They got married in Erie (the photos are all so amazing I get emotional seeing them both looking so young and so madly in love) and then went off on what they called their "permanent honeymoon." They loaded up the VW, packed what they wanted to take and drove to Huntington.

With their garage apartment and the various jobs they could dig up and do for a while, they lived life to the fullest. They spent their money on necessities, because the really big splurges in life, for them, were the waves, the art and the love. As long as you can eat and pay the rent, those things can carry you a long way.

Mrs. Louvier, who lived in the house, was an accomplished artist and my mom took great interest in her techniques and her creations. She was inspirational to Mom, and she took a great amount of interest in what my mother was doing, as well. After about a year, Mrs. Louvier insisted that my mom should let her take a few of her pieces to a shop where she sold a lot of things. She'd tell the owner that she vouched for Mom, and that they could take the pieces on consignment for a month. If the oil paintings didn't sell, they'd take them back. They sold in a week.

Dad was surfing small waves as he kept working at rebuilding some strength and stability in his knee, while also doing his various jobs, and Mom was really excited about the art. Life was truly good. And then Mom got pregnant. They always insisted to me that getting pregnant made a good life even better. I believed them, but there's also always been a part of me that felt like maybe that was true or maybe it wasn't. Having a kid changes everything, and right up until she found out she was expecting, SoCal was providing everything they ever wanted.

I was delivered at 11:53 pm on June 29, 1969, after a good 14 hours of labor, according to my mom. Why are babies so often late? Probably because we had it so good in there. Lay around all day, get fed without any effort and get to know your parents' voices before you ever see them. I'm sure the sound of the surf was already wired into my brain, too.

Mom and Dad stayed in the room over the garage for the first few months I was around, because Mom basically put everything aside to nurture and care for me. I was a healthy boy, by all accounts, and while I wasn't a big fat baby, I was a long one. I checked in at a little bit over 23 inches. As I said, as babies you're used to lying around for nine months, so you get measured in length, not height.

Again, looking back it's hard for me to fathom that my arrival actually made life better for my parents. Dad had to dial up the work and cut back on the surfing because my mom quit everything, including her art. I was the sole focus of her attention.

Before my first birthday, they decided to make a move to be ready for when I started doing radical stuff like walking and talking. They loved the garage home, and loved the owners, but it was too small for three of us. Dad found a small home that was for rent, another few blocks further off the beach and another few blocks away from the pier, but those were sacrifices he knew he had to make. It was another old home, dating from the 1940s or earlier, wood frame, and nothing to rave about other than the fact it had two bedrooms, so I could have a nursery. Rent skyrocketed up to $200 a month, so pennies were going to have to be carefully watched.

Apparently, I was a pretty precocious little kid. I crawled earlier than normal, at around five months, and took my first steps at 10 months. I began talking with single words at around the same time I first walked, and Mom swore I was talking in real sentences by 18 months. I guess I'll always just have to believe her.

My dad said he was really interested to see if I had any natural ability for sports. By the time I turned two, he was softly throwing toys to me and I was catching most of them. When I was three he took me to a gentle spot on the beach. We drove there in the VW bus, of course, and he had me wade out a little by myself. He said I showed no fear, which he thought was a bad thing. You don't have to be deathly afraid of the ocean, but you better respect it. On that same day, he put me on his board, right in front of him, and we rode a little wave. He said he stayed seated, so he could hold me, and it was a tiny little wave, but I was laughing hysterically, shouting, "More, more, more! Surfing! Surfing!"

It seems like I remember that, but I'm sure it's just because of how many times I heard the story and how often we did get to the beach. It's hard to remember the first time when you start so young.

That was all pretty standard stuff for me, right up until kindergarten. I didn't have any siblings but I had my mom all day. When I was somewhere around four she started to paint a little, but even that was impacted by having me around. The house had a small detached garage, but there was no way she'd be going out there while leaving me by myself, so my dad spent weeks cleaning the place out, putting down some carpet and other rugs and making it safe for me. Mom didn't want me getting anywhere near the paints or paintings, though, so they kind of fenced off a play area. I remember watching her a lot. I loved finger paints but I was a typical sloppy little kid with them. She took her brush and made real things appear. It fascinated me.

By then, though, more changes were coming. I'd be heading to kindergarten as a 5-year-old and two major things came together to cause another move. My folks thought the schools around the house were OK, but not great. I think they had that "new parent syndrome," where they both believed their little boy was so special he'd be bored if surrounded by "normal" kids. I'd never really been around other kids much anyway, so who knows?

The second part of the equation was the owner of the house, our landlord, letting Dad know that he wanted to sell the place. We needed to go, and this time we left Huntington altogether. Dad went further south, down beyond Laguna.

He had a friend from the board shop and the bar who had made the move all the way down to San Clemente, which is actually the furthest point south in Orange County. Basically, after San Clemente you have Camp Pendleton (a giant military base) and then there's just a couple of small beach towns between you and San Diego. It seemed like a long way to go, but his buddy convinced him he could get Dad plenty of work and the surfing was great.

His friend was right. San Clemente has some seriously righteous surfing, including the legendary area known collectively as Trestles. The swells aren't huge, but they are incredibly consistent. How big is surfing there? It was actually a high school sport in San Clemente. To me, at that age, San Clemente was just another place to live.

Dad found a house for rent in San Clemente similar to the one we'd left in Huntington. It was hardly a mile or so off the beach, while the board shops, surfer bars, and all the other fun stuff that comes with a surf town were all within walking distance. He always told me, "I thought I was a Huntington guy from the first time I went out there after high school. San Clemente was as bitchin' a surfing scene as there was. It was like it was straight off the cover of a Beach Boys album. I loved it."

I remember the move, and how stressed out it made both Mom and Dad, or as I thought at the time, it made them act really weird. Like not even smiling. They generally smiled all the time, and were obviously happy, but the move made things quiet for a while, and I didn't understand it. Maybe, once again, I thought it was my fault.

After we got settled, in late spring of 1974, life was better. Dad again carried two jobs, one at a board shop and the other cleaning pools. Mom was getting back into her art more steadily, and I was getting ready for kindergarten.

With me going off to school in the fall, Mom decided to look for a yoga job while she also ramped up the painting in the hope of landing some consignment deals with a studio in Laguna Beach, which is like the epicenter of the art world in Orange County. She was still in contact with Mrs. Louvier, the woman who had lived in the house where we rented the garage, who had some good contacts in Laguna, so Mom was energized. I was a combination of nervous and excited about kindergarten. Other than playing with some kids in various parks, I'd never really been around the same group of children for long periods.

When school rolled around, I was presented with more new clothes and shoes than I'd ever seen in my life, and on the first day both Mom and Dad drove me to Las Palmas school, a few miles from home. In those very early years one of them would always be in charge of getting me to school and back home later in the day. I'm sure it took quite a bit of juggling, in terms of the VW and jobs, but they never got me there late and I rarely had to stand outside the school for more than a minute before the Vee Dub arrived.

I liked kindergarten, I liked being with other kids, and I loved my teacher, Mrs. Denton. We had a good mix of ethnicities in the school, but that was hardly something I even noticed. It's hard to grow up in Southern California without being around all kinds of people who don't look like you. My mom and dad were always clear about one thing, even before I went to school. They said, "We're all the same on the inside. Like, imagine if we painted four bottles of apple juice different colors. They all look different, but they're all apple juice."

They also used us as an example of how little it meant to be well off or rich. Dad would say stuff like, "As you go through school, you're going to be around a lot of kids who get dropped off in fancy cars, or who have nicer clothes than you do. And if you ever go over to their homes you might be surprised by the houses they live in. Just remember, none of that buys happiness. Your mom and I will always give you every ounce of love we have, and our lives will all center around happiness. That's what matters the most."

In terms of school itself, I have vague memories of kindergarten being about 90 percent art class. We did start to officially learn the alphabet and how to read, but my parents had been all over that since I started to talk, so I was way ahead of what Mrs. Denton was teaching.

We didn't have organized sports to get involved with yet, so no baseball or anything like that. At recess, we mostly just ran in circles and kicked big inflated red rubber balls around. At home, my dad was starting the process of playing catch with me. He still had one of his old fielder's gloves and he scraped enough cash together to buy me my first real baseball glove. It was a miniature version of a Rawlings glove but I remember how big it felt to me at the time, like it weighed my arm down. When I was three and four I'd had one of those dime-store gloves, which were made for really little kids and just cheesy vinyl replicas. With those, about all you could do was catch the ball with your palm up, then hope it stayed in place. With the real glove, as a 5-year-old, I was learning how to catch baseballs the right way.

And if you're wondering if I just used the word "baseballs" loosely, since I was still such a little kid, I did not. Once he got me that first toy glove my dad never wanted me to start off with tennis balls or anything soft. Just like the ocean, you can't be afraid of the ball but you have to respect it. I took a few off the chin.

While I was enjoying running around the Las Palmas playground or making "art" with popsicle sticks, at the same time being a year or more ahead of my kindergarten classmates in terms of reading and writing, my mom was in the middle of what she always called her "own personal renaissance." She couldn't paint fast enough, the ideas wouldn't stop flowing, and Mrs. Louvier gave her the big news that one of the most respected studios in Laguna would take six of her pieces on consignment. When Mom told them what she thought they should be priced at, the staff laughed. They priced each piece at $300, twice what Mom had thought, and told her they'd sell fast. They did. And right around then, she landed a yoga job that paid pretty well, too.

13

My dad was also working hard, but he always made time to surf. Whether it was Lower Trestles or T-Street in San Clemente, or down at San Onofre, he considered surfing his lifeline. Since the knee wouldn't allow him to do much of anything that had high repetitive impact, he could swim, ride a bike or surf. Between him and Mom, we started to have enough money to actually buy a few things. The first such thing was a second car.

My mom needed something big enough to carry framed art in, and she'd not only need to be my personal school bus driver in it, she'd also have to get up to Laguna Beach fairly regularly. So, my dad found a VW bus for her. What else would fit the bill so well?

Hers was light blue with a white roof, but I don't think it had the smaller windows on the roof edges so I don't know for a fact what year it was. It also did not have beach towels pinned above the windows to act as curtains. I'm sure it either didn't come with a back seat or she took it out, because my memories of that bus are almost all centered around riding back there, on a big fluffy rug she cut to fit over the rubber floor. Seat belts? Car seats? Hadn't heard of them, at the time.

Once my kindergarten adventure came to a close in early summer, it was time to spend lazy afternoons at the beach. Sometimes Mom would come too, and we'd spread out a big blanket to watch Dad surf while she cut up pears, oranges, and cantaloupes for us to eat. Other times, I'd go with him and ride along on his board. I even began to stand up with him holding me steady, just to get a feel for how he maneuvered on the waves. When I wasn't out there on the water, it always seemed like there were enough other kids and their moms on the beach to hang out with. It was a surfing community, and the VW buses were lined up in the parking lot. It was not, on the whole, a terrible way to spend your early childhood. I had no idea that most other little kids didn't grow up like that, even the ones that grew up just a few miles inland. The only concept I had of cold air was what I felt when I opened the refrigerator door.

My hair was long, it was bleached out blond, and I lived in baggy shorts and sandals. Yeah, I was that kid. Dirty feet and all.

When the summer ended, it was time for me to go to real school. First grade at Las Palmas Elementary. And a whole lot of new stuff was about to happen.

CHAPTER 4

Eric Olson

I wish I could say that my family is really unique, but we aren't. I bet if you averaged out every characteristic of all the families in Roseau, we'd be a great example of what our home town is about. Parents who married young, had 4.5 kids, worked hard all their lives and stayed true to their roots. Children who rarely missed a day of school, ate their vegetables and the dinners put before them, respected their mom and dad and got good grades. And, of course, all five of us Olson kids played hockey from the time we could skate and put on the gear. If Roseau was the location for a TV series, people would think it was fictional. It's not. I grew up there. It's just Roseau.

My great-great-great grandfather and grandmother came to Roseau in 1879, as 20-year olds from Sweden. There's some debate in the family as to where they lived in Sweden. Some Olsons claim it was Stockholm, but my dad always said they were wrong, and it was Malmo. That was important to him, for some reason, but I never really cared. I just knew we were Swedish. Many other Swedes and Norwegians came to America back then, and they ended up in Minnesota. That was a good thing. Scandinavian is a nice way to grow up.

My mom and dad went through the Roseau school system together, so they knew each other from the age of five or six. To actually go to school, they also went to the same place from kindergarten through 12th grade. To this day it's still one large school connected by hallways lined with lockers. There are no separate elementary school or middle school buildings. There aren't enough students to justify that. You just "graduate" to a different part of the school when you would have been going from elementary to middle to high school. And all the kids share the same cafeteria and gym. They do use them at different times of day so that the second-graders aren't eating lunch with the high school seniors, and somehow it works. And for all the years I went there, I never had to remember the combination for the lock on my locker. No one had locks on their lockers. Why would you mess with someone else's stuff?

My upbringing was pretty simple. My dad had taken over Olson Hardware after his minor league career was over in 1962. He knew he wasn't going to get out of the minors, and he and Mom already had David Jr., who was about to turn three. On top of that, Brent and Jon were on the way. My grandfather was only in his mid-40s, but he had a heart condition and needed to cut back, so Dad and Mom left pro hockey behind and went home to Roseau. For the next three years my dad helped my grandfather run the store while he learned the business. Right about the same time, Betsy was born in February of 1965 and then I came along in June of 1966.

I never got to know my dad's father. He passed away when I was nine months old. When I turned one, my dad was in total charge at the hardware store while Mom went back to work, part time, at Polaris. My grandmother Evelyn, on my dad's side, became a nanny for Dave, the twins, Betsy and me. It gave her a reason to go on, after losing Grandpa at such a young age and it made us very close. My dad told me often that if he would've let Grandma Evelyn just stay home she would have had no purpose, and that spending those days with us really rejuvenated her. She got some help from my grandparents on Mom's side as well. Gail and Doug Erickson were always around, and it surprises me now just how young everyone was. Back then, Mom, Dad and my grandparents all seemed to be "old people" to me.

My folks were still kids, just 28 years old. They had five children and they owned a business and a house. My mom's folks, who definitely seemed very old, were still in their 40s and still working full time. Grandpa Doug worked at Polaris and Grandma Gail worked at the school, in the principal's office. That sort of stuff seems unbelievable now. Today, I'm nearly as old as my grandparents were back then. It doesn't seem possible.

We had a three-bedroom home in town, with a small den my dad turned into a fourth bedroom by the time I was three. When my mother wasn't working a few hours a day, she was our head chef, our tutor and the lead driver, in terms of our hockey transportation. Dad was mostly at the store, and my siblings were all used to helping out there. I would be, too, as soon as I was old enough. I can still close my eyes and smell the place. Hardware stores and bakeries are the two best smells on any Main Street.

I was skating as soon as I could walk. All of us were, but just like walking it takes a while for a little kid to get good enough at it to avoid falling down every few steps. I was six when I first hit a rink with miniature gear on and a little stick in my hands. It was the start of youth hockey, but at that age it was kind of similar to youth soccer. You know the scene, when all the kids go out on the field at the same time and when the whistle blows they all just chase the ball in a mob. It's basically the same, at that age, in hockey. They could talk to us all they wanted but none of us were really listening and although we'd all skated and we watched our brothers play, we had no clue what we were doing. Positions? Responsibilities? Rules? Who needs 'em? Those coaches must have had an enormous amount of patience.

I was small. I didn't skate particularly fast or even all that well. I had kind of mastered the art of skating backward, but it had taken me at least a year to do it without coming to a complete stop first.

On our first day of team hockey, at the mites level, the coach said to me, "You'll be on defense." That's how it went. The best and fastest skaters were forwards. The slower ones were defensemen. The bigger kid who couldn't skate much at all was the goalie. Kind of like the catcher in Little League. It turned out, most of those labels stuck with a lot of us for a long time.

My oldest brother, David Jr., is a little more than six years older than me so even as I was getting out on the ice for my first youth hockey experiences, he was already 11 and playing real hockey. Brent and Jon were nine then, and Betsy was seven. Throughout my youth, when we'd play pick-up hockey or just skate around, it was Betsy who was my protector. My brothers felt it was their responsibility to pick on me. They were all pretty big. Definitely bigger than the other kids their age. I was smaller than just about all of the kids I was around. Betsy threw more than a few checks on the guys to let them know she'd be looking out for me.

I don't remember much about that first youth hockey practice, or much of anything that first year. One thing I do remember was David Jr. telling me, "You're a defenseman. Your job is easy. Just stay between your man and the net." Dave would be telling me that for decades.

To do my job, I was going to have to master the art of skating backward and really smooth out the transition where you go from skating forward to backward on the fly. I don't recall exactly when I did it for the first time, but I remember how proud I was of having accomplished the feat. My hockey career would not have lasted long if I had to come to a complete stop to get going the other way. So I worked on it every time I could get on the ice. I practiced it in my socks on the wooden floor of my room, too.

I wasn't real fast and I wasn't big, so I didn't have a lot going for me those first few years. I just loved the game. By the time I was in early elementary school we were going to Roseau Rams games at the one and only Roseau Memorial Arena. Built in the 1940s, it has an arched wooden ceiling held up by huge wood beams. With a capacity of around 1,500 it held only a few less fans than the number of people who lived in Roseau, and it always seemed packed on game nights. To me, it was like going to an NHL game and the Winter Olympics all rolled into one. The players on those teams were men, in my eyes. The crowds were enormous, and really loud. And it was all happening right in the little town I lived in. Right in Roseau.

Roseau had won the Minnesota state championship in 1946, 1958, 1959 and 1961 before I was born. Those '58, '59 and '61 teams all beat big schools from the Twin Cities to do it. From little Roseau to the mountain top. The year I was born, they finished as state runner-up to International Falls. That must have been a heck of a battle between those two northern-tier schools.

In 1971, when I was just a few months shy of my fifth birthday, the Rams finished as runner-up again, but that time they lost to Edina from down in The Cities. Roseau versus Edina. Do the math and it should be impossible. But like in the movies, sometimes the underdog bites pretty hard. Roseau isn't a movie. It's real life.

It's real life with drafty windows and a wood-burning fireplace in the winter. Deep snow that comes early and stays late because very little of it melts until April and it gets packed down on the streets. It's boot hockey out there in the street, with "goals" that were just mounds of snow we'd pile up. If neighbors in their cars would come through, the first of us to see the car would yell "Tin can!" and we'd get off the road. The neighbors would almost always drive around the piles of snow so we wouldn't have to build the goals back up again.

It's sitting on the cold vinyl bench seat in Dad's truck waiting for the engine to warm up, with the windshield completely frosted over until the heater can generate a bit of warmth. The side windows would never clear on a really frigid morning. The defroster didn't have enough strength for that. And we'd sit there quietly. Dad never talked much in a social way. He was a pretty serious guy who took care of the store and made sure all of us had the things we needed.

It's a thing we call hotdish. In the rest of the country, most people call that a casserole. In Minnesota we call it hotdish, and there are all sorts of different kinds that are favorites in different parts of the state. You take a protein, a starch, a can or bag of veggies, some creamy soup and usually something crunchy, and it goes in the oven. My mom's favorite included ground beef, canned peas and carrots, cheddar cheese, diced potatoes and cream of mushroom soup, all mixed together and then completely covered by tater tots. That actually doesn't sound very appetizing, but it was great. Hotdish helps get you through those cold winters.

It's going to school bundled up in layers, from long johns to a huge coat with a hood, plus a stocking cap under the hood with the full knit face mask. Your nostrils freeze with every inhale and your breath looks like the exhaust from a steam engine. When it's really cold, way below zero with the wind howling out of the north, we'd often walk to school or to the rink facing backward. We knew the route without even looking and it kept our faces a little warmer.

Heading home at night, when I was a bit older, I'd walk home but make pit stops on the way. I'd walk from the rink to the first diner and stop in there for a minute to warm up. Then down to another diner or open business. If it was so cold I needed another stop, there was the bowling alley, where everyone was carousing and smoking. It seems like everybody smoked back then. Mom would always know I'd stopped in there to warm up because I came in smelling like cigarettes, but it didn't bother me. And it almost never failed that someone in the bowling alley would buy me a hot chocolate before I headed back out to get home.

In the winter, we were lucky to get eight hours of sunlight but we spent almost all of it at school during the week. On the weekends we'd be outside or up at the rink all day. Next to the Memorial Arena is the North Rink with another indoor sheet, and that ice was available for open skating a lot of the time. They only ran the Zamboni once or twice a day though, so after a few hours of skating the ice would get covered in the snow we were kicking up. We'd have to push the heavy scrapers around ourselves to keep it clear. Sometimes we'd have shootouts and the losers had to scrape the ice.

In the summer, we only had about eight hours of darkness and could play outside as long as we wanted, or until Mom made us come in. Street hockey, basketball, baseball and riding our bikes kept us busy and entertained. All it really seemed to be was fun. In Roseau, we had a lot of fun. It was a great place to grow up.

We went to the Rams hockey games each winter, and even made the big trip in the family car over to Warroad when the Rams played the Warroad Warriors. It was a huge rivalry. After those games, a little kid like me would stay up all night. Too much excitement, especially if the Rams won.

By third grade I had only one goal in life. I wanted to play for the Roseau Rams. I really never dreamed of anything beyond that. I only wanted that dream to come true, even if it took me until my senior year at Roseau High to make it happen. I wanted to grow up as fast as I could so I could wear the Roseau jersey. Except we don't call them jerseys. We call them sweaters. It's a hockey thing.

I actually would dream of it at night. Me putting on the Roseau sweater and skating out onto the Memorial Arena ice. It was the ultimate goal. Just playing any level of hockey in Roseau was neat. Playing for the Rams would be a dream come true. It would be a miracle.

I had a lot of work to do. I knew, at a very young age just getting started in mites, that I'd have to outwork and outsmart the bigger, faster, and more powerful players.

Looking back on it, I think I have to admit that I was mature beyond my years. That had a lot to do with our parents, our grandparents, and our collective upbringing, because my brothers and my sister were very similar to me. We all got good grades, but without having to put much effort into it. We did our chores and pitched in at the store. I really don't think my parents had much to worry about, when it came to us. We were very responsible kids. Probably pretty boring, too.

What strikes me now, thinking about what I was like at the very start of my hockey career as such an undersized kid, was that I somehow knew what the answer would be if the question was "How can I be a Roseau Ram some day?" The answer was I'd have to outwork and outsmart the bigger and more powerful players. If I did that coming up through squirts, peewees, and bantams, maybe I could make the varsity and be a Ram someday. That would be something I could always be proud of, and Mom and Dad would be proud of me too.

Those two words "outwork" and "outsmart" were in my mind almost every day. Just skating around with my big brothers, I figured out how much it irritated them when I wouldn't back down from their attempts at intimidation. They'd yell, "Geez, ya pipsqueak. Stay down when we hit you or we'll pound ya harder."

That was the key. Be smart, don't give up. Do the work.

I was up for that. I had to be. I made a promise to myself that I'd be a Ram one day.

CHAPTER 5

Brooks Bennett

It was time for elementary school! I went into first grade totally amped up and with almost no fear. I'd gotten along great with the other kids in kindergarten, even though at that age you don't really socialize much. It's not like you make any real friends when you're five. But you do learn how to play with other kids and how to follow the teacher's instructions. Every now and then Mrs. Denton would have us work in groups on a project, and I seemed to be a natural leader at that, whether or not popsicle sticks were involved.

In first grade it all seemed a bit different. Yeah, we were all just a year older but it's that time in your childhood where a year makes a massively huge difference. These days, on my birthday I'm just a year older and wanting time to slow down. Back then, in school and on the playground, we were all becoming little people. I even knew some kids by name!

I also seemed to be kind of a natural in the classroom, although I'm stunned that I can't remember my first-grade teacher's name. I guess Mrs. Denton made a better impression the year before.

A lot of that natural ability in school was due to some seriously stout DNA and the rest was probably just the way my parents raised me before I went off to sit at a desk in a classroom. They were never timid about teaching me how to read, spell, and write, or how the world worked.

My dad told me, "We made the conscious decision to talk to you totally like adults, and to teach you real stuff, not just colors or shapes or baby talk. Mom had read a million books while she was pregnant with you, trying to map out a plan on how it was all going to work. One thing she latched onto was speaking in adult voices. Baby talk can go on way longer if the parents are speaking that way, too. It was amazing to watch you grasp it and learn. You beat every benchmark, from crawling, to walking, to talking. You were a little man in a hurry. A pretty cool little dude, too."

The thing I remember most about the early years of elementary school was how much fun it was. I really looked forward to going to school each day because I was good at it and I loved to learn. I don't recall many times, all the way through elementary school, where the teacher was saying something that I just couldn't get. I always seemed to get it and it never seemed like work.

A few big things happened by the time I got through second grade with Miss Rotter. (See, I remember her. What was wrong with my first-grade teacher?) After each school year there was summer vacation, and I spent a lot of it with my dad or both parents at the beach. Living within walking distance of the Pacific Ocean is one of the most awesome things. I had no idea how lucky I was, because it's all I knew.

The summer after second grade I was riding a lot of waves with Dad, standing on his board with him, and he kept riding slightly bigger waves until it became obvious that we were going to wipe out at some point soon. He'd taken it really slowly with me up until then.

I'd been playing in the water since I could walk, and I could already swim pretty well. When you're that young and you've already spent that much time in the ocean and on Dad's board, you just adapt. It was like walking. I don't remember walking for the first time just like I don't remember learning to swim, or figuring out how to paddle around and body surf a little. I think I do remember the first time Dad rode a big enough wave that it kind of folded up on us and we went down. To this day, I'm 99 percent sure he did it on purpose. He said I dove off the board right with him, went under, tumbled once or twice underwater as the wave kept going, and then came up laughing. Yeah, that sounds like me.

Once it was time for me to surf on my own, Dad took me to the board shop where he worked and showed me a new thing. It was called a boogie board. They hadn't been out long, but the shop carried a few and to me it was like getting an epic new toy. I also got my first wetsuit, because having my own board meant spending a lot more time in the water and SoCal ocean water is pretty cold. If you're just riding on Dad's board for 15 or 20 minutes, it's not that big of a deal but Dad knew it would be tough to get me to leave the water once I had my boogie board. Lying on it, I could learn how to technically surf and that lets you ride each wave much longer. That's how you learn to drop into the face of a wave and ride the curl. The next step would be a standard board and by then it was just a matter of learning how to get up on it by myself. I know I clearly remember that. I'll never forget it. By the end of that summer, the boogie board felt totally natural, and Dad would even let me take his board out by myself. I was a complete surfer dude by the age of seven. And yeah, I still had the long stringy hair, the dirty feet and the flip-flops.

Something else big also happened that summer after second grade. I played baseball.

It was the youngest league for kids where I could play actual games with a pitcher and a full field of players. T-ball existed then, but we didn't have a league in San Clemente so all of my baseball experience to that point had been just my dad and me. Dad built a tee for us out of plywood, PVC pipe, and some rubber hose. When we weren't surfing or playing at the beach we were at a park where there were ball diamonds with dirt infields.

21

He'd tee up the first ball for me and then he'd hobble out near the pitcher's mound and tell me to swing. He had marked each base with an X in the dirt and I'm guessing they were probably about 45 feet apart. Still seemed like a long way for a little guy like me, but it was killer fun. What was it like to hit a baseball and run until he tagged me, limping along on a knee that was still killing him but laughing all the way? It didn't get much more fun than that. And he'd hit me grounders and pop-ups before we'd play a bit of catch. Each time we'd go to the field, we'd back up a little more, making the tosses and the catches just a little bit harder. Then he'd throw me something that I guess you'd call batting practice. He just lobbed them in underhanded, but it was a good way to get the hand/eye coordination going, to hit a moving ball. It was some serious quality time with my old man. Life-altering, I think.

So, I was pretty prepared that summer after second grade when we started playing in the youth league. A lot of those kids were being taught how to play while I already knew how. And I knew most of the rules, too. I was a baseball sponge and couldn't soak it up fast enough. I don't think we pitched at that age, which is odd because you'd think I'd remember every second of it. By my recollection, the coaches pitched to us. I'm sure that's how it went, because we did get to swing the bat a lot and make contact and run the bases. If other kids were on the mound, I think we would've just been standing around a lot while some poor catcher chased all the wild pitches. Either way, we played baseball and I loved it. I loved surfing too, but it's a total loner sport once you're able to do it. Though it's a sport that's mostly one-on-one individual plays, what I loved about baseball was the team thing and the magic that has to take place for the team to work. It didn't hurt that I was obviously the best player on the team, even at that age. Again, just like with surfing, my dad had me ready to go way before almost all the other kids.

And looking back on that now, my dad amazes me more and more. His knee was still a mess, but him limping whenever he'd try to jog was all I ever knew. He hobbled along almost like a horse galloping, trying to get the most out of his right leg while the left one wouldn't cooperate. He never complained. He never really ever mentioned it, except for the times when it would swell up on him and he'd have to actually sit still for a while, with an ice pack on it.

Elementary school at Las Palmas was grades one through six, and it seemed to rush by so fast it all flows together like one big memory now. School was fun, man. For an only child who had never really interacted with other kids before, I think I'm lucky that I liked it so much. I could've been very introverted, but again — my parents. They had me ready.

I was popular. My teachers were great, and my grades were all A's and B's. I don't believe I ever got a C at Las Palmas. And what a life it was. Our school was pretty typical for that era and that part of the country. All the "hallways" were outside, with something like a carport roof over them. To get from class to class (we started doing that in fourth grade) you walked outside. Same thing for lunch in the cafeteria or to get to the little gym we had. It seemed like every kid in school was into all the same stuff, and the bike rack outside the main building was jammed with BMX models all tricked out and painted in wild colors. Skateboards were everywhere and by the time I was 10, right after fifth grade, a bunch of my school buddies and I were regulars at the beach, with our boogie boards or standard surf boards. After school, we could get home, grab our wetsuits and boards and still get to the beach in time for an hour of surfing before dinner.

We were pretty good for being 10, or at least we thought we were. We talked about carving and shredding and ripping and hopping on the smaller waves we could handle. We were learning the sport and learning how it worked socially, all at the same time.

There's a lot to surfing that people from the rest of the country don't know, and it's all very social and very territorial. It actually has a name, and it's called "localizing." Surfers have their favorite "home beach" most of the time, and they get to know one another. There's a very real pecking order at just about any beach, and it's the ocean version of having "turf" that's yours. You don't just show up at a new beach and act like you own the place. Doing that, or cutting guys off by dropping in when it's their turn next, will get you some seriously mean looks at the least, and probably a few choice words. It can be really intimidating.

It helps to have someone who brings you out and makes you part of the group, but you still have to remember the etiquette and stay out of the way to earn your stripes. My dad had been fortunate that summer after high school to be living with that guy who was a regular at Huntington Beach. He took my dad with him, introducing Dad to all of his friends while letting those guys know that this "Barney" (surfing lingo for a complete beginner) was from way out east in Pennsylvania and that he was going to teach him how to surf and he's a totally cool dude. That got the rest of the group to kind of buy into helping Dad out, instead of hazing him or making him wait forever before trying to catch a wave. When everyone is trying to help you, that's when you get some seriously good time on the board. Otherwise, you have to defer to the better surfers a lot, and take what they let you have.

When it became obvious that Dad had a natural knack for it, he was part of the group. Before long, he had a nickname and I think that's a sign of real respect, right there. They called him "Tricky," which was short for "Tricky Ricky," because he was never afraid to try any new move they showed him, and he was damn good at most of them.

The same thing happened for Dad in San Clemente, because his buddy who had moved there from Huntington got him known and into the local group. Dad was my "sponsor" in that way. I was "Tricky's kid" from the first time I sat on his board to ride with him during that maiden voyage on a one-foot wave. By the time my buds and I were all 10, we were known and part of the group, but you still had to respect the etiquette and show the veteran guys who the boss was. They were the bosses, and we were the kids. We really looked up to those dudes, and some of them were true badasses on their boards. We could only dream of someday surfing that well.

All during that same period, baseball was also a huge deal to me and I was playing as many games and innings as we could find, in local youth leagues and on official Little

League teams. Just like my buddies and I were really getting stoked with our surfing by the time we were all 10, the same thing was happening on the field. During those elementary school years, I honestly don't recall not being the best player on any team. By the time I was 10, people were telling me I was the best player in that whole area in south Orange County. I could hit, hit with power, play a mean first base, and I was turning into a pitcher. I would always play first when I didn't pitch, but it was those days on the mound that got me so fired up I'd be dressed and ready to play three hours before Dad could even drive me to the park where we were scheduled.

Even then, I was the tallest kid on the team by a few inches. I was skinny as a pencil but I was tall and lean and really "loose" in terms of my flow and coordination. At 10 or 11 I looked like a pitcher, my dad said. Fluid mechanics, nice balance, great arm speed, and a smooth follow through. When I got a bit older he said, "You were effortless, dude. So smooth you looked better than 90 percent of the kids in high school. And the ball came out of your hand so damn easy, with a real downhill plane. I'm telling you, I'd never seen anything like it from a kid your age. You'd get a lot of hits and bang some home runs playing first, but that was nothing compared to you as a pitcher. You were born to be a pitcher."

Up through sixth grade, I have no idea how hard I was throwing. I was just throwing, but when I moved on from fourth and fifth grade, I started to understand that pitching is different than throwing. I wasn't allowed to throw a curveball yet, but I must have been throwing pretty hard because the first time I accidentally had a ball slip out of my hand a little, and it came in slower, the batter missed it by a foot. I figured out the whole changing speeds thing in a hurry. When you throw hard, sometimes throwing a little slower is even better because the batters are a little intimidated and they're cheating a bit, starting their swings a little early, trying to catch up to you. It's pitching.

I think it was sixth grade when I pitched a complete game and at the end of it my dad rushed up to me and gave me a huge hug. I had no clue what that was about, until he said, "You just pitched a no-hitter!"

I truly had no idea. I'd walked a few guys, hit one or two, and some other guys made solid contact but apparently they were ruled errors. To me, it seemed like a normal game with some guys on base. I knew I'd shut them out, but I had zero idea that I hadn't given up a hit. Sometimes that's a good thing. It's why, as you get older, you understand the superstition about never mentioning a no-hitter to the guy who is throwing one.

During those years, things were really about to make a big change at home. Mom had been doing a lot of painting and she was selling a ton of pieces. Damn, she was really good. I was so proud of her, and to go to a showing with her to see a dozen or more of her works on display in some fancy Laguna Beach shop with pendant spotlights illuminating her art like it was in a museum, well that was just the most bitchin' thing ever. Then, at one of those shows, a woman introduced herself to Mom. She was the executive director of a new five-star, super-luxury hotel that was in the initial planning stages and was scheduled to be built in Irvine or Anaheim or somewhere up there. Somewhere where you couldn't walk to the beach.

24

The woman told Mom she'd heard of her work and loved the show. She asked my mom if she'd possibly consider a full-time commission to do all original paintings for the hotel's 100 guest rooms, the lobby, and restaurant. According to my mom, she was so stunned by what she was hearing she could hardly reply. All she said was: "You're actually going to have original pieces of art in the rooms?"

They had a long talk and then continued it for a week or two. It was going to pay Mom a ton of serious money. More money than either of my folks had ever had. Maybe even more money in one year than they had made, collectively, their whole lives. What worried Mom were two things. First, she wondered if she could even do it and keep the quality up to her standards. Second, we'd probably need to move. She was going to need a full professional studio, so it wouldn't hurt to be up there near where the hotel would be built and the developer was located. They gave her a three-year target to get it all done. It would be a challenge, but it was a chance to do something epic and get paid very well to do it. It could change our lives for the better but also maybe for the worse. She really worried about me and my dad being able to deal with it. I mean, she absolutely loved us more than she loved money. It had always been that way.

She and my dad each talked with me about it for days. Then, they'd try to double-team me but my mom always came back for more to keep talking. It didn't surprise me that my dad was good with the whole thing. He always put her first. I wasn't sure what to think, and I'm sure I was selfish about it and probably pushing back like a brat. I had my friends, my board, my school, and I lived in the coolest town on the coast. And then my dad reminded me of one key thing. He said, "We don't have to do this, and we absolutely won't if you don't want to. But if we move up there you'll be going from decent baseball, where you're way better than the other guys your age, right into one of the best baseball areas in the world. Big leaguers come out of Anaheim and that part of Orange County. You'll be playing with the best. And you're going to have the chance to play as much ball as you want. They have leagues almost year-round up there. And I promise, we'll throw the boards on the VW and come back down here any time we can get away. Whattaya think, dude?"

He had me at "They have leagues almost year-round."

My mom took the gig. We'd be moving as soon as I finished sixth grade. For an only child who had never had much interaction with other kids until he was five, I'd be starting all over again in a place where I didn't know anybody. Heck, I'm not sure I'd even been to Anaheim before. It was like 40 miles away. Might as well have been a million miles. It's not like we had the money laying around to go to hop in the VW and drive up to Disneyland on a whim. My Disneyland was the beach. It was free!

But Anaheim here we come. Let the adventure begin!

CHAPTER 6

Eric Olson

As I went through the Roseau school system, I didn't know enough to even compare it to anywhere else. Life was very routine and it seemed like everyone in town was pretty much alike. The richest people in town weren't all that rich and the poorest weren't all that poor. And we all kind of looked the same. Polaris was the big magnet that kept people employed and that allowed the downtown area to be full of small, family-owned businesses, just like Olson Hardware. It was a great place to live. It still is.

I remember having a conversation with a teammate when I was about 10 or 11. I said, "Do you think it's possible you could grow up here and by the time you graduate from high school there would be someone in town you never met?"

We agreed that it was probably possible, but we didn't think it was very likely. It sure seemed like you knew everyone in town, from the mayor to the school custodian.

Throughout the elementary school years I played as much hockey as I could, and the whole "outwork and outsmart" thing never left my mind. I stayed smaller than average all the way through. Well, to be honest I guess I'm still smaller than average, but I never let that stop me. Instead, I let it motivate me.

When you're from a town like Roseau, you end up playing a lot of sports. A glass-half-empty kind of person would say there's nothing to do there. They would be wrong. Most of us saw it as "there aren't any stupid distractions" in our town, so we found ways to have fun. We played baseball, we learned to golf, some played football and others played basketball, and I ran distance events in track, figuring it would keep me in shape. Almost all of us played hockey. And there's not a lot of population turnover in Roseau, so you end up doing all of that stuff with the same small group of kids for a long time. There are a lot of people I still know and stay in touch with that went through every level of school with me, from kindergarten to graduation as high school seniors. I don't live in Roseau full-time anymore, I live down in Florida, but I go back a lot and when I do there's a real comfort to it. It doesn't change much, and neither do the people.

In terms of hockey, by the time I was in the middle of the elementary grades I could already begin to see the traits of certain guys I played with. Some were gifted and even by that age you could tell they'd be stars on the Rams varsity in a few years. Others played just because it was fun and all their friends were doing it. They didn't have any ultimate hockey dreams. It was just fun to play. And then there was me.

Playing for the Rams was all I ever dreamed of. I'd keep playing other sports because that's what we all did, and I did well in school, but the dream of being a Ram was something I thought about every single day.

I worked at my defensive game relentlessly. I had to be a pest on the ice, I had to outskate every opposing forward to get to pucks in the corners. I had to get the puck out of our defensive zone quickly but accurately. A stupid blind pass from the behind the goal or in the corner often turns into a goal for the other team, but taking too much time to get it out can get you boxed in or run over. You have to learn how to anticipate where your teammates are and where they're going to be. The more you play together, the more everyone gets to know that.

In practice, I drove the other kids crazy. I only had one speed and that was maximum effort, whether we were practicing against our teammates or playing real games. I never let up until the whistle or the end of my shift.

I don't know how good I would have been if I'd been a bit bigger or more naturally gifted. I got by on max effort, and a lot of those other kids didn't even know what their max effort was. They thought they were playing hard and skating fast, but there was more there. Every day in practice, I tried to give it everything I had just so I could see what that was like. Then I'd try to get it to a new level the next day. If you lined us up and put a $10 bill at the far end of the rink, at least eight guys would get there before me. But make it five times down and five times back, and I was going to outwork them to get that 10 bucks. Max effort was what it was about, for me. That was my key.

Something one of my coaches said when I was at the peewee level, so I was probably 11 years old at the time, let me know I was on the right track. He had spotted my max effort work rate, and at the end of a practice he brought all of us out to center ice and said, "Guys, Eric Olson here is trying to show you something. That something is effort. It takes zero talent to work hard. It only takes determination. If you are determined to be the best you can be, each and every day, you'll be a very good hockey player in the end. You have to want to, because if you don't you're not emptying the tank. There's still more in there. I want you to empty the tank."

I was proud, but also a little embarrassed at what he said. All during those years, I could see the reactions from my teammates during practice, and I think it made us all better. I hope so, anyway. Most of them were bigger and faster, some of them were obviously really talented, and yet the little pesky defenseman was winning the battles.

Year by year I got a little bigger and I skated a lot better. By sixth grade I was one of the better skaters on the team. Not the fastest, but fast enough and tough enough. When my brothers would skate with me, they'd still try to rough me up a little but they also saw how hard I worked and that made them part of the process. They were always way beyond my level, being so much older, so when we'd skate together they would give

27

me tips on what to look for in an opponent. They would show me how a typical forward goes after the puck in the corner or carries it up ice, and they'd drill it into my head the best way to defend that. I can't tell you how many times I heard Dave, Jon or Brent say: "One thing really good defenders do, that I have a hard time with, is this technique..." And then they'd show me how to do those things.

It was great to have three brothers around, who were also like extra coaches, during those years. Dave made the varsity as a sophomore, so from third grade to fifth I was watching him play on the Rams. When he graduated, he got an offer to play at St. Cloud State, so he followed my dad's skate tracks down there.

Everything Dave did was just more motivation for me. Jon and Brent made the varsity as juniors, so they missed playing with Dave by a year. That would've been pretty neat, to have three Olson boys on the team at once. The funny thing was, they didn't seem to have the same fire as Dave. They loved the game but what they really loved was actually playing the game. They did all the same workouts on the ice and off, the workouts we call "dry land" during the off-season. Dry land can be brutal and boring, because the season always seems to be a long way away, and Jon and Brent just found ways to get through it. They didn't go all in.

I was developing fast at that point. Each year was a huge leap up and I was proud that I had closed that original gap where I was too small and too slow. I think the varsity coaches were keeping an eye on my whole class. We had some really good players in the group that would become the class of 1984.

As those years passed, nothing much changed in town or around the Olson house. I still love that. We'd have cookouts in the summer, we'd play ball, we'd ride bikes and we'd help out at the hardware store. When we were very young, most of it was just busy work. If it meant counting all the screws in a drawer and then putting them back in at least we were getting used to the fact you had to pay attention and help out. And Dad would always smile when I'd report back by telling him, "There were 52 screws in drawer number six" as if I'd solved all his inventory problems. He'd say, "Great work. Now go count drawers seven and eight and let me know what you find in those."

In terms of hockey players to look up to, there was no shortage in Roseau. Right when I was at a real impressionable age, from 11 to 13, Neal Broten was playing for the Rams and they went to the state tournament for three straight years. Neal then went to the University of Minnesota to play for the Golden Gophers, and after college he played for parts of 17 years in the NHL, for the Minnesota North Stars, the Dallas Stars, the New Jersey Devils, and the L.A. Kings. But one thing he did outside of all that happened in 1980, and he'll always be associated with it.

His coach at The U was Herb Brooks and 1980 was the year the Winter Olympics were in Lake Placid. Herb was the coach of that team, and Neal made the squad. You don't have to be a huge hockey fan to know how that panned out. The USA team won the gold medal, and beat the Russians as part of their run. That group will always be known as the "Miracle On Ice" team, and a Roseau boy was part of it.

Neal's two brothers, Aaron and Paul, also went on to the NHL, where they had great careers. Neal and Aaron are both in the US Hockey Hall of Fame. That's a whole lot of hockey greatness coming out of one Roseau home. Their parents, Newell and Carol, still live in the same house. When I go back, I make a point to stop by. Newell is always happy to share a beer and some stories out on the front porch.

Did I want to be like Neal, Aaron or Paul? To be honest, I never even considered it. They were great on a scale I couldn't imagine. I never even thought about playing in college until I was closer to 13 or 14 years old. All I wanted to be was a Roseau Ram, and that seemed like a steep enough mountain for a smaller defenseman to climb. The fact that all three Broten boys played for the Rams when I was growing up idolizing those players and teams is something I can see now as making a huge impression on me. At the time, I didn't know any different. I thought every little town had hockey teams like ours and players that good.

When the Roseau-Warroad rivalry games happened, my naive feeling that every school team was like the Rams was only reinforced. The Warriors had great teams and great players too. Dave Christian played for Warroad and then went to the University of North Dakota. In 1979, UND played the Gophers for the national championship. UND lost, and it was Neal Broten who scored the winning goal for the Gophers. A year later, Christian went from being a rival to a teammate with Neal on the "Miracle On Ice" team. It's amazing to think about all of that now.

All I wanted to be was a Ram. And as I was nearing high school, I had a feeling I could do it. In eighth grade I was still only about 5 feet, 6 inches tall and maybe 135 pounds, but I was strong. I was still sticking with my daily belief that I'd have to outsmart and outwork everyone, and still trying to play every shift at max effort, whether it was practice or games.

Just like my coach in peewee said, you have to want to empty the tank.

CHAPTER 7

Brody Bennett

Once our family decided to move up to the Anaheim area, a whole bunch of details had to be worked out. I was only heading into middle school at the time, but my dad had already been scouting out the best high schools for baseball and he drove me up there to see Canyon High. It looked awesome to me, and when he showed me a list of the players who had gone there and who went on to the pros, I was all in.

So, even though they had enrolled me at Cerro Villa Middle School, which is about four miles from Canyon, my parents looked for a rental property right near the high school. I could ride my bike or they could drive me to Cerro Villa, and then by the time I got to high school I could walk every day. Mom and Dad found a house for rent just three blocks from Canyon, and it was unlike any home we'd ever had.

First of all, it wasn't a small 1940s bungalow. It was way more like a suburban "Brady Bunch" type of house. It was split level, it had three bedrooms, a nice living room, a two-car garage that was actually attached, and a kitchen more than one person could be in at the same time. It seemed really foreign to me. This was the kind of house those "other kids" lived in. The kids who dressed really nice and whose parents dropped them off at school in expensive, cool cars. It was nice, though. I'll be honest and admit I got used to all the space, having a nice big bedroom, and finally having a TV. My folks never had one in Huntington and they were used to that, so they never got one in San Clemente either. I guess I never knew what I was missing. I'd seen "Mork & Mindy" and "Good Times" over at friends' houses, but not in my home. Having a TV was pretty bitchin'.

Dad told me once that the original rent on the place was like $650 a month. He said he almost choked when he heard the figure, but Mom reminded him that they could afford that now and it would be a great place for me, so he kissed her on the cheek and signed the lease.

We moved there in the first week of June that summer, right after I turned 12. I didn't know a single kid within 40 miles, but I was happy to see that we had some other kids in our neighborhood who looked like they might be about my age. They didn't look

30

anything like surfers, but I saw them shooting hoops in their driveways and riding their bikes. I remember feeling like an outsider, because I still looked like a kid who went to the beach every day. I got some funny looks, and I felt something I'd never really felt before in my life. I felt a little shy and intimidated, and I guess I felt out of place, too.

To help get me acclimated, my dad got me onto a summer youth baseball team that was about three weeks into its season. He took me to my first practice and stayed around to watch. Within about 10 minutes I could tell these kids were all better than the dudes I played with in San Clemente, but I didn't really think they were any better than me. After I met the coach, I told him I was a pitcher who could also play first base, and he shook my hand and asked me to throw to him from the mound. It's goofy that I remember that first practice like it was a week ago, but I have no idea what the coach's name was. I probably didn't even know it back then. He was just "Coach" to all of us.

I got loose and then threw about 20 pitches to him. When we were done Coach told me to go out in the outfield and join the rest of the kids, who were playing catch. Coach then went to talk to my dad. When I got out to the outfield I was still feeling that gnawing pain of shyness, but one of the bigger kids came right over to introduce himself and that broke the ice. One by one, they all came over. They asked where I was from, where I was going to school, and stuff like that. Only a few of them had ever been to San Clemente, and I remember one of the guys actually asked, "Where is that? Is it in California?" But, and this was big, in just those few minutes standing out there in the outfield, I had about 15 new friends. I was going to have to learn their names in a hurry, but they all accepted me immediately. It didn't hurt when one of the taller kids, who might have even been taller than me, said, "I was watching you throw to Coach. You throw really hard, dude. How do you do that?" I said I didn't know. I just threw the ball.

On the ride back home, Dad told me that Coach was peppering him with questions about me. He said, "Your new coach basically sounded like he felt the best pitcher he'd ever had on this team just fell into his lap and he was trying to find out if this was all for real. You blew him away, dude."

For the rest of the summer, I had a ton of fun. It seems now like we must have played 30 games that summer, but I bet it was really only about 15 or 20. I pitched about once a week, so I figure I threw in about 10 games, always as the starter, and when I didn't pitch I played first base. It was the best baseball I'd ever been part of. My dad had been right about that. It was way better than San Clemente. It didn't have a beach, but the level of baseball was totally way better. It actually looked like baseball, and the infielders on our team made plays I'd never seen before, as if they actually expected to catch the grounders no matter how hard they were hit. I was 12 years old, and my eyes were wide open. It was my favorite game at a whole new level.

And the best part was that I was still the best player on the team. The coach said I would've been the center fielder if I wasn't a pitcher. During batting practice I caught everything out there, and it was the first time I realized I was actually pretty fast because we turned something that's usually boring, shagging grounders and fly balls, into something really fun. We'd always have a contest to see who could catch the most balls during BP, and I could outrun just about all the other kids. According to Coach, since I was going to be his best pitcher he'd only let me play first base when I wasn't on the mound. He didn't want me making any long throws from the outfield because he was afraid he'd mess up my mechanics or hurt my arm.

I don't remember my record from that year. I don't even remember our team's record, but I do remember striking out a lot of guys and winning a lot of games. I still wasn't throwing a curve yet (Dad wanted me to wait until I was 14), but I already knew some tricks about changing speeds and I was learning about location. At 12, I was learning as fast as I could and it felt like pitching. That made it even more fun.

Then September rolled around and it was time to go to school, and that was like a loop back to when we first moved to the area. Cerro Villa seemed huge to me, and it was full of kids I didn't know. Not one guy from the summer baseball team went there. I was pretty intimidated that first day because it wasn't just a new school, it was a whole new area. It was still SoCal, but it felt and looked really different. And then I realized that these other kids came to Cerro Villa from a variety of elementary schools, so none of them knew everybody on the first day. We were all new kids.

Being in a controlled environment like that helps a lot, and it always had since kindergarten. We all had to get to know our teachers and one another, and having your name called out during attendance helped everyone put a name to a face. I'm sure we were all pretty quiet for a few days, but the teachers were cool and the classes were easy. Pretty soon, I felt like I fit in, and I noticed that I kind of naturally changed my look to be more like the rest of the dudes in my class. My mom had always cut my hair, although that didn't happen very often, and I asked her to neaten it up a bit, and maybe even show some of my ears. I guess it was time to grow up a little, but deep inside I'd always think of myself as a surfer. Dad and I even went back down to San Clemente twice before school started and I was totally stoked about that. We were both stoked, actually, but I totally remember being a little surprised that it didn't crush me to put the boards back on the VW and go "home" to Anaheim.

Dad also knew there was one more big benefit to living in Anaheim, and he planned on doing as much as he could for me in terms of that. We could go see the Angels play. It's hard to believe this now, but when we went over to see them (they were called the California Angels then) at their gigantic stadium, it wasn't just the first Major League baseball game I'd ever seen. It was the first baseball game I'd seen that I wasn't either playing in or only watching because we were waiting to play our game next, on that field.

It was totally incredible. The stadium was awesome, and it still had the original A-shaped scoreboard out in left field, with the huge halo around the top. A few years later the NFL's Los Angeles Rams would move to Anaheim and the stadium would be enlarged by expanding the upper deck so it completely enclosed the whole place. When that happened, they had to move the "Big A" to the parking lot, where it still is and it still looks stupid there, and the whole stadium seemed to lose its vibe. But that first night, the vibe was so electric I almost couldn't stand it.

We had a great time that night, watching Bobby Grich, Rod Carew, and the rest of the Angels playing the Cleveland Indians. I don't remember the score or who won, but I remember being in awe of the whole thing. And then a few days later the Major League players went on strike. I was crushed.

When the strike ended, in early August, we made one or two more trips to see the Angels and by then my dad had me "scouting" the teams more than just watching. We were both looking for how the strategy of the games went, and how the pitchers attacked each hitter. It was right then that I began to understand how totally mental the game can be. I mean, every player in the big leagues is incredible, so something has to separate the winners from the losers. It was a lot for a kid my age to absorb, but I sort of got it and understood it.

With my mom getting going on her commission to create all that artwork, she agreed with my dad that it would be best for me if he took that first summer in Anaheim off just to help me get settled and into the groove in our new town, new home, new school and new teams. It was awesome that he did that. He made it all so much easier, and the bond we'd always had somehow got even stronger. It could've been a real bad time for me, but it ended up being fun and having him around so much was a big part of that.

After school started, he began to look for a job but bartending didn't seem right anymore and there weren't surf shops on every block around Anaheim. He for sure wasn't suited for sitting behind a desk and carrying a briefcase so he went and applied at a place not too far from home. I never would've dreamed of him doing that, but it made sense. He's a people person. The dude is instantly popular and he loves getting to know new people. So, of course, he applied for a job at Disneyland. And he got one, working in the park. His first job was in retail, working in a souvenir shop on Main Street. When he started, Mom and I both went to Disneyland for the first time. Like my first game at Angels Stadium, it was another rad moment for the surfer kid from San Clemente.

I was 12 years old and as much as we'd moved I still hadn't really "gotten around" much. I saw my first Major League game and visited Disneyland for the first time all in the span of two months. Mom and I had a blast and it felt great to me, because I'd been doing a lot of accelerated growing up right about then. Everything I'd ever known was different, and it wasn't all easy, but going on the rides at Disneyland and just experiencing the place made me happy like only a kid can be happy. It was great to just be a kid again, at least for that day. I think I was laughing the whole time, and Mom was too.

Mom and I even strolled through the store Dad was working in and she winked at him. He said, "If I can help you folks in any way, just let me know." Mom answered, "Oh we're just looking, but thank you. You're a very nice man!" When we went back out onto Main Street my mom said, "That was awesome. I never saw him as a Disney guy, but he fits the part perfectly." I thought it was hilarious. I had never seen my dad in anything but the clothes he wore at home or in board shorts and sandals. He looked pretty funny with his bright blue uniform on and his hair all combed. He'd gone to an actual barber to get it cut and it turned out he cleaned up pretty nicely. Who knew?

Middle school turned out to be more than OK. It was fun and the teachers were great. My classmates were actually fantastic and I got to know them fast. At that age, boys like me were also noticing the girls in class a lot more. You're still a few years away from going on dates, but it wasn't long before classmates were whispering about which guys liked which girls and vice versa. Lots of notes got passed in the classroom too.

I had crushes just like any guy, but there really wasn't one girl I pretended to be boyfriend and girlfriend with. Those sorts of "relationships" were popping up all over the place, but I think I had a lot of my dad in me then. I guess I still do. I just liked people, and wanted to be friends with everyone. I could see the kids who paired off, and before long they "broke up" and usually started nasty rumors about each other. I wanted nothing to do with that.

I played in a fall league that year, but my dad and I decided that I'd take those two months off from pitching. As he said, "The way I see it, there's a finite amount of pitches in your arm, whether it's your shoulder or your elbow or both. Let's not use them all up this early. Have fun at first base." I did have fun, and I met a lot of new guys on the fall team. There's a lot of cool stuff in the game, but in my case the coolest was probably that baseball provided instant friends. I loved that as much as I loved the game.

My dad loved working at Disneyland, and he really liked it when they'd switch him around to a new job. He wanted to learn it all and he was bent on being the happiest guy in the "Happiest Place on Earth." Mom was working on her art for the hotel, and life was good that first year at Cerro Villa, which everyone called CV for short. My folks weren't always available to get me to and from school, though, so my BMX bike got a lot of mileage put on it. I could get to school on back roads with sidewalks on the days Mom and Dad were both working. I could be trusted to get myself to and from and had my own key to the front door. My mom made it a policy that on those days when I was a latchkey kid, she'd take off a little early from the studio to try to be home by 4.

By the spring, it seemed like I'd always been there. I was popular, I got good grades, and I had a group of buds who lived near me. Lots of driveway hoops and Wiffle Ball games, for sure. And living so close to Canyon High made it real easy to cruise our bikes around the school and the little park next to it, kind of dreaming of the day we'd be Canyon Comanches. It was only a year away.

By that summer, the baseball strike from the year before seemed like ancient history, and we went to a number of Angels games again. I tried to soak it all in every time we went, no matter where we sat. Then, a few weeks before July 4th, Dad had another surprise for me. We were going to Dodger Stadium on July 4th to see the Dodgers play the Astros. To say I was a little jacked up about that would be putting it mildly.

It was a day game on July 4th, and my dad had bought some tickets up at the top of the upper deck. I didn't care where we sat. The Angels' stadium impressed the hell out of me, for sure, but nothing prepared me for Dodger Stadium. It was the most beautiful thing I'd ever seen.

It turns out my dad picked that particular game to be the first Dodgers game I'd see, and for a reason. When we got there he said, "Wait until you see who's pitching for Houston today." It was Nolan Ryan. I hadn't heard of half the players on the Astros, but even my surfing buds back at the beach had heard of Nolan Ryan, because he'd pitched for the Angels before he went to Houston. Heck, my mom had heard of Nolan Ryan and I didn't think she knew the names of any pro athletes.

I watched the master at work that afternoon, and all through the game my dad and I were talking about how Ryan went about pitching. Dad kept pointing out how balanced and under control he was with his delivery. It wasn't just compact; it was absolutely the same on every pitch. He made it look effortless and he got a lot of drive from his strong legs, the way he'd bring his left knee up and kind of peek around his left shoulder. Then he "drop and drive" by bending the right leg while pushing his whole body forward. His throwing action was magic to me, and his follow-through was perfect. What really got me, though, wasn't his fastball. He rushed that pitch up there so quickly that even I, sitting way up high in the upper deck, could tell it was special, but Dad said, "Just watch him, don't watch the pitch. Zero in on Nolan, and then tell me what the pitch was."

I made a circle with my right thumb and fingers, like a little telescope, and I put it to my eye so that all I could see was the pitcher's mound. All the pitches looked like fastballs to me, and after I called that out eight or nine times Dad stopped me and said, "Four of those were curves." Dad said my eyes got big and my mouth dropped open before I said, "What?" I wasn't allowed to throw a curve yet, but I'd seen some kids my age messing around with them and the delivery was always way different. Nolan Ryan's fastball and his curve looked a whole lot alike coming out of his hand. No wonder he struck out so many hitters. He made you speed up to even have a prayer of making contact with his fastball and then he'd drop the hammer on you with the curve. Then, you'd walk back to the dugout. He shut out the Dodgers that day, and struck out 10.

This might sound a little over the top, but it's for real. That afternoon watching Nolan Ryan changed me. Before the fifth inning I realized something I'd never even thought about before. I knew I wanted to pitch in the big leagues. At some point during that game, it all became totally real. I'm not trying to say I had a vision or heard voices or anything, and it's not like I decided right then that I'd work my butt off to get better every day. I'd just never really contemplated being a professional baseball player before that afternoon. I never planned for much of anything, up to that point. It was the first real long-term goal I ever had. Might as well go big, I guess.

My second year at CV flew by, and I was actually voted President of our Student Council. I'd never been elected anything before, so it was a pretty big honor and I had a lot of fun doing it. I had turned 13 in June and played summer ball and fall ball again, and when January rolled around my dad found the best team in the area for me to play on the next spring. We didn't have a school team, so he found the squad that was at the top of the elite level. I was the best pitcher on the team, but not necessarily the best all-around player. We had some guys that were really in a different universe, and it was awesome to play with them. It was totally clear that I was moving up to whole new levels of play every time I joined a new team.

What this all meant was I was getting to be known around the area. My dad talked to the head coach at Canyon and told him about me. He came to see me pitch once that spring, and after the game he let me know I'd have every shot to make the Canyon varsity as a freshman. I might have to be the third or fourth starter, or even become a reliever, but if I could earn my way on the team he wouldn't hold me back.

I played summer ball on the same elite team and it all just came so easy for me. I was learning how to hit spots and change speeds at a new level, even without spinning a curve. I found I actually had better control if I took a little off my fastball. When I was throwing it as hard as I could it would sometimes get away from me a little and I'd walk too many guys. By throwing around 90 percent I could hit the catcher's mitt almost all the time. It helped that my 90 percent was still a lot harder than what most other kids were throwing at that age.

I also got to spend a lot of time with my mom that summer. Dad was working long days at Disneyland and I really enjoyed going to her studio to watch her work. It was close by, in Yorba Linda, and there was a little shopping center just around the corner. There was a taco joint there that blew my mind. I think I must have been going through a growth spurt because I seemed to be hungry all the time and I could demolish a dozen of those 25-cent tacos.

At the studio, I was just amazed at what Mom was doing. She had multiple paintings going at once, and she'd perfected a method for creating all the pieces. She had about a dozen basic designs, but she'd always mix it up a little on each one, so that no two paintings were exactly the same. She'd let me come up with new ideas, too, and then she'd plug those into the next painting. It was awesome to watch. I can remember thinking how lucky I was to have such incredible parents, and at the same time I was thinking about how I was going to pitch in the big leagues and the first thing I would do would be to buy them a house. They'd never done anything but pay rent, and I was going to change that. It was a dream that was still a long way off, but by then I was kind of "brimming with confidence" in terms of my pitching ability. OK, maybe I was a little cocky. I knew I was good.

When the summer league ended, I had a few weeks off before my freshman year at Canyon started and my dad had a surprise for me. He said, "Your mechanics are about as good as any I've ever seen, so we ought to get you started on the basics of a breaking ball. I always said let's wait until you're 14, and we did that, but you're way ahead of everyone else, man. I just want your mechanics to be as flawless with your curve as they are with the fastball."

I already knew how to hold one, and which finger to put the most pressure on, and I'd be lying if I said that I'd never messed around with it at practice. I just threw them real easily to avoid putting any stress on my arm. I think Dad had me paranoid enough to keep me from really trying to snap one off.

We'd go play catch and I'd ramp them up a little more every day. He really focused on two things. First, I had to have the same release point as my fastball. Second, I had to keep my arm flow the same and not try to yank the ball too much. It's hard for kids that age to get real good spin on the ball and most of them compensate by twisting their arm at the release point, and that puts a lot of strain on the elbow. Dad's message was, "Just trust your arm and your mechanics. It will take you a year or two to get the kind of spin that will make it a real curve. Don't cheat now. It's a process, dude. Follow the process."

I was about to go to high school. I had a hard fastball and had developed a funky kind of change-up by gripping the ball deeper in my hand so that it was maybe 10 miles per hour slower with the same arm action. I was about 5-foot-10 and a solid 135 pounds. I couldn't wait.

CHAPTER 8

Eric Olson

As eighth grade came to a close, all of Roseau and Warroad were paying close attention to the USA Olympic hockey team. Neal Broten was representing my town and Dave Christian was the pride of Warroad, but both of them were part of something none of us will ever forget.

I had been playing with Paul Broten for years, because we're the same age, and it was a thrill to be friends and teammates with a guy whose oldest brother made the Olympic hockey team. Both Roseau and Warroad were buzzing with pride, but I don't remember there being a lot of anticipation. Back then, the Soviet Union and many of the other European countries had found ways around the "amateur" designation for the Olympics. The Soviets kept their core group together for many years, and they did that by making the players members of the national military. They were actually fully professional hockey players, and they were the best team in the world – NHL included.

The USA team, on the other hand, was made up of real amateurs, and young ones at that. They were all college kids. They honestly didn't stand a chance against those European and Scandinavian teams. Because of that huge mismatch, nobody really expected anything from them. We were excited to know Neal and his family, but the Brotens didn't even go to Lake Placid for the tournament. Neal's dad once told me, "It was an expensive trip, and hotel rooms were almost impossible to find. Plus, we thought they'd be lucky to even come close to winning a game. Nobody expected what happened, except maybe Herb Brooks, but I don't think Herb really thought they'd win a medal, much less the gold."

And Herb Brooks was the key to the whole thing. Most Americans are familiar with the basics of the story, especially those who have seen the movie *"Miracle"* starring Kurt Russell, who played such a realistic Herb it was like watching the real thing. He was tough on those guys and put them through the ringer for months. They played 61 games to prepare for the tournament, and no American team had ever prepared like that or pushed themselves that hard to be the best team they could be.

When they got to Lake Placid, they were the youngest team in the tournament. We mostly hoped they wouldn't get creamed, and there was good reason to worry they would. Their last exhibition game had been against the Soviets at Madison Square Garden just days before the games started. The Soviets won 10-3. It wasn't that close, either.

So, we were proud and we were excited, but we had no expectations. We were able to watch on TV, and I know just about everyone in Roseau and Warroad was crowded around sets in various living rooms or public places. We didn't get many channels, and some of them didn't come in very well, but ABC was one that gave us a good picture and they broadcast the Winter Olympics that year.

The young USA team started out playing Sweden, another world hockey power. We were stunned to see how well Herb had coached the young guys. They stayed right with Sweden but were down 2-1 with less than a minute to play in the final period. When University of Minnesota Golden Gopher Bill Baker scored with only 27 seconds left, the towns of Roseau and Warroad about exploded. That tie was more than we'd ever dreamed of.

Herb had pushed those guys so hard, and when they came out of the Sweden game with a tie, I think they began to believe. Neal Broten told us, after he got back home, that they knew they were good. They knew they were better than anyone had ever expected an American team to be. But, until the tie with Sweden, they couldn't help but have some small doubts. They were college kids playing the best hockey teams in the world. Teams full of grown men who had played together for years. Until 1980, the young American teams rarely played more than a few exhibitions before the Olympics and because of that they didn't play much like a team. Hockey relies on close-knit teamwork. Herb's concept was to play them and push them so hard they'd have to become a team and a family, and it worked.

In the next game at Lake Placid, they stunned Czechoslovakia 7-3. The Czechs were considered, by all the experts, the favorites to win the silver medal. Then came wins against Norway (5-1), Romania (7-2), and West Germany (4-2) to send our boys to the medal round.

The first game in the medal round was against the Soviets. I don't think I'll ever forget a single minute of it. My parents, my sister, and I were sitting around the TV in our living room, with a fire in the fireplace, after eating another hotdish masterpiece my mom had created. Brother Dave Jr. was off at college, no doubt watching in his dorm, while the twins Jon and Brent were at someone else's house. On the black-and-white screen, we could tell the arena was packed, and I'd never seen so many American flags flying in one place before. Right before the USA team took the ice, Herb Brooks gave a speech in the locker room. I bet every kid I grew up with in Roseau could recite it for you to this day.

He said:

"Great moments are born from great opportunities, and that's what you've got here tonight, boys. One game. If we played them 10 times they might win nine. But not this game. Not tonight. Tonight we skate with them. Tonight we stay with them, and we shut them down

because we can. Tonight, we are the greatest hockey team in the world. You were born to be hockey players - every one of you - and you were meant to be here tonight. This is your time. Their time is done. It's over. I'm sick and tired of hearing about what a great hockey team the Soviets have. Screw 'em. This is your time. Now go out there and take it."

Until the day I die, I will always believe that was the greatest pregame speech in the history of sports. I still get chills just reading the words.

The odd thing was the game was scheduled for the late afternoon. ABC asked to have it moved to the 8 p.m. slot for prime time, but the Soviets wouldn't agree to that. So, ABC taped the game and showed it to America that night. If you think you watched the USA-USSR game "live" on TV as it happened, right here in America, you're wrong unless you were in the control room. ABC, though, kept a tight lid on the final score and then put it on the air that night as if it were "live" on television.

In the final seconds of the first period, with the USSR leading 2-1, Warroad's Dave Christian fired a long shot on Soviet goaltender Vladislav Tretiak, the greatest goalie in the world. Tretiak stopped it, but he gave up a big juicy rebound. It looked like the Soviet defensemen figured the period was over and they let up, but when Mark Johnson streaked in and pounded the puck into the net right before the buzzer, with just one second left on the clock, I think the whole world stopped. We went crazy. Goals like that, when you outhustle a better team and put the puck in the net with one second left, are the goals that win you medals and championships.

The American kids went on to win that thriller of a game 4-3, with team captain Mike Eruzione scoring the game winner and then running on the tips of his blades around the boards, but there were still 10 long minutes left against the best team in the world. Goalie Jim Craig came up huge time after time, and the USA team played at their absolute best. They left nothing in the tank. They emptied it. We were so nervous that the Soviets would come back and break everyone's hearts, but the boys who were "born to be hockey players" didn't buckle. As the clock wound down to just a couple of seconds left, announcer Al Michaels said the words he will always be known for: "Do you believe in miracles? YES!"

And a lot of people think that win over the USSR was for the gold. It wasn't. The Americans had to beat a great Finland team for the gold medal. They did, and our boy Neal Broten brought the medal back home with him. It was one of the neatest things I'd ever witnessed. It still is.

Paul Broten reminded me that the city of Roseau gave his parents a new TV so they could all watch the Olympics with a better picture. When that happened, his dad went out and splurged on a Sony Betamax video-tape machine, and he recorded all the games. Then, after the Olympics, ABC sent Neal and all his teammates each a full set of broadcast quality tapes, so they'd always have every minute of their gold medal performance on the shelf.

Neal scored two goals in the tournament, one against Romania and the other against West Germany. I like to tell people that the entire town of Roseau got the assists on those goals.

A few weeks later came my next big moment in life. I graduated from eighth grade. That meant one very important thing to me. The next time I went to school that fall, I'd be a student at Roseau High. That was one warm and beautiful northern Minnesota summer I could barely stand. I just wanted to get back to school. And no, we didn't have any summer training camps or even unofficial workouts. Basically, we went fishing, played golf and just messed around. Back then, it wasn't like it is now where kids get all this specialized hockey training year-round. There were some summer camps, but they cost way more money than a typical family from Roseau could justify.

So we all played lots of sports and I think that was a good thing. We didn't get to play hockey until October, when they finally installed the ice at the Memorial Arena and the North Rink. While there was ice, skating and playing was just about all we thought of. Once they took the ice out in the spring, we found other things to do.

Summer always seemed to go by so fast in elementary school. You wanted it to slow down, but once the end of July came around it was like the whole summer vacation was on fast-forward. The summer of 1980 was just the opposite. I had fun, and I did do some running and worked out doing push-ups and sit-ups just to keep getting stronger, but all I could think about was the fall.

Roseau High had two teams. The A team, which was the varsity, and the B team. The B team was basically the junior varsity, and incoming freshmen were expected to compete for a spot on that JV roster. Even Paul Broten planned on playing on the JV that fall, and he was already a great offensive player. There was an open tryout for the varsity, but I wasn't surprised when Paul said he wasn't even going to attempt it. He said, "The varsity team is so good and so deep, we'd have no chance. I'm going to make sure I make the JV and have as good a season as I can. Next year I'll aim for the varsity."

Making the move from Bantams to the JV wasn't going to be that big of an adjustment, actually. I'd been playing with almost all of those guys since we were little kids, and we'd all grown up and gotten bigger and better as a group. We were pretty good, too. My "outwork and outsmart" philosophy had stayed with me, and motivated me every step along the way. I was still small, maybe 5-foot-7 that summer, but I was playing the best hockey of my life. Not good enough to be a varsity Roseau Ram yet, but I knew I could make the JV.

By sixth or seventh grade, head coach Gary Hokanson was keeping a close eye on the guys in my class. By eighth grade it was getting to be pretty obvious that we had some very special talent. Paul was our best offensive player, Tom Pederson was the best defenseman (I wasn't close yet, at that time), David Drown was really good, and Donny Johnson was already a heck of a goalie. In total, though, our whole group entering high school that fall was good. We were Roseau good.

Once September finally rolled around, it was time to go to school. It was time to live my dream. It was time to play for the Roseau Rams, even if that meant the JV. The sweater said "ROSEAU" on the front. I was determined to wear it.

41

CHAPTER 9

Brooks Bennett

The first day of high school at Canyon was one of those moments a kid never forgets. I'd had some orientation meetings before the first day, but to head to the high school campus and arrive at my original home room, with quite a few of the kids I'd gone to Cerro Villa with, felt like the biggest job promotion ever. It was like I never really thought about the elementary school I went to, and the jump to middle school in Anaheim wasn't as much of a thrill as it was stressful, with the move and everything. The first day at Canyon, just a few blocks from our cool suburban home, was a very big day.

Maybe you're just too young to think about big moments in elementary and middle school. You just go where you're told and follow instructions. And you're still so young things like high school or college are too far away to really even consider.

I totally remember how I felt on that first day. Putting my books in my new locker. I can remember the smell of the new books and the clang of the locker door. I recall memorizing the combination on the lock (and keeping it on a slip of paper in my wallet, petrified I'd forget it and get laughed at). Meeting the new teachers and the kids seated around me. I also always equated the first day of school with the smell of all-new clothes. To this day, when I put on a new shirt, it reminds me of the first day of school. I remember thinking in that first hour of the first day, "Damn! I'm in high school! How cool is this?"

Classes weren't hard, they really never had been for me, but stuff like math and science was a lot more technical and challenging. As the science got harder, I didn't struggle but I had to really focus on it to keep getting A's. What I noticed right off the bat was that I had a thing for numbers.

In middle school, math was moving into algebra and some other difficult stuff, but it all made totally perfect sense to me. To me, numbers are like puzzles. If you arrange them the wrong way, they fall apart. If you see how the flow goes and why they go together, it all becomes a solid unit. It was just easy. I don't know how else to say it.

It's weird how we're all wired a little differently, right? I was OK at English and in creative writing classes, but I wasn't a great writer and it never came as easy as the numbers did. I prided myself on being good in all my classes, and I knew a lot of kids who were just the opposite of me. They were already awesome writers, history buffs, or artists, but they were stumped by math or science. I guess the kids who master it all are the ones that go on to Harvard or places like that. In my world, nobody had all the skills. We all just mastered a few and got by in the others. Strengths and weaknesses. Just like in baseball.

We had some fall ball at school, mostly practice but a few games, and that was the time for the coaching staff to make evaluations about who was going to contribute on the varsity and who would be on the JV once it all started for real in January. It was way different in a lot of ways.

For one thing, it was the first time in my life I was on the field with guys as much as three years older than me. Up until that fall, it was totally rare for me to be on a team with anybody who wasn't my age, and usually that only happened because someone had a weird birthday that just barely fell on the other side of the guidelines. Even at the first practice, I could feel how different it was to be out there doing drills with juniors and seniors. They looked like men to me. They had facial hair! The dudes had muscles! They made plays I'd only seen on TV or at Angels games! It was thrilling. And looking back on it now, I can remember being really impressed with the level of skill I was surrounded by, totally stoked to be out there but not at all intimidated. I still had all that Brooks Bennett confidence.

I did make a conscious decision, though, to just be quiet and do my work. That felt like the best way to fit in at the time. I did what the coaches asked me to do and tried not to screw up.

Our head coach was a guy named Gary Hansen, who had gone to Canyon, then on to Cal State Fullerton, and then played a few years in the San Diego Padres organization. He was smart, he was calm and he was definitely in control. I was only about 95 percent intimidated by him, but by the end of the fall workouts he put his arm around me and said, "Brooks, you're going to be a big part of this program and I don't see any reason your time on the varsity shouldn't start during your freshman year. But promise me one thing. Do it all the way I want you to do it. You're going to get impatient and want it all, and that's a good thing. I'm telling you right now that we're going to take our time with you, and prepare you for how good you can be, not how good you are right now. Be patient. Follow instructions. When I slow you down, it's for a reason. When I push you, that's for a reason too."

I made that promise. And, at that moment, I could start to see the future because Coach's history at Fullerton meant I'd get a stout recommendation from him if I kept getting better. Coach loved to tell us all about the place, as if he was almost recruiting for them. Looking back, I think he was, in a subtle sort of way. Fullerton has one of the best NCAA Division I programs in the country. Going to Omaha for the College World Series wasn't a dream for them. They expected to get that far. And they expected a bunch of players in each junior or senior class to get selected in the Major League draft.

Just a few months earlier, the future had no real definition for me. It was just kind of "out there" and I wasn't sure what it held for me in the end. After one semester of high school, I could see how it might go and how that could get me to the big leagues, and how that would allow me to buy that house for my parents while I was living my biggest dream. Some nights I had to force myself to stop thinking about it when I was in bed and needed to sleep, because just the thought of the whole road ahead of me got me so wound up I'd be awake for hours. I thought about it every single day.

At home, things were going along pretty smoothly. Mom was cranking out the art for the new hotel, which still hadn't broken ground or even gotten the permits to be built yet. That kind of worried me, but Dad said, "Hey dude, they pay her every two weeks and she's loving the hell out of doing this. I don't really care if the place ever gets built."

Dad was enjoying his work at Disney, and even though he was never going to be a character in a costume, like Mickey Mouse or Goofy, he liked to tell me how much he felt like he was a member of the cast, and how at work they weren't called employees. They were called cast members. He said everyone who worked there felt that way, like they were all putting on a performance no matter what job they had. He was happy, and that was all that mattered to me. I gave him some crap about it from time to time, but only in a kidding sort of way like saying, "Say hi to Mickey for me today." If he was happy, and my mom was happy, then I was happy. I'll never forget how, when I was a little kid and we didn't have many possessions, my parents would tell me that there would always be a lot of love in our home. They were right.

Even in that first semester of my freshman year, I felt like I was growing up fast. I could be trusted to walk home after practice and either do my homework or hang out with friends, maybe shooting hoops in someone's driveway, until one of my parents got home. That's more Bennett DNA right there. They brought me up that way, and I never even understood why other kids would get into trouble. If someone in my circle of friends wanted to do something they knew was bad, just to be rebellious, I'd stop being friends with them. Making my parents proud of me meant just about everything to me.

By Christmas break, it felt like I'd been at Canyon for years. I fit in, I got good grades and I had close friends both in the classroom and on the ball field. The whole high school experience was awesome. I totally dug everything about it.

When we got back to school after the break, things got serious with the baseball team. The practices got more intense, and I got to pitch in a few intrasquad games before the season started. I didn't strike everybody out like I had against kids that were all my age, but I didn't get hit hard either. Even by the seniors.

I kind of figured I had the varsity made, but Coach made it official when he gathered us on the field to announce the roster. He left me until last, when he said, "And our final varsity player this year will be our only freshman. Brooks Bennett, welcome to Canyon High Comanche baseball." I got a round of applause and a bunch of pats on the back and handshakes.

My dad was working at Disney until about 9 that night, and I about went nuts waiting for him to get home. I was able to tell Mom when she got home from the studio right around 5, and she gave me a huge hug and I think I saw a tear in her eye, but I knew it would mean more to Dad. He was going to be totally proud of me, and I knew he'd be stoked for both of us.

When I heard the VW pull in the drive, I met him at the door and Mom was right next to me. He said, "Hey dude, hey my love, what's up with this welcoming committee?"

I just said, "Dad, I made the varsity. I'm the only freshman on the team." He didn't just get a little misty. He started seriously crying, and that got Mom and me going too. We had a group hug for the ages. Dad was speechless.

Before I went to bed, and after he'd composed himself a bit, he came to my room and shook my hand before giving me another hug. He said, "I'm damn proud of you, dude. I've seen this coming since we went out on those San Clemente fields by ourselves. I swear I knew it when you were 2. And you still have so much more to come. Your mom and I are with you all the way. Just keep up what you're doing, keep hitting the books and take care of that arm."

The next day, during batting practice, Coach was roaming around the outfield while we were shagging balls, and when he approached me he asked, "Brooks, have you ever pitched in relief?"

I said I hadn't. I was always the best pitcher on any team I'd been on so I was always a starter.

He nodded his head a little and said, "I've been thinking about this a lot. Any other freshman pitcher I've ever had on this team has gone to the bullpen. I don't think I want to do that with you. I'm planning on making you a spot starter, which means you won't be in the regular rotation but whenever the games stack up I'm going to give you some starts to keep everyone rested. I'll always give you a couple of days' warning, and I'll get you as much work as I can. The best thing we can do for you, this year, is to get you the ball as often as possible while still protecting you a little bit. Is that OK with you?"

I almost laughed.

"Yeah, that's OK with me," I said, with a grin. "I'll do whatever you want. And when you give me the ball I'll do the best I can. I know I can get better, but I'm ready to show you and the guys everything I have. Coach, I'm totally stoked to be on this team." Sometimes the surfer in me just had to make an appearance. Coach laughed and said, "I'm stoked too, dude."

The next huge milestone in my life came the next day. We had our physicals and when it was my turn to be measured the school nurse said, "Six feet tall, 149 pounds."

Holy crap! I was 6 feet tall.

I hadn't really been paying too much attention but I had noticed my jeans all seemed to be getting a little shorter. I figured they were shrinking. They weren't. I'd shot up to 6 feet from 5-foot-10 in about four months.

It didn't take too long for me to fully fit in with the older guys, who treated me great. I think they could tell I had some talent, and once I felt confident in that I started coming out of my shell a little. It felt like a family in no time, and we had some guys that could really play. Again, a whole new level of talent, and this was the single biggest jump I'd ever made.

After a few weeks of practice, we opened our season at home against Villa Park. I sat on the bench and cheered for the guys, and I think we won. It was just cooler than hell to wear the uniform and be a part of it.

And wearing the uniform is a totally big thing. It was really that freshman year when I started to understand how much I loved the uniform, and the process. When you're a kid, you just throw it on and go. The pants might not fit, the hat may be too big, but it didn't matter. As a freshman, I was surrounded by these older guys who took great pride in wearing the Canyon uniform, and in the locker room I watched as they carefully got dressed. They did it slowly, step by step. Then they looked in the mirror to make sure it was all sharp.

I figured out my routine in a hurry, after watching the other guys. After getting undressed, the first thing we'd put on is what we called "baseball underwear." They were tight cotton thigh-length briefs. Compression shorts hadn't become a thing yet, and you wanted some protection from getting a rash from your jockstrap. We'd have to scour the stores to find them, because I think they were really designed for old guys who wanted a combination of briefs and boxers. Kind of halfway in the middle, or a bit of both. We all wore baseball underwear. Then your jock, then your baseball undershirt with the correct colored sleeves. Then, the most meticulous part of the process: putting on the socks.

Most of the time as a kid we wore regular tube socks. For a long time that's all we wore. Then, by middle school, we started wearing stirrups over those but a lot of the guys were kind of cheating by wearing tube socks that already had a long stripe down each side. I hated that. And, Coach made it a team rule that we'd all wear stirrups and sanitaries, or "sanis" for short, so I was stoked to have the classic look. Sanis were the long socks that went up to your knees, made of thin white cotton material. But, they had no elastic at the top to hold them up.

I'd put my sanis on and then pull the stirrups on over them. I liked a little of the arch of the front of the stirrup to show below the bottom hem of my pants. Some guys on other teams were wearing longer pants by then, but Coach wanted us to all look the same. I dug that.

So the million-dollar question was: "How do you keep your socks up?"

You'd pull the stirrup up to near your knee, and then fold the top of the sani down over it. That was all above your calf, so if you could secure the socks there they would generally stay up. Some guys used big, thick rubber bands but I didn't like the way they felt. It was like they were cutting off my circulation. I'd fold the white sani over my stirrup then run a roll of white athletic tape around my leg there a couple of times. Worked like a charm.

Then the pants, carefully pulled up over the socks you just put on. Then the jersey. A lot of schools were wearing pullovers then, and a few were still wearing the pants with the elastic waistband instead of a belt, but our coach liked the classic look. So did I. Buttoned jerseys and a belt. When the look was complete, I'd check the mirror and smile. I looked like a ballplayer. Up until then, I looked like a kid playing ball. As a freshman, I looked like the real deal. It gave me goosebumps, and the whole lengthy process of slowly getting dressed became one of my favorite parts of the game.

And you thought it was easy, right? This is complicated stuff!

A few weeks later, the schedule stacked up a little, and on a Monday Coach Hansen pulled me aside during BP and said, "Hey, man. We have four games this week. I want you to start the game over at El Dorado High in Placentia on Thursday. They're pretty good, so it will be a good test for you. To be honest, everyone we play is pretty darn good, so I expect to see your best stuff."

My first thought was: "I wonder if I'll get any sleep between now and Thursday."

Before I would start on Thursday we had another game on Tuesday, which meant I got to be the guy who charted all the pitches that day. The next starter always got that duty, and it's a great assignment to get. First of all, it means you're starting next, which is cool, but it also really helps your focus because you have to pay attention to every pitch and mark its location in little boxes on the page. We had one of those four-color pens so you could chart fastballs, curves, change-ups and whatever the guy's fourth pitch was, if he had one, in different colors. To be honest, I needed some help with the focus thing. When you're a starter, you know which days you'll be playing and when you're not going to play. On those days when you're in the dugout, it's easy to let your mind wander.

As I watched my teammate Gary Heinz dominate the other team (I have no idea who we played) I was impressed in a lot of ways. He was a junior and he didn't throw real hard but he had fantastic command. I could see that come to life as I looked at the boxes I was filling in. Everything was off the center of the plate. Nothing went right down the middle. Those guys didn't have much of a chance against him.

I did get some sleep on Wednesday night, but it wasn't very deep. I couldn't stop thinking about what was going to happen the next day. I'd already told Coach that my plan was to keep it really simple. My curve still needed a lot of work and I knew I couldn't paint corners with it or totally keep it down in the zone. So, I was going to attack them with my fastball and use my pretty good change-up as my offspeed pitch.

I have no memory of that day in school. I imagine I didn't pay much attention to what was being taught. I do remember carefully and slowly putting my uniform on in the locker room, and getting on the school bus to head over to Placentia. We had a nice field at Canyon, but if anything the field and ballpark over at El Dorado were even better. As I got off the bus my heart was already racing.

I remember being really nervous, even as I was doing my routine "warm-up" stuff well before game time. I was really pumped up, and I think Coach could see that. Before I started throwing in the bullpen he put his arm around me and said something like, "You look like you're pretty jacked up. I want you to jog to the other foul pole and back, really slowly. We need to get your feet on the ground."

That was great advice, and it did help. I would go on to do that same thing before every game I ever started, and I'll never forget that slow, methodical jog around the warning track.

We were the visitors, so I finished up my warm-ups just as the El Dorado pitcher threw his first pitches in the top of the first. Then I walked toward the dugout trying to take deep slow breaths. When I took a seat on the bench, most of the guys came by to shake hands and say stuff like "Have a good one, Brooksie" or "You belong here, BB. Have fun out there."

When we took the field, I stood on the rubber to make my eight warmup tosses, and home plate never looked so far away. It's weird how that works. In the bullpen it feels like you can hand the ball to the catcher. Out on the mound, he looks like a dot in the distance. I think it's a combination of nerves made worse by the spatial difference. It's the same 60 feet, 6 inches, but it really does look farther away on the real mound.

Somehow I threw eight balls right to my catcher. After I threw the last one, and he threw the ball to second, I spotted Dad and Mom in the stands. They were both standing and clapping.

When the leadoff guy stepped in, my catcher signaled by putting down one finger. That's pretty much the universal sign for a fastball. I took a deep breath, focused on his mitt and threw my first pitch as a high school freshman on the varsity. It went all the way to the backstop and hit the chain-link fence about 10 feet off the ground. It made a stout racket, too.

Holy crap was I embarrassed. I felt like I was out there on the mound with all those people watching and I had just discovered I was naked, like in a bad dream. The problem was, it wasn't a dream. My catcher came out to bring me the ball and said, "Slow down BB. You don't have to throw 100 miles an hour. These guys can't hit your stuff."

The next one was a strike. I ended up striking the kid out with a change-up he couldn't touch.

We won the game, although I can't remember the score. I do know my pitching stats, though, because I wrote them on the last ball I threw, with a ballpoint pen.

- 7 innings pitched
- 4 hits
- 0 runs
- 8 strikeouts
- 2 walks
- 1 hit batter

I was 1-0 in my high school career.

With that first one out of the way, I really felt better my next time out. Coach kept his word and got me a start about every six or seven games. I ended up getting five starts and I won them all.

As a freshman I totally held my own. I wasn't the best pitcher on the team by any stretch, because the curve was a work in progress all year. I threw one to a big kid from El Modena High that's still going. It orbits the planet about twice a day.

48

All in all, it was freaking spectacular to have a season like that as a kid who was just about to turn 15. I have the stats in a scrapbook my mom made for me.

- Games: 5
- Starts: 5
- Innings: 30
- Record: 5-0
- K's: 31
- Walks: 10
- Hits: 18
- HR's: 1

After the last game I pitched, Coach motioned me over to the fence next to the dugout and introduced me to a guy. He said, "Brooks, this is (I don't recall the guy's name) from the Texas Rangers."

I think he was the first scout I ever met, and what struck me was that he was dressed like he should be on the golf course. A bright sport shirt with khaki slacks and loafers. He had on a Panama hat. I shook the man's hand and heard him say, "We're going to keep an eye on you, Brooks. You have a chance to be a heck of a pitcher in a few years. Keep working on that curve and let's try to cut down on the walks a little bit. Keep up the good work, son."

Wow. After the scout left, Coach said something along the lines of, "He's seen you pitch three times. I didn't want you to know until the season was over."

A few days later we had our final face-to-face meetings with Coach Hansen, and during my 15 minutes his big push was all about focus.

"You beat two of the best teams in the conference this year, and in those games you were locked in," he said. "Some very good hitters who will be playing in college next year couldn't touch you. But there were a couple of games when the other team was just OK and you sailed through the first couple of innings, and then you'd lose your focus. It was like it was too easy for you, and maybe that's a good problem to have, but we've got to work on that."

He couldn't have been more right, and I knew it. I could feel it when we'd be playing a really good senior-dominated team and it was like I had tunnel vision. Nothing mattered more than throwing strikes and changing speeds. And then we'd play a team that wasn't as good, and the challenge wasn't there as much. On those days, I'd become a thrower by the third inning. The mental side of the game was way harder on me than the physical side.

Coach finished the meeting by asking me, "Do you have any idea what your fastball velocity was this year?"

I really didn't and we didn't chart that in our books because as a team we didn't yet have a radar gun. The scouts did, though, and Coach said, "The guy from the Rangers and another scout from the Giants showed me the notes they'd written down. In your last

49

game, you were hitting 93 pretty regularly. I think those guys are worried I'll overwork you and you'll break down before they can sign you after your senior year. I told them you and I were on the same page. Let's just work on your pitching, your curve and that focus. You can make a lot of money playing this game, if we keep you healthy."

I played summer ball again, probably making another six or seven starts, but I approached it way differently. I decided stats didn't matter in the summer, so I was going to use that team as a place to help me work on things, especially the curve ball. If it got hit, so what? It went well, and with that relaxed approach I felt like I got a lot better.

Mom was doing great with her art project. She really had the whole process down and was ahead of her timeline enough that she could bug out of the studio in time to catch a lot of my school games in the spring. Summer ball was mostly day games though, since we were out of school, so neither Mom nor Dad got to many of those. That was OK by me. It didn't feel like Canyon High baseball so the vibe wasn't as strong.

Dad was still at Disneyland and they did offer him a higher paying job in the security department. It was totally behind the scenes, though, and he loved his job because it had him right out in the middle of the fun, surrounded by people. For him, it was all about the people. So, totally like my dad, he turned down the promotion. He wanted to keep wearing the brightly colored uniforms and interacting with humans. Staring at security monitors and racing around the park in the tunnels and other areas the public never sees meant nothing to him, no matter how much they paid him.

We got back to school after summer ended and it all felt awesome. Being a sophomore is way more than just being a year older than you were as a freshman. To use a math analogy, it wasn't like 365 days later. It was like 365 days squared. I felt right at home.

Fall ball was great, and I could see that I'd be a much bigger part of the pitching staff in the spring. We lost two really good pitchers to graduation, and both had gone on to play college ball. So, while I was feeling more at home at Canyon, they were starting over as college freshmen trying to make the varsity. That's not easy at Fullerton or Cal Poly Pomona, where those two guys went. That's sort of like the circle of baseball life. For most of your career, there's always the next level.

School was still pretty much smooth sailing for me. Basically all A's and it wasn't that hard to get them. The biggest challenge was English literature. That was seriously more complicated than calculus.

When the holidays rolled around my mom was about 75 percent done with her contract, cranking the originals out a couple per week. Dad took us to a private Christmas party for Disney cast members and that was cool. All the costumed characters were in attendance too, and you can probably imagine how bitchin' the ice carvings were.

When we got back to school we cranked up practices, and when I had my physical I found out I had grown to 6-foot-2 and weighed a stout 160 pounds. I was the starter for our first game and pitched regularly, about once a week. I'm not sure how hard I was throwing (Coach never told me that stuff during the season) but I felt like I was pitching a lot more than throwing, anyway. I was trying to keep my mechanics pure and make the delivery as effortless as possible. When you ramp it up too much, you lose a lot of command. It was obvious to me that I could throw at about 90 percent of my max and still get guys out, because it allowed me to hit the corners more. The curve was coming along, too, and the change-up was killer.

That season seems like much more of a blur than my freshman year for a couple of really big reasons. First, as a frosh I was soaking it all in and burning as many details as possible into my memory. Sophomore year, it was just about pitching and getting better, and I knew my focus was a little sharper. I'd still have a few games where it came too easy and my mind would wander, but the difference was I'd realize it during the game and usually could make the correction.

The second big reason was Mom. About halfway through the spring she started having real bad headaches. At first we thought it was migraines, or maybe it was just being around the paint and oils so much. They weren't too bad at first, but they got progressively worse through March and into April.

To make things worse, the hotel developer finally struck out on the financing, and the project was stopped. Mom had finished about 90 percent of her work. She got her last paycheck and that was it, but she wasn't as crushed as I thought she'd be. After all, the paintings she did were all going away anyway. The developer sold them to a big national luxury hotel chain. We never found out which chain, but for years after that I'd always check out the artwork in hotel lobbies whenever I'd stay in a nice place. I never saw a single piece she did.

And the headaches got worse. By the middle of May she couldn't take it. Dad took her to the hospital because he didn't want her to go through it anymore. They ran tests and couldn't figure it out. Then she had a seizure during one of the tests and they ran her over to intensive care. I was at school, and when the principal came into one of my classes to get me, I'll never forget the look on his face.

I didn't have a driver's license yet, much less a car, so the principal himself drove me to the hospital. I found my dad in the waiting room outside intensive care and he looked really shaken. I'd never seen him like that in my entire life.

All he said was, "They're working with her now. She had a seizure during an episode, right at the time they were running some tests. They're not sure what this is all about."

The whole thing was a mess and my head was spinning. The look on my principal's face had scared me enough. The look on Dad's face petrified me.

I finally got to see Mom, and although she looked awful she was at least pain free and able to talk to us.

"They're not sure yet, but I'm going to be here for a day or two getting more tests," she said. "Can you guys handle bachelor life for a couple of days?"

My dad made it clear that he wasn't going anywhere. He drove me home and then went right back. I felt so sick to my stomach I thought I was going to throw up, but he called me from her room and told me to hang in there.

"She's going to be OK, bud," he said. "We'll get to the bottom of this and get it fixed for her. You get yourself to school tomorrow."

The next day I sleep-walked through classes, but I did have my end-of-season meeting with Coach Hansen.

51

My stats were pretty good.

- Games: 10
- Starts: 10
- Innings: 62
- Record: 9-1
- K's: 72
- Walks: 18
- Hits: 49
- HR's: 2

Coach praised all the improvements I'd made, saying, "We talked about all of this a year ago and you really got after it. You're the best pitcher in the conference, and probably in the region, so just keep trying to get better and good things are going to happen for you. I know what you're going through with your mom, so focus on that and put your glove and spikes away for a while. Your family comes first. Remember that, Brooks. You're a wonderful young man who loves his momma. Take care of her first, and be there for your dad. You could probably use a summer off, anyway."

I appreciated that, but I had no idea what was coming in the very near future. It was the biggest challenge of my life to that point.

CHAPTER 10

Eric Olson

The fall of my freshman year just would not come soon enough. I was chomping so hard on the bit to make the B Team it seemed like time was standing still. To make it worse, back then we still had almost nothing in the way of off-season facilities, so we weren't just waiting for school to start. We had to wait all the way until October, when they could install the ice.

As a hockey player I knew I was still undersized, but I didn't let my height and weight get me down. I didn't obsess over it, either. I was what I was, and at about 5-foot-6 nearing 140 pounds, that's what I was. We didn't have our heights marked on a door frame at our house like a lot of kids in Roseau did, so I didn't really pay too much attention to it. I knew, deep inside, that the dream of being a Roseau Ram was right there in front of me, and I'd just have to keep working my butt off and keep getting better.

It was one of my twin brothers who gave me the phrase "win every race" and it stuck with me. When the puck went into the corner, I had to win the race to it. If I was playing the point in the offensive zone, and the puck was ringing around the boards in my direction, I had to win two races. First, I had to win the mental race and instantly decide if I was going to pinch and try to hold the puck in or get back to play D. Then I had to win the race to the puck or to the defensive zone. Win every race.

I couldn't exactly rough anybody up out there, so it was still all about getting there first, being a pest and never leaving anything in the tank. I took that so far that just getting off the ice after a shift was a race. The faster I could get to the bench, the faster we could get fresh legs on the ice. All of it was a race.

There was another race going on at the time and it was between me and the day the ice would be installed at the Memorial Arena and the North Rink next door. It felt like a race stuck in the mud because time just would not pass.

The school year finally started, and again that's another thing in Roseau that's different than what a lot of kids experience. The actual school was a building I had known and attended since kindergarten. In the fall of 1980 I just moved to a new hallway and a new locker, in a different corner of the overall school. It didn't feel much different, and to be honest I can't really imagine what it would feel like to spend six years in an elementary school and then have to switch to a whole new school for two years, before having to switch again for four years of high school. I just walked the same path to school and back home each day, ate in the same cafeteria, and played basketball in the same gym.

In terms of our home life, that was changing a little, too. With David Jr. off at St. Cloud State, Brent and Jon graduating from the high school that spring, and Betsy a year ahead of me, we were all getting to be grown up enough that Mom thought it was OK to add some more hours at work and, at the same time, take the load off our grandparents. We didn't need a lot of oversight by then.

I can't totally speak for my older brothers, especially with Dave down in St. Cloud learning about things college kids learn about, but I think it's fair to say we were all good kids and could be trusted. Betsy and I looked out for each other. OK, she still looked out for me. She was taller than me and always would be and on any given day could still whip me on the basketball court or the golf course. I can close my eyes and remember the exact sound her driver made when she teed off. It was the purest click, and mine didn't sound quite like that. Her form was darn near perfect.

Jon and Brent were finally coming to the end of organized hockey. They were good, and could've gone on to play at a small school, but that just wasn't in their hearts. They liked hockey a lot, but they didn't live for it. They each had girlfriends at the time, and they really didn't want to leave, so they decided to stay in Roseau and get jobs. That was a real difference between us. I couldn't imagine life without hockey, and I was just about to get my chance to live my dream as a Roseau Ram. They graduated from high school and just left it behind, other than some pick-up games and alumni stuff.

Jon and Brent enjoyed their last summer after school, and near the end of it they both went to work for Dad at the hardware store, which finally gave the man who raised us a chance to slow down a bit. He'd been running the show there my whole life, and it was beginning to show in the lines on his face and a lack of the nonstop energy I thought he would always have. The perfect man was starting to look tired, and a bit beaten down.

It would be the first time any of us would work there during the day when school was in session. For my brothers, it was a way to ease into life after school, because we had all helped out there as kids and they could keep living at home. I think they planned to stay there and take it over from Dad someday but, like a lot of Roseau kids, if it was time to do something different Polaris was always just down the street.

Me? All I could think about was hockey and, when I could fall asleep, I dreamed about it.

September seemed to take about a year to end. School was fine, like it always was, but now I was at least eating in the cafeteria with other high school guys and girls. That was the one major thing I couldn't help but notice. After nine years of eating off trays with a bunch of other young kids, as a freshman I could find myself sitting next to guys

54

who were over 6 feet tall or near girls who were definitely not "little girls" anymore. I hadn't really paid much attention to girls up until then. Hockey was more important, I guess. But hey, some of them were kind of cute. That's what's unique about freshman year. It was kind of strange to be feeling so much older, to actually be in Roseau High, while all of a sudden I also felt really small and young at the same time. That gap, from 14 to 18, is a huge chunk of your life at the time and those are years where you change about as much as you ever will.

I also noticed that a lot of guys around my age were starting to go through growth spurts. They'd come to school looking like they did the year before, but by the next month their pants would be too short and they'd be an inch or two taller. I kept waiting on my own growth spurt, but it never seemed to happen. I didn't know it at the time, but at that point in my life I was already within three inches of being as tall as I'd ever be, gaining about an inch every year after freshman year. I would never be more than a bit over 5-foot-9.

Mercifully, they started to build the ice about a week into October. Even that process felt like agony to me, but it was a fun type of agony. Making good ice is a slow process, and since we were going to be playing games on it, the process was even slower and more detailed. It wouldn't just have to be a smooth sheet of hard ice. It would need to be white and have regulation lines, circles and dots on it.

Word shot around school the morning they started to spray the first coat of water on the refrigerated floor. Guys would duck out at lunch or between classes and come back with updates like, "Second coat of water going on right now. The white will go on late this afternoon!"

"The white" is the white paint that goes on after the first couple of sprays. It's not easy making good ice, because you need to have it exactly the right thickness, your refrigeration unit has to be working perfectly, and it doesn't hurt to have your building located in a cold climate. Keeping good ice when it's hot outside is not easy. We rarely had to worry about that.

Once the white paint is mixed with water and sprayed on, it freezes white and you're getting close. Once it's fully frozen, you can start painting the lines. That's where patience and artwork come in. It's not that much different today than it was when I was at Roseau. It's all done by hand, very carefully. All the lines have to be straight, the circles have to be perfectly round, and the dots need to be where they have to be. When it's first completed, it looks incredible. Then, every time the ice is cleaned by the Zamboni throughout the winter, the lines and circles get just a little bit less distinct and it all looks a little blurry. And once the ice is all in, it isn't as thick as most people think. The first day when skates hit the surface, it's usually about an inch or inch and a half thick, with the white and the lines way below the surface, maybe at the eighth-inch mark. You don't want skate blades to be able to cut deep enough to get to the paint.

When we heard late in the afternoon that they had flooded the last layers and were about to run the Zamboni over the Memorial Arena ice one last time, about 20 of us sprinted the few blocks over to the building to see it. It was like seeing the decorated tree and all the gifts on Christmas morning. I clearly remember feeling a tingle run from the back of my neck down my spine. I'd waited my whole life to be in a position to play hockey as a Roseau Ram, and there it was. All summer it sat there, just a gray concrete floor. Right then, it became a hockey rink. Our hockey rink. It was the neatest thing I'd ever seen.

And here's a funny side story about making ice. If you watched the 1980 "Miracle on Ice" Olympics you might recall there were two hockey venues, and that sometimes the USA played on a perfectly white sheet of ice, but when they played in the main Lake Placid arena the ice had big swatches of blue in it. According to the hockey producer at ABC, he wanted to add some blue dye to the white to make the rink look more "telegenic" and not so overwhelmingly bright. At the time, a lot of Americans didn't know much about hockey, and it was a tough sport to televise because of how white the ice was. The cameras at the time couldn't handle the contrast. But, they didn't get the blue on very evenly and it just looked odd. The rink that hosted the USA vs. the Soviets and the gold medal game against Finland had big blue splotches all over it. That's one detail they didn't get right in the movie "*Miracle*." They showed the rink as being fully bright white.

A few days later at school, the varsity held their open tryout but I don't think any of us freshmen went to that. If Paul Broten didn't go, and he has always said he didn't, then I can't imagine any of the rest of us thinking it was worthwhile. The varsity was stacked, and very deep. None of us had a chance, especially a 5-foot-6 defenseman.

A few days later, we had our first practice for the B team. You could call us the JV, too, because the terms were basically interchangeable. As I wrote, the adjustment to the B team wasn't that big of a leap because almost all of us had been playing together for a lot of years, and getting better together over that time. One difference was having sophomores at practice. With the varsity being so good, only the very best sophomores made that team. We had at least five or six with us on the B team, back for their second year, so that marked the first time I ever played hockey with guys who had already worn the Roseau sweater.

On the first day of practice, I remember a bunch of the sophomores being pretty unfriendly once they saw how I played. More than once I heard "It's just practice" or "It's only the first day, take it easy kid." The guys my age just looked at me and smiled. A number of them skated by and said, "Just do what you do, Oly."

I don't remember a lot of the actual drills, but those things really don't change that much over the years. Lots of down-and-back skating, lots of pylons to skate around, and then the coaches would break us down and begin to work on plays. How to enter the zone efficiently and without being offside. How to clear the defensive zone without giving up the puck. How to stay in your lane but be willing to hit an open spot on the ice if the play was there. Up until then, just about all the way up through youth hockey, the coaches were more focused on the fundamentals and they didn't want us freelancing too much. It was more "You go here, you go there, and you guys stay back there" because we weren't experienced enough to really ad lib and find open spaces. Early in the weeks of practice that freshman year, we were already seeing the game at a different level and gelling as a team that could handle the fundamentals while we learned how to stretch the ice and get behind the defense.

I was never much of an offensive defenseman, and mostly that had to do with my size and with a series of coaches who figured that forwards scored, the D-men stayed back, and the goalie was your last line of defense. They preached that so much I was basically afraid to go forward too much. I mean, what if I went forward and the other team got behind me? Those are usually races you can't win.

I got my first taste of how different it was going to be when I was put on the first unit for the power play as the only defensemen out there. Just little ol' me and four sophomore forwards. I'd man the point, but we were learning rotation plays that moved us all around so I had to get out of my comfort zone quite a bit.

I was also on the penalty kill unit, but I expected to be out there, where winning the races and blocking shots would be the key to keeping the puck out of the net.

After three or four weeks of practice, and a lot of conditioning, we were getting close to our first game. When the uniforms were handed out, I held my sweater in my hands like it was made of gold. There it was. It seemed to glisten and almost glow as I held it out in front of me. The word Roseau was across the front and the number 11 was on the back. The number thing was just random, but I liked it and I knew right then I'd try to keep it on the varsity if I could. Of course, I'd have to make the varsity at some point, but by the start of that freshman season I was gaining confidence daily.

We opened at home against Thief River Falls. Everything about that day is still pretty clear in my head. I remember it being a Friday and there being a lot of handmade signs in the hallways at school. We walked like nervous zombies through our classes but being the JV we had our final class turned into a study hall, because the teachers knew we'd be useless as students. The varsity was opening at home too and we had to play our game before they played theirs, so by 3:00 we were absolutely wired.

The Roseau Memorial Arena feels really massive when you're inside, because of the arched ceiling of huge wooden beams. But the areas under the grandstands, where they put the locker rooms, are really pretty cramped, especially when a full roster of players are all getting dressed at the same time. It gets kind of steamy in there, and as we got closer to heading out onto the ice for warm-ups, I think we were all soaking wet with sweat. It was the kind of sweat that comes from nerves, excitement and a hot room. We couldn't wait to get out there.

When it was time to go out for warm-ups, I think I was shaking. I'd been walking on skates since I could walk at all, but it felt like my ankles were wobbly as I walked down the rubber runners in the cramped hall and out through the door and into the bright lights. When I went out on the ice, I did the typical little "hop and run" step to get going and all of that seemed to go away. We skated furiously around our zone, going faster and faster, before we started passing pucks around and taking shots at our goalie, Don Johnson, who must've sensed these shots were coming in a little harder than they did at practice. I know we all felt like we were shooting harder.

I took a moment to look in the stands and I found Mom, Dad, Jon and Betsy. Brent drew the short straw and stayed at the hardware store to close up. With the varsity playing right after us, there weren't going to be many customers anyway. As I nodded and they clapped for me, BAM! A puck hit me right in the skate and about knocked me over. It was from one of the sophomores, and as he skated by he said, "Game's out here, Olson." I got the point.

We finished our warm-ups, they played a scratchy version of the national anthem, and the few hundred people who were there to see the new Roseau JV stood and sang along. And then they dropped the puck. I was out there to start, playing defense on the right side. I remember our forwards winning the draw and heading off to the other end. I glided up the ice, basically scared to death that some Thief River kid was going to get behind me and score before I even knew what happened. All those youth coaches had really drilled the whole "stay at home" thing into me.

When Thief River got the puck and came toward us, they shot it in and I had my first race. I beat their forward to the puck and got it back out of there. No one even touched me. I'd handled my first puck in my first high school game, but my shift wasn't over. Our guys were flying up the ice and I trailed. I remember it like it was yesterday. They had the puck deep, and then behind the net. I was at the blue line and I crossed it, officially then in enemy territory, on the right point.

When the play shifted to the left corner, most of the players couldn't help but slide that way. And one of our forwards saw me, wide open at the top of the circle. He fired a diagonal cross-ice pass and I never even thought about it. I stopped it and fired that puck on the net. I never had any intention of scoring. I was just trying to get it on goal to create a rebound. But a crazy thing happened. It went right past the goalie and into the net. In the first minute of my high school career I had scored a goal. The one guy on the ice who was least likely to score a goal had made it 1-0 Roseau. I remember letting out a big "Woo Hoo!" and that wasn't something I planned. It just came out. It was neat to be mobbed by all the guys, too. "Attaboy Oly!" sounded sweet.

OK, so here's the funny part. I know we won but I don't remember the score. That was the only shot I took, and I don't recall ever getting beaten (too badly) on defense. It was still the same hockey I'd always played, but it was different. It was better. I won most of the races, and I emptied the tank to a level I never knew was there. I was a Roseau Ram, and I knew I belonged. I don't think I fell asleep that night until 3 or 4 in the morning.

That JV winter went by in a blur. For the first time in my life I wasn't looking forward to spring or summer vacation. I just wanted to keep playing, no matter how cold and dark it was. How cold and dark was it? Well, on the rides in our school bus to places like Thief River Falls, Bemidji, Brainerd and even Warroad, just 20 short miles away, the bus would never warm up. It was drafty and cold. It had to be. It had a lousy heater and when it was 10-below outside and all the windows were rattling from the gaps in their frames, it was going to be cold.

If it was cold on the way over, it was bizarre on the way back. We'd all still be sweaty and overheated and the bus would fog up almost before we were on the road. The driver had to put every ounce of heat on the windshield just to see, and the windows by our seats would fog up and then freeze solid. So much so that if it was a long ride back (Bemidji is one of the closer rivals, and it's a solid two hours and 20 minutes south) the ice on the windows could get as thick as a quarter-inch or more, and it always felt like it was hard to breathe in there. We'd put our hands on the windows to try to melt the ice, and if you did that starting when the ice wasn't too thick, you could keep a hand-shaped open spot clear. Not that there was that much to see out there on a dark northern Minnesota night, but it was something to do to pass the time.

We rode the bus a lot. During the regular season we never spent the night anywhere, and four-hour rides back to school were pretty regular. We could generally fit the varsity and the JV in one bus, because we only had about 15 guys on the JV, but we also loved it when our band came along for away games. When they did, we'd caravan with a couple of school buses and a trailer for their instruments. Those games were great.

In the end, I think I played well. I scored one more goal late in the season, but I concentrated on my defense and I could feel how much better I was getting week by week. I was getting stronger, and in much better condition, too. When you're just little kids, the coaches don't work that much on the conditioning. You're just kids, and it seems like you're never tired. But once we got to high school, we found out just how "in shape" we could be. They skated us a lot. And we got better and faster.

I think our record was around 15-5 or something like that. In today's digital age, it's hard to believe that stats were kept on handwritten sheets of paper. When you're on the JV, you felt lucky if anyone kept the score. It's hard to find those records, and they might not even exist anymore, but I know we won most of our games and our coaches really worked hard with us.

After our final game, Coach Hokanson from the varsity came in to talk to us in the locker room.

"Boys, you did a great job this year," he said. "I've been watching, and I like what I see. There are going to be some open spots on the varsity next year, and I can already see that a number of you are going to be ready to make the move up. But here's the thing to remember, boys. Just like this year, there are going to be more guys wanting to fill those spots than there will be spots available. Some of you will have to come back to the JV. The ones who work the hardest might just be up with us. Stay in shape, get those grades and work on your moves. We'll leave the ice in as long as we can and you're all free to use it whenever the lights are on."

The varsity, that year, made the state tournament once again, but lost in the first round. It was going to take forever for October to roll around again.

CHAPTER 11

Brooks Bennett

We thought Mom was doing better, and for a while I guess she was. Maybe it was just Dad and me hoping she was. She came home and had a couple of good days, but then another horrible headache smashed her and it was kind of hard to be in denial. Something was wrong.

The most beautiful and vibrant woman I've ever known couldn't get out of bed. She couldn't stand any sort of bright light at all. She just had to lie there in the dark. There was no way she could take showers. She couldn't wash her beautiful auburn hair, and it just fell flat instead of tumbling so gently on her shoulders. She was a naturally gorgeous woman who hardly ever wore makeup, and she was the sort of person who had a glow about her. Right then, though, the glow was gone.

I was totally worried and before long I couldn't even sleep. Nothing in my wonderful love-filled life prepared me for something so scary. I worried about my dad, too, because he was so full of fear and I'd never seen him like that. Those deep, soulful James Taylor eyes looked different and confused. He wanted nothing more than to be by her side and make her better, but he needed to keep working because without Disney we'd have no medical insurance. Dad and I hugged each other each day, when he'd have to head to his job.

Mom seemed to bounce back from each episode, and that gave us hope, but I don't think she ever recovered all the way back to how she was before each one hit. Every horrible headache left a little less of her. It was horrifying. Just a couple months before, I was pitching in big games for Canyon High and life was perfect. Then it all just fell off a cliff.

When the next one hit, Dad took her to the best medical center in Orange County, and they kept her for a week. I was by then just getting to be old enough to get my driver's license and I could've used Mom's VW to go see her every day, but with all that was going on we just didn't have the time or the energy for me to go take the test. All I could do was visit her when Dad could pick me up and take me along.

I was with him the day a very stern-looking doctor, wearing a starched white coat and wire-rimmed glasses, came in to see us. I think my heart stopped, because I could just tell he had bad news. I don't think any of us were breathing.

He started talking, quietly at first.

"Mrs. Bennett, we're still not totally sure what's going on but we've ruled out standard migraines," he said. "Those are horrible enough, but this is certainly worse. We're relatively sure it's a brain condition, and if it's brain cancer or we find any sort of tumor within your brain, those are not easy things to overcome. We're going to do what we call a CT scan. It's a relatively new machine that can give us a look around in there without having to do any dangerous surgery. It's totally painless and safe."

You think you're prepared for moments like that. You are never prepared for moments like that. I had just turned 16 a few days before. I can't imagine any 16-year-old who loved his mother as much as I did could ever be prepared to hear that. My dad tried to lift us all up. His positive outlook on everything had carried us through so much, maybe it could help us now.

"Look, this is a good thing," he said, with a forced smile. "This scan will give us answers. If we have answers we can address the problem. We have access to phenomenal doctors, and if they can pinpoint what's wrong, they'll fix it. We're gonna fix this. It's gonna be OK."

They scheduled the scan for the next day.

Dad was scheduled to work that day, but his supervisor generously gave him the day off with pay. We were at Mom's side by 9 in the morning. At 11 they wheeled her away and headed for the CT scan room. Why on earth do I remember that the gurney had a squeaky wheel?

Dad and I waited. It didn't take that long, actually, but during stress like that a half-hour goes by very slowly. We hardly spoke at all, which is definitely not like us. We mostly just stared at the floor with our elbows on our knees.

When they wheeled her back in, I think both Dad and I figured the doctor would be there too and give us the answers we were craving. Maybe spell out a course of action to make her better. Instead, the nurses just dropped her off and said the doctor would be in to see us in an hour or two. More waiting, but at least this time Mom was with us.

She said it had been super easy. She just kept still while the machine did all the work. There were a few comments from the doctor to the nurses, she said, but that they were all medical and technical. Her most pointed comment was, "They're real professionals. I could tell they're very well trained to keep emotion out of it. I couldn't tell if they were thrilled or mortified."

A couple of hours later, the doctor came in with that same stone-face look. He had news.

"Mrs. Bennett, we saw a mass in your brain during the scan, and analyzed it a bit more after we were done," he said. "It's not too big, but it's in a really tough place. If I was the only specialist in the world, I'd still have a hard time calling it anything other than inoperable. The risks associated with going in there are enormous.

61

"Here's my recommendation. There's one place in the United States that is ahead of everyone else in terms of these kinds of things. I'd strongly recommend that you go to the Mayo Clinic."

I blurted out, "What's that? How far is it from here?"

"It's in Minnesota," he said. "Rochester, Minnesota. It's the best medical center in the world."

My mom had her eyes closed. My dad and I looked at each other like we were two mannequins. Just blank faces. The doctor might as well have said "It's on the moon." We were too stunned to comprehend what he'd just said, on so many damn levels.

Mom is really sick. It's something in her brain. They can't operate. There's no pill to make it better. They want her to go to Minnesota. It was too much to absorb in the span of five minutes.

The doctor left us and we all shared a hug. As he always was, Dad was the rock.

"There you go," he said. "Now we have some answers. Now we can move forward and fix all of this. If the Mayo Clinic is the best place for you to go, my love, you're going to the Mayo Clinic. We'll make it work. I don't know how yet, but we'll make it work."

She just nodded. I just stared up at the ceiling, as if that might help me keep from crying. When the first big tear rolled down one cheek, there was no stopping it. I felt like a 5-year-old who had lost his mommy at the grocery store. It was the biggest, scariest challenge our little family had ever faced.

I should take a minute here to write about a subject I really haven't touched on yet. That would be grandparents. To be honest, they weren't really part of my life. I never met my mom's parents. They were pretty old when they had her. I think they were 40 when she was born, and she came 11 years after her only sister. By the time my mom and dad were getting married, her folks were over 60 and in bad shape.

My mom's mother died just a month before I was born. Both of Mom's folks smoked like the chimneys at a power plant and no one much cared about nutrition. They ate a lot of heavy, fatty stuff, according to Mom, and that had a lot to do with her being so health conscious. She watched her mom and dad start their decline when she was still in elementary school and her way of rebelling was to get into healthy foods and avoid cigarettes. She needed to be her anti-parents, I guess.

After her mom passed, her dad went only four months later, not long after I was born. With me being just a baby, Mom couldn't even go home for the funeral and she'd missed her mom's services too, because she didn't want to fly when she was that far into her pregnancy. There's also the fact we were pretty broke back then. Mom liked to blame it on inconvenience and timing, but I don't think there's any way around it that she really couldn't afford to go.

My dad's folks weren't much different, but they'd at least had him at a younger age. I met them once, when they came out to California, but they were like distant strangers to me. They didn't even look like anyone I knew in SoCal. And they talked funny, too. To me, it was like they were from another country. My dad's father died when I was 6, of a heart attack, and his mother suffered from severe dementia before she passed about six years later.

I remember when my grandfather died, and it was strange to see my dad clearly crushed by it but also sort of defiant. He told me, in harsh words, that his parents had never condoned the California thing. They'd offered no support of any kind. They basically erased him from the family until that one time they came to visit. That was supposed to be a healing trip but I remember being very nervous and upset about it, because no one smiled the whole time they were there.

We never once went back to Erie to see anyone. Dad always said, "I don't belong there" and I think there was a ton of lingering resentment from parents, siblings, cousins and friends back in Pennsylvania. Like they felt my mom and dad selfishly deserted them. All my parents wanted was a better life but a lot of people back there had the mentality of "This is the home we have. This is where we're from" and never left. I don't recall, at any time in my life, hearing much about communications with anyone back in Erie.

So I never knew any different, but I think it was hard on both Mom and Dad that she was so seriously ill and there really wasn't much in the way of family to help ease the pain. It was just the three of us. We were all we had. And now we were going to have to figure out how to move to Minnesota.

At first, Dad was totally overwhelmed by it. I had no experience seeing him looking that confused and, well – mortal.

"I gotta look on a map, just like you," he told me. "I think Rochester is like 50 miles south of Minneapolis and St. Paul. Those are called the Twin Cities. Did you know that?"

I told him I'd heard of them in geography class but I didn't know much about them. I think I asked: "Are they really like totally identical cities?"

He said he didn't think so, but they were really close to each other. And St. Paul was the state capital. That rang a bell from geography class, too. I was going to have to do a lot of research, but we also had to be in a hurry. Mom needed to get to Mayo quickly.

Dad wasn't close to any of his distant relatives either but he could remember having a cousin who also left Erie to take a marketing job with General Mills at their headquarters in Minneapolis. His name was Don, and Dad said he was really smart and destined to be somewhere else too, but they barely knew each other and Dad hadn't spoken or corresponded with him since he was in high school and Don was at Penn State.

I'm not sure how you found people like that back then. We'd never heard of Facebook or Google. I think I remember Dad saying he called 411 information and asked for the Minneapolis and St. Paul area. He asked if any Don Bennetts showed up there. There were numerous Don or Donald Bennett listings. He wrote down all of them.

Can you even imagine that? He had a cousin he hardly knew and hadn't seen for decades. The last time he'd seen him was right before the guy got a great job at a Fortune 500 company and then moved to the Twin Cities. Dad had to start calling all those numbers just to see if one was a cousin. It had been like 20 years since Don moved there. I wouldn't have bet on Dad's odds. I didn't like the odds of the guy even still living in Minneapolis. Heck, he might not be alive.

Dad started the calls when we got Mom back home. I helped her into bed and we talked with the shades drawn. I told her how much I loved her and how she and Dad meant everything to me. I told her she had no idea what a wonderful life they'd given me. I wouldn't trade it for millions of dollars and a mansion. I wouldn't trade it for anything. And growing up with very little in the way of money or possessions had made me understand that all that stuff was worth nothing. The love and care I had in my house was priceless.

And then I did my best impression of my dad, telling her, "We're going to beat this. We'll get the best help in the world and you're going to be OK. I just know it." I'm not sure if I sold that or not, but she gave me a look that was mostly "You're just like your father" and that meant the world to me.

It wasn't worth talking about the fact Dad would have to quit a job he loved that also provided benefits. How we were going to be able to pay for her care was way beyond a mystery to me. I figured Dad would somehow make it happen. He always did. Mom needed the care. We needed Mom.

When I came out of her room I heard him talking, and I eavesdropped from the hallway for a while. I heard a lot of "OK, thank you anyway. Sorry to bother you. Have a great day" responses before the sound of the wall phone being hung up.

I don't know how many numbers he had written down, but the calls just kept going, and they kept getting him nowhere. I went to my room.

I don't know if it was subconscious or what, but I swore I could hear his voice elevate even though my door was closed and he was down in the kitchen. I waited for him to hang up and then sprinted down there.

"I did it dude, I found him," he said. "He's still in the Twin Cities but not in Minneapolis anymore. He lives in the suburb of Bloomington, and five years ago he left General Mills to open his own marketing and promotions agency. He said it's a challenge but he's doing well."

My dad then excitedly told me about the rest of the call. He said Don was interested in why he'd tracked him down and Dad had to say, "Well, it's not a good reason at all but I need some advice from someone I can trust in Minnesota."

He told his cousin about Mom and Mayo Clinic. He told me that his strategy was just to ask for advice, not ask for any favors. He said, "When you ask for advice, you'll learn in a hurry who wants to help or not, and you don't put them on the spot."

He said Don was great, and very understanding. Dad told him that he was going to try to find a furnished apartment in Rochester, and he asked him if he knew what high schools had good baseball programs.

"I told him that I didn't think Rochester was the place for you," Dad told me. "The competition isn't going to be good enough playing all the teams from those small towns down there. I told him I want you to go to school in the Twin Cities and if he could tell me which schools had good programs I'd be able to call the coaches and tell them about you, maybe get you enrolled right away.

"I told Don I'd handle all of that," Dad went on. "And, it was my hope that after

64

the coaches heard about you and talked to your coach out here, they'd be willing to find a family that would host you. Hopefully a family that included another Bloomington baseball player your age. Do you think you could do that?"

I impulsively said, "I know I can do it, but that's not the issue. It's just that I don't want to do it. I want to be with you and Mom. I don't care if the competition isn't as good in Rochester. That just means I'll strike out more guys and win more games. I want to be with you!"

He said, "Look, man. This is the most important thing you can do right now. Mom is either going to get better or she's not, and you can come down to spend as much time in Rochester as you want. But dude, you are THIS CLOSE to being ready for professional baseball. You're going to be lost in the woods in Rochester. The scouts will all find you in the Twin Cities.

"Don is going to dig into it for me. He said he'll call me back tomorrow with some recommendations. This is going to be hard for all of us, and we're all sacrificing just about everything right now, but I want you to succeed. It's what you're here for. It's what you're destined to do. You were born to be a pitcher and we want you to have the best opportunity to be the greatest pitcher you can be. Will you do that?"

I told him I couldn't handle that decision right then and there. I needed to process it and think about it. He gave me a hug and said, "Yeah, you're right. We've handled a lot lately, changing our lives in too many ways. Let's all think it through, but Mom has to get to Mayo. That part we know."

I went to bed early, but I stayed up very late. I don't believe I fell asleep until close to 6 in the morning. I'd never felt such pressure in my head. Everything was out of control, including the health of my incredible mother. All the answers seem wrong and awful. It was like: "What did we do to deserve this? Why my mother? Why us?" It felt like I was spiraling down into some very dark place.

Sometime after I looked at the clock at 5:30, I sensed an answer. A wave of what I can only describe as "peace" came over me, and I don't use the term "wave" frivolously. When you're surfing on nice gentle waves, it feels like they're caressing you. They're holding you. It's a corny term but you really are one with the waves. After about two hours of sleep I got up when I could hear my dad talking on the phone. When he was done I went downstairs. He said, "Can we talk?"

I just nodded. Throughout most of the night the thing that had kept me up the most was knowing he was going to want to talk. Until 5:30 in the morning I just wanted the whole nightmare to go away like some magic trick.

"I just got off the phone with Don," he said. "Basically, the guy is a saint. Here's the deal…"

My dad then proceeded to tell me many things, in a jumbled sort of order.

Don's new company was based in Bloomington. He lived there, too, in a roomy house made roomier by the fact he'd gone through a divorce a couple years ago. John F. Kennedy High, in Bloomington, had a great baseball program, playing top competition. Kent Hrbek, a young star for the Minnesota Twins, had gone to Kennedy and in just three years after graduating he was in the big leagues. Most importantly, Don said to my dad, "I don't know about finding a family for Brooks to stay with, but I know there's a full bedroom with an attached bath here at my house. It's a mother-in-law suite that's a whole wing of the house and it's sitting empty. He's more than welcome to stay for as long or short as you need. He's family. He's welcome here."

Dad looked me in the eye and said, "Again, just like the move up here to Anaheim, you don't have to do this. But Mom has to go to Rochester. Would it feel better for you to stay here with another Canyon family, or go to Minnesota and live with my cousin? Think about it."

I didn't have to. I'd decided during that late night that we all had to be close to one another and I couldn't possibly stay in California. That was the peace I felt. The nightmare was awful, but it was reality.

"No, Dad. I know what to do," I said. "We're all going to Minnesota together, and Bloomington is where I should be. I need to get my driver's license as soon as we get there, so I can come down to Rochester whenever possible. What am I gonna do for a car, though?"

Dad had the answer. "Don has a second car you can drive. I would bet it's pretty nice, too. Sounds like he did very well at General Mills and now his agency is taking off."

I decided to call Coach the next day. The timetable for this deal was really short and he wasn't going to like what I had to say. And, not only was I leaving, I was going to ask him to call the coach in Bloomington to let him know I was coming and what my skills were.

The next day, Don called again with more saintly news. He'd taken the initiative to contact Mayo and he asked them a lot of questions my dad needed answers for. He let them know the circumstances and asked how the clinic handles patients like my mom, and the cost for the care. There were options, it turned out.

One option was charity. There were a number of independent charities that worked hand-in-hand with Mayo to help establish funding for families with no insurance. Mayo itself had such a charity. There were applications and time-consuming evaluations, but it was possible.

Another option was something called "experimental treatment and evaluations." Most of the fees could be waived if the patient agreed to participate in some experimental research projects. Don said the Mayo people were pretty clear about one thing. Everyone needed to know right up front that research like that has to have patients that are trying experimental treatment, as well as those who are the control group. That's a fancy way of saying some patients would think they were getting the new treatments when they actually weren't. There was no guarantee that my mom would be getting the experimental treatments.

Don had also asked about furnished apartments near Mayo, and it turned out there were plenty of them. A lot of other families were in the same position as us. People needed to be near the ones they loved. I remember thinking it was a gruesome way to be a landlord, but there really was a need.

While all that was going on, we had other important things to do.

I called Coach and let him know. He was sad to see me go, but he said, "You take care of your momma, Brooksie. You're doing the right thing. You're a fine young man. Now, I'll talk to the coach at Kennedy and tell him he just got about 10 wins smarter with you joining his team."

We both got a laugh out of that. I needed one.

Dad called our landlord and let him know the situation. He told me he said to the owner, "Look, I know we're not giving the sort of notice you need and we're basically breaking our lease, so I don't expect the deposit back. And honestly we can't move our furniture, so you can have that too." The owner of our house said, "I couldn't sleep at night doing that. You're free to go as soon as you can, and I'll bring the deposit to you tomorrow, plus I'll bring some cash and we'll figure out what your furniture is worth. I'll buy it."

We were surrounded by a bunch of saints.

There was just so much more to do, and so little time. But Dad had one more surprise for his only son.

"Listen dude," he said. "We're getting up at first light tomorrow. We're grabbing our boards and our wetsuits and heading down to San Clemente. We need a few hours in the water. It's like medicine for us. We need to surf one last time. Are ya in, dude?"

I was very in.

CHAPTER 12

Eric Olson

When the JV season ended I did something that was pretty rare for me, up until that point in my life. I rested.

Growing up through all the youth hockey levels it seemed like we all had endless energy. After my first season in high school I could tell it was different. I woke up the day after that final game and didn't want to get out of bed. That was not an Olson trait, trust me. I could tell I was tired and my muscles finally told me "Take a break." It wasn't just the physicality of the games, and that JV season was the most physically rough season I'd ever had; it was the way I approached practice, too. I went flat out every day, and I wound myself up with that will to succeed. That morning, my brain and my body got together and convinced me that the best thing was for me to spend a few weeks recovering.

I mostly just went to school and came home, or maybe hung out with my dad and brothers at the hardware store. When our season ended it was still winter in Roseau, even if the calendar said spring, and I would go skate a few times a week at Memorial Arena or the North Rink, but for me that was taking it easy. I wasn't doing down-and-backs or any skating drills. I was just keeping my edge and skating, like a lot of kids do on a Friday night at the local rink.

Once the weather warmed up, it felt like my body was bouncing back right along with the temperature. It was time to get busy again. And it was time for my twin brothers to have a talk with me.

Jon and Brent asked me to go golfing with them right after the course opened in late spring. I thought that sounded great, but I didn't know they had a plan for me when they asked.

As we shook the rust off and played our first round of the year, they spelled it out to me. Jon went first, when he said, "All right, you gotta listen to us. We both saw something in you on the JV we've never really seen before. You're a heck of a hockey player, and you can be the real deal if you put everything you have into it. I know how hard you work, but Brent and I want to help you take it to the next level."

Then Brent said, "You work your butt off, but we don't really have much in the way of off-season stuff here. We want to be your trainers. We'll figure out ways to get you stronger and maybe a little bigger. We never had the chance to do stuff like this, but we want to help you. You can go a long way in this sport if you get stronger. We want to put a full program together for you. Can we do that?"

I was honored, and thrilled, that they'd even been thinking about me much less coming up with a plan to help me. Betsy and I were really close, but my three brothers had always been kind of their own group. It was like the family was two sets of kids, with the older boys being the first set and Betsy and me being the tight pair that followed them.

As it turned out, the seed that grew into this plan the guys had hatched was based on a bit of good luck. One of the guys they'd played with as a Ram went off to continue playing at St. Cloud State, and he left a basic set of weights and other workout gear in his garage. When he came back from school that spring, his parents let him know that parking their truck in the garage was a far better use of that space, now that he was off to college and not using any of the equipment. He offered everything to Jon and Brent for almost nothing, but even "almost nothing" was more than they had. Dad only paid the guys minimum wage, just a bit over $3 an hour at the hardware store, since they were still living and eating at home.

I didn't know any of this at the time. My brothers wanted to make sure they could do it right before asking me, and they secretly went to Dad and told him what they wanted to do. He loaned them $50 to buy all the weights and accessories and told them he'd take it out of their paychecks $5 at a time. For Dad, that was really generous. He wasn't ever interested in handouts or gifts for things we didn't earn. It was pretty black and white for him. Even a loan that he'd settle by taking it out of their paychecks was out of character, but it felt great for all three of us to know he supported the effort we were making.

Jon and Brent went and picked up all the stuff and brought it home after I agreed to have them train me. It wasn't anything glamorous or high tech, even for that time, but I could use it to lift weights in a number of different ways. There was even a bench for doing leg presses. There were also a bunch of ropes and big, wide leather belts we had to figure out. Brent realized what they were for.

"This is resistance training," he said. "You put this big weightlifter belt around your waist and one of us will hold the end of the rope. Then you try to do wind sprints with us holding you back. This'll be great! Timmy Johansen was a year ahead of us, and his parents spent the money to send him to a two-week skills camp down in Brainerd. He told us the resistance training made him at least a step quicker on his skates."

We all messed around with it and tested it out, and then we set it up in our garage (thanks to Dad helping out in that way, as well, just by allowing us to do that). Brent said, "Don't screw around with this stuff by yourself. You can get seriously hurt really easily doing that. Give us a day or two and we'll map out a schedule and a list of all the things we're going to do between now and October. We know all the techniques that

69

work the best because those were the things a lot of our teammates did. And they were the things we avoided like the plague."

A couple days later, we actually sat at the kitchen table, like having a business meeting, and went through their plans. We'd gradually build up on the weights, and we were going to start pretty light. Lots of work for the biceps, pecs, shoulders, lower back and legs, focusing mostly on the calves, quads and hamstrings.

Jon said, "We have to work on your core a lot, too. All the guys on our team that were in the best shape were ripped. They'd always tell us, 'Get strong in your core and everything else follows.' We never listened, but looking back on it those guys were the strongest on the ice, especially fighting for pucks in the corners. You're going to do a lot of sit-ups and squats."

They also mapped out a way to make me quicker. There's a big difference between being fast and being quick. I was getting to be a faster skater, but I knew I had a lot of work to do on being quicker with the first few steps. Getting to your top speed as quickly as possible, in as few steps as possible, was the key. I was fast enough to be a good player, but there was a lot more in me if we worked on that quickness. It could make me a whole new hockey player, even if I was never taller than 5-foot-9.

We got started and did a pretty good job of sticking to their schedule all summer. We'd alternate what we were doing each day, whether it was weights, exercises or the resistance stuff, but we'd run every day. They were great about that. They never said "Go run two miles and then do some sprints." They did all of the running with me, and they spotted me on the weights, pushing me to do more, more, and even more. Dad let them set up their schedules at the store so that at least one of them could work with me each day. At least twice a week I'd get both of them.

It turned out to be a pretty terrific thing, and not just in terms of getting stronger. We Olsons aren't exactly the most open people when it comes to showing emotions. We're a close family, at least as far as I can tell because it's the only family I've ever had. But there wasn't a lot of hugging and kissing going on. Let's just say we were "Minnesota reserved," something we got from our folks and the people around us. I think one way to describe us collectively would be "stoic." To my folks, the best way to show love was to keep a roof over our heads and keep us fed. Doing all this work with my twin brothers was really neat. I was honored.

The twins were absolutely great about the entire effort, and that wasn't lost on me. They were having fun and putting me through my paces, but they never slacked off or let me slack off. I remember thinking during the first week that they'd stick with this for another week or two and then they'd lose interest and it would be over. That didn't happen. They were as dedicated as I was.

The first time I put that belt on and Brent held the rope was really strange. I'd never done anything like that, and it surprised me how hard it was. I got in a sprinters stance and Brent yelled "Go!" And then I tried to run and almost went nowhere. It was like running in molasses. I knew I had a lot of improving to do.

With the weights, we'd do bench presses, squats, curls and deadlifts. Every week we'd try to add just a little weight. We did a ton of stretching and other exercises, to keep loose and not all muscle bound. And yes, my core and I got to know each other well. The first week I think I did 25 sit-ups. By July I was doing 100 at the start of each workout and another 100 at the end. And the crossover sit-ups were like crunches. Right elbow to the left knee. Left elbow to the right knee. Don't let your feet touch the ground. It was brutal. I guess I just felt like if I got done on any day without feeling like I had to throw up, I needed to up the pace and the reps the next day. Empty the tank.

We also had a whole plan for working on quickness, and only some of it was resistance. Brent even rigged up an old truck tire by tying the rope to that. The tire couldn't subconsciously ease up on me, and they both admitted they'd done that early in the summer so I wouldn't get discouraged.

I'd get down in a stance and concentrate on the first five steps. "Get quicker. Get quicker. One more time. Get quicker," I'd say to myself, sometimes out loud.

Around midsummer, Jon came home from the store with a stopwatch and that really helped. It was the first time I could actually see the results in numbers and not just in how it felt. Our technique with the tire was just to work on those first five steps, but we'd do at least 25 reps of those before taking a break. After a month, by the end of August, I was a full half-second quicker than the first day we used the watch. The guys could see it.

"You're not just quicker to the fifth step," Brent said. "Your steps are visibly quicker. We can see it. You're jab stepping and really pounding it better. It's working!"

Another way to work on your quickness without having to wear a belt and drag a tire around is to run hills. That's more natural resistance, and you have to concentrate on pounding your legs like pistons and getting your knees up. There was only one problem. We didn't have any real hills in Roseau. We did have stairs, though.

The school buildings and Memorial Arena stayed open during the summer, and all we really needed was about 8 to 10 steps. They'd do them with me, and we'd time ourselves. It was hard at first, but it got quicker and easier in a hurry. It was like "Boom-Boom-Boom" on those stairs. We'd run into some of the other guys from time to time and they'd join us. The first day that happened and two guys who were going to be seniors that fall joined in, I blew them away. It was obvious how much quicker I was. I could hear them mutter things like "Wow" to each other as I pounded up those stairs. They looked strong, and they were, but their legs were much heavier and slower.

I remember Jon, on that first day the seniors joined us, saying, "Think this is working?" I just laughed and said "Oh, ya."

By the fall, we had to cut it back quite a bit because school started. Before I'd come home from school I'd sprint the stairs at Memorial Arena, because there were too many kids in the hallways of the school. I'd get that work in, then head home and hit the weights a bit before dinner. And speaking of dinner, it was my mom who noticed it first. She said, "You look great, like the best shape of your life, but you're eating like a horse, you know." I guess I needed the fuel.

Finally, the ice went in at Memorial Arena and the North Rink, and just like the year before it was like Christmas day for all of us on the hockey team. When practice

71

started, I couldn't wait to see if all the work we'd done had actually paid off. I didn't have to wait long.

At our first practice, Coach stopped me and said, "What on earth have you been doing? You're a totally different guy, and in a good way."

I told him about my brothers, our training and the schedules we kept and all he said was: "I asked you to keep working hard but I never thought I'd see this. I wish the rest of these guys worked this hard. The more we practice and you leave them in your dust, all huffing and puffing, they're going to figure this out. At least I hope so. Great work, Oly. Keep it up, son."

To be fair, more than a few of the guys didn't have the benefit of the free time I'd had all summer. Some had to work on the family farm or carry full-time jobs to help out at home. My advantage was my parents and my brothers. They allowed it to happen. And with Dad letting my brothers buy the equipment and use the garage, we were a step ahead of most of the other guys.

Two weeks later, Coach announced the varsity roster and he called my name first. I'm not going to say I was completely surprised, because I'd more than held my own in practice, but I sure wasn't expecting to be the first varsity player announced. All I could say as I skated out to the circle was a quiet "Wow" almost under my breath. Then I sprayed Coach with a little ice as I skidded to a stop. Every other player that was called did the same thing, but instead of spraying Coach they sprayed me. I looked like a snow man when they were done, and I never stopped smiling. I loved it.

I clearly remember thinking this was the greatest moment of my life. I've always been honest and straightforward with people when I tell them that since I could lace up skates all I ever dreamed of was being a Roseau Ram. I never had any aspirations beyond that. I didn't care if it took me until my senior year to play in a varsity game. I just wanted to be able to remember it and say I was a Roseau Ram. And if I got to play against our rivals over in Warroad, all the better. As a sophomore, I had done it. I made the varsity. And it was obvious to me that I hadn't just squeaked onto the roster. I was going to be a big part of it.

If the nerves and excitement I had felt a year earlier making my debut on the JV were off the charts, I'm not sure there was a chart for the start of my first season on the varsity. I felt a lot of things that day. Pride, nervousness and a little fear of the unknown were all mixed in there. I'd been practicing with the team for a number of weeks and knew I fit in, but soon a group of strangers would be on the ice with us and ready for a battle against a team they wanted to beat very badly. Everyone wants to beat Roseau. With all the workouts we had done through the summer, I had officially "bulked up" to 165 pounds, but I was still just 5-foot-7 and a half. If there was ever a half-inch to be claimed, I'd claim it.

A bunch of the guys from the year before were back on the JV again, and as good as I thought we were on the varsity I didn't see how many of them would ever break through. We had a group of sophomores who were all going to play a lot for a long time. Most of us would play together for the next three years, and as we moved on only the best of those guys who played a second year of JV would join us when older players graduated. I remember that a few of the guys, who were sophomores when I was on the JV, just quit when they didn't make the varsity as juniors. They were realistic enough to know it was over. It wasn't easy to make the Roseau Rams. I was proud to have done it.

The guys around me were proud of it, too. We took it seriously and we took it as a responsibility. From our head coach Gary Hokanson to our assistant coaches Gary Ross and Jeff Olson, right down through the roster to our student managers, Tracy Ostby (who we all called, and still call, Bobcat) and John Dorwart and our stat guy Brian Haugen. From superstars like Paul Broten to a little undersized defenseman like me. Guys like Tom Pederson, Jon Helgeson, Bruce Helgeson, Scott Vatnsdal, Donny Johnson and every other guy on the team. We were a proud family of Rams.

We opened the season on a Friday night. I noticed one thing that was very different from the year before. As the day went on, I could feel my focus sharpening. It felt like tunnel vision. I kept seeing plays developing and could go through my reads and reactions to what the other team came at us with, or what I could do to jump into the offense without leaving us exposed too much in the back. All day long, as I sat through classes, it was like a movie was playing in my head. Basically, it was agony to wait through the day just to get to the moment I'd been waiting for my whole life.

When the JV played their game before ours, the enormous thing I'd just accomplished really hit me. When I put the Roseau varsity sweater on in the locker room, with the number 11 on the back, I took a second to stop and appreciate that. Looking around the room at seniors, juniors, and our group of sophomores, I got a little emotional. At least for me. I didn't shed a tear or anything, I was too focused on playing the game, but I remember feeling a vibration in my neck that made my head shake a little, and I got a little dizzy. I don't think I'd ever been that nervous before a hockey game. I sat back down and took a few deep breaths.

Two seniors must have seen that, because they both walked by me like they needed to urgently go get a drink of water, and as they passed me they just tapped me on the shins with their sticks. And then more guys, some of them saying, "Have a good one, Oly" or "Here we go boys" even though I was the one they were talking to. It meant more to me than any of them could have imagined. And it calmed me down.

When the JV game was over and the ice was cleaned, it was time to get out there for warm-ups. The place was packed. I'd never experienced anything like it. All those years of youth hockey and my season on the JV, we played in front of people but it was mostly the families of the guys on the team. These were people from Roseau and the surrounding area. They were hockey fans coming out to see us and cheer us on. There were 1,500 of them filling the seats. My head was spinning as I skated with the guys. It felt like I was going 100 mph.

It's funny that so many of my clearest memories are "firsts" of some sort. That whole day of my first varsity game still seems like it was yesterday. The next 20 games each season? They all blend together. Lots of rinks, lots of fans, lots of bus rides on a very cold bus. But the first game? Like it was yesterday.

I was on the third defensive line. I'd have to keep working my butt off to move up to the second or first line at some point during the season, but I was incredibly proud to be on that third line. I'd get to play plenty of minutes there. The first two lines would need rest every period.

I was on the bench as the game started, joining my teammates by shouting "Let's go boys" to the starters and ourselves. My heart rate must have been 150. About two minutes into the game, the first line came off the ice and the second line jumped over the boards. About a minute and a half later, an assistant coach walked behind the bench and tapped me and my left-side defensive partner on the shoulder. "Here we go boys, you're next. Stay tight and protect the goalie. Go, go, go!"

I jumped over the boards like I'd done a million times. The puck was in the offensive zone so I skated out to about the red line at center ice and looked around. When one of the other team's forwards got the puck and started racing up ice with it, he was coming straight at me. He was fast. He seemed faster than anyone I'd ever faced in my life. I was skating backward when he made a sort of juke to his left and then tried to cut in front of me to his right. I never saw that move on the JV.

All that quickness training paid off.

Instead of skating right by me, which I kind of expected him to do after he'd put that move on me, I just put my feet into gear and stayed right with him on his left elbow. I remember putting my stick under his a little, then I popped his stick up off the ice and I took the puck away as I curled sharply to my left. As I looked up ice I saw my forwards tearing toward the blue line. I wristed a pass to my left winger and put it on his tape. After three passes, tic-tac-toe, our center scored right through the goalie's "five hole," which means right between his legs. The place went crazy. I'd been in the Memorial Arena during games when the crowd about blew the historic roof off, but I'd never been down there on the ice to hear it. It was deafening.

I didn't get an assist because of the multiple passes that happened after I passed the puck up ice, but I didn't care. In my first shift as a varsity player, I'd stripped the puck from a really fast opponent and set up the goal. My teammates knew what I'd done, and they let me know. The coaches did, too.

We won that night. I didn't get on the scoresheet but I played a lot of minutes and held my own. I felt I was varsity caliber. It was the same game I'd always been playing, and I felt like I belonged. I was a third line defenseman, but I'd earned it and I belonged. It didn't surprise me that I didn't sleep much that night. I was a Roseau Ram.

As the season wore on, I learned some valuable lessons. For the first time in my life, I think I got a little overconfident. We'd worked so hard all summer, and I knew I was in the best shape of my life, but I was surprised more than a few times against good teams. I was stronger, and quicker, and just as motivated, but some of the forwards I played against were at a level I'd never seen before. I had always thought of myself as an underdog, but even so I still knew I could outwork and outsmart most other guys my age. Playing against juniors and seniors was different. And the physicality in the corners was a huge step up. As fit as I was, I took a beating and it wore me down. By the end of the season it felt like I was sore all over and really tired.

Because of all that, my dream of moving up to the second or first line never happened that year. I stayed on the third line the whole season. I had good games and questionable games, maybe even a few really bad games, but I kept plugging.

I don't remember our final record and actually can't even find it anywhere. I think I played the whole year so focused on my own play and my responsibilities I didn't process the bigger picture of wins and losses. I know we didn't make it to the state tournament, so the season ended too early for Roseau fans.

Coach met with me after the season ended, and he was really honest. He said, "Eric, you do everything you can possibly do to be the best hockey player you can be, but a lot of the bigger players are eating you up. You're strong, but they're strong too and they're a lot bigger than you. If a guy is strong and then has four or five inches on you, it's going to be tough."

He told me to get some rest and then get back after it with the offseason training. He asked if some of the other guys could work out with me that spring and summer, and that sounded great to me. We could all motivate each other, and if Jon and Brent wanted to come back and train us all, we'd become a better team. The one thing I couldn't control was how tall I was.

I did my best to rest up after the season ended, but the truth was I could barely do anything other than rest up. I was not only stiff and sore, I was exhausted. I could hardly get up to go to school in the morning, and that wasn't like me.

Finally, I woke up one morning and getting up was impossible. My throat was killing me and I was alternating between broiling and shivering. My mom took my temperature and it was a solid 102 and on the way up.

I ended up having a full-blown case of strep throat that knocked me flat for a week. I'd never had a sore throat that bad, and had hardly ever been too sick to go to school. I missed a full week of classes, but I was so delirious it all just seemed to run together in a blur of thermometers, lozenges, aspirin and cold wet towels for my forehead. About midway through it, Mom decided she had to get me to a doctor and he confirmed what we already had guessed. Strep throat, and a serious case of it. He gave me some prescriptions, but he also gave me a stern warning.

"You can't go at it this hard without wearing yourself down, Eric," he said. "The body needs time to recover, all year long, not just after the season ends. You used up all your natural resistance by working so hard your body never got back to normal. You're going to need to find a better balance from this point forward."

A lot of it was mental. As the season went on and I kept running into bigger and stronger guys, I panicked that I was getting soft. So, if we played three games in a week I'd try to get in some brutal workouts on the other four days. It was like I felt I needed to punish myself for that puck I gave up in the corner that turned into a goal, or the time I got creamed into the boards like I'd been run over by a truck. I had to get my head wrapped around the fact that I needed to be in my best realistic shape, but not the best shape in the history of hockey. I needed to find a way to stay sharp and strong, but stay healthy.

I began to feel better, but the illness was severe enough that even after I beat the symptoms I still had no energy. There you go. That's your body telling you to recover.

We did get back into the workouts once mid-May rolled around, and Brent and Jon were still really into it. Now they had anywhere from two or three guys to six or eight on any given day. We still had a lot of teammates who had to work summer jobs or be on the farm, so we could never get everyone there, but it was great to have a group of guys all pulling together for the same goal.

When fall finally came, and we started practice, it was obvious that my class was already dominating the team. We had 17 or 18 juniors on the team. There really wasn't much room for anyone else. Paul Broten was clearly already a star, just like his brothers before him. He was the best offensive player I'd ever played with, or played against in practice. It was valuable to work hard in practice, just to try to stop him.

Once the season started, Jon and Brent and I sat down to figure out how to not have a repeat of how exhausted and overworked I was by the end of the prior season. The rule was that I was only going to do limited workouts a couple of days a week. We still had practice on days when we weren't playing, and I should go all out in those just like I always had, but no more brutal workouts on top of it. The idea was to save most of that for the off-season, and then find a way to maintain my fitness during the hockey season.

We were good, and getting better. Memorial Arena was packed for nearly every home game. When we went on the road, you could tell it was a big night for the other team. They knew we were good, and that put a target on our backs. A lot of those games were rough, with some strong trash talking, but we did better than hold our own. I think we ended up 18-6, and that included the section tournament, which we won. When you win your section, you get to go to the state tournament, down in St. Paul.

If just making the varsity had been a lifelong dream for me, going to the Twin Cities to represent Roseau in the state tournament was an even bigger thrill.

I don't think people outside of Minnesota have any idea of the importance of the state high school hockey tournament. The whole state watches, the crowds (back then at the old St. Paul Civic Center) were like NHL crowds, and the honor of just being there made you feel like you were in the Stanley Cup, the Super Bowl and the World Series all rolled into one. There's nothing like it that I know of anywhere else. St. Paul embraces it, and it's the experience of a lifetime. To be 17 years old and feel like a celebrity hockey player is beyond neat or cool. It's unbelievable.

It's an eight-team tournament, but there are various banners you can win. Obviously, you'd love to go home as state champs. Runner-up is pretty good, too. If you lose your first game those two options are out, but you're not done playing yet. You then have a chance to win two more games against other first-round losers to be the consolation champs. It might not come as a surprise that only state champ and runner-up banners get hung in the Roseau Memorial Arena. Getting to the final is always the goal for the Roseau Rams. That junior year, 1983, all we played were big schools from the Twin Cities. We lost to Sibley High from the St. Paul area, then beat Bloomington Kennedy to make it to the consolation final. We lost to Edina there. As big as Edina is, and as good as they always are, I doubt they hung up that banner either.

One other thing happened during that junior year. I finally noticed girls. I knew they were there, of course, and I'd been attracted to a few, but hockey was everything. I was really about as single-minded as a teenager can be. It was hockey, 24/7/365. If I wasn't playing or working out, I was thinking about it.

I'd known Carol Jorgensen forever, it seemed. That's the way it is in Roseau, especially at school. You spend all 12 years of school with a lot of the same kids. Not too many families move away, and only a few move in. So, you start out as little kids and you go through all the clumsy or klutzy phases together. I steered clear of most of the drama, which I think started around sixth grade when a lot of flirting started to go on. By my junior year, though, I kept noticing that I stared at Carol a lot. And I tried to find ways to bump into her in the hall or at lunch. As it turned out, she'd had a crush on me since seventh grade, but I was never smart or aware enough to notice. By 11th grade, I had a crush on her.

She'd already been coming to all of our games, and some of our away games, but it was neat to know she was up there rooting for me. A pretty girl, rooting for me. She could make me laugh, too, and that was magic. No girl had ever cracked me up before, other than my sister Betsy.

Carol was about 5-foot nothing, so I even felt kind of lofty standing next to her. She had soft brown hair that fell straight to her shoulders, with bangs that were cut straight across, just above her eyebrows, and her hair always seemed to shine. Her dark brown eyes almost looked as black as the pupils they surrounded. She definitely stood out with those looks in Roseau, where the Scandinavian heritage in our town made for a lot of blond hair and blue eyes. I learned she was only second generation Roseau. Her parents had moved up from the Twin Cities to work for Polaris, and while her dad was Swedish, her mom was mostly Italian. It was a beautiful combination. She was smart, very polite, extremely popular and she smelled nice. What's not to like?

We began dating that year, although in Roseau that means maybe you go bowling or grab a pizza. I had my driver's license by then, but my mom had a car and my dad had a truck, and that was it. If I wanted to borrow one, I was fourth in line behind my twin brothers and my sister. And there really wasn't anywhere to drive to, so we never thought about it much. It was a classic small town, with a great little downtown area, and for just about anything we wanted to do we could walk or ride our bikes to get there. At least until it got really cold in the winter.

Both of our sets of parents approved, and Betsy told me I was the luckiest boy at Roseau High. She said Carol was the best catch at school. We were both good kids, too, so that gave us a little more freedom than the few kids in town who might not be as trustworthy. It was a lot of fun, and I could tell I was growing up fast.

What I could also tell was that I was NOT growing taller very fast. By the end of my junior year I had sprouted up from 5-foot-7 and a half all the way to 5-foot-7 and three quarters. I wondered if I'd ever see 5-foot-8, and if I didn't I wondered if I'd get to play any more hockey after my Rams career was over.

Yes, I was starting to allow myself to think about that. We were a good team, and some of our guys were real prospects for even the elite college programs. The University of Minnesota was watching us, as were Minnesota Duluth, North Dakota, Mankato, Bemidji, St. Cloud State (where both my dad and oldest brother had played) and some other schools. After our junior year, I got letters from all of them, just letting me know they were watching and interested. Although we had an Olson legacy at St. Cloud, I dreamed of going to "The U," as we called University of Minnesota. I think I didn't want the comparisons at St. Cloud State. But man, I couldn't see being a Golden Gopher at under 5-foot-8.

I played some guys who were 6-foot-4 or 6-5, but generally those really tall guys were pretty slow. The guys who were 6-1 or 6-2, and fast, were already a handful. I couldn't imagine what it would be like to play NCAA hockey where almost all the players would be like that, or even bigger and better. Again, I never aspired to do that. I had only wanted to be a Roseau Ram. But getting those letters opened a whole new world of dreams for me. If I could just grow a little…

As we headed toward the summer, another thing that was starting to happen around school was the thought of playing junior hockey. I was pretty intrigued when teammates David Drown and Donny Johnson began to mention that they'd been hearing from the Des Moines Buccaneers of the USHL (the United States Hockey League) and they said they'd told the Des Moines team about me.

Junior hockey is really a unique thing in just about all of sports. It's basically just like minor league pro hockey, but you don't get paid. The teams are made up mostly of 18- to 20-year olds, just out of high school, and the teams line you up with families in town, known as billet families. You become sort of a surrogate kid for them. Various teams in the league concentrated on different parts of the country, and Des Moines was the team that focused a lot on our area in northern Minnesota.

In juniors you work out every day, play three or four games a week, ride the bus a lot, learn how to be a responsible young adult and how to be a great teammate with mostly a whole new set of guys. It provides great experience, and it's great hockey at the next level, but the best part is you get to keep your college eligibility because you're not getting paid. It seemed like that might be a good next step for me, especially if the other guys went. But first, we needed another summer of workouts and we all needed a great senior year. With all those colleges watching us, and with the Des Moines junior team interested, it would be good to finish high school strong.

We worked our butts off again that summer, and by doing that we really had come together as a group. It was like we were all brothers, and we pushed each other to be as good as we could be. I'd known since sophomore year that our class was going to be a solid bunch, and we were. As incoming seniors, there were 18 of us on the varsity roster. That's pretty incredible, actually.

Carol and I were getting a little more serious, but I think I always held back a little. I really liked her, and I never had any thoughts of dating anyone else, but hockey always came first. There must've been a part of me that was worried about letting the relationship get too serious. Fear is a great motivator, and fear of failure on the ice was something that was always on my mind. There's no doubt that our relationship was a wonderful thing, but the dark side to it was my fear of it being a distraction.

She definitely had an interest in what my plans were, and I couldn't fault her for that. I had an interest in what my plans were going to be, too. I just wasn't sure yet. If I had a good season, I'd have options. It was still my hope to go to The U and get my degree there while playing for the Gophers, but that wasn't totally up to me. I'd have to earn that scholarship. With other schools staying in touch with me, I'd have some good choices once the season was over, but the Des Moines thing was also something I was thinking about.

As we got back to school that senior fall of 1983, Carol was definitely getting a little frustrated. If I was going to college, she wanted to go to the same school. If our relationship wasn't going to work out, she had to start planning her life without me. I felt the pressure, and that didn't help how we were getting along. I still adored her, and I'd say by then I knew I was in love with her, but there were so many loose ends out there and I wasn't sure what any of the answers were. Plus, most importantly for me, we had a hockey season to play.

I had to focus on that. I had to put all my attention into the game I loved. My teammates were like my brothers, and we'd all come so far together. I knew that wasn't fair to Carol, but I also knew it was my responsibility to my teammates, my family and myself. We could do great things that would change our lives. I just hoped my relationship with Carol could survive that. I didn't want to break up with her at all. I figured maybe she could put up with where I needed to be, in terms of focus, but in my heart I knew that was a lot to ask. It was too much to ask.

When we took our physicals before the season, I got a big surprise. My so-called growth spurt had finally happened. I was just a tick short of 5-foot-9. And I was up to a solid 173 pounds, thanks to the muscle mass we'd been working on for three years.

As we practiced prior to our first game, I could tell how good we were. The fact we had so many seniors on the team just made us better. When you play with the same guys for that many years, it's going to have a really positive impact on how well you play together. It felt like we could almost play blindfolded, because we knew one anothers' tendencies so well. I didn't have to look to see where Paul Broten was. I knew where he was and where he was going. It was just a matter of us executing as a group. If there's one emotion I can remember from that time, just before the season started, it was a bit of fear. We were good, but nothing was going to be handed to us. We had to earn it. What if we didn't?

I was on the first line by then, and I was playing the best hockey of my life. We came out of the gate strong, and never let up all season. The games against Warroad were incredible, and as I recall we beat them both times. I believe we ended up 19-4 and we won our section again. We were going back to St. Paul.

This time, our coaches decided we weren't going to stay in downtown St. Paul. It was fun to be down there, with all the hoopla that went on as part of the tournament, but it could also be distracting. So, we broke with tradition and stayed in a suburban motel. Basically, all there was to do was either sit in our rooms or go to the rink. I think we all kind of liked that, actually. It was a bit of a "been there, done that" in terms of being downtown, surrounded by the other teams, all the fans and our families. It felt good to just focus on hockey. We truly believed we could win state and add our class of 1984 to the list of teams that had brought the trophy home to Roseau.

And then we got absolutely blitzed by Edina in the opening game. They were good, that's for sure, but we played terribly too and when we got behind it just snowballed on us. When it ended at 7-0, I was just glad it was over. We were embarrassed, defeated and humbled. Playing the consolation games didn't even seem like anything we'd want to do. We were there to win state.

We had a team meeting and talked about responsibility. It was a real moment of clarity for all of us. We'd played together for so many years, and 18 of us were facing the end of our Roseau careers. We owed it to our school, to our town, to our families and to ourselves to go out as strong as we could. We had to put the disappointment of that first game against Edina behind us.

We beat St. Cloud Apollo 3-0 in the consolation semifinal. We faced Burnsville, another strong suburban Twin Cities school, in the consolation final. As we took the ice, 18 of us knew it would be the last game we'd play as Roseau Rams. And we ended up getting to play a few more minutes than expected. We beat them 9-8 in overtime, when Sean Bucy scored the winning goal. We celebrated and hugged each other. It wasn't the state championship, but we'd done ourselves proud by showing up and playing as hard as we could to get that consolation banner. It would've been easy to quit and just go through the motions. I was really proud of how we handled that. I've never forgotten it.

All the schools that originally contacted me had stayed in touch. Once the tournament was over it all ramped up to a new level, though, and my head was kind of spinning as to what my next big choice in life was going to be.

I got a call from one of the assistant coaches at The U and he was blunt. He said, "Eric, you're going to be a heck of a hockey player. We'd love for you to be a Golden Gopher, but I'm not going to blow smoke at you. You'll have a hard time getting minutes for at least your first two years here, and that's if you keep improving and working hard. It won't be easy for you. Just let me know what you're thinking after you make your decision. We can bring you in on a partial scholarship but that's all we can do for now."

St. Cloud State offered me a large scholarship. Bemidji State made a big push. But my mind was made up. I knew what was best for me and my career. I needed to go play juniors. Des Moines made offers to me, Donny Johnson, Sean Bucy and David Drown. We could all be going into the USHL together.

Carol and I had to have "the talk" and as soon as I made up my mind we sat down and did that.

"I love you Eric," she said with a hint of a tear in one eye. "But I'm going to get a college education. I can't go to Des Moines with you and I'm not going to stay here and just get a job at the bank. I can do more than that. I want you to succeed and live out your dreams. Hockey has always been your first love. You need to stay true to that, OK? I'm going to St. Cloud State. We'll both end up wherever we end up. I want nothing but the very best for you. I adore you."

Everything she said was absolutely right. It was crushing in a big way, but it was right. I had to go. I had to stay true to my dreams, even if my dreams had always just been to play as a Roseau Ram.

I called the head coach of the Des Moines Buccaneers and committed to him that I would play. College could wait.

It felt incredibly strange to know I'd never play for the Rams again. I know my teammates felt it too. It was going to be very hard to say goodbye to all of them. Donny, Sean and David were going with me, but from that point forward I'd only play pick-up games or socialize with the rest of them. I never considered that I might play against a couple of them in just a few more years. Until then, I had never considered anything other than being a Roseau Ram.

CHAPTER 13

Brooks Bennett

There was so much to do and so little time to do it, but Dad and I kept our promise to hit the waves one more time before we left. We loaded our boards on the VW and headed for San Clemente. I had only been back a few times since the move to Anaheim, and I'd grown quite a bit, so there were some surprised looks on the faces of the dudes who remembered us. How many remembered us? Basically all of them. They hadn't changed a bit, and were really stoked to see us. I heard a lot of "Man, look at you dude!" comments.

In the VW on the way down, Dad had said, "I don't think I want to get into any details with anyone we still know down there. I'm just going to tell them that we're moving to Minnesota and leave it at that. If anyone presses for an explanation, I'll say there's an opportunity there I can't pass up. I want it to be a happy couple of hours for everyone. No need to bring all those guys down."

I agreed.

We surfed, we shared hugs with too many guys to count, and we shared a deep, long hug ourselves, before loading the boards back on the VW when we were done. We made a stop at the board shop where Dad had worked and left all of our surfing stuff there. They promised to keep it all for us and have it ready whenever we got back. I could only hope that we would, someday. I had a feeling it was the last time we'd ever do anything like that. I couldn't know for sure at the time, but with the weight of the planet pushing down on both of us, and the huge challenge we would be facing in just the next few days, surfing didn't seem like the sort of thing that we'd be doing again anytime soon.

Looking back on it now, the next week or so must have been manic and crazy. I really don't remember much of it, but it's mind-boggling to think that we had to get all of our personal belongings packed up, get the bus ready, sell Mom's VW, settle up with our landlord and then hit the highway for a 2,000-mile trip with Mom along with us. Somehow we did it. I remember Dad getting pretty scientific about figuring out how to pack what we were taking. It wasn't much.

I also remember Dad buying an air mattress and making a small bedroom in the back of the bus. I'd ride up front with him when Mom wanted to lay down or sleep, and when she was feeling good she'd sit up there and I'd hang around in the back. My dad had to drive the whole way. I can't imagine that.

What I also couldn't imagine was the scenery. If moving from San Clemente to Anaheim had felt like a jarring experience, my brain had no way of processing what I was seeing. I mean, I'd never so much as left SoCal in my entire life. It was a whole new world. Amazing stuff.

I remember leaving California and seeing the "Welcome To Nevada" sign, then feeling my heart break just a little. That sign made it all real. We weren't turning around and going back. Then we drove through Las Vegas that first afternoon and I couldn't comprehend what I saw, with all the casinos and hotels. Finally, after driving through stark desert landscapes and huge mountains, we got to Salt Lake City and found a motel outside town. Mom had done really well. Dad had, too. He was our hero.

I recall the next day being an absolute marathon. Mom was tired from the first day, and she slept much of the time. I sat up front with dad, with a map open, and I'd go check on Mom regularly. It seemed like we were going so far it was impossible to still be in the United States. As a SoCal boy, I guess I didn't really grasp the size of the country or the planet. I thought Dodger Stadium was a long way from home.

I remember driving through the mountains of Colorado, coming into Denver from the west. It was one snow-capped peak after another until they all blended into a mass of mountains, and then bam, we came out of one pass and there was Denver ahead of us. And as we ccme down into Denver, I could tell there wasn't much out there beyond it.

That night we made it as far as some little town in Nebraska. I have no idea where that might have been. I just remember it being a small, L-shaped motel with a gravel parking lot and about a dozen rooms, where you parked right in front of your door. It had an Old West sort of feel to it, as if you could've tied up your horse to the railing in front of the room just as easily as parking there.

Mom was really tired by the third day, but I remember her really being a trouper. She knew she needed to rest and keep the stress level low, so most of the time she was on the air mattress in back. We'd stop at rest areas, almost always in the middle of what I considered nowhere, and make sandwiches or cut up some fruit. By that third day it seemed like an endless journey, and without the majestic scenery of Utah and Colorado, it seemed like a trudge. Somewhere out there in eastern Nebraska or maybe Iowa, I remember turning to Dad and saying: "I've never seen anything so flat. This is agony."

He laughed and said, "It's a big country, dude. The first time I drove from Erie to Huntington Beach, I was mesmerized by the scope of it, just how huge it all was, and how many different types of landscapes and vegetation I was seeing. I actually researched it a lot, ahead of the trip, because I thought it would be a great learning experience, and it was. It's America. But even here, where it's flat, there are things to notice. What are they growing? Why is that town there? There's more going on than you think."

From that point forward he was my tour guide, pointing out the various crops and the railroad towns. In the mountains, it was so overwhelming I had basically just sat there in silence, marveling at it all. In the plains, I learned you had to look deeper. That was just like Dad. He was always wanting to teach me. It got me through the trip.

That third day was definitely long, but when we got to Des Moines and made the turn north, I felt another one of those "this is real" pangs in my gut. We were headed straight to Rochester where we'd hook up with Dad's cousin Don, who was going to meet us there the next morning.

As we entered Minnesota, I finally asked my dad a question that had me really worried. I hadn't had the nerve to even ask up until that point. I didn't want to add to anyone's stress.

"How are we going to pay for all this, Dad?"

As he drove, he turned to me and said, "We're going to be OK. There are some grants we can get, and we might do the experimental treatment deal. But beyond that, your mom and I have saved up quite a bit of money. She got paid really well for all that artwork, and I made steady money at Disney, so much so that we put almost all of your mom's income away. We never really changed our lifestyle all that much. We paid the rent, bought the food we needed, and made sure you had the clothes and baseball gear you had to have. Other than that, we put almost all of it into a savings account. It's a lot of money. When I closed our bank account in Anaheim, I wired about $57,000 to Don. He's holding that for us until we get settled and get some accounts set up there. I've got about $8,000 on me in cash."

I couldn't believe it, in two ways. One, I had no idea they'd put that much money away, but looking back that's exactly what they would've done. It was never about money or having tons of nice things. It was about happiness. Two, the whole idea of wiring all our money to a guy my dad hadn't seen in decades scared the crap out of me.

All I asked was, "Dad, are you sure you can you trust him?"

He said, "No, not a hundred percent, but I'm putting my faith in him. He's been a saint so far. I believe in him and his kindness. I think we'll be fine. There are times in life when you have to trust your instinct, and my instinct about Don is that he's a good man. And he's family."

It was late in the day when we pulled into Rochester, and we were really weary. I'm not sure how Mom did it, but she got through it without a single complaint. She was tired and resting for most of the trip, but she'd had no episodes. We were all worried about that when we took off from Anaheim. What if we were in the middle of nowhere and she had a big episode or a seizure? It was like she'd willed that away. The doctors in Anaheim had also prescribed some medications to help make the trip easier for her. That's why she slept so much, for sure.

Dad had planned ahead and booked a room for us at a nice motel near Mayo, and I remember how much better it was that we didn't have to drive around looking for a place. He normally didn't like being tied down to a schedule or forced into making it to specific places. For the first two days we'd just driven as far as we could. It was a relief to pull in the motel and know all we had to do was check in. No worry that there wouldn't

84

be a room, or haggling over the price. I don't remember much about that night, other than how tired we all were.

The next morning there was a knock on our door pretty early. It was Don. I could instantly see the resemblance, and my dad and Don shared a hug that just got deeper and stronger by the second. I'll never forget that moment. I wasn't sure what to do, and I awkwardly just kind of stood back and kept quiet. Don and my dad were almost exactly the same in terms of height and build. They looked almost like twins, but wearing very different clothes. Don was wearing loafers, slacks and a golf shirt that looked brand new. I didn't see much of that at the beach or in school. Dad had on a pair of long board shorts and sandals.

Don had my dad's eyes, too. Those James Taylor eyes. They clearly ran in the family. Just like Dad, he was a handsome guy with those eyes. They were both clearly Bennett men.

Don seemed like a great guy, and I liked him instantly. But, we had all sorts of details to get through and the plan was to get Mom checked in at Mayo by that afternoon. It was all pretty boring for a 16-year old kid, as they talked about bank accounts, grants for health care, and the decisions that needed to be made for Mom. Would we rely on grants and go for the best possible care, or would we go the experimental treatment route? I don't remember the specifics of the conversations, but I do remember feeling really calm around Don. He wasn't like my dad. He was serious and really unemotional and businesslike about everything. Dad was passionate about everything he did. Don kept the emotions out of it. He seemed to be the voice of reason, and he'd done a ton of research for us.

Mom was in bed sleeping at the time, when Don looked at me and my dad and said, "There's something I've just recently made a decision about that I need to share with you two. It's really important that you be honest with me."

We were both like "Sure, whatever you want" but he had a really serious look on his face.

"Look, my ex-wife and I didn't get a divorce because we couldn't get along," Don said. "We got along great, and she's one of the most wonderful people I've ever known. It's just that I finally looked in the mirror and told myself it was time to stop living a lie. You both need to know this. I'm a gay man. I always have been. I knew it by the time I got to high school. I just couldn't or wouldn't admit it. It's time to be myself and stop living that lie. I need to know if you're not comfortable with this."

He continued, "I'll totally understand if you're not comfortable. It's a hard thing for anyone to grapple with, whether it's me or you. If we need to find Plan B, I can do that. I'll work with the school to find a family with a boy on the baseball team, and you can live with them."

My dad said, "Are you kidding?"

Don said, "Uh, no. I've thought about this for most of my life. Gay people rarely kid about it." Dad laughed a little, and so did I.

"That's not what I meant," Dad said. "I meant are you kidding that you think we might be too uncomfortable with that? I have no problem with it, and I don't imagine that Brooks does either, although he can speak for himself and it's up to him. We're all family."

I'm not going to say that I didn't have a little mental flinch when Don told us that. I certainly wasn't expecting him to say it. I mean, if you would've asked me all the things I'd think this guy would say right after meeting me, it would've ranked in the bottom 10 percent. It took me by surprise for sure, but the one thing it didn't do was make me uncomfortable to the point of wondering what we should do. So, I chimed in.

"Don, Mom and Dad raised me to understand everyone is different in a lot of ways, but deep inside we're all the same and we all need to be true to what we are. People are people. You can be a good person or a jerk, no matter what your sexuality is. Back in Anaheim and down in San Clemente I knew at least a dozen guys who I figured were gay, even if they weren't open about it. Mom and Dad have always been around a lot of gay people, so it's nothing new. It's never been an issue for me. I guess I should ask if having a straight high school kid in your house will be an issue for you."

Don nodded, laughed a little and looked enormously relieved. He said, "Oh, a teenager living a totally different lifestyle? I guess I'll do my best to deal with that. No, seriously, of course it's not an issue for me, and I'm relieved we're all on the same page. You know, I hear some friends these days talk about how they've 'come out of the closet' by going public. I don't get that. A closet seems like a nice cozy safe place. It felt more like a prison to me. I wanted out of the prison."

We'd all been doing a lot of hugging. The next one was all three of us and it lasted a while.

When that was all sorted and behind us, it was time to get Mom to Mayo. Again, I really don't remember much about the process and the paperwork. All I remember is that I had never thought to visualize what Mayo Clinic might look like. The word "Clinic" makes it seem like it could've been in a strip mall. It wasn't. It was enormous. It was like its own city.

I remember being part of it for some of the process, and during the rest of it I sat outside a number of offices while Mom, Dad, and Don met with staff people. Then we took her to her room. It wasn't much different than the hospitals I'd been in, but there did seem to be a vibe that was totally different. People don't move in at Mayo Clinic because they broke a bone or had a fever. It was all very serious stuff, and the staff all seemed a lot more engaged and focused than the emergency room doctors and nurses I'd met, who were just plowing through their day taking care of as many people as possible, one crisis at a time.

We got Mom situated, and Dad decided he was going to stay with her that first night. Don took me back to the motel, where he had reserved a room too, and we had dinner together. All I remember about that dinner is how kind and thoughtful he was. He never talked down to me like I was just a kid, and he always looked me in the eyes. He spoke softly, but he always had a serious tone. Basically, I could tell he really cared. If any of my buddies were to ever ask me about Don, I could sum him up by saying, "He's a really great dude."

I remember covering a lot of important ground over that dinner. For a kid like me, it was about as serious a conversation as I'd ever had. We had bank accounts to open, both in Rochester and Bloomington. Back then, you just had an account at your local bank. I don't remember being able to bank from any branch like we do now. ATMs and online banking were science fiction back then.

Things had seemed pretty overwhelming ever since the decision was made to move to Minnesota. It was still overwhelming, but Don seemed to have such a handle on it I felt calm. It was like, "OK, this is going to work out. This is totally going to be fine."

The next day, Don and I met Dad at the furnished apartment Don had lined up for him. He'd even had a phone line installed so we could all stay in touch. Then he took Dad to a bank in Rochester and helped him open checking and savings accounts, using the cash we'd brought with us. The next day, Don and I would drive up to Bloomington and he'd do the same for me, while he also wired the $57,000 my dad had sent him to the new account in Rochester. It was all very complicated, and it kind of made my head spin. All this was going on and I still needed to get up to Bloomington to start my new life there!

I needed to meet the coach, move into Don's house, get a driver's license and buy some clothes. It was summer, but I knew winter was out there somewhere. The heaviest coat I owned was my Canyon High letter jacket. That was it. I didn't own a pair of gloves or a stocking cap, and I definitely didn't own a pair of boots that would get me through the snow.

I think I was still a bit in denial about even being in Minnesota, and that was an easy trap to fall into in Rochester. It could've been any medium-sized town in the middle of America. It just had a huge, world-famous medical center at its core. We'd driven across much of the country, which was definitely a jolt of mental overload, and while this part Minnesota certainly didn't look like California it also was just kind of vanilla. Other than Mayo, there was nothing remarkable about it. I wasn't sure if that was good or bad. I just tried to stay focused on what we were doing and what had to be done. The fact I didn't see any igloos or guys ice fishing was a bit of a relief, I think.

The next morning we dropped by Mayo to see Mom and Dad. It was right then, in her room, that I finally understood the scope of it all. I had never left my parents to go live somewhere else with someone else. I had never left my mom knowing things could go very wrong for her, very quickly. I'd never had to walk away from my dad, my hero, at such a critical point for all of us. I was 16 and I felt about 10. A big part of me just wanted to curl up and cry, and maybe kick my feet and yell "I'm not going! I want to stay here with you. I'M NOT GOING!"

I remember looking at my dad and realizing I couldn't do that. I had to hold it together. It wasn't easy, and there would be plenty of nights in the near future where it was almost impossible, but it had to be done. Don and I said our goodbyes to them and headed north in his car. His car, by the way, was the nicest ride I'd ever been in. It was a big solid Mercedes Benz sedan. I quietly sat in the front passenger seat and stared out the window as we drove north toward the Twin Cities. I had one big suitcase with me.

That was my whole life, in one gray Samsonite my dad had owned since his first trip from Erie to Huntington Beach.

As we drove north, I looked out the window a lot. Rural Minnesota wasn't SoCal, but it was pretty in its own way. Lots of trees and lakes, and lots of towns that all looked safe and clean as we passed by.

We kept driving, but not much farther. That was a relief. I totally did not want to be too far from Rochester and until we made the drive that day I wasn't sure how far away Bloomington was. When we passed Burnsville Don said, "We're only a few minutes away now. Once you start playing for Kennedy, you might pitch against these guys in Burnsville. They're always good."

When we got to Bloomington, we got off the highway and made a few turns, driving down streets surrounded by beautiful houses. It really didn't look anything like SoCal. The first time we passed a bright red fire hydrant that had a tall, yellow stick attached to it, pointing straight up, I had to ask what that was about.

"That's a snow marker stick," Don said. "When the snow gets deep in the winter, the fire department needs to be able to find the hydrants."

The only thing I could say was, "You gotta be shitting me."

And then we pulled into a big circular drive in front of a gorgeous two-story brick home.

"We're here!"

I just muttered, "Wow."

I walked into Don's home with my head spinning. I'd never set foot in a place that big or that nice in my entire 16-year life. The richest kids I knew in Anaheim didn't have houses like this. I was blown away and basically speechless. Don kept asking what I thought and I couldn't utter much more than "Incredible" each time.

He gave me a tour and then showed me to my part of the house, the place he'd referred to as a "mother-in-law suite" on the phone. She must've been one heck of a mother-in-law. It was enormous, and totally private. It was like it was its own little home attached to the bigger house. It was connected to the house by a hallway, but it had its own front door, too. There was a huge master bedroom, a full bath, a living area and a kitchen. He had it all furnished and decked out, right down to dishes and silverware. Until we moved to Anaheim, this mother-in-law suite would've been bigger than any house we'd ever lived in. And it was nicer than all of them put together.

Don showed me around the suite and made it clear that it was all mine. He'd expect me to keep it clean and neat, but it was all mine. He said I should consider the whole house my home, and he hoped I'd feel free to go where I pleased and hang out wherever I wanted, but it was up to me. If I wanted privacy, I could just stay in my part and not feel pressured to do anything else.

He showed me the phone line he'd had installed. My own private phone with my own number. The guy thought of everything. He thought of things I wasn't smart enough to even consider.

"Make all the local calls you want, and I'll pay the bill for any long distance calls to your mom or dad," he said. "Now, get unpacked and let's get busy. We have a lot to do."

I unpacked all the belongings I'd brought with me, which didn't take long, but mostly I kept staring at this whole new world I was visiting. It was like I couldn't believe it was real.

Our first stop was the bank where Don had his accounts. When we walked in, everyone knew who he was. Dad had given me a thousand bucks to open checking and savings accounts, and that was way more money than I'd ever had. I put a hundred dollars into the new checking account and nine hundred in savings. While I was doing that, Don wired the $57,000 to Dad's new account in Rochester. My dad had been right about trusting this guy. My dad was almost always right.

Then we went straight to the DMV. I took my birth certificate and remember thinking it was a great thing my dad was in charge of how we packed. I probably wouldn't have thought to bring my birth certificate. I'd never needed it for anything, as far as I could recall.

"You need to pass this thing on the first shot," Don said. "Are you ready for that? You're going to use my car for the driving part of the test."

I figured I was ready. Driving an automatic would be a first for me, but that just made it easier. Having driven the VW around the neighborhood and on parking lots, I had the advantage of having driven a bigger car that had a balky stick shift, so the Mercedes didn't seem totally intimidating. It was easy to drive.

I passed the written portion with ease. Then I aced the driving part. At the end of one day I'd moved into what I considered a mansion, gotten bank accounts set up and earned my driver's license. Kind of a big day, although the thoughts of Mom and Dad never left me. I guess I discovered that I was pretty good at compartmentalizing things. The good stuff went here, and the bad stuff stayed over there. I was 16 and hadn't really had a lot of bad stuff in my life up until then. I remember thinking: "This is your next big challenge, dude. Deal with this, and stay focused."

I didn't sleep much that night. I don't know, maybe I didn't sleep at all. It was all so confusing and crazy. I was surrounded by all this luxury, Don was maybe the nicest person I'd ever met, and I was about to start a whole new chapter in another world. But Mom and Dad weren't there with me in this place called Bloomington, Minnesota. That side of my brain and heart were aching. How could all this stuff be happening at once? I was worried to death about both of my wonderful parents. Nothing I'd ever experienced in my damn-near perfect life prepared me for this. If I did sleep that night, I know I cried myself into that state.

The next day we went over to Bloomington Kennedy High. First stop was the principal's office, where Don helped me fill out the paperwork to get enrolled. School would start in about two months. Then we met in the gym with the baseball coach. His name was Fred Lund.

Coach Lund seemed like a great guy and he was young, too. He'd gone to Kennedy and played college ball before coming back to coach. This would be his first year as the head coach, and you could tell how excited he was. I think he was also excited to have me join the team.

"Your coach at Canyon told me all about you," he said. "If you're half as good as he said, you'll be a huge part of this program. Are you going to play any summer ball?"

I told him I didn't know. All of this stuff had happened so fast, from Mom's first headache right up until this meeting in the gym, I never really thought about summer ball.

"Hey, if you want to come here and workout unofficially, or lift weights, or do anything, you're welcome to do that. I'll introduce you to a couple of our catchers and maybe you can throw to them if you want. Other than that, baseball is really the least important thing in your life right now. Take care of the rest of it first."

That was good to hear, but there was definitely a part of me that needed the sanctuary of baseball. When I was on the mound, not much else mattered. It was my safe place, I guess. I told him I'd look forward to meeting the catchers and everyone else. Maybe he could design a throwing program for me, just to keep my arm in shape before fall practice.

"I'll do that, no problem," he said. Then he added, "I'm going to guess that our fall practice program probably isn't what you're used to in California. It's pretty informal, and it's just September. We'll work with you to make sure it's what's best."

I told him I was just another player. He didn't need to do anything special, and I really didn't want him to. I just wanted to meet the guys and blend in. It was that whole "instant friends" thing that baseball provides. At that time, I needed the friends. I needed them badly.

When we got home that afternoon, Don took me out to the garage at his house. Time for surprise number 112 or something like that. The garage had two doors, one big two-car door and one single, so it had three stalls. He parked his Mercedes on the big side and I hadn't thought much about what was in the single side. He lifted the door. It was a 1984 Toyota Corolla. It was nearly new. It didn't have a ding on it and it only had about 6,000 miles on the odometer.

"What the heck is this?" I asked him.

"Well, I told your dad I had a second car you could drive," he said. "Truth was, it was an old Saab that had some sentimental value to me, but it wasn't going to get you around very well, especially if you're wanting to get down to Rochester a lot. It needed a ton of work, and Saabs are expensive to work on. So I bought this.

"I got it cheap, so don't worry about it. I have a longtime friend who owns a string of dealerships, and I asked him a favor. I told him what I was looking for and he found this car at an auction within days. Apparently, some people buy nice cars and conveniently forget to make the payments. It was a repo, but it's just like new. It's all yours to drive. Take care of it!"

How many times could this SoCal surfer kid be speechless in the same week?

The next couple of days were a blur. Don took me shopping and I filled a cart with clothes for fall and winter. I felt like an astronaut getting ready to go to the moon. I'd never owned anything like that heavy winter stuff, and never had anything as nice as the school clothes I picked out. When it came time to pay for it, he pulled out a credit card.

"Hey, I need to pay for this," I said. "You're doing too much as it is."

"Well, you didn't bring your new checkbook. So, you're going to have to pay me back over the course of the next four months," Don said with a chuckle. "Plus, you didn't deposit nearly enough into your checking account to cover this. Heck, I'm not even sure you know how to write a check. We ought to work on that tonight, as well as how you keep track of what you've written and what you've deposited. It's called balancing a checkbook. It's just one more part of being an adult."

What the heck, I thought a hundred bucks was more than I'd ever spend at one time. It turned out that winter clothes were kind of expensive. Who knew? I didn't. I had a lot of learning to do. Money had never really been part of my life. It was never the focus at home, but we had everything we needed. I honestly didn't know if a good winter coat cost $10 or $110. Insurance? Never thought of it. Budgets? What are those? It was time to grow the hell up.

Don needed to get back to work running his marketing agency, so I spent a couple days just driving around the area, getting to know where everything was and the easiest ways to get to school, while I also got comfortable in the car. One day, I drove by the old Metropolitan Stadium, which was right there in Bloomington. The Minnesota Twins had moved into the new Metrodome in downtown Minneapolis just a couple of years before. The old stadium was basically abandoned and about to be torn down. I was thrilled just to see it. Even as a SoCal kid, I knew who Harmon Killebrew was. Rod Carew, too. And Kent Hrbek, that Bloomington Kennedy alum who was starting to make it big in the Major Leagues as a local kid on the Twins.

While I was going through all this wonder and awe, the other side of my life was always there. I called my dad every night. Mom was doing OK, he said, and the doctors were fantastic. They were brilliant, but the key thing is that they really cared. The term he used to describe how they approached my mom and her illness was "invested." They were totally invested in her, and my dad could sense that immediately.

"This was the right thing to do, dude," he said. "These people are the best and they have the best resources in the world."

He said he'd talked it over with the staff and the best thing to do was to apply for some grants to cover most of the cost. They'd help him expedite all of that, and allow him to pay off the upfront costs over time. The doctors said they believed Mom needed the best of everything, and that the experimental treatment wasn't the way to go for her.

"The doctor was real honest about it," Dad told me. "He said the experimental stuff might not work anyway, and if she was put in the control group and just got placebos, she might not survive a year. The prognosis isn't great, Brooks. How often can you get down here?"

That was kind of a shock to my system. Dad sounded OK, like himself, and there I was feeling like I'd just moved to Beverly Hills. Everything seemed to be going well, but to hear him use the word "survive" shook me. It didn't fit. I felt enormously guilty that

91

I'd been enjoying this new place and new experience while he was down there dealing with reality. I wasn't sure how to keep compartmentalizing it, because now it seemed way more dire. Baseball was important. It could take me places. It could make Mom and Dad's lives way better. But these were my parents. The two incredible people who raised me their own way. They made me everything I was and would ever be. I talked to Don about it, and we decided I'd go every weekend. He'd go with me the first time in the new Toyota, but after that I'd be on my own. A week earlier, I'd never driven more than a block at one time, or around a parking lot. Now I was going to be commuting 85 miles, each way, on highways every weekend. Maybe it was a good thing that all this stuff happened so fast. It didn't have time to fester or build up. In a blink, we all went from perfectly happy to dealing with it.

Before we headed down to Mayo on that Saturday, Coach Lund called an informal meeting with the team, or at least the guys who were around during the summer, and he introduced me to all of them. I think word had already gotten out about me, because they all seemed to know I was from California and apparently I threw hard. They were really friendly and all seemed like good guys, although a lot of them had names I'd never heard of before. Jorgensen (like it's spelled with a Y not a J), Gunderson, Sjogaard and other names like that. Different world, right?

They all stood around me asking questions. What part of California? Did you surf? What's it really like out there? Did you go to Disneyland all the time? Are you an Angels fan? Ever seen snow? Think you can handle the winter here? The answers were, Southern Cal, yeah I grew up surfing, it's nice and almost always warm, my dad worked at Disneyland so yes to that, big Angels fan, only seen snow in the mountains, and I have no idea about handling winter but I guess we'll see.

Two catchers were eager to help me stay in shape and they wanted to figure out a schedule with Coach, so I could get some throwing in despite not playing American Legion or any summer ball. We'd throw on Monday, Wednesday and Friday for the rest of the summer. Nothing too hard or strenuous. Just a nice throwing program to keep us all sharp.

Don also asked if I'd like to make a little money. Of course I would, considering I had made basically no money at all to that point in my life. I just wasn't sure what he was thinking.

"Look, I pay a lot of money to have a landscaping company come cut the grass and trim the hedges," he said. "I'll fire them tomorrow and pay you to do the same thing. They aren't that good anyway. Want to do that?"

I said sure. I mean, I'd never mowed a lawn or trimmed a hedge in my life either, but I thought I could figure it out. I was encountering a lot of "firsts" in a short period.

All within the span of just a couple weeks, I'd moved from SoCal to Minnesota. I'd seen my mom go to Mayo Clinic where the doctors weren't sure if they could make her better. I'd moved in with my dad's cousin Don, and he gave me what felt like a mansion of my own, not to mention a car. I enrolled at a new school and met my coach and teammates. I was learning my way around Bloomington and would soon be driving to Rochester as often as I could. And, I had a job mowing Don's lawn and keeping the landscaping neat and tidy. It was all mind-blowing. And conflicting. And scary. Yeah, kind of heavy on the whole scary part, but I felt this determination inside me. This was a challenge. Just like facing great hitters. Stay focused, do what you do best, learn everything you can to overcome it.

Life can meander really slowly when you're in your comfort zone. I learned it could spin-out like an out-of-control race car when you had to get out of that zone. I was way out of the zone, but I was determined to overcome it.

I also really needed to see my mom and dad. It had only been a week since I left Mayo with Don, but it seemed like a year.

Don had me drive, so I could learn the route and get comfortable in the car. He said I was a natural, and he liked how focused I was.

"Most teenagers can functionally drive just fine after only a few days behind the wheel," he said. "But way too many aren't mentally ready for it. They're too distracted and they don't realize how serious driving a car is. It's life or death, and I don't say that lightly. You're doing great. Keep it that way, bud."

We went straight to Mayo when we got down there, and when we walked into Mom's room I was stunned by how bad Dad looked. He was a shell of himself. He looked like he hadn't slept in a week or eaten anything. Mom, the sick one, looked pretty good actually. It was like totally surreal. My mom looked great, and we had a wonderful conversation about everything I was doing up in Bloomington. She honestly looked so happy to hear about the house, my new school, my new teammates, and the fact I had an actual job. OK, it was mowing the lawn for Don but I had taken on the responsibility and would be getting paid.

Dad was strangely quiet. Any new doctor walking into the room to meet my mom and dad might have thought my dad was the one who was seriously ill.

Don stayed and chatted with Mom for a bit, so Dad and I could go for a walk around the building. I didn't waste much time.

"Tell me what's up, Dad. You look terrible and I've never seen you so quiet. Are you OK?"

"It's hard, dude," he said. "I've never dealt with this kind of thing. I've been so fortunate to live my life with you and your mom. I can't sleep, I don't have an appetite, and it all just seems too overwhelming. I've never felt this way before. It all just sucks. I don't know what to do or how to fix it. I'm feeling a lot of 'Why me?' or 'Why us?' stuff. I'm not sure I have a purpose right now, because I can't seem to fix anything. It's hard. I'm in a dark place and pretty lost."

"Dad, I need to tell you something," I replied. "You have one job here now, and I don't mean to be a hard-ass but it's kind of critical that you do it. You absolutely have a purpose. It's keeping Mom's spirits up and helping her get better. You've always been our rock. I call you my hero for plenty of good reasons. Now I have to be up in Bloomington while you're here dealing with this by yourself. Mom needs you. The real you. I do, too. Find that guy for me, please. Find him. Bring him back. She needs her hero, and so do I."

He just started bawling, right there in the hallway, and he grabbed me like he'd never let go. I was so worried about him, but when he composed himself enough to speak it was straight from his heart.

"My God, you're everything I wanted you to grow up to be, dude. You've gone from being a kid to a man in a blink. This is the circle of life. When I needed someone to tell me how it is, and how it has to be, you were the guy who just did that. I'm so damn proud of you. Thank you, Brooks. Thank you. I'll make you proud."

That conversation would always stay just between us. Father and son. We even went to the cafeteria and got something to eat. He said it was the first food he'd put in his mouth in four days. Those James Taylor eyes looked just a little bit brighter.

CHAPTER 14

Eric Olson

We didn't slack off that summer after our senior season. A bunch of guys got together to run, do resistance training, pound the stairs and push each other. We had a small group of us going to Des Moines to play juniors, and at least a few other guys going straight to college, whether it was The U (that's where Paul Broten went) or other state schools. We had such a rare thing, with all those seniors on the '84 team, and nobody wanted hockey to end. Guys were going to do everything they could to keep playing, but we'd never forget what we were in our hearts. We were Roseau Rams.

I'll admit it felt strange to know I was working out and still a hockey player, but when practice would start for the Ram's '84-'85 season I wouldn't be part of it. What I had to look forward to was a whole bunch of "firsts" for me. First time leaving home. First time living with a family that wasn't mine. First time playing at this new level. First time in Des Moines!

I still didn't have a car, although my dad would let me use his truck from time to time. Some of the guys and I would go fishing or hunting, and usually one of them would drive, but Dad was good about making sure I could pull my fair share of that. And, Carol and I weren't totally done either. I'd borrow the truck and we'd go on long drives out in the country and even up to Winnipeg once, just to do some shopping at a real mall, before she went off to college and I headed south to Des Moines.

It's not like either one of us had been looking to break up. It was just that Des Moines was pulling me one way and St. Cloud State was pulling her another. So, even though you wouldn't say we were still dating, we still loved each other and we weren't afraid to do some things together. We both knew it was the last summer of our lives that would seem like all the ones that came before. At the end of the summer of '84 both of our lives would change and we wouldn't be seeing a lot of each other. I don't recall much of it being sad or anything like that. We just hung out together and spent some valuable time with each other. By the end of that summer, it would be over.

When August rolled around it all started to get a lot more real. Carol would be leaving first, heading down to St. Cloud to get moved in and all set up with her classes. That last week she was home was different than anything I'd ever experienced. Hockey had always come first, and that fall it would come first again, but just knowing that the only girl I had ever been serious with, or gone on dates with, was leaving Roseau (and me) gave me an ache in my gut so bad I thought I was sick. On her last day in town, I was just walking in circles. It was the first time in my life that I questioned what I was doing. It was also the first time I ever felt a little bit lost. When Carol and her parents drove away, hockey seemed secondary. I had never felt that way in my 18 years of life.

I think what got me grounded a bit was when school started at Roseau High. All of that was so familiar, and even though I had graduated and was out of there I'd always be part of it. And with our team almost all moving on, there would be 18 slots to fill on the varsity. The whole town was kind of excited about that, and probably a little nervous too. Me and all of my buddies were interested in how it would all shake out. Roseau didn't usually have such huge turnover on the varsity, but our group had been special and nearly the whole roster was going to be up for grabs.

Right around the same time, those of us heading down to Des Moines were getting ready to go. None of us had ever done anything like what we were about to do, and the team had sent us letters telling us when to be there, what to bring, and how to find the Des Moines Ice Arena once we got to town. It's funny now, but looking back on it I realize I'd never packed like that before. The longest I'd ever been away from home was when we went to the state tournament in St. Paul.

On the day we had to leave, there were definitely some nerves. Even for stoic Minnesotans it was pretty emotional to say goodbye to our folks and leave town for this big adventure. We drove to Des Moines in two vehicles, sticking together the whole way down through Minnesota and then into Iowa. I remember it seemed like a long trip, and that our moms had made us sandwiches and given us coolers full of soda and juice so we wouldn't stop at the first McDonald's we saw. We didn't have a McDonald's in Roseau. I remember we left first thing in the morning, right at sunrise, and I don't think we got to Des Moines until real late in the afternoon. I don't recall if we talked a lot on the way or didn't say a word. I just remember looking out the window for most of the trip.

We followed our directions and headed straight for the arena, and I do remember thinking that Des Moines reminded me a lot of St. Paul. It was a big city, to us, but not scary or overwhelming.

Having just completed our entire youth hockey and high school careers in Roseau, where Memorial Arena is about as old school as it gets, the Des Moines Ice Arena looked pretty modern to us. It was a big, rectangular box of a building, like a lot of the rinks we played in with the Rams, and really kind of "nothing special" as I recall. It's not like we were in awe when we walked in to meet the staff. We had just played in front of huge crowds at the St. Paul Civic Center arena a few months earlier at the state tournament, so there was nothing intimidating about it. When we got inside, it all looked like stuff we were familiar with. It looked like a real arena, and it probably held about twice the fans as Roseau Memorial Arena did.

We met the staff and all the coaches, then a bunch of our new teammates. It was all kind of a blur for us. We'd played together for most of our lives. And here all at once we were meeting new people and new teammates from all over the place.

Someone phoned our billet families, who were "on call" that day because no one knew exactly when we'd get there. David Drown and I would be living with the Warners, and when they showed up to meet us I could tell it was going to be good. They were quite a bit younger than my folks, and had two boys who both played youth hockey. I guess the boys were probably around 10 and 12 that first year. Their names were Bobby and Clint, with Bobby being the younger of the two. They both had red hair and freckles. That's the memory that sticks with me the most from the moment the family came to the arena to meet us.

We had to be back at the rink first thing the next morning to get our physicals and sort out the locker room and our gear, so we followed the Warners to their house. I absolutely remember Dave and I being a little nervous, because neither of us were normally very talkative and on that short ride we never stopped yapping.

Once we got there, the Warners showed us to the basement of their house, and they had it all set up for us. It was fully carpeted and we had two beds, a full bath, our own refrigerator, a couch and chair and our own TV. Heck, it was a lot nicer than my room at home!

David was one of the tallest guys on the Rams, and I was one of the shortest, so it cracked everyone up when Mr. Warner said, "Looks like we got Mutt and Jeff this year!" I was never really sure who was Mutt and who was Jeff. I'm guessing I was Mutt.

After they showed us around, we all sat around the kitchen table upstairs and John and Mary (Mr. and Mrs. Warner) laid out how it all worked.

"Basically, we just gained two sons," John said. "You guys are just part of the family. We work around your practice and home game schedule to make sure you have the meals you need, and you get the lower level. But, this entire place is your house. We're here to make you feel at home and comfortable. You can count on us for anything you need. We'll help you keep your fridge stocked and you can hang out down there if you like, but you're always welcome up here with us."

John showed us around our room and how things worked down there. There were a few more firsts for us. There was a microwave on the counter. I'd seen and used them before, but we'd never had one at home. And when he turned on the TV we discovered another thing Dave and I had never had. The Warners had cable! It was basic, and it actually worked by putting the TV on channel 3 and then pushing buttons on the box that sat on top of the television, but it had about 24 channels and we'd never seen anything like it.

I don't remember sleeping much that night, though we'd made about a 600-mile trip that day. I remember laying down and thinking: "I was at home in Roseau this morning. Seems impossible." It was actually pretty hard to comprehend. It felt like a long way from home.

The next morning we headed to the arena for physicals, meetings and all the other things that happen before a hockey team ever takes the ice for its first practice. At my physical, I was measured at "just a tick over 5-9" as the nurse put it. Something like 5-foot-9 and an eighth of an inch. Not enough to be called 5-9 and a half. I remember thinking "This is probably what I am. I'm 5-9. I'm always going to be 5-9. Deal with it."

I weighed in around 170, and that's what I was listed at in the program that year, but I could tell it was a different 170 than my senior year at Roseau. I'd worked out hard during the summer, but it wasn't as intense as my high school summers. I'd call those high school summer workouts more "desperate" than just intense. I was still in good shape, and as strong as I'd ever been, but there was no getting around the slight difference in how hard we all worked.

When they handed out gear and uniforms, we were given our sweaters and there was no negotiating for numbers. The returning players all had first choice, so they could wear what they'd worn the year before or change to pick up a new number that was available, and for the rest of us it was basically whatever was left in your size. I got number eight.

We had a series of meetings, got a full tour of the building and put all our gear away in our lockers. Then, the coaching staff gave us the standard pre-season pep talk about how hard we were going to work, what our offensive and defensive philosophies were going to be, and things like that. It all sounded pretty good to me, and the guys in the room looked like really good athletes, so I bought in. Then they sent us all home to get fully situated with our billet families. Just like us, a lot of the guys got in late the day before, so we still needed time to turn our rooms into homes.

I really didn't know much about the United States Hockey League before I got there. I wasn't even sure where the other teams were located. In 1984 you couldn't Google it on your phone. So, it was a good thing they handed out schedules to us before we left the building.

The USHL had 10 teams in '84-'85, and we were all mostly midwest based. There were actually two teams in the Twin Cities, which seemed like a good thing. The Minneapolis Jr. Stars and the St. Paul Vulcans were the two teams. I had no idea what the Vulcans nickname was about, and hadn't watched enough TV to that point in my life to make the mistake of thinking it was something about Star Trek. I made a promise to myself that I'd learn more about that when we got up there.

Besides the two Twin Cities teams, the league also had another Minnesota team in Austin, a small town in the southern part of the state and home to the SPAM factory and Hormel's headquarters. Even up in Roseau we knew about Austin and SPAM, because we ate a lot of it, mostly in hotdish dinners our moms whipped up. There were four other teams in Iowa, based in Dubuque, Waterloo, Sioux City, and Mason City. There was one team in Wisconsin, based in Madison, and a team beyond the Canadian border in Thunder Bay, Ontario. That would be one really long road trip but it didn't look like the other bus trips were going to be that bad. Thunder Bay was about as far from Des Moines as Roseau, but over on the north shore of Lake Superior, up past Duluth.

Preseason training started the next day. The thing I remember most clearly is that there was that group of guys back from the year before, who picked their numbers first, and our group of guys who were new. I think the room was split pretty evenly. The only people in the room that I knew were my teammates from Roseau, and a couple of other guys we'd played against. That was something I had never dealt with in my life. I knew almost all of the guys I played with in Roseau from the first time we ever laced up skates. I remember everyone in the room being outgoing and trying to act relaxed and confident but it was really strange to be with a big group of guys from all over the place.

Before practice started, the coaches had us go around the room to introduce ourselves, including where we were from. There were four of us from Roseau, and I remember a lot of the other guys nodding when we spoke. There were one or two players from Thief River Falls, so we knew them because we had played against them, but then we heard guys saying "St. Louis" or "Madison" or even towns in Colorado, Ohio and California. It was an interesting group. I'd never been part of anything like it.

At that first practice, we mostly just skated and talked strategy, then scrimmaged a little. We hadn't really talked about who would end up on what line or who would be playing alongside whom, but the coaches put up a sheet with some pairings and lines written on it, and off we went. The first time I hit the ice I knew I could play there. And even though I was just meeting most of the guys, I sure wasn't going to stop playing the way I had always played. I still had that "outwork and outsmart" attitude, and I gave it everything I had from the first whistle. And yes, I got some looks from the veteran guys who weren't used to a little defenseman being such a pest and a hitter, especially during the first practice. I did get some "attaboy" comments from the coaches, though.

Since most of us were strangers, another funny thing that happened was the hockey habit of creating nicknames. I don't think there's any other major sport where nicknames are such a big part of the culture. Before I ever got to Roseau High I was "Oly" to my teammates. Dave Drown was "Drownsie," which was an example of the fallback position of just adding "sie" to anyone's last name.

Even on the first day, you could hear the "Jonesie" and "Clarksie" and "Woodsie" nicknames out on the ice. Funny thing was, they all immediately called me "Olsie" not "Oly" and it stuck. All year long, I don't think I ever heard anyone say, "C'mon Eric." It was always Olsie.

We got into a nice groove in just a few days, and by the end of the first week it all felt normal. We had a great billet family, and discovered their boys had a table-top rod hockey game in the den upstairs. Those games got intense within 24 hours, and the kids were a lot of fun. I could tell they really looked up to us and were proud to have two Buccaneers living in their basement.

We'd go to practice, work out a little, and come back home to a nice home-cooked dinner. It was really comfortable and helped erase a lot of stress.

I thought our team seemed pretty good. It was clearly a different level than high school, because these were basically all the best players from their various high schools, and a lot of the guys on the team were big and strong, but I held my own. I didn't have any doubt I belonged.

Our first game was at home against the Mason City team, and it was pretty neat for us first-year guys to put our game uniforms on and make our debuts as junior players. We had a decent crowd, and the buzz was good, but it sure felt different than a Roseau Rams opener. We weren't pro hockey players, but we'd all left home to take this next step. It felt like being a pro. In Roseau, hockey was life. It was everything. The Roseau crowd was full of people who knew you and watched you grow up. That night in Des Moines, I was just No. 8.

I was on the second line, which was good. On my first shift, I raced to the corner to battle one of the Mason City guys for a loose puck. I'd done that a thousand times, and I usually won those tussles. Except this time when I got to the corner, the guy turned around, and hit me right across the chest, holding his stick with both hands spread apart. The referee just looked at us and kept skating. It missed my throat by an inch. I thought, "OK, this is different" and, honestly, it actually did faze me a bit. This really was playing at a different level, and it was going to be a rough level to conquer.

Very few guys on any high school team get the chance to play juniors or college hockey. If you took the juniors route, it's a battle to get out of that level and earn a pro contract or a college scholarship somewhere. It was a different kind of desperation that I could almost taste. It felt like we were fighting for our hockey lives, and it was just the first period of our first game. That night, we got creamed by a tougher team.

As it turned out, that happened a lot. All winter. We weren't very good, even at our best, and we were downright awful on other nights. We looked good in our uniforms, but we weren't all that fast, we weren't all that tough, and our defensive system was full of holes. And for me, the system was way different than how we'd done it in Roseau. It had me out of position a lot, away from my strengths in the corners and in front of the net. Plus, it was hard to understand and adapt to. For the first few weeks, I think we were all just kind of shell-shocked. After that it seemed like we were just numb to all the losing.

We made a lot of bus trips. At least it was a real bus, not a school bus, so it was a lot more comfortable and insulated from the winter weather. No more solid ice on the inside of the windows on a cold winter night. We stayed in motels, we grew very fond of our billet families and our fans, but we got beat a lot. You could say we got beaten into submission. It all kind of blurred into one long winter of defeat. We played 48 games, which was way more than any of us had ever played in one season of high school or youth hockey. Our final record was 7-37 with one tie and three losses in OT, which means we were really 7-40 with one tie. We won seven entire games. We finished dead last in the USHL. 10th place, out of 10 teams. It felt like we were lucky to get the seven wins and the one tie.

It was really a grind. It was all hockey, no school to worry about, but there's not much reward in it when you're not only getting beaten but also getting beat up almost every night. I'd never experienced anything like it, and I don't think many of the other guys had either. Our head coach, Ivan Prediger, clearly hadn't. He resigned during the season and one of our assistants, Jim Wiley, took over. We didn't win much for him either.

My family came down to the Twin Cities from Roseau for a few games, when we played up there on our first road trip, and once more when we were in Thunder Bay. It was wonderful to see them. By then, though, it was already clear that we weren't very good. I remember an odd look on my mom and dad's faces after the first time they came to see us play the Vulcans in St. Paul. I'd never seen that expression before. They looked worried. My dad just said, "How are you dealing with all this, son?" That was a big question, and I wasn't sure which part of it he meant. How was I dealing with losing? How was I dealing with the grind of junior hockey? How was I dealing with being away from our little home town we all loved so much? All I said was: "I still love the game, but I hate losing." The next time we came to the Twin Cities nobody came down. I don't think they liked losing, either.

That same first trip to St. Paul also taught me about their team nickname, the Vulcans. When our bus pulled up at the rink before the game, someone on the left side of the bus yelled "Look at that" as he pointed out the window. There was a vintage old 1930s fire engine parked right by the player's entrance, and it had "St. Paul Winter Carnival - Vulcan Krewe" painted on the side. There was a group of men in long red capes and funny red hats, with big black boots and stuff that looked like soot smeared in V shapes on their faces. And before the door to our bus even opened they were yelling at us and firing up the siren on the engine.

I thought: "That's the strangest Fan Club group I've ever seen," and it was like running a gauntlet to get through all those soot-smeared faces as we lugged our gear past them. It was loud, too.

Once we got inside I saw Coach talking to one of the St. Paul staff members, and when we got in the locker room Coach told us all about the Vulcans. It wasn't a fan club; it was part of the annual St. Paul Winter Carnival. The Vulcans were a major part of some big drama that happened every year. I was pretty clueless.

I'd heard of the Winter Carnival, and I knew it was a big deal, but didn't know many details about a big showdown at the end of the huge parade that wraps up the weeklong celebration, between a group that represented the north and the Vulcans, who represented the south. It happened every year. The red Vulcans wanted to bring heat and summer back to Minnesota. The others, dressed all in white, wanted it to be winter forever. I guess the Vulcans always won. So, those guys were the actual Vulcans for that year's carnival, gearing up for the big battle. They weren't a fan club. The team was actually named after them. Pretty neat, I thought. You learn something new just about every day.

I worked hard, and focused on my job all year. I couldn't single-handedly fix all that was wrong with us, and while I did score three goals and "racked up" a grand total of eight or nine assists, what I worked hardest on was never letting up, and that took every ounce of will I had. I'd never experienced such failure in a team sense, but I wasn't going to let that bring me down. Every night, I brought everything I could and I emptied the tank. I was playing hockey. I owed it to the game.

As the season wound down, I thought a lot about the experience and what the future might hold for me. All the losses had been tough to take. I wasn't sure if I'd lost 40 games in my entire life up until that point. I probably had, but doing it all in just a few months was really hard to absorb. Going to the rink had always been one of the most exciting things I'd ever done. By the middle of that first season in Des Moines, I admit it was hard sometimes to even get motivated enough to go. We knew we were probably going to get creamed, and it wouldn't be unusual for one of the boys in the room to leave the rink that night with his bell rung. We didn't talk about concussions then. You just shook it off. You had to be tough. Hockey players are tough. You got your bell rung. Shake it off and get back at it.

The losing created so many new questions. Did I even want to keep playing? At 5-foot-9 was there a future for me? Was I wasting my time? Should I just enroll at St. Cloud State so I could be with Carol? Maybe I could make the team as a walk-on. I didn't have any of the answers, but I knew I was a bit homesick and ready to get back to Roseau for the summer. It was a stark difference between the Des Moines Buccaneers and my dream days of being a Roseau Ram and how much it meant to put on that sweater each game. Like night and day.

This was much more mercenary than passionate. We were all looking out for ourselves, mostly. We got along well, and pulled for each other, but not one guy on the team had lived his whole life to that point with his greatest dream being to one day wear a sweater that said "DES MOINES" across the front. We were all trying to keep playing. And as much as we liked Des Moines, we were all trying to get somewhere else. I just didn't know if a "somewhere else" existed for me.

After the last game, we had our one-on-one debriefing meetings with Coach Wiley, and he made a world of difference to me in that sit-down. Looking back, I'd say it was life-changing but I don't know if either of us knew it at the time. I would not have been surprised or argued if he had said, "Thanks for your effort, Olsie, but I don't think you can play at this level," I just would've gone home.

Instead, he said, "Olsie, I don't think you realize you were our best player this year. Just because we lost a lot, and just because you're not a scorer who could carry us on your back, doesn't mean you didn't stand out. You played your butt off every night, during a season where I could feel the fight drain out of the rest of the guys a little more after every game.

"You know, Olsie, here's how I see it. As an athlete or a person, you don't grow and get better without adversity. If it all comes too easy, you get complacent and you think it's automatic, but you haven't really earned it. You earned a lot of stripes this year. You kept after it, you were a great teammate, and everyone on this team looks up to you. You're a huge part of what I see in the future. I'd love to have you back next year. You can go a long way if you keep this up."

That really lifted my spirits, which had been so low those last few weeks. It was literally a physical reaction. Like when people say it felt like a ton of bricks were lifted off their shoulders. I actually felt it. I'm sure I was slumping and looking down when he began to talk, but by the time he finished I was sitting up straight and staring right at him. A lot of what I guess you could call false guilt just evaporated.

Right up until then, I hadn't been able to shake the thought that I was supposed to be the lockdown defenseman and we were getting creamed every night because of me. I thought it was all my fault. I thought I'd hit a level where I couldn't make it. I was barely out of Roseau, still a kid, and still remembering the high of going to the state tournament. Instead of feeling that, I was to the point of feeling almost nothing. I was in Des Moines wondering why I was there. I was also wondering if it was all over. If it was, it was a lousy way to end a career, but I had a feeling I could accept that. All I ever wanted to be was a Roseau Ram. Basically, I'd already accomplished everything I had set out to do as a hockey player. But that competitive fire inside of me wasn't quite out yet. The embers were still lit.

Without a second of thought, I shook Coach's hand and said: "I'd be honored to come back next year. Count me in. I want to see if we can make this team better, and maybe even turn it into a winner. Thanks for everything, Coach. Everything you just said really means a lot to me."

He nodded and said, "You needed to hear it. It's been tough on all of us. Easily the worst hockey season of my life, and I'm sure you can say the same. By the time you get back here in the fall, you're going to be the leader of this team. Don't be surprised if the rest of the boys vote to sew that captain's C on your sweater. They all look up to you. They will follow you, Olsie. Just keep leading by example. Have a good summer. I know I don't have to tell you to stay in shape, but have some fun, too."

We went back to the Warners' house and packed up our stuff. It was pretty emotional to say goodbye to them. They were such a kind, giving and caring family, and we'd grown really close. Heck, I'm pretty sure it was more emotional to say goodbye to them than it was to leave our own families when we left Roseau for Des Moines to start the whole adventure in the first place. Lots of hugs and the two Warner boys, Bobby and Clint, were doing all they could to hold back tears. I think we were, too.

We got in Dave's truck and drove home. On the way I had plenty of time to think about everything that was swirling in my head, and that included seeing Carol again. I felt I'd done a good job of focusing on hockey the whole season, but we did share a few letters each month. I was happy to do that, and eager to see her again, but I couldn't shake the feeling that the tone of her letters had changed a little in the last couple months. It wasn't anything specific, just less personal and more just "what I did today" and details about her classes.

While the season was still going on, I was able to be the same focused guy who was so serious about hockey it cost him his girlfriend. Hockey had to come first, even on a bad team that barely won any games.

On that 10-hour drive north, I was, once again, all questions. Who would I work out with during the summer? Should I take some time off or get right back to it? Maybe I ought to be fair to my dad and brothers by working at the hardware store part-time. Maybe I'd see Carol and it would all become perfectly clear.

I just wanted to get home. I figured the answers would come.

CHAPTER 15

Brooks Bennett

When I started working out with a couple of our catchers, enough time had passed since the last time I touched a baseball, not to mention even having thrown one, that we decided to start out like it was the first day of practice. Three days a week, it was me, Carl Slaten, and Mitch Moore, who were both going to be seniors. Coach would come by at least once a week, just to see how we were doing.

The first day, we started out just playing catch, nice and easy, on flat ground. We wouldn't graduate to the mound for at least a week. It was like starting over for me, and that last game I pitched for Canyon High totally seemed like years before. It had really only been about four weeks, I think. Maybe five. Baseball hadn't been that far out of my mind since I was a little kid. Maybe ever. And on that first day together, we all decided that for the first week we'd get together every day, just to get in the groove a little quicker.

It felt great to be out on the field with those guys. Getting to know them, getting to know Bloomington, and enjoying the Minnesota summer weather, which was kind of fantastic. After we'd throw, we'd get some running in. Mostly jogging from foul pole to foul pole, which ballplayers call "running poles." We'd do four or five sets of those. Then we'd follow that up with some sprints. I could tell I was out of shape compared to how I'd always been, year round, out in California. I needed to do some serious work to get back to being the player and pitcher I had been for so long. I was just stoked to the max to be outside on the field. It's always been my sanctuary.

When we'd get done with each day's workout, we wouldn't just hop in our cars and go home. We'd sit in the dugout, taking our sweet time as we switched shoes from our spikes to our sneakers. We'd talk and ask each other a ton of questions. Neither of the catchers had ever been to California, and they wanted to know all about it. I did my best to fill them in with as many details as I could.

In return, I really wanted to know more about Minnesota. I was still pretty sure I might just curl up and die during the winter, but they actually made it sound like fun.

The thing I heard the most was: "It's not that bad. You'll get used to it." It was all about

104

wearing layers, they'd say, and winter was when a lot of the sports fun could be had. They were all about going to Minnesota North Stars games at the Met Center, which sat next to the abandoned Metropolitan Stadium right there in Bloomington. Apparently, our high school hockey team was pretty good, too. Just about all the guys went to the home games. They even went to a few University of Minnesota Golden Gophers hockey games each winter, up at the campus. I'd never been to a hockey game in my life, but they insisted I'd be hooked after one period.

There were Vikings games to go to at the Metrodome, and I knew if I got to one of those it would be another first for me. I'd never been to a professional football game.

There was snowmobiling, ice fishing, even skiing. Going to the indoor sports events sounded fun. That outdoor stuff sounded crazy. Ice fishing? Are you kidding me? They'd just laugh and say, "Just wait. You'll understand. We don't let winter get us down or slow us down. There's always stuff to do. We'll show you the ropes, California boy."

A couple days later, after working out, we all piled into Mitch's car so those two guys could give me a grand tour. I'd been learning my way around Bloomington just fine, but I was nowhere near ready to explore the two downtowns on my own. We headed to St. Paul first, then drove over to Minneapolis, only about 15 minutes away. My eyes were wide open.

SoCal in general, and Los Angeles for sure, aren't as much about a big downtown area as they are about sprawl. The whole L.A. region is just nonstop humanity that goes on forever. My dad took me up into the hills above Anaheim once on a super clear night, and it looked like a movie scene from up there. Nothing but lights for as far as you could see. And from that vantage point, all you could see was not even a tenth of the whole L.A. area.

I saw quickly that the Twin Cities were nothing like SoCal. Two different downtowns, with Minneapolis being about twice as big as St. Paul, but they really acted like the hubs on two wheels. The suburbs spread out all around them, and overlapped in the middle. That's where the fairgrounds were for the Minnesota State Fair. When we drove by that, the guys said, "We're taking you to the State Fair this August, right before Labor Day." I couldn't fathom why I'd want to do that. All they said was "You'll see."

The first thing I noticed in downtown St. Paul was the skyway system. It seemed like almost all the office buildings were connected by these glass-enclosed walkways that went over the street. On that day, we got there in the afternoon and even though it was a really nice day, you could see all the workers walking back and forth inside the skyways.

When I said something like, "Wow, look at that," Carl said, "My mom works in that building right there. She says it's just convenient to use the skyways during the warm months, because you don't have to wait at stop lights or deal with wind or rain. In the winter, the skyways are a lifesaver. There's a whole world in there. She calls it the 'Skyway Ecosystem.' Shops, restaurants, even doctors' offices. And you can't even see the tunnels from out here. A lot of buildings are connected below ground, too. In the dead of winter, you can pretty much get anywhere you want in either downtown without going outside."

If St. Paul was fascinating, Minneapolis blew my mind. It was way bigger, way taller, with skyways literally everywhere. They drove me by the Metrodome, with its huge white inflated roof, and my eyes about bugged out of my head. I'd never seen anything like it. Mitch said, "The Twins are on the road right now, but next week we can get cheap tickets to a game and come up here. Are ya in?" Sure!

We drove over to the U of M campus, which was way cool. The whole time we lived in SoCal the only real college campus I'd been to was Cal State Fullerton. It was kind of vanilla and unremarkable. U of M was more like a classic Ivy League school, like the ones I'd seen in movies. From the first second we were on campus I was in love with the place. I remember getting back in the car with the guys and saying, "Man, it would be cool to go to school here."

Carl said, "Yeah, it's a great school and they have a very good baseball program. Dave Winfield and Paul Molitor both went to The U." That stunned me. I had no clue. If Dave Winfield and Paul Molitor both had gone to The U and played ball there, then went on to superstar careers in the big leagues, there had to be hope that being a baseball player in Minnesota could work out OK. It was a really big day for me. It changed my whole perspective on the Twin Cities. For the first time since I moved into Don's home, I was starting to feel really stoked about living in Minnesota.

When we got back down to Bloomington, we stopped at a McDonald's. As we sat at a table eating Big Macs and fries, Mitch finally broke the ice. We had not yet spoken about my mom and dad.

"Coach said your mom is down at Mayo, but that we shouldn't bring that up," he said.

I nodded and smiled and said, "Well, thanks for doing exactly the opposite."

I filled them both in, with as many details as I could. I hadn't talked to anyone but Don about it since I got to Bloomington, but these guys were becoming my buddies really fast and I felt like I should let them know how it all went down.

I told them about Mom's artwork, about Dad working at Disneyland, about surfing, and about how I grew up and how super close we were from the earliest times I could remember. I told them how they raised me and what our homes were like. Then I told them how Mom started getting the headaches, and how bad it got.

"The doctors out there didn't know what to do," I said. "They just knew it wasn't good, and the best shot my mom had was to get to Mayo as soon as we could. We literally packed up everything and moved within about a week. It was crazy."

And I told them about Dad searching through all the phone listings, hoping to find his cousin Don. And how he found him, and how incredible Don was, and now I was living in his house driving a car he bought for me, and mowing his lawn.

They both listened to all of that with their eyes wide open, not saying a word. When I finally quit talking, they both just said, "Wow."

I said, "Yeah, well that's how I feel too. This has all happened since the end of May and early June. It's been insane, but it also feels like we're doing all we can for her and my dad really didn't want me down there in Rochester. He wanted me to play for a good school up here in the Twin Cities. He was afraid the scouts would never see me down there. And then he found Don in Bloomington. So here I am."

As soon as we were done working out on that first Friday, I raced home to Don's house, took a shower and drove down to Rochester. I met Dad at his apartment and we went over to see Mom. He looked a bit more upbeat. Mom still looked better than he did, though, and she was the sick one.

Basically, they still didn't know enough to have any idea what the treatment was going to be. They were trying different approaches to just treating the symptoms with pills, at the time. Some worked, some didn't. They were fast-tracking the grants to get some funding, she was holding her own, and it was all pretty much a waiting game at that point.

I just felt lucky to have my parents around me again. The prior few weeks had been like a tornado in our family. It was all spinning too fast and everything seemed out of control. It felt great just to sit around and talk to them again.

Sleeping on the couch in Dad's apartment wasn't the greatest thing, but I didn't mind. I was kind of sad when Sunday afternoon rolled around, but I knew I needed to get back up to Bloomington. I was living there for a reason. The reason was baseball.

On Monday, Mitch and Carl met me at the field, and then another car showed up. And another. And another. Word had spread about what we were doing, and some of the other guys wanted to be a part of it. By the end of that week, we had a dozen guys out there throwing and running. We even started to throw BP to each other, just so guys could swing the bat a little.

Many of the guys had part-time summer jobs, so they tried to fit their schedules around our workouts. Some others had gotten on local summer ball teams or American Legion clubs that ranged from lousy to pretty good, but they only played a couple of games a week. Still, it was a great way for this SoCal guy to get to know my new instant friends.

Coach came by a few days later, and he said, "OK, Brooks. This is a first. I've never seen any of our guys work out on their own, as a group, after our season was over. You're going to be a pretty good leader here, son. They're already following you."

That day, Mitch said, "OK, Carl and I want to go see the Twins play this week. Want to go see them play Cleveland on Wednesday night?"

I was all in on that. We went up to Minneapolis and parked Mitch's car a few blocks from the Dome. We didn't have tickets, but it was like that back then. You couldn't just jump on the internet and pick out your seats, so you either made a special trip up to the stadium to buy them in advance or you just showed up and got them before the game at the box office. The Dome was huge, and the Twins averaged filling only about half of the seats on any given night, so it was no problem. We bought tickets for seats out beyond the left-field wall.

Getting into the stadium was my first strange experience. To keep it inflated, they had to keep all the doors sealed. So, getting in meant going through big revolving doors that were like airlocks. Once inside, it was interesting, I guess, and very different from my Angels Stadium and Dodger Stadium experiences. OK. it wasn't just interesting. It was completely bizarre.

I'd never seen an artificial turf field. I'd seen them on TV, of course, but never in person, so before we went to our seats we walked right down to the front row by the Twins bullpen, just so I could get a close look at the turf. It didn't look much like grass, other than it was green. It was also my first time seeing sliding pits at the bases instead of a dirt infield. And the roof! It was white. I guess it had to be, but the first time a fly ball was hit anywhere near us, I couldn't see it after it got up high with the roof as the backdrop. White ball on a white fabric background? It was strange. No wonder the Twins outfielders rarely took their eyes off any fly ball. It would be hard to pick back up again.

The guys had already prepared me for what right field looked like. Out there, the sideline football stands had to be pushed back for baseball, kind of like your high school gym can be altered by collapsing the bleachers up against the wall. That made the Dome's playing field have more of a standard ballpark shape, but they didn't want all those folded up blue seats visible as a wall out there, so they covered the whole area in a big tarp. Twins fans called it "the Baggie" and that's what it looked like. Just one more bizarre thing to see! Artificial turf, sliding pits, a white roof, and a giant Baggie in right field. This definitely wasn't SoCal anymore.

The Twins won that night, although I don't remember the score or all of the players. They seemed pretty good though, even for big leaguers. I clearly remember Kirby Puckett, Kent Hrbek and Tom Brunansky on that team. I'd heard of them, and as a Bloomington Kennedy graduate, Hrbek was already a local legend.

We were sitting in what were considered "cheap seats" in the Dome, but all that really meant was that we were out beyond the left-field fence. There were no bleachers in the Dome, it was all seats. A sea of blue seats. It was neat to be that close to the left fielder and it was a cool perspective to watch the game from, especially compared to the nosebleed tickets my dad and I always got at Angels games. One of the Twins cranked a long homer out toward us, but it landed a couple rows in front of us. That never happened in the upper deck at Angels Stadium. And one other thing about the Dome. It was really loud in there. It was just a Wednesday night during the early summer, and when that home run came out to where we were, I'd never heard anything that loud at a ballgame. We couldn't hear ourselves talk.

When the game was over, and we'd eaten our Dome Dogs, Carl said, "Now you get to experience another Metrodome highlight." I soon learned what that was. They used the revolving doors to get the crowd into the Dome, since people show up over the course of an hour before the first pitch. Almost everyone, though, leaves the stadium around the same time. So they allowed fans to use big standard doors, and when those were open you literally got "ejected" from the stadium. All that forced air was rushing through those doors so fast you took one step to get through and all of a sudden you were staggering outside. It took me five or six steps just to get stopped, because the air pushed me out with a stout amount of force. I'm not sure you could have even done it in reverse. It was rad, and I laughed out loud when we did it. That Metrodome was a bizarre place.

We had fun that night, and we had fun all summer. The workouts went great, and all of the guys were happy to be out there. My trips to Rochester continued every weekend, and Don and I were getting along perfectly at the house. He took great pride in showing me how the lawn mower and hedge trimmer worked. I took an equal amount of pride in how I kept the place looking. And he was paying me enough so that I never had to ask Dad for any money.

And, my suite was my home. Don and I would watch some TV together in the main living room, and he'd cook some amazing meals a couple times a week. He was a master on the grill, out on the back patio. The best way to summarize it would be the word "comfortable" but that's a totally crazy understatement. I'd never lived in a house as nice as my suite, and I'd never met anyone quite like Don. My dad had been right. He was a saint.

Mom was hanging in there, although they were still swapping out medications to treat the headaches and the couple of seizure episodes she had. I think Dad was getting into the groove of being down there and supporting her every day. He was mostly out of his funk by then, and the specialists were keeping them posted on everything they learned. By early August, I was getting ready to head off to a new school and Mayo was ready to let them know what was coming next. They were going to try some sort of radiation treatment to see if they could shrink the mass on her brain. That sounded about as scary as anything we'd dealt with. I think the summer had been pretty calm up until then. Now I needed to get ready for school and Mom and Dad needed to be ready for the next dose of drama.

Right before school started, Mitch and Carl reminded me of something they'd talked about on our first grand tour of the Twin Cities. They wanted to take me to the State Fair. I still wasn't totally sure why we'd want to do that. I'd never been to any kind of fair, state or otherwise, but I'd learned by then to trust those two guys, so off we went. This SoCal surfer will admit he'd never seen anything like it.

The place is huge, and the crowd on the day we were there was the largest gathering of people I'd ever seen in one place. There were at least 100,000 people there. Heck, it could've been twice that. It was packed.

The whole place is set up like a city, with blocks of permanent streets and buildings filled with exhibits. And of course there were rides, including a Ferris wheel, an indoor boat ride, and a giant slide. According to Carl, the fairgrounds sit there mostly empty for 11 months a year, then it becomes like the third-largest city in the state for 12 days.

We had a great time, and I learned one key thing about the Minnesota State Fair. Basically, you eat your way through the place. We never stopped eating, and a lot of it was various kinds of food on sticks. A lot of bacon was involved, too. Corn dogs, chicken wings, little sugar-coated donuts they call "mini-donuts" and another thing I'd never seen or eaten before. They're called "cheese curds," which sounds awful but they're really good. Just little wads of some sort of melty white cheese, battered and deep-fired. Totally rad!

There were too many exhibits to see, and none of them were things I'd ever thought

I'd enjoy. Never in my life had I said, "I want to go see an entire barn full of sheep" or "I wonder what giant sculptures made out of butter look like?" It was wild, but it was great. I was feeling more at home in Minnesota by the day.

Less than a week later, I showed up on the first day of school as a junior who just transferred to Bloomington Kennedy from some foreign land called California. I felt a lot of eyes staring at me. I was 6-foot-3, I still looked a little different than all the Bloomington kids (some part of the surfer in me would always be visible, my entire life) with my hair still bleached out a little as if I'd just surfed Trestles the day before, and it was still pretty long. Also, the guys I'd been working out with had clearly spread the word about my pitching. Even the teachers treated me a bit differently than any of the instructors I'd had in SoCal. It was a little weird, but in a way it was kind of comforting. I was getting a lot of attention, but it felt good. Like they cared.

About halfway through that first day, I realized something. It was the first time I'd ever gone to school where all of it was indoors. When I'd told Carl and Mitch about how our "hallways" in SoCal were outside, they thought I was yanking their chains. It was weird to walk into the school in the morning and stay there all day.

As I went from class to class, I got a little overwhelmed by how many people I was meeting and shaking hands with. It was a big school, and there was no way to learn all those names on the first day. I wished they would've worn name tags, but they already knew each other. I was the new kid, but I think coming into it as a junior helped. At least I wasn't the new kid who was the youngest guy in school. I had some street cred being a junior and being taller than almost everyone else.

One thing I noticed right away was the "look" of the kids. It was very different from Canyon and other schools in SoCal. Out there, everything seemed to be to the extreme. Whether it was the whole "valley girl" thing, or punk rockers, or stoners, surfers, and jocks, or just the way kids dressed and acted, it was always a show. At Kennedy, everyone just looked "normal" to me. Very clean cut, I guess you'd say. And there were a lot of cute girls with blonde hair and blue eyes. They might have all been looking at me like I was a weird foreign exchange student, but a lot of those girls were cute and everyone was really friendly. Everyone I'd met in Minnesota was friendly. You can kind of slink through life in SoCal without making eye contact if you want, but in Minnesota it seemed like you never stopped saying hello to people. Everyone was really outgoing, and really nice.

I could tell immediately that the actual school stuff would be easy. It always had been. Over the course of the first week, and then the first month, I got to know a lot of the other kids and it all just settled into being normal old school. It was my 11th year of real school, or 12th if you count gluing all those popsicle sticks together in kindergarten.

We did have a short fall baseball program although it was informal without coaches and we didn't play any other teams. We just worked out, took BP, threw in the 'pen, and shagged flies. The guys were good, probably better than I'd anticipated for a bunch of guys in Minnesota, but not as good as the slick players on the Canyon High team. Our summer throwing had me pretty much ready to ramp it up on the mound once we started the workouts, and it was all still there. The fastball was popping, the changeup was nasty, and my curveball was finally getting some bite. When I threw BP, nobody seemed to have much of an answer for what I was dealing.

I remember thinking that the oncoming winter couldn't come at a worse time. All I wanted to do was start playing games. I liked Minnesota so far, and I liked the school, but this whole winter thing was bugging me and it hadn't even started yet.

And then they started the radiation program with Mom. Our principal excused me from school for a day, since Mayo was starting this deal on a Thursday. I got down there Wednesday night and then Dad and I spent all of Thursday with her. They moved her to a different room, in a wing where all the equipment was, I guess. I don't know. I never actually saw any of that stuff. I could only imagine what the equipment looked like. A couple of old horror movies came to mind. Dr. Frankenstein might have played a role.

I went back to school for a day and then headed back down for the weekend. When I saw Dad, he pulled me aside.

"Look, before we go see your mom I need to fill you in and prepare you a little," he said. "This is pretty potent stuff they're doing, and it can really rough her up. So they're medicating her pretty heavily until they see how she handles it and if it's working. It's non-invasive, since they can't really get in there with an operation, but it's really powerful. She's not going to be like she normally is. And she'll probably lose her hair pretty quickly."

I thought I was ready, but I wasn't. They basically had her doped up and she could barely open her eyes when we went in. She was also white as a sheet. I could tell she knew it was me, but that was about it. She tried to squeeze my hand but I could barely feel it. I didn't know what to do or what to say. I just gave her a bit of a hug and then Dad and I sat by her bed for a while.

When we went back to his apartment, Dad laid it on the line for me.

"This is a longshot, Brooks," he said. "It's going to be really a tough go and the doctors were straight with me about it. They think it has maybe a 20 percent chance of doing any good. It's the only chance she's got. They've been kind of preparing me for a few weeks now. I keep hearing lines like 'We'll keep her comfortable' and 'We want to ease her pain and stop the seizures' way more than anything approaching 'We're going to fix this and everything will be fine.' I guess they're trying to lower my expectations, but I have to agree with one thing. I don't want to see her in pain anymore."

I just nodded my head and tried not to cry. I think Dad was all cried out. The whole damn thing was so surreal it felt like I was living some movie script instead of my previously wonderful life.

Back at school, we only had one week of fall practice left, so I headed back up on Sunday night and filled Don in on everything. He told me he was really impressed by how well I was holding up and dealing with all of this. I told him I felt like I was doing a hell of a job of faking it.

Within a few weeks, Mom was completely bald. She was still heavily medicated, too, and I started to understand Dad's line about not wanting her to be in such horrible pain anymore. I'd had a hard time understanding that, but then I got it. This was about her.

111

Not about what we wanted or the life we'd shared that was so happy all the time. At least they were keeping the headaches mostly at bay.

Somewhere near the middle of October, I got up one morning to go to school and Don yelled at me, "Put on a coat, Brooks." I slipped one on and went outside, and then I felt and saw something I'd never experienced before. I could see my breath, and it was COLD! I was shivering, even with a coat on. Then I got to school and saw I was pretty much the only guy wearing anything heavier than a sweatshirt. It was like 35 degrees. I'd learn quickly that 35 can feel like a warm day in Minnesota. It was the coldest day I could remember in my life, and some kids were still running around in shorts. Crazy.

As we closed in on November, it was getting legit cold. The first day the high never reached 32 was nuts. Then, by the end of the month we were getting down into the teens at night. I learned pretty fast about that whole "wearing layers" thing. T-shirt, long-sleeve shirt (maybe even flannel), sweatshirt and coat. Wear gloves too. And a beanie hat. And real shoes. I'd stretched the flip-flop thing out until the end of September. It was going to be a while before I'd wear them again.

In the early part of November, Carl and Mitch kept another promise. We headed to the Met Center to see the North Stars play the Montreal Canadiens. I didn't know crap about hockey, and I didn't know much about the NHL, but I sure as hell knew about the Canadiens. They were the Dodgers, Yankees and Red Sox all rolled into one historic franchise.

As opposed to the Twins game, there weren't really too many cheap seats at the arena. We sat up at the top of the bowl behind one of the goals. I knew right away that I needed to be closer the next time we came, no matter how we scrounged the tickets up. What was happening on the ice was insane, it was really fast, and it was way cool. And these great athletes were doing it all on skates! The guys were right. I was hooked on hockey after one period.

When I got home, I was telling Don how cool it was. He said, "Yeah, it's awesome right? My agency owns season tickets. They're really good seats right down by the glass. Just pick out a game and you and your buddies can use them." OK. Awesome!

Then came an important call from Dad. It was the middle of November, and he said "Brooks, I've got some news. It's getting smaller. Not by a lot, but the doctors say any shrinkage is a great sign. For the first time, they feel a little optimistic. I could hear it in their voices. This round of treatment is over, too, so they're going to really lower the meds. Can't wait for you to get down here this weekend."

We rambled on for a good 30 minutes and it was the most animated conversation we'd had in months. I couldn't wait to get down there either.

Mom looked so much better. Just getting her off the heavy meds made a world of difference. She was alert and able to hold a conversation, although quietly. We talked for a good 20 minutes before she needed to get some more rest. That rest was actually prescribed by the doctors. Without it, she wouldn't have the strength to keep fighting the fight.

Dad and I went to dinner and he was a new man.

"These last few months have been hell, but I think we're turning a corner, dude," he said. It was the first time in months he'd called me dude. When you're talking about your wife and mother of your only child being close to death, dude doesn't seem appropriate. It meant a ton to me, just to hear it.

We talked about our plans for the future, and one thing he said kind of surprised me. He said, "Look, I know you want to be down here every weekend, but you don't have to do that now. She's getting better, and they hope that continues. Plus, it's about to be real winter soon, and you've never driven on snow. I'm sure Don will give you some pointers, but I can remember winters in Pennsylvania that were pretty terrifying and I've already heard how bad the highway between here and the Twin Cities can be when it really comes down with the wind blowing. Snow is one thing, but the wind is worse.

"Until you get comfortable with it, just stay home a few weekends after the snow flies. I'll call you every day. I just don't want to put you in any danger if the roads get bad. Have you met any girls yet?"

OK, that last part cracked me up, but I could tell it was a way to ease the jolt of being told I didn't need to be there every weekend. I laughed and said, "First off, snow doesn't have a chance against me but I'll get with Don and get some lessons. Second off, half the school is girls, so yeah I've met a few. They're all pretty cute, too."

"Great," he said. "Ask one of them out. Use one of these rare free weekends to have a date. Go to a movie. Eat a pizza. Have some fun."

That last line got me a little. I'd been having fun. Carl and Mitch were already my best buds, and everyone up there was nice. Baseball was back in my life. Don was fantastic. My suite was luxurious. And all that time, Dad had been down in Rochester in a cramped studio apartment, having to deal with this while my Mom, the woman I loved the most, was in such pain.

He could see it in my eyes, as I shook my head. Dad was always that perceptive. I swear he could read my mind. He always could.

"Hey, man, I didn't mean what you're thinking. I sent you up there, and Don brought you into his home. You can't feel guilty about that. You wanted to stay here, but I wouldn't let you. I sent you up there, OK? It had to be this way, and now it looks like it's working out. Be a high school kid, and get ready for next season. The scouts are going to be all over you."

I didn't have much choice but to accept what he'd said. It made sense, but I still felt guilty. I had to get back up there and get through the winter though. There was no escaping that.

I spent Thanksgiving with Don, who invited his friend Robert to join us. Don had told me about Robert, and I was eager to meet him. From the first second, he seemed like a great guy and he was absolutely hilarious, so we hit it off immediately. He was a doctor, and although his specialty wasn't anything related to what Mom was going through, he was really interested in all the details and the procedures, especially some of the experimental things they were trying. I could tell within minutes that he'd be the sort of doctor who would have a great bedside manner. Lots of compassion and direct eye contact. My thoughts were with Mom and Dad, but it was a great day with a huge feast. It was family.

Winter. It didn't really hit until mid-December. At that point, I was already cold every day but a lot of the guys were telling me winter was actually late that year. Then I woke up on a Monday to go to school and it about knocked me over. It was seriously cold. Couldn't have been much more than five degrees. And the snow was coming down almost sideways in the wind. I went outside just to experience it, and within a minute I was covered in snow. Don was standing at the door laughing. I guess it was pretty funny.

I think we got about eight inches that first snowfall, and a lot of it came down while we were at school. No one even talked about classes being canceled. We just went on with our studies, and I looked out the windows a lot.

When I got in my car to drive home, I was a little worried about it. Then I left the parking lot and two giant plow trucks went by, clearing the snow off the road. It was kind of amazing to watch, and the roads were already pretty clear. I figured out right then that Minnesota knows how to handle snow.

When I got home, Don introduced me to another piece of important equipment he owned. It was something called a snowblower. He had a whole collection of regular shovels, but his driveway was pretty long and I didn't see the two of us shoveling our way to the road, after the snow finally quit. He fired up that snowblower and showed me how to use it. Basically, it was a lot like the lawnmower. It was kind of fun, really. And it took just enough energy to keep you warm. It was 5 degrees and there was snow everywhere, but I realized I wasn't really cold. My toes were, a little, but other than that I was fine. Maybe I would get used to it. Maybe I already was.

I think the hardest thing to get used to, that first winter, was how short the days were. Up there, in the northern part of the country in December, it gets dark by 4:30 in the afternoon and it stays dark until after you get to school in the morning. That bothered me more than the snow and the cold.

By that time, they were allowing Mom to come in for treatments, tests and other procedures on an outpatient basis. She moved into Dad's little apartment but still had to go meet with the doctors a lot.

For Christmas I went down there to be with them. Mom was looking a lot better, although her hair hadn't really come back yet. She did, however, proudly point out that she had a little "peach fuzz" coming in.

We had promised to only get each other one small gift, but Dad kind of lied to me. He gave me a fairly large box that had a new pair of Puma spikes and a new Rawlings glove in it. I gave Mom something I'd picked out just for her. It was a calendar with pretty photos of Minnesota scenes on it. The pictures were beautiful, but an equally important part was the lower pages with the months and the days printed on them.

"This is Minnesota, and you're going to love it," I said. "You've been here all these months and all you've ever seen is the parking lot below your room. We're going to go see these lakes, waterfalls, parks and lighthouses.

"And all these dates — 365 of them! They're going to help us all look forward, Mom.

Look at these pages full of days we have to look forward to. And next year, I'll buy you another calendar. Every year, I'm buying you a calendar. We shouldn't let any of these days go to waste." We all cried a little, but I meant it in a positive way. We had to believe we were going to have all those days.

After the new year, school got going again and Coach called a meeting in the gym for the whole team.

"This is the hardest part for all of us, as you guys know," he said. "We're back in school, baseball is already ramping up down south in Florida and Texas, and I'm sure Brooks can tell you that his former teammates in California are probably taking BP on their field today. We're still months away from that.

"So it's on us to be ready. It's on us to work as hard as we can on our throwing programs, and on our BP program. We'll hit the weights a little too. The difficult part is going to be keeping our legs in shape and building up our capacity to go flat out. There's not enough room for all of that in the gym, and we have to share it with the basketball teams anyway.

"I've talked to Principal Brendell, and he agreed to a couple of things. We can put the batting cage up in the gym three days a week. And the whole school will stay open until at least 6 each night. We can do some running in the halls. We'll start for real around February 10. Our first game is scheduled for April 10. I hope the weather lets us do that."

I'll admit, I felt a little homesick for SoCal right then. He was right. My former teammates were already getting on the field out there. They'd have their first game in early March. It wasn't going to be easy getting through the rest of that winter, but as Coach said, it would be "on us" to get ready.

Winter kind of fell into a routine, and school was actually really fun. Like I said before, the hardest part was how short the days were. When it was finally mid-February, we started our practices in the gym and did our running in the halls. It was unreal, in a lot of ways. Just crazy to think we were getting ready for a baseball season by throwing and hitting on a basketball court and running just outside the classrooms, while the piles of plowed snow out around the edges of the parking lot were about 6 feet tall. At the end of the first week, Coach brought us together for another meeting.

"Guys, I've got some big news for you," he said, with a smile on his face. "This has been developing all winter, but it just became official and now I can tell you. There's going to be a non-conference tournament before our regular season starts, and we're going to be part of it along with five other schools. It will be in late March."

No one said a word, but if life was like cartoons I'm sure we all would've had question marks circling over our heads. How in the world could we play a tournament in March? He let us know.

"Guys, the tournament is going to be in the Metrodome!"

We all started yelling and screaming, and high-fiving each other. It was totally nuts, and he completely blindsided us. We had zero clue up until he said that.

"We don't have the schedule worked out yet, but right now it looks like it will be a three-day tournament, and it's round-robin so we'll play all the other teams," he said. "We'll play two seven-inning games a day, I'm sure. In the end, there will be a championship game on Sunday afternoon. There are still a lot of details to work out, but we're going to start the season indoors on a Major League field. That ought to give you something to shoot for."

I guess so. It sounded incredible.

After the meeting, Coach pulled me aside and said, "Brooks, you're going to start the first game at the Dome, but I'm not letting you go more than 50 pitches. I don't really care about winning or losing up there; this is not about that. I want you to be our featured starter in that first game. It will be a heck of a way to introduce you to the other teams and whatever scouts are there."

Our next practice was the following Monday, and you could tell the intensity level was off the charts. We still had about five weeks until we played at the Dome, but it felt like we were training to play by the end of the week. I had to consciously keep reminding myself to stay with the throwing program and not try to air it out yet.

A week or two later, we got more info. The tournament would include us, Edina, Eden Prairie, Cretin, Mahtomedi and Stillwater. All the schools except Stillwater were in the Twin Cities. Stillwater was a separate town just to the east of St. Paul, on the St. Croix River.

Basically, this tournament was going to showcase the cream of the high school crop. Just to be in the thing was a high honor, and Coach made it clear that not only would there be scouts there, but college coaches too.

Meanwhile, Mom's hair was starting to grow again and she was making incredible progress. So much so that the conversations were turning to "What are we going to do when they release you completely?" Ever since the move, I hadn't even thought of that. I hadn't dreamed it would come to that.

She still had another couple of weeks down there, and the specialists were really interested in how it was working and how well she was bouncing back. I guess you'd say she was kind of a case study for them.

Mom and Dad had both decided that we'd be staying in Minnesota. Mayo wanted to keep track of her on a monthly basis, but at least they could move into an apartment up in Bloomington and we'd all be together again.

It was all a bit of a blur, but it was a great blur to be a part of. Mom was getting better. School was great. Baseball was about to happen. And, I was going to open the season for us at the Metrodome!

Bring it on. Bring it all on!

As we got into March, it was clear Mom was going to be released from the outpatient deal at Mayo pretty soon. We had to put those wheels into motion to find a place in Bloomington so we could all have a home together again.

Dad said, "Look, you concentrate on baseball. Be ready for that first game at the Dome. I'll find a rental place for us, and get everything situated. If Mom is ready to go to a ballgame, we'll be there. If she doesn't have the energy for that, you can bet your ass I'll still be there. This is pretty damn cool, isn't it dude?"

It was cool. And Dad found a furnished two-bedroom apartment only about a mile from Don's house. I made sure Don understood that his landscaper and snow removal guy still wanted to keep his job.

When the big day came, Mom and Dad drove up to Don's first. She looked pretty good, and had better energy, but she still had a long way to go. We had lunch with Don and Robert, and in the end the hugs were totally amazing, and for good reason. There were many weeks and months before that moment when I was pretty sure the hugs were going to be condolences, when it was time for me to leave Don's home.

When I asked Don when he wanted the car back, he just laughed. "It's your car, man. I bought it for you. Take good care of it. We'll get the title changed over to your name because I'm going to sell it to you for one dollar. Make sure you keep it insured, OK?"

Did I ever mention that Don was a saint?

Looking back, I don't know what life would've been like without him. I'm sure we could've found a family that would take me in, but living in my suite at Don's home was an incredible experience. He was a phenomenal man with a heart of 24-carat gold. I was happy that I'd still get to see him when it was time to mow, trim, or snowblow.

In the meantime, I had a date to get ready for. It was going to be at the Metrodome. Talk about stoked!

CHAPTER 16

Eric Olson

The summer of 1985 was the strangest stretch of time in my entire life, up to that point. It was like I'd gone away to play in Des Moines and when I came back home, everything was different. Nothing had ever been "different" in my whole life in Roseau. There was no denying it felt different. Or maybe I was just different. Probably a bit of both, I guess.

I had been gone about six months, and it felt strange coming home. I'd never been away for more than a short string of days. When I got back it seemed like the town was the same but everything else was slightly altered. Or, like I said, maybe it was just me. I'd grown up a lot being down in Des Moines. I felt a lot older when I got back. And I felt a bit like a stranger, which is about the most peculiar thing any Roseau native can feel. I'd spent 18 years of my life absolutely tied to this town. It was *my* town. And now I felt like I was visiting. Part of it might have also been "How'd this entire town get along without me for six months?"

Even our home life was different. Betsy got a job working in my mom's department at Polaris. Only Jon was still working with Dad at the hardware store, because Brent had also gone to work at Polaris. It paid a lot better than working at the store, and it allowed Brent and Jon to rent a small house in town and live on their own. I could tell that Jon's plan was to take over the store someday, and keep it in the family. David was out of college, with a degree in business administration, and he was living in St. Cloud. He'd made a lot of friends there, and landed a job with Polaris as a regional sales and marketing rep, covering central Minnesota. Everything felt really odd.

Carol came back home that summer, but even that wasn't the same. There was a distance between us that just didn't seem comfortable, which was different than the summer before. We knew then that we were going our separate ways, but we were such close friends we could still just be relaxed and have fun together. Not this time.

We got together at her house when she got home but it felt like a big invisible gorilla was in the room with us. We had never had any trouble just talking, but it felt like neither one of us knew what to say. She filled me in on school, her classes, her roommate, and that sort of stuff. I told her about the season, and all the losing, and my billet family. And then there was silence.

I finally said, "OK, tell me what's really going on. This is too awkward."

Thankfully, she got right to the point. "I'm seeing somebody," she said. "He's a nice guy. I like him a lot, and he treats me really well. Plus, he doesn't play any organized sports. He played hockey, but only through high school. He's planning on being a reporter. He's a journalism major."

I asked her how serious it was, and she had a look on her face that made it clear she was about to cry. When the first tear rolled down her cheek, all I could do was give her a hug.

She said it was "pretty serious" but they'd only been dating for a couple months. He was from St. Cloud, so he was already home for the summer, and she admitted that she wished she could go back down there but she'd promised her folks she would come home to Roseau.

I told her exactly how I was feeling, as bluntly as I could.

"Look, we're always going to be friends. You're the only girl I've ever felt this way about, but we both knew our lives were changing when we left Roseau last fall. I just want you to be happy. You don't need to worry about me. You can call me anytime. You can come see me whenever you want. You'll always be in a special place in my heart."

And then, maybe trying to be a little funny, I added, "I still have my mistress, you know, and that's hockey. I'm still playing. I think there's a good chance I'll play the next two years in Des Moines and then go to college. I never really thought about playing college hockey, but I think I can do it. We both still have paths we're supposed to follow. I love you, babe. Just be happy."

We ended up seeing less and less of each other as the summer went on, but that conversation had kind of taken us to the level where we needed to be. We both wanted the other to be happy. No expectations, just support. We needed to support each other in these new lives, and the independence came with that, I guess.

A few days later, I went up to the school just to see what was going on there and I ran into the hockey coaches. They immediately asked me if I was going to do the same sort of workouts I'd done before, and I said I was. Then, one of the assistant coaches said, "You think you might want to have some of our younger guys work out with you? Like, kind of lead them through what you're doing and help them out?"

That sounded great. I knew my brothers had moved on and probably couldn't help me much, so having some of the newer varsity players around would keep it all going and it would be good for them, too. I liked the way it made me feel. A graduate now, but still in contact and still part of the program. I'm not sure I'd ever felt like that sort of leader, with guys who looked up to me as a Roseau Ram who went on to play in the USHL. It was neat, and it got me through the summer.

The guys were all younger, of course, and my year in Des Moines had made me even more serious about how I approached staying in shape. At first, I was kind of stunned to see how they acted, goofing around a lot. I remember thinking, "These guys are so immature. They're not taking it seriously" and then my next thought was, "They're just kids. It's my job to show them how to do this."

We'd start each day, no matter how many guys showed up, with me running through what the drills were going to be. I always said, "Look, I'm not your coach. You have great coaches who can make you better players. I'm here to show you how to be in the best shape so you can be the best player possible. You're Roseau Rams. That's a lot of responsibility, so take it seriously. Let's get to work."

As the summer wore on, the workouts ramped up and the guys started to see why they were doing it and what the workouts were doing for them. Once that happens, you flip the page from "this is just a lot of hard painful work" to "I'm getting quicker and stronger" and everyone starts to take it more seriously. That happens when you see actual results.

Summer in Roseau is spectacular, so that helps. My golf game was getting better, the workouts moved along, and I finally got to the point where I was counting the weeks and then the days until I'd head back to Des Moines. I'd be doing it as the lone Roseau guy that second season, and the team had a bunch of new recruits they had brought in, so I was looking forward to it a lot. I could tell how much I'd mentally grown since that first trip to Des Moines. A year earlier I was nervous, a little scared, and happy to have a few friends going with me, while I was still not sure it was the right thing to do. This time, I didn't feel anything but ready.

Finally, it was time to say goodbye to Carol again, when she left to go back to St. Cloud. It was different than it had been a year earlier, when I was pretty lost and sad to see her go. We'd managed to stay friends, but I figured that's all we'd ever be, or at least I hoped that. I wished her well, gave her a quick hug, and then mentally shifted gears to start the process of getting ready for another year in the USHL. More than anything, I just hoped we'd be a better team.

My big challenge for getting back to Des Moines was the fact I still didn't have a car and I had no Roseau teammates to get me down there. Dad came to the rescue when he bought a new truck and handed down his old beater to me. It was a Ford F-100 and it had about 150,000 miles on it, but he took great care of it and had never really had a problem with it. We even changed the oil and put new tires on it just to be safe.

It all came together in a hurry, just like it had the year before. The Roseau High kids were excited to get on the ice just about the same time I was scheduled to head down to Des Moines. We had one last workout, with maybe a little extra effort on everyone's part, and said goodbye. We were all in a similar boat. A year earlier, after our 18 seniors had graduated, the Rams were looking to almost completely restock the roster and that process was still ongoing. After going 7-40-1 in Des Moines, the Buccaneers were doing the same thing. There would be about 10 of us back for another year there. The rest of the team would be new guys.

It's interesting how maturity changes just about everything about you. A year before, I was nervous as hell about just riding along with Dave when we drove down there. It seemed like such a huge trip, for a lot of reasons. In 1985, I just said goodbye to the family, loaded up my gear and hit the road in the truck. I was back down at the arena late that afternoon, and it felt a lot like home. At least a second home. Yes, Mom did make me sandwiches and stock some soda and juice in the cooler. That all came in handy.

I'd already heard that I'd be living with the Warners again, and was excited about that. I'd have a new roommate, but I wouldn't find out who that was until I got all squared away. Turned out it was a guy named Randy Goodrich, and he was from Denver. We were both defensemen, and Coach had let us know that we'd be on the ice together a lot. We'd have plenty to talk about all winter, talking hockey and explaining our different upbringings. I thought that was a good thing.

We went through the same preseason process we'd done before, but this time Coach Wiley and his staff were in charge from the get-go. After about two weeks, we were ready. We seemed like a better team, but I remembered clearly that I had thought we were pretty good after preseason workouts the year before. It's hard to tell until guys in different uniforms show up to play you.

Everything was great with the Warners, and the boys, Bobby and Clint, were growing up. The table-top rod hockey games were a lot faster than the year before, when Dave and I were slowing it down so they boys could be competitive.

A few days before our opener, at our arena, we had a meeting to discuss a bunch of details and to cast our votes for the captain and assistant captains' roles. The coaches said they reserved the right to overrule if they didn't think we'd picked the right guys but they didn't do that. I would be wearing the captain's "C" on the front of my Des Moines sweater. That was another first for me, and I was proud of it.

There were a few adjustments in terms of the teams in the league, but all in all the bus rides were going to be about the same. The Minneapolis and Austin teams had dropped out, but we picked up a team in Rochester, Minnesota, so we'd have a nine-team league. At least we couldn't finish 10th again!

And, as we plowed into the 48-game schedule and rode the bus all winter, we still weren't very good. Not as bad, but we struggled all year just to get a "W" every now and then. I didn't let it affect the way I played, and Coach was good about keeping us all positive and working hard, but we still lost way more than we won. In the end, we finished 11-36-1, so we picked up an entire four wins over the year before. Personally, the key for me was emptying the tank every game. If I could look back on the season and know I had done that, then that was all I could do.

A lot of it was exactly the same, but this particular group of guys seemed more willing to hang in there and buckle down than the '84-'85 group. We never got too down on ourselves, and we just kept fighting to improve. By a long shot, it was a better experience than the year before. I managed to pop a few goals into the net along the way, and I could tell my defense was continuing to get better. Coach Wiley knew my strengths, and instead of trying to implement some complicated and crazy schemes, he had us keep it simple. As the year went on, we understood it more and it was at least more fun.

Randy and I were paired up on the first line a lot, and we quickly formed that bond you need, where you don't have to look to see where your partner is, because you already know. He was about 6-foot-1 and he liked to hit, so I think my quickness and my toughness in the corners meshed pretty well with his game. Neither one of us liked losing, but we enjoyed playing and rooming together.

Probably the highlight of the year was something I didn't know about until after it had happened. We'd been up in St. Paul to play the Vulcans for a two-game set, and after the second game, on the way back to Des Moines in the bus, Coach came down the aisle and found me in my seat.

"Come on up to the front for a bit," he said. "There's something I have to tell you."

I'll admit that worried me a little. Anytime the coach wants to see you, whether it's in his office or in the seat next to him in the front row of the bus, there's more to worry about than to be instantly optimistic about.

When I sat down he said, "I didn't want you to know this until we were done in St. Paul."

I just looked at him and said, "OK. What?"

"Well, the Gophers had some coaches there watching us, and they were there to watch you. They've followed you since your senior year at Roseau. The two assistants who were there told me they're interested. Sincerely interested. They think you need one more year in Des Moines, and if you keep improving and getting stronger, there's a good chance they will make you a scholarship offer."

I wasn't really sure what to say other than "Wow. I had no idea."

Coach said, "That's why I didn't tell you and didn't have them talk to you. I'm sure the head coach, Doug Woog, would be the one to talk to you directly, when the time comes. I didn't want you to try to do too much if you knew they were there. You've still got a way to go, but I wanted you to know they're watching you. You've never needed motivation since I met you, but this news ought to help you turn the dial up another notch."

It sure as heck would. All I ever wanted to be was a Roseau Ram. Nothing more. Then, the chance to play juniors in Des Moines came along and as rough as it had been, teamwise, it was a great experience for me to play with and against a lot of really talented big guys. I knew I was getting better.

As I'd told Carol over the summer, I really thought I'd play three years in Des Moines and then I might have a chance to play in college. That would be a mile past the end of my wildest dreams, but even then I was thinking in terms of maybe Mankato State or Bemidji State. Those are two great programs, but the Golden Gophers at The U were the cream of the crop. That was, literally, one possible step from the NHL. That thought actually made me laugh and get goosebumps at the same time. I might as well have been thinking, "If I keep getting better, maybe I can be an astronaut." It was that crazy.

We finished up with those 11 wins, the 36 losses in regulation, and the one "L" in overtime. We finished ninth. Last place again. A lot of the guys seemed exhausted and over it, and the memory of the year before was still clear in my head. When Coach got us together for our final meeting, he had a bunch to say but then he surprised me when I heard him say, "You got anything for the boys, Oly?" And yes, with all the new guys on the roster my nickname just organically switched back to Oly. It sounded way better to me than Olsie. I actually couldn't stand that.

I stood up and looked around the room.

"Boys, I know this look on your faces, and this feeling. It felt just like this last year. I'd never had a losing season in my life, and we won seven entire games last year. It was brutal, and a lot of the guys just quit making the effort and started mailing it in by midseason. They couldn't take it.

"We never did that this year. You guys busted your butts every night, and I was proud to wear the Buccaneers sweater and to have the 'C' on it. We're better, and we can still improve. If we keep this squad together, we can be a lot better next year. Don't quit on me if you're on the fence, but don't come back if you know you don't want to do what it will take to move up in the standings. I'm absolutely not coming back here to finish last again. I'm coming back, but we're moving up. Thanks for the effort boys. There's still more to give. There's more in the tank. Have a great summer."

They actually clapped. That was another first for me. I'd done some pregame rah-rah stuff of course, almost every game, but I'd never stood before the room and given a speech. And they clapped, which was cool.

Before we all packed up and headed out, I think almost every guy on the roster came by to shake hands, share a hug maybe, and tell me I'd been a great leader. It meant the world to me.

The next morning, I packed up the truck, said goodbye to the Warners and to Randy, who had been a great roomie and had become my closest friend on the team. We'd shared all those stories about Roseau and Denver, and both promised to make a trip to the other guy's hometown that summer, just to experience it. I really wanted to do that, because I'd never seen mountains and had never been anywhere close to Colorado. I hoped I'd have a chance to show him around Roseau, too.

And then I got in the truck and drove home.

I found it really interesting that it didn't seem as odd and different, this time. This time, I just kind of fell back into the Roseau rhythm. It was good to be home.

I also remember the first few days back in the house, with Mom, Dad and Betsy. That part was comfortable, but for at least a week I couldn't relax. It's hard to turn off that full season of intensity and just do nothing. On top of that I was seriously tired and sore. When you're getting your butts smacked 37 times in a 48-game season, you're kind of a mess when you slow down and feel it all. So, I relaxed as best I could and helped out at the store.

I saw Carol when she got home from school and I couldn't help but notice she had a different look on her face. She seemed really happy to see me, and I was happy to see her. We had only traded a few letters throughout the winter, and we hadn't kept each other up on any personal stuff. I didn't have anything to really share anyway. Some of the guys dated local girls in Des Moines, but I didn't have any interest in that. I was there to play hockey. Once again, the game came first.

When we did get together for lunch, she was a lot more upbeat and engaging than the year before, and I wasn't sure why. It didn't take long for me to say, "So, how are things? Still dating that guy?"

She shook her head, and kind of grimaced and smiled at the same time. It was really an odd look and I didn't know what to make of it.

"He wasn't the right guy for me," she said. "It just took me a while to figure it out. He's a good person, and really kind, but there was no real spark there and I don't think he had a lot of ambition or passion for life. I thought he wanted to be an award-winning journalist, but it kind of became clear that he just wanted to write for the local paper and have a job.

"I think I was just taking the easy way out, to have something different since you and I were going in our own directions. I feel a lot better about it now. There's no rush. I'll meet the right guy, and until then I'll just enjoy school and all the friends I've made. Want to play golf this summer?"

I laughed and said, "So you're ready to whip my butt on the golf course now? We'll do that whenever you want. I'm glad to see you so happy."

She asked me more about my winter down there and what my overall plans were.

"It was brutal to lose that much again, but it felt great to be a real leader and to have a whole team listening to me," I said. "It meant about as much as anything I've ever experienced in the game. I committed to going back for one more year and I think we'll be better. Hopefully a lot better."

Carol then said, "And what comes next? This will be your third year in juniors. Think you'll go straight to the North Stars and win a Stanley Cup?"

I laughed and said, "How'd you know that? Geez, word must have gotten out about my million-dollar offer, huh. Actually, The U is watching me. They want me to play one more year in the USHL and then they think I might be ready to be a Gopher. Babe, all I ever wanted to be was a Ram. Then I was a Buccaneer. To even think about being a Golden Gopher is just crazy. But I'm going to give it everything I have. I think I can do it."

She was beaming. I always loved how she looked when she was truly happy, and at that moment she was radiant and beautiful. Those dark eyes seemed as big as hockey pucks. I remember clearly, at that moment, I was struck by how much she cared. She was like that. She really cared about other people and about me. And I thought, "I'm never going to meet anyone else like her."

"I'm so happy for you," she said. "You seem to have more confidence than ever and you were never really short of that. You're so fired up about this I know it's the right thing. I'm fired up for you. Keep being my friend, OK? Stay my friend forever. I know what your first love is, but you're still allowed to have friends. We're always going to be friends."

I felt the same way. It was a world away from the weird uncertainty of the year before. I'd known then that our friendship could make it if neither one of us did something rash or stupid, and somehow we'd gotten through two years of it. We'd always be friends. I knew it. I couldn't let someone that special just drift out of my life.

After about three weeks, I knew it was about time to kick in the workouts again, but first I had a promise to keep. I called Randy and said, "Before I jump back into my offseason stuff, I want to drive out there and see Denver. You up for that?"

He was all for it. By then Randy was living in an apartment with a buddy, and they had a pull-out couch in the living room so I could claim that for a few days. I serviced the truck, scanned all the maps and plotted my course. Any route I took was going to be a long one, but the one down through Sioux Falls, South Dakota, looked the easiest and it gave me a target for spending the night. I was off before sunrise.

I drove straight west to North Dakota, then down through Grand Forks and Fargo. At around 4 that afternoon, I arrived in Sioux Falls and checked in at the Holiday Inn. It was the first time I'd ever checked into a hotel by myself. I didn't have a credit card, so I paid with cash. I remember when I did that I thought, "You know, it might be time to go to the bank and get a MasterCard or a Visa. Time to grow up a little."

I had thought about driving a little farther, but it had been a pretty boring trip to that point so I decided to have dinner and call it a day. I'd be in Denver after about nine hours of driving the next day, and so far you could not have guessed that I was heading for the mountains. It was all really flat.

When I checked out in the morning the clerk asked me where I was headed, and when I told him, he said, "Well, you're going right through Mitchell to get there. It's the next big stop going west from here. You should stop and see the Corn Palace."

"What's a Corn Palace?" I promptly asked.

"I'll just let you go there and see for yourself. It's worth it. Get off the highway and go find it in the middle of town."

I did that. And when I got to the Corn Palace I was shaking my head and laughing. It's a full-size high school gym and civic events center, built in the late 1800s, and the entire ornate exterior is covered in corn cobs. I went inside, just to check it out, and it was a nice gym, actually. It was the middle of summer, but you could still smell the buttered popcorn. That's a smell that you can find in just about any high school gym. The whole place was one of the strangest things I'd ever seen. Of course, that's not saying much. I was the kid who made his first trip to far-off Des Moines just a couple of years earlier, and here I was in the wilds of South Dakota looking at a palace made of corn.

I left Mitchell behind and went down through Nebraska, which made South Dakota look absolutely bumpy, and the epic scope of the trip sunk in. I was feeling so much more mature and like an adult after two years out there in the USHL, but as I was driving it hit me how far away from home I was, and how desolate it was out there. It was a little intimidating, but I loved it. It was an adventure.

Once I got to Colorado, I expected it to look like all the photos and movies I'd seen of the Rocky Mountains. Instead, it looked like Nebraska. And for a long time, too. I thought maybe Randy had pulled a prank on me. "Come to Denver, it's amazing!" And yet there I was in Colorado and I could see forever across the open plains.

And then finally, like I was seeing a mirage, I saw something on the horizon that looked like a series of low clouds. When it hit me that I was actually seeing snow-capped mountains, the hair on my arms stood up. And there was the Denver skyline. A huge downtown full of big buildings right at the foot of the mountains. With every mile, it all became more real. It was one of the coolest things I'd ever seen. And just earlier that day, I thought the Corn Palace was one of the coolest things I'd ever seen.

Randy and his buddy lived in Englewood, just a little south of downtown. I followed the directions I'd been given while trying not to have a wreck as I drove down the big highway that runs north and south right through downtown. Mile High Stadium was just off to the right. It was the most impressive sports facility I'd ever seen. It was gigantic. Another "hair on the arms" moment. This wasn't Roseau. It wasn't even Des Moines.

Randy's place was nice, and his buddy Rick seemed like a good guy. They'd played high school hockey together, and Rick went straight on to Colorado College in Colorado Springs. The program there was really well known, but they were in a bit of a down period with the current team. Rick could've gone to Des Moines with us, but he felt like Colorado College was desperate to improve and he thought the tough NCAA competition would be good for him. I really couldn't relate to that, yet. I was still only hoping to play college hockey someday.

I stayed for maybe four or five days, but it seemed a lot longer than that. We crammed a lot in, however long it was. They showed me as much as they could, all around Denver and then through the mountains out to Vail. My head was on a swivel during that side trip, so much so it felt like three quick and burly forwards were coming at me full speed, three on one. I couldn't see enough of it and couldn't soak it in fast enough.

Vail was unlike any place I'd ever been. It was tucked into gigantic mountains, with a fun little downtown and ski resorts all around (and above) it. It was summer, but it had a real mountain feel I'd never felt or experienced before. With all the pine trees and the low humidity, and the fact your brain can hardly understand the size of the mountains towering over you, it felt completely different to me. Almost alien. There's a fresh smell to it that I've always equated with the mountains since that exact moment, when I got out of the truck and inhaled. I've been back numerous times over the years, and I have never forgotten how it felt and smelled that afternoon. Pine needles and fresh air.

It was a fantastic few days. A real highlight of my life. I was a long way from home on my own, with new friends. That's as unlike Roseau as anything I'd ever done to that point. It was fantastic.

Before I left, Randy and I hatched a good plan. He'd keep up his end of the "show me your hometown" agreement by coming up to Roseau, but he'd do it about three weeks before we were supposed to report to Des Moines. He'd stay with us at the house and work out with me and the Rams guys before we drove south to Iowa. I planned to make him throw up if I could. I wanted him to see the kind of work I had been putting in every summer. It was the kind of work that gave a 5-foot-9 defenseman a chance to play in the USHL and survive it.

I also told him to stop in Mitchell to see the Corn Palace.

I made the long trip back home without any problems, and I knew once I got there that it was time to ramp up the workouts again. Just like the summer before, I'd have anywhere from four to six Rams varsity guys with me, and we pushed each other pretty hard. They were mostly juniors by then, and they'd had a taste of the workouts the year before, so we all got after it pretty hard. Just to be on the level, I can't say honestly that I liked the workouts. I mostly hated the workouts. It's hard stuff and it's painful. But I sure loved the way I felt after each one. It's like the old line: "It hurts like hell to bang your head against the wall, but it sure feels good when you stop."

We all knew why we were doing it, so the guys bought in and pushed each other. I still had the old set of weights my brothers bought all those years before. And the weightlifting belts with the rope and tires attached. It wasn't glamorous, but it worked.

I saw Carol way more than the previous summer, but it was still just having fun and being friends. My best friend, for sure, but that's what it was. My mistress was waiting. Hockey always came first.

Carol left town first, for St. Cloud again, just like the years before but this time it was a little different. The hug we shared had some meaning. I wasn't really sure what she was trying to tell me without saying anything, and I didn't want to guess or ask, but that goodbye hug was meant to tell me something. It lasted a while. A long while. She gripped me a little harder as it went on. And it made me smile.

About three weeks before it was time to head back to Des Moines, Randy showed up, as promised. When I went to Denver, we tried to cram in as much sightseeing as possible in just a few days. He got to see most of Roseau in about an hour, but he swore he loved it.

"There's a vibe here, man," I remember him saying. "I love it. I've never experienced anything like it, and I absolutely love it. I can see why you and so many other guys stay attached to this place. It feels like hockey."

I showed him the school, we ate lunch at the Roseau Diner, he loved the hardware store and the fact it had stayed in the family for so long, and Roseau Memorial Arena just blew him away. "Coolest damn rink I've ever seen" was what he said. I agreed with that statement.

The ice hadn't been installed yet, so the high school guys were still working out with me and they got after Randy as much as I did. I don't think we got him to puke, or if we did he hid it well because I never saw that, but in our year together in Des Moines I'd never seen him much more than a little winded. He was in good shape, but our goal was to take him to another level. He was on his knees a few times those first few days. Doing sprint bursts pulling a tire will do that to you.

He improved fast, and after a week he said he could feel a huge difference. I recall him also saying, "It's a good thing we're working this hard, because the way your mom feeds us would be a really bad thing if I was just sitting around."

He learned about hotdish, as well. On the first cool day near the end of September, that day where you can feel the north wind a little and you just know what's out there, Mom made her tater tot hot dish and I thought Randy was going to eat the whole thing. "Where has this been my whole life?" he said, although his mouth was full.

We stayed after it as hard as we could until it was getting to be time to hit the road.

Sprints, stairs in the arena, weights, and all the resistance stuff. When I asked him how he felt, all he could say was: "I thought I was in good shape last year. This is a whole new world. And I want to move to Roseau."

I cautioned him on that last bit, reminding him that 25-below-zero with a good north wind whipping the snow into your face isn't something you can appreciate until it bites you. And it bites hard.

When it was time to head south, we were both ready. We each drove our trucks, since we'd be heading in different directions once the season was over, but making the trip for the third time made it all familiar to me. And, we were happy to hear that we'd be staying with the Warners again.

When we had our first practice, Randy and I were clearly in better shape than most of the other guys. We had a good group who had come back from the season before, and the new recruits seemed pretty fast and strong too, but you just never know. I learned that lesson the first two years there.

The USHL had all nine teams from the year before back again, plus we added a team in Omaha called the Lancers. We'd be back to a 10-team league and I was adamant when I was telling the guys that we weren't going to finish 10th. We weren't going to finish ninth either. We were moving up. We were determined to make the playoffs. Eight of the 10 teams would go to the playoffs, which probably makes it sound easy. We'd finished dead last two years in a row. The playoffs seemed as lofty as those mountains around Vail.

I got the captain's "C" again, and Randy earned one of the "A" letters as an assistant captain. It felt a lot like home, and the Warners made sure of that. Looking back on all three years there, I can understand now how fortunate I was to have landed with them that first year. They made the experience what it was. They weren't just a wonderful and supportive family. They had lived up to the words they told us that first day in '84. We were part of the family. That's exactly how it felt. Really great people, and I've stayed in touch with them to this day.

As soon as the season started, I knew we were better. The fight and the effort was great, and after about eight games I think we were right around .500, at 4-4 or something. With each win, we got a little more confident. With each loss, we were a bit more determined.

And the first time we went to Omaha to play those guys, we all got a reminder of just how hard the game can be. They were totally disorganized and overmatched, which is probably what you'd expect of a new team thrown together right before the season. It was like playing against a high school JV team. We creamed them, and that look on their faces was familiar to all of us. We'd made the big step up and improved a lot, but those Omaha guys were living that same tough lesson we'd all been through. They finished dead last that year, and unbelievably they did it by going 0-46 with two losses in OT. That had to be tough.

Right before our first road trip up north, where we'd play Rochester, St. Paul, and Thunder Bay, Coach Wiley called me into his office before we got on the bus and said,

"At least two Gophers coaches are going to be there for the St. Paul games. They want you to know they'll be there, and I've agreed to let them meet with you after our first game. Can you handle that?"

I knew I could handle it. We had to play Rochester first though, with one game there before going on up to St. Paul, and we learned that we weren't as good as we thought. They were big, strong, and fast. Easily the best USHL team I'd ever played against. I remember thinking, "These guys are at a different level. This has got to be what playing against the Gophers is like."

Little did I know that Coach Woog himself was there in Rochester to see that game. He'd thrown me a little head fake by only mentioning they'd see me in St. Paul. I didn't know he was in town, but I was happy when I found out a couple of nights later when we got up there to play the Vulcans. I'd played well, against a very tough team.

I remember staying with all my normal pregame stuff for that first game against St. Paul. I hadn't told anybody at home about The U guys coming to see me, and no one had made the trip down from Roseau. That was probably a good thing. I didn't need any more distractions. I just wanted to stay focused because, as far as I knew at that time, I believed this was going to be Coach Woog's first look at me. He didn't tell me about being in Rochester until we met after the game.

St. Paul was a good team, but I thought we were better and after that tough game against Rochester it was easy to keep up that intensity and take it to the Vulcans a little bit. We won easily, I scored a goal, and I think we even shut them out. I remember thinking I'd played two of my best games in a row as a Buccaneer.

After the game, I got showered and Coach took me out into the hallway. I was expecting one or two men to be out there. I think there were six or seven and I did a complete double-take when I saw that Paul Broten was in the group. My former Roseau teammate was in the middle of his junior year. Two of the other guys were clearly current players, as well. The first one to introduce himself was Coach Woog.

"It's a pleasure to meet you Eric," he said. "I have to admit I told your coach a little white lie. I was in Rochester a couple of nights ago, but I didn't want you to know that. Word had gotten around about how special that group is down there, and how big and physical they are. I wanted to see how you stood up to that. Now we'd like to talk to you about being a Golden Gopher."

You know, it doesn't really matter how much you think about it, or consider it even remotely possible, when an NCAA head hockey coach from a place like the University of Minnesota says, "We'd like to talk to you about being a Golden Gopher." It's more than a little stunning. All I could say was: "That would be fantastic" or something appropriately dumb like that.

Our team hotel was only a few blocks from the rink in St. Paul, so Coach gave me permission to walk back there after meeting with the guys from The U. There was a restaurant right by the arena, and we all headed there.

We sat around a table the restaurant had set up for us in a back room, and that just made it sink in a little more that being a Gopher was a big thing. All Coach Woog or one of the assistant coaches had to do was call the restaurant and tell them they wanted a private place to recruit a new player, and it was done.

Coach Woog was in charge, but these guys had obviously done this tag-team deal before. He wanted Paul and the other players to fill me in on the school and the culture, and the experience of going to The U and being a Golden Gopher. They were really positive about the whole experience, and I was glad to hear them talk as much about the school as they did about the team and the level of play. It was great to see Paul again, too. He'd come back up to Roseau fairly regularly during the summers, but just for a few days at a time.

What no one needed to tell me was how many great NHL and Olympic players had been Gophers. Around Minnesota, those guys were legends as I was growing up. Guys like Paul's oldest brother, Roseau's own Neal Broten, or Steve Christoff, Rob McClanahan, Eric Strobel and Bill Baker. The U was well known as a pipeline to pro hockey. I could hardly comprehend the idea of actually going to school and playing there.

Within just a few minutes, the reality of it sunk in. They weren't there just to talk to me. They weren't there to see if I'd like to maybe walk on and try to earn a spot. They were there to recruit me! Like they needed to convince me to be a Gopher. When that sunk in, it was hard for me to concentrate. I couldn't turn that thought off in my brain. The University of Minnesota was putting on a full-court press to recruit me.

I guess they said all the right things, but mostly I remember Coach Woog talking about the Rochester game and what that showed him.

"Three years ago, when you were coming out of Roseau, you weren't ready to play for us," he said. "That Rochester team is on a level with just about every team we play. You might still be 5-foot-9, but you play like you're 6-3. We want you at The U. We can give you a scholarship if you'd like to play for us."

"It would be an honor," I said to Coach Woog. After that I was kind of dumbfounded. I really had not anticipated the meeting being anything more than a chance for them to get to know me. It turned out they'd done all that homework. They knew everything about me, and I would imagine Paul put in his two cents on his former Rams teammate. They liked what they saw. Honestly, the rest of the meeting might have lasted 15 minutes or an hour. I don't know. I remember there being some details, like a National Letter of Intent and some other paperwork that was going to have to be taken care of after the USHL season, but mostly it was just a blur. My head was definitely spinning.

When we all shook hands and said goodbye, Paul took the time to say, "Let's be teammates again." I walked back to the hotel and went up to see my roomie. Randy knew where I'd been. When I walked in he said, "Well, what happened?"

I just shook my head and said: "Son of a bitch, they were there to recruit me. They offered me a scholarship. They want me to play for the Gophers. I thought they just wanted to meet me and maybe size me up a little. I can't believe it."

Randy's first response was something along the lines of, "You said yes, didn't you?"

I told him about Coach Woog being in Rochester on the sly, about Paul and the other two players that were there, about the hard sell they were giving me, and about how stunned I was when they asked me to come to school there and join the program.

There were a thousand people I wanted to call at once, but it was getting late and I decided not to wake anyone up. The news would be just as good the next morning. And then Randy had a surprise.

"I was under strict orders to keep this a secret, but now I have to tell you," he said. "The University of North Dakota has been after me. At first, they were talking about me playing one more season in Des Moines, but now I guess they want to make me a scholarship offer. They're coming to the games we have in Sioux City in a couple of weeks. Sounds like we might be playing against each other next year!"

The whole thing was surreal. What I remember the most about that night was just a sense of disbelief. I honestly couldn't process what had just happened. And my roomie was going through the same thing.

We had another game in St. Paul the next night, and I don't recall getting a lot of sleep. In the morning, I made all the phone calls and spread the word with my family. Yes, I called Carol too and she literally screamed into the phone. I told Coach about the whole thing, of course, and he was really thrilled for me. Once we were at the rink and getting dressed, Coach Wiley came in the room to make what we thought was just a typical pregame speech. It was, for a bit, but then at the end he added one more thing.

"Boys, I've got one more piece of news for you," he said. "Eric Olson received a scholarship offer from the University of Minnesota last night. He's going to be a Golden Gopher. Boys, that's how good we can all be. If one of your teammates is able to move on to that level of hockey, we're a damn good hockey team. I know not every one of you will get a chance to play college hockey, but I'm going to push you all to do what Eric has done. When he got here, he wasn't ready to play NCAA hockey, and certainly not for a team like the Gophers. And now he's done it. You should all be motivated to hear that. Congratulations, Oly."

Lots of stick taps and shouts. Lots of high fives. It was quite a moment.

A few weeks later, when we went on our road trip to Sioux City, the UND staff was there to meet Randy. They offered him a scholarship and he accepted. These two Buccaneers were moving on up to college, and we'd be going from teammates to rivals at two very good schools.

As the season went on, we were definitely better. We kept staying right around the .500 mark, and at the end of the season we finished 23-20 with two ties and two overtime losses. We finished in sixth place, and we made the playoffs. We got swept by a good Madison team, but we made the playoffs. I was really proud of what we had done as a group.

When it was all over, and it was time to pack up and hit the road, the goodbyes were a lot more emotional. I didn't know if I'd ever be back in Des Moines again. Saying goodbye to the Warners was especially tough, and I think everyone was crying. Saying goodbye to the staff, the arena people, a bunch of the fans, and my teammates was rough, too. Des Moines had made a great second home for me. I liked it there. I loved my teammates. We had accomplished so much that third year, and it was really rewarding.

After Randy and I loaded up our trucks to head home, that parting was easier because we knew we'd be playing against each other soon.

All I said was, "See you next winter, brother. May the best team win."

And then I drove home.

CHAPTER 17

Brooks Bennett

As the tournament in the Metrodome got closer, I was so stoked about starting our first game my biggest challenge was "slowing it all down," as Coach would say. The tournament was right there on the schedule. The dates weren't going to change. Trying to make it get here faster was useless. I needed to stick to the program and get prepared at a pace that would have me ready to go when I took the mound at the Dome. We all did.

School was fine, winter never wanted to end, and practice was what excited me most each day. I actually had a calendar hanging on the wall of my bedroom at the new apartment, and each day I'd put a big X through that box before going to bed. I drew a big red star in the box for Friday, March 28. That would be the first day of the tournament. I'd be pitching. The whole freaking concept was out of this world. If having to leave SoCal to move to Minnesota had been crazy, the idea that I'd be pitching on the same mound the Twins used at the Metrodome was totally off the hook.

We did have a wooden practice mound in the gym at school. It was basically just a wedge- shaped thing, made out of thick plywood, with a pitching rubber bolted into the top, and it was covered in some sort of heavy-duty carpet. About the only thing I clearly remember about it was that the carpet was worn through right where most guys landed with their front foot. And it wobbled a little, to the point where I was so distracted by the little lurch it would make I had to bring some thin shims to school to keep the thing balanced. I don't know why nobody else thought of that. It did, however, give us all a chance to throw on a downward slope. You wouldn't want your first day on the mound at the Metrodome to be the first time not throwing on the flat gym floor. That would not be rad.

Everything was good at home. The little apartment was nothing compared to my former suite at Don's house, but it was fine for the three of us. Mom was doing well, regaining a lot of strength and energy, and the visits to Mayo were going better than anyone had expected. She still needed to get down there two or three times a month, as I recall, but with each visit she said the doctors were getting more and more confident

133

that they'd taken the right approach and she had a chance to be fine for a long time. She was just turning 40 then. She had a "long time" to go and a lot to do. She was even talking about doing some painting. I never thought I'd hear those words from her again.

Dad was talking about getting a job. Nothing too major, nothing too stressful, and something that could be really flexible so that the Mayo trips would never be a problem. And, just like at Disney, he wanted to interact with the public. He wasn't in a big hurry. We'd been living the same frugal lifestyle we always had, but I think he needed to clean the slate a little and have something to do other than worrying about Mom. The better she got, the more he needed to have something to do. I was busy with school, practice and clearing Don's driveway each time it snowed. For a guy who had never experienced winter before, I was getting to be an expert with the snowblower. And I realized I wasn't going to freeze into a statue when it was below zero. Carl and Mitch had been right. I got used to it.

Finally, we got to the week of boxes on the calendar that ended with the big red star. I thought we were ready. Or, at least I hoped we were. All of the teams in the tournament were going to be in the same situation. None of us had been outside yet. And, well… I guess we still wouldn't be outside during the tournament because the Metrodome field was inside. So basically, the difference was being in a gym versus being on a field. That was still totally a big adjustment.

Each day that week, we ramped it up a little more to simulate game action. No more standard BP just throwing it over, with each hitter getting 15 hacks at straight fastballs. All of the pitchers, myself included, started throwing like it was the real deal. The catchers gave us signs, we mixed up pitches and locations, and we did our best to strike the hitters out. That was good for us and good for them. I think it was Tuesday that week when I threw my last session. That would have me ready to go on Friday.

And in case you're wondering, yes — it is different throwing inside the batting cage. We had a screen in front of us that protected us from most line drives, but the whole thing is just claustrophobic. And it's loud in there, too, being inside the gym. For a guy like me, who had spent his whole life pitching outside on a real mound actually made out of dirt, the whole thing was kind of crazy. The catcher and hitter seemed really close, the netting on the sides of the cage made it feel totally too narrow. And even that little screen we had could let you down. The cage was right up against a wall in the gym and any line drive hit to what would be the right side of the field could push the netting out enough so that the ball would hit the wall. Ricochets were not fun. But, it was all we had and we needed to get the work in. Nobody got killed, and only a few guys got some bruises out of it, so it was OK.

When Friday finally came around we were all buzzing. I don't recall what all the team vs. team match-ups were or even the times of the three games, but I remember we all got out of school a little early to take the bus up to the Metrodome. That makes me think we had the first game, which would've been around 4 o'clock, I'd guess.

I'm pretty sure we opened the tournament against Edina. That's a really affluent area in the suburbs and it's a school with a tremendous athletic program. Bloomington has some really nice parts but a lot of it is just middle-America normal and comfortable and the schools were really good but not elite. It was a big deal to play Edina, because they were always good. And if they're always good, the scouts and college coaches will pay attention. I'd have my chance to show off a little.

When we got to the Dome, we entered near a loading dock area, and I remember hearing one of the guys saying, "This is where the Twins come in and out. I've stood right there by the fence to get autographs."

I don't know what locker room we used, but it was really big so I'm guessing it was one of the football rooms. We shared the place with the Edina team and all got dressed really fast. Like totally faster than normal. We were all just amped up to get out on the field and look around. It was the first time I'd worn the Bloomington Kennedy uniform. I couldn't help but take my regular look in the mirror. I looked like a ballplayer. I looked pretty bitchin', too.

We walked down a stairway, oddly enough, to get to the field. Then into the visitors' dugout. I was trying my best to not only look cool and comfortable, but to actually be that way. I didn't want to be too psycho about where we were playing and who might be watching. So, I combined two things I wanted and needed to do. I jogged out to the right field corner to do my few easy jogs from pole to pole. And that gave me a chance to be by myself and take a look around.

It was still early, maybe 45 minutes before the first pitch, and there were only a few people in the gigantic stadium. It was a sea of dark blue seats. I stood out by the baggie in right field and stared at it for a bit. Then I jogged to the left field corner and back, and even that was a revelation. The Dome was so huge it looked like a mile jog to get to the other corner, but it really wasn't any farther than I'd run at Canyon before games. I was calming down, and soaking it in at the same time.

As the guys loosened up I sat on the bench and just collected myself. It felt like we were totally in some old Roman coliseum getting ready to have a gladiator battle. I'd been in some high-pressure situations at Canyon and during summer ball, but looking around at everything inside the Metrodome, from my perch on the bench, was something completely different. I don't get goosebumps very often, but I had them then.

None of us had any idea if a crowd would show up, other than our parents and friends. So, I didn't really pay attention to that until Mitch and I walked down to the visitors' bullpen to start the process. I remember just looking down at my feet as we walked. I was probably subconsciously not wanting to even think about where we were. It felt a bit like a quadruple whammy of ways to be too fired up. My first game with my new school. I was starting. We were playing one of the best teams in the state. And we were in the Metrodome. I took the deepest breath I could.

I then looked back toward home plate and noticed that there actually were some people there. Hard to say how many, now, but maybe a couple thousand? Maybe more? It was enough to make me a little more nervous.

I didn't know if Mom had made it. We left that up in the air when I took off for school that day. I knew my dad was in there somewhere, and I also knew there was no way he'd wave or make himself seen. He wouldn't have wanted to distract me at a moment like that.

Mitch and I started with a routine we'd been doing the previous summer. Instead of going straight to the mound, he went out into right field and I stood on the foul line. With each throw, he'd back up a step or two. Pretty soon, it was legit "long toss" as we called it. It was a great way to get the blood flowing and get my arm loose. Just let it all hang out and fire rockets at him.

Then he came back in and took his spot behind the plate. Another good thing about long toss is that it makes the 60-feet 6-inches look a lot closer. It felt like I could hand the ball to him. As I started firing them in for real, I knew the fastball was popping. I felt a sense of calm come over me. It was like "They can't hit this."

We got the curve going, and the change-up. Finally, we walked slowly to the dugout just as our lead-off hitter got in the box. It was finally happening, and it was damn cool.

I really don't remember a lot of specifics about what our guys did on offense, and I've never seen a box score from the game. I don't think we scored in the top of the first, but I remember picking up my glove and walking out to the mound in great detail, like it was yesterday. I can still feel the sensation of scratching a little dirt out from in front of the rubber, thinking, "OK, this is definitely the nicest mound I've ever been on." It should've been. It was a Major League mound!

After I threw my warm-up pitches and the guys threw the ball around the infield, I looked around a bit. It was all just surreal. When I took the ball and looked in to get my first signal from Mitch, I knew I was focused. It was like tunnel vision. All I saw was him. Strike one, and the fastball popped when it hit his mitt. Strike two, swinging this time and the dude was way late on another fastball. Strike three. A change-up that dove into the dirt and he missed it by a foot. I remember thinking, "OK, this is going to be fine."

When the next batter stepped out of the box after strike one, I did notice something in the stands right behind the plate. There must have been two dozen radar guns pointed at me. That didn't phase me. I remember thinking, "Well, let's give 'em a show."

Coach was true to his word about protecting my arm. We were on a pitch count, so the fewer I could get through an inning with the deeper into the game I could pitch. In the end, the baseball I still have had the stat line written on it with a ballpoint pen.

- 5 innings pitched
- 57 pitches
- 12 strikeouts
- 0 walks
- 0 runs
- 0 hits

Apparently we scratched out two runs while I was in the game, because the final score was 2-0 and I got the win. It was a seven-inning game, and I don't remember who came in to relieve me, but they obviously got the job done to hold onto the shutout.

It would've been a huge deal if the reliever had not given up any hits either, because it would've gone in the books as a combined no-hitter, but that clearly didn't happen. All it ended up being was a huge win over a tough team, and pretty much total domination.

When we walked up the stairs to the locker room we were sharing with the team we just beat, I got a lot of handshakes and pats on the back from the Edina guys. I heard "That was some bad-ass stuff" from more than a few of them.

Coach didn't want to do anything more than have us get showered and back on the bus as soon as possible, out of respect for the other team that was in the same room with us. We did that, and shook a few more hands on the way out.

When I could see that spot by a fence where one of my teammates had said he had stood to get Twins autographs in the past, I spotted my dad and my mom at once. I ran over there before getting on the bus. We'd gone through so much together, and I'm not exaggerating when I say I never thought any of this would happen. That I'd be pitching in Minnesota. That I'd be pitching at the Metrodome. That Mom had survived, and was there with us. All three of us were pretty good at crying. We had developed that skill over the past year. I don't remember what either of them said, I just remember them crying while all my teammates watched from inside the bus.

I wiped my tears away and told them I'd see them at home. It was time to get on the bus with my new band of brothers. We were a team. It felt really good.

When we were rolling through downtown Minneapolis, Coach stood up and told us how proud he was of all of us. And then he walked back to my seat and handed me the ball, which he'd already written the stat lines on. The guys gave me a standing ovation, and that's not all that easy to do on a rolling school bus. I felt at home. I felt like I was on that bus with my family.

The whole ride back to Bloomington was like a totally Zen thing. Pride, happiness, contentment, all of those things. It felt like I had earned what I did that day. It wasn't an easy road to get there, believe me.

When we got back to school, Coach pulled me aside and said, "I could barely get back up to the locker room after the game. There must have been a dozen pro scouts there, and at least as many college coaches. Boy, did they all want to know about you!

"One of the scouts asked me if I knew how hard you were throwing. I only said, 'Hard enough, as far as I could tell.' He said it was a consistent 93-94 and the ball was coming out of your hand so easy he couldn't believe it. He said it was clear there's lots more. You're going to have a lot of attention paid to you this season, Brooks. Just keep doing what you're doing."

I don't remember much about the next two days of the tournament. I knew I wasn't going to pitch so I just watched and pulled for my teammates. I'm assuming we didn't win the tournament because I figure I'd remember something like that. I do recall a big, strong outfielder for one of the other teams hitting an absolute bomb over the baggie in right field and into the upper deck. We all kind of looked around with wide eyes, mouthing the word "Wow" to each other. But I also remember thinking: "That's a big-league home run. I can get these guys out. Maybe I can get big-leaguers out some day, too"

Going back to practice in the gym was torture. We had some games scheduled in early or mid-April but Coach was quick to warn us that those might not happen. He said, "Boys, we're going to prepare to play every one of these games. We'll be ready to go on game day. But in my years here we've never played every April game. It might be 70 degrees, or we might have a blizzard. So don't let it get you down if we have games scratched. It's part of being Minnesota tough."

At home, things were good. Mom was doing well, and Dad was itching to have something to do. He'd mapped out the finances before we ever moved, so it wasn't really about making a bunch of money. It was about interacting with people and keeping busy. Don had actually offered him a job at his agency but Dad wouldn't even consider it. It sounded way too much like corporate work and it "smacked of nepotism" as he put it. So he got a job as a vendor.

Yes, a vendor. At the Metrodome for Twins and Vikings games and Met Center for North Stars games. As he put it, "It's a physically active job, which I like, and it's all about dealing with the public. It'll be fun."

I'd learned by then to never question what he wanted to do. He had priorities, and money was never one of them. Walking up and down the aisles selling beer, peanuts or hot dogs seemed like something he'd totally dig. I got that.

I don't remember much about that span between the tournament and our first regular season game, but I do remember that day. We were lucky. It was about 55 degrees and mostly sunny. That's what you'd call a "bonus day" for April in Minnesota. We played some other school I can't remember, and I started. We won. I struck a bunch of guys out and it felt easy. I'm not trying to say that Minnesota hitters weren't good, like the SoCal kids. Some of them were really good. Like, I'd never seen a ball hit as far as that one dude hit in the Metrodome. But I'd really filled out and gotten stronger, and it just felt effortless. Whether it was Mitch or Carl behind the plate, I trusted what they signaled and just threw it where they wanted it. I don't know what else to say. It just felt easy.

We lost a few games to weather, but the April blizzards didn't happen that year and it finally warmed up. I didn't mind it when it was chilly, like in the upper 40s or in the 50s, and by the time we were playing in May it was in the 60s, which felt positively hot. At Canyon, if we ever played a game at 60 degrees we'd have all been wearing jackets. You adapt.

Dad was having the time of his life as a vendor at the Dome, walking up and down those aisles selling whatever they gave him each night. He was really happy. Mom was happy, and doing great. I was happy. It was a really good time.

All I remember about how the season ended up was that I did well, and as a team we were pretty good, too. We went to the regionals or sectionals, or something like that, but lost a tough one when our starter couldn't get out of the first inning without giving up big runs. We got blown out, and it was over.

In SoCal, you play so many games for so many months. It's almost like pro ball in that regard. It's a long season and it grinds on for what seems like half a year. In Bloomington, we crammed a whole season into two months.

My mom kept the official stats in a scrap book for me.

- Games: 9
- Innings: 76
- Hits: 40
- Runs: 6
- Strikeouts: 90
- Walks: 12
- Record: 9-0

The new kid from SoCal was named First Team All-State and I got my picture in the Minneapolis paper. And the phone started ringing. And the letters started to arrive.

We got calls from the Rangers, Twins, Cardinals, Angels, Dodgers, and a few more I'm sure. I was still untouchable as a high school junior, but they all wanted to talk to me and my folks, to dig a little deeper and get a better idea of my background and makeup. They all said they'd be watching closely during my senior year.

We heard from the University of Minnesota, and one of their assistant coaches even came down to Bloomington to meet with us at the apartment. That was way cool, and I'll be honest and admit that the letters or calls I got from other colleges (probably 15 to 20 schools) were all kept pretty much in a separate pile. If I was going to go to college to play, I wanted to go to The U.

That summer, I discovered something else about Minnesota that's really unique. Rather than work out informally, like we did after I moved there, Carl and I signed up to play summer ball and instead of American Legion ball we went a different route. The high school season had been regimented and sometimes stressful. We just wanted to stay in shape and have some fun. In Minnesota it's called Town Ball. From little towns to big suburbs, all over the state, these teams are what tie communities together. It's a big deal, and a lot of the towns have absolutely awesome ballparks for their teams to play in. Some of the teams are made up of wannabe guys and never-were players, but in the Twin Cities suburbs the teams were really good. Kind of All-Star teams, basically, because many of them were made up of a couple of the best high school kids and a bunch of college players as well. There'd always be a few older guys too, who had grown up there or played some minor league ball, so it was a good mix and it was a lot of fun.

We played for a team in Shakopee, not too far west of Bloomington, and we had teammates from Edina, Eden Prairie, and quite a few from the smaller colleges in the area. I remember our coach treating me with velvet gloves, which makes me think he'd gotten word from my high school coach to take it easy on me. I'd pitch once a week, if that, but it was a ton of fun. And again, instant friends came with it. That's one of the things I love about the game the most. Instant friends.

That was a cool way to spend the summer, and way better than just playing catch and running poles or sprints. When I wasn't pitching, I kept myself busy keeping the scorebook and got to know a whole bunch of new guys.

When school started again, I just got back into the rhythm of it and kept my grades up. It was always on my mind that I might not get drafted, or I might not at least get selected in the early rounds of the draft, and if I wasn't a top pick then going to The U was my goal. If I was going to attend such a prestigious college, I'd want to get the most out of it and get my degree. School had always been pretty easy for me. I wanted the challenge.

The winter dragged on. I kept clearing Don's drive and walkway, and Mom and Dad were doing fantastic. Some nights, Dad and I would sit in the small living room of the apartment and play mental pitching games. He'd say "OK, first batter is left-handed, likes the ball down."

I'd say, "Heater up to start him out. Then away to see if he'll chase. Then throw the change in the dirt." We could do that for hours.

Finally, practice started. A few weeks later, our first game was scheduled against Cretin. I'd be pitching. I remember that morning in crystal-clear detail. I was amped up to get the season going, but the first thing I heard when I woke up was rain. It was coming down pretty hard, but it was also raw and cold out there. Like, probably around 40 degrees. Even Minnesotans consider that miserable. I had already adapted enough to know the drill. Most Minnesotans will take 10 degrees and sunshine over 40 degrees and rain.

The rain let up, and then quit as we went through the school day. Coach got the call from Cretin that the game was on. It was still damp and cold, and a strong wind made it much worse. For one of the few times in my life, I would have preferred not playing.

We rode over there, I went through all of my routines and got ready. Even with the lousy weather, there was a big group of serious looking men in the bleachers behind home plate. I couldn't tell who was a scout and who was a college recruiter, but there had to be 20 of them, and an equal amount of radar guns.

It was still wet out, even though the rain had stopped. They'd done a good job on the infield, and it was playable. They'd had a tarp on the mound, so it was fine. It just felt miserable. I struck out the first guy, and then the second hitter tapped a ball toward first base. I took off to cover and got the toss from my first-baseman in plenty of time to beat the runner, but my footwork was a little off. Instead of landing on the front or middle of the base with my right foot, I hit the back side of it. And with the base still being wet, I slid right off and went down in a heap.

I rolled my right ankle a bit, and was already worried about that before I hit the ground. But then the real problem made itself clear. When I rolled my ankle, I also had apparently hyperextended my knee. Two injuries on one play, all thanks to a wet base and bad footwork.

As I sat there on the damp grass with my teammates and my coaches surrounding me, all staring in disbelief, all I could do was shake my head. Both injuries were painful, for sure, but what crushed me was the fact it was my second hitter of the year. My senior year. What the hell?

We didn't have a trainer who went to away games with us, but Cretin had one on staff and he spent a long time with me out there on the grass while everyone else stood there quietly. It seemed like forever before two guys helped me up to see if I could put any weight on the leg. I really couldn't. Between the ankle and the knee, it was like a war of pain going on. I hopped over to the bench with my arms around two of my teammates. No one was saying anything. The Cretin trainer advised Coach to get me to a hospital for better analysis.

Dad wasn't there for that game. There was no way Mom was going to sit out there in that weather, so I guess he just stayed home with her. While I sat there on the bench wanting to cry, someone called Dad to let him know. We put ice on both injuries and I sat at the end of the dugout with my right leg stretched out on the bench. I kept hoping I'd wake up from this nightmare, but it was all real.

Once Dad got there he took me to the ER at a hospital near home, and I was still in full uniform. When the doctors saw me, they called in a few other specialists to take a look. The diagnosis was basic and, I think, pretty much based on speculation.

The ankle part was easy. It was a "high ankle sprain" and those are pretty bad. Like four weeks minimum before I could run again, much less pitch. The knee was the big worry.

I remember hearing this: "It's definitely hyperextended, which isn't too bad and you can recover 100 percent from that. But what we don't know is how the ligaments and your meniscus fared through this. X-rays don't help us there, and we sure don't want to cut you open just to look around. We advise you head down to Mayo Clinic where they have the latest internal imaging machines. They can look around inside your knee and get a better read on it."

Talk about full circle. We'd moved to Minnesota so that Mom could go to Mayo. And now, just short of two years later, I'd be going. My stuff was nothing compared to what Mom had gone through, but I thought it was crazy that now I'd be going there too.

They wrapped the ankle as tightly as they could, slapped a knee brace on me and handed me some crutches. I'd never used those things in my life, but if I wanted to get back to the car I was going to have to learn pretty fast.

The hospital got us set up with Mayo and I needed to be there a couple of days later. They wanted some of the swelling to go down before they did the images. I was relegated to my bed at the apartment, or the living room sofa. I couldn't play ball. I couldn't even go to school yet. They didn't want me doing anything until after the Mayo results came in.

Don came to the rescue once again. When he found out about the injury and the need to head down to Rochester, he insisted we use his big Mercedes sedan so I'd have more room. It was bizarre to head back down there. I'd made that drive so many times I thought I could do it blindfolded. But this time, both Mom and Dad were in the car too, and I was splayed out in the backseat as best as I could. It wasn't exactly comfortable, but I couldn't imagine making that painful drive in the VW or the Corolla.

We got checked in, got seen, and had the images taken. Basically, we were in and out of there in about an hour. We'd have to wait for a phone call to hear the news a day or two later.

When the call came, the bottom line was that nothing was torn in my knee, but the anterior cruciate ligament and the medial collateral ligament were both severely strained. Considering the alternatives, that was a good thing. At the time, ACL or MCL tears could end a career. The surgery and technology just wasn't as good then. But, the strains were bad enough to require at least a month without putting any weight on the leg and then a few more months of rehab to build the strength back and get anywhere close to normal.

After two hitters, my high school career was over. Freaking over.

For a while, it was all sort of a haze from that point.. After a week at home, I could get around enough to go back to school but I obviously couldn't drive myself and it wasn't that easy to even get in a car with the brace on.

The principal called and said, "Brooks, we're all concerned about you and we want you to handle this the right way. Your grades are outstanding, and we only have about six more weeks of classes. We'll let you do it from home. Just do what you can, as best as you can, and let's see you walk across the stage on graduation day. Even if you're still on crutches."

That was like a blessing and a curse. I really couldn't imagine going to school, or even getting there each day, and had no clue how I could sit at a desk. But school would be my safe and happy place. It would be as important as any therapy I'd undergo on the actual knee. So, I was kind of trapped at home and that totally stressed me out.

I shouldn't have worried about it.

The next day, Coach came over along with Carl and Mitch, and they brought all the books from my locker. Between the three of them, they'd bring me my assignments after school every day, but more importantly they'd hang out for a while and keep my spirits up. I think by the time graduation was getting close, every guy on the team had been to the apartment at least once. They kept me sane! I would've gone nuts being cooped up in there by myself for that long.

The ankle started feeling better within a couple of weeks, in terms of the throbbing pain that was always there even when I was on the sofa. I couldn't put any weight on the leg at all for four weeks, so the rest of the recovery was still a mystery that needed to unfold.

After about four weeks (or was it years?) I finally started therapy. That first day at a Bloomington clinic was the first time I had put my right foot on the ground since the injury. I had no idea what would happen, or how bad it would hurt. I was thrilled to feel that it wasn't that bad. Even that first day, I was walking down the hallway at the clinic with a walker and I felt like I could've done it without that assistance. It really wasn't that bad. I knew I'd be fine. It was just a matter of time.

They insisted I stay on the crutches for at least another two weeks, and I almost obeyed them. When I was by myself, I just couldn't resist walking around and testing it out. By the time graduation happened, I walked across the stage without the sticks. It wasn't the prettiest stride anyone took, but I did it. I was going to be OK.

142

Two other things happened right around then that were more important to me than any of that. During the first week of June, the Texas Rangers surprised the hell out of me by selecting me in the 30th round of the draft. They'd been watching me since that first scout said hello back at Canyon. Their midwest scout called and said, "If you can get a scholarship to a good school, I'd advise that you accept that. We drafted you because we believe in you, and we're all hopeful the leg will fully recover. But we can't offer a signing bonus of any more than $2,000 in that 30th slot."

That bonus, of course, wouldn't make a dent in a college education if I signed a pro contract and wanted to go to school on my own. I knew then that I'd be going to college.

In the end, I had offers from University of Missouri, University of Iowa, University of North Dakota, Illinois State, and even Cal State Fullerton. That last one was tempting as hell. But, I also heard from The U and they were behind me 100 percent. A scholarship and a top notch training staff. If I accepted their offer, I could start working out with the trainers immediately. It wasn't a hard decision to make.

I was home. I was a transplant but I was a Minnesotan. I was going to The U and I'd be a Golden Gopher. If it was good enough for Dave Winfield and Paul Molitor, it was sure as hell good enough for me.

I was stoked. Mom and Dad were over the moon. But, looking back on it now I remember a bit of a numb feeling coming over me. This was a huge deal, getting a full college scholarship at a great school with a fantastic baseball program, but it's not like I broke down in tears like I did when I made the varsity at Canyon High. The knee injury must've really taken something out of me, mentally.

I mean, let's face it, the whole last two years were just nuts, and emotional, and crazy. Even after missing my whole senior season it all still felt like a weird dream. SoCal seemed a million miles away. Minnesota was feeling more and more like home. But there I was committing to the Golden Gophers and there wasn't a lot of emotion in it.

We were a very emotional family. Maybe we were all just spent. But the good news was we'd all be in the same place. I'd be living on-campus, but I'd be 20 minutes from home. Dad was talking about finding a house to rent, instead of the apartment, so that Mom could paint again in the garage. My knee was feeling better and I knew my arm would still be strong. I should've been jumping up and down and hugging everyone in sight. Instead, I just felt this sense of a mission, I guess I'd call it.

I was born with a golden arm and raised by two incredible people who always had their priorities straight. I'd had a setback, and it cost me a chance to turn pro right out of high school. Yeah, I would've done that if I'd gone in the first couple of rounds like most people thought I would. As a junior, I heard one scout say I might go in the top 10 picks!

So it was like a big train chugging down the track, and all of a sudden the knee thing happened and the train had to pull into a siding and wait.

I was excited about The U. I was looking forward to getting there that summer to start working out with their training staff. It just didn't totally sink in yet. For a kid my age, I'd had a lot to deal with in a short amount of time.

Sometimes life takes you to a 3-0 count and you're sure a fastball is coming right down the middle. And then it's a curve instead. You have to react and deal with that.

So I had a mission. I had to follow the program and get 100 percent better. I had to get my arm back in shape. I had to succeed. It had all been pretty easy up to that point. Not a lot of drama when it came to striking kids out. Now, I was taking a big step and I had to make it work.

It had never felt like I was faced with any sort of major responsibility in my life up until then I was just along for the ride and striking people out. Now I was on a mission.

CHAPTER 18

Eric Olson

I did all my summer training stuff again, prior to heading down to the Twin Cities to start my career at the University of Minnesota. I might have even pushed it a little harder than I ever had, but all these years later it's hard to know that.

All I clearly remember is that something inside me was excited and confused at the same time. For a guy who never dreamed of doing anything other than being a Roseau Ram, I was already well beyond that after the three years in Des Moines. Now, I wasn't just heading off to college, I was going to The U to be a Golden Gopher. It was hard to figure out, but I sure was ready to get there and see how I would do.

Carol and I had a good summer, and I guess the best way to describe it is that we just seemed to have an unspoken understanding that what we had was special, but we both had really important things to accomplish and we each had to focus on that. She was on track to graduate from St. Cloud State with her bachelor's degree in business administration. I had a college hockey career staring me in the face, and hadn't even thought of what I was going to major in. We had to have a lot of trust that whatever was meant to be, for us, would be. It seems strange now that two college kids could have that kind of maturity, but we'd grown up in Roseau and that was the sort of mentality our parents instilled in us. Be focused. Follow your dreams. If it's meant to be, it's meant to be.

I knew, by then, that what I felt for her was real love, and I had never loved anyone else. I hoped she felt the same way and I was pretty sure she did. We just had to see if it was meant to be. Plus, St. Cloud was a lot closer to Minneapolis than either Roseau or Des Moines. She could actually come down to see me play and, when I had some days off, I could do something I'd never done before. I could visit her in St. Cloud.

Late in the summer, after I'd been doing all my workouts with the Roseau guys, it was about time to get down to the Twin Cities to get acclimated, registered and all set up at The U. I remember being pretty nervous about it. Actually, really nervous. I mean, going to the USHL was a big adjustment from Roseau, but I kind of went into it blindly and then we lost all those games the first two years, so a lot of it was just a matter of keeping my head down and getting through it. This was the Golden Gophers, one of the best college hockey programs in the country. I knew it was a huge step up, but I was also excited about the school and the culture.

I had been thinking that, whenever my playing days were over, I'd like to get into coaching. Being the captain at Des Moines had a lot to do with that, and leading the younger Roseau players through my summer drills made it even clearer to me. I had no idea if I could play at a level that would even get me on the ice as a Gopher, so I wasn't really able to process the idea of when my playing career would be done. Why not put myself on a track to be a coach? I seemed to be a good leader, and the thought of it kind of excited me, so I decided to major in physical education. Being a P.E. instructor was a great way to get a coaching job. I was a good all-around student, and definitely wanted to get my degree, but a business or marketing degree didn't seem like what I was supposed to do. I came to believe that I was destined to teach and lead hockey players. After all, I'd already been doing that.

At home, right before I left, my family was being their normal version of supportive. Not a lot of hugs and kisses, but some encouraging words and plenty of advice. I don't think I needed the advice. I knew why I was going to The U just as much as I knew why I was going to Des Moines three years before. I wasn't a party guy. I took this stuff seriously. I'd put 100 percent into my hockey. But the whole "advice routine" was one I was used to, because it's what my mom and dad always did. They couldn't help but be parents. The best approach they had was to tell me what to do and what not to do. And yes, when it came time to leave, Mom gave me a cooler full of sandwiches and soft drinks.

I drove down the day before my packet of information instructed me to be there, and got a hotel room just outside the Twin Cities. I wanted to be on campus first thing in the morning. I don't remember if I slept much that night, but I bet I didn't. It was a pretty big deal to be going to the University of Minnesota, and it was ten times bigger to be doing it as a Golden Gopher hockey player. If I could make the team and take just one shift as a Gopher, my name would go in the all-time stats along with guys like Neal Broten, Bill Baker, Rob McClanahan, Buzz Schneider, Mike Ramsey and other greats. And, of course, Coach Herb Brooks. I couldn't conceive of doing anything as great as any of them, but being able to say I played for the Gophers seemed like a huge mountain to climb. If I could get to the top, I'd enjoy the view.

I got out of bed at the crack of dawn and did something I'd never done before and never really thought of until then. I got in my truck and drove to college. I remember thinking that was pretty special. Up until maybe a year earlier, I was never 100 percent sure I'd go to college. Maybe I'd just go back home and work in the hardware store. In terms of hockey, I'd already done more than I ever hoped for.

I somehow found the residence hall I'd be living in, Pioneer Hall, and it was a good thing the athletic department had sent me a detailed map of the campus in order for me to do that. For a guy who spent every year of school in one building back in Roseau, the University of Minnesota campus looked really intimidating and complicated. Not to mention it also was huge. I'd memorized my route from where I parked to Pioneer Hall and was pretty proud of myself when I found it.

Back in those days, there weren't any dedicated athletic facilities with dorms, workout facilities, and cafeterias all set up for the teams, but a lot of the scholarship athletes stayed in the same dorms. We were about a week ahead of the rest of the student body, so it was mostly just athletes from various sports hauling in their boxes and finding their rooms. Just about everyone was arriving at the same time, so my head was spinning being surrounded by all these guys from such a famous Big 10 school. I still just felt like a kid from Roseau, and it seemed like I was surrounded by grown men.

After getting the details sorted out, it was time to find my room. My most vivid memory of Pioneer Hall was that, to me, it was like a maze. It seemed to be made up of endless hallways and lots of turns and corners. Now, I can look back and remember it all clearly and easily, but that first day I was a bit lost. OK, I was totally lost.

My itinerary indicated I had a hockey team meeting in a campus assembly hall around mid-morning. It was my first time navigating my way around the classic Big 10 campus, but it was a neat feeling knowing I was there as a Gopher and not just as a visitor. I was part of it. I was a University of Minnesota Golden Gopher. And I had a map!

I saw Paul Broten at the meeting and he welcomed me to the team and to the school. Just two Roseau guys acting like all this was normal. That actually helped me a lot. It calmed me down.

After the meeting I headed back to Pioneer, which was way out on the edge of the campus about as far away from the athletic arenas and training facilities as it could be, carrying a bunch of binders and folders the coaches had given us, and I went back there to kind of soak it all in. I remember this like it was yesterday. After I walked in, I turned the first corner with my head down and I actually ran right into a guy coming the other way. He was tall and lanky and I think my forehead hit him right in his chest. I dropped most of what I was carrying, and felt like a moron. Like a little kid who just ran into a senior in the Roseau High cafeteria, spilling my lunch tray all over the floor.

I apologized, of course, and so did he. Then he helped me pick everything up.

"Hey dude, sorry about that," he said. "I didn't see you coming and this is my first day in the dorm. Still trying to find my way around. My name is Brooks. Brooks Bennett. I'm on the baseball team."

I introduced myself and told him I was on the hockey team.

"Cool," he said. "That's rad. I'm from southern California and only saw my first hockey game like a year ago. I loved it. Stoked to meet you, dude."

I had never heard anyone talk like him. I wasn't sure what half the words meant. But something about meeting him seemed, I don't know, maybe important or something. I just had an instant feeling that we might end up as friends if we kept running into each other.

About an hour later, Paul Broten came and found me and asked if I wanted to go to lunch. I'd never been to the cafeteria, or the "dining hall," as they called it, so I was happy to have a tour guide to show me the ropes.

When we walked in, there were a lot of athletes in there, all chowing down. It was a bit intimidating but I was with a senior who was a star hockey player and who was part of one of the greatest Minnesota hockey families ever. I really appreciated that Paulie did that for me. He didn't have to. We hadn't seen much of each other since the end of our last Roseau season, but he was looking out for me.

We grabbed some grub and took our trays to a table. We saw one with only one guy sitting at it, and it just happened to be the same baseball player I'd literally just "bumped into" in the hallway. Brooks Bennett.

I introduced Paul to Brooks and we all started talking. We told him about Roseau. He told us about Southern California, his story about moving to Minnesota, and how he got hurt the first day of his senior season at Bloomington Kennedy. He knew enough about hockey to understand the Broten family, and how Paulie's brother Neal was on the "Miracle On Ice" team, and we knew enough about baseball to know that he had to be pretty darn good to earn a scholarship after basically missing his whole senior season of high school ball. I heard the words "cool" and "stoked" and "rad" more times in one lunch than I had ever heard in my life. And I liked the guy. He was different. He wasn't from Roseau. He wasn't a hockey player. He was a cool dude from California and it was like a breath of fresh air. My initial impression had been correct. I could definitely be friends with this guy.

He picked our brains about hockey and Roseau, and what it was like growing up like we did. He told us about his parents, and them being hippie surfers and artists was how it was for him as a kid. And about moving to Minnesota "for his mom" as he put it without explaining much. I remember wondering what that was about, but I didn't pry. It was all eye-opening, like a peek into a foreign country. I was kind of mesmerized.

I really liked the guy. He was easy to like. I'm not sure how anyone wouldn't like him.

I needed to get back up to my room to fill out a ton of paperwork the coaches needed from us and hopefully, to meet my roommate who hadn't checked in yet when I put my stuff in the tiny little dorm room. He was there, and was trying to organize his stuff but that was really hard. I'd never been in a bedroom so small, and it sure was different than living in the Warner's basement in Des Moines. His name was Sean, and he was from a Twin Cities suburb. Like me, he was an incoming freshman but in his case it was as a true freshman. He'd just graduated from high school the prior spring, so I was three years older than him. He was also a defenseman like me, so I'm guessing that's why they put us together.

He seemed like a good guy, and when I told him I was from Roseau his eyes got pretty wide. I'd gotten used to that response over the years. Being from Roseau, as a hockey player, you just about always get a reaction like that. The town and the Rams have a reputation.

I was in a different world, and it was pretty darn neat to experience. I couldn't wait for school to start and for practice to begin. When we would hit the ice, I'd get a quick idea of whether or not I really deserved to be there. I'd understand in a hurry if I belonged at this level or if I'd gotten into something I couldn't handle.

I was up for it.

CHAPTER 19

Brodes Bennett

Once I made that walk across the stage to get my high school diploma, my knee was feeling a lot better and the ankle was fine. I was in near constant contact with the Gophers coaching staff, and they advised me to enroll early and take a couple of summer classes so I'd officially be a student. That way, I could go see the athletic trainers every day and get treatment and therapy for the knee. Sounded cool to me, so I signed up for a couple of courses in the "general studies" area, which is like stuff you'd need to take in addition to your major if you wanted to graduate. I definitely wanted to graduate, so I was stoked to get started.

I'm not totally sure what the two classes were, looking back on it, but I know one was in the English department, and I think it must have been a creative writing class. I remember the teacher was a cool dude, and some of his "tricks of the trade" on how to write stuff that flowed and was balanced have stayed with me to this day. The other class was in the science department, and I remember lots of rocks were involved. Must've been geology, I guess. They were both fun, and both easy, and they got me kind of tuned in to the campus and college life at a time of year when there were fewer students around.

I went to the training room five days a week, and they worked me pretty hard. There aren't any shortcuts if you're coming back from a serious knee injury. You have to want it and you have to work for it. Until I was 100 percent, I didn't even want to throw and the trainers absolutely didn't want me to. All the focus was on the knee.

At home, everything was really good. Mom was doing very well and still hitting her targets when she'd go down to Mayo for check-ups. She got back into painting but not with the mad passion to sell everything. I think she was just enjoying the process again. Dad was having a riot as a vendor at Twins games in the Metrodome. He was such a people person, so that didn't surprise me. Since I was born, my dad's entire resume consisted of working in board shops, bartending, cleaning pools, working at Disneyland, and being a vendor at ballgames. That was him. He was the coolest damn dude in the world. As always, it wasn't how much you made, it was how happy you were. He knew what was important.

I lived at home that summer, and just drove up to campus when I'd need to go to classes or work with the trainers. And Dad did actually find us a rental home. The apartment was nice but it was on the bottom floor of a two-story building and the guy upstairs might actually have been Frankenstein. It was totally noisy, and I'm not sure when the guy ever slept.

The house wasn't in Bloomington. It was in Burnsville, which is basically right in the same area. I had pretty much a 30-minute straight shot up to campus every day, driving right by the airport. It was a nice suburban house, a brick ranch style with three bedrooms and an attached garage. It also had a basement that was partially finished and Dad promised to find a way to turn that into an art studio.

I'm guessing the place was probably built in the '50s or early '60s, but it was nice and it was quiet. The neighborhood actually reminded me of the house by Canyon High. Lots of kids, nice families and good neighbors.

Dad also decided it was time to retire the VW bus. It was the only vehicle he had owned throughout my entire life, and he worked on it a lot to keep it going. If you did that, and kept it serviced, those VWs were pretty indestructible. But, he'd learned the hard way that it didn't have much of a heater (that never really came up in SoCal) and, with all that empty space inside, it was totally hard to get it warm in the winter. I think he sold it for $500. It might have been less than that. A Volkswagen surf bus wasn't exactly a hot commodity in the Twin Cities.

Don helped hook him up with a car dealer friend, and Dad bought a used Honda from him. It was a Civic, probably a 1984 or 1985 model, but it only had about 20,000 miles on it so to Dad it was like a brand new car. I just remember that it smelled good. The bus had a certain VW aroma, some of which might have been left over from the surfing days, if you know what I mean. I remember him taking me for a ride in the Civic, and saying, "I had to learn how to shift all over again, dude. This Honda has such a smooth clutch and transmission it's like a dream. I had to baby the VW, and carefully nudge it into each gear. This is like luxury."

At school, the two classes were great and my therapy was trucking along just fine. The hardest part for me was taking it as slowly as the trainers wanted. I felt good, no pain whatsoever, but the patient is usually the lousiest judge of strength and mobility. After being off that leg for so long, I needed to build all of that back up. No jumping off the examination table and running sprints, and still no throwing at that point.

As the real school year approached, I got registered for fall semester classes, mixing in a few more general studies classes with two basic accounting courses. I hadn't firmly decided on a major yet, but accounting seemed to be the best fit, since I'd always understood the concept of how numbers work. I was still pretty confident I would eventually play pro ball and hopefully make the big leagues. Knowing how all the digits meshed, and maybe having a little background in some tax stuff, would be a good thing. I remember thinking, "I'll take these two Accounting 101 courses and see if I like it."

Around that time, I also learned where my dorm would be and by then I'd already gotten a pretty good idea of where everything was on the big campus. It was cool to be there. I dug it a lot, and was proud to be a Gopher. About a week before I'd be moving into the dorm it hit me that the whole thing was even more real. Like totally real. After that weird, out-of-body feeling I had when I committed to the school, I was finally feeling a lot more stoked. From SoCal to the Twin Cities. From Canyon to Kennedy. And now I was a Golden Gopher on a beautiful Big 10 campus.

I told Mom and Dad all about that, sort of flushing it all out of me before it was time to move up to campus for real. Up until then, I'd either still been numb to it or maybe just in denial about the injury, but I hadn't let myself really enjoy much of anything for months. And now, as the fall semester approached and about 35,000 other students would be pouring into the school, I was amped. I felt excited. I felt a lot more like me. I just remember my dad looking at me, right in the eyes, and nodding a little as he gave me a little closed-mouth smile. I knew that smile. He was proud of me. And I was proud of him. None of this would've happened without him. I don't recall if Mom cried, as I let it all out, but the odds are pretty stacked that she must have.

I drove up to campus on move-in day so excited it was all hard to believe. It was weird, because I'd been on campus all summer, but fall semester and move-in day meant something completely different. Now it was all going to be totally for real, and I'd be getting to know a ton of other athletes and students. All summer, I just went to my two classes, saw the trainers and went back home. I really didn't get to know too many people. I wouldn't have any choice now.

As soon as I got there, I saw a ton of kids with boxes and crates and all the things they thought they'd need out on the curbs getting ready to find their rooms and get moved in. I mostly brought clothes, some bedding, my favorite pillow and my baseball stuff. I figured if I needed anything else, I could always go home and get it.

I remember the campus seemed like a totally different place. It was so quiet and relaxed all summer, and now it was almost overrun with students and teachers and all kinds of activity. Plus, in my case, there was the baseball team. We had a meeting that morning, after getting our room assignments.

I'd be living in a dorm called Pioneer Hall, way down on the edge of campus. Back then, they didn't have completely separate dorms and cafeterias for athletes, so we were mixed in with regular students, but that was cool by me. I wanted the whole college experience.

I did see on a list that my roommate would be a guy named Brian Raabe, who was also on the baseball team and an incoming freshman. The one thing I remember most is wondering how to pronounce his last name. Ray-bee? Rayb? I wasn't used to names that had two "A's" right in the middle, and I wanted to be ready when I met him. After all, this would be the first time I'd ever had a roomie! I thought that was pretty weird and unique to me at the time, but looking back on it now I understand it was the same for almost all the new freshmen. Athlete or not, most of us had never shared a room with anyone before, except maybe a brother or the family dog. I was stoked about it, but not completely sure how it would go.

I didn't have time to dwell on it much. I had a baseball meeting to get to and I was anxious to get there. Like I said, those first few days in the fall on campus were all a total swirl of new stuff, and it all just flew by me more than I controlled any of it. I was just trying to be where I was supposed to be.

Our meeting was up on the north side of the campus, right by the baseball field. It was a long walk up there, but it felt good to be strutting around a big college as a baseball player and full-time student. It was time to start my college baseball career, even if it was just a meeting.

A few guys had been in and out of the training room with me that summer, so I knew them a little but I was so focused on getting better I wasn't really there to socialize. The legendary John Anderson was the head coach, and I'd only met him briefly. His assistants had handled most of the direct communication with me, but as I walked into the meeting he clearly knew who I was. He came straight over and shook my hand, then asked how I was doing. I told him the knee felt great, and I was sure I'd be able to contribute in the spring if he thought I was ready.

Just as we were gathering around the coaching staff to hear what they had to say, one last player came jogging up from behind us, looking a little frazzled. I was close enough to hear him talk to a coach and say his name was Brian Raabe. That's my roomie! We didn't have time to talk then, but we'd have plenty of time once we got back to the dorm. I was just wondering why he was late. And by the way, when he checked in I learned it's pronounced "Robbie" so I was all good to go when we met as roommates.

Overall, I was a little afraid of there being some freshman hazing, or stuff like that, because I was clearly one of the youngest guys there and I was already tagged as the SoCal surfer dude, but they were all great. One by one all the guys introduced themselves and welcomed me to Gopher Baseball. It felt awesome. Instant friends, once again.

We left the meeting with binders full of stuff, and schedules for fall workouts and winter training. One of the first things I did, after the meeting, was to dig out our regular season schedule just to see what that was going to be like. It was stout, and I actually got goosebumps just looking at it.

We would open in late March with a week-long road trip to Arizona, playing in Phoenix against some smaller schools that were also getting away from winter, and then going down to Tucson to play three against the University of Arizona. I figured we would not have even been outside yet, at that point, before we got out there to play some warm-weather powerhouse teams.

When we would get back in early April, we'd get right after it with home games but they wouldn't be at Siebert Field on campus. Until it warmed up, we'd play at the Metrodome! Scanning down the schedule, it was crazy to see opponents like Florida State, Iowa, Iowa State, Purdue, Illinois and all those other big schools. I knew college would be a huge step up from Kennedy High, and even from Canyon, but just looking at that schedule was a total wake-up call. To me, it looked big league.

I clearly remember that my first thought was that I couldn't wait to get home to show my dad all this stuff, and the schedule, and then I remembered I wasn't going home that night. I would be spending my first night in the dorm. Yeah, that felt pretty weird, but all of this was a huge move for me and I was ready for it. I could call him from a pay phone.

After the meeting our advisors worked with us on our final registration stuff, getting our schedules locked in so we had time between classes and time to get to workouts every day. I had only picked up my paperwork for the dorm at that point, and hadn't been over to the room yet. I headed over there immediately. It seemed like everything was in a hurry, like in a bad dream, and I remember this nagging feeling that I had to hustle up or it was all going to get away from me.

I got checked in and headed up to the room with my two suitcases.. Brian had just gotten there, too, and we shook hands. Not only had I never had a roommate before, I'd never had a room that ridiculous either. It was really narrow, but it was goofy long. After we introduced ourselves, Brian looked around and said, "This place is like a bowling alley." From that point forward, that's what we called it. We lived in the bowling alley.

There I was. I was moved into my dorm at Pioneer Hall. We had dubbed our room the bowling alley. I had a roomie who seemed like a great guy. It all felt good. So I asked him why he was a little late to the meeting.

"Man, that was awful," he said. "I hardly know my way around campus at all, and I had just signed into the room here but needed to get to the meeting. I got completely lost. I think I walked by the basketball arena three times before I finally stopped and asked someone for directions. What a way to start my college career, right?" We had a good laugh over that. The fact he'd tell the story that way made me realize I'd scored a good roomie. He was honest about it. I never did like guys who pretended that nothing was ever their fault. Brian was a cool dude.

We didn't have much time right then, but we shared the basics. Brian was from a town called New Ulm, in southern Minnesota. He was a second baseman. And he was clearly a smart guy. Not a bad way to start the long process of "having a roomie" as a baseball player. If you keep playing, you'll have a bunch of guys you share a room with, whether it's a dorm, a hotel or an apartment. Some great, some good, some obnoxious and some who snore. I still had a lot to learn.

I had to go back down to the lobby to meet with one of the assistant coaches, who was going to give me a new training schedule for the knee, and we were going to sit and talk for a while about how we'd keep up that routine while we also looked ahead to the day I'd begin throwing.

On my way down the hall, I turned a sharp corner and POW! I completely ran into another guy who was carrying all his books and binders to his room. I remember three distinct things about it. His face hit me right about in the sternum and, as little as he was, I remember thinking I'd obliterated him. But he never budged. He never even took a step back. If anything, I kind of bounced off him. Finally, he dropped all of the stuff he was carrying. I felt totally bad about it, like a moron.

I scrambled to help him pick everything up while I basically just kept saying "I'm sorry, man" the whole time. After we got all situated again I stuck my hand out and said,

"I'm Brooks, on the baseball team. Brooks Bennett." Of course, we'd just gotten all his stuff picked up so he had to shuffle it all in his arms to even shake hands, but he smiled and said, "Nice to meet you. I'm Eric Olson, on the hockey team." This whole incident seems crazy now. We literally ran into each other, and we seemed to sense we were both athletes. I mean, a ton of the other kids in Pioneer Hall were just regular students, but we seemed to sense we were brothers. Weird. I still don't get it.

For some reason we both felt the need to stand there and talk for a bit. I'm guessing it was because we felt an equal amount of embarrassment for having plowed into each other in the hall. It was like, "If we talk for a while, we'll forget about what happened."

I told him I was from SoCal and a pitcher. He told me he was from a little town way up north called Roseau and he was a defenseman. There's a chance I might have heard of his home town when I was in high school, if the guys around me were talking about the state hockey tournament, but the name didn't stick. Had you asked me at the time, I would've guessed it was spelled Rozo.

Eric seemed like a cool guy though, and he was really straightforward. Today, I'd say he didn't have any pretense about him. Back then I just remember thinking, "This kid is from the middle of nowhere, and that's kind of cool. In SoCal, I couldn't have grown up any further from the middle of nowhere. I was in the middle of everywhere."

I also remember thinking, "My dad would tell me to get to know this guy. We're totally different and that's a good thing. I can learn a lot from him and understand how other people are brought up and how they lived." Plus, there was no getting around the fact he was honest and polite. I never liked hanging with the guys who screwed around or broke the rules, and if I had one worry about college it was that I'd be surrounded by wild guys like that. That stuff just wasn't me. It wasn't in my DNA.

Eric seemed really genuine. I was looking forward to telling Dad about him.

We went our separate ways and not long after the meeting about my therapy, my coach told me where the dining hall was. I hadn't noticed how hungry I had gotten. With all the excitement, I hadn't eaten all day.

I walked over there and got a tray full of everything that looked good. Then I found an empty table and started chowing down. I remember looking around and thinking, "Holy crap, I'm in college. This is pretty rad."

I'm not sure why eating lunch brought that thought to my head but I think it was because everything else I'd done so far that day was based around the start of the school year. My first real semester as a full-time student athlete. A full load of classes. A roommate. Finding my way around. And it hit me that lunch was something I'd be doing every day from then on. I was in college. I was a Golden Gopher.

Out of the corner of my eye I saw two guys walking toward me, and one of them was the dude I'd just plowed into. Eric asked if they could join me and I said, "Sure, dude, have a seat."

He introduced the other guy to me. Another hockey player, of course, but probably the best player on the team, according to Eric. His name was Paul Broten. The last name sounded a bit familiar. When Eric explained the Broten family from Roseau, the last name rang a bell.

Like just about everyone else in the United States I'd followed the 1980 Olympics and the hockey team's "miracle" tournament, even though I was just a kid. A guy named Neal Broten was on that team. I remembered that last name as much as ones like Craig, O'Callahan, Johnson, McClanahan, Strobel and Eruzione. Paul was Neal's youngest brother. That was super cool. Neal was the oldest Broten boy, and he had played at The U before going on to an epic NHL career. He went straight to the North Stars after the Olympics, too, so I'd clearly seen him play at the Met Center. Maybe that's why the name was so familiar, because looking back I'm not sure how much of the Olympics I actually watched and how much I just absorbed later as it became clear that the team was so special. The third Broten boy, Aaron, was the middle brother who had also played at The U and then had gone on to the NHL, as well. Just three hockey-crazy brothers from this little town called Roseau. I was eating this stuff up as fast as they dished it out.

We spent a good hour and a half there at the table. They were really interested in my upbringing, my parents, surfing, and how I got to the U of M. I glossed over a lot of it, including my mom having gotten so sick, because I didn't want to overload them or me. I liked that they didn't press for more information when I kept it short. It felt like respect.

I was more interested in where they were from, what their parents were like, and about Roseau. I couldn't believe the town really existed. Talk about a place like nowhere I'd ever been. For a bit, I thought they were making it all up and yanking my chain, but as we kept talking it was totally obvious that it was for real. While I'd been growing up surfing, they'd been totally focused on hockey in a tiny little town in the middle of nowhere. While I had one decent jacket for those cold winter mornings when it might be in the low 50s, they were laughing when they told me about walking to school when it was 20 below zero. My first two winters in Minnesota had seemed plenty stout to me, but Roseau was, apparently, a whole different deal. I just kept shaking my head and saying, "You gotta be kidding me." They weren't.

For the second time that day, I remember thinking, "My dad needs to hear all about this. This is the sort of stuff he loves. This is why he's worked with people in every job he's ever had. Everyone is different, and these guys are cool."

It was a hell of a first day.

CHAPTER 20

Eric Olson

It was more than pretty neat when school started, just to be on the U of M campus learning my way around. I always liked school, and at college I could pick what classes I wanted to take so I loaded up on stuff that sounded interesting to me and I started my physical education major. I felt like a college student, and that was good.

The funny thing was — and this was something it took me a while to wrap my head around — I should've been a college senior. I didn't feel like a senior; I felt like a new student. I felt like a freshman, but those three seasons of Junior Hockey in Des Moines had me entering school three years later than everyone else.

And that carried over to the hockey side as well. On the day of our first team meeting I'll admit I was pretty nervous. This was the Golden Gophers. Any list of guys who played here over the years can look like an NHL All-Star team, and that also includes the coaches. Coach Woog was on his way to being a legend. Coach Brooks would be a legend forever.

The meeting was in the locker room at Williams Arena, where we'd play our home games. Today, the Gophers have a modern and spacious dedicated home called Mariucci Arena, but when I was there we played in what was the "back half" of Williams, where the basketball team also played. Right before I got there, they started calling the hockey section of the arena "Mariucci" to honor longtime Gopher coach John Mariucci, but when they opened the new arena in 1993 he got the title all to himself in a brand-new sparkling building. It would've been nice to play there, but timing is everything.

I loved the architecture of the old place because it has a huge arched ceiling just like Roseau Memorial Arena, only a lot bigger. The whole place is really gigantic, but the basketball arena filled about two-thirds of it and the hockey part was kind of crammed into the back third. Since our seasons ran at the same time, we needed our own places to play, and they got the bigger part. The hockey rink was squeezed into a space that could barely hold it, with big floor-to-ceiling walls right behind each goal while the spectator seats were only on either side of the rink. It was unique, to say the least.

They also call Williams "The Barn" and that's easy to understand when you get there. It feels like a barn, or a big field house, but on steroids. It's a giant arena but it has a midwest kind of down-home feel to it. Not a lot of pizzazz, but great atmosphere.

So, as I walked in for the first meeting, I felt intimidated. Was I really good enough to play for the Gophers? Were these guys going to be such a huge step up from Juniors that I'd feel like I was starting over? Could I make it?

And then I saw Paul Broten and I calmed down. I'd played all the way through high school with him. He was a great player, but I never felt in awe of him or any of our guys up there in Roseau. We were all talented, and we were a team.

It hit me like a slap to the cheek, right there, that I belonged. I was a Gopher. I could play with these guys. And I realized the three seasons at Des Moines were really important in terms of making it all happen. I wasn't good enough, coming out of Roseau High, to play at the University of Minnesota. I wasn't there yet in terms of my skills.

Had I not gone to Des Moines I would've ended up at St. Cloud, or Bemidji, or Mankato, or some other school, and that's OK. Those are great schools and great programs. But by playing Juniors for three years, and living through and learning from all the losing we did there, I grew as a player and a leader. I didn't grow much as a human, though. I was still just a tick over 5-9 and I knew I was going to stay there. But, the work I'd put in up to this point, and the work I was willing to do going forward, would make me a Gopher.

As I looked around the room, it surprised me to see how young most of the guys were. It was the first time I'd ever sensed that in my life! Even in my last year at Des Moines, it never really struck me that I was older than a lot of the guys. We all seemed the same age. As a Gopher, I had just assumed that I'd walk in the room and feel like I was a kid among men. I was old enough to be a senior, one of the leaders and one of the "old guys" but I was only a freshman in terms of school, and I definitely felt like a freshman. But, a lot of my fellow first-year guys, the ones that were true freshmen, looked like boys to me. That was another realization that eased the intimidation factor and raised my confidence level. I remember thinking, "A lot of these guys are going to have to be at their best to play with me."

I also caught myself looking back on that night Coach Woog, his assistants, and Paul recruited me after a Des Moines game in St. Paul. They wanted me. They were pitching me. I deserved to be in this room with these guys.

In the meeting, Coach was talking and I was listening but my brain was spinning. I was ready to lace them up and get after it right then and there. I usually didn't have any problem focusing on whatever was being said or taught, but on that day my head was going a mile a minute.

I remember quickly getting into the swing of things on campus and with my classes. I'd run into Brooks Bennett pretty regularly in the dorm or during meals, and we'd always take the time to talk and compare notes on what was going on in our sports. The baseball team had a fall practice schedule designed to get in as much as they could before winter hit. We were already getting ready for the real thing. Those were good conversations, and I liked the guy. Maybe it was because we were so different. We "totally were" different, as he would say. We were about 180 degrees apart in most ways, but I could tell he was a really good person. His parents were definitely different from mine, but they'd raised a heck of a son. I remember him telling me, "I can't wait for your season to start. I'll be at every home game, dude." I think I said, "That's cool" or something like that, but I know I was thinking, "Really?"

As we trained, it didn't take me long to realize I was ready. Those years at Des Moines taught me a lot, but they also toughened me up quite a bit. I'd always been the pest, even at practice, digging in the corners and treating each drill or scrimmage like the real thing. Practice like you play. Those are words to live by.

I wasn't sure what line I'd be on, or how much ice time I'd get, but during training I sure seemed to be getting a lot of the reps and that made me even more confident. I'd outwork the other guys in terms of getting the weights done and I knew I could outwork them on the ice. After that first meeting when I was a little intimidated, I don't recall ever feeling that way again. I was a Gopher. The guy who only ever dreamed of being a Roseau Ram, who then went on to play at a high level in the USHL, was a Golden Gopher. Some dreams, I guess, come true. This one was already beyond the wildest version of what I had hoped for.

I didn't spend a lot of time in our dorm room. My roomie was a quiet guy and a true freshman, so we didn't have a lot in common but we got along just fine and he was very respectful. That's a good thing when you share a room that's so small it feels more like a cell. I'd go to the library to study, or hit the weights a little extra, or just walk around campus and the area around it, which is known as Dinkytown. There were lots of places to hang out and meet new people, and the whole area had a neat college vibe to it.

Carol and I stayed in near constant contact, but even then in the late '80s it still usually had to be done by mail. It wasn't much fun to talk to each other on payphones when other people were standing in line, tapping their feet, waiting to use the same phone. I'd say we traded at least two or three letters a week, and we were plotting our first chance to get together. It would have to be at The U rather than St. Cloud, because our hockey workout and practice schedules weren't going to give me a chance to go up to see her. And our first home game was coming up in just weeks.

As I remember it, we went up to Eveleth (about halfway to Roseau up on Minnesota's Iron Range) to play an exhibition game right before the season started. I know we won easily, and I played a regular shift, but I don't remember the score or even who we played. It was an exhibition game so it didn't feel all that real. It was like practice but with guys wearing different jerseys on the other side.

We opened the real season on the road. We played a couple of games against Colorado College out in Colorado Springs, followed by a couple against the University of North Dakota in Grand Forks. It was a good way for me to ease into it without the pressure of a roaring crowd at home. On the road, we were the bad guys. We were the team every other college in the region wanted to beat. It's easy to put your head down and just do the work in games like that. We were good. It was the best hockey team I'd ever played on. We could beat anyone. And everyone wanted to beat us.

159

Unlike Roseau and Des Moines, I don't remember much about the first game or my first shift. I know I was on the second line, and got lots of minutes against Colorado College, and I never once felt overmatched. I wasn't the best out there, but I could hold my own. In the second game on that trip, I found Paul on a breakaway and got my first assist. An actual point for the record books, as a Golden Gopher. That's the kind of thing that sticks with you as a memory. I don't remember many other details about that game, but I'll never forget my first college assist.

That opening road trip was really special for me, and not just because it was my first time on the road playing college hockey. The trip I'd made to Colorado to hang out with my Des Moines roomie Randy was still fresh in my mind, and it was one of the highlights of whatever travel I'd done to that point in my life. Colorado Springs is south of Denver, but it all looked the same to me and if anything the mountains seemed to tower over the town even more down there. It brought back a lot of memories. Great memories.

And then we were going to Grand Forks to play North Dakota. I hadn't heard much from Randy, but the last time I saw him he was planning on playing there. I was really looking forward to that.

When we got to Grand Forks, I looked for Randy on the ice when we came out to warm up, and he was doing the same thing in my direction. All we could do was stop at center ice and shake hands to say hello, but after the game we met out in the tunnel and caught up on things for a bit.

After the second game, we met out there again and had a great conversation. He had played really well in both games, and they were close and hard-fought. We won both, and that's the first indication I had that we might be special. North Dakota is a great program, and they were hard to beat no matter where you played them. To go into their rink and take two from them was not easy to do. Before we got on the bus to head back to the Twin Cities, Randy and I met up and he said, "You're doing great, man. Just keep doing what you're doing. The sky's the limit, and I'm not kidding. I'm not blowing smoke, dude. You're as good as anyone I've ever played with. Good luck the rest of the way, buddy." Another one of those moments I'll never forget. It's one thing to think you're doing a pretty good job. It's another to hear it like that, from a person I respected so much. He's a good guy.

After those road games, we came home to open at our place against Northern Michigan. We killed them on opening night. I think it was 10-2, or something that lopsided. I had a bunch of hits, a few blocks, another assist, and the icing on the cake was a shot I took from the blue line that ricocheted off a defender and into the goal. My first NCAA goal. We were rolling. We were gelling as a team. And after the game, Coach Woog gave me the puck. I still have it. My first NCAA goal.

The best part of that opening weekend against Northern Michigan wasn't even the games or the goal. It was the fact my folks and my brothers and sister all made the trip down, and Carol came in from St. Cloud. They were all there, and all so supportive.

I usually don't like to talk about my personal relationships in too much detail, but maybe now's the time to start. Carol and I were developing something very special, even though we'd never so much as spent a night together. We'd barely done more than make out a little in my dad's truck during high school. We worked on being friends for years, and we worked on trust and honesty just as long. We were as close as two people could be, considering we'd spent so little time actually with each other since the last day of high school. It hadn't been easy, but maybe that's a good thing. It was all a big test, I think. We passed, and we knew it. The letters were actually getting pretty romantic, and I knew I was very much in love with her.

That made the opening weekend kind of hard. I was thrilled my family was there, and I needed to find time to be with them even though we had morning skates followed by the games. I wanted to spend some quality time with Carol, too, but there was hardly any way to do that. We couldn't exactly "go back to my room" since I had a roomie, and she really had nowhere to stay without getting a hotel room. My folks had figured that out, though, and they got two adjoining rooms at a nearby hotel, so Carol could share the other half with my sister, Betsy. I guess Mom, at least, understood how serious it was getting to be. She was the one who organized the trip and the rooms, without even telling me.

Out of everyone, though, I was the one who was able to share the big moment the least. Getting as far as college hockey made that part of the deal. I knew that. Hockey got me there. It was providing me with a college education. It was my responsibility, and Carol knew it, too.

"Don't worry about anything. I just wanted to come see you and watch you play," she said. "We'll have all kinds of time to be together and do normal stuff, just the two of us, after the season. You have to stay focused. But don't you dare forget that I'm up there in the stands watching that little defenseman who pestered every kid from Warroad to Thief River as a Roseau Ram. And now you're a Golden Gopher. I couldn't possibly be any more proud of you."

She got it. We both got it. It would have to be that way, and if I went on to play any more hockey after college, it would stay that way. But, we'd been mature beyond our years since high school. I really felt we could make it happen. I knew we could. It was meant to be. That gave me a ton of confidence just to work on my game and be a good teammate. At that age, a lot of the guys on the team were going through a string of girlfriends, or "temporary girlfriends," and they always seemed to have a lot of drama in their lives, dealing with those relationships. I didn't have to worry about it. I could concentrate on being the same pest I'd been since I could skate. Carol had my back. We were going to make it. I was already in love with her, and it was only getting stronger. I didn't just love her; I appreciated and respected her, too. She was a rock. My rock.

At the dorm, sometime around then, there actually was some drama. My roomie wasn't playing much at all. He wasn't even getting many reps at practice. He was really down about it, and I didn't know what to do. I thought he was pretty good, although he was a true freshman who acted and looked even younger than that, but I also knew he wasn't going to make it. He quit the team before we'd played six games.

161

I remember walking in one day and he was putting his stuff in cardboard boxes and duffle bags. I didn't know what was going on.

"They don't think I'm good enough," he said. "I think I am, but that doesn't matter. I'm going home and I'm going to find a school that wants me. I don't have to be a Gopher. I just want to be a hockey player."

He had a few tears in his eyes when he told me that. And then he took all his stuff and left. It was a really weird and empty feeling. We hadn't even gotten all that close and all of a sudden he was bugging out and I felt really bad about it. We were, after all, a team. He was my teammate and my roommate. I was kind of stunned.

The next day, one of the assistant coaches pulled me aside and said, "Hey look, that was a lousy way to start your college experience but you're a guy who can deal with it. You can handle anything. We've put in a request that you just stay in the room by yourself for at least the rest of the semester. You might get to fly solo all year if they don't try to force someone else on you, but being a hockey player protects you. They're not going to put another non-athlete freshman in with you."

I told him I was fine, and the roomie situation would actually be good. I was never a party guy, and I was serious about school and about hockey. I was sad for my roomie, but happy to have the place to myself. He and I said we'd keep in touch, but we didn't. I never saw him again. If he played on any other college team we had on our schedule, I don't remember it. Growing up in Roseau, you never really experience anything like that. Everyone was always around. Nobody just up and left in the middle of an afternoon. We had some guys come and go in Des Moines, but no more than a couple ever left in the middle of the season. My roomie didn't make it three weeks.

The season got into a groove and I was loving it. As a high school kid, Roseau was amazing, playing in the Memorial Arena and being followed so intensely by the whole town. Des Moines was very different, but it was a learning experience I really needed and it got me out of my Roseau shell. The U was something else, completely. I never dreamed of it. I had never really considered it. But there I was putting the maroon and gold sweater on for every game, proud as heck to have the big M on my chest. The crowds seemed enormous. The electricity was beyond anything I'd ever felt. It was a mile past my wildest dream, and I was loving every second of it.

And then we played Northern Michigan again, but this time at their rink in Marquette, up on the Upper Peninsula of the state. It was remote, and it reminded me of Roseau. I remember really enjoying the ride on the bus. It felt like home, and it felt like hockey.

They beat us on the first night, and it was our first loss of the season. We'd started 8-0, and had just swept a pair from the Wisconsin Badgers, who were a big rival from the state next door. We were flying high until Northern Michigan knocked us down a step. We played them again the next night, and it was clear the intensity level was ratcheted up a lot in our locker room. Guys were mad. Half the team seemed to be stalking around the room at any given moment, just itching to get out there and play. We all wanted to get back at it with those guys and put another win on the board.

The game was just as intense. Northern Michigan was amped up too, having beaten us once already. I just remember the game seemed to be at an all new level of fast. Guys were flying, and everything was happening so quickly it was the first time I'd felt like I could hardly keep up. Not in terms of conditioning, that was never a problem, but in terms of the flow and where guys were on the ice.

We ended up winning that night in a very close game, but I never saw the end of it. Early in the third period, I was cutting across the rink at center ice, weaving as we pushed the puck into the offensive zone, and I guess I had my head down. I never saw the Northern Michigan guy right ahead of me, skating the other way.

It wasn't a cheap shot. I don't think he saw me either. We just collided at full speed. I'd been hit at full speed too many times to count up until then in my career, but I could tell this one was different the second it happened. We were both flying and hit knee-to-knee, which any hockey player knows is a bad thing. I had all my weight on my right skate and the other guy's knee hit me flush, right behind the kneecap on the side of my leg. I knew it was bad before I hit the ice. The other guy wasn't in much better shape than me.

I struggled just to get up and limp to the bench. Guys were yelling, "You OK, Oly?" but I couldn't even respond. The pain was unlike anything I'd ever felt, at least for a bit. Then, it all began to go pretty numb.

I'd been banged up and bruised playing hockey since I was old enough to lace up my own skates. Bruises are just part of the game. You don't play defense and win all those corner battles without getting banged up, but I couldn't recall even missing a shift, much less being truly injured. And there I was on the bench trying to process it, with trainers and coaches all in my ear asking questions I couldn't answer.

I remember they finally convinced me to go back to the locker room to get "looked at" as they put it. When I got up to walk there, I almost fell down. My right leg just wouldn't work.

I guess I was more scared than anything. I was petrified. I'd never been through anything like it, and I had no experience with something like what had just happened. I limped back to the room, sat on the training table for a second, and then fell onto my back, with both arms over my face. I don't recall if I was crying, but if I wasn't I was sure close to it. The pain had returned after the short walk, and all I knew was that it wasn't good. It wasn't good at all. It was just plain bad.

For the first time in my life, after all those dreams had come true, I was seriously injured. And we were in Marquette, Michigan. I felt about a million miles from home.

CHAPTER 21

Brooks Bennett

I dove into school as if I was jumping into a pool the quickest way I could, like it was a race. It was a really cool thing to experience. I had a full schedule, including some legit accounting classes, and dashed from each one to the next, excited to be there and eager to absorb it all. I was also learning to navigate the big campus. During the summer, I had only carried two classes, which were in the same hall, so the full load in the fall made it a new and bigger challenge – finding new buildings, navigating the shortest routes, and exploring strange hallways – but I was up for it. Within just a couple of weeks, it felt like I'd been there for a full semester. Plus, we had daily baseball workouts and weight work to do. There wasn't much spare time.

But there was time to hit the cafeteria at the dorm and I found myself running into Eric from Roseau quite a bit. His buddy Paul Broten was around a lot, and I got to meet a lot of the other guys from the hockey team. I was looking forward to seeing them on the ice!

Mostly, I picked their brains about the sport they played. It was totally foreign to me when we got to Minnesota, but I was instantly impressed by the fact it was played on skates, it was really fast, and they weren't afraid to run into each other. Now, I wanted to know the strategies and the techniques they used. It was pretty rad to hear how they all synced up to work together on the ice and actually had planned plays. To a new fan like me, it all looked sort of crazy and made up on the spot. I had no idea they practiced all these moves and plays for months, or even years.

They did make it clear that a lot of what happens in a game is based on repeated practice and knowing where the other guys would be, but it wasn't always run exactly the way they practiced it. After all, there was another team out there trying to stop you from doing what you wanted to do, so you had to improvise to get around them. With all that repetition, though, they knew what their teammates were capable of and how they might adjust to the pressure. It was really cool to eat up what they were dishing out.

I quickly got to know, or at least hear, a lot of their lingo too. One thing you can always expect from hockey players is that none of them seem to be called by their actual names. You never hear them talk to a teammate by saying "Hey Joe." They all have nicknames, even if it's just a shortened version of their name with the letters "sie" added to the end. Had I played hockey, I would've been Brooksie for sure, but maybe even Bennsie. My baseball teammates usually just called me BB or Brooks, although for some reason it was my coaches through the years who usually called me Brooksie.

Early on, I could tell the hockey guys and baseball guys got along well. It seemed like most of the hockey players I met had played a lot of baseball, and that made sense since the seasons are opposite. Why not play ball during the summer when you're growing up? And, they were as interested in me as I was in them. I think they kind of dug my story and my background, too. Absolutely none of them were SoCal surfers, I'm positive of that, so I'm sure they found it pretty crazy.

I'd see Gopher football players from time to time (they were mostly impossible to miss) but there didn't seem to be much interaction. Same thing with the basketball guys. You might get a "hello" or a "hey man" but that was about it.

As for the baseball team, we had a limited amount of time to do our work outdoors so we pushed it pretty hard. I'd learned at Kennedy High that you might get to be outside through October, and even early November could be possible, but by then you're feeling winter in the air.

They had me on a nice, steady throwing program, ramping it up in bullpen sessions and then throwing some live BP, where there's a catcher calling pitches and you're trying to get real batters out by mixing up the selection and changing speeds. The ball was coming out of my hand nice and easy, and everyone seemed happy enough with how it was going. I was happy too, and the knee basically felt fine. No issues at all. I was really looking forward to the couple of intrasquad games the coaches had lined up as the final part of our fall program. I'd been told I'd be starting one of them.

As the practices ramped up and my velocity came back, I was getting totally excited about the intrasquad games. I'd faced some good hitters in high school, especially out at Canyon before we moved, but I'd never faced a college hitter, and I'd never had college players playing behind me in the field. And that's a good point to make, about how things change as you move up. Yeah, the hitters are better and harder to fool, but guys start making plays behind you that you've never seen before. It all kind of evens out. You give up a few more hard-hit balls, but the outfielders often track them down or the infielders make diving plays. It gives you more confidence as a pitcher. Just challenge the hitters, and count on your guys to bail you out every now and then.

I don't remember if it was late October or early November, but I started the first intrasquad for the "gold" team (against the "maroon" team, of course) and it was pretty brisk out there. Coach Anderson told me before I warmed up, "Hey Brooks, let's just go a couple of innings, OK? No sense in straining anything or pushing it too hard in this weather." I was fine with that.

I have no memory of my exact stats from that start, but it went well and I struck a few guys out. I don't think they enjoyed hitting my stuff in that weather. I got a round of high-fives when I came out. It felt great, and the best part was the fact my dad was there. I didn't know it until after my two innings were done, but then he came down by the dugout and found me. He does cry a lot, but I don't think he did that day. He just gave me a huge hug and looked me right in the eye, doing that little nod he does to show how proud he is. After that, he stood back a little and stared at me from head to toe, still nodding. I know exactly what he was doing, because I'd already done it in the mirror. He was looking at me in my U of M practice uniform, and just soaking in the thought of that. He's the best.

Speaking of Mom and Dad, it was weird to be so close to home but not really see them for at least the first month. I wanted to be a full-time student and stay on campus, experiencing all of that. I'd met some local guys who would rush home every weekend, but I wanted to get immersed in it all before I went to see my folks. That's what made my dad's appearance at the intrasquad game even more special. I hadn't seen him in two months..

And one of the elective classes I took was Art Appreciation 101. I'd always been amazed by the things my parents did, especially my mom with her oil paintings. As a little kid, even, I'd sit in the studio and watch her start with a blank canvas. And then she'd just pick up a brush and keep going. It always shocked me to see what would emerge by the time she was done. Very modern, very impressionist, very complex, but each piece would open up the more I looked at it and become something I never saw the first moment it was done. I loved that.

I wanted to get a better understanding of methods and styles, so the art appreciation class was really a lot of fun. I was totally stoked to get there each day it was held. We sat in a small, dark theater, so the instructor could put up slides of various works on the screen. We studied many of the masters, learned the different styles and "schools" of art (a fancy term for various types of painting within the art world, like cubism or impressionism) from over the centuries, and the whole thing just kept me connected to Mom and Dad, even though we weren't all under the same roof anymore. It was cool, and I still remember a lot of those works we studied and the artists' names who had created them. That stuff really sticks with you when you enjoy it that much. That's one of the really bitchin' things about college. You get to pick subjects you like and really get into them.

After we wrapped up those intrasquad games it was finally too cold to be outside, so we had a few meetings and then began the real offseason. No more official workouts until the new year, and even then we'd be exclusively inside. We did have a weight room, so at least we could stay strong and, hopefully, in shape. January seemed like a million miles away, though.

I felt like I'd come a really long way in getting to know my new teammates. They were all great, and wanted to know all about my story, so I focused on asking all the same questions right back at them. I felt like part of the team in a hurry, and my roomie Brian was totally cool. A really good guy.

I think it was just a few days after the end of our practices when I was walking into the dorm and I came upon Eric. I was stunned to see that he was on crutches and a team doctor was with him. I couldn't believe it. He was on his way to a full exam to figure it out, but he took the time to tell me about the collision he'd had on the last road trip and how bad it felt. He knew that I'd just gotten over a knee deal, and I told him, "I'll help any way I can, dude. I just went through this. It's tough, but you'll come back stronger than you've ever been." He appreciated that. Then off he went on those damn crutches. I remember looking at the palms of my hands and remembering the calluses I built up from my time with those awful sticks. He'd have those calluses soon enough. And man, he looked like hell.

Right around that time, a bunch of my teammates and I went over to the Metrodome to see the Gophers play football. I don't remember who they played, but they must've won because I clearly recall having a great time. We even walked over there from campus, which was a totally fun "college experience" for me. It's not a long hike, but the Dome was in downtown Minneapolis so we had to cross the Mississippi River bridge to get there, and there was a long parade of students doing the same thing. Today we would just Uber or take the Light Rail, I guess.

The Dome was packed and it was loud. I'd been to a few football games at Canyon and Kennedy, but that was basically a few hundred fans on aluminum bleachers. You could hear the cheerleaders easily. At the Dome, it was insane. The place was rocking and full of maroon and gold. Yet another cool new college experience for this kid. My school. My team. In a gigantic stadium filled to the top. I do remember soaking that in at one point during the game. Like, "This is totally happening. When we were in SoCal, I never would've dreamed this …"

We went to a basketball game or two as well, at Williams Arena, and that was rad. I'd seen college basketball on TV but I hadn't seen very many basketball games in person other than a couple of times at the Canyon and Kennedy gyms. Those were fun, in their own way, but nothing like the Gophers. The first thing I noticed when we walked in at Williams was that the basketball floor was raised up. The benches were about two feet below the level of the floor. It was weird, and I'd never seen anything like it. I'm not sure why they did it that way, but it sure added to how unique the building was.

Oh, and there was something else I learned at both the football and basketball games. It's the line "Ski-U-Mah" and it's near the end of the U of M fight song. It's pronounced "Sky-Yoo-Mah" and I asked a couple of guys what it meant. The universal answer was "I have no idea."

So, of course, I did some research at the library. Turns out, a U of M athlete in the late 1800s (picture that) saw some native American boys from the region having a canoe race on one of the major lakes in Minneapolis. The team that won yelled something that sounded like "Ski Yoo" and the U of M guy figured it must be some reference to victory, or triumph, or something like that. He told his teammates about it and they decided to add the "Mah" to the end because it rhymes with "Rah" and that was always in every fight song.

Over the years, the fight song evolved and the end of it goes: "Rah, Rah, Rah, for Ski-U-Mah, Rah-Rah-Rah-Rah. Rah for the U of M." Pretty technical, huh.

Anyway, as the years went by some people started looking into it and it turned out Ski-U had nothing to do with winning and it wasn't even a real phrase. It was more of just a slang bit of whooping and hollering. Kind of like kids today might yell, "Woo Hoo" after seeing or doing something good. But it's still in the song and on a lot of sweatshirts and other merchandise, and everyone sings it at the games.

I was really looking forward to getting to a hockey game, too, but I hadn't seen Eric in a day or two and I was wondering what was up with him. I had gone to see him in his room after his exam with the doctors, but he seemed really out of it, at the time. I was hoping he was OK, but back then we didn't have cell phones or email. I didn't want to bug him too much, so I was hoping we'd just run into each other. I mean, that's how we met in the first place, right? But then I figured I owed it to him to check on him in his room, every day for at least the first week. It had to be lonely and depressing to be pretty much stuck in there.

The next day I stopped by his room around dinner time to see if he needed anything. He gave me an update.

It wasn't good, but it could've been a whole lot worse. He had what they called a Grade 2 sprain of his medial collateral ligament. A Grade 2 sprain sounds like it's just stretched, but actually it means there was a slight tear to the ligament. The dreaded MCL injury. The doctors didn't think it would need surgery but the rest alone, to let it heal, was going to take four to six weeks. He also had a pretty bad bone bruise from the collision, and that's what hurt the most. I know too well how frustrating that is. He was pretty down about having to be off the leg for that long, and he knew he'd have to get back in shape and strengthen it once it was healed. It might easily be a couple of months before he was back on the ice. That sucked.

I did get to a game with a couple of my teammates and it rocked as much as I thought it would. The hockey rink was jammed into one end of Williams Arena back then, and the whole place was a lot smaller and tighter than the basketball side. It was a bit claustrophobic, but it was loud and I could tell instantly that the Gophers had a real home-ice advantage there. They were a very good team, as in one of the best in the country, and then they had that loud snake pit of a rink to make the other teams even more intimidated.

I recognized a bunch of the hockey players I'd met through Eric, so that was cool to watch guys I actually knew. The only downer was that Eric wasn't playing. I bet it drove him nuts.

With fall baseball over, I just put my head down and went to my classes. There was homework to do for all of them, and I actually dug going to the library to do a lot of it there. It was quiet and serious, with no distractions. It felt like everything I always thought college would be like.

I finally did head back down to see Mom and Dad a couple times, filling them in with all the stories about school, baseball and the other sports. My mom gave me a full report on her health, and everything was going great with her. We'd sure come a long way from those dark days at Mayo. We talked about that, and how weird it was that we were all living in Minnesota just because she'd been so sick and needed to go to Mayo. That was more than just traumatic. It was brutal and heartbreaking. But we'd all grown to love it in the Twin Cities and didn't see any reason to leave.

Dad and I had a big laugh when I told him I'd gone to a Gopher football game at the Dome. He shook his head and said, "Dude, I was there! I work those games whenever I can. You didn't even tell me."

I was kind of shocked, actually. That's how much I was deep into the college thing. A bunch of guys said, "Let's go to the football game" and it just happened. It didn't even occur to me that Dad might be working there on that day. I was embarrassed, but I think he got it. Even still, I wanted him to understand that I wasn't ignoring him. I was just a college kid going to a football game with his new buddies. I was also an idiot.

"That would've been so rad to see you there," I told him. "If you had come up our aisle it would've blown my mind. I would've introduced you to all the teammates who were there with me. They know all about you and Mom. It would've been an honor to have them meet you."

He just laughed and said, "You're at college now, dude. That's cool. Live that life and get the most out of the experience while you can. But next time you go to the Dome, you better let me know and maybe I'll find a way to get to your section. And you better buy what I'm selling, too."

I did go home for Thanksgiving, and that was phenomenal. We had dinner at Don's house and it was great to see him and be back there. Robert was there, too, and it was fantastic to see him again. It was awesome to have Don, another actual family member, to share all the same stories with, about how it was going for me at The U. His eyes were wide and he was really into hearing about it all. That's the kind of guy he is. He's pretty special.

I brought a teammate with me for that. We had a shortstop named Dean "Deano" Franklin, who was from Chicago. He didn't have a car on campus, and didn't want to waste two days taking a train or a bus back home, so I invited him along.

I had never pried too much with Deano about his family or his upbringing, but I got the impression they were not well off and that the scholarship to The U was as big a deal for them as it was for my folks. I really didn't think Mom had it in her yet to put on a big feast at the Burnsville house, but when I heard Don was hosting the dinner it was a no-brainer. I asked Deano right away, and he was really happy to get the invite. Not only did he dig the feast (it was amazing, of course) he also instantly fell in love with my folks and Don and he couldn't stop staring at Don's house. When I showed him the suite where I'd lived for so long, he just shook his head and said, "You gotta be kidding me."

I told him, "Yeah, that's pretty much what I said when Don showed me around here. Look dude, I grew up in everything from a room over a garage to some small rental cottages, before we finally rented a real suburban house when I was in middle school. But none of them were anything like this. I was kind of blown away, too. My parents have never owned their own house. All we ever did was rent, and they're living in a rented house now."

169

I made sure Deano got a decent version of the whole story. From the days spent surfing to the fact we didn't have a TV until I went to middle school. I wanted to make sure he knew I never had a silver spoon. I wasn't one of those guys. I just was lucky to come from a very loving place and it never mattered to me what our furniture or cars were like.

Deano had the time of his life with us, and we became way better friends after Thanksgiving. SoCal is a really diverse place, and I'd had tons of friends who didn't look like me, or who came from totally different backgrounds. One thing I had noticed about life at The U was how the number of white kids was a pretty big percentage of the enrollment. Lots of Scandinavian looking dudes and girls, with that brilliant Minnesota accent, just like the one Eric had. "You betcha, don'tcha know." I was happy to have an African American teammate to hang out with. As my dad always told me, "Experience life, dude. If you only hang out with people just like you, you're not learning anything." I always looked past skin color and background. I just looked at the people. He was a cool dude and we could teach each other a lot about our lives. And he was a helluva shortstop, too.

It was only a few weeks between that Thanksgiving break and the Christmas break, so I wrapped up my semester finals and scored a straight-A report card. Lots of effort had gone into that, and lots of accounting homework, but I actually loved it. I was damn proud of those grades.

I hit the weight room over at our practice facility near our ballpark about three days a week but that was getting to be more and more of a challenge as every week went by. It was getting seriously cold and our dorm and the baseball facility could not be much farther apart on a very big campus. You had to bundle up in layers and then change clothes after you worked up a sweat, but it seemed to me that the whole team was serious about it. And sessions like that are another way to really get to know your new friends. There's no structure to it, and no drills to run, just a leisurely trip through the weights while talking to other guys and pushing them on.

I'd seen Eric once or twice after Thanksgiving and he was about ready to start some light skating, so that was good. The second time I saw him we were close to final exams and he was planning to go home to Roseau for Christmas. I wished him a Merry Christmas and told him, "Keep working, dude. I want to see you on the ice right after we get back from the break."

I honestly didn't think that was realistic, but I could already see how much improvement he had made and that he was right on or even a little ahead of the schedule they'd prepared for him. He told me about his therapy, and it was clear that he was a "by the book" guy who didn't cheat on his workouts. He worked hard.

Christmas was great, and it was time for me to finally slow down a bit from all the "college experience" things and just relax with my parents. I was proud of how I'd handled that first semester, and still loving every day of it. But I'll admit it did feel good to just turn it all off for a few days and relax with Mom and Dad. I felt like a totally different guy from the one who had started his full-time college career just a few months before. That was a cool feeling.

170

Mom and Dad bought me a really nice new winter coat and ski gloves as my only gifts. I didn't really have the ability to buy them much of anything so we had already decided that they'd get me one important thing and my gift to them would be just being there. The coat was a big warm ski jacket and the gloves were high-tech for that era. The timing for that could not have been better. We'd already been below zero a couple of nights in December and I will admit that life on the U of M campus seemed a whole lot colder than what I'd experienced my first two Minnesota winters, when I'd mostly just dash from the school to my car and hurry home. College life, on a big campus like The U, is all about walking. The wind just seemed to howl through there and I hadn't really had a coat warm enough for that. After Christmas, I felt invincible!

Just a couple of days after Christmas, Eric was back and I took him down to see my folks and have a nice home-cooked meal. He really enjoyed it, and I think he loved my parents. I could tell they loved him too. That was the "Parents Official Seal of Approval" for picking good friends.

We got back to school in early January and I started a bunch of new classes. Another set of accounting courses, Art Appreciation 102, a creative writing class, and one other one that I don't even remember now. That last one must not have been all that great, I guess.

We went to work immediately with spring practice, despite the fact it was actually the dead of winter, and fitting my class schedule around that was a bit tricky. Fortunately, we had great academic advisors working with us, and we found ways to carry a full load of classes in the morning, keeping the afternoons clear. Once we'd start traveling, I was totally not sure how it was going to work but all the guys I talked to said it always seemed to go OK and recommended taking some books on a road trip.

We had our winter workouts at the Bierman Center, which was right next to our ballpark, Siebert Field. Bierman was a great facility for winter workouts, with plenty of room for hitting in cages, throwing off temporary mounds, taking grounders, and hitting the weights. The one thing that was nearly impossible was for the outfielders to take any fly balls or really stretch their arms out. It was crowded in there, but the coaches had it all well organized and it felt great to be back in action, even if it was inside. And yeah, I was stoked to be a Golden Gopher and couldn't wait to get out there for real.

As the opening road trip approached, we ramped it all up and my arm felt great. The fastball was hopping and my off-speed stuff was going right where I wanted it to. Pitching indoors like that, though, can give you a false sense of security. Everything is controlled. There's no wind, the temperature doesn't change, there aren't any divots or holes on the artificial mounds, and the ball definitely popped louder in the catcher's mitt. It actually echoed a bit in there. It made you feel like you were throwing 100 miles per hour. I was, at that point in spring practice, probably in the high 80s.

I also knew the first road trip was going to be monumental for me. We were opening the season out in Arizona, and I had never so much as set foot on an airplane before. This SoCal boy was going to fly for the first time. I wasn't worried at all; I was basically just jacked up to experience it.

171

Around the same time, Eric finally got back into uniform and began playing again. That was cool, and I was amped up to see him on the ice. I knew all the details because we'd made an agreement right after we got back after Christmas break. We were in the dining hall, and Eric said, "Hey, let's compare our schedules and make it a routine to get together for lunch on at least one day each week. I want to know everything that's happening with you and the baseball team." That's what we did, and it was great to share stories and keep each other up to speed.

I couldn't go to his first game back, which sucked for me. I had a big test coming up in one of my accounting classes and as much as I was dying to go, I knew I had to study. "Cram" would be more like it. All the baseball stuff was having one negative impact on me. It kept me out of the library during the afternoons, and although I was still doing well in all my classes it was a lot harder to fit all that school stuff in. Classrooms all morning. Baseball in the afternoon. All I had left was nighttime after dinner. The walks to the library, to and from the dorm in the dark, could be a bit stout. It was a good thing I had that serious winter coat and gloves my parents gave me for Christmas.

About a week before we were set to leave for our opening trip to Arizona, we had a team meeting followed by a pitchers meeting. The team meeting was all about travel rules, hotel rules, roommates (Brian was going to be my road roomie, so that was cool), and other stuff like that. I remember one of the assistant coaches talking about how we'd travel. We'd have matching warm-up suits and small U of M carry-on bags. We'd all look alike and we'd be expected to represent the university in a first-class way. I thought that was cool.

He made a huge point of telling us one key thing: Bring your game glove on the plane. Strap it to your carry-on.

Gloves are the single most "personal" thing a baseball player has. Once you break in a glove, it fits to your hand and your hand only. It's bizarre how weird it is to put on someone else's glove. Your first thought is: "How does he even play with this thing?" As the coach said, "If any checked bags get lost, we can piece together a uniform and find a pair of spikes that fit you, but you're going to want your glove." This was stuff I never even considered. It was like a class called "Rookie Initiation 101."

At the pitchers meeting, we got the lowdown on how the season was going to start. Limited innings, lots of relievers if we needed them, and a five-man starting rotation that could be adjusted if double-headers started to stack up. I was going to start the third game, so I guess I was the No. 3 starter. I had the confidence that I could be the stud No. 1 guy, but coming into a Big 10 school and being the No. 3 guy as a rookie freshman — well, that was pretty cool. I was amped up.

You better believe I sneaked a peek at our schedule while the meeting was still going on. We'd be playing Grand Canyon University in my first college start. That's a private school based in Phoenix. I'll admit I had never heard of Grand Canyon University. I had no clue what to expect.

A few nights later, the hockey team was playing at home and Eric was in the lineup. A bunch of us walked over to the arena for the game, and it was fantastic. I'd gotten to know this guy since the first day in the dorm, and I'd become a big hockey fan at the same time. Now, I finally got to see him play. That was way cool, and for me it really added to the intensity of the game. It was like I had a real rooting interest beyond just pulling for the Gophers.

Let me tell you about Eric and his style. He was really good. He outworked everyone. He's about 5-foot-9 but he played like he was 6-foot-3. I still hadn't seen that much hockey in my life, but I had definitely never seen anyone play defense like him. There was no let-up. There was no fear. And for a guy coming back from a serious knee injury, that was really impressive. It seemed like every time he was on the ice he was in the middle of everything. I remember thinking, "If I could skate and I played hockey, I don't think I'd want to go into the corner if it was going to be me and him battling for the puck. He always wins and I bet I'd take a beating in the process."

And maybe this is a good time to tell you about Eric as a person. The guy I'd only met in the fall when we showed up to move in Pioneer Hall and plowed into each other. He's mostly quiet, but when he speaks it's really worth listening to. He doesn't just ramble on about nothing. It's like he's paying by the word when he talks, so he's being as efficient as possible. He comes across as super serious and very mature. I couldn't even imagine him going out and partying, but I could easily picture him doing extra sit-ups and push-ups in his dorm room. That makes him sound boring, but that's not it at all. Like I said, when he spoke it was always worth listening to, and when he wanted to he could be hilarious, in a very dry way.

When I bugged him for more stories about growing up in Roseau, it was like listening to an audio book. It was all so rich and colorful, and it seemed like an alien planet to me. The day I met him I could just sense that he was a good guy, a caring guy, with no bravado or any kind of attitude. What you see is what you get. For some reason, I just really enjoyed being around him and sharing our different histories. They could not have been any more different. And Eric and I could really not be much more different, but I felt a friendship almost instantly. I really cared about his hockey career, and he clearly felt the same way about my baseball stuff. Bottom line, I knew the day I met him he was a special guy. A guy you could trust. A friend. In high school, I felt like I was a pretty lousy judge of character. Some of the guys I thought were fun to be around ended up doing some crap I didn't want to be associated with. I got to where I didn't trust too many people. This was a guy you could trust.

After seeing that game, we took our time before going back to the dorm and I caught up with Eric when he came out of the locker room. I hope I wasn't acting like too big of a fanboy but I probably was. I just raved to him about his game and how he plays. He seemed kind of embarrassed, actually, but I made it clear I was totally impressed. That was a fun night.

Right after that, our departure day finally arrived for the baseball team. I was taking some accounting books with me and I tried to figure out what to pack in terms of clothes because we were going to Arizona after leaving Minnesota. I wasn't totally sure what to take, but one of the older guys told me, "Hey, it may be nice and warm during the day, but when the sun goes down out there in the desert, it gets cold. Even for us. Take a sweatshirt or a light jacket." Strong advice, right there.

When we got to the airport, we went to a special counter for groups and all stood around in our matching maroon warm-up suits with gold stripes and an embroidered "M" on the chest with the word "Baseball" stitched underneath it, while waiting for the coaches to sort out the tickets and boarding passes. I thought we looked first-class, and everyone was really calm about the whole thing. I was doing my best to act like them but I was buzzing, man. I couldn't wait for it to all happen. And the whole bitchin' trip was starting with a flight on an airplane. How cool is that?

I know some big college programs use chartered flights now, but that was never the case back then. We flew on regular commercial flights and would often end up scattered all over the cabin among the regular passengers. I didn't care.

I remember I had an aisle seat when they handed out the boarding passes. I only knew that because Brian looked at mine and told me it was on the aisle. He had the window next to me. I knew I couldn't be shy. I had to ask him and divulge my big secret. I hadn't told anyone I'd never been on a plane before.

"Hey roomie, this might be hard to believe but this will be my first time on an airplane," I said. "Any chance you'll switch seats with me? I'd be totally stoked if you'd let me have the window. I want to see everything. I'll make it up to you." He just chuckled and said, "Sure rooms. You take it. Buy me lunch sometime."

The flight was amazing. I'd never seen the tops of clouds before. I'd never seen anything like what I was looking at. I guess "mesmerized" would be the word.

When we landed, we headed through the Phoenix terminal and gathered at baggage claim to get our personal suitcases. The team managers would gather up the duffel bags and equipment and get that on the big charter bus that was waiting for us at the curb outside. Just stepping out there and feeling that warm desert air was awesome. I remember thinking, "Air travel is magic, man. It was 5 degrees when we got on the plane, and now it's about 80 and all I did was sit there for three hours."

The whole thing is still etched in my brain. I'd played plenty of away games in high school but we'd never gone on a real road trip. We rode on school buses, not jets and big charter buses. And we never stayed in hotels. That first trip was all a thrill for this dude. When we got to the hotel, Brian and I got our keys and went up to our room. The only hotels I'd ever stayed in before were actually small roadside motels, during our long drive to Rochester from SoCal. I'd never been in a hotel that had a lobby and a restaurant before. Crazy, right?

We were going to be in Phoenix for a few days playing games, and then we'd head down to Tucson for three more days to wrap up the trip. In all, I think we were on the road for a week, not counting the days traveling back and forth on the plane. My head was spinning, but I had to focus on the game.

We opened up against a small school from Utah. I think it was Southern Utah State, or something like that. As we got ready for the first game (it was a double header) I put my Golden Gophers uniform on for the first time. We wore old uniforms for the

174

practice games in the fall, and had worn these new jerseys and hats for Photo Day, a few weeks earlier, but this was the first time all of us were getting dressed in the full deal to go out and play. And those headshots we took would be used throughout the season and in the Media Guide. I remember I looked a little scared, not cocky at all, in my photo. On that first day in Arizona, we all got dressed and admired each other, and of course I couldn't help but look in the mirror. College baseball, baby. University of Minnesota. Those boys from Utah didn't stand a chance.

Normally, the guy who is pitching the next game charts pitches the day before he throws. But since we were playing two against the Utah team that day, the coaches wanted that pitcher, a good guy named Kent Billings, to stay focused and just watch. I volunteered to chart both games. It was a good way to stay into it and look for tendencies, for both teams in terms of their pitchers and ours. If I could spot anything one of our pitchers was doing that was working against him, I'd tell the coaches. I might be a rookie freshman, but I wouldn't hesitate to do that.

We handled the small school easily in the first game. I don't remember the score but it wasn't close and I thought we looked pretty good for it being the first time we'd been outside. I figured we'd bomb them again in the second game. I think we all felt that way. Lesson learned. They creamed us. Our starter couldn't get anyone out, we booted ground balls, we threw the ball all over the ballpark, and we actually did look like a team that was playing outside for the first time. It was pretty deflating. I remember we were all stunned. "How did that just happen?" Well, it's Division I college baseball. Even the small schools are good. You have to be ready. If this was hockey, I'd say we all just cruised around without hitting anyone or skating hard. Eric would not have approved. I was due to pitch the next day.

I never had a really superstitious game-day ritual. Some guys won't talk to anyone if they're starting, and want to be left totally alone. I'm not like that. Never was. I joked around on the bus, I took my time getting dressed, I checked the mirror to make sure I looked totally bitchin', and then I went out and did my slow jogs from pole to pole, just getting my heart rate down and trying to relax. Was I nervous? Hell yeah. But I felt the same way at Canyon and at Kennedy. I was pretty good at overcoming it.

We were playing Grand Canyon. They looked like normal guys over there in their dugout. I figured I could handle them. The coaches set the lineup, so I had no input on who my catcher would be, but I was thrilled it was a guy named Cory Branson. He was a senior and anytime I'd thrown to him on the side it was pure joy. He was an amazing receiver, and made it look effortless. No stabbing at the ball or making jerky movements. It was like he just reached out and guided the ball into his mitt. And when I pitched in the intrasquad, he called a great game. He was everything a rookie freshman could want, and I suspect that's why he started. I was in good hands.

When we took the field, I threw my eight warmup tosses and took a deep breath. This was college. Kind of a big deal. And I walked the first guy on four pitches. No wild ones, most of them just missed the corner, but it was four straight.

That woke me up and I decided to see if those Grand Canyon guys could hit my fastball. No more nibbling the corners, trying to be cute. Just go right at the next guy. And the next guy. And the next. Nine straight strikes. Nine straight fastballs. Nine straight loud pops in Cory's mitt. They didn't make contact. After my first college inning, I had given up no hits, walked one, and struck out three.

And that first game was kind of up and down like that, but mostly good. I gave up a couple of bloop hits, walked another guy or two, but struck a lot of guys out. After four innings, the coaches told me that was it. We were leading 3-0.

Here's the thing about a team. You're all in it together. If a guy boots a grounder and a run scores, you pick him up. When you leave a game with a shutout on the board but the bullpen guys come in and give up five, you give 'em a hug or a pat on the back. We were all going to need each other a lot throughout the season. That's what happened in my first game. We lost 5-4 to a school I'd never heard of. Since I left with a lead, I got what goes in the stats as a "no-decision" because a reliever got the loss. After one college game, I was 0-0 with a no-decision.

We played three more games in the Phoenix area and then rode the bus down to Tucson. Just like on the plane, my nose was pretty much stuck to the window. Arizona is a stark place, but the desert is beautiful in its own way.

I was set to pitch the second game down there, against the University of Arizona at their beautiful stadium. Unlike Grand Canyon, I'd definitely heard of Arizona. They are, year in and year out, really good. Like REALLY good. They expect to win, and any season that ends without a trip to the College World Series is considered a down year. Yeah, I was pitching against them.

I wasn't aware of it at the time, but there were some guys who went on to greatness on that Arizona team. Maybe it's a good thing they were just anonymous players to me that day. It's better that way. So, I had to look it up but as far as I can tell that lineup had three future big league stars on it. Kenny Lofton, Trevor Hoffman and J.T. Snow. They all played a long time in the show, and at a very high level. Funny thing about Snow was that he was from Long Beach. We never played against each other in high school, but it tells you something about the level of competition in SoCal that I had never heard of him and I'm sure he never heard of me. If J.T. Snow played high school ball in Minnesota, everyone would've known who he was before he was a sophomore.

Anyway, enough of that. I went through my routine, with the jogging and light toss before warming up, and I clearly remember not being nervous at all. I think I felt a ton of pressure before the Grand Canyon game because it was my first college start and I felt like I absolutely should beat those guys. Against Arizona, I think my mentality was, "Just go after 'em, dude. Fire your best shot. Make them beat you. Don't worry about it. And if you get them out, you've really done something."

It was like that. They were just uniforms in the batter's box to me. I struck out the side in the first inning. It went really well, and I was proud of my performance. I only gave up a couple of hits, allowed one run on the hardest hit ball I gave up (OK, it was pretty much a rocket into the gap and a "Welcome to College Ball" moment) and then left after five with a 2-1 lead. Then, it was Grand Canyon all over again. Arizona never quit, and they were definitely very good. We lost 4-2. I had another no-decision.

The entire coaching staff and most of the guys were all really supportive. I'd thrown the ball well, had good command and looked like I belonged out there. Just a freshman throwing darts. Did I "deserve" a better outcome? No way. Nobody deserves anything on the baseball field. That's why the game is hard. All you can do is your best.

We flew home the next day and Brian let me have the window again. I already felt like a seasoned traveler. I'd done more firsts in that one week than in most of my life combined. I guess I never realized what a sheltered life I'd had up until then. Crazy to look back on that. When we got off the plane, it was snowing and about 20 degrees. Welcome home, dude. This is where you live now. You're a Gopher.

That weekend, after a couple of off days with just practice, we hosted an annual tournament at the Metrodome. Now that was cool, to be back there again after that game with Kennedy. The Dome was our part-time home field. We wouldn't play at Siebert Field until the weather warmed up. Again, I had to look this up because I really didn't remember all the teams in the tournament. It was us, Florida State, Washington State, Iowa, and Maine. We lost to Florida State and they pretty much dominated us. We then lost to Maine and Washington State in very close games that went back and forth. Three straight losses, and I was up next.

My game was against Iowa. Five innings, a couple of scratch hits, but one big bomb over the "Baggie" in right, with two runners on. When I left, it was a 3-3 tie. You can guess the final outcome. We lost 7-6 and I got my third no-decision. Three games, and I was still 0-0.

After that, it's all just a blur to me now. We played so many games it was crazy. Even in SoCal, I never came close to playing that many games. I think our regular season was something like 59 games. We had road trips to Ann Arbor to play the University of Michigan, Iowa City to play Iowa, Champaign to play the University of Illinois, Omaha to play Creighton, and West Lafayette to play Purdue (yeah, I looked that all up just to be sure my memory was right on). After that we'd go back to Ann Arbor for the Big 10 playoffs. In all, we played 66 games in two and a half months. By the time the season was over, I'd seen enough hotels, planes and buses to not even notice.

I did finally get a W in my column, but it took until mid-April and it was one of the best games I'd ever pitched in my life. We were in Iowa City playing the Iowa Hawkeyes, and it was the final game of the road trip. I had taken my first "L" against St. Cloud State at the Dome in a tough game we lost 2-1. I pitched seven or eight innings in that one and was feeling pretty "stretched out" for going all nine if I could. I was totally mad at myself for losing that game, though. I had never had a losing record since the first day of high school. 0-1. Damn.

At Iowa, I was just plain dealing. Complete game. Nine innings pitched. Four hits. Twelve strikeouts. No runs. We won 1-0 for my first college win, and to get it I had to make it to the finish line myself. I couldn't wait to call Mom and Dad when we got home. I was pretty amped up on the bus heading north. We had phones in our rooms

177

but Brian and I hadn't bothered to get ours connected yet, so when I got to the dorm I had to stand in line to use the pay phone and I remember really needing to go to the bathroom, but I didn't want to lose my place in line. That's the sort of detail you never forget. Man, I had to pee so bad. When it was my turn, we only talked for a minute, but I rattled off all the details and I knew that sniffle on the line when I heard it. Dad was crying. It took all the self-control I had to not join him while three guys stood in line behind me, waiting to use the same phone. Right after that call, I told Brian, "Dude, we need to get our phone hooked up."

We went on a long winning streak in early May and then went to the Big 10 tournament in Ann Arbor. It was a whole new level of intensity and really cool. We lost the first game to Michigan State but then plowed through four straight wins to earn a spot in the NCAA Regional. I contributed. I pitched against Ohio State and went the distance again. One run allowed and 13 strikeouts. By that point, I was 7-2 on the year, so the 0-1 losing record was ancient history. And I was throwing darts.

The regional was held in Fresno, California, at Fresno State. I'd never been there. Heck, the whole time we lived out in SoCal I'd never been out of the massive L.A. and Orange County area. One last road trip for us. We lost two straight and were done. It was kind of fitting, I guess, that my last start ended up in yet another no-decision. We were leading Fresno State 7-4 when I came out after six. I'd been a little wild and walked way too many guys, so the coaches wanted to be careful with me. We ended up losing 10-8.

It was a long flight home. After the Big 10 tournament, I know we all felt we were good enough to make it to the College World Series. I'm sure that was just wishful thinking. We were good, but there were some holes in our lineup that gave us problems. Yeah, we were good, but we weren't College World Series good.

My roomie Brian had played really well all year. He was a prospect for sure, and had been a solid starter as a true freshman all year. Deano, my buddy from Chicago, had made a lot of progress too. He could just flat play in the field from the first day, but his hitting needed to improve and he worked his butt off all year to do that. I was proud of him. I was proud of the whole team. We had bonded as brothers, and it was rad to see how far we'd gotten. It was rad to see how far I'd gotten!

In the end, and I had kept my own stats just to make sure the team had them right, my numbers were:

- 13 games (all starts)
- 67 innings pitched
- 53 hits
- 3 home runs allowed
- 22 earned runs allowed
- 2.95 earned run average
- 65 strikeouts
- 13 walks

The only stat that bothered me was the 22 earned runs. Every time I'd give up a run I felt disappointed in myself. I could get better. I was determined to get better.

The whole thing went by so fast. It was kind of a jolt when it ended. And at the same time, I'd kept my grades up pretty well and had to go right to finals when we got back to school. I aced most of them.

Oh, and I met a girl. A really cute and funny girl. More on that later.

CHAPTER 22

Eric Olson

When the game ended in Marquette, after I had gotten hurt, we still had to get back to the Twin Cities on the bus. By then, the pain in my right knee was as bad as anything I'd experienced in the game of hockey, or for that matter in my life. It was going to be a long ride.

Heck, it's a long ride even if you're not hurt. I remember, when we were going up there, that it seemed to take forever. You think, "Well, how far can it be? The eastern edge of Minnesota up to Michigan's Upper Peninsula?" About seven hours, as I recall. After the game, the ride back was an overnight trip. By then I could hardly walk.

One of the trainers found some crutches for me, and they put on a basic elastic-style brace on the knee, but back then those things were really only about as good as an ACE bandage. What the trainers didn't have was much in the way of pain relief. Literally, just some stuff that basically only tore my stomach up, probably because I took it without any food. So not only did I have a horribly throbbing knee; I also had a horribly throbbing stomach. The stomach pain would ease up, but the knee was another story.

I got on the bus, and the guys were good about giving me two seats so I could extend my right leg out, but it was pretty bad and the pain was relentless. It was a long, dark, quiet ride. I remember it like it was yesterday. Everyone else was sleeping. The motor just droned on and on, taking us back home through the darkness. Just a flash of light every now and then when a car or truck would pass going the other way. And I was wide awake, feeling every bump in the road.

I'm not exaggerating when I say it was the most difficult moment in my hockey career. About an hour into the ride a trainer came back and took the brace thing off. He then wrapped my knee in bags of ice, and covered that with an ACE bandage. The ice numbed everything. That was a good thing.

After another hour or so, the ice had melted and leaked pretty much all over the seat I had my leg on, and the ACE bandage was soaked. And everyone was asleep. The whole thing wasn't just painful, it was depressing.

The same trainer came back a little while later and took off the ice packs. They had a cooler full of more ice for me, but he said, "Let's just let it rest for a bit. We'll put another ice pack on in an hour or so. I won't forget about you."

I'd been hurt before. We all get hurt. If you play hockey all the way through high school, you're going to get banged up and hurt. It's just part of the game. Being injured is a different thing.

I'd ridden on a frozen school bus from points all over Minnesota, just to get back home to Roseau after another tough game against yet another team that could think of nothing better than beating the Roseau Rams. Most of those times, you were just tired. Sometimes, though, it was different and there were specific aches or pains, from a hard hit into the boards or catching a skate and twisting an ankle, and that bothered you the whole way home. The ride home from Marquette was far worse. I thought it would never end.

I remember I needed help to get off the bus. I hadn't really used crutches much before then, and after the ride my leg had just about locked up. Basically, a couple of guys had to carry me off the bus, down those narrow steps with one guy holding me under the armpits and another by my legs, being extra careful with the right one. It wasn't pretty.

The bus had taken us back to the rink, of course, and I lived all the way across campus. The trainer who had been checking on me during the ride said, "Just wait right here. I'll go get my car and I'll drive you down to Pioneer."

When we got there, he helped me up to my room and I collapsed on my bed. A few minutes later, before the trainer left, there was a knock on the door and it was our team doctor. He had called the medical staff before we left Marquette and they had some prescription pain relievers waiting for me. He was my delivery guy. When he gave me one he said, "Take it easy with this stuff. It will help you sleep and it will numb you up pretty good, but you can't take more than two a day. And drink lots of water."

I was OK with that. I really just wanted to get some sleep, and I knew I couldn't do that with my knee throbbing. I'd never really taken anything stronger than aspirin to that point in my life, so it was an all new thing to this Roseau boy. I just hoped this new pill would be kinder to my stomach than the one they gave me for the bus ride. The doc and the trainer left, I laid down, and drifted away.

It was early Sunday morning when I went to bed, probably around 5:00 a.m.. I slept until about noon. The knee woke up with me, reminding me it hadn't been a dream. It was not fun. I was groggy, and the whole thing seemed like some sort of hallucination, but once I felt the knee saying "Good morning!" it all came back to me.

The doc came to my room not too long after that, and sat down by my bed.

"As soon as you're ready, we need to get you over to the medical center and have pictures taken of this," he said. "We need to take a good look at it, and when we move it around it might be pretty painful, but we need to know what we're dealing with.

"I don't think it's just a knee sprain. Those hurt, but generally guys can even walk on them with just some bearable pain. Even torn ligaments sometimes aren't that bad unless

181

you stress the area. There's got to be something else going on here. Could be a bone contusion. Could be a fracture of the patella. We need to find out what it is."

I didn't want to wait. I got up, still in my sweat suit from the bus ride the night before, and I hobbled out to his car.

The evaluation was pretty intense, but I wanted to know what was going on as much as they did. The consensus was this: Grade 2 sprain of the MCL and a deep bone contusion. The good news was this: The bone thing was just pain. It would go away. Nothing was cracked or broken in there. The Grade 2 didn't need surgery. It just needed rest. Maybe four weeks, maybe six, but I had to stay off it. All in all, that was about as good as it could be. Had it been a full ligament tear, I would've been done for the season.

The medical staff also fitted me with a real brace, but the problem with that was how tight it was. It needed to be tight to keep the knee stable, but that also pressed on the bone bruise. As soon as they put it on I just about screamed. They agreed to give the bone bruise four or five days to calm down, if I'd promise to stay completely off the leg during that time. Then, if the bruise got better we could put the heavy brace on. They just wrapped it with a new ACE bandage and it all sounded like a fair trade to me. I'd just have to get better with the crutches. I wasn't worried. I'm a fast learner.

Then there was the problem with school. We had about two weeks of classes left before Thanksgiving, but it didn't seem possible for me to get to class, much less sit at a desk, for at least a week. Our academic advisors promised they'd talk to all of my instructors and work it out. Obviously there was no online stuff then, so if I was going to do the work I'd need some help just getting it to me. I didn't want to get behind.

Once I was back from the examination, I knew I had some phone calls to make. I needed to call my folks and I really needed to talk to Carol. As far as I could tell, no one in Roseau knew I was injured and Carol couldn't have known, unless her ESP was alerting her of something.

I had the phone in my room hooked up by then, but first I walked down the hall on my crutches to the bathroom and could tell I was getting better at using those things already. Then I called Mom and Dad, collect, of course (does anyone under 30 know what a "collect call" was?) and told them all about it. Their reaction didn't surprise me. No hysterics or emotion, really. Just very matter of fact. Dad said "Do what they tell you, follow the rules, and stick with the process. You'll get better."

That's much of Minnesota in a nutshell. We all played hockey. We all got bruised and nicked up. Suck it up, buttercup. Gut your way through it but follow the rules and do what they tell you. Do the right thing. Truth is, by being at The U, I had about the best care I could possibly have. Top notch doctors and specialists who knew a thing or two about sports injuries. My guess is they probably averaged one knee injury like mine, or much worse, per week during football season.

It was great to talk to Mom and Dad and hear their voices. We didn't talk about Thanksgiving at all because I hadn't planned to be up there with them anyway. We had home games on Friday and Saturday right after the holiday and I figured I'd be focused on those. It was too far to drive just to be there for dinner on Thursday. With the knee, there was no question. I couldn't go.

After I got off with them, I called Carol. It was clear she had no idea what had happened. She just sounded happy to hear from me and said, "So how did it go up at Northern Michigan?"

I filled her in on as many details as my foggy brain could process, trying to reassure her that I was OK and it would all be fine, and that I just needed to stay off it and rest. She listened to everything I said, and replied, "OK, well I'm coming down. I can be there in a few hours. How do I find you?"

I was still a little goofy from the pain pills and just stressed out overall from the whole ordeal, and I realized that as much as we had talked about it and I'd described the campus to her, she'd never been to the dorm. When she came down for the first home game with my family they stayed in a hotel. I tried to give her directions, but I guess I wasn't making a lot of sense.

"Listen, I'll find it," she said. "I'll ask someone if I need directions, and I'll find it. What floor are you on?"

She's pretty resourceful and self-sufficient. I really didn't need to worry about her finding me. Somehow she would. I did have one moment of clarity, though.

"Look, it's fantastic that you're coming down and I can't wait to see you. I really need to see you. So let's pick a time and I'll find one of the guys who will go down to the front door and meet you. It's kind of hard to describe how to find my room."

It was late afternoon when we talked and she thought she could get there by 6:00. I just needed to find a volunteer to meet her at the door. I shouldn't have worried about it. When I got off the phone there were a couple of guys waiting for me in the hall. They must have heard me on the phone because they knocked and came in as soon as I hung up. The room was a small typical dorm room, so they had to kind of crowd in, but they wanted to check on me and see how I was doing. Then a couple of more guys showed up.

The good thing was I didn't have a roommate so there was more space than usual in there. They were all concerned about what the doctors had said, so I told them all about it. I promised I'd be back, and better than ever, and I hoped six weeks might be the time frame. That would put us just after New Year's Day. We all decided that was my goal. Make it back on the ice as soon as possible after the new year.

Two of the guys offered to wait for Carol at 6:00, so I showed them the photo of her I carried in my wallet. Then I said, "You guys are the best. Thanks for coming by, and thanks for finding Carol for me. Now I need to lie down."

They left and I just crashed on the bed again, being extra careful with the knee. Even just trying to lift the leg up and onto the bed hurt, and I wasn't supposed to bend it if I could help it, so everything was an effort. I think I fell asleep in a minute. I'm not sure what time it was, but it was starting to get dark so probably around 4:30. The next thing I knew there was a knock on the door. It seemed like I just fell asleep. It was 6:00.

Carol walked in, with the two guys who had met her. I thanked them sincerely, and they said, "No problem, Oly. You've got a winner here. Heck of a girl. We're not

183

sure why, but we think she likes you. Must not be too much to choose from up there in Roseau." Teammates are the best. That was the first time I'd laughed in 24 hours.

They took off, and Carol came over to sit on the edge of the bed. We hugged. We hugged for a long time. It was like we were hugging as hard as we could. It reminded me of that fall day when she went back to St. Cloud State for her junior year. We'd gone through what could've been the end of us the first year, heading off to different places to follow our own dreams. But things had changed and so had we. That hug in Roseau was the deepest and most emotional thing I'd ever felt with a girl. This one, in my room and stuck on the bed, was even better.

Did you ever have a moment in your life when everything changed, in terms of being in love and knowing what your future was going to be? That was it. It kind of overwhelmed me, and I really had to hold back the tears. I'm not a crier. None of us are in my family. Stiff upper lip and all that. But that moment, that hug, made it all clear to me. This was my partner, my rock, the love of my life. I was pretty glassy eyed when we pulled away from that amazing hug and looked at each other. I just stared into those gorgeous, dark brown eyes. She then gave me a kiss. It was beyond anything I'd ever felt. It wasn't two people pressing their lips together. It felt like two souls joining. I know that's kind of "deep" but that's what it felt like. I'm not sure if it was the hug, the kiss, or the pain pills, but my head was spinning.

"I'm so glad you're here," I said, somewhat coherently. "Nothing could be better than to have you here. I love you, Carol. I love you so much. Not like 'love you' or 'love you too' at the end of a phone call. I love you with all my heart."

And then she started bawling. I'd rarely ever seen that out of her. We were a lot alike in that way. We were both kind of Roseau stoic. We knew we cared about each other. We knew it was something unique and special. We respected each other so much it was almost insane, and we knew we were in love. But at that moment, with the crutches leaning up against my bed and my aching knee in an ACE bandage, it all came out.

"Gosh, I'm sorry," I said, shaking my head and wiping away my own tears as if I'd done something wrong. "It must be the pain pills. I didn't want to get all mushy on you."

She wiped her eyes and said, "If you ever apologize again for being yourself, I'm going to make that knee feel like a walk in the park. I love you, too, Eric. I always have. I think I was in love with you by the sixth grade. There's no place else on Earth where I want to be other than here, with you, in this miniature dorm room. Thank God you pissed off your roommate and he quit school. Good plan!"

And there it was, my second laugh in the last 24 hours.

I've often thought of that night, that hug, and that kiss. Why was it so special? Do other people experience anything even close to what I was feeling? At the same time, it kind of blindsided me and it was something I knew was in there. I'd just never felt it all flood out of me like that. Maybe it really was the pain medication.

Almost all the guys I knew and played with went through girlfriends on a constant basis. The typical question would be "Are you dating anybody?" and the answer was "Yeah, there's this girl. She's pretty cute." It seemed like it was just something you did, but it wasn't anything I ever did. I was all about hockey. I'm sure a lot of guys wondered about me. I never thought about it. I was massively in love with hockey. But on this night, with all that emotion, I knew I was absolutely in love with this girl.

We were still having our "moment" with Carol sitting there on the side of my twin bed, when there was a knock on the door. She got up and answered it, and I could hear a guy's voice say, "Oh, damn. Sorry. I was looking for Eric. Is this his room?" I knew that voice. It was my surfer baseball buddy Brooks.

I yelled, "Come on in, man" and Carol opened the door fully.

"I'm really sorry, dude, I thought you might be alone and need something," he said. "After I saw you earlier today I was worried about it. How are you?"

My only reply was, "You saw me earlier?"

"Yeah, remember. I saw you in the hall when you were headed out to get examined. You had the doc with you. You were pretty out of it."

All I could say was, "Wow. I kinda remember that now that you mention it."

I introduced him to Carol and I could tell he wasn't just worried about me, he was also worried that he'd interrupted something between us, but I was really honored that he'd sought me out to check on me. That made two people in my room who had never been there before.

Brooks was nice enough to ask if I was hungry, and it hit me just then that I was. Carol had brought some snacks for her drive, and she said she'd stopped at a McDonald's when she got close to campus because she wasn't sure what any of the options were going to be for food, but I hadn't eaten since before the game the day before. It had been about 28 hours since I'd had a bite of real food.

Brooks went down to the dining hall and got me a couple of deli sandwiches so I could have one right then and save the second one in my mini-fridge. Man that tasted good.

Brooks only hung out for a bit, and then he promised to keep looking in on me each day. The fact that he'd just gotten over a bad knee injury himself was kind of reassuring, I guess. He'd be a good resource for getting better without hurting it worse.

Once he was gone, I put my head back on the pillow again, feeling the knee throb with each heartbeat. Carol sat next to me and we just held hands for a while. I needed the rest and I just wanted to be quiet, at that point.

And then I said, "You know you're staying here with me tonight, right?"

Carol smiled a little and said, "I kind of figured that. I'm sure as hell not driving back to St. Cloud!"

I still had bunk beds in the room, and for a second I was afraid she was going to insist on sleeping in the other bed.

"It would really be great to spend the night with you. This bed is tiny, but we can make it work."

She just nodded and smiled.

Fact: With a terribly painful knee and very little mobility, this particular night will always be one I'll remember as the first time I shared a bed with any female other than my sister. I needed the sleep, and it was a bit uncomfortable, but I was so at peace. She kissed me, ran her fingers through my hair, and said, "You just sleep. I'm going to try not to stare at you all night."

When I woke up I had no idea what time it was. I think it was still dark outside, but the thing I clearly remember was the fact I was on my back and the love of my life was tucked in next to me on that little bed, and we had our arms around each other. Maybe that's why the knee didn't seem to hurt so bad.

Carol needed to head back to St. Cloud early that day. I'd never been so sad to see her leave, but I was so happy she had come down to check on me. That "welfare check" flipped a switch for both of us, I think. It all went from someday to today. I never doubted anything about our relationship after that. That moment, when I woke up and she was still in my arms just like she was when we drifted off to sleep, was all I needed to realize this was it.

I actually started doing some therapy and rehab that day, too. That first week we concentrated on everything other than the right knee, just to keep me toned a little bit. Arm work, chest, back, and some work with my left knee. Until I could put weight on it, which would be about a week, we couldn't do anything else, but it was good to work up a sweat.

Brooks kept dropping by, mostly in the evenings, and I think I saw him every day that first week. That was when we finally had the time to just talk about our lives and how we were raised. We'd spoken about that stuff, but never in great detail. It was really interesting to hear how he grew up in California, how his parents were more or less hippies, and how important surfing was in his life. That to me was like sitting down with an alien and hearing about his planet. And the alien said "rad" and "stoked" a lot.

My teammates were great, too. Bringing me food those first few days when just getting to the dining hall would be a dangerous thing for me, and keeping me up to date on what was going on with the team. We had gotten home from Marquette on Sunday, and on Thursday they were leaving on a road trip to the East Coast. It was Boston and Providence, if I remember right, but since I wasn't going it was another sad deal. Depressing, really. They were going off to someplace I'd never been but always wanted to see. I was stuck there in the dorm with my crutches.

After that weekend, though, the team was home for a long string of games. It seemed like a long time to me then, but I looked it up and it was just four games over the next two weekends. By the first weekend, I could get around enough on the crutches to head to the arena for the games, and that was fantastic and awful at the same time. It was great to be there, and be in the locker room with the guys before the games, but terrible to have to watch from the press box. I was a good spectator when I was a little kid just dreaming of being a Roseau Ram. I discovered I was a terrible spectator when I was supposed to be out there on the ice as a Minnesota Golden Gopher.

By that time the bone bruise had calmed almost all the way down, so that was a huge relief. I could wear the big bulky brace instead of just an ACE bandage, and we finally began to do the rehab on the knee. Just had to get past the bone bruise to get to that point. Once I had the green light, I was all in.

Thanksgiving was right in that time period, too, and it was actually as good as it could be for a guy who couldn't even imagine it when we got back to school after the injury. We had a bunch of local guys from the Twin Cities on the team and a few of them invited me to their houses for dinner. I went with one of my defensive partners named Chris Carlsson, who I really liked and got along great with. It sure was great to get off campus, and his family couldn't have been nicer. Plus, the turkey dinner was fantastic. Absolute comfort food. The dark mood was definitely beginning to lift.

Carol had offered to come back down and find some way to have a Thanksgiving meal with me in the dorm, even if it was just turkey sandwiches, but by then Chris had made the invite and I knew Carol really wanted to see her family back in Roseau. I let her know that her getting to see her family meant more to me than anything else. I really wanted to see my family too, but there was just no way.

For a while, the trainers wanted me to stick with the crutches, but we were already doing some walking at rehab, and it really didn't hurt that bad. I learned one thing. When the pain goes away, that's when you really have to listen to the doctors and therapists. It's easy to overdo it and hurt it again. It was so tempting to just put crutches in the corner and walk around Pioneer and the campus, but I knew I had to follow the program. It hadn't taken long before using the crutches felt like something I'd always done. Like I said, I'm a fast learner.

Over the next couple of weeks we progressed to some light weights with the knee, as well as some stuff they called "isotonics" or something like that. It wasn't weights; it was just resistance training against big heavy rubber bands, or sometimes the trainers themselves pushing against my ankle when I was trying to use my knee to raise my leg. I was making great progress and feeling better every day. I was even back in class by then, and hadn't really gotten too far behind.

The guys went on another road trip without me, to Denver, and by then I was finally doing some running and skating. I had a long way to go, fitness wise, but when the team left for that weekend I got permission to go all out. I had the rink to myself for three or four days, and skated as much as I could. The knee was actually feeling really good, considering, and it was getting stronger by the day. The real issue was my cardio fitness. I'd never been off my feet, doing nothing, like I was forced to do right after the injury. It's amazing how fast you get out of shape when you can't skate or run.

When the team got back, they didn't want me out there for drills or practice yet. So I skated for a couple of hours each day after they were done. I was getting close.

I just skated and skated and skated. I shot pucks out of sheer boredom, but that had an added benefit too. I'd never been what you'd call a "sharpshooter" with the puck. I could get it to the goal in a hurry and in the general area I was shooting at, but those days by myself on the rink gave me a chance to sharpen up those skills a lot. When you're by yourself out there, doing endless "up and backs" on the ice and firing pucks at the net, you do that thing you did as a little kid. You start imaging scenarios and game winning goals. Anything to get through it.

There was a long Christmas break, about two weeks if I remember right, and my goal was to get home for at least a day or two. I could drive by then, but I'd only driven around the Twin Cities a little bit and I wasn't sure how it would feel to make the six-hour drive north. I was a little sore when I got there, but I put the brace on and was happy it didn't feel any worse than it did. It was awesome to see Mom, Dad, my brothers Dave, Brent and Jon, and my sister, Betsy. Carol was home, too, so we got to spend a few hours each day with each other, at her house or mine. I think, by then, both of our parents were understanding that we'd gotten a lot more serious about each other. There was just a look in their eyes. I think they approved, but there was a bit of "what took you two so long?" in there too.

A lot of Roseau neighbors also dropped by the house to say hello. Talk about medicine for the soul. I'd missed it. A lot. It was home. It was like I'd never left. And Mom made hotdish, so there was that!

When it was time to get back to campus. I wasn't really sad to leave. I was ready. I'd taken three full days off from skating and I was antsy to get back on the ice. I needed to keep pushing it, because I had a plan.

Right after the first of the year, Boston University was coming in for two games. That's a huge deal, and they were always good. I was still in street clothes for those two games, but I'd circled the next weekend on my calendar. North Dakota was going to be at our rink for two weekend battles. My plan, my goal, was to be dressed and available for those two games. Without the brace. I'd been practicing with the team for a couple weeks by then, but everyone was trying to avoid any collisions that would set me back. I needed to play in a game.

When I got hurt, the docs were figuring four to six weeks for me to get back out there, in a game. They were a little off. I was finally skating hard at six weeks, but had so far to go to get back in game shape. If I could play against North Dakota, and not just play but go all out and actually help the team, that would be almost exactly eight weeks. It seemed like a year.

I pushed it as hard as I could. All those days of running stairs at Roseau High, or pulling that old tire around doing sprints, all came back to help me. I knew how to push it. I knew where the limits felt like they were. And I knew how to get through those limits and take it one step further. And then another step. And another. I knew by the Monday before the North Dakota games that I'd be ready. The coaches and trainers were watching, and they all impressed by what I'd done. I remember one of the trainers saying, "I never told you, but I wasn't sure you'd play again this year. Healing the injury was one thing, but a knee needs lots of rest and everyone gets out of shape in a hurry. I've never seen any other player here work it as hard as you have. You're an animal."

By Wednesday of that week, I got the word I'd be dressing for both games. On Friday night, it would be really limited. Only a few shifts per period. Just get back out there to feel game action. If it all went well, we'd push it harder during the game on Saturday.

That Wednesday was actually a big day all around. I got the news I'd be suiting up and playing, and Brooks dropped by my room again with an idea.

"Hey dude, want to come have dinner with me and my folks at their place?"

I said, "Sure, that sounds awesome. But you need to tell me, what kind of food do former hippies eat?"

He just laughed, and said, "Well, I've heard all about Minnesota hotdish since the day I got here, so maybe Mom will try to do something like that. Don't worry, we won't be eating twigs and weeds with granola for dessert."

On the way down to their place, he finally got into some detail on his mom's illness, and the time she spent at Mayo Clinic. He'd only mentioned it in passing, saying stuff like "My mom was pretty sick and needed to go to Mayo, so we just moved here." He told me about the long trip in the VW bus, about how he moved in with his dad's cousin in what he thought was a mansion, and all the days and nights he and his dad thought they were losing her. It was like nothing I'd ever heard before.

Then he asked me about Carol, and how that was going. We hadn't talked much about girls before, so it was all news to him. I told him about growing up in Roseau, and that we were the same age so we went to school together from first grade through our senior year of high school. I did my best to explain how our relationship worked, but it's a hard story to tell because most guys can't relate to it.

They'd always say, "Wait, you're just friends, but more than friends, but really just friends?"

Then I told him that, literally, five minutes before he knocked on the door and met her, I'd just had "the moment" where it hit me how important it all was.

He first said, "Wow, what a story. I don't even know anyone I went to first grade with. Not one person. I can't imagine growing up with a girl and finally falling totally in love with her three years after high school."

But then he added, "And guess what, I'm dating a girl now and she's really special. Met her in an Art Appreciation class. It's like we've known each other forever, but it's only been a few weeks. I've had crushes before, and gone on group dates when it was just a bunch of guys and girls all going out together, but never anyone exclusively. I can't say I'm in love with her yet, but I'm totally stoked by the whole deal. It's like we're made for each other. I haven't even told my parents yet, so that will happen tonight. Crazy, right?"

Yep, pretty crazy.

I was kind of surprised by the house his parents lived in, even though Brooks had told me about it and all the other homes he'd lived in growing up. He kind of prepared me for something basic, but it was nice, and his parents were incredible. I'd never really met anyone quite like them. They were so, I don't know how to put it. They were just so loving, to Brooks of course, but also to me. I felt like a stepson within minutes.

He had told me about his mom being an artist, but seeing four of her oil paintings hanging on the walls in the house was unbelievable. I'd never seen anything like them. What a talent. And then I remembered how he said he'd met his new girlfriend in an Art Appreciation class. I could understand how that would appeal to him.

And Brooks was thrilled to see what his mom had created for dinner.

She said, "We learned all about hotdish when we moved here, and this is my California spin on it. It's basically a tuna casserole but I added some extra vegetables that

I promise won't kill you, then put tater tots on top just to make it qualify as Minnesotan." That got a laugh out of me.

"You hereby qualify" was my reply.

It was fantastic. The whole night was fantastic, and everyone was really interested in my story, my background, and the injury. Such great people. I could see Brooks in both of them. When he told them he was dating a girl he met in Art Appreciation they both just glowed, and I think I saw a tear or two from both of them. In unison, they both shouted, "We need to meet her as soon as possible."

I said, "Yeah, me too!"

All I remember about the next day, which was the Thursday before the first North Dakota game, was that it lasted forever, but I felt great at practice. That gave me a lot of hope.

On game day, I got there early and saw North Dakota get off their bus. I spotted my Des Moines roomie Randy and we talked for a bit. I had to bring him up to speed with the injury, because he hadn't known about it.

I said, "Yeah, and this is my first game back, so take it easy on me."

He just winked and said, "Not a chance."

It was fantastic to go through all the rituals and be in the room with the guys as we all got dressed, taped up, worked on our sticks and got amped up for warm-ups and the game. I felt like part of the team again, and the guys were great about making me feel that way. It seemed like I was flying during warm-ups, as if I had jet engines on my skates. Adrenaline will do that for you. During the national anthem, I was rocking back and forth on my skates and nervous as can be. It didn't so much feel like my first game back; it felt more like my first game ever.

I only played a couple of shifts per period, but it was great to be out there. Took a couple of big hits in the corner, but delivered a few as well. And we won, which is always a big thing against North Dakota.

The next night my ice-time about doubled. I didn't feel any bad effects from the night before, and still had a ton of energy. That made me happy, because you never know how much you're in game shape until you actually play in games. I even clanged one off the post that just missed going in, and had two assists in a big win. We creamed them that night. I was pretty much over the moon in the locker room after that game, and saw Brooks and a couple of his baseball teammates in the hall afterward. We were getting to be really good friends, and honestly he looked kind of emotional when we hugged out there.

There were no setbacks after that. I credit the trainers and doctors for making that happen. They had a plan and I stuck to it, even when it was getting frustrating as the weeks ticked by. I felt like I was back in my top form and life was good again.

Starting with that first North Dakota game, we had only 14 dates left in the regular season and they were pretty much a constant flow of home and away. We went to Maine, Massachusetts, up to Duluth, then to Madison, Wisconsin, and finally back up to the Upper Peninsula of Michigan, but this time to the town of Houghton to play a tough

Michigan Tech team. It was mid-February by then, and we still had plenty of snow on the ground in Minneapolis, but man there was a ton of snow up there in Houghton. It's right near Lake Superior, so when it snows there it's heavy and deep from the lake effect. It was piled up on the sides of the road so high you couldn't see the sky from the bus. It was an amazing place to visit.

At home, we played Colorado College and Denver. We finished 29-7. I looked that up.

We played Colorado College again, at our home rink, in the first round of the WCHA (Western Collegiate Hockey Association) playoffs, and handled them easily. And guess what? I put one in the net during the first game, but with a final score of 7-0 a lot of us scored goals. Still, it was great and the guys made sure I knew how great they felt about it, on the ice right after the goal, on the bench, and in the room afterward. When you feel that happiness, all that hard work seemed like it never happened.

Then, we got to play the next round in St. Paul, at the old Civic Center arena. The same place the coaches and Paul Broten came to meet me and recruit me to be a Gopher when I was with Des Moines. My parents came down for those games against Minnesota-Duluth and Wisconsin, and Carol even made it in for the Duluth game, although it was an odd Sunday game and she had to drive back to St. Cloud that night, so all we could share was a kiss and a hug out in the hall after the game. We played well, and I felt 100 percent by then, but we lost to Wisconsin in a tight one after blasting Duluth in the first game. We did move on to the NCAA playoffs, though, and got to play the first round of that at home, playing Michigan State twice. Two tight games, lots of heavy hitting, an assist in each game for me, and we beat them twice, 4-2 and 4-3.

The NCAA championships were in Lake Placid, of all places. That was really a neat trip, to see where the Olympics were played and where the Miracle on Ice happened, just eight years before. That was legendary stuff for all of us, and Paul Broten got to play where his brother Neal had made the Gophers and the Roseau Rams proud, winning the gold medal. Since Paul had gone straight to The U after Roseau, this was the end of his final college season. It seemed like a fitting place to end it.

To me, it was like a trip to a foreign country, to be in that little village where so much history was made. Maybe it was more like an amusement park. I just remember that all of us were soaking it in and maybe a little distracted by being there and imagining the whole Olympic Village craziness, and the USA hockey team taking it all. We lost to St. Lawrence and Maine in two straight. My freshman season was over.

Paul's college career was over. Soon after those games in Lake Placid, Paul signed with the New York Rangers. He'd play one season in the minors, out in Denver, and then went on to play 322 games in the NHL for the Rangers, Dallas Stars and St. Louis Blues. Another Broten boy making Roseau proud. Between Neal, Aaron and Paul, the Broten boys played 2,169 games in the NHL.

Honestly, when Paul signed it was the first time in my life I thought I might have a real future in the game. I'd known Paul my whole life, and he was really good, but I knew I was on a fairly even level with him, all the way back to youth hockey. Most of the time, year after year, I just kept my head down and worked as hard as I could. All I wanted to be was a Roseau Ram. And then I got to play juniors in Des Moines, and grow up a lot doing that. And the University of Minnesota, where so many future superstars had played. If I could do that, and keep improving, maybe there was a chance I'd play against Paul again, in the NHL. It seemed a little crazy, and when Paul signed I remember thinking, "Don't get ahead of yourself here. There's still a lot of work to do and a lot of college left. Stay focused."

Focus was always the big thing for me. I had tried not to think about all that had happened while we were playing that last stretch of games. Today I'd say I was "living in the moment" but I don't think I knew that term back then. I felt like I had blinders on, though. Just playing one shift at a time, one game at a time.

I had missed 12 games right in the middle of the season. I'd suffered some pain like nothing I'd ever known before. I worked my butt off to get back in the lineup and contribute to the team. And I finally understood I was deeply in love with the most wonderful girl in the world. That last part, with Carol, was something that actually had to overcome all that hockey focus. Somehow, we were finally making that happen.

Man, a lot happened that first year at the University of Minnesota. I'll never forget it.

CHAPTER 23

Brooks Bennett

As for my new "girlfriend" (I wasn't ready to call her that yet), the whole thing was a little confusing but it was mostly fun. There was obviously a part of me that was holding back. I knew she really liked me, and I thought she was fantastic, but every time we'd come close to taking the next step I'd retreat a little. Like, we'd see each other every day for a week, and start to feel really close, and all of a sudden I'd start coming up with excuses for not getting together. I didn't really understand it then, and I still don't to this day. It was like I was a puppet on a string and every time things would get kind of serious some mysterious puppet master in my head would pull me away, like I wasn't even in control of it. I'm really used to being in control, and I wasn't. It was weird. Through all that, though, she was amazing. What was mostly holding us back a little was me.

Her name was Donna. She was from the Twin Cities, up on the north side in a town called White Bear Lake, and she was totally cute. She'd been a cheerleader in high school, and she looked the part. Straight, shiny blonde hair that practically glowed in the sunlight, beautiful blue eyes, amazing body, really fit, and those eyes seemed to sparkle like a movie star's when she smiled. I dug the hell out of her and my heart actually raced every time I'd see her, especially when she wore those tight tank tops and running shorts, but I needed to get my head straight or I was going to drive her away. It was obvious that those spells, where I'd just chicken out or try to pull back, really frustrated her. They frustrated the hell out of me too. I don't know, maybe I was just in such uncharted territory I didn't have a clue how to handle it. One day it was exciting, the next it was scary.

I'd been on dates, or at least group dates, and I'd had my share of crushes, so that wasn't totally new, but seeing one girl so often was definitely something else. I guess I was a mama's boy. And a daddy's boy too. I knew I was really charged up about her, but it was like I was trying to go somewhere totally new without a map.

We finally had a long talk about it one night, right before classes ended, and I did my best to spill my guts to her. I was just honest about it. That's how my mom and dad raised me. If something is bugging you, be honest and get it out there, even if you don't totally understand why you're feeling whatever it is you're feeling. Talk it out. You can't make any progress if you hold it in.

It was a good conversation, very open and raw, and the hug and kiss at the end of it sent chills through me. Now that was something I'd never felt before. If I had a gauge on my dashboard that measured my level of love, it was a five out of 10 before that moment but it clicked up another notch or two right then.

We just made a pact that we'd be totally straight with each other, and that we would only see each other and not date anyone else, but we'd try not to feel any pressure to show anything other than what we were really feeling. Just be honest. That was the mantra. I could deal with that. I was excited about it.

We both took a couple of summer classes just to get some credits, plus I totally dug the vibe on campus during the summer. When I did that before my first full freshman semester I loved it. We both lived at home during the summer, though, so we had to make the effort to see each other. We went on dates at least once a week, and it seemed like we were finding a way to make it work. It was cool. Me, in a relationship! Another first.

As for baseball, back in the early part of my freshman season as a Golden Gopher, a couple of coaches asked me what my plans were for the summer. To be honest, I hadn't really thought of that yet. I mean, I was just focused on getting that first season of college ball under my belt, hoping I was ready for that level of play.

I'd played Town Ball in Shakopee during the summer after my junior year of high school, and I guess I just thought I'd do that again. Summer ball was definitely something I missed about SoCal. Out there, the summer teams were great. Probably better than your high school team, because they were loaded with the best players from a bunch of schools. It was pretty much an elite level of play. Town Ball in Minnesota was way fun, but I probably needed something at a higher level if I wanted to keep developing.

Coach Anderson asked me a question I'd totally never heard before. He said, "What do you think about going to play this summer in the Alaska League?"

I think I just shook my head and said, "Um, what's that?"

I knew there were some high-level collegiate summer leagues around the country. Some of the guys on the Gophers talked about going to Cape Cod to play in a league out there, and they said it was the best of the best. Another teammate talked about playing in a league in Illinois, that a lot of big leaguers had come out of. I'd never heard about a league in Alaska.

The more the coaches told me about it, the more it sounded rad. A ton of big-leaguers had played there, and I'm not talking about guys who were just average. Tom Seaver, Frank Viola, Dave Winfield, the list goes on and on. And it's in Alaska! How stoked can you be?

Coach Anderson had a relationship with the manager of a team in Anchorage, called the Glacier Pilots, and he was sure he could get me on that team. It sounded like I was all set. Instead, it ended up being the "great summer experience that never happened."

About a month before the Alaska League started in June, the Glacier Pilots decided to not play that year. By then, it was too late to hook on with any other team up there. It still bugs me to this day that playing in Alaska didn't happen. It sounded really cool, and it would've been a great thing to do.

So, even though it was a huge step down from the Alaska League, I decided to just go back to Shakopee and play another summer of Town Ball. I might have been the only Gopher to do that. I'd make the best of it, I'd live at home with Mom and Dad at the apartment, and I could keep seeing Donna. All good things. Would I have jumped at the chance to go to Anchorage? Absolutely, and I was bummed that it didn't happen. But there were benefits to being home. I knew that.

The Town Ball talent level could range from very good to very bad, and it wasn't going to be much of a challenge for me but I needed the innings and I needed to keep working on my breaking ball and change-up. Coach Anderson and I decided I'd use the summer as something like an instructional league. I wasn't going there to throw gas and strike everyone out. I wanted to become a better pitcher. I wanted more weapons.

I met with the head coach of the Shakopee team, the same guy from a couple of summers before, and kind of laid it all out for him. I wasn't going to be there to throw 95 and run up my stats. I'd mix the fastball in, but I had to keep working on my off-speed stuff. And not too many starts or innings, either. The Gopher staff made that clear to me: "Get your work in, keep developing your breaking ball and change-up, and stay in shape."

The Shakopee guys were cool with that. I'd go to all the games and would help the other pitchers any way I could. I wasn't being a diva. I'd be a good teammate, but I just wouldn't throw that many innings and when I did it was going to be "school" for me instead of "win at all costs." OK, sure, if it came down to winning a playoff game and I had a guy 0-2 with two outs, the fastball would make an appearance. I mean, winning is winning, right? I needed to throw hard here and there anyway, just to keep my velocity up, but the off-speed stuff was the focus.

I don't remember much about the season, other than it was a good bunch of guys and we had fun. I worked the program we'd laid out, and the off-speed stuff was getting sharper and better with each game. I think there's no doubt I had pretty much always relied on the fastball to get me through almost anything, and even though I did work on my breaking ball and change-up I'll admit that I'd never been totally 100 percent dedicated to either one. Whenever it came to a big moment in a game, when I had to get an out, I always felt like I had to throw my best stuff. I didn't want to get beat using a pitch that was just average.

At first that summer, I got hit around a little, throwing so much offspeed junk, but it got better and better and I started to "have a clue" about it before long. The key is always the release point. If you're altering that to get the offspeed stuff to work, that's a sure way to get bombed by any smart hitter. I'd always look back on that day at Dodger Stadium with my dad, when Nolan Ryan was pitching. By just focusing on Nolan, I couldn't tell what pitches he was throwing. They all came out of the same release point with the same arm slot. That's a lot to aspire to, but great motivation!

195

I'd mix in one good fastball just to keep the hitters nervous, and then it was totally fun to buckle their knees with a breaking ball or pull the string with the change so they'd be out in front of it by three feet. They'd be so worried about the heater they couldn't dial it down for the slow change. It was awesome. Pitching is cool. You get to where you feel like you can dictate how bad each hitter is going to look, and when a guy does square one up and lace a shot into the gap, you try to learn from that. Like, "Never throw a change-up to a guy with a slow bat. You're just helping him out. That's the guy you bust inside with the heat." Lessons learned.

One downer that summer was when I heard that my buddy Deano, my teammate who had shared Thanksgiving with us, had left school. He was transferring to a smaller college down by Chicago. He was a good player and a great guy, but he hadn't played much at all and was stuck behind some really good infielders who were all the same age. I can imagine how that would be a mental challenge, just wondering if you'd ever get a chance to play. I never got to say goodbye to him, and haven't heard from him since. I'm not even sure where he went to school down there. I hope he got a chance to be the star of their team, though.

I kind of lost track of Eric right around then, too. I knew he planned to go home to Roseau for the summer while I was playing Town Ball. It's not like we had cell phones and could just text each other every week. Finally, somewhere around July, I called "information" (remember that?) and got a number for his family home. I wasn't sure how many Olsons lived in Roseau, but I got lucky. It was his house. He wasn't home, but I left a message with his dad, who had answered the phone. A few hours later, Eric called me back.

He was back home for the summer, and was not only working out but also leading workouts for the high school hockey team. That sounded just like him. He was one of the most dedicated athletes I'd ever met. It was good to catch up, and we talked about getting back to school in the fall and seeing each other then. He talked a lot about his girlfriend, Carol, and how great that was going. And all that added up to me asking, "Hey, dude — how far of a drive is it to get up there? I'd love to come up for a day or two just to see this place I've heard some much about."

I headed up there about a week later. I had a start for Shakopee, followed by three days off and then one more game that I wasn't going to pitch in, and I got permission to miss that one. I really had no clue how far of a trip it was, but I'll summarize it by saying it was a long drive. Probably around six hours but it sure felt like more than that. When I was about halfway there the thought occurred to me that I'd never driven that far by myself in my life. How crazy is that? Those drives down to Rochester were it, in terms of distance. Of course, I'd ridden in the VW all the way from California but I wasn't driving then. It was cool to be out there in totally different surroundings and scenery, going such a long way. I guess I had no idea Minnesota was so "tall" as a state. It felt like I'd never get there.

I hadn't really been north of the Twin Cities before, so the landscape and the small towns were all new to me. It was cool! Thick pine forests, lakes around every corner, cabins and boats everywhere I looked. I had to concentrate on the road because the scenery kept distracting me.

I had a map, so it was no problem getting up to Roseau, but then I'd need to follow the directions Eric gave me on the phone in order to find his family's house. I think he told me there were three entire turns after I got to town. It was a different world.

I don't think I was 10 miles out of town when it still seemed like I was in the middle of nowhere. When I rolled into Roseau, my eyes were wide open as I looked around. To me, it was like this little town was straight out of a movie. A classic old downtown area full of restaurants, diners, stores and offices. Driving toward Eric's home it was clearly so different from anyplace I'd ever lived. All the homes were pretty old, mostly wood frame, but all of them were well kept and classic, with most of them having huge mature trees in the yard and big front porches. It was exactly one million miles from SoCal. It was at least a half-million from the Twin Cities.

I parked on the street in front of their house. Then I went up and knocked on the door. A pretty girl answered it, saying, "You must be Brooks! We've been waiting for you. I'm Eric's sister Betsy." She then stuck out her hand.

Eric was up at the school working out with the Rams team, she said, adding "Let's go up there." I told her I'd drive and she just laughed, and said, "We'll just walk."

It was only a few blocks, and it was a gorgeous day. I remember that like it just happened. The air felt different up there. Definitely less humid and even though it was the "Dog Days" of summer, I swear I could feel just a slight tinge of cooler air keeping it so comfortable. It's funny, and probably weird, but I do remember thinking the air seemed "delicious" to me. Clean, pure, and as delicious as a cold glass of water on a hot day.

On the way, Betsy said, "Eric has told us all about you. You're from California, you used to surf, you're a pitcher on the Gopher baseball team, and everyone thinks you're a 'cool dude' because that's how you talk. Did I miss anything?"

I just laughed and said, "No, I think you got it covered. By the way, Roseau is really bitchin'."

"It's a neat place to grow up," Betsy said. "Not much to distract you around here, that's for sure. We look out for each other, we keep the shops and restaurants open even though there's only something like 2,500 of us here. It's a little ecosystem all by itself, I guess. We've got the Polaris factory to keep people employed, and we all just get along and enjoy it here. Even in the winter."

By then, we were at the school and it was another vision unlike anything I'd ever seen. Kindergarten to senior year all in one place. Again, a million miles from the outdoor hallways at Canyon and a half million from the modern buildings at Kennedy.

When we went inside I could hear the voices. Guys shouting and clapping, and I swear I could smell the sweat. Down the hall, there they were. A group of about a dozen young guys, drenched and breathing hard. They were doing sprints up the steps at the end of the hall. And Eric was right there, doing the same drills and shouting at them to work just one step harder. Those were his exact words and they stayed with me. "C'mon, one step harder! Take it up a notch! One step harder!" Words to train by!

197

Eric finally saw us and told his guys to take a break. He came over, hardly breathing heavy at all compared to the high school kids, and welcomed me to Roseau. "I see you've met Betsy, my partner in crime growing up."

He said he had just another 20 or so minutes with the guys and then he'd be done. It didn't surprise me at all that he would put that workout at the top of his priority list. Betsy said, "We'll just stroll around a bit so I can show Brooks some of the town, and then we'll see you at home."

We walked down the main road for a bit, and then came to the Roseau Memorial Arena. I stood there and stared at it, after hearing so many stories about how cool it was. She said, "The doors are usually open, let's go inside." It was mind blowing in there. The big arched ceiling, the huge wooden beams, the grandstands, the rink (there was no ice that time of year), all the championship banners hanging from the top, and we even walked around and saw the locker rooms. I just turned to Betsy and said, "This is about the most bitchin' thing I've ever seen. So stoked you brought me here." She giggled a little. I think because I said "stoked." I should've mixed in a "rad" too. Might have blown her mind.

On the same parking lot, right out in front of the arena, was an old brick building. Betsy pointed it out and said, "That's the American Legion Hall. 77 steps from the doors of the arena to the side door at the Legion. A good bar, great food, and all your friends. You should see this place on hockey nights!" This was like a lesson from another planet. I'd actually never even heard of American Legion Halls, but apparently they're everywhere in small town America. Another rad introduction for this former SoCal dude.

We walked around the small downtown area, and she was waving and saying hello to basically everyone. Then we got back to their house just as Eric was getting there from the school.

Eric's mom was home, but I think his dad was still at work. I knew he owned a hardware store in town, and one of his older brothers worked there too. They'd be home in time for dinner. Another brother worked at Polaris, so he had a regular schedule. I think the oldest brother wasn't living at home anymore. I had a lot to learn if I wanted to understand the Olson family tree.

We toured the house, and although it wasn't very modern it sure was inviting and warm. I loved the vibe of the place. It was a lot like San Clemente, just a lot bigger. There was a feeling of family in that house, from the second we walked in. Then Eric said, "I'll show you around town" and we headed outside. I wasn't going to be fooled twice, so I figured we'd be walking, but Eric said, "Jump in my truck. It's easier that way, and I'll take you over to Warroad too."

It was so cool. I saw the golf course, the Polaris factory and office, a couple of main streets where it seemed like every business was a place you'd want to stop in and visit. I don't remember seeing any big national chains, like McDonald's or Taco Bell, but there were too many small restaurants and diners to count. I don't know, it just had a charm to it unlike anything I'd ever seen. I loved it.

We headed over to Warroad, which was a 20-minute drive. As we were pulling into town, I finally got a taste of exactly where we were. At an intersection, there was an arrow pointing to the right by the word "Warroad" and an arrow pointing left by the word "Canada." And next to that was "6 miles" or something like that. We were basically on the Canadian border.

Warroad was cool too. I knew from Eric's stories that the two high schools were big rivals, and the two towns were in a way, too. Just like Roseau had Polaris, Warroad had a huge factory and the headquarters for Marvin Windows. I wasn't much into housing construction at that age, but it only took one look for me to figure out that Marvin sold a lot of windows. The place was huge.

Warroad was only about half the size of Roseau, but it was a really cool town too. And the high school had a first-class hockey rink and arena. You can easily get a feel for why those two towns produce so many great players. Even at that point in the summer, you could taste how much hockey meant to everyone.

After my tour, we headed back to the house and I met his dad and his twin brothers. I'm sure Eric had told me that two of his brothers were twins, but maybe I didn't process that. When I met them, I'm sure I did a double-take. No pun intended. I'm guessing they were kind of used to that.

I think Eric's mom wanted to give me the full experience, and she whipped up a dinner for this SoCal kid that I'll never forget. Hot dish with tater tots that was to die for, fresh green beans from the garden, and a giant jug of iced tea. It was totally awesome.

We talked for hours during dinner and then after in the living room. They were peppering me with questions about my folks, how I grew up, what it was like in SoCal, and then we got to why I ended up in Minnesota. I think Eric had told them a little of what he knew about my mom, so I filled them in as honestly as I could. When I was telling them the stories of the long drive across the country, and getting Mom into Mayo when things looked really bad, I think Eric's mom had a tear roll down her cheek.

And that told me all I needed to know about the Olson family and about a town like Roseau. There was no pretense. There was no "fake support" or anything like that. They might be stoic and not very outgoing, but they really cared. They cared about a guy they just met. It was just another moment when I realized how glad I was that I lived in Minnesota. Yeah, I missed the hell out of surfing, but I couldn't see going back. This felt like home.

Eric and I stayed up pretty late, talking about all kinds of stuff. It was great. A little earlier, Carol even came by for a bit and we had a laugh over me knocking on the dorm room door and interrupting a "moment" they were having after Eric got back from the road trip they'd been on when he got hurt. We talked about both of our injuries, and how hard it was to rehab from those, but even that was good. We shared one major trait, and we talked about that. We'd never quit when times got tough. We both stuck to the program and came back stronger. And after Carol left, I said to Eric, "She's the real deal, dude. What a great girl. Don't screw that up!" I'm sure my own thing with Donna played a part in my wording. I always felt like I was screwing it up.

That was a fantastic trip. It meant a lot to Eric that I'd come up to see him and meant a ton to me just to see it and experience it. When we first got to the Twin Cities from SoCal I felt like I was in a different world. To get a taste of Roseau and Warroad, and small-town Minnesota in general, was like seeing and feeling the real thing. It was so rad. And just making the effort to get up there and see Eric kind of cemented our friendship. It was special, and I know we both understood how different we were from each other, but that's exactly why it was so special. We could each hear about and experience a whole different kind of life and upbringing.

When I got back, it was almost time for school and fall ball to start. I registered for more accounting classes and remember that I signed up for one elective course that semester. It was Psychology 101. Maybe I wanted to be able to analyze myself, who knows? It just seemed like an interesting thing to study.

Brian was my roomie again, which was great, but we had to find other housing because at The U you had to move out of the dorm after your freshman year. The good thing is the whole area around campus is covered with rental homes or apartments. We got together with four other guys and found an old, drafty four-bedroom frame house a few blocks away on a side street, and with six of us in there we could afford it and still have enough money to actually eat. It's not easy to find a house near campus, and the competition to land a lease is stout, but two of the guys had lived there the year before and the landlord liked how they took care of things, so he kept the house for them. When a landlord finds a good situation, like renting to athletes and good students, they're eager to keep that going and not get any surprises. But here's the most hilarious part. On the day we were all moving into our rental house, I was unloading my car and heard someone come up behind me. It was Eric! Get this: He lived with three other hockey players, directly across the street. His roomies had moved in at the beginning of the summer, and we hadn't even talked about what we were going to do for housing or who we'd live with. We just totally ended up living across the street from each other. That was freaky, but rad at the same time.

Donna and I got together for a pizza, and what I remember about that night is how I kept thinking about how being with Eric and Carol had made a real impression on me. Their story, about knowing each other since they started grade school and then just being close friends for so long, was unlike anything I'd ever experienced. But to see them together and to see how they interacted and had such obvious love and devotion for each other actually reminded me of my parents. There was so much love and such deep support for each other. I had to wonder if I was capable of that. I told Donna all about it, and I said, "I must still have some growing up to do. In a lot of ways, I've been through a lot of hard stuff with my mom, but I've also lived a super-cool life with the most amazing parents a guy could have. But I'm just starting this whole serious dating thing and here I am about to start my sophomore year in college. I think I have a lot of catching up to do. Can you be patient with me?"

She said, "I'll do the best I can."

I think that was her way of gently telling me not to screw this thing up. I got the message.

Donna was a journalism major, and really smart. I dug that about her. No messing around, no going to college just to have fun. She had a plan, and she loved to write. She told me she had kept journals since she was 10 years old, but no one else would ever see them. She had dreams of working for a newspaper and writing books. And she was funny and totally cute. What's not to love?

We all got rolling again with school and practice, and it felt way different from the year before. Just knowing my way around, getting to know some other students who weren't athletes, and understanding how the baseball program worked all made it seem like I'd been there forever.

I also made a conscious decision to drive down to Burnsville and see Mom and Dad more than I had as a freshman. I was trying to immerse myself then, to be a full-time college student, and I didn't get down there enough. I think my relationship with Donna, and really getting to know Eric and Carol, pressed a button somewhere in my head. It was the button that made me realize that all of these relationships were precious. Don't screw them up! That was my new mantra. Don't screw it up.

It was winter again in a flash. More classes, more time in the library, more workouts over at the practice facility, and then all of a sudden it was Thanksgiving. And man, that house really was drafty. Once it got down into the 20s, not to mention lower than that, the old furnace had a hell of a time keeping the place warm. I had a floor vent right next to the head of my bed, and some nights I'd drape my blanket over the vent and hold it in place with a shoe to send whatever warm air there was under the covers.

I also asked Donna to come down to my parents' home to meet them for Thanksgiving.

My mom did the best she could to put on a real Thanksgiving feast in what had then become a comfortable, warm, family home, and honestly it was really great. They loved Donna, and she was amazed by them. She was completely fascinated by my mom's art, and she was kind of melting talking to my dad. I think his approach to life mesmerized her. By that time, Mom was back to work creating magic, and had some space in an art studio in the town of Eagan. She was selling a lot of paintings again, and she looked totally vibrant. It was hard to even connect the dots back to when we thought we were losing her. Donna clearly had never met anyone like my dad. The dude was so smart, so real, so honest, and such a great and supportive father. And he worked as a vendor at the Metrodome! He's unbelievable.

Basically, she loved them and I think Mom and Dad dug her a lot too. I don't think it, actually, I know it. My mom gave me a hug when we left and whispered in my ear: "She's a winner".

I think that was another "big step" for us as a couple. It was a big step for me, I know that.

Eric was hard at work getting ready for his season, but we kept up our routine of meeting for lunch at least once a week, usually on Wednesdays, and I was looking forward to his season as much as he was. I was a huge fan by then. Gopher hockey was a great way for any U of M student to get through the winter. I was starting to understand why so many local guys raved more about winter than they did about summer. It was like: "Yeah, we spend the summer playing golf or boating on the river, maybe do some fishing on the big lakes, but winter is where it's at. We look forward to winter all summer." I originally thought they were nuts, but I was starting to understand it. Plus, our rental home was actually closer to the rink than Pioneer Hall had been. It was on the north side of campus, just a few blocks away, and all the houses and trees blocked a lot of the crazy winter winds, so it even felt a little warmer up there when you were outside.

After Christmas and New Year's Eve it was time to get serious about pitching again. The workouts ramped up, my throwing program was in place, and it all felt good. I didn't feel like the new kid anymore. My teammates were great, and the incoming freshmen looked up to me. That was rad all by itself, but really cool. I took it as a sign and knew I'd do all I could to help those new guys adapt and adjust to Big 10 baseball as a Golden Gopher.

Our schedule for that year (which was 1989, just for the record) was quite a bit different than the year before. We'd open at the beginning of March, but we were going to Miami instead of Arizona. We had a three-game series with the University of Miami. We knew when we saw it in print that we'd have a huge challenge on our hands. They were very good, and we'd be showing up down there without having been outside yet. Plus, the coaches told me early on in preseason practice that if all went well getting ready, I'd be pitching the opener down there.

We all gathered around to look at the schedule. We'd heard about it for months, in bits and pieces, but until you saw it on a piece of paper it was like it wasn't real yet. After Miami, we had a weird gap of about 10 days off and then we'd hit the road again, this time out to California. We were going to play UCLA, Long Beach State, USC, Pepperdine, Chapman, Loyola Marymount, and UC Irvine, over the course of eight straight days. Most of the guys were kind of stunned. That's a big road trip, and keeping up on our classes wasn't going to be easy. Plus, those were some seriously stout teams to play after having just been in Miami. To me, a big thing I was thinking of was that I'd be going back to SoCal for the first time and how bizarre that would be. I wasn't sure if I was thrilled about it or nervous. I think I was both.

The rest of the schedule was pretty much like the year before. We'd open at home with the big invitational tournament at the Metrodome, playing Oklahoma State, Georgia Tech and Arizona. Even though we were playing indoors, I had to wonder what being in Minnesota in March was going to be like for those guys. It wasn't the dead of winter, but it could easily still be snowing. It hadn't been that long since I showed up and experienced it all myself, after coming from a place where we thought 50 degrees was cold.

After the tournament, our schedule showed a long string against other Minnesota schools, then our Big 10 games against the same cast of characters like Michigan, Iowa, Indiana, Northwestern, Illinois, Wisconsin and Purdue. It would go by fast. When you play that many games in under three months, and go on that many road trips, it flies by.

I took another psych class that semester because I'd really dug the 101 introductory course. It was cool, and pretty enlightening. Other than that, just more accounting and I was flying through that stuff. Me and numbers. We get along fine.

As the trip to Miami closed in on us, I was ready. The fastball was hopping and the off-speed stuff was so much sharper than my freshman year, I think every coach and catcher said something about it. Looking back, maybe it's good that the Alaska thing fell through. That's a much more serious league and winning was important. I would've been there to win for the Glacier Pilots, not work on my breaking pitch and change. With Shakopee, it worked out great for everyone. I still either won or pitched great in all my starts, but I got to work on what I wanted.

Like the year before, I was heading out on a road trip to more unknown places. Miami? Never been close to there but I'd sure seen the movies and TV shows. Brian and I were talking about what to pack but neither one of us had any experience with Miami or even Florida. Would it get cold at night like Arizona? We didn't know. I think Brian was the one who asked the coaches, and they actually called the Miami staff to get a feel for it. We would not need jackets or sweatshirts.

We got on our flight early one morning and I took the aisle seat. A year earlier, I had to beg a little bit to get the window, because I'd never flown before and I wanted to look out the window. After all that travel as a freshman, I realized the aisle had one even bigger benefit. You could get to the bathroom without having to wake anybody up or step over them.

I remember getting off the plane and just about suffocating. It was still just early March, but it was at least 50 degrees warmer than Minnesota. The sun was bright. The sky was a deep blue with a few puffy clouds, and man, it was humid. I think my shirt was stuck to me by the time we got on the bus.

The University of Miami is south of downtown and Miami Beach, so we never got to see any of that on the bus ride. Our hotel was near campus in Coral Gables. Still, one thing I vividly remember is getting off the bus at the hotel and smelling the ocean. I couldn't see it, but I could smell it. Pretty cool.

We hung out at the hotel, got some swimming in and had a team dinner in the banquet room. We had our meetings, got our agendas and went to our rooms. Was I fired up? Sure. Was I too fired up to sleep? That's funny. Before big games I was almost always really calm. I think I slept great. No memory of insomnia or tossing and turning. If I was thinking about anything it was whether or not we'd have a chance to do any sightseeing, especially up in Miami Beach.

Coach had arranged for us to have early BP and practice in Miami's ballpark, about four hours before the game, and looking back on that I think it was really gracious of them to let us do that. Running around out there would help us get used to being outside, and it would help us burn off a little of the nervousness. As the starter, I just did some nice easy laps, pole to pole just like I'd done since my days at Canyon, and then I shagged fly balls.

When we took the field to play, I was in a solid place. I knew they were good. We didn't really have any scouting reports on them but we knew they were always good, year after year. They were something like 52-15 the year before. As we got ready for the game, we were undefeated in 1989. We were 0-0.

I wasn't nervous at all. I knew I'd probably have a five-inning limit unless I really kept my pitch count down, so I was just focused on being as efficient as I could be. I wasn't really familiar with any of their players and I couldn't see into the future to see which ones of them would play Major League ball, so I wasn't intimidated. Years later I'd realize how good they were and how good they could be, as a number of them did go on to the big leagues, but on that day I just told myself, "They're just hitters. They've never seen you. They don't know what you've got. Eat 'em up."

And I did. Struck out the leadoff hitter on three pitches. Fastball in, fastball away, change-up in the dirt. Got out of the inning one-two-three.

I pitched five innings, gave up a few hits but nothing major, and left with the score still tied at 0-0. In the end, neither bullpen was great. We scored four runs and gave them a battle. They scored five. A "no-decision" for me, but a great start to the season for us, against a team we should've been totally overmatched by.

We lost again on Saturday, getting pretty much blown out as I recall, but then we oddly had Sunday off. The coaches had arranged a surprise tour for us, and that was awesome. They didn't have to do that. They could've locked us down at the hotel and told us to stay put, but they hired the big bus for the day and we went up to Miami Beach. They did have some rules, though. We hadn't really seen the sun for months, so no lying on the beach. We'd go as a group and get a good look at this famous place, and then they had lunch all set up at a restaurant right on the main street. It was phenomenal. We were all glued to the windows as our driver steered that bus up the busy street. The old Art Deco hotels were super cool and their pastel colors made me think of Mom and her art. All the huge resorts on the beach side of the road were like nothing I'd ever seen before. We had a great lunch, they let us walk around for an hour, and we headed back, hopefully with no sunburns. A great day. Seems like I remember every minute of it. The kid from SoCal was really getting to see the country, and I stuck a toe in the Atlantic Ocean just to make a point: Now I'd been in the water on both sides of the country.

We lost the last game, although it was another close one. I don't remember the score but I know we were in it until the final out. We were 0-3 and I'm pretty sure I'd never been on a team that was 0-3 before, but considering we'd just come down from frozen Minnesota I thought we did well.

We got back home, put our jackets back on, and concentrated on classes and practice for a week. It was odd to have like 13 days off after playing three games, but the trip to California was coming up and we all needed to get ahead of our classwork to be ready..

Donna and I saw each other nearly every day during that time off. In January and February we had gone to a bunch of hockey and basketball games together, but the hockey guys were into the playoffs when we had that gap in our schedule so we didn't have a chance to see Eric play one more game. It was cool that she was really into sports, and we always had a great time cheering on the other Gopher teams.

Eric and I did our lunch deal once a week, so we got together twice during that span at home, and he was really having a great season. It was cool to see how well he had bounced back from the year before. There was no sign of him ever having been injured, and he was already the glue that held the defense together.

Finally, it was time to head to the airport again, in our matching travel sweats, and head back to my old home. SoCal, here I come.

I had to look it up, because it's all kind of a blur now, but our first four games out there were all going to be north of where I grew up. We'd play UCLA first, then Long Beach State, USC, and finally Pepperdine, which is near Malibu. Pretty weird, I know, but I'd actually never been to Malibu. It was way cool, and man, what a place to go to college. Kind of like taking classes in paradise.

I pitched the first game, against UCLA, and we stomped them. That short series with Miami had us ready to go, I think. I would bet the UCLA guys thought they had easy pickings that day. A team from Minnesota that was 0-3 coming in to take on the mighty Bruins. We got our first win, I think it was 12-3 or 12-4, and I pitched six good innings. Four hits and none of them really hard. Eight punch-outs and — get this — no walks! We were 1-3 and I was 1-0. That was really fun. I clearly remember how rad it was and how happy and relieved we all were on the bus after the game.

I also remember we stayed at one hotel for those first four games. It was easier to find a place kind of in the middle of all those schools and just commute to the games. I have no clue and no memory as to where that hotel was, I just remember battling LA traffic each day to get to the game.

I also remember Long Beach State bringing us back to earth. After beating up on UCLA, maybe we were overconfident. They spanked us pretty hard.

I know we beat USC, another team that was always good and had a history of sending a nonstop stream of guys to pro ball and the big leagues, and we scored a bunch of runs. I decided, at that point, that we were pretty good. It was tough to open against Miami in what was the dead of winter for us, but we were over that by the time we got to SoCal. We could beat any of those teams.

After the Pepperdine game, which we also won, we headed down to a hotel in Anaheim to be more centrally located for the last four games of the monstrous road trip. I have a memory of it not being too far from Disneyland, on Harbor Blvd. If the sight of those old pastel hotels on Miami Beach made me think of Mom, just being near Disneyland made my heart ache a little for Dad. I remember being on the bus and having to stare out the window so nobody would see a couple of tears run down my cheek. He would have loved to be along on that trip. To see me play college ball in SoCal. To be back where we lived when life was so simple. It seemed like a totally different life from the one I was living at the moment.

We beat Chapman College and then got our butts kicked by Loyola Marymount. Don't get me wrong, they were good, but we were better. Kinda like when we went into Long Beach State and weren't ready for them. We just got pounded by a much smaller school after having beaten some of the best teams in the country. The next game was UC Irvine, and I was on the mound.

We bounced back. I was dealing and my curveball wasn't just breaking, it was snapping. Like it was falling off a table. It was kind of eye-opening for me. Like, that's what a good breaking ball is supposed to do. Our guys were pounding the ball, and we played spotless defense. By then, we were on Day 7 of the road trip and had played a game each day. That's a lot of big-time baseball so early in the season, but we were getting better. The final score was 9-1, I believe, and they didn't score until I was out after seven innings. Just three or four hits, 10 strikeouts, no runs allowed, for me. I was 2-0 with a no-decision against Miami and then earned wins over UCLA and UC Irvine. We were 5-5 and starting to erase that 0-3 hole we started in.

We finished up with one more game against Loyola Marymount and got back at them for having beaten us up just a couple of days before. It was time to head home.

I think we were all ready to get back to Minnesota, but it had been a fantastic trip. We'd played some truly stout teams and had some great games. We'd had the chance to get out of the hotel a bit on nights after day games, and that was really cool when we were staying in Anaheim. It was a much more walkable area, and we found cheap food and fun times around there. That sort of stuff really bonds a team, and we were all 10 times closer as a group than we had been the day we headed to Miami. It was a good bunch of guys.

One of our catchers, who was really the best I'd ever played with to that point, was Dan Wilson. The SoCal road trip really cemented our trust and approach. He was a stud, just a great receiver. He hit well, too, and I knew by the time we were heading home from SoCal that he had a big future ahead of him. I was pretty sure he would play in the big leagues, and at that time in my life and career I think that was the first time I had ever felt so sure about any player. I was finally at a level where guys I was playing with or against were top prospects. Dan was definitely a top prospect. It was a joy to pitch to him and he was a fantastic guy. A lot of catchers are just the target. A few stand out as total partners in the whole pitching experience. It was like we were in it together.

Dan had also played in the Cape Cod Summer League and he told me all about it. I remember thinking, "Well, if everyone in that league is as good as him, it must be a hell of a league." He also spent one summer playing for the USA National Team, against teams like Cuba, Japan, Korea, Mexico and others. He said he knew they were good, but at the time the guys were just teammates like on any other team. Well, Bret Boone, Fernando Vina, Jeromy Burnitz, and a bunch of other future big leaguers were on that team. I guess they actually were pretty good. Must've been a totally rad experience for him. And let's not forget, Dan Wilson was on that team too!

Like me, Dan had been drafted out of high school but in the last few rounds, and that's how we both ended up at U of M. We needed a bigger stage and time to develop as players a little more. We'd both be eligible for the draft again in 1990, after our junior year, and I was sure he'd go high. I wasn't sure about me, but I knew he'd be a very high pick. Catchers are a valuable commodity. They're pretty much like quarterbacks, because they run the show back there. Nothing happens until they give you a sign and set up for the pitch. Great catchers are rare, and he looked to me like he'd be great.

We got back home and hosted the tournament at the Dome, and that started the engine for the rest of the season. It was going to be pretty much nonstop from that point forward. We played four games in the tournament and went 2-1. That's not a typo and my math isn't wrong. I pitched the third game against Arizona, and we started a little late after the game before ours went into extra innings. I was pitching well, and we were playing really well against, yet again, a great team, but we were tied after nine innings at 5-5. I pitched seven innings and gave up two runs, my first runs of the year, but both teams were struggling to break the tie.

There was a time-out called, and the umpires asked both head coaches to come to the plate. When Coach got back to the dugout he said, "Arizona has a flight home they have to make, and we're running so late they're in danger of missing it. We're calling the game now and it will be a tie."

So there you have it. I played a part in a major college baseball game that ended in a tie so one team could get to the airport on time. You see something new every day! Another no-decision for me. I was 2-0 but felt great about how I had pitched in all four games. My confidence was higher than it had ever been, and I was dealing and getting strikeouts with the off-speed stuff as much as I was with the heat. I was stoked for real.

The rest of the season did, indeed, fly by with some games against non-conference teams and our Big 10 schedule. The one thing I remember clearly, though, is that for the first time in my life I was struggling to keep up with school. Even when I was hurt in high school I was able to get the work done, but we were playing four or five games a week, with half of them being road trips, so it was really hard to cover the material and do the assignments. In that regard, deciding to be an accounting major worked against me. Numbers don't let you fudge the results. Those numbers are kind of sticklers for that sort of thing. Being a communications major would've probably been easier.

Our advisors had done a great job working with our instructors to make it all work. In my case, I'd get all the lesson plans and take my books with me on the road. I just had to make the time to find a quiet place and focus on the work. The instructors allowed me to turn everything in on the first day we were home from each road trip. Accounting instructors are kinda like the numbers they teach us about. They're sticklers.

Games at home, games on the road. Series after series against the Wolverines, Hawkeyes, Hoosiers, Illini, Badgers, Boilermakers, Cyclones, and Wildcats. I can't lie and say I remember every game. I don't even remember every road trip, but in the end we finished up at 31-22, plus that one tie.

One of the best parts of that season was having both of my parents at a lot of games. They weren't going to come to many (or any) games if I wasn't scheduled to pitch, but they were great about getting there when I was, whether it was at the Metrodome or Siebert Field. My dad didn't have to skip work when we played at the Dome. We were lucky to draw 1,000 people for those games, so there really weren't any concession guys in the stands. He got to be a fan, and I always found them after each game to give them each a hug and thank them for coming. My dad had that little nod and smile down pat. I saw it after every game they attended. It said: "I'm proud of you." Always meant the world to me. There was no one else whose pride I wanted to earn more than his.

I pitched in 12 games, always as a starter. It was a good year. I ended up 8-1, with my one loss being 2-1 at Indiana.

- 12 starts
- 3 complete games
- 94 innings pitched
- 106 strikeouts
- 26 walks
- 68 hits
- 1.94 ERA

I was sad to see the season end, but I was totally stoked about how it had gone. And even more stoked when we finished up our last homestand against Purdue, and after the game Coach Anderson told me there was a guy who wanted to see me.

I came out of the dugout and though I didn't know the man, I knew he was a scout. They all seem to have the same look about them. The fact he was carrying a note pad and still had a stopwatch in his hand was kind of a giveaway, too.

We shook hands (I do not remember his name but I wish I did) and he said he was with the Texas Rangers.

"Hey Brooks, you know we've been following you since high school out in California," he said. "And even though we didn't plan on you signing at the time, we thought enough of you after high school to draft you. We believe you're everything we thought you'd be. We'll stay on top of you next year, and when that season's over you'll be eligible for the draft again. Have you thought about that?"

I said, "Well, sure, that would be awesome, but I try not to get ahead of myself. It would be an honor, but all I've really thought about this year is winning every time I go out there. I'm really happy with my stuff, and I think I can keep getting better."

We talked a little more, and he asked me to fill out a small information card, so they'd have all my up-to-date details, and then we shook hands again. As he was leaving he stopped and said, "I'm new to the Rangers and new to this area. When my scouting director hired me he said I was getting a gift in Minnesota. The team really thinks highly of you, and your family, and now I do too. You take care of yourself young man. I'll see you next year."

What do you think my first thought was? If you said I wanted to call my dad as soon as I could you'd be right. We had two more games to play in the next two days, before the season was over, so I didn't drive down there, but I called him as soon as I got back to the rental house. I told him all about it.

After he got emotional, and I did too, I had to say, "Let's not focus on this. I have another summer and a whole season to play next year. If it doesn't happen, I'll still have my senior season after that and I'll have four years of tuition paid for by then. I might even have my degree, so any signing bonus would be just that. A bonus."

He got all practical on me and said, "I know that. But you've worked your whole life to get to this point. Don't try to put it completely out of your mind. Use it as motivation. It's all right in front of you, man. Your mom and I love you. We'll support you in anything you do."

He always had words of wisdom.

I wasn't going to tell Brian or any of the guys on the team, but when Brian got back to the crib the first words out of his mouth were: "That was a scout you were talking to after the game, right?"

I told him a bit about it, but not all the details. The key thing was that the Rangers had always been on me, since I was a kid at Canyon. When a team follows you that closely, even drafting you after a senior season in high school when you basically didn't pitch, you appreciate that. If I let my mind wander, and I'll admit I did a few times after our season was over, the thought came to me that if I did get drafted, I hoped it would be the Texas Rangers. Of course, you don't have any choice in the matter in terms of the draft. Any Major League team could draft me if they were interested. The Twins might draft me, and they'd certainly seen me enough. The Angels could take me, and that would be way cool. But the Rangers had done the legwork. If it was going to happen, I hoped it would be them.

As much as it flew by, it had been a long season. I needed to finalize all my classwork, enroll again in a couple of summer classes to catch up a little, and for the first time ever I felt like taking some time off. I'd pitched nearly 100 innings and that's a lot for a 19-year old arm. I didn't turn 20 until a month after our season ended. Just a puppy.

I talked to the coaches and we all decided I should just put a summer throwing program together, using some of our freshman catchers to make it happen. It would be good for me and good for them, and I wouldn't run the risk of catching a line drive up the middle with my forehead. Pitching is a dangerous deal, and I'd had a few whistle by my ears since high school. I needed to stay in shape but stay fresh.

As for me and Donna, we were doing great and I think I was holding up my end of the bargain on the whole "grow up a little" deal. We just stayed honest. And we took more than a few momentous steps behind closed doors, if you know what I mean. My mom and dad had both always been open and honest about sex, and using protection and birth control. I knew all about it, and I had sure heard a ton of stories from the guys, but up until then I hadn't met a girl who could pull me away from baseball and my family. It was all for sure new and different, and a lot of fun. That's kind of an understatement, I guess. Fun doesn't really describe it. It was amazing.

My dad "had a talk" with me about it one night after Mom had gone to bed. He said, "So it must be getting kinda serious with you and Donna, right?"

I played a little dumb. I said, "Serious? LIke in what way?"

That threw him off a little, and he shook his head as if to clear his thoughts. Then he said, "You know, serious. In bed."

I almost laughed, but I didn't. That was just so sweet of him to bring it up. I told him it was indeed getting serious, and we were being really careful, but for me it was all stuff I'd never forget. I'd remember every moment of everything we were doing.

He just said, "I don't have to tell you to be good to her. She seems like a great girl, and you guys are a really good fit. I know you'll be good to her. You don't know any other way to treat people, and she seems really special. You can talk to me about anything you want, anytime you want to. Right?"

Right.

I don't want to get too graphic (that's not me) but it was, well, how do I put it? It was an ongoing adventure. Donna had clearly had some experience in that sort of thing, and I not only didn't mind that, I actually appreciated it. She lovingly brought me along and taught me a lot. I'd made out with girls, even done a little "touchy feely" with a few, but this was way beyond that and I loved the fact I was aching to please her. I was such a newbie, but she was patient and supportive. For the first time ever, I was learning my way around a whole new territory. Again, if you know what I mean. I also think I was seriously falling in love.

It was wonderful. Donna was wonderful. Life was wonderful. The future looked wonderful, too.

CHAPTER 24

Eric Olson

After our hockey season ended in Lake Placid, I concentrated on school and talked to Carol as often as possible. I wanted to get caught up on anything I was behind on, in terms of classes, because I still had it in my head that I wanted to graduate on time. Carol was graduating in just a few weeks at St. Cloud. I wasn't 100 percent sure what that meant for us, but I had a few ideas. We'd have to talk about it after she walked across the stage to get her diploma.

I decided to stay at school for at least part of the summer, where I could continue to work with our trainers and keep getting stronger. I could pound a few extra classes too, which was not a bad idea. I couldn't stay in the dorm, you only stay there for your freshman year, but three other guys who were doing the same thing had a line on a rental house just off campus, and they asked me to join them. Finding decent off-campus housing is really competitive, but you have an advantage if there's a group of you and you start the lease in the summer, when far fewer students are around. You can rent bigger homes and combine your rent money, while in the fall most students are lucky to find one person to room with and they're all scrambling for small apartments. It's like an Easter Egg hunt. You don't want to be late.

Although Carol had changed her major once and her minor twice, she graduated on time. It would have shocked me if she hadn't. She had her degree in business administration with a minor in communications. I guess if you're going into the business world, you need to know that stuff but you also better know how to communicate. I was really proud of her.

We needed to talk about her plans for the summer, and at first I was a little surprised to hear what she wanted to do but after thinking about it I knew it was the right thing for both of us. She was going home to Roseau for one last summer before adulthood. She wanted to be with her family in her hometown. She'd almost certainly be leaving Roseau when she landed a job, and she'd be putting out resumes all summer. We knew we'd have to be flexible. I still had a lot of school left and the possibility of playing maybe

211

a little more hockey after my college days were done, whether it was in the minors, or Europe, or who knows? The NHL? Whatever the options, I wanted to keep playing until everyone told me I couldn't. So, there were far more questions than answers. She promised to come down a few times during the summer, and she was really hoping to land a few interviews with some major Twin Cities companies. It was a very mature decision, but I expected nothing less from her. I supported her completely.

The rental house was probably what you'd expect it to be. Not unlike Animal House, I guess. It was on a side street not far from campus, old and beat up, it needed repairs and a coat of paint, there were some rotten boards on the porch, and it came with some shabby furniture, but it gave us all a home and a place to sleep, plus we could walk anywhere we wanted to go. I don't remember exactly how much the rent was but between the four of us it was manageable. We still had our tuition, fees, and books covered by our scholarships. I think all four of us took out small student loans, just to pay the rent and have some money for food. Nothing huge, maybe just a couple thousand dollars. It was nice to have bank accounts so we could all write rent checks and pay the phone bill.

The house wasn't really any farther from the campus core than Pioneer Hall. It was just on the other side of campus, which made it about the same walk to the rink and most classes. The four of us got along great, and even cooked some meals and grilled some burgers in the back yard that summer. Our plan was to just keep renting it month-to-month until we found something better, but "better" probably wasn't going to be in our price range. If "better" didn't happen, we could just keep extending the lease. We worked out a lot, took a few classes, and I made a point of working with the trainers three days a week. I'd committed to myself that the knee wasn't just going to be OK, it was going to be stronger than ever.

Carol did come down twice, when she had interviews at General Mills and Dayton-Hudson, a department store chain that also had a subsidiary at the time you might have heard of. It was a fast-growing discount chain called Target. She said they both went well, but it would be weeks before she heard anything. It was fantastic to see her for a few days each time, and since I had my own room she could stay with me. I think the house kind of scared her (she's still a neat freak) but she understood that four college hockey players probably weren't going to spend a lot of time sweeping and dusting. We felt like we'd done a lot if we made our beds or did the dishes.

Just a few weeks later, she got offers from both of the companies she'd interviewed with. General Mills offered her a real entry-level position on one of their cereal brands, where she'd do market research. Dayton-Hudson, though, made a strong offer with much better pay. She'd go through some training, then become a junior analyst for business development. She wasn't sure at first, with General Mills being a much bigger national company, but what swung her over was that General Mills was on the west side of Minneapolis, and that area was quite expensive. She might have to live 20 miles farther away to find a place she could afford. Dayton-Hudson was right in the heart of downtown. She could probably find a nice safe affordable place not too far from The U.

My advice was, "Do what's best for your long-term career," but she made my heart skip a beat when she replied, "I think I need to do what's best for my long-term life. It's a great job with a great historic company, and the Target brand is growing fast. Plus, I want to be near you, not an hour away. An hour is way better than six hours, but it would still keep us apart too much. We've already been apart too much." I knew I loved this girl.

As the summer came to a close and my classwork became a full load again, Carol made the move to Minneapolis. Dayton-Hudson even had an orientation program to help new hires meet others interested in being roommates. She found a girl from Iowa, who had gone to Iowa State, and they decided to live together. They found an apartment just off University Avenue, not far from campus, and they could take a bus to work everyday. I got to meet her new roomie, Charity, right after they signed the lease. She was a really nice "down-home" girl, so I felt good about that. It was a small apartment, but it had two bedrooms and nice enough furniture, so it would be fine for them. My girl was starting her career, and we could see each other a lot.

Now here's the next strange thing about my friendship with Brooks. My buddies and I had spent the summer in the rental home, and I don't think any of us were really planning on finding anything that was a step up, so we got all moved in and comfortable, making it our own. Right before classes started, we saw some cars across the street. Directly across the street. And a bunch of guys who sure looked like Gopher athletes carrying stuff in. And there was Brooks. He and a group of other baseball players had rented the house directly across the street. What are the odds of that?

I dashed over there and caught him just as he was pulling a suitcase out of his car on the curb.

"You have to be kidding me, right?" I said while his back was turned.

He spun around and said, "Whoa, dude! What are you doing here? You live around here?"

"Well, yeah. Right there, actually, with three other hockey guys. We're going to live across the street from each other!"

He just yelled "Wow!" and gave me a big hug.

"This is going to be great, neighbor! I'm so stoked."

We talked about the neighborhood, places to eat nearby, and ways to get on campus either in your car or by foot. It was fantastic. It was also crazy, but that's how things had worked for us since the day we literally ran into each other in the dorm as incoming freshmen.

We promised to share our class schedules with each other, and vowed to keep up our weekly lunch meetings. No more dining hall to make it easy, but if our schedules worked out there were plenty of dive bars and restaurants nearby. There was a place called the Big 10 just a few blocks away where you could always get a good burger, and a beer if you were so inclined.

As it turned out, our schedules meshed pretty well. We both had really easy Wednesdays, with the middle of the day free. We'd just need to decide on a place to meet, or maybe just make tuna sandwiches and eat at one of our houses.

Classes were going well, Carol was getting adjusted and thriving in this new business environment, and we got together at least three or four nights a week if she could. She'd never had a job like this and I wasn't sure how she'd handle it. She handled it by diving in and working whatever hours were necessary. Some nights she got home at 6, and others it was more like 10. She helped study new trends in retail shopping, looking for what was going to be "hot" in L.A. or in New York, where all those trends seem to start. Her focus was on women's apparel, which is a huge part of department store sales. The funny thing was, she's a Roseau girl. Her idea of a "hot new outfit" was a new pair of jeans and a nice sweater. She was never a big fashion type at all, but that's what she was studying and analyzing. She was determined to make her mark at Dayton-Hudson.

Practice started up right about then, and I was getting fired up for my sophomore season. We had a good team, with an interesting schedule ahead of us. It started out with typical opponents like Wisconsin, Denver, North Dakota, Northern Michigan and UMD. But right there on the schedule, in the middle of December, was a quick two-day tournament. We'd be playing Western Michigan and Michigan Tech, but that wasn't what had me excited. We'd be playing the tournament in Anchorage, Alaska. Seeing Alaska sounded really neat to me, but I hadn't factored in that it's basically dark almost all the time that time of year, up there.

We got off to a good start, with a string of wins all in a row. I was playing well, and the knee was fine. Got a couple of assists in a big win over North Dakota and my defense was where I wanted it to be. I was locked in, total hockey mode, even learning a few new defensive techniques from the older guys and always trying to get better. I don't think Carol minded, really, because she was locked in too, total business mode. We were good at making time for each other but we always knew what the priorities were.

Early in the season, we went back over to Marquette to play Northern Michigan. This time, I didn't get injured and I played well, but the long ride home was a reminder of what I'd gone through just a year earlier and how far I'd come to get back, better than ever. All those memories of that awful bus ride coming back were firing in my head as we rolled down the dark roads of the Upper Peninsula on the way home. I didn't sleep a wink on the return trip.

The Alaska trip finally happened about 20 games into the season. It was already pretty cold and dark in Minnesota, so the thought of going up to Anchorage was really something unique and I was definitely looking forward to it.

We flew out on a Friday for the weekend tournament, and we took off in the morning. It's a long flight from Minneapolis to Anchorage, but it was also December. It was the middle of the afternoon but it was pitch-black when we got there. It wasn't much colder than Minnesota, but I remember being disappointed because I really couldn't see anything. It didn't look much different than most of the places we'd been going. As far as I could tell, we might have been in Duluth or St. Paul. I was hoping to get a look around the next day.

Again, I got disappointed. It snowed like crazy on Saturday, so not much to see. Before the trip I had scoured come encyclopedias to see photos of Anchorage, with the huge mountains easily spotted off in the distance but it was a no-go for that. It was dark again in mid-afternoon, so my dream trip wasn't going so well.

We didn't play all that great, either. One loss and one tie. I did, however, score a goal against Michigan Tech on Sunday. That was, honestly, the highlight of my trip. We flew long hours to get to such a unique place, so far away, and basically saw nothing more than the hotel and the rink at Alaska Anchorage. And we never even played the host team. The flight home was just plain long.

You get to that point in the season where it all just takes on a life of its own. You've got classes to juggle, a girlfriend to see, roomies to exist with, and games every weekend at the least. Lots of bus rides and airplane flights too, which means more bus rides at the destination and more hotels. Pretty soon, if you keep your head down and focus on what needs to be done, you're nearing the end of another long season and you can't believe it's almost over.

We did make one short weekend trip to Boston, which I had missed the year before when I was hurt. That was neat. We had a chance to walk around and experience the history of the city, and I got to check that off my list of places I'd always wanted to go.

In the end, we finished at 34-10-3. We advanced through the WCHA tournament, then swept two games from our rivals Wisconsin in the NCAA quarterfinals, and then were in the NCAA national championships, held right in our backyard in St. Paul. We'd accomplished a lot and were proud of what we'd done. We beat Maine in the first game and then Harvard broke our hearts in the next one, beating us 4-3 in overtime. Just like that, it was over.

Just a few minutes earlier, you're jumping over the boards late in the third period and it's just another game, another part of the season, another thing to focus on. And then they score in OT and it's over. No more games. No more wins. No more hockey for another year. It's hard to deal with.

I scored four goals on the year, and had at least 15 assists (the official scoring wasn't as advanced as it is now), but what I was most proud of was my defense. All those endless hours and days up in Roseau, making sure I was fit and tough, making sure I knew the techniques and could focus on getting to the puck first, being certain I could control it and get it out of the defensive zone safely, that was all paying off. Outsmart and outwork. In that regard, nothing had changed since I was a little kid. It felt good, but it was more than hollow that we went so far and came up empty in the end.

And then, probably about a month or so after the loss to Harvard, Coach Woog called me into his office. I couldn't think of anything I'd done wrong, but you still get a little nervous when the coach wants to see you. I sat down and listened. He was looking me right in the eye.

"The Boston Bruins and New York Rangers have both called me in the last two days," he said. "They're obviously interested in you, and I think the calls were more about you as a person, your work ethic, your personality, things like that. They've obviously had scouts here to see you play. I just told them the truth.

"Look, I've never once told a player to stay in school and not sign a pro contract just because I want you here. I'm not going to start doing that now. There may be some other teams interested too, but if they don't call we won't know, so there's that to think about. But I do care about you. You're a great kid and can be a great hockey player at any level. I want you to be ready to go to the next level and I want you to get your degree. If you do play pro or you don't, you'll make a helluva coach someday, and that degree can help you land a coaching job. The NHL entry draft is in two weeks, so I guess we'll see. However it goes, Oly, I only want the best for you. You've been a rock here for two years. We're fortunate to have you here. Good luck!"

I got up, we shook hands, and I walked out of his office. People often say "my head was spinning" at a huge moment like that, but for me it really felt like it was. I was dizzy, lightheaded, whatever you want to call it. I couldn't really process it. I mean, I just finished my sophomore year. I still felt like a kid playing with grown men. And at least two NHL teams called to talk to Coach about me? Me? I couldn't wrap my head around it.

All I could do was go for a long walk. I couldn't go back to the house because it would be impossible to see the guys and not tell them. I figured I had to tell Carol and my family, but should I? What if I got everyone all excited and nobody drafted me? What if those two teams had already called two dozen other college coaches to talk about guys that were also on their lists? There was no guarantee it was going to happen. I know I was in shock, and deep down I figured it wouldn't happen. I wasn't sure what to do.

So I went for that walk. I wandered around campus. I tried to sort it all out, but that was impossible considering I didn't know how it was going to turn out. I stopped at a pay phone and called Carol at work. All I said was, "Can I come over to your apartment tonight? There's something big I need to tell you."

I shouldn't have said that. She went nuts. "What is it? What is it? Tell me." All I said was, "It's good, but I want to tell you in person. There's a lot to explain." She vowed to get out of work right on time and be home by 6.

It was only the middle of the afternoon, so it was going to be a long wait for me. It was all bottled up inside me. I figured I'd call my parents after I saw Carol. We only had one phone in the rental house and it was in the living room, so I still had to figure out who I'd be telling what. I just kept walking.

I dropped by the house first, and thankfully only one of the guys was there. I just said, "Hey, man," and went straight to my room with my head down. I lay on my bed and just let the thoughts swirl. I finally was calm enough to start thinking clearly.

My first thought was to not get excited. I was still a long shot to get drafted. My second thought was that I still needed to keep improving and The U was as good a place as any for that. My third thought was that we were a good team, and we had a chance to win the national championship next year. I was beginning to feel pretty sure that no matter what happened I was staying in school, at least for another year. Plus, as a P.E. major, I really wanted my degree. If I was going to have to start a coaching career at the high school level, I'd need to be a teacher as well. I wasn't sure, and obviously no one else knew about this but Coach and me, so my mind might change. But right then, in my room, it seemed pretty clear to me. I'd stay in school. I'd stay a Gopher.

One loose end was that I didn't really understand how the NHL draft worked and how long the team has a player's rights. I knew it was complicated, because the Entry Draft is for players of different ages and from different countries, but I thought I'd heard once from Paul Broten that the team that drafts you when you're in college controls your rights until 30 days after your college eligibility is over. I wasn't sure, so I had a lot of learning to do.

I went over to Carol's around 6, and she really had a worried look on her face. She said, "I couldn't concentrate on work after you called me. Sit down right now and tell me what's up."

"Well, Coach Woog called me and asked me to come over to his office. I was kind of worried, but when I got there he sat me down and told me the Boston Bruins and New York Rangers had both called him to ask about me. They've obviously scouted us and maybe they liked me. They wanted to know what kind of person I was. You know, kind of a background check."

Her beautiful brown eyes were so big I thought they were going to pop out of her head. And her whole head was kind of vibrating. Her long, dark straight hair was actually shaking a little. I can still see it just remembering it.

We were face-to-face in two chairs at their little dining table, and she reached out to grab both of my hands. All she could say was, "Oh, my God, Eric. Are you for real? Is this real?" A tear rolled down her cheek.

I downplayed it as much as I could.

"Look, they scout 10 times the number of players they're going to draft, so who knows. I'm not expecting it, but it's an honor they called to ask about me. I'm just taking it as that. The draft is in two weeks, so we'll see.

"And listen, these teams draft underclassmen and even kids out of high school just to control their rights. It doesn't mean they want me to sign and suit up in Boston or New York. If I get drafted, I'm pretty sure the team will control my rights until I'm done with college. I took a long walk after meeting Coach and the thought that kept coming back to me was that even if they do draft me, it will probably be better for all of us if I stay here at least one more year. I need my degree, we have a great team, and you're here. But what an honor it would be to get a call telling me I've been drafted. These next two weeks are going to be agony."

She looked stunned. It was a lot to absorb all at once. All I could say was, "Let's just wait and see what happens. I've already decided to take a full load of classes this summer. I want my degree, even if stupid hockey gets in the way."

I could tell she wanted to know more, but I really didn't have much more to tell her. I needed to know more, too. I suggested we just have dinner and talk about her job for a while. I wanted to clear my head and get back to normal life, if we could.

We moved to the couch in their little living room and, for the first time, I looked around the small apartment she was sharing with Charity, and it struck me how completely different it was from the rental house I was in with my teammates. It was very new, very modern, and absolutely perfectly clean and neat. Not a thing out of place.

Not a single dish in the sink. A flower in a vase on the counter. I remember thinking she had landed the perfect roommate.

Carol said, "I'm going to make dinner. Do you want tuna casserole or a big salad?"

I opted for the salad, because my mind was still racing too much to wait for her to actually cook something. It was delicious. The fact she had a hard-boiled egg in the fridge and all the lettuce, onions, cheese, and dressing ready to go didn't surprise me, but it sure made me happy. It was a dinner to remember. We ate and just kept staring at each other, shaking our heads.

And I kept saying to her, and to myself, "Hey, this is probably not going to happen, OK? Maybe next year if I have a good season, but they were just doing research, just like you do at work. It was just research."

When we were done, I said, "Look, I have to go to the house and call my family. And I'm going to have to let on a little to my roomies. I can't have the phone conversation right in front of them if I don't."

She immediately said, "Bull. I'm calling your house right now and handing you the phone. You don't need to share this with anyone else. Keep a lid on it or it will consume you."

She picked up her phone, dialed long-distance, and I could tell Betsy answered on the other end.

"Hey, Bets, it's Carol. Eric is here with me and he needs to share some amazing news with you all."

She handed me the phone and, honestly, I was glad it was Betsy who had answered. She and Mom were the only ones home at the time, but Dad was due home any minute. I did the same "downplay" routine, just giving Betsy the few facts I had and trying to keep the expectations low.

She put Mom on the phone and I had to go through it all again. And then Dad walked in and it was the same spiel for a third time. My parents were both exactly as I figured they would be. Calm and wise.

"Whatever happens with hockey is great, but you get your degree, Eric," Dad said. I told him I would, and I planned to get it early. I asked if they'd please keep this just within the family. I didn't want a bunch of people sitting on pins and needles if I didn't get drafted. I'd still be a Gopher anyway. That's not a bad thing. I never dreamed I'd be a Gopher, or a Buccaneer for that matter. I just dreamed of being a Roseau Ram.

When I left, Carol and I had another one of those hugs. One of the deep, heavy ones. The ones that don't want to quit. It went right through me. All I could say was, "This is going to be some kind of adventure. We just don't know what kind yet. I hope you're with me on this thing, no matter what."

"I'm with you no matter what. If you get drafted, we'll figure out that path. If not, I still could not be more proud of you or more in love with you. You've earned every bit of this. Every single bit."

It was funny. I went home and had no problem not telling the guys. That time with Carol and my chat on the phone with my family kind of grounded me. My head wasn't spinning anymore. What a day!

The next two weeks are kind of a blur now, looking back. I signed up for not just a full load of classes, but one extra, too. I still needed time to get to workouts with the trainers, but I was pretty good at having the discipline to make it all work. Just keep your head down and do it. Don't mess around. Don't lie on the couch. Don't sleep in. Do the work. It's just like hockey.

Finally, in early June, Coach Woog called and said, "I think you might want to come over here to my office. Can you do that? Right away?"

I'd have to cut a class to make that happen, but I called the instructor and let him know. I rarely ever cut classes and I never did it without calling first. I hustled over to Coach's office. It was a warm June day and the sky was a deep, dark, impossible blue without a cloud in sight. Campus was beautiful, and I loved how uncrowded it was in the summer. Funny how those things stick in your memory. I don't remember everything, but I remember that sprint over to Coach's office like it was yesterday.

I sat down by Coach's desk, and he said, "The draft is going on right now. If it's going to happen, they'll call me. Want a Coke?"

I passed on the Coke. I really didn't like soft drinks that much, but I thought it was hilarious that he said that. It loosened me up.

We started talking, and I told him what I thought I wanted to do. I could tell he was relieved, but just like he would typically do he said, "Well, let's just see how this goes." And then his phone rang.

I heard Coach say, "Yes sir. Is that right? Well that's tremendous. I have Eric right here with me. You've selected one helluva hockey player. Would you like to tell him yourself?"

I held my breath.

Coach put his hand over the phone and said, "This is the assistant general manager of the New York Rangers," and then he said a name I still don't remember. I learned later that right at that time the Rangers were in a complete turnover and hadn't named a new GM yet. And they had a new coach coming aboard as well, but he wasn't announced yet either.

The conversation was pretty much one-sided. I just listened. The man said something like: "We're right in the middle of the draft right now, but I wanted to let you know we selected you as our third pick just now. We can talk soon about what's best for you and for us, but I want to get our new staff in place and we'll take it from there. As of this minute, your rights are ours until your college eligibility is up, and we're thrilled to tell you that. We think you can not only play in the NHL, but be an impact defenseman. Once our new GM is in place, we'll sort it all out and plot out a plan for the future. But congratulations, Eric. We're going to be proud to have you in a Rangers sweater someday soon. Stay in shape, stay focused, and we're going to send a Rangers sweater to Coach Woog for you. This is a legendary organization, playing at Madison Square Garden. You can be part of that legend if you keep working hard."

All I could say was, "Thank you. It's an honor. I'm speechless, but this is beyond any dream I ever had."

I just kind of slumped back in my chair and looked at the ceiling. Coach said, "You OK?"

"Yeah, I just really can't believe what I just heard."

He said, "You've earned this, Oly. You're one helluva worker and one helluva hockey player. On top of that you're a great teammate for everyone in that room."

He told me to be patient. The Rangers were in a bit of a mess after letting a bunch of coaches and executives go. It kind of surprised me they could even get through the draft without a GM or a head coach, but I was obviously on their short list.

I was still just shaking my head.

I ran back to the house, actually wondering on the way if there was any chance I could make either of my afternoon classes. My roomies weren't home. That was a lifesaver. I called home and no one answered. I forgot it was the middle of the day. Everyone was working.

So I called Carol in her office and she had that sound in her voice that meant she was really busy but she took my call anyway.

"I know you're busy, but I just talked to the New York Rangers. They picked me in the third round. I can't believe it."

There was a brief moment of silence on her end, which kind of spooked me. Then she said, "You're being honest, right? This isn't a gag?" I told her it was true, and that I couldn't even comprehend what had just happened.

She asked what I was going to do, and I said, "Nothing, for right now. They're doing a total overhaul of the front office and coaching staff and don't actually have a GM or head coach right now. It'll all sort itself out, and the guy I talked to seemed to expect me to stay in school for at least another year. But, hey, I am now the property of the New York Rangers! Unbelievable, right?"

She was crying. I was dizzy. Life sure had taken a whole new turn.

It was very unlike me, but I skipped my afternoon classes. There was no way I could focus. I'd have to make up the work.

Not long after I hung up with Carol, the phone rang and it was the Gophers Sports Information Director. I guess Coach Woog must have called him to tell him the news. He wanted to interview me and put out a press release. I don't remember a single word of that interview, but it didn't take long for the news to spread.

When my roomies got home, they knew. When I went to work out, the trainers knew. I was sure, though, that my parents and family didn't know. I called again, and Betsy answered.

"Hey, New York Rangers in the third round."

She screamed. She actually screamed.

"I think they just want to control my rights for another year or two, and that's fine with me. I can sign with them anytime until my eligibility is up. No hurry. I have to focus on what I'm doing here. Can you tell everyone?"

She said she would. Dad called me at the house that night. Same message: Keep working hard, stay in school, get your degree.

Carol came over as soon as she could leave work. She knocked on the door and one of my roomies answered it. Luckily, he wasn't in his underwear.

I was in the kitchen, making a sandwich. She came up from behind and hugged me. I turned around and she said, "Hey, Ranger!"

I smiled and said, "I'm still a Gopher, but someday! Can you even imagine playing in Madison Square Garden?"

We made plans to have dinner at her place, and maybe even have a glass of something to celebrate. Neither one of us were big drinkers but I was never opposed to a toast when something important happened. Carol said, "I'll take care of everything. You just have to be there by 7:30." She dashed back to her apartment to get it going.

I had one more call to make, but rather than pick up the phone, I just walked across the street and knocked on the door.

One of Brooks' roomies answered, and I could see Brooks behind him. Brooks saw me and yelled, "What's up, dude? C'mon in."

I walked up to him and said, "Third round. New York Rangers!"

"What? Really? Guys, my buddy here just got drafted by the New York Rangers!"

Everyone came over to shake my hand or pat me on the back. Brooks was just staring at me, shaking his head a little. And a huge smile came across his face. He walked over and gave me a hug so big I thought I might pass out.

"Are you gonna sign? Are you going to New York?"

I told him everything I knew, about the front office and the fact they just wanted to control my rights for the next couple of years. I'd be staying at The U for at least one more season, and aiming to get my degree as soon as I could.

"That's cool. It doesn't work that way in baseball. You either sign or you don't and then you're a free agent again. None of us can even be drafted until after junior year. Sounds like the NHL has a whole different angle on it.

"Damn, dude! I'm so proud of you and so happy for you. This is amazing, and I'm glad you're sticking around another year. Maybe next June we'll both be signing pro contracts. Would that not be the coolest thing ever? We better both work our butts off to make that happen."

Work our butts off, indeed. That was the plan.

CHAPTER 25

Brooks Bennett

A few of us stayed for the summer after that sophomore year. There were only three of us from the house who actually stayed, so we finally all had our own bedrooms. That was sweet. I'd never shared a bedroom with another guy until freshman year at the dorm, and even though Brian was a great dude and didn't snore (much) it was still hard to get used to. I was stoked to have my privacy again. And this kept us in control of the lease, so that was another reason to do it. On top of that, I took a few more accounting classes and got into my throwing program.

None of us had jobs during the regular school year. There wasn't time for that, with all the baseball, road trips and full loads of classes. I mooched off Mom and Dad quite a bit, but they actually brought it up first and were happy to at least give me enough money each month to eat and socialize a little. That's all I really needed, but I felt terrible about it. They'd given me everything a son could want when I was growing up, and sacrificed so much to do it. So, after sophomore year I applied for a government-backed student loan. I didn't want to get into a big hole with it, but it would be great to not have to lean on my parents for money, like I was still in middle school or something. I think it was $5,000. It was way more money than I'd ever had at one time, but I also thought it was good training. I had to watch it, take care of it, and not waste it. An accountant would need to know how to do that.

Sometime around June, Eric came over from across the street and he told me some incredible news. Just hours before, he'd been drafted in the third round by the New York Rangers! Whoa! I didn't even know that could happen. All I knew was baseball and its draft rules. In baseball, you could be drafted after your senior year in high school, then if you went to a junior college you could be drafted after each year there. If you went to a four-year college, you couldn't be drafted again until after your junior year, and then again after your senior year. The team that drafted you only controlled your rights until the next draft. Then you went back into the free agent pool again. The hockey thing kind of blew my mind, and man I was stoked for him.

Eric was really funny about it. I could tell he was excited, but he seemed nervous too. He didn't stay long, but he explained to me how it all worked. The NHL has one big "entry draft" to select amateur players, and that includes junior players, college guys, and players from other countries. It's a huge worldwide deal. They can start drafting them as early as right after high school, or out of the junior leagues, or any time in college. Then, they had the rights to that player for a long time. In college, in Eric's case, the Rangers would control his signing rights until after his senior season, and he'd just finished up his sophomore year, just like me.

He was talking fast, but I remember getting the gist of it. He didn't think they wanted to sign him right away anyway, so he was 99 percent sure he was staying in school for at least one more year. That sounded great to me, in a sort of a selfish way. I liked the guy and liked being around him. I loved learning about hockey and really admired how hard he worked. The dude was an animal. I don't think I worked 50 percent as hard as he did. Maybe not 25 percent.

I remember telling him, "Well, if they want to sign you after next season, and I'm lucky enough to get drafted next year, maybe we'll sign our first pro contracts together. Would that be rad, or what?"

I didn't mention the word "Rangers" floating in my head. Maybe we'd both sign with teams called the Rangers. One from New York and the other from Texas. That would be just like us, right? Background-wise, we were as different as oil and water. We met when we literally ran into each other at the dorm. But I think we kind of fascinated each other because of how different we were in terms of our upbringings, but also how much the same we were in terms of our sports. We were both raised well. It's not like one of us was crazy, or the other was a huge party animal. We connected on those levels. We were good students, and we were nice to people. I absolutely aspired to be in a deep relationship like he had with Carol. I really admired the guy. We loved the sports we played, whether it was hockey or baseball. We appreciated that we were getting a great college education because we excelled at our sports, and we took that responsibility very seriously. We were Gophers, and proud of it. Playing the game was the happiest place we could be.

It's just that I had no control over who might draft me, and no team had control over me, so we'd just have to see. I didn't want to get ahead of myself. Heck, maybe the Yankees or Mets would draft me and we could both end up in New York. There was no way to know. In some way, maybe the next great coincidence would happen, just like when we ended up living across the street from each other without ever talking about it.

Once summer was over, it was time to get serious again about school and fall ball. It's funny how summer on campus feels like almost a vacation. When all the new freshmen show up on "move-in day" and the rest of the student body comes back, the whole place changes. Just walking around becomes more of a challenge, especially with all the new kids trying to learn their way around campus. I was always willing to help when they looked really lost and panicked. I totally found myself walking through campus actually looking for freshmen who looked lost. It was the least I could do.

Donna and I were on a solid course, but she was deep into her journalism major and a really dedicated student, so that took up a lot of her time. I was taking a full load of classes in the fall as well, and I added a finance class to my schedule. By that time, I figured I was going to play pro ball as long as nothing horrible happened during my junior year. And if I could sign and play professionally, maybe there was a chance I'd make it to the big leagues. Just maybe. But if I did, it would be good to understand how rich guys or big companies handle their money to protect it and make it grow. I was good with the basic accounting numbers, which never lie and really don't change, but I needed to know more about the finance side and what's the best thing to do with that money. The numbers are numbers. They go in boxes and get added up. The finance side was strategy and analysis, and up until then I never really understood that. I was amped up to learn, though.

As part of her journalism program, Donna wanted to get into sportswriting, because she totally loved sports. The professor set up a mock newsroom and gave different students different "beats" to cover, and she was assigned Gopher women's basketball that fall and winter. Like a real reporter, she'd go to the games, interview the coach and players afterward, and file her story. There was no email then, so she couldn't exactly file it like you would today, with your laptop. She'd have to turn it in as a complete story the next morning, after writing it on a typewriter. It was kind of an honor system thing, but she really worked at it. She always wrote the story as soon as she got back to her apartment after each game. She knew it was good practice for the real thing. She'd lived at home and commuted from White Bear Lake the year before, but for junior year she and a girl named Rita, who she shared classes with, found an apartment within walking distance of campus. They were both in journalism and both dedicated, so it was a good fit.

And since she was going to basketball games on campus, I could go with her. That was fun, and I helped out any way I could. I'd chart the score and stats so that she could concentrate on the flow of the game and see the big picture. She said it was totally a lot harder to see it all when I didn't come along, but she needed to do that often because in real life there wasn't going to be a helper sitting next to her, doing part of the work. She was going to be a great reporter, if that's what she decided to do. I was so impressed.

The leaves turned red then fell to the ground, and not long after that they were replaced by snow. I was a veteran of this sort of stuff by then. I knew it was coming, and it didn't scare me. It's just life in Minnesota. Bring it on.

At the house, we had two new guys join us when two of the original guys moved out after they found an apartment. I guess we weren't good enough for them. The new guys were good dudes, both from out of state, and they had been around as freshmen but I don't recall that they played much. One was a shortstop named Michael Miller from Peoria, Illinois, and the other was an outfielder named Jake Hurst from Terre Haute, Indiana. As the house rookies, they shared a room. I think we even had a few pictures on the walls by then, and a new big fluffy rug in the living room. The landlord had even put in a pot-belly wood stove out there, and that made a big difference once the real cold stuff hit. OK, I'll admit we did use some real logs but we started each fire with one of those fake logs wrapped in paper. None of us had the patience to grow a fire from scratch, but if you started with the fake log you could then just throw another real log on when the fire got low.

Once the holidays came and went, Donna and I each bought one Christmas present for each other (I bought her a bracelet and she got me a new scarf and some matching mittens, so I think I came out ahead on that), and then it was time to ramp it up and get serious about practice.

Our 1990 schedule was really bizarre, actually, and we had to be ready for it. We were going to open up on the road again, of course, and this time it was back in Arizona, but only for three games against the University of Arizona. And it was really early. Like still January, as far as I recall. Even in Arizona, it was going to be pretty chilly in late January. Then, after we played those games we were going to come back home for almost a month off. No games, just practice. Crazy. The way the schedule laid out, we'd then go to Austin, Texas, at the end of February to play the University of Texas for three, then to Lawrence, Kansas, to play the University of Kansas for three. And that was the first weekend in March! Just looking at the schedule, when they handed them out, I knew that trip to play the Jayhawks had a chance to be brutal. Kansas in the first week of March? That didn't sound good.

After Kansas, the schedule showed us on another huge road trip. Eight straight days out in San Jose, playing a bunch of different schools from all over the country, as well as San Jose State. The funny thing was we didn't play Stanford when we were that close to Palo Alto. I thought maybe they didn't want to play us, but then I looked at the schedule again and noticed we played them the next game, at home, after that road trip was over. Stanford would be our first opponent in our annual tournament at the Metrodome. Crazy, right? It all looked nuts to me. But we had to be ready. It was in writing; it was all set up. We had no choice but to dial it up and be ready.

I was going to pitch the opener in Tucson. I'll admit I had the feeling I was the ace of the staff by then. It was an honor I'd take seriously and be proud of. When you're the ace, there's a huge responsibility to live up to that. If you don't perform, you can crash the whole team and the entire season all by yourself. I took every practice and every throwing session as seriously as any game I ever played.

We took off for Tucson on the Friday before our first game, which was Saturday against Arizona. It felt like the first road trip of the year when we went to the airport and all got on the plane. You could look around and spot the new guys. Their eyes were wide open and they were really fidgety. I guarantee I looked like that just two years before. And we all looked bitchin' in our travel sweats, with our gloves attached to our carry-on bags. People knew who we were. As we walked down the concourse I don't think we walked 10 feet without hearing "Go Gophers!"

We'd been to Tucson before, during my freshman year, so that was all pretty familiar. Once again, when we got dressed to play on Saturday it was our first day outside. First day hitting in a real batter's box. First day throwing off a real mound. First day running the bases. And all we were doing was playing the Arizona Wildcats. They'd sent a huge list of guys on to pro ball and the big leagues. Back then, in 1990, they'd already played in the College World Series 14 times and had won it three times. So, it was a big-time program. They were always good. And yeah, I looked all that up.

Once again, I'm proud to say I wasn't nervous. My mindset was the same it's always been. They're just hitters. They don't know me. I don't know them. May the best man win, each at-bat.

It felt great to be outside and to be digging a spot out in real dirt, right in front of the rubber. All three games were day games, so the time between getting to our hotel in Tucson and then playing the next day was a blink. I was on a pitch count, but I made it through five innings. Gave up a couple of unearned runs (can't blame infielders for not making all clean plays when they haven't been on a field yet that year) but left with a lead. We ended up beating Arizona 11-8 and I imagine they were wondering how that happened. I wasn't. I knew we were a solidly good ballclub.

I recall us going 2-1 against them, out there, and then we flew home to do nothing but go to classes and practice for more than three weeks. That was tough. We'd been outside playing the game we love against stout competition, and now we had to go back inside and trudge through the snow to get to class.

Right at the beginning of March we went down to Austin, yet another place I'd never been before, to play the Longhorns. I started the first game, and after that month off it was like being the Opening Day starter twice in the same season. Twice in four games! We stayed a few miles from the University of Texas, rather than downtown. Coach told us about the entertainment and music district in Austin, and I remember him saying, "Look, I trust you guys but 6th Street in Austin is a wild place and it can be a huge distraction. Let's just focus on baseball, OK?"

I pitched well. I was happy with it. For a few innings I absolutely dominated, but man they were good. I gave up one run and left in the sixth down 1-0. They tacked on two more and beat us 3-0. All things considered, that was a nice showing by us, but I got the loss. I was 1-1.

OK, so then after that excursion we did the Lawrence, Kansas, trip to play the Jayhawks. Who the heck scheduled that for the first week of March? It was as bad as I had thought it would be when I first saw the schedule, in terms of the weather, and I pitched the first game. It might have been 40 degrees, maybe, and cloudy. It actually smelled like it might snow. To make it more fun, the wind was howling and it felt much colder. I had never pitched in weather like that in my life, even at Kennedy or Siebert Field. I wasn't sure how it was going to go, but I made sure I had a nice warm jacket in the dugout each inning. I actually got used to it after the first inning, and settled down. Ended up going six scoreless innings and struck out a bunch of guys who didn't seem really interested in hitting my stuff in that weather. We ended up winning 4-3 and my record went to 2-1.

A couple weeks later, we headed west to San Jose for that big string of games out there. Again, I pitched the first one, against the Washington Huskies. We scored 13 runs, which allowed me to be really aggressive, and I had six strong innings. I don't know how many I struck out, but it seemed like a ton. And then I noticed what might be a troubling thing for our team. Our relievers were giving up more than a few runs. We ended up winning that game 13-6. I was 3-1.

I pitched one more game on that road trip, beating Brigham Young. Again, I think I made it to the sixth inning with only one run allowed and a bunch of K's, and then the bullpen had to hang on to win 10-9. Holy crap, that was stressful. I was 4-1.

After that, we got into the grind of the regular part of the schedule, at the Metrodome, on the road, then at Siebert Field once it warmed up. I was basically dealing, but we were giving up too many runs late in the games. Seemed like they all ended up being cliffhangers.

What a season it was. For the rookies, it was a hell of an initiation to Big 10 baseball. It seemed like we were on the road constantly. Keeping up with the school work was massively hard. Keeping up with Donna was just as tough. Even keeping up with Eric was difficult because his season was still going for the first part of ours. He and I seemed to always be on the road at alternate times. It was hard to get together for lunch. And for my parents, well, that was just pretty much impossible. When we were back at school, I had so much stuff to catch up on it was nonstop school work. I'd be at the library until they closed the place on a lot of nights. The best thing was when Mom and Dad and Donna would come to home games I was starting. I felt like I pitched just a little bit better when they were there, but I pitched pretty well all year.

Final numbers:

- 14 starts
- 3 complete games
- 2 shutouts
- 10-3 record
- 90 innings pitched
- 65 hits allowed
- 18 earned runs
- 113 strikeouts
- 39 walks
- 1.80 ERA

It was about as good as I could do. I felt great about it. But, we didn't get to the World Series and didn't win the Big 10. I actually finished on a down note by being the losing pitcher in the final game of the year at the Big 10 tournament. We lost 6-4 and I gave up two earned runs. Maybe I was running on fumes. It had been a truly exhausting season.

At least five times throughout the season, I was approached after games by scouts. I asked every one of them for a business card. I wanted to know who was watching. The Cardinals, Twins, Red Sox and Dodgers were among the teams who had guys watching

227

me. Then, late in the year, another scout asked Coach if he could see me and he shook my hand. He was with the Rangers, but he wasn't the guy I met the year before. His business card listed his title as something like "National Cross Checker."

I wasn't really sure what that meant, but I had an idea. I asked one of our coaches about it and he said, "That means you're on their draft board, and you're probably on it pretty high. That guy is one of their best scouts, and he goes out to see all the prospects the regional scouts have submitted, to figure out what order they're going to try to get them in. That's a big deal, Brooksie."

The cross-checker guy only asked me one question. He said, "Have you thought about whether you'd sign this year, or are you waiting until after your senior year?"

I said, "Yes, sir. I've thought about it a lot. I'm absolutely 100 percent committed to my degree, and I'd be giving up my scholarship to sign this year, but if I go high enough I guess that would pay for the rest of my education. I'm not ruling it out. I'd be honored to be drafted this year. And I'd be honored to play for the Rangers."

If that sounds a little formal, it's because my dad walked me through that response. He said, "You don't want to scare them away, but you want them to know they have some competition with the Gophers and your scholarship. They won't lowball you if they know there's something they have to beat. But tell them you'd be honored." I think I said it all correctly to the man.

The season was over. My prospects looked pretty good but you never know. The only thing I feared about the draft was maybe getting picked by a team that didn't have a good staff or farm system, and if they had a tight budget that could cost me too. I'm not greedy, and money has never meant much to me, but if I was going to walk away from a free education at the University of Minnesota, I'd need a decent signing bonus to pay for the classes I had left. But yeah, I wanted to get drafted and I wanted to sign. They just didn't need to know that.

I cranked up my classes. I saw Donna as often as we could get together. And I waited. Our season had ended in the middle of May. The MLB draft would be the first week of June. It was tough to focus, but I got through it and aced all my finals. I had maybe six more classes to get through in order to get my degree. We'd just have to see who'd be paying for it.

Those three weeks seemed like three months.

When the first day of the draft was a day away, Coach Anderson called me and said, "Look, I don't have any idea where you're going to go, but you're going to be selected. I've done this a long time and rarely have I talked to this many scouts about any player. This year we have two. They're all over your catcher Dan Wilson, too. So stay home tomorrow until you get a call. You don't want to be out having a burger and miss the call that says you've been drafted. Got it?"

I got it. But seriously, how rad is it to get a call like that from your head coach? Insanely rad is the answer.

I went over and saw Eric and told him about it. He was as jacked up as I was. And I asked him what he thought he was going to do with the New York Rangers. He said, "I don't know yet. It's still kind of out of my hands, but if they make me an offer that's legit and it tells me they really want me, I'll sign it before they pull it away."

Maybe my crazy dream of us both signing within a week of each other could come true. The part about us both signing with the Rangers was something I couldn't control. But to say I wasn't over-the-moon stoked about all this would be ignoring the truth. I was going crazy with anticipation. I'd never felt anything like it before.

For once, I really didn't sleep well that night. Before starts, I typically slept like a brick. This time I tossed and turned and couldn't turn my brain off for hours. When I finally did sleep, it wasn't deep. I woke up a dozen times and finally got out of bed around 7.

Two of my roomies were still around for the summer. They were in charge of keeping the lease on the house no matter what happened to me, and they'd registered for a few classes to make up for what they missed during our crazy baseball schedule. Those two guys knew what was up. They actually made an awesome breakfast of scrambled eggs and bacon for me before going to class. I'd bought some deli meats and bread and figured I had enough food to get me through a day or two. To be clear, it was completely possible I might actually get drafted the next day, but I had no clue. Back then, the draft went as long as 30 rounds and it could take up to three days to complete it. I sure hoped I'd go on the first day, but had no way of knowing.

The clock was ticking so slow I was going insane. It got to be noon. And then 3 o'clock. Nothing. I was pacing like a caged animal. I had totally no appetite. I'd never been that nervous about anything related to baseball. Whether it was chasing a ball around a dirt field with my dad, or playing youth ball, or playing at Canyon and then Kennedy, I just played. It really never made me more than a little nervous. As a Gopher, I felt like I belonged from the first day. And through it all, the whole adventure was under my control. I could play for who I wanted, and go to school where I wanted. Now I was completely out of my control. I had nothing to do with it.

And then the phone rang. I about jumped out of my skin but I remember thinking, "If this is someone calling for one of my roomies, I'm going to tell them he's not here and hang up."

I answered and heard, "Is this Brooks?" I confirmed that I was.

I don't remember the guy's name but he said, "Brooks, I'm an assistant to our head of scouting and our general manager, Tom Grieve, here at the Texas Rangers. I just wanted to let you know that we selected you with our second pick in the draft. Congratulations, Brooks. I hope you want to be a part of the Rangers family."

As much as I'd been waiting for that moment, and as much as I always seem to have a good comeback, I felt speechless. I stammered out a response that was something along the lines of "Well, that's just awesome. I'm stoked. I'm stunned too. This is great. Now what do we do?"

He said they had to finish the draft and within three days they'd call me with an offer. If I accepted, they wanted me to report to one of their minor league teams immediately, but first we had to get the contract signed. For a second-round pick, they weren't going to mail it. A scout would come see me and bring the contract with him. We'd sort out the terms before the scout came, and we'd sort out which minor league team I'd be going to. It would all be finalized before I signed.

All I could say was, "Yes, sir. That sounds great. I'm looking forward to it. And thank you. You don't know how much this means to me and what it's going to mean to my parents. This is a huge thing. I can't wait to be a Ranger."

My dad would probably say I shouldn't have said that last sentence, but I couldn't help it. Since I met that first Rangers scout at Canyon I'd wanted to play for them. It was a dream. And my dream of being fellow Rangers with Eric actually freaking came true.

Insane. Completely insane.

I was actually shaking, but the first person I called was Coach Anderson. I told him about it and he was so supportive. He said, "If they make you a fair offer for a second-round pick I just got about 12 wins dumber as a coach, but I'm thrilled for you, Brooks. You earned this. And guess what? Your boy Dan Wilson went too, in the first round to the Reds with the seventh pick in the draft. You two guys really did us proud. Keep me posted, and congratulations!"

Then I called my parents. My dad answered, and he knew what day it was. He just said, "Well… did you get a call?"

I could barely hold it together. As a matter of true fact I don't think I did hold it together. All I could spit out between the tears was "Texas Rangers. Second round" and then all hell broke loose between the two of us. He just kept saying "Wow" and then I'd hear a few more sobs before he'd say "I'm so proud of you" and cry some more. I was sure glad none of my roomies were home.

When we composed ourselves a little more, I told him the details: 16th selection in the second round. We'd talk numbers and terms in the next few days, and if that all worked out they'd have a scout come straight to Minnesota in person.

I said, "Dad, if that works out and the scout is coming with the contract, I want him to come to your house. I want to sign it there with you and Mom next to me, and Donna too if she isn't in class. That would mean the world to me."

I could tell he lost it again, and all he said was: "It would mean the world to us, too, man. Absolutely. We'd be thrilled."

My third call was to Donna. She wasn't home. She and her roommate had an old-school cassette answering machine and all I said on the message was: "Big news. It has to do with the Texas Rangers and your boyfriend. Call me!"

She called a few hours later and just said, "I'm coming over. Is that OK?"

After I left the message on Donna's answering machine, I called Eric and told him. He's normally just an even-keeled guy. Never too high and never too low. I was stunned when I heard him scream "FANTASTIC! Woo hoo!" He came over right away.

By then my roomies were home, too. Hugs all around. They were all stoked that Gopher teammates had gone in rounds one and two. I was a little stoked too.

Donna showed up with a bottle of Asti Spumante or Prosecco, or something bubbly like that. I said, "Hey, the contract's not signed yet!" But she immediately said something like, "You just got freaking drafted in the second round by the actual team you wanted to play for. We're having a toast. And we'll have another when you sign. They're going to make a big offer, I know it. They want you. They've always wanted you. And now they have you on the hook. They took you second out of all those rounds they still have to complete. They're not going to let you get away."

We grabbed some plastic cups, popped the cork, and all enjoyed the bubbly goodness. My roomies were proud of me. Eric was proud of me. Donna was proud of me. My parents were crying.

My gosh, people talk about dreams coming true and it always just sounds like a cliche or a Disney movie. My dream was coming true. I still get chills and goosebumps thinking about that day. I have them right now, as I'm typing this.

My dream was actually coming true.

CHAPTER 26

Eric Olson

The New York Rangers stayed in touch regularly, but they hadn't settled their front office and coaching positions, so there was really no news. I made up my mind that I was staying in school.

The start of my junior year really felt like a heavy responsibility on my shoulders. It kind of felt "do or die," but that really wasn't the reality of it. The New York Rangers owned my rights all the way through my senior year and a month beyond, but in my head there was the recurring thought that I needed to force them to make a decision after that junior season, and it wouldn't go away. I felt like it was all on the line, and I had to dig back into those youth hockey years, and the high school years, and the Des Moines years, and find the next level.

Up until I was drafted I had never seriously considered the option of playing in the NHL, but there it was and I wasn't going to blow it. I was going to put everything I had into having the best season possible as a Gopher. I would outwork everyone, even my teammates, and if it wasn't enough for the New York Rangers, then it wasn't enough. I didn't want to look back on it and think I'd let it slip away because I didn't put enough into it. That would be a letdown to my parents, my sister and brothers, and the whole town of Roseau. I didn't really know if it would be a letdown to Carol. We'd been connected since elementary school. I don't think she ever saw me as a potential professional hockey player until I was finally playing major college hockey as a Gopher. It wasn't like she was after that at all. She just wanted a loving relationship with a man she could trust and a guy she could have a life and a family with. I wanted to be that man, but by that point I also didn't want to let her down. I wanted to see how far I could go. And I wasn't sure how far that was. So, give it everything you've got!

I enrolled in a full load of classes for the summer and that would leave me just a few classes short of my degree. My promise to my parents to get my degree, and hopefully get it early, was on track and I wasn't going to fail in that regard.

I hit the training room every time I could, and continued to work with the therapists to keep the knee, and every other part of my legs, in the best possible shape. Next level, next level, next level. Always looking to get one step quicker.

Carol was thriving in her job and our relationship (speaking of "next level") was already there. By then, I knew I wanted to marry her but we'd only danced around the topic when talking. I wanted to see how the season went and what would happen with the Rangers before actually asking her if the answer was yes or no. I felt 99 percent sure the answer would be yes, but that one percent is enough to make a guy nervous. If New York would offer me a contract, I'd ask her the next day. Maybe the next minute. That was the promise I made to myself. If I signed and went away to play, we would have a tough time as a couple. I never saw her as a housewife. She had a career going and was so smart it would be idiotic to assume she'd quit and just come follow the hockey player. We'd danced around that conversation too, but it seemed too big of a challenge to even address at the time. Why talk about what we'd do if I went pro when I had no guarantee that it would happen? Plus, I just don't think we wanted to think that far ahead. I had my junior season to play. She was already being handed more and more responsibilities at work. They were talking to her about a promotion within the company to work for the Target chain, which was expanding nationally. As we'd say in hockey, she was killing it.

When training started for the season, I got a phone call from Coach. He told me that Neil Smith, the new GM of the Rangers, had called him to check on me. They also finally had a new coach, Roger Neilson, and they asked Coach Woog if they could speak with me. They didn't have to do that, but it was a professional thing to do and I know Coach appreciated it when they called him first to see if it was OK. He told me to be home that evening, even if it meant skipping a workout. I called Carol at work and told her about it, and she said she'd do all she could to be there with me. I had no idea what they wanted to say, but if the GM and head coach of the New York Rangers wanted to talk with me, I'd make sure I was there to answer.

Carol got to the house around 7. There were only three of us living in the house at that point, and I asked the other two guys for some privacy in the living room. They were happy to head to a nearby bar for a burger and a beer.

When the phone rang, I answered right away and heard, "Is this Eric?" After I said yes I heard, "Hey, Eric. This is Neil Smith, the general manager of the New York Rangers. Our new head coach, Roger Neilson, is here with me on speaker. How are you?"

I'm pretty sure I said I was fine. All I could think about was what they were calling to tell me.

"We're getting our ducks in a row here, and feel we're going to make some great headway with our hockey team and the whole Rangers organization," Smith said. "I'm sure you know Paul Broten is on our roster, and we've talked to Paul about you. He was really positive about what you can do as a pro. Our scouts have seen you quite a bit, and I got the same reports from them. We wanted to tell you directly that we'd like you to go ahead and play your junior year at Minnesota and if all goes well we can talk about a contract right after that, next spring. Are you OK with that?"

I only paused for a second.

"Of course I'm OK with that. I had planned on that all along and think it would be the best for me. I'm getting close to my degree and that's important. My Gopher teammates are important too. I'll tell you right now that I'm going to give it everything I've got to make it impossible for you to not sign me. It would be an honor, sir."

I remember they both talked a little more, but I don't recall a single word of that. I just remember the world "contract" and my vow to make it impossible for them to not offer one.

Carol was only hearing my end of the conversation, so as soon as I hung up the phone I had to blurt it all out and fill her in. I finished by saying, "So, I have another season as a Gopher for sure. It's going to be my best season ever. Our world is going to change if this happens. Can we handle that?"

All she said was, "We can handle anything."

As that season began, I could tell it was different. I was a leader and a frontline player. I was counted on to do the right things on defense and help the team in all areas. I think I was also the oldest guy on the team, and that was pretty obvious to me when I saw the new freshmen come in straight from high school. To me, Roseau High seemed like a lifetime ago. These guys were just kids, but they were good hockey players.

Brooks and I stayed in touch all the time. We still lived across the street from each other, and that was a really good thing. It's easy to get kind of locked in to your group when you're playing college sports. It's like a fraternity, and you have your brothers. Having a best friend who was in a different group, like a different fraternity, was a really important thing for me.

It was pretty neat to see him grow into his relationship with Donna, too. Our upbringings were so different, and I knew he hadn't really had many girlfriends before her, but I could see a lot of change in him as we talked about it. He was constantly picking my brain about Carol and how we'd gotten to where we were. I think he was looking for a road map. I was happy to be as much of a guide as I could be, but I was always honest about the fact every relationship is different. Every person is different. You can't force it to be what you dream it to be.

As for the hockey season, it was just another blur. We seemed to always play the same schools every year: North Dakota, Wisconsin, Northern Michigan, Michigan Tech, Minnesota Duluth, Colorado College, on and on. We did go up to Maine to play them at their rink in late December, and I remember telling the guys, "This is a different type of cold. I grew up in cold weather, but this is bone chilling. It's such a wet cold." I didn't like it much.

We were good. We got off to a rough start, losing a few games, but like we always seemed to do we got our skates under us and we went on a few hot streaks. It all went by so fast.

School was going by fast, too. By the time we were beyond the holidays and into the second semester I was basically done with my degree. I took a couple of additional communications classes just for fun, and because they were free with my scholarship, but I was done with my physical education bachelor's degree and it was great to finally just be a hockey player and not so consumed with school. I had done what I wanted to do with that. I'd played three years of major college hockey and I'd gotten my degree a full year early.

In the end, we went to the WCHA Final Four but lost to Wisconsin after we'd beaten North Dakota. That was a heartbreaker. The Minnesota-Wisconsin rivalry is real, and it's not just college hockey. The two states seem to compete for everything, in all walks of life. You haven't experienced sports until you've been in the middle of a Packers-Vikings game. To lose to them in the WCHA Final Four was tough to take.

We got through the first round of the NCAA playoffs, and made it all the way to the quarterfinals, but lost to Boston College to end our season. I think we ended up around 26-16, so maybe we weren't quite as good as we'd wanted to be, but we were still proud of the effort.

The next step was either going to happen or not, but I couldn't stop thinking about it.

I had a good year. Actually scored six goals, had about 20 assists, and played my usual pest-style of defense. Get there first, win the battles, get the puck back up the ice. It's funny, because that exact theme had been in my head since I was just a kid. I was just playing with much bigger kids at that point.

Once the season was over, we had about another month of classes and I checked in with my advisors to make sure my math was right and I really was on track to get my diploma. I was proud of the fact that my chief academic advisor said, "In all my years working with the hockey and football teams, I can count on one hand how many athletes graduated early. I can count on one finger how many graduated a full year early. That's you."

I finally had a chance to get to a couple of Gopher baseball games after we were done. I saw Brooks pitch once that spring, and he was dominant. It was like he was just toying with the hitters. I knew right then that he'd be drafted in June, and probably pretty high. He looked so confident on the mound, and he was not just overpowering, he was pitching. He could absolutely overpower a college hitter, but he didn't rely on that. He hit spots, changed speeds, and fooled them all the time. It was incredible to watch.

His mom and dad were there. They came to just about every home game he started, and we sat together that afternoon at Siebert Field. They were so interested in the hockey season we'd just finished, and wanted to know what I was planning on doing. They knew New York had picked me the year before to control my rights, and I told them I thought, or at least I hoped, that they'd offer me a contract pretty soon.

On top of that, I told them that I just knew in my heart that Brooks was going to get drafted again, and would go high in one of the first few rounds. Brooks had often told me about "that look" his dad would give him when he was proud of what his boy had done. He'd smile a little, with his lips closed, and nod slightly. I saw it right then, when I gave him my input on how Brooks was doing. I wasn't a baseball scout, but I knew dominance when I saw it.

Brooks and I met at a nearby pub that night for a burger. We ate like college maniacs but then settled in with a few soft drinks and just talked. And we talked. And we talked some more. It was about as in-depth as any conversation we'd ever had.

We talked about his parents, and what it was like to grow up with them as an only child. That's obviously another thing that's totally different about us. I couldn't imagine growing up as an only child. I also couldn't imagine growing up in Southern California, or SoCal as he calls it. And I sure as heck can't imagine riding on my dad's surfboard or watching my mom paint.

He told me a lot more about his mom's illness, and how much they knew they were losing her until Mayo Clinic tried the new procedure on her. I only got to know her after she was better, so it was hard for me to even envision it.

And we talked about Donna and Carol. At one point, he said, "You know, I really like Donna. I think I'm in love with her, but it's weird. I mean, she's gorgeous and funny and a really rad girl, but I'm not sure what it's supposed to feel like when you think you might want to marry someone someday. How am I supposed to know that?"

I told him I didn't know. Everyone is different. With Carol it's just been a bond for so long, and we overcame the uncertainty even when we were in different places for years. But once we knew, we both knew. I don't know if he got that. I wasn't sure I got it. We just knew.

Then we got into the differences between hockey and baseball. I told him how impressed I was with how calm he was on the mound. How he'd walk to the dugout after striking another guy out like he expected that to be the outcome. Just so calm and confident. That just blew me away.

I told him how hockey is so different. It's about getting as wound up and wired as you can because you're going into battle and you need every ounce of focus and energy. Everything needs to be high-speed and max effort.

He said, "You know, pitching is like meditation to me. I just fold my brain up and let my inner pitcher out" or something like that. He was a pretty deep guy.

We talked for hours. And we shared a hug when we went to opposite sides of the street to go home. He was big on hugs. I already knew that.

Around the first week of June, two life-changing things happened. The Texas Rangers drafted Brooks in the second round. I absolutely knew that would happen, and he came over to tell me at my house.

He said the Rangers were going to make him an offer within a few days and that if it all went well they were going to have a scout hand-deliver the contract. Brooks said he wanted to do that at his parents' house.

Two days later the New York Rangers called me again. It was Neil Smith, the new GM. He made me an offer. For the first time in my life it felt like my heart was beating out of my chest.

It would be what they call a "two-way contract," meaning I'd start in the minors, at a minor league salary, but if I got called up the contract would convert to NHL money and if I went back down it would go back to minor league pay. None of that bothered me, but my

Roseau upbringing also calmed me down enough to know I needed to talk to my family, Carol and Coach Woog. I told him how honored I was, but asked him for 24 hours just to let the important people in my life know about it and weigh in on it. This is hard to believe now, but back then the minimum salary for rookies in the NHL was only $25,000. In the minors, playing in Binghamton, New York, in the American Hockey League, it would be more like $1,200 a month, and only during the season. The money didn't matter to me.

When I hung up, I'm pretty sure I was hyperventilating a little. I'd never felt that light-headed and woozy before. All I ever wanted to be was a Roseau Ram. I never thought I'd be a Des Moines Buccaneer. I never imagined being a Minnesota Golden Gopher. And now the New York Rangers were offering me a contract, even though I didn't know the specifics of it yet.

It was the middle of the day, so I couldn't call my folks for a few hours. I did call Carol, and told her about it.

I gave her what details I had and said, "Can we make this work?"

She said the same thing she'd said when the Rangers drafted me: "We can make anything work. We made St. Cloud State and Des Moines work. We learned a lot about ourselves doing that. We'll make it work."

I called Coach Woog next and after he congratulated me he said, "Look, you're not going to get a huge offer. It's all about how much you want to play professionally. Once you make it to the NHL and earn a spot there, you'll make more than you ever dreamed of up in Roseau. And let me tell you, they're probably going to send you to the AHL and when you get there it's another new level, especially in terms of how physical it gets. You'll be playing with other rookies just getting started, but also with 30-year-old guys still just trying to hang on. It can be rough."

On a different subject, he said, "If you say yes, would you consider signing the contract here at The U? I'm sure the sports information department would like that to be on TV."

Then he added, "And hey, don't you know that pitcher on the baseball team who just got drafted by Texas?"

I told him Brooks and I had become really close friends, and that he was a good guy.

Coach said, "Maybe we could get the school to arrange a press conference to have both of you sign on the same day. That would be pretty good for both teams, in terms of recruiting. Would you consider that?"

I told him that sounded like a really neat idea, and yes I'd consider it. But, Brooks had told me it would mean the world to him to sign at his parents' house. I asked him if we could talk again the next day. If we both got offers that were right, maybe he'd go along with that idea.

I talked to my parents not too long after that, and for one of the first times in my life, I think I sensed some real emotion from both of them. My mom might have actually cried a little. My dad was still Mr. Practical, but with me graduating early he had no reason to advise me to not sign. Then they put Betsy on the phone and she was screaming again.

I told them I was going to speak to the Rangers again the next day, and if everything lined up right I'd sign. And we might even do it at a press conference on campus. And once I signed I'd go to New York to go through that process, in front of the media. I guessed there might be more TV cameras and tape recorders at that one. It was all pretty heady stuff.

Mr. Smith called me the next day and told me what the offer was.

It would, indeed, be a two-way contract and he made a big deal out of the fact my NHL salary would be $27,000, a little above the minimum. I'd need to come there for the announcement at Madison Square Garden and would be involved in some rookie camps that summer. I'd also go to training camp with the Rangers, just to get my feet wet and maybe play in an exhibition game or two, but they planned on sending me to Binghamton in the AHL for the season. I could get called up anytime.

I told him the university really wanted me to sign my contract in front of the Twin Cities media, and he said, "We can do that. We'll send you a contract but it won't be signed on our end. You can sign that in front of the Minnesota media. Then we'll fly you here and you'll sign the one that has all the signatures on it."

New York. Madison Square Garden. The New York Rangers. Life was about to change, and in a big way.

CHAPTER 27

Brooks Bennett

I only had to wait a couple days for the draft to be over, but it seemed like an eternity, and I totally had no idea what to expect or really how to handle it. I didn't have an agent to help me with any negotiations, because at that time if you hired a registered agent you'd lose your college eligibility. You could have a relative, like a brother or father, sit with you as long as they weren't registered with Major League Baseball as an agent, or you could hire a real one and roll the dice. My dad and I decided it would be best to maintain that college leverage and keep that option open, so he'd let me talk to the Texas Rangers and he'd just give me his advice. But, and he made this clear, this whole thing was my moment and my decision.

The day after the draft ended I was at the house when the phone rang, and one of my roomies actually picked it up. I remember him saying, "Yes he is. I'll get him for you."

As he handed me the phone he silently mouthed the words: "It's the Rangers!"

I said hello and heard, "Hello Brooks, this is Tom Grieve, the general manager of the Texas Rangers."

We exchanged the normal "How are you?" stuff then he got down to business. I don't recall the exact wording of it, but it went something like this:

"Brooks, we drafted 60 players in this draft. That's a lot. That's why it took a while to get back to you. As the GM, I don't call all 60 players. We have the scout who reported on each player get in touch and offer the contract. But I'm calling you and pitcher Dan Smith, who we drafted in the first round, because we're intent upon bringing you into the Rangers family.

"I know school is important to you, and we not only understand that but appreciate it. It's part of your makeup and we like that. If we can make the finances work for you, will you come out now and sign as a professional baseball player with the Texas Rangers?"

I had mostly expected that sort of thing, so I responded, "I'm totally ready to be a pro, and I'd be more than stoked to be a Ranger. But I have at least another full semester of classes and that's critical to me. How do we make that work?"

Mr. Grieve got right to the point.

"Here's the deal. We had the 16th selection in each round. In that slot, in the second round, the average signing bonus would be about $75,000. That's good money. You'll get it all at once after you sign. So, we're going to offer you $80,000 and on top of that we're going to sign another contract that obligates the Rangers to pay your fees, tuition, books and everything else you need at the University of Minnesota so you can get your degree. The agreement is that you take the maximum amount of classes when you're not playing, to keep it all like it was when you were on scholarship. We don't pay that to the player, we pay it directly to the school, so it's like your scholarship will just continue. We'll have to see your transcripts to see what you have left, and we'll sort that out. It's on us.

"As for your salary, those are set and all rookies make the same amount. As you move up the ladder, your pay will generally go up."

All I could say was, "Wow, that's a fantastic offer and it totally gets me where I want to be."

Then he said, "Brooks, this is a drop in the bucket compared to what you can earn if you're as good as we think you are. You can make millions. You've got a big league arm and a great head on your shoulders. We love your makeup and your family. Do we have a deal?"

I said, "I thought I was going to have to say, 'Let me talk to my dad,' but we already discussed this and yes, we have a deal. I'm honored. Mr. Grieve, I can't thank you enough."

He said, "My name is Tom. Call me Tom. I'm going to have our national cross-checker, Billy McIntyre, bring the contract to you in Minnesota. We won't do this by mail. You met Billy after one of your games this year. He'll be calling you to set it up."

"I'd like to do that at my house, with my mom and dad there. That would mean the world to me," I told him.

He said that was no problem. Then he asked me to get my transcripts to him as soon as possible so they could figure out the scholarship part of the deal. I promised I would.

He finished up by saying, "Brooks, we're probably going to send you up to Butte, Montana, in the Pioneer League, first. That's pretty much entry-level rookie ball, and probably not even close to the level of Big 10 baseball, but we want to get you acclimated to pro ball for a bit. I don't think you'll stay there long, but it will be a good way to ease into professional baseball. After a few starts, if all goes well, you'll probably be promoted to a higher level. Welcome to the Rangers family."

I was shaking when I hung up. And then I'm not ashamed to say I broke down and cried. Not little tears, either. A real cry, with sobbing and all. The dream came true and it was better than I ever imagined.

I had to get my act together to call my dad, and I knew that would be a replay of what I just did. My one roomie who was home, the guy who had answered the phone, just came over and hugged me. He said, "I don't know what the Rangers guy said, but I saw your reaction and heard a bit of your side. I'm assuming this is pretty good stuff, right?"

All I could do was nod.

"You earned this, Brooks," he said. "You earned every bit of it. All the guys respect you so much and look up to you. This gives us all something to aim for. Congratulations, roomie. You're going to be a freaking Texas Ranger." He may, or may not, have used the word "freaking."

It was bizarre. It was the biggest moment of my sports life and I couldn't wrap my head anywhere near around it. It was totally overwhelming. It was like an out-of-body experience. I didn't know what to do! It seemed like I had a million calls to make, a trillion things to do, and I wasn't sure how to do any of it.

I did the only thing I could think of. I went for a short walk, just a few blocks, but I needed to clear my head. It was warm. It was sunny. All the old oak trees in the neighborhood were full of bright green leaves. I was in board shorts, a T-shirt, and flip-flops. All at once, the surfer kid in me welcomed the new pro ballplayer into his life. It was like a total "full-circle" moment that tied it all together. And I swear I didn't dress that way on purpose. It must have been subconscious. The two major parts of my life just melded into one.

When I got back to the house, I called my dad. The waterworks flowed again. It was hard for either of us to talk, and when he put my mom on the line it all flowed one more time.

When we all got composed enough to actually speak, I told them the offer and that I had agreed to it. My dad was on the line then, and through the sniffles, he just said, "That's amazing."

I blurted out, "I got so much to do right now, Dad. I love you. I'll give you more details as soon as I can. I feel like I have a ton of work to do."

I called Donna next. She was silent when she heard the numbers. Like she totally couldn't believe what she was hearing. She promised to bring another bottle of something bubbly to the house that night, and she kept that promise. Before I left, we'd have to have the talk about how we could hold it together with me being gone and so far from home.

I called Coach and told him, and he was thrilled. Then I called Eric.

"Dude, I'm going to be a Ranger, just like you," then I gave him a quick overview of the contract.

He said, "Hey, look — what do you think about both of us signing our contracts here at school, as a way to thank the athletic department and our two sports? Coach Woog really wants to do that and he asked me about you. I know you want to sign at home, but you can have your mom and dad right there with you."

That blew my mind, and I wasn't sure what to think, but I said, "Let me think about it. Doing it at school might be a cool thing to do. And crap, my catcher Dan Wilson went in the first damn round. Maybe he'd join us too. Let me talk to my coach and my parents. Give me a night to sleep on that."

I didn't really l need a whole night. Within a couple hours it hit me.

The University of Minnesota had believed in me, even after my injury in high school.

They provided three years of an education at one of the best schools in the country. An education I could never have afforded. They handed me the ball in the biggest games. The U changed my life. If sitting at a table in front of the local media and signing my contract would help the school and the department with recruiting, I wasn't just good with it. I owed it to the university. I called my dad back and told him about that, and that I wanted them right there with me.

He totally got it. He said, "You know, we just want what's best for you and it's totally like you to want to thank the school for all they've done. Let's do that, man. For sure."

I called Eric next, and told him I was in for the signing at school. The Texas scout would be there with the contract, and my mom and dad were happy to sit right in front of me.

He then said, "Funny thing is, New York wants me to sign at Madison Square Garden, along with some other draft picks, but they agreed to send me a dummy contract I can sign at school. It's just blank. I'll sign the real one a couple days later in New York."

And then I said, "Let me see if Dan Wilson can make it, too. Talk about a rad recruiting effort, to have a first and second-round pick at the table for baseball."

I called Coach Anderson and told him all about it. He said Coach Woog had clued him in but at that point I hadn't committed. He was psyched about doing it and said he'd talk to Dan to see if he could be there, too.

Rangers scout Billy McIntyre called me later that day to see where he should go. I told him about the U of M wanting us on campus and that we were trying to get Dan Wilson to be there too. The only request I had was: "Can you bring me a hat? I think that would be a solid thing to have once we actually sign the contract."

And then I got a call from Coach Anderson telling me the Cincinnati Reds wanted Dan in Cincinnati to sign his contract and put on the hat and jersey. As their first pick in the draft, that was priceless publicity. That put a dent in our plans.

Next, Eric called me back and said New York had pushed up their plans and they wanted him at Madison Square Garden in just a matter of a couple days. The whole grand scheme fell apart, as grand schemes often do.

I called Coach and told him about it, and at that point I just wanted to go back to what we originally were going to do. I'd sign at home. The U could absolutely send a photographer, but it didn't make any sense to try to promote the second-round baseball pick when the first-rounder couldn't be there. He was disappointed, but he understood. My mom and dad acted disappointed, but I think they were relieved. It was always the right idea to do it at home.

I called Billy McIntyre and got him all set up. He'd be flying in three days later.

The day before I was going to sign, Eric had to be in New York. He asked me for a ride to the airport that morning, and that made me laugh. We were both about to become professional athletes and he wanted a ride. He had a truck, but he had no clue how to park at the airport and didn't want to stress over that. I understood.

When Eric's big day arrived, we met right after dawn in the street and gave each other a hug and Eric said, "We talked about signing together a year ago and that almost

242

happened, but I guess when the stakes get pretty high you don't have full control of this stuff. Enjoy every moment of it at home, and by the time I get back from New York, you might already be gone to your first minor league team. If I don't see you before you go, once you get settled, you've got my number so keep in touch. I'll have all sorts of rookie camps and training sessions throughout the summer, but we'll probably overlap here a bit when you're done and I haven't left for preseason yet. We should have plenty of stories to share."

We sure should. The world was spinning so fast it was hard to keep up with it all.

The Rangers had called to tell me they had to change the signing date to make sure Billy McIntyre could make it on time, so I'd be signing the same day as Eric, just in two different places

The day after I dropped off Eric, Billy McIntyre flew in from Dallas and came straight to my parents' house. Coach Anderson was there, too, and he brought a school photographer with him. The sports information director had put the word out to the Minneapolis-based Star Tribune and the St. Paul Pioneer Press, and each of the papers had a photographer there as well.

We all sat at the dining room table and Billy surprised me by not just having an official Texas Rangers hat with him, but also a white home jersey, with BENNETT on the back over the number two. It was all surreal. I'm pretty sure I giggled like a little girl when he handed me that jersey and I put it on over the nicest shirt I owned.

After Billy showed me what to do, and where to do it, I scribbled my autograph in all the appropriate places and we shook hands. Everyone shook hands. Even my dad, who would much rather hug, shook hands with everyone in the room, including my mom I think.

Dad really held up well. A few little tears ran down his cheeks when it was over, but he held it together and so did I.

I would need to be in Butte in just a couple of days. No time to mess around. Pack some clothes, fill a duffle bag with all my gear, and get on a plane.

I flew to Salt Lake City and then made a connection on a small prop plane up to Butte.

I'd never seen any place like it. As we approached, my nose was plastered to the window. It looked like something out of an old western movie.

I didn't know much about the place. I'd read a little in an encyclopedia and knew it had been a huge copper mining town a long time ago, and that's why the team was called the Butte Copper Kings, but in a lot of ways the whole town looked like it was in a time warp. Just an old western copper town built at the foot of the mountains, just below where the old mines were. Talk about cool! Butte was so cool I was mesmerized.

I took a cab to a motel, according to my instructions, and learned I'd be rooming with the pitcher who went one round higher than I did. The Rangers' first-round selection was Dan Smith from Creighton University. We introduced ourselves and sat down in the room to get to know each other a little.

We talked about college ball, and I told him about town ball and how big a thing that is in Minnesota. He said, "I know all about it. I'm from St. Paul."

Blew my mind. Crazy, right?

He told me he'd played for the USA National Team in 1989 after his sophomore year and again, sparks came out of my ears.

"Wait, you played for the national team? My catcher at Minnesota was Dan Wilson. You guys played on that team together, right?"

He said, "Oh, yeah. What a great guy and a great catcher. I knew he went to the U of M but for some reason I hadn't added that all up yet. Man, we had some great players on that team. That was a phenomenal experience, to play against all those other national teams on a tour that took us all over the country. It's almost like you and I already know each other."

The next morning, we headed out to our home ballpark, Alumni Field, and it was a sight that matched the rest of the town. Just old-school as hell, and pretty little. It didn't look to me like it could hold more than 1,200 people, with just one covered grandstand behind the plate and some bleachers on either side of it.

We met our manager, Bump Wills, who had played for the Rangers in the big leagues and whose dad was Maury Wills, one of the all-time greatest Dodgers. We met our new teammates, and we got dressed in workout clothes they provided and put our fancy Copper Kings uniforms in our lockers. Then we walked out to the field for our first workout. Bump pulled Dan and me aside and told us how it was going to be.

"We're going to treat both of you guys with a lot of care while you're here. Hopefully, you'll move up the organization pretty fast, but while you're here I want you to stay within yourselves, just do what you already know how to do, and stay healthy. You don't need to impress anyone. You already impressed our scouts and front office, so just do what we tell you and pitch."

We had a meeting in the cramped clubhouse to learn how this was all going to happen. As I looked around, it was surprising to me that all the guys looked to be about my age. I had expected a few more players who had signed out of high school, but almost everyone was in the 20- to 21-year-old range.

The Pioneer League was pretty spread out. You'd think a league that had most of its teams in Montana and Idaho would be compact, but Montana is huge.

In our division, we had Salt Lake City, Idaho Falls, and a team called the Gate City Pioneers which, we learned, was actually based in Pocatello, Idaho. The other division had Great Falls, Helena, Billings, and Medicine Hat, which was up in Alberta. Yes, for real.

After the meeting, Bump pulled us aside again and had the general manager of the Copper Kings with him. The GM, who if you put a million dollars in front of me today I couldn't come up with his name, said a couple of things.

"I know Bump told you about our approach to your pitching. Look, we're a minor league club and we like to win, but we're in charge of the Texas Rangers' valuable property, and you two guys are the biggest pieces. The last thing we want is for either of you to walk off the mound holding your elbow or shoulder in your first month in the Pioneer League. We're going to be careful.

"Also, after the first week most of the guys will move to homes with host families, or get together and rent apartments. I wanted you both to know that we want you to stay in the motel together when we're at home. We'll cover it. We don't know how long either of you will be here, so there's no reason to sign leases or put down deposits. That sound OK with you?"

Sure it did. Dan and I were already clicking with all the things we were learning about each other, and the motel wasn't The Ritz but it was fine. I'd stayed in worse. I'd seen worse ballparks, clubhouses and towns. It was all new and different, in a strange part of the country, but I made the decision to learn as much as I could and enjoy it.

After a few days of workouts, we opened at home. I think we opened against Gate City, which we learned was an independent team with no Major League affiliation. Dan would pitch the opener, and I'd pitch the second game.

They weren't very good. When the Rangers had told me that the Pioneer League probably wasn't going to measure up to Big 10 baseball, that was obvious when it came to the Gate City team. They might have made a good town ball team in Minnesota, on a good day. Dan took care of them with little effort and went five innings. We had a nice little crowd, too. Maybe 1,000 people.

The next night was my turn, and I went through all my normal routines. I decided to treat it like one of those starts at Shakopee, when I was working on the fine art of pitching instead of just blowing hitters away. I'd show them the fastball, and then carve them up. It was a little too easy, to be honest. They let me go five and I gave up one hit and no runs. I struck out a bunch and didn't walk anybody. I would've liked to have pitched more, for sure, but that was the limit. It seemed odd to both Dan and me. We'd just finished our college seasons and were in prime shape, but the Rangers' rules were the rules.

We went on a road trip to Pocatello and Idaho Falls, and I pitched the final game of that trip. Idaho Falls was a Braves farm club. They were a lot tougher, and I did give up a few hits, but no runs. We rode through the darkness to get back to Butte, arriving there in the middle of the night. Welcome to the low minor leagues. It's a lot of things but it's not glamorous. I gotta say, though, it was rad. I was playing minor league baseball and getting paid to do it.

And speaking of getting paid, that was a little weird at that time of my life. They'd advised Dan and me not to set up bank accounts in Butte, because they didn't know how long we'd be there and that could get complicated. We were all on the same rookie salaries, about $800 a month, so after taxes the check would be around $660. The Butte team paid us, and the checks were drawn on a local bank, so many of us would just go to the bank and cash the checks. I'd probably never had more than $40 in my wallet or pocket at one time to that point in my life, but in Butte I was strolling around with close to $1,000 on any given day. It sure makes picking up the lunch tab or buying a new shirt a lot easier. As for my bonus, I still had my checking and savings accounts Dad and I set up when we first moved to Minnesota, at a bank near Don's house. The Rangers would send my bonus check there and Dad would put it in savings and just let it sit there until we figured out what was the best thing to do with it.

The hardest part of the journey was staying in touch with Donna. I was in a motel where they charged ridiculous amounts of money for long-distance calls, and I sure wasn't going to call her collect. So we resorted to actually writing letters. Maybe one or two a week, but they were mostly short little notes. I'd just fill her in on what was going on and she'd do the same back to me. One of the guys had a Polaroid camera and I bought a pack of film for it and had him take pictures of me in my uniform. I sent one of those to Donna and another to my parents. I hadn't heard if we'd have actual baseball cards made, so I wanted to be on the safe side. At least I could justify the cost of the stamps. The phone charges were just stupid.

I ended up pitching in five games over the course of about a month. I was 4-0 with a 1.98 ERA and 40 strikeouts in 29 innings. But after that fifth game, they called me into Bump's office. I was being promoted to Gastonia, North Carolina in the South Atlantic League. Gastonia is just outside of Charlotte, so I had a lot of flying to do just to get there. I was happy I'd gotten to see a lot of that part of the country, although I was sad I never made the road trip up to Medicine Hat. Bump had told us it was a great ride and a neat place.

When I walked back out of his office, they called Dan in, right behind me. When he came out, we were both smiling and everyone in the clubhouse figured out what was going on. The Rangers were bumping him up three levels, skipping their two Class A teams and sending him all the way to Tulsa in the Double-A Southern League. We had flights out in the morning, so we had a lot to do, but we circulated around the room and wished all the guys, many of whom we were still barely getting to know, good luck.

What an awesome experience that was. I wouldn't trade it for anything. I was stoked to have played in the Pioneer League and honestly believe every new pro player should play at that level to get started. It was bitchin' and I'll never forget it. And yeah, Butte was cool. I'll always be proud to have been a Copper King!

But I had to get to Gastonia.

Dan and I were on the same early morning flight to Salt Lake City, and then we'd split up there to get to Gastonia and Tulsa. At the huge Salt Lake airport, I wished him luck. With no cell phones then, it might not be until the next spring that I'd see him or talk to him again. He was making a huge jump. Guys in Double-A are close to the big leagues, and some have already been there.

From the Salt Lake airport I called my parents, collect, and told them the news. The one thing that kept that from getting out of hand emotionally was the fact I had to dash to my next flight and I still wanted to call Donna and Eric. I had to leave a message for Donna, but got Eric on the phone and he was jacked up about it. He'd already been to Madison Square Garden to sign his deal, and he'd taken part in a few rookie camps. All he said was, "It's way better hockey, but I can handle it. Facing the actual NHL guys this fall in camp will be where I get a real feel for it."

246

When I got to Charlotte, one of the equipment managers picked me up at the airport and we went straight to the Gastonia ballpark. It was also classic old-school, but about twice the size of the Butte park. A really neat place, and the clubhouse was a lot bigger. I never really saw the town that day. The ballpark was right off the highway from Charlotte. But North Carolina sure did look a lot different than Montana.

I met the manager, Orlando Gomez, and then worked my way around the room to meet all the guys. They clearly knew I was coming and that I was the Rangers' number two pick in the draft, and they were all great. The equipment guy had a uniform waiting for me and my name written on athletic tape across the top of my locker. The uni fit like a glove. That still meant a lot to me. I had to look like a ballplayer, not a pretender.

Two of the guys came over and said, "We have a spare bedroom at the house we're renting. Do you need a place to stay?" I said, "Sure," and that was a nice box to check off the list of things I had to do in order to survive.

Orlando and I met in his office. I don't recall there even being a pitching coach on that team. What he said was pretty close to what Bump had said in Butte. They were going to use me as a regular starter but didn't want to stretch it out too far. I tried to tell him I was good to go, but all he said was: "I do what Texas wants me to do. We'll track pitches, so we'll do it that way, not by innings." Sounded fair, I guess.

I knew nothing about the South Atlantic League, although I learned that first day that most of the guys referred to it as "the Sally League," for short. I grabbed a schedule to see what was in store for me.

There were six teams in each division, and they were all Major League affiliates. No patched-together independent teams in the Sally League. And unlike Butte, where the season didn't start until after the draft in June, these guys had all been playing since spring training started in March. They already had more than 70 regular season games in the books. They were a close-knit bunch. Playing every day for months will do that. I was stoked to be there, but decided I'd just lay low for a bit until I got to know them all.

I sat in the dugout that first night. I think we were playing Asheville. I just wanted to soak it in and check out the level of play. It was way better than the Pioneer League, but maybe still not as good as some of the college ball I'd played. Schools like USC, UCLA, Texas or Miami were incredible.

The South Atlantic League was also considered a standard Class-A league. Most organizations had two Class-A teams but considered one to be their "advanced" A team, which played in a tougher league. The Rangers advanced A team was in Port Charlotte, Florida, in the Florida State League. I'd already heard about how tough that league was. Maybe it was a good thing I took the step to Gastonia first.

I think I started on my fourth night there, on a long homestand. I do know we were playing Charleston, West Virginia, that night. They were a Cincinnati affiliate, so guess who was there! Yep, Dan Wilson, my former Gopher catcher. It was great to see him, and face him for the first time.

I think I pitched pretty well. No real nerves that I remember. I got through five without a scratch and only gave up a couple of hits. I struck out a bunch, and punched out Dan on a change-up. I mean geez, he caught that pitch every game. He had to know it was coming, but it still fooled him. He shook his head at me as he walked back to the dugout.

It was another whole new part of the country to see and experience, and the bus rides weren't bad. Lots of cool little ballparks and rowdy fans. It was a real step up and it felt like what I always thought minor league baseball would be like. Most fans have watched the movie *"Bull Durham"* and that's really what it was like, in terms of fans, ballparks, and buses. Almost exactly like that.

Donna and I kept sending letters. There's a thrill when you walk in the clubhouse and there's mail in your locker. I never got over that.

By the time I'd gotten to Gastonia from Butte, they were down to their last six weeks or so of the season, so maybe another like 40-some games. I got 10 more starts.

- 11 games started
- 65 innings pitched
- 79 strikeouts
- 10 walks
- ERA of 2.20

I think I handled it well. When it was over, I was looking forward to getting home. The guys at the house had saved my room for me and I was going to load up on classes. The Rangers had taken care of the tuition and fees, as promised, so it was up to me to carry my end of that bargain.

As for the baseball card I was hoping for, that didn't work out too well. Both teams had them made, but in Butte it happened after I left and in Gastonia it had already happened before I got there. I'm not even in either club's official team photo. Timing is everything, right?

All in all it was just a rad year. A great college season. Getting drafted so high by the team I was hoping to play for. A big bonus. My first taste of pro ball out in Butte, and then a quick promotion to a new level in Gastonia. It was, by far, the most baseball I'd been a part of in one year. I couldn't wait for spring training, but I had work to do.

When I got home, my bonus was in the bank and like the "Mr. Money Bags" I'd been out in Butte I brought a few thousand more bucks back with me in cash. It was so much more money than I'd ever had, not even counting the bonus.

For school, I wanted to complete a couple more finance classes. Having tens of thousands of dollars in the bank will make you pretty motivated to totally understand what you're doing with it. The money was kind of nerve wracking, actually. Scary a little bit. But I'd never gotten much joy out of spending money just to spend it. I wasn't raised that way. It was all about having what you need, not everything you want.

What a year.

CHAPTER 28

Eric Olson

Well, the whole "sign our contracts together at school" plan fell apart in the space of about one day. New York wanted me and a couple of other new players at Madison Square Garden three days earlier than we originally talked about. We'd also tried to get catcher Dan Wilson from the university's baseball team, because he was Cincinnati's first-round pick, but the Reds wanted him there right away to sign in front of the local media. So that just left Brooks, and I know he really wanted to sign at home with his mom and dad anyway.

I had to get to New York in a hurry. No problem for a Roseau boy, right? I'd been to Boston on a road trip, and a couple other big cities, but nothing like New York.

Someone from the New York Rangers called me, I think it was the traveling secretary, and he said he had the whole itinerary ready, plus my flight information, and a list of what I'd need to bring. He asked if he could FAX it to me. I know it's odd, but a bunch of college hockey players who lived in a rental house did NOT have a FAX machine. Hard to believe, right? I told him I'd find a number that worked so I could go pick it up.

I called Coach Woog but he wasn't in. I talked to his secretary and she gave me the FAX number for the office and told me to give the green light to the Rangers. She'd call me when it came in.

I did that, and an hour or so later she called me back and said it was there. I basically jogged to the office to get it. Before I even left I held it in my hands to stare at the New York Rangers logo at the top, and it had a whole bunch of information on it.

My flight was leaving in two days, and early in the morning. I had no idea how I was going to get to the airport. I needed to bring a suit and some nice casual clothes, including a sports coat. I had all that, but it wasn't exactly top-of-the line or brand new. It would just have to do.

The pick-up information for La Guardia airport was interesting. There would be a hired driver waiting for me at baggage claim holding a sign with my name on it. We wouldn't have to wait at baggage claim, because the team urged me to pack efficiently and carry my bag on the plane. Once I hooked up with the driver, he'd drive me to the hotel they had set up for me and two other guys. You might have heard of it. It was the Waldorf-Astoria.

The memo also informed me that the two other rookies were Edvin Vertanin from Finland, and Lars Karlsson from Sweden, who they drafted ahead of me. They'd be flying in from home, so they would land at JFK airport and we'd all get to the Waldorf in our own hired cars. Once we got settled, we'd meet in the lobby around 6 p.m. for a nice dinner with Neil Smith and Roger Neilson. The sports coat would be needed for that.

The next day, the press conference would be at noon and the three of us would be introduced to the New York media, then we'd sign our contracts. I had a flight home that night.

I had basically 36 hours to be ready and I still needed a way to get to the airport. I called the one guy who came to mind first, who had a car.

"Brooks, I gotta get to New York Wednesday morning early. Any chance you can give me a ride to the airport?"

He just said, "Sure, happy to do it dude. The Texas scout isn't coming in until Thursday now, so I'm free. I can't believe you're going to New York."

I said, "Not only that, but they're putting us up at the Waldorf-Astoria and sending hired cars to the airport to pick us up. And they're taking us out to dinner after we get in that day. The press conference will be the next day. It's crazy, and intimidating too."

I told him I'd fill him in on the details on the way to the airport.

I had a suit that needed to be pressed, some pants that needed ironing, a sports coat that needed the dust cleaned off of it, and my only pair of dress shoes that needed to be polished. And I had a ton of phone calls to make.

I talked to my family, filling them in on what details I had, and I called Carol. She was excited as heck, and like me she'd never been to New York. She said, "Memorize everything you see, hear, and even smell. You can tell me all about it when you get back. Anything I can do for you to help you get ready?"

I said, "I hate to even say this, but I don't own an iron. Do you have one? I might need lessons too, if you do. I'm useless. Stupid hockey player, I know."

I was at her place an hour later and she said "Just watch me. I'll do it this time big boy, but you're on your own in the future. It's not that hard." Everything looked brand new when she was done. I even did OK on the shoes.

I spent the next day packing and worrying. It was one thing to sign a contract with an NHL team. That's big enough and stressful enough all by itself. But to fly to New York, get driven to the Waldorf-Astoria, then sign in front of the New York media at Madison Square Garden was a completely different thing. It felt like I was going to the moon. It didn't seem real at all.

Carol and I had a nice tuna casserole dinner that night. That was our comfort food and we made it whenever we were a little stressed. We stared at each other and talked really quietly, as if any loud noise might break the dream. It was odd, but it felt right. Plus, I was worried I wasn't going to sleep well that night, so the whole thing was maybe a subconscious way of keeping myself calm. We sat on her couch. We held hands. And I remember laying my head back against the wall and exhaling deeply. All I could say was: "I can't believe this is happening to me. I never would've dreamed this."

She squeezed my hand tightly and put her head on my shoulder. A lot of the stress melted away. And all of a sudden, I was exhausted. I gave her a huge hug, about a dozen kisses, and said goodnight. A big tear rolled down her cheek.

My alarm went off at a ridiculous hour. I had a 6 a.m. flight, so Brooks was going to be ready to leave at 4:30. We met outside in the dark and headed for the airport.

I remember saying, "You know what? I have never flown by myself. I've only flown with the team, and everything gets taken care of for us. We go as a group, they hand us our tickets, we get on the plane, and a bus is waiting at the other end. I'm not even sure where to go when you drop me off."

He said, "I'm the same way. I've never flown on my own. What airline are you flying?"

It was Northwest, and my itinerary told me that I needed to go to the main ticket counter and show them my ID. They would print my ticket and point me in the right direction for the gate.

Brooks dropped me off at the curb and we shared a hug. "Good luck, dude," he said. "Knock 'em dead in the Big Apple, and enjoy the next two days. Try to burn it all into your memory banks. You won't want to forget a minute of what's about to happen."

It all worked out, as things normally do. I'm not going to say I wasn't a bit stressed, but I got my ticket and was shocked to see I was in seat 1-A, in first class. The Rangers were really taking care of us. I got to the gate and asked the agent if she thought I'd be able to see New York City out the window when we were coming in to land. She said, "I don't know. The flight attendants might have a better idea about that. I've flown in there a bunch and sometimes you see Manhattan and sometimes you see Queens. I think air traffic control decides that."

When I got on board, I found my seat (it was kind of hard to miss, being the first row on the plane) and tried to relax. It was just beginning to turn light outside, and getting a little sleep wouldn't be a bad thing. I honestly didn't know anything about first class, other than we always walked through it to get to our seats in the back on road trips. Turns out, the seats are way bigger, there's more leg room, and the flight attendants are hovering over you just about all the time. We even had breakfast served. Not the greatest omelet I ever had, but it was a legit hot meal. After that, I actually fell asleep.

A couple hours later, I woke up when I felt the plane slow down. A flight attendant came by to check on my seatbelt, and I asked her if she thought I was on the right side of the plane to see New York.

"I'm not sure yet," she said. "There are three major airports in New York and air traffic control moves us all around the area to keep all the planes separated. Sometimes we even go north of the city and then come down the Hudson River right alongside Manhattan before we circle around the tip of the island to get to La Guardia in Queens. That's a great view, but the pilots might not even know which way we're coming in yet. Keep an eye out!"

As it turned out, we were routed a different way and Manhattan was outside the windows on the other side. I'd have to see it first at ground level. The rest of the adventure was just about to begin. Was I nervous? The answer would be yes.

I found my way to baggage claim and spotted a guy in a dark suit holding a sign that read "Eric Olson" so I walked up and introduced myself. He said, "Follow me. Welcome to New York."

We got to where all the hired cars were parked and I honestly didn't know what the term "hired car" meant. Was it just some guy's personal car? Was it really just a taxi? No on both counts. It meant I'd be riding in the back seat of black Lincoln Town Car.

We left the airport, and even the area around La Guardia, in Queens, was like nothing I'd ever seen other than in the movies. And then, not too far ahead, just about all of Manhattan was laid out in front of us. It was something my brain couldn't comprehend. So much city, so many skyscrapers, all crammed into such a small area. The next thing I knew we were heading into a tunnel to get to Manhattan. There are bridges, of course, to get over the East River, but we wanted to go straight to Midtown and the tunnel was the way to do that. When we came out on the other end, it was like the movie had completely changed locations. You could barely see the sky. It was as if you were at the bottom of a canyon, but the cliffs were buildings. On the streets, it looked like madness. Yellow taxis everywhere, and every driver seemed to be constantly honking their horn. The sidewalks were packed. The traffic was stacked up. This was when my driver said, "The easy part is over. Now we have to get to the Waldorf, and it's only about 10 blocks away."

I was trying to act cool, like I did this every day, but I know my head was on a swivel and I was dumbfounded. It took us a solid 20 minutes to go those 10 blocks, and the honking never stopped. It was like bumper cars at the carnival out there, and it didn't take long for me to figure out one of the taxi drivers' best tricks. If they want to change lanes, they can't be shy. Just get the nose of the taxi out there and pretend you don't hear the honking. Finally, we pulled up at the Waldorf. I asked if I owed him anything, and he said, "No, it's all been taken care of. I'm not supposed to talk about people's jobs, but I know why you're here and I just want to say good luck. I'm a huge Rangers fan."

I checked in, and that experience was another new level for me. A doorman in a crazy outfit held the door open while he said, "Welcome to the Waldorf-Astoria, sir." There was a front desk that looked like it was out of an old movie. The lobby was like a museum. Certainly nothing like the Holiday Inns we stayed at on road trips, and I always thought those were nice.

I went up to my room and held my breath when I opened the door. I didn't know what to expect. It wasn't huge, but it was luxurious beyond anything I'd ever stayed in. And it looked right down on Park Avenue, out in front of the hotel. It was yet another "pinch myself" moment.

I hung up my clothes and thought about a nap, but I was wired. It was also only about noon, so I had a lot of time to kill.

252

I went back down to the lobby and spotted a concierge desk across from the check-in area. I told the woman I was in New York for the first time and wanted to take a walk to check it out, but had no idea where to go. I asked her for some advice.

She pulled out a small map and showed me where we were, on Park Avenue at 50th. Then she said, "You can't get lost if you watch the street signs. Just get back to Park and 50th. If I was you, I'd head up here to Central Park; it's just a couple of blocks. You can walk around the park for a while, and then maybe walk down Broadway toward Times Square. You'll pass a lot of famous theaters and restaurants. If you go all the way to Times Square, it can be a little crazy for a first-timer. Lots of people trying to sell you stuff and most of it is fake, so just keep walking and don't even respond to them. There's lots to see just in this small part of the city. Enjoy the sights!"

Going from the airport to the car and then into the hotel, I hadn't even noticed what a beautiful day it was. Maybe 75 degrees, white puffy clouds on a royal blue sky. It was fantastic. Had it been a rainy or gloomy day, my whole first impression of New York would've been completely different. Maybe that was a good omen.

I did what the concierge recommended, going up to Central Park and walking around in there for a while. The park is so big and such a main part of Manhattan. It was neat. Then I found Broadway and walked south down the crowded sidewalks. Here's something I figured out right away. There are so many people, all busy and all trying to get somewhere, and they don't have time to make eye contact or say anything. They just stare ahead and walk. And so many of them looked really important in expensive suits and carrying leather briefcases. It was all a blur to me. As I got close to Times Square I remember thinking, "I'm not going to go that far. I'll have plenty of other times to see stuff like that. I'll just head back over to Park Avenue."

And the concierge was right. All I had to do was walk east to Park and then north a few blocks to get back to the hotel. My walk had been maybe two hours. I figured I'd just relax in the room until we were supposed to meet at 6. I was even a little sweaty from the walk but didn't have that many changes of clothes, so I hung up what I was wearing and took a shower. Then I put on the Waldorf-Astoria bathrobe and laid on the bed. I never slept, I was way too nervous about being late, but I zoned out pretty well. It had already been a big day, and Brooks dropping me off at the airport already seemed like a week ago. But it was about to be a much bigger day, having dinner with the other two rookies, the GM, and the head coach.

I got up and got dressed around 5. Khakis, a white shirt, and my blue sports coat. I hoped I looked the part. A kid from Roseau hanging out at the Waldorf all dressed up. I remember, at that point, thinking, "Gosh, tomorrow I have to wear a suit. I hope I remember how to tie my tie."

I'm always pretty prompt. On this day, I wanted to be a little early. I got down to the lobby around 5:45 and immediately saw two guys standing around who had to be hockey players. And if that was the case, they had to be the two guys I was going to sign alongside.

I walked up and said, "Are you Edvin and Lars?"

"Yes, yes, yes we are," one of them said. I introduced myself and we did the best we could to have a conversation while we all nervously waited.

I asked them where they flew in from, and the answers were Helsinki for Edvin and Stockholm for Lars. They had just gotten in a few hours before. And I thought I was tired flying in from Minneapolis.

Seconds later, two gentlemen in very expensive suits arrived. They walked right up to us and introduced themselves. It was Roger Neilson and Neil Smith. After all the handshaking, they said, "Let's go, we have a private table reserved for the five of us."

We followed along through the maze of the Waldorf's main level and ended up in a dark and swanky restaurant. Back to the rear of the room was a large table set up in a recessed area, and we could have the curtain in front of us closed if we wanted. Mr. Smith said, "It's OK, just leave it open."

Before we could even look at our menus, Mr. Smith said, "Boys, let's just get the business out of the way first so we can enjoy our dinner. Tomorrow we'll have contracts drawn up and ready for you. They will be two-way contracts, and the NHL side of that will be $27,000 if you make it up here to New York, and that's $2,000 over the league minimum. We want all three of you to start out at Binghamton in the AHL. It's a tough league and it'll be a challenge for you, but we wouldn't be signing you tomorrow if we didn't think you could succeed. When you do succeed, there's a lot more money to be made and a lot more hockey to be played. Lars and Edvin, did you understand all that?"

They nodded and replied with the same "Yes, yes, yes.".

"OK then, tomorrow you officially become part of the New York Rangers organization. Tonight, we're going to eat well. Order anything on the menu you want! And tomorrow morning, feel free to either eat breakfast in the main restaurant or call for room service. Just sign for it, and add a tip. We'll cover all that."

Up until that moment, I could count on one finger the number of times I'd had filet mignon. I ordered that. Everyone ordered steaks, of various sorts.

We ate like kings, and we had some fun conversations about Roseau, Finland, and Sweden. I told them about my Swedish heritage the best I could, and how Minnesota is heavily populated with Scandinavians. The guys spoke pretty good English, fortunately. We also heard great stories about the history of the Rangers, and how these two men, Neil and Roger, were intent on getting the team back to the glory days. I believed them.

They told us about Madison Square Garden. The three of us had never been there, so the plan was for a hired car to pick us up around 10:30 the next morning and take us straight to the private players entrance. When we got inside, they'd have a staff member waiting to give us the full tour of the place. Easily one of the most famous arenas in the world.

And until that moment, I had no idea that Madison Square Garden sits on top of one of the biggest train stations in the world, Penn Station. No idea. Zero. That's nuts. I thought it was just an arena, but in New York the real estate is so precious and so expensive, apparently they do things like that, building up and over instead of spreading out. I couldn't wait to see it.

We were stuffed from the huge dinner, and we shook hands with Neil and Roger. My two new about-to-be teammates were obviously exhausted, so we all shook hands again and headed to our rooms. I neatly hung up my clothes, and got in bed. I fell asleep in five minutes.

I had set an alarm for 6 but I didn't need it. I think I woke up at 4 and kept checking the clock every 15 minutes. Finally, I was staring at the clock when it went from 5:59 to 6 and the alarm went off. Time to get up.

I took a shower, put on my suit slacks and my white shirt, and called for room service. I ordered scrambled eggs with bacon and toast. It showed up around 30 minutes later. I do believe that was the first time I ever had room service.

When it was delivered, I signed the check and added a 10 percent tip. And 10 percent of the bill was $2.90 because the scrambled eggs, two strips of bacon, and two pieces of toast came to $29. My eyes almost fell out of my head. I'd never spent more than $5 for breakfast in my life, and most were twice the portions. I remember thinking, "Geez, I hope they meant what they said. This is ridiculous." Well, it's New York. It's the Waldorf.

I managed to put a good knot in my tie and headed downstairs around 10. Lars and Edvin were already down there. We all looked a little (a lot?) out of our normal hockey lives in our suits, but we looked sharp too. It was going to be another huge day. The car showed up right on time, and off we went, with all three of us in the back. Nervous energy? About a 12 on a 1-10 scale.

We saw the Garden from a block away. The big, round building is impossible to miss. The driver had obviously driven some hockey or basketball players before because he knew the plain unmarked garage door at the bottom of a slight ramp was where we had to go. The door went up, and we drove into the building.

A young member of the Rangers staff was waiting for us. These guys didn't miss a beat. So far, everything was perfect and right on time. It was like clockwork.

We got out and met our host, a young man named Trevor, I think. He said, "I'm going to give you the best tour. Just follow me." We walked down a long, curved interior walkway, past storage rooms, auxiliary rooms, the ice refrigeration plant, the New York Knicks' offices, and finally turned a corner in front of the Rangers' offices. We went inside and it was a beehive. The season had just ended a month or two before, but everyone was busy. Our guy walked us around but mostly we just tried to stay out of everyone's way. They were definitely working hard. That's a good thing.

We went back out into the concourse and passed the Knicks' locker room. We went in there for a look and it was a bit of a surprise. It was nice, and their lockers were great, but it was small. I mentioned that to our guide and he said, "Well, they only have about 15 players on their roster, and they don't wear pads, so they don't need as much space." Their training room was really nice, and the coach's office was top-notch. I was just surprised an entire NBA team would dress in that room.

Back out into the bowels of the building again, and we came across the promised land. The Rangers' locker room. It felt like walking on hallowed ground. We were all really quiet when we entered, hoping we weren't breaking any tradition or rule by being in there before we had even signed our contracts. Trevor (if that was his name) said, "Don't worry about it. There are no players here right now. In a few hours, you'll actually be Rangers and you'll belong in here. You'll be part of the family. It's fine."

It was awesome. A big room, big lockers, fantastic training room, a full weight room, and all the best stuff. The three of us were kind of mesmerized. Another moment when it all didn't seem real.

Then, the last piece of the big puzzle. We followed the rubber runners on the concrete floor that took us out to the arena, the same way the Rangers did every night. And when we popped out of that tunnel, there it was. We were at ice level, although there was no ice installed at the time, looking up at Madison Square Garden soaring above us. All three of us just said, "Wow."

It seemed enormous on a scale I'd never seen before. I'd played in the St. Paul Civic Center, and a lot of the college rinks we played in were plenty big, but I'd never seen anything like the Garden. We literally just stood and stared. Spinning around trying to soak it all in.

That's when the newest revelation hit me. All my life I wanted to put on the Rams uniform and come out on the ice at Roseau Memorial Arena in front of 1,500 crazy fans. Then I got to play in a real arena, down in Des Moines, although the atmosphere wasn't nearly as great as it was in Roseau. Then came The U, playing for the Gophers, and that was the highlight of my career up until this point.

I remember thinking, "I have to play here. Somehow, some way, I have to play here. This is what I've worked so hard to do for so many years. I must play here. I must."

As we looked around we stood there mostly in silence. The lights were on, and I noticed that the seats were different colors in horizontal bands. I asked our guide about that and he said, "Those are different sections. It helps make it easier for fans to find their seats."

I said, "Those seats all the way at the top. They look blue, or maybe black. They're so high up, how can anybody even see the game from there?"

He replied, "Those are called 'the blues' and the real hardcore hockey fans sit up there. Tickets aren't cheap, and many of the lowest seats in the house are owned by very rich people or major companies. The hardcore fans from the outer boroughs can afford those seats up there, and they are diehards. They create a ton of the atmosphere on game nights. Once you play here, you'll appreciate them. They love the game and love the Rangers, but yeah, those seats are way up there."

I asked him how they got to the games if they were regular blue-collar fans and he said, "That's the beauty of being part of Penn Station. They can take a train here, or take the subway right into the station as well. That's how we do it around here. Public transportation gets everyone around. Did you have a chance to ride the subway yet?"

I said, "No. I took a long walk and passed a million subway stations, but I wasn't ready for that yet. Seems like a good way for a kid from Roseau to get lost."

"You'll figure it out. Next time you're here, get a subway map and just get a feel for which lines go where. It's a whole different world down there, underground, but it works and New York would come to a standstill without it."

At that point, we needed to get back to the office to get ready for the signing. After all we'd done and seen since we arrived, this part of it seemed easy. I was going to be happy just to do it and get it done.

We met up with Mr. Neilson and Mr. Smith and got prepared to go out there to the media room. They had regulation Rangers sweaters (jerseys) for us, with our names on the back and the number 90 on each one, to signify the year, and they had hats. I asked when we were supposed to put that stuff on and they said they'd hand them to us when we were introduced and had signed our contracts. I wondered if I was the guy asking too many questions.

We filed in. We sat down. And we squinted. I couldn't tell you how many TV cameras were out there, but they all had bright lights on, pointed right at us. It sure looked like the room was full.

GM Neil Smith spoke first. After welcoming the media, he spoke about how excited the team was to sign us, then introduced Lars and Edvin, giving quite a bit of background on each one of them. They had both played a lot of hockey for only being 19.

I came last and he said something like, "And we're really happy to have selected Eric Olson, from the University of Minnesota, last year. He played one more season for the Golden Gophers this past year, and now he's here with us. He's a heck of a defensemen and has excelled at every level. He's also from one of the most well-known hockey hotbeds in the United States; Roseau, Minnesota. This little town near the Canadian border has produced a phenomenal number of top-level hockey players, including the Broten brothers and our own Paul Broten. When we watched Eric play, we could see the Roseau influence. Those kids are hard workers and relentless players. That describes Eric perfectly."

An assistant brought out our contracts and put them in front of us. We each signed on the appropriate line.

Then they brought out the sweaters and hats. We did the best we could putting those on over our suit coats, and then put on our hats. From that point forward, for the next 10 minutes, we all stood there and it was just a nonstop series of camera flashes and bright lights.

The team had a few one-on-one interviews for us, and I thought they went well. One guy holding an ABC microphone asked me: "So, do you think you can play at this level?"

I gave him the honest answer. "All my life, since I put on skates as soon as I could walk, I've been working at getting to the next level. I dreamed of being a Roseau Ram, and that worked out. I had some college offers, but wanted to go play junior hockey so I went to Des Moines, to take it to another level. When I was done there, the University of Minnesota offered me a scholarship and a chance to play at yet another level, for one of the best college programs in the country. I've never backed down. I've always worked as hard as I can. I'm not going to change that now. I'll do all I can to get here and play for this incredible franchise in this historic building, in the Big Apple."

I'm pretty sure that was the best answer I'd ever given in an interview. It should've been. I was from the heart.

Before we left, the Rangers staff loaded us up with information about rookie camp. It would be in July and would take place in Rye, New York. I had no idea where that was, but they assured me it was just up a parkway from New York and they would take care of everything. After my first experience with the team, I was confident they would.

When it was all wrapped up, I was taken back to the hotel to gather my stuff and get ready to go to the airport. The driver actually waited for me at the curb. I changed out of my suit and into my khakis, threw everything else in my bag, and headed back down to the car. What a whirlwind couple of days it had been.

La Guardia was quite an experience as an arrival airport, but it was pure mayhem for departures. Lines everywhere, people cutting in line and jostling for position, and basically just madness. I quickly realized that being a polite guy from Roseau wasn't going to get me to the gate. I remember thinking, "I'm a long way from home," as I tried to navigate and get to my plane. I finally made it, and found myself in seat 1-A again. The flight attendant came by to see if I wanted anything to drink before we took off and I wasn't sure what that meant. My flight out to New York was at 6 in the morning, so orange juice was my choice then. This time, I did something I rarely did. I asked for a beer. And it was free. First class is a nice place to be.

By the time we were at cruising altitude, they brought us a meal and I wolfed that down. Other than the huge dinner the first night, and the room service in the morning, I hadn't eaten much. As soon as she took the tray away I put my seat back and fell asleep.

I didn't have a ride from the airport, so I took a cab back to the house near campus and it took about all the cash I had left to pay the guy. I'd just signed my first professional contract but I had no money to speak of.

At that point it struck me that the New York trip was kind of like a "fantasy land" for me. The Waldorf, the dinner, the hired cars, all of that. Once I left I was just Eric Olson again, with no money in my pocket. And from that point forward, especially going to Binghamton, it would be a lot more like Des Moines than New York.

I got back to the house and the guys were all eager to hear about it. I did the best I could to describe it all but my mind was pretty worn out. Carol came over a bit later and we sat on the ratty couch in the living room. We were quiet again, just like before I left. I told her everything I could remember. She held my hand and stared at me with those big brown eyes. They were always the most beautiful eyes I'd ever seen. On a night like that, they were a little more spectacular.

All she said was, "What an amazing life experience. It sounds magical and insane all at the same time. And now you're a professional hockey player. You left here two days ago as the same Eric from Roseau. Now you're a pro. Don't you think that's amazing? Do you realize what you've accomplished?"

At that point, I'm not sure I did. It was such a blur of a trip doing all sorts of things I never dreamed of, and it hadn't really sunk in. And signing my name on a complicated piece of paper was supposed to be the focus of it. Funny how the least memorable thing was the most important piece of the whole trip.

I was done with school, but I wanted to keep living in the house and do my workouts with the Gophers. Being a few blocks from Carol was important too.

I worked out every day, pushing it as hard as I could, always thinking about the rookie camp coming up. Another new level. Another new challenge. Another chance to prove myself to any doubters who still thought I was too small.

When it was time for camp, they flew me back to New York but it was to a different airport. It was called Westchester County, in White Plains, and it was a much smaller and easier place to navigate. It was also really close to Rye, where the camp was going to be held. I did as I was instructed and took a cab to the team hotel, which actually happened to be a Holiday Inn. I felt a little more at home there, and it relaxed me.

We had roommates, and mine was Jimmy Carfalo, from just north of Boston. He'd gone to Harvard, so we'd played against each other but it wasn't like we got to know each other doing that. Jimmy was there for the camp on an amateur tryout. We connected all the dots and then scanned our itineraries to see what was about to happen during the week.

Rooming with Jimmy was another calming thing. I'd just played against the guy. We weren't all that different. I belonged there. I knew I could hold my own.

Lars and Edvin were also there, and it was good to see them. I was eager to see how they played.

The next day would be the first day of my pro career. The funniest thing was where the rink was located. It was at an amusement park called Playland. Seriously. I guess it was actually a pretty famous and historic park in that part of New York and it had been around for many years.

We all piled on a bus in the morning, and headed over there. It was bizarre to drive by the amusement park to get to the facility, which ended up being a really nice little arena with a great sheet of ice. The locker rooms were fine, and we had Rangers uniforms to wear. We had a string of meetings, then a light lunch, and we got dressed for an afternoon skate, just to shake the cobwebs off.

The next day, we were at the rink by 9 and ready to go by 10. They ran us through some drills, we did a lot of skating, and then took a break. We'd have our first scrimmage in the afternoon. They split us up into two teams, and actually had us in different locker rooms, to make it a little more game-like. I was on the "home" team so I wore a white Rangers uniform. The other team wore the blue road jerseys. We all wore the red Rangers breezers. Wait. I can't believe I'm this far into telling this long story and that's my first reference to breezers. They are the big baggy shorts hockey players wear, and they're held up by suspenders. Sorry about that. Such a thing is key knowledge, in my mind.

Anyway, dressed up like Rangers we hit the ice for a full scrimmage. Edvin and Lars were on the other team, and they were both left-wingers so I'd get a real close-up look at how well they skated and what their skills were like.

I was on the first defensive line, playing the opening shift, and I actually was a little nervous. You just never know what it's going to be like until you're out there and they drop the puck.

I shouldn't have worried. I don't think that first rookie scrimmage even measured up to a Gopher game against North Dakota or Wisconsin. Everyone was trying to impress the coaches, so there was a lot of hitting and a lot of shooting, but it was kind of a mess. None of us had ever played together before.

My way of impressing the coaches was to do exactly what I'd always done. Be a pest. Get there first. Win the 50/50 battles, control the puck, and get it up ice. I took some hits, but I'd taken worse. I have no memory about which team won, but I knew I'd played well and played my game. I think a lot of the guys were trying to elevate to a new game, and that didn't help them.

As for Edvin and Lars, they could skate very fast, and stick-handle very well, but they were really shy about getting hit. They'd give up the puck to avoid a big check into the boards. They were just 19, and they had a long way to go.

The whole week went well, and when we did our exit interviews before we all scattered to go home, the coaches were really nice and complimentary to me. They said I'd played just as I'd been advertised. They also said Binghamton was going to be a whole different animal, but I had the skills and discipline to be very successful there.

There was a second rookie camp in August, at the same place, and it went well too. I felt really at ease by then. I knew my way around and knew most of the guys.

It would be about a month and a half before the real training camp opened, right back up there in Rye, and for that I'd be with the real Rangers. Of the NHL. The National Hockey League. Madison Square Garden is such a huge facility, and it hosts events all year round, so they don't put the ice in until just before the NHL season. Playland it was.

I was eager and a little nervous about that. I'd be sharing the locker room and, hopefully, the ice with guys like Brian Leetch, Mike Gartner, Brian Mullen, John Vanbiesbrouck, Mike Richter, and of course my Roseau buddy Paul Broten. The fact Paulie was there gave me hope. We had played together since we were little kids. If he could play for the Rangers, maybe I could too. But (and it was a big "but") the level was not just going to be new. It was going to be the best in the world. The world! Just thinking that way made my head spin.

Before I left, the coaches let me know that I'd get a lot of ice time during preseason games. They wanted to see how I'd handle it, against superstars. They also said, "Look, these are the best hockey players on the planet. Don't put too much pressure on yourself. Just play your game. We'll see you back up here then."

I couldn't wait.

CHAPTER 29

Brooks Bennett

It was great to get back to school and see my roomies again, and I was actually a little late for the first week so I dove into those classes like I was possessed. I can't even tell you how rad it was that the Rangers would cover my last semester like they did, and I was absolutely determined to get it done on time.

One of my first priorities was to get down to see my parents and tell them everything I could remember. We hadn't talked much over the summer but I sent them letters and a Polaroid photo of me in my Butte Copper Kings uniform. Mom had a fantastic pot roast dinner waiting for me, and it struck me that this was the first really good food I'd had in months. In Butte and Gastonia you might have a pocketful of money but lunch was really the only full meal you could count on, since most games were at night, and fast food was sadly the easiest route to go.

It was great to spend time with them, and yes, Dad gave me the standard closed-mouth smile and the slight head nod. I never got tired of seeing the "I'm proud of you" move on his part.

I went over to see Donna the next day, and that was a little weird. It was maybe a lot weird. It seemed like I'd been gone a really long time, and I felt like a different person when I got back after all those experiences, but it had really only been three months. Weird how time messes with you like that, right? In three normal months at school nothing really changes. Go away to play baseball every day in Montana and North Carolina and it seems like an eternity and everything seems different.

We talked and said all the right things, and she seemed interested in whatever stories or details I could tell her, but it was weird. Like, we were starting over? I didn't know. Like, we were drifting apart? Maybe.

I had such a small track record with deep relationships I wasn't sure what to make of it. It's not like I had years of experience in how things were supposed to be or how to get it back on track if it seemed a bit derailed. Talk about totally out of my element!

When I went home that night, I remember lying in bed thinking, "Look, dude. She's gorgeous, smart, and funny and everyone loves her. She's got a group of great friends who are just as pretty and just as much the focus of attention wherever they go. I went away to throw baseballs for a living and she was here without me. It's not like I could expect her to sit in her apartment and knit for three months. She's young, and she craves having fun. Every guy in Minneapolis has been hitting on her and filling her full of compliments. You need to figure this out."

My plan was to buy her flowers the next morning, which was a Saturday or Sunday, and surprise her with them. I'd never done that.

I bought the flowers and headed over to her place with no clue as to whether she'd be home or not, but excited to let her know that she'd be the focus of my attention again now. If she wasn't home, I'd leave the flowers with a note. I was home. Everything was going to be great again. The summer had been fun. Pro baseball is fun. But I'd been loyal the whole time, just concentrating on pitching, and I wanted to dial us back in, to where we'd been before I left.

As I walked up to her apartment, a guy was walking out. His eyes got a little wide when he saw me and then he just looked away as we passed on the sidewalk. You want to feel a sense of dread and paranoia all at once? Try that on for size. I knocked on the door.

Donna answered the door. She was laughing when she did it, and then her face totally changed and her eyes got wide. All she said was, "Oh, hi, I wasn't expecting you."

I went inside kind of puzzled about the guy who had just left, and equally puzzled why Donna was only wearing a tight T-shirt and shorts, and didn't seem to have anything on underneath. I handed her the flowers.

"Well, I brought you these and wanted to surprise you," I said as I showed her the roses. "Looks like I did."

She really had no response. I'd never been so uncomfortable around a girl in my life. I think I knew what was going on, but I kept trying to find better explanations for everything that had just happened. A guy had come out when I walked up. Her roommate wasn't there. She was dressed like she'd just thrown some sexy things on. Add it up, idiot.

She walked me to the sofa and we sat down. She stared at me right in the eyes, and a tear rolled down her cheek.

"I'm so sorry, Brooks," she stammered. "It just happened. A lot happened while you were gone for so long. I don't know what to say. I'm just sorry, but I can't erase it or make it go away."

She'd been partying and meeting guys since right after I left. She'd dated more than a few of them. She'd been seeing this guy for a month, and she swore she'd told him she had to cut it off because I was back from pro ball. She also swore he was the one who insisted they have one last night together and she didn't say no. I guess my timing was either totally perfect or terribly awful, depending on how you look at it.

I just sat there, and when she was done I said, "Wow. I had no idea."

She said, "Look, I really want us to get back to normal. I need to focus on that and you need to focus on your career. I want to share it all with you, and I'll be there through the ups and downs, but I don't think there will be many downs. The future can be great for us. I want that."

I hate to say this, but when I heard those words I remembered my bonus money in the bank, and all the money I could make in the big leagues if I got there. I didn't believe a word of it. I felt like a meal ticket and I definitely didn't like that. What bond we'd put in place before I left wasn't just broken. It was shattered.

All that flashed through my brain was that this momma's boy totally needed to talk to his mother. I just said, "I gotta go. We'll talk later."

I went back to the house and called my mom. All I said was, "Can I come see you right now? I need some relationship advice pronto. This totally sucks."

She said, "Of course. Your dad is here too. Do you want it to just be me, or can he be here for you, too."

I said I'd love for him to be there, and that I was on my way.

As soon as I got there we sat at the dinner table and Mom said, "So what's going on?"

I said, "I just found Donna with another guy. Well, I missed that by seconds actually, which is probably a good thing. He was walking out as I walked to the door to surprise her with some flowers. When I knocked, I think she thought it was him coming back for something because she was laughing when she opened the door. When she saw it was me, all the color drained out of her face.

"But that's not the worst part. She told me she'd been dating guys all summer, and had told the dude I saw that she had to break it off because I was back in town. Then she put on the big puppy-dog look and tried to convince me that it would all be OK, and that she wanted to be a big part of all my success. She didn't ask me to forgive her, though. She just said she was sorry it happened. It was pretty much a 'I don't know how, but it just happened.' Like she had no control over it."

My mom said, "Wow. That's awful."

And my dad chimed in, "This is just me talking, Brooks, but this is not the girl you thought she was. She broke your trust and she did it on purpose. This was no accident. She cheated on you. Plain and simple."

I told them I could tell the money was more important than the relationship. And that bummed me out huge. The whole thing sucked.

"This is all new for me, but the truth is I don't think anyone has ever cheated on me," I said. "You guys never did, and I don't remember ever being fooled like this whether it was a girl, or money, or grades, or anything. It crushed me to add it all up and think of what was going on while I was playing this summer. Everything in her letters was nothing but lies. It was all lies. How do you trust anyone again, after something like this?"

My dad said, "It's going to take some time. But maybe you're right to be extra cautious now that you have your bonus and your career is taking off. People will tell you all sorts of lies to get close to you. We've got your back, and we'll never lose your trust or confidence because we aren't capable of acting that way. We promise you. Just take some time to decompress. And spend some time with Eric before he leaves for hockey. He's a guy who's on the same career path as you, with all the same dangers. You can trust him."

I said, "I totally get that. I've got to get over it and concentrate on school right now. I owe it to the Rangers to get my degree after this semester. I basically just walked out of her place and said I'd talk to her later. I'll do that. I'm going to break up with her. There's no other option. It's weird, but I don't feel sad. I just feel mad. How can any person be like that?"

What stunned me is that nobody cried. My folks looked so caring and so understanding, and pretty heartbroken. But not because Donna cheated on me. They were heartbroken that I had to go through this. But we all held it together.

I finished it up by saying, "I'm still so damn naive. This was a big lesson. You guys gave me the greatest gift anyone could get. You loved me and raised me right. It's hard for me to even understand that people will want to take advantage of me. I have to keep my circle as tight as I can. I still can't believe it. All those damn letters were lies."

The next day I called Donna and asked if I could come over. When I got there, I got right to the point. We never even sat down.

"I can't trust you anymore, Donna," I said. "You betrayed me, you lied to me, and you did it for a whole day after I got back! It's over. Good luck with everything. I have a life to live and a career to conquer." She turned on the waterworks for effect, I think, but I just turned and walked out. It wasn't fun, but it felt like a weight off my shoulders.

I told some of the guys about it, and one of them said, "Do you know who the dude was that came out of her apartment?"

I said I didn't recognize him, but he definitely recognized me.

He said, "Let's find him and kick his ass."

I shook my head and said, "Guys always get that wrong. The dude is just a guy. She's gorgeous. She led him on and never said no. It's not his fault. It's her fault. I don't understand why guys want to go kick another guy's ass when their girlfriend cheats. That's backwards. And I'd never lay a hand on her. I broke up with her and walked away. That's all I can do."

I called Eric and we got together for a beer that night. He needed to leave for preseason with the actual New York Rangers in just a week. I couldn't comprehend that. We talked about all we'd gone through, and got right down to the point where it seemed all wrong how we were paid. I spent the summer in the low minor leagues playing for peanuts, but I got $80,000 up front to do it. Then I made all of about $800 a month to actually play. He was going to camp with the actual New York Rangers and hadn't been paid a penny yet. He'd go to the minors and make pretty much the same peanuts I made in Butte and Gastonia, maybe a little more, but if he ever got called up to the Rangers his contract called for him to make only $27,000 in the NHL.

I said, "How in the hell are you supposed to live in New York on that kind of money?"

He replied, "I have no idea. I guess I'll just hope it happens at some point and then we'll see what we'll do. It would sure be crazy to be in the NHL and not be able to pay

264

the rent anywhere near Manhattan. I could be an actual NHL player who has to ride the subway from Queens."

We had a great long conversation. I told him about the Donna drama and let him know that I'd learned a lesson. People were going to try to take advantage of me, and I couldn't let that happen. I warned him that it could happen to him too, and he needed to be careful.

"Believe me, I've already felt it," he said. "I'm so lucky to have Carol. We've known each other all our lives and she never fell for me because I played hockey. I think, in a lot of ways, she might have preferred that I just got a job at Polaris and we could have a nice house and raise a family. But I trust her because I know I can. What I have actually experienced is a string of guys I grew up with, or met here at school, who all of a sudden are acting like we were best friends. I knew them. I might have even liked them. But we weren't best friends. When it feels fake like that, I can smell it. I'm just like you.

"You know, trust is everything to me and I think there's a lot of Roseau in that. We all trust each other. We don't lock our doors. What's mine is yours. Now that I'm out here in a much bigger world, trust is going to be really important but there are going to be people who try to earn it and don't deserve it. Was that deep?"

I told him it was spot-on. I got it. I knew it. I just felt it happen to me.

He said, "Honestly, if I ever put my trust in someone and they took advantage of me it would just break my heart. I'd feel like a fool, and I'd be so disappointed. I'd also be pissed off to the max. I don't know, man. It's hard to find people you trust. I hope the next girl you meet is all about that, but be careful."

We said goodbye, and I wished him well. It might easily be 10 more months before we'd see each other again. I asked him to call me when he got to New York for preseason, just to fill me in on being in the locker room and on the ice with real NHL players. And then we'd have to figure out how to stay in touch. The U.S. mail might be utilized.

I got on with life. I buried myself in my books and my classes. I had a fun time running and lifting some weights with some Gopher teammates, and that was good for my soul, but I didn't dwell on any of it. I had a promise to keep with the Rangers and school was most of my focus.

The Rangers did ask me one baseball favor. Tom Grieve called and said, "Focus on school. Don't pick up a baseball until December. You threw more innings this year than at any time in your life, and you did it at three different levels, from college to rookie ball to A-ball. Just give your body a rest and get that diploma."

I agreed, but I knew it was going to be hard to not pick up a ball. I figured I could still do the running and the weights, but I promised I wasn't going to throw until December.

Eric did call from New York once preseason started, and he was talking a mile a minute. It was way cool to hear it all. He said their preseason camp was actually north of the city and the rink was part of an amusement park, the same place they'd had their rookie camps, but it was good to be out there and not in the middle of Manhattan. Being in the locker room with all those guys who were already NHL regulars was way intimidating, but they were great to him. In practice, he said, when he'd be his usual pest on defense, they respected that. He said one forward actually thanked him after practice one day, telling him he was pushing all the rest of the guys instead of taking it easy. It was all cool to hear. He promised to call again if he got in a preseason game.

Sure enough, just a week or so later, he called to tell me he'd played in an exhibition game against the New York Islanders. I asked him what it was like and he said, "It wasn't a dream come true because I never dreamed of this stuff, but I can tell you one thing. It was *fast!*"

It was just absolutely rad to hear all that, although when he'd rave about certain players he was playing with or against, most of the names didn't register with me. I had become a hockey fan, but I was lucky to know two or three names on the Minnesota North Stars. I had never really followed the NHL.

He did get sent to Binghamton in the American Hockey League, and when he got there he called me again. He was sharing an apartment with three other guys and they had a phone, so I could call him any time I wanted and he'd call me with regular updates. It was kind of eerie how this dude, who I'd literally run into in Pioneer Hall on the first day of school, was living such a parallel life with me, even though we were so different. What are the odds? It was crazy, but even then I could tell we were bonding. He was such a good dude. Amazingly good dude. And I knew he was going to be a star.

As we closed in on the end of the semester, I was on track. I'd have my degree in accounting, with a minor in communications. I'd also taken some finance courses to learn more about money management. It was a stout schedule to make it all happen in three and a half years, especially considering how much traveling we did on road trips each spring. I was proud of it.

The one bad thing about graduating a semester early is that you don't get to put on a gown and a funky hat with a tassel to get your diploma in front of your family. That only happens in June. I wouldn't be home in June, so I'd just get my diploma from the university and frame it.

That happened at the end of December. I was a college graduate. I actually took it to my parents and gave it to them. I told them I was going to be moving around so much the next few years I might lose it. I wanted them to have it. I couldn't have done it without them. Their moral support and the way they raised me gave me the strength and focus to do it. They were so proud, but probably no prouder than I was. It was a huge accomplishment. I wasn't just a college graduate, I was a scholar/athlete who had graduated early from the University of Minnesota. Crazy.

Even with my degree, I wasn't really a financial planner of any sort. I was still just a strict accountant. I put numbers in boxes. So dad called his cousin Don and asked for some advice. Don told him about his finance guy, and raved about his investment skills and his integrity. He'd been working with him for 20 years. His name was Jack Karlsson.

We met Jack, who was an agent for the investment firm Edward Jones, and Dad and I both felt good vibes. He was smart, he had a client list that was long and prestigious, and we both felt good about what he could do. It felt right.

And, as much as my dad and I are both pretty progressive in our thinking, we knew we were both really conservative and safe when it came to money. Living the lifestyle he had followed, where money came so far down the list of important things, I could understand that and it totally had rubbed off on me. I didn't want Jack to risk much of anything. Just put it away in some safe investments and let it grow a little. No restaurant investments, no car dealerships, no fancy condos. Just keep my money safe.

We did decide to put $20,000 in my savings account and $5,000 in my checking account. We'd trust Jack with the other $55,000 and if my career went where I wanted it to go, there would be more to trust him with in the future. I had given Dad power-of-attorney over my accounts when I left to go play in Butte, so he could move my bonus money in and out of accounts. He still had access to my funds if I needed anything, and could wire the money to me. My little Corolla was still running great, and I actually planned to drive it to Florida, but at some point I might want something bigger. I also had to pay rent in Port Charlotte once the season started. With three or four other guys sharing whatever apartment we could find, that wouldn't be too expensive, but I needed access to money to make it happen.

We also decided I needed a credit card. I'd be doing some traveling myself and it would help to have a card to check into motels with or use at restaurants. I got a MasterCard with an enormous credit limit of $2,000. The bills would go to Mom and Dad's house and Dad could write the checks to pay it off each month. Jack urged that really strongly. He said, "If you cut corners and don't pay the whole balance each month, the interest is going to bury you. Just be vigilant every month. Never leave a balance. In a couple of years you can get an American Express card and they don't even give you the option. You have to pay it off each month." Sound advice.

Just around that time Tom Grieve from the Rangers called and asked me to start my throwing program. The team sent a small binder to me and it outlined everything I was supposed to do on a weekly basis, step by step. It was rad to have it all outlined in such detail. I was amped to get to the gym and get to work.

Coach Anderson offered to let me work out with some freshman catchers, and that was fine. I could throw to them and they could learn a little about catching professional pitches. But we had to take it slow. I hadn't touched a baseball in almost four months. I don't think I'd ever gone that long without pitching.

It felt great. It was sublime. My happiest Zen place, right there on the mound, although it was made of wood and covered in Astroturf. My mind was totally clear. Donna didn't exist. I had no more classes to dash to. Baseball was all that mattered. I can remember thinking, "It doesn't get any better than this."

I got my contract and signed it right away. It was for the Rangers' advanced Class-A team in Port Charlotte, Florida, and I got a raise all the way up to $1,000 a month, which is only paid during the season. You go to spring training for free.

I'd already been told that I would go to the minor league camp for spring training, then stay in Florida to start the season in the Florida State League. They expected me to do well there, and if I did then a promotion to Double-A Tulsa would probably happen.

267

I couldn't wait to get there. I'd need to be down there in early March. It was time to ramp up to the next stage of my throwing program, so that I'd be ready to rock as soon as I got outside on a real mound.

I stretched out the program, started popping the fastball, snapping the curve and mastering the feel for the always tricky change-up. I was ready.

I packed my duffle bag with all my gear, filled a suitcase full of clothes for warm weather, threw in some board shorts and flip-flops, and was ready to leave.

My first spring training was about to happen, but I had a three-day drive ahead of me. It was 22 degrees when I left. This time I had to really say goodbye to the guys in the rental house. When I came back, I'd have to be on my own. It all seemed totally ridiculous, completely exciting, and very heavy all at the same time. It wasn't lost on me where I was going, and where it could take me. It was going to be big.

CHAPTER 30

Eric Olson

When Brooks got back from his first summer of pro ball, we got together over a burger and a beer and caught up on everything. We were lucky to even be able to do that, because I had to get ready for training camp back in New York and he was diving right back into school.

We talked about a lot of stuff, including what it was like for him to be out in Montana and then North Carolina in the minor leagues. It struck me then that the financial comparison felt a little unfair. I'm not going to say I was jealous, because I don't know if I've ever been jealous a day in my life, but it was an odd feeling. Envy? Maybe. I didn't like the feeling. I should be above that. I should never let stuff like that bother me, but it did a little.

The truth was, I'd worked my butt off almost every day since the first time I could skate. I had to overcome my size to even make it as far as the Roseau Rams. I was still proving people wrong and outworking them to get to where I was, about to leave and attend the New York Rangers preseason training camp. I'd signed a two-way contract which, in the minors, would pay me about what an hourly McDonald's employee makes, if you took into account all the time hockey players spend practicing, getting ready, warming up, playing, riding the bus, and the other stuff that has to happen. And, if I made the Rangers NHL roster I'd be getting paid $27,000 per year, and even that would be prorated if I got called up in midseason.

Brooks was naturally gifted. He was a great pitcher, and he did put the work in, but he never really had to overcome much of anything. He was great from Little League on up. And he got a check for $80,000 just to sign his contract with the Texas Rangers. He was actually making less, per month, than I would in Binghamton but that signing bonus was huge. I'd never dreamed of that much money, and I know he hadn't either.

I don't know, it surprised me a little when I felt a little pang of whatever it was. Like I said, I didn't like the feeling. I was embarrassed to feel that way. I was proud of him and happy for him, but there was no denying the idea that hockey players had it a lot tougher than baseball guys, and for that we got paid less.

He also told me about his girlfriend Donna cheating on him, and how he broke up with her almost immediately. He told me how much it felt like she was just with him for the gravy train, wanting to be a Major Leaguer's wife.

We talked about being careful, about not trusting everyone who pops up and tries to be close to us. Being a professional athlete is awesome, but there are a lot of people out there who will take advantage of you. I'd seen it myself and I hadn't even played my first pro game yet. I was so lucky to have Carol, and I knew it. There was no sense of that with her. She and I had been friends since grade school. She never once even talked about what life would be like for her if I made it to the NHL. Not once. As a matter of fact, I'm not even sure she looked forward to it. She was really proud of me, but it's a tough life for the wives. Hockey players travel half the time, and even when the team is at home there's practice or morning skates before games. I knew enough guys who had made it to the top to know they were rarely at home for months on end. Carol might've liked it better if I just had a regular job and we stayed in the Twin Cities so she could concentrate on her career. She was already making way more than I was going to make no matter where I played during the upcoming season.

The deal with Donna made me feel really bad for Brooks. He didn't deserve that. He'd treated her like a queen and would never have done to her what she did to him. When he told me that all he ever did out in Butte or in Gastonia was concentrate on baseball, I believed him and knew in my gut that it was true. The fact that he'd had a girlfriend at all surprised me. He was never into going out and chasing girls. Almost every hockey player at The U did their share of bar-hopping and flirting with girls. Maybe flirting is putting it too lightly. Let's just say they "chased" them pretty hard.

Drama like he went through with her is the kind of thing that can change a guy's life and his outlook. Trust can be easy when you're young and naive, but it is such a difficult thing to regain once it's broken. He seemed like he was focused though, and ready to crunch the school work for one more big semester. I guess I just felt confident that he'd be OK, and being dedicated to school and baseball wasn't necessarily a bad thing. We promised to stay in touch and I'd call him once I got to camp.

I had a lot of details to wrap up before I would head to Rye, New York. The Rangers sent out a series of packets listing where I had to be, when I had to be there, what the agenda was for the first couple of days, and other things. It was great to know how it was going to work, but what I didn't know was how long I'd be with the team in camp. At some point, unless some really bad things happened to the regular defensemen on the Rangers, I'd be going to Binghamton. I just didn't know when. They told me I'd get to play in a few preseason games, so that was something big to look forward to, as well as just being in the locker room with so many great NHL players.

I talked to my folks and to Betsy a few days before I left. I made sure to tell my mom and dad how much I appreciated them for everything they'd ever done for me. That's about as "emotional" as we ever got in the Olson family, but I meant it a lot to me. With

Betsy, it was mostly light-hearted. She said, "OK, you've worked damn hard for this so don't screw it up now little brother."

All I could tell her was that my plan was to NOT screw it up, and I thanked her for all those years of street hockey and pick-up games when I was a kid. I also said, "I can't really believe I'm about to put on a Rangers uniform and share the room and the bench with these guys. It's unbelievable."

Carol and I had dinner together just about every night the week before I flew out. I think we only went out once, and that was for a greasy pizza. Every other night she cooked and I helped. It felt like home that week, like an anchor. I'll never forget that combination of comfort about being with her and the excitement about getting to New York. It was like both sides of the emotional scale happening at once. I was also becoming a pretty good assistant in the kitchen, but she worked magic.

On the night before my early flight, we had tuna casserole. That was definitely our dinner of choice when something big was about to happen. It was fantastic. I was all packed and ready to go, with a suitcase full of winter clothes, my giant duffel bag filled with my gear, and a half-dozen sticks. Hockey players are kind of hard to miss in airports.

I spent the night with Carol on my last day at home, and she was going to drop me at the airport for my 6 a.m flight. We stayed up pretty late, talking about everything. She was absolutely a star at her job and had been told a promotion to a bigger role with the Target division of the company was about to happen. She needed to stay in the Twin Cities and concentrate on that, but she was also getting close to having a full week of vacation days. As soon as I got to Binghamton I'd scan the schedule to see if we had any homestands long enough for it to make sense for her to come out there. I sure hoped we could do that.

At around midnight, I turned to her and said, "I gotta ask you something. I don't have a ring, but I sure hope we can get married. Would you take me as an option? I love you, and I want us to be together forever."

She didn't just shed a tear. She started crying and it just got bigger and bigger. I had actually wondered if getting to be a little older made her more emotional, but I think it was much more related to us being more in love and me being more open with her. She had taken the lid off her emotional side.

Leave it to me to wonder if the tears were because she was going to say no. It took a while, but she finally stopped sobbing and said, "I was wondering if you'd ever ask me. I think you just asked me. Did you really just ask me?"

I said, "I did. Will you marry me?"

"Of course I will, you dummy. I love you so much and I'm so proud of you. Don't worry about the ring and we don't have to tell the world about this until you save up some of your salary and can buy me one. Buy the cheapest one you can find. There will come a day, not too far ahead of us, when we'll be able to buy whatever we want."

I said, "You're so good at your job and you're going to be a superstar at Target. This won't be easy, but if I make it to the NHL we'll cross that bridge then. For now, let's just know we're unofficially engaged, OK?"

"I love that," she said. "We're unofficially engaged, but in my heart it's as official as it can be. I love you."

I think we might have slept an hour that night, if that. My instructions from the Rangers told me to take cabs to and from every airport, but Carol was absolutely insistent that she take me instead. She wanted to drop me off and seal it with a kiss at the curb. That sounded way better than a taxi.

I was wound up tight as we went to the airport. Excited too, but definitely nervous. We had another one of those epic hugs at the curb, and I stared into those beautiful dark brown eyes just trying to burn the image into my brain forever. It was hard to let go, but I had a huge adventure ahead of me. The last thing Carol said was, "Be yourself. They won't be able to keep up with you."

I flew into Westchester County and took a cab down to Rye. My instructions were to head to the rink first, to drop off my gear with the equipment managers and get signed in, and then head over to the same Holiday Inn we'd used for the rookie camps. The place was an absolute beehive when I walked into the lobby. I think it was obvious I was a player, but I didn't recognize a single guy. To be honest, this was all new and pretty intimidating. A lot of them were big. Almost all of them looked really old to me. It struck me then that I'd never really played with too many guys who were more than a year or two older than me, and most of the Gophers I played with were younger than I was.

I finally saw Edvin and Lars after I checked in and we talked for a bit. They were the only two people I had recognized. We spent about an hour down there, and some of the other guys who had been in the summer camps came by. It was starting to feel more comfortable. Then Paul Broten came walking in, and everyone was yelling greetings to him. It was great to see Paulie. I don't think I'd seen him since our last game of his senior year at The U. He'd spent about a year and a half in the minors for the Rangers, but had gotten into maybe 30 NHL games in '89-'90 so he knew all the guys and he was, after all, a Broten. It was fantastic to see him, and it once again gave me that boost of confidence that I could do this. And that was just when I needed it the most. Standing around that lobby with all those NHL veterans made me feel about 5-foot-4 instead of 5-9.

We had a team dinner that night, and most of the veteran players came over to where all of us rookies were seated to introduce themselves. My gosh. Brian Leetch, Mike Gartner, Kelly Kisio, Brian Mullen, John Vanbiesbrouck, Mike Richter, and a parade of other guys I'd watched on TV. They were all really nice and very welcoming. Richter asked me if it was true that I was from Roseau, and I was stunned he even knew that. When I said yes, he said, "Well, there's obviously something in the water up there. Bring more of that Roseau vibe to this team. Between you and Brots, we'll have a big advantage. Welcome to the Rangers, Eric."

Then he said, "So what do the boys call you? Oly?"

"Oly, Olsie, or 'Hey you' all work. I'm not picky. Thanks for asking."

I thought I was floating.

I'll never forget the next day as long as I live. We rode a couple of buses over to the rink and found our lockers. With so many guys in camp, we were using both locker rooms and I was interested to see if all the rookies or guys who had just come up the year before would be relegated to the smaller room. We were, but I was thrilled to see that there were a few veteran guys in the room with the rest of us, although Lars, Edvin, and I were stuck in the back corner where it was hard for all of us to get our gear on and get dressed at the same time. I didn't care. I was in the New York Rangers locker room. Brian Leetch was in our room, as was Brian Mullen and my Roseau buddy Paul Broten.

I remember shaking some more hands, introducing myself, and then giving it 100 percent of my focus to not just sit at my locker and stare at the other guys, and the Rangers uniforms hanging in front of us. It's just a locker room. It's just a uniform. They're just hockey players. That was my mantra. I'm not sure I was completely able to do that, but I did know that looking the part, acting like I belonged there and not seeming like a wide-eyed rube, was an important key to fitting in and not being intimidated.

I recall going out on the ice once we were all dressed, and having a meeting with the staff out there. I also remember thinking, "I'm so glad we had rookie camp here. At least the rink is familiar and I know my way around."

That first day we just did drills, and the first time my name was called to go out on the ice I was worried about skating. Seriously. It was like "what if I forgot how to skate?" when I jumped over the boards. Fortunately, I still remembered how it was done.

It was all a blur after that. I got out there a lot, and took a few hits from some of the biggest and strongest guys I'd ever played against, but I'm pretty sure I held my own and did some good things. As the day went on, my confidence came back and it was just hockey. Hockey with guys who were big and fast, but it was the same game. I knew I'd have to step it up to yet another level, but I felt I could do it. I felt like I belonged. That was a huge thing. I was in NHL preseason camp and I felt like I belonged. No one took it easy on me. I belonged.

We worked out for about a week, did some scrimmaging, and got in better game shape. I relished that last part. When we were doing down-and-backs it was my goal to lead the team on every lap. I felt it all coming back quickly. I belonged.

Finally, we had our first preseason game, against the New York Islanders on Long Island. I wasn't in the least bit nervous. I remember that clearly. We rode in two buses down next to what I guess was the East River, and I made sure to grab a window seat. I remember soaking it all in as we drove south, then over to the island somewhere near Queens. Then up the island to Uniondale and the Nassau Coliseum. I don't recall who I sat next to and don't think I said a word. I was in a different world, literally and in my mind.

Was it a thrill to meticulously get my gear on and get dressed in the visitors' locker room? Yes. I remember my heart racing a little. Was it crazy to jump out on the ice for warm-ups and skate just as fast as I could to get the nervousness out of me? Beyond yes. I was in a huge NHL arena, and the New York Islanders were skating around and taking shots at the other end of the ice. Pat LaFontaine and Brent Sutter were probably the two biggest names on that team. Just 10 years before they had won four straight Stanley Cups, but from what I'd heard and what I saw on the ice, they were a much different team by the time I got there. Still a strong NHL team, but nothing like that dynasty from '80 through '83.

I had a New York Rangers uniform on, with my name on the back. My number was 45. Funny that I still remember that? Not in the least. Wouldn't you remember every detail of something as important as that?

By the time warm-ups were over, I was just playing hockey again. The nerves were gone. The anticipation was huge. All I wanted to do was get out there and see what it was like.

I just watched and shuffled around on the bench as the veterans jumped over the boards and others came back to find a place to sit. In hockey, it seems like you're always moving left or right on the bench as guys come and go, but it's so ingrained in you since childhood you don't even notice. It just happens.

The veteran guys got a few shifts in, and as the first period was coming to a close an assistant coach tapped me on the shoulder and said, "Next shift, you're in for Moller."

Randy Moller was a longtime NHL defenseman. He'd played for many years with the Quebec Nordiques. I'd been paying attention to him in practice, because he had all the "stay at home" skills I craved. When he came scraping to a halt in front of the bench, I hopped over. I was on the ice. There was a game being played. It was all very real.

It's like it was yesterday. My head was on a swivel. My feet were constantly moving. I got into position and the Islanders had a big rush coming up the ice right at me. Their center and wingers were swerving in and out, and I just concentrated on the puck and their movement, while skating backward. They dumped the puck into the corner and I turned to race after it, getting there first. I suspected I was about to be creamed from behind, and I did take a good hit, but I kicked the puck out to my stick and carried it behind the goal. I spotted one of our forwards making a break for the other end and sauced him a pass. I put it right on his tape. He was off to the races with help on his right and fired a shot. Goal. An NHL goal. Preseason? Sure, but it was amazing to be a part of that. An assist on my first shift. What a deal to be in the celebration and get so many stick taps, hugs and "attaboy" shouts. What a deal. It was hard to believe it really happened. I'll never forget a moment of it.

We lost that game. I don't really dwell on that part, but it was an experience like nothing else I'd ever done. I played a few more shifts and didn't make any glaring mistakes. I took a few hits and survived, I pestered the hell out of any Islander who was near me, and I even delivered a few good checks. One was so good the Islander I smashed into the boards slashed me on the back of the leg with his stick once we separated, and for that he got a two-minute penalty. It was all good.

When we got back on the bus to head back to Rye, my head was still spinning. As it turned out, Randy Moller was sitting next to me, and all he said was, "You did great, man. Keep it up. You can play here."

I called everyone after that game. My family, Carol, Brooks and even the guys back at the house. Seemed like every conversation started with: "We played the Islanders tonight, and I got a few good shifts in. Got an assist on my first shift and even drew a slashing call on a guy I ran pretty good into the boards. It was incredible."

Practice went on. We played another couple of preseason games, with one being against the Bruins in Boston Garden. I try to never look like a small-town kid who is out of his element, but that was insane. The Boston Garden. So much history there, and even though it was an exhibition game, the place was packed to the rafters. I got a few shifts in and did OK, trying not to notice exactly where I was playing. It was impossible, though, to keep that out of my mind. For one thing, I'd heard that the Boston Garden ice surface was smaller than other rinks, and that was instantly noticeable when I hit the ice for the first time. It was nearly 10-feet shorter and a few feet narrower than NHL specs. It was really weird. Huge hockey players skating full speed with 10 fewer feet to cover heading to the other goal. And the crowd seemed to be right on top of us. And all those Bruins and Celtics banners hanging from the rafters. It was incredible. Just one more thing I'd never experienced before.

After that game, when we got back to Rye, Coach Neilson stopped me and said, "You're doing really well, Eric. I'm proud of you. You can play at this level. We just don't have room for you right now so we're going to go ahead and let you head up to Binghamton so you can play regular shifts and get that experience. That was the plan all along, but it was a hard decision to make because you've done everything we hoped to see. Lars, Edvin, and a couple of other guys are going too. Just be here in the morning to get your gear and we'll have a van waiting for you all. Thanks for everything you've done. We'll see you back here soon."

I thanked him as sincerely as I could. Just being able to suit up and play for the Rangers was the thrill of a lifetime.

The next morning, we gathered our stuff and loaded it all into a small trailer behind the van, which was one of those "vans for rent" things. Like an oversized taxi with half the charm, but there was room for all of us and our stuff. A day before I'd been on a luxury motorcoach with an NHL team. Now, I was in a creaky old van with vinyl seats, crammed in there with four other guys, heading to Binghamton, New York. American Hockey League, here we come!

It seemed like a long ride, but it was probably only a few hours. Maybe it was the thought of leaving the NHL team to head to the minors, or maybe it was the bone-jarring suspension on the van, but it seemed to take forever.

When we got there, we were surprised to see a very modern rink, called the Broome County Arena. Everything about it was first class, and it seated around 5,000. We hauled our stuff in and met head coach John Paddock, as well as the trainers and equipment guys. They got us situated in the locker room, and since we were players coming there from the Rangers, we actually got nice centrally located lockers. It was still morning, so none of the guys were there yet. There would be an afternoon practice in a few hours.

We signed a bunch of stuff, and met with the GM who gave us some tips on what part of town we should probably live in. The problem was, none of us had come up there with a car, so we weren't sure how we were going to get around. The team offered to put us up in a motel close to the arena for a week, though, so we had some time to sort that out.

Binghamton seemed OK as we arrived. We really didn't get to see too much, but it looked like a typical old town that was trying to reinvent itself. The arena was obviously a big part of that. It was right downtown and still surrounded by a bunch of closed businesses.

The first thing I did after we checked in was grab a schedule. I didn't even know what other teams were in the league. It was quite a slate of games. We'd play 80 in total, and the other teams were located as far north as Nova Scotia and New Brunswick, and as far south as Baltimore. There were teams in Massachusetts, Connecticut, Pennsylvania, Ontario, and four other teams in New York. I liked that the league was kind of geographically condensed, and there'd be new places to visit that I'd never been to before.

As soon as I looked at the schedule and saw who the other teams were, I started looking for any kind of homestand we might have. That was my shot at getting Carol out there for a few days. There were a couple I noticed right away. We'd be home for six days in mid-November and then for five days in late January. I was hoping she could come for that first one. Having her there would be a very good thing, even just for a few days.

Our coach seemed like a good guy. John had played a ton in the minors and got some time in the NHL as well. It was going to be his seventh season as a head coach in the AHL. He was pretty no-nonsense when we met, and his basic message to all of us was: "Do the work, stay with our system, and never quit." I was all for that.

Before we left, the GM gave us a list of some rental properties we could look at, and I saw a four-bedroom house on the list. We all agreed we wanted to see that first, but we still had no wheels. The GM said, "If you guys want to borrow my car for a few hours, you can go look at apartments and that house. Then you're going to have to figure something out in terms of a car."

We had to be back at the arena in just two hours, so we called the landlord of the house and asked if we could come by. It was an old place, but to me it felt just like our rental home at The U, and there would be plenty of room for all of us. If we split the rent it would only be about $100 a month for each guy. We signed on the dotted line immediately. As we drove back to the rink, Lars said, "Why don't we all go in together on a used car? Just an old one, you know? Maybe spend $100 apiece on it so no big deal."

Sounded like a plan to us. We'd do that the next morning.

Back at the rink, the guys were showing up and it seemed like a really interesting mix. Definitely some older guys, who maybe had been up and down with NHL clubs a few times, and some younger guys, too. A couple of them looked like babies to me.

We got dressed and hit the ice. Coach walked us through our training plan, diagrammed some offensive and defensive schemes on the glass, and we got to work. The defensive stuff was right up my alley. I felt confident about it.

It went well, just doing drills and a lot of skating that day. I felt like I was in good shape and ready to go. I didn't feel intimidated at all, and I think that was because I'd literally woken up that day back in Rye at the Rangers' camp. I knew immediately that I could play in the AHL. It might be rough, and I might take a beating, but I could play there.

I called Carol and my parents from the motel that night, collect again, of course, and filled them in on everything. I hadn't even had the chance to give them anything in the way of details after I learned I was being sent down, but I'd prepared them for that so they weren't surprised. The first question everyone asked was: "How's Binghamton? What's it like?" My answers were, "It looks OK. The arena is actually really nice, but we haven't seen much of the town yet. Five of us did sign a lease on a house, though. It's furnished and it's pretty good. Now we have to find a car."

There were a couple of used-car lots within a block of the motel, so early that next morning we walked down to see what we could afford. Not much, but we did find an old Ford Fairmont, maybe 13 or 14 years old with 100,000 miles on it. We took it for a drive and it ran fine. The brakes were a little iffy, but it was solid inside and out. There was just barely enough room for all five of us, but the sticker in the window said $995 and that sounded good. I don't think Lars had any clue what a decent used car would cost, but $200 from each guy didn't seem too painful. We'd all pooled some cash and thought we could go as high as $1,000 so we offered the guy $900, on the spot. He came back at $950, saying, "You guys are professional hockey players, you can afford more than this." I told him we were all rookies and let him know what our contracts paid us, then I said, "Meet us in the middle. $925 cash money right now." Just like that, we had a car! And if any of us got sent up, sent down, or sent home, it wasn't going to be a huge financial loss.

Practices went fine for a couple more weeks, and we were getting to know each other, both on and off the ice. The "on the ice" part was critical. You have to know the tendencies of the guys, especially the wingers and centers. How fast do they skate? Where do they like the puck? Will they come back and help on D or are we all alone back there? We were jelling as a team.

Our uniforms were very similar to what New York wore, with a few touches that were different. We had a Binghamton logo of some sort on one sleeve and an AHL logo on the other, but the same color scheme as New York. White home jerseys, blue on the road, and red breezers. Also a very similar RANGERS in block print, on a downward diagonal on the front, and our names and numbers on the back. It was neat to see that stuff hanging in my locker.

We got settled in the house, with Edvin and Lars sharing one room so that the other three of us each had our own. The other two guys were Guy Larose from Hull, Quebec, and Daniel Lacroix from Montreal. They both spoke heavily accented English and mostly talked to each other in French. There are a lot of French Canadian hockey players, so I actually looked forward to seeing if I could absorb any of the language.

My bed might have been the least comfortable thing I'd ever tried to sleep on, and I remember thinking, "Once I get a few paychecks under my belt I'm going to have to buy a new mattress. I'll be in traction if I keep sleeping on this thing." We also got a phone put in and all got checking accounts at the same bank. All the better for pooling our money for groceries, beer and rent.

Once the phone was in I excitedly called Carol. My first words were something like, "Hey, we have a phone and I'm paying for this call!" I told her the dates of that first, mid-November homestand, and she was really happy to hear that. She could come in on an off day, see us play two home games, and then head back home. She'd be there for five days with me. That sounded like heaven.

Her first question was: "How do I get there?"

I wasn't sure, but I promised I'd figure it out. As it turned out, she could fly from Minneapolis to Syracuse, and then take a little commuter plane down to Binghamton. If she took an early morning flight out of Minneapolis, and came in on that off day, I could pick her up before we practiced or skated. It was great to know I had that to look forward to.

We opened the season on the road in Hershey, Pennsylvania. The team there had one of the greatest nicknames in sports. They were the Hershey Bears. Cracked me up. When the bus got there, you could easily sense what was the biggest business in town. The street lights were shaped like Hershey Kisses, and when we got out of the bus we could smell chocolate.

We lost that night, in front of a packed crowd in Hershey, but we played well. We had to get right on the bus after the game to get back home, where we'd have our opener the next night. It was a quick way to get a feel for what kind of bus league it was and how many short turnarounds we'd have. The next night, we won our home opener against a team called the Capital District Islanders, based in Troy, New York. They were the New York Islanders AHL affiliate, and I'm sure I was playing against a few guys who were in camp with them when we went up to Long Island for our first NHL preseason game. We won 8-1 and I picked up an assist. I remember not even thinking about the crowd. I knew they were there, but I never really paid attention. According to the box score, the attendance was 3,193. That seems a bit light for your first home game, but as the season wore on it picked up a bit and a little over 4,000 ended up being pretty average for us. I think we got close to selling it out a few times, and the fans were great. As I remember, the biggest home crowd we played in front of all year was about 4,800 and the biggest crowd on the road had to have been around 7,500 in Springfield, Massachusetts, right near the end of the season. I do recall one really snowy night up in Newmarket, Ontario, when they announced the crowd at around 1,000. I don't think there were 100 people there. We could hear them talking behind us.

After our opener, I remember going on a road trip to eastern Canada. Looking at the schedule, I see we played four games in five nights against Halifax, Moncton, and Cape Breton.

We were pretty good, and we were getting better by the game. I was dialed in and feeling good about how I was playing. I'll admit I was also thinking about November 15, when Carol was going to arrive.

By the time she got there, we'd already played 17 games and it seemed like I'd been on the team forever. We all got along great, no attitudes at all, and even the games we lost were solid efforts.

On November 15 Carol got in around noon, and the hug and kiss we shared at the little Binghamton airport were ones for the ages. We were so busy playing and practicing I hadn't really had time to stew over missing her, but the second she walked down the stairs from that little airplane I knew how much I had.

She looked gorgeous. She was the prettiest girl in the world. And I was the luckiest guy.

She wasn't horrified by the rental house, so that was good. And by then I had been paid and did spend some money on a new mattress and new sheets. As she said, "This is way better than your rental house on campus. You guys are doing OK here."

She got to see me play in two games, on back-to-back nights, and even though it was November it wasn't overly cold or snowy yet, so when I had to go to the rink for a morning skate she walked around town just to check it out. My roomies loved her and she thought they were pretty neat guys, too.

It was really sad when her short visit ended. I remember thinking that maybe I shouldn't have invited her. I was kind of all focused on hockey before she got there and as she got back on her plane I was really crushed. She was crying. I wasn't, but it was close. Man, I loved that girl.

Starting the next day, it all spun back up to full speed. It was nonstop. Home games followed by bus rides, followed by road games and more bus rides. Generally we played four games a week, and some of the bus rides were long. It was easy to run yourself into the ground.

As the long, cold, snowy winter settled in, it just became a marathon that seemed to never end. From the day Carol left, on November 18, until the end of the regular season on March 31, we'd play 61 more games.

Was it rough? Sure. There were some goons in the league, and guys trying to literally "fight their way to the NHL". I was not a fighter. I think I dropped the gloves twice all year and barely held my own.

The checks were hard and sometimes could be vicious. The slashes, even the ones they got away with, were painful. Blocking shots was a necessity, and I'd try to keep the puck in front of me any way I could.

The older guys in the league had a ton of experience, but they didn't scare me. They were a step slow by that time in their careers. The guys that scared me were the young wingers and centers. Some of those guys could absolutely fly, and I'd never seen stick-handling like that.

About halfway through the season, I remember a local reporter asked me what I thought it was like, compared to college. I said: "When I first got here, I didn't think it was even as good as the hockey we played at Minnesota, but now that we've been around the league it's pretty obvious this is a new level. I've caught myself getting beat too often, and that hardly ever happened in college. I'm getting up to speed now. It's like the game is finally slowing down and I feel a lot better about it, but this is a tough league in every way. The schedule is tough, the travel is tough, and the other teams are tough. Definitely a new level."

We ended up 44-30-6, so we were pretty good. We went two rounds in the playoffs before we were eliminated. I know I held my own. I wasn't the best defenseman in the league, and might not have been the best one on our team, but I handled it all pretty well. I could sense the rest of the guys had confidence in me, and that meant a lot.

At the time, I wasn't really aware of who our best players were or how far they'd go. One of my fellow defensemen was Peter Laviolette, who had already been up with the Rangers before I played with him in Binghamton. He was good, but never stuck very long in the NHL as a player. Instead, he became one of the best coaches in the league. He was the head coach of the Carolina Hurricanes, New York Islanders, Nashville Predators, Philadelphia Flyers, and as I'm writing this he's the head coach of the Washington Capitals. He led the Hurricanes to a Stanley Cup championship in 2006.

Tie Domi was with us in Binghamton, too. Unlike me, he was definitely a fighter. He was our chief protector and would drop the gloves if you looked at him funny. One super tough guy, but a great teammate. He'd end up playing 16 years in the NHL, with the Rangers, Winnipeg Jets, and then a long time with the Toronto Maple Leafs.

My buddy Paul Broten even spent about eight games with us in Binghamton. I have no memory if that was just a demotion to get him back on track or a rehab assignment. I remember he looked really good playing for us, and then he was back in New York. He eventually played seven years in the NHL.

It was a great experience. I learned a ton about how the game has to be played at that level. I learned how to take care of myself even better than I had before. It was exhausting. It was a full winter of nicks and bruises and pain, but I never missed a game. You always wake up the next day and think you're broken all over, but you keep going.

I played in all 80 regular season games and all 10 playoff games. I somehow scored six goals and helped out with 18 assists. I have no idea how many shots I blocked but I'll have the scars from a number of them for the rest of my life.

Hockey is a tough sport. All the way around. And I'd just gone through seven nonstop months playing professionally, one step away from the New York Rangers.

When we were eliminated, we had exit interviews on our last day at the rink. Coach Paddock was as "to the point" as he always was, but he told me something like, "I don't think you'll be back here next year. You can play in the NHL. Let's put it this way, I like you a lot and you're a great teammate in the room, and I'd love to have you back on this team, but I hope I don't see you next season. Get some rest, and then get after it. You can do it."

We shook hands and I tried to be funny. I said, "Well, then I hope I don't see you either! I'm just kidding. I've enjoyed every day of this, and you're a heck of a coach. Thanks for everything."

And yes, we sold the car. For $500. Basically we rented a beat-up old Ford Fairmont for seven months and it only cost us a combined $425, and that was split up between five guys. Can't beat that!

I think I went home with about $3,000 after all the rent, food, taxes and other expenses. It was more than I'd ever had in my life, but I had something I wanted to spend at least part of it on. I needed to buy a diamond ring.

I couldn't wait to get back to Minnesota. I couldn't wait to get back to Carol.

CHAPTER 31

Brooks Bennett

I got really lucky with the weather when it was time to head down to Florida. It was early March, and I'd already learned that March is one of the snowiest months in Minnesota, in terms of total inches. That's because it's starting to warm up a little. When it's 5 degrees and snowing, it comes down as fluffy white powder. When it's 29 or 30, it comes down wet, heavy, and thick. Getting a foot of snow in one day is not rare for March, or even for April. Those are the blizzard months.

On the day I left, with my little Corolla stuffed to the roof, it was 22 degrees and sunny. I remember that, because I took it as a good omen.

I've always been a map nerd. As a kid, my dad got me into geography and we'd scour maps of different countries, and then look them up in the encyclopedia to see pictures of what they really looked like. He even went to a thrift store and bought an old globe for a couple bucks. We'd spin that thing and then do the research together.

My love of maps really came in handy when we drove from Anaheim to Mayo Clinic and I was the navigator. I had an atlas and a bunch of folded state maps with me, sitting up there in the front passenger seat of the VW. Part of that was to make sure Dad didn't get lost, but more than that I just liked knowing where we were and following our progress from town to town.

In my mind, things were more fun before GPS, although I had some friends who actually couldn't read maps. They somehow didn't have the ability to see the route from above and maps looked like a bowl of spaghetti to them. They could only see the world horizontally. Ask them for directions and they'd say, "Go down the road to the McDonald's and turn left." They couldn't have told you if left was north, south, east or west. I saw everything from above, just like looking at a map. I still geek out on it. A good map is rad. The whole world is on there!

My plan was to drive to St. Louis the first day and find a hotel somewhere beyond the city so I wouldn't have to fight traffic the next morning. On Day 2, I was aiming for somewhere south of Atlanta, maybe even Valdosta if I felt like going that far. On Day 3

I'd make it all the way to Port Charlotte. I'd be there two days early, before the official opening of camp, because I wanted to be able to recharge a little and not be road weary on my first day down there. It was a big trip, and way farther than I'd ever driven by myself, but there was a huge prize at the end of it. Spring training in Port Charlotte at the Rangers' complex.

The big league guys were already there. They report at various times through February and a lot of them show up early just to get to the warm weather. I'd scanned the Rangers' roster, and man, it was totally stacked. They had some serious horses on that club. In the field, they had guys like Julio Franco, Juan Gonzales, Rafael Palmeiro, Gary Pettis and Ruben Sierra. On the mound they had Kevin Brown, Kenny Rogers, Calvin Schiraldi, Bobby Witt and the one and only Nolan Ryan.

They would be practicing and playing preseason games over in the spring training stadium. We'd be on the complex out beyond the outfield. I knew that because the Rangers had sent me a map! See. Maps are important. Before I ever got there, I knew where to park, where the office was, and how to get to the minor league clubhouse. Maps, baby!

Anyway, I had no idea if I'd ever see any of those big league guys, much less get to meet them. As rad as it would be, if I ever ran across Nolan Ryan I'd probably be totally tongue-tied. It's likely I'd just say hi and keep walking. It sure would be cool, though, to tell him about my dad taking me to Dodger Stadium and having me focus just on Nolan's delivery, trying to guess the pitches. They all looked exactly the same to me. His release point and delivery never changed. That's one of the reasons he's Nolan Ryan. That was one of the most important learning experiences of my baseball life.

As I pulled out of the Twin Cities I knew there was no direct interstate between the Twin Cities and St. Louis, so I had my road atlas out and had to beat my way down a bunch of state or federal highways passing through a bunch of little towns. I got there earlier than I thought I would though, so I kept going. At St. Louis, I'd have to cross over into Illinois, and when I approached downtown I saw the Gateway Arch for the first time and about wrecked my car staring at it. I'd never seen anything like that, and I remember thinking, "I'm in a hurry now, and need to keep going, but at the end of the season, I might have to stop and go see that up close."

I drove across the Mississippi River and I was pretty mesmerized by that as well. It sure as hell didn't look like the same pretty Mississippi that flows by downtown Minneapolis, right by campus. In St. Louis, it's wide, it's muddy, and it was flowing like crazy with big barges going both ways. This was turning into quite a little tourist trip.

Somewhere east of St. Louis I decided to stop for the night. I saw a Days Inn right off the interstate and got a room there. It was the first time I'd used the new MasterCard and that was a big-boy deal. Money in the bank, a card in my wallet, and checking into a motel by myself. I doubt I paid more than $25 for that room, but I felt like a big spender.

The next morning I got back on I-64 heading east, until I caught I-57 and took that south for a while. Then I went southeast on I-24, which would take me down to Nashville. About an hour or so south of Nashville, I hit a spot I'd seen on the map and read about in an encyclopedia. It was Monteagle, and for Tennessee it's a totally steep and seriously big mountain. A little scary actually. Once you're past there you're in Chattanooga, and that's where I would pick up I-75, which would take me all the way to Port Charlotte.

I spent that second night just past Atlanta in another Days Inn. There were nicer hotels around, but my Bennett upbringing wouldn't let me blow extra money for a few hours of sleep. My Bennett mindset wouldn't even allow me to buy a nicer or bigger car for this trip. Why should I? The Corolla ran great and never let me down.

The third day was another marathon. I was getting pretty worn out by the trip, and my butt hurt a little. But, I was stoked to get down to camp. Port Charlotte is just north of Fort Myers, pretty far down the Gulf Coast. I expected to get there at night, so I'd have to find another roadside motel for one more sleep because the team office wouldn't be open. They had dorms for the minor leaguers and, starting the next day, I'd stay there. This whole adventure would have been amazing if it was just a vacation, but with it taking me to spring training it was a thousand times more special. It was close to midnight when I hit Port Charlotte and started looking for a motel. The Days Inn was sold out. Foiled! They recommended a Holiday Inn just a few blocks away. Probably twice the cost of the Days Inn, but I didn't have much choice. It was late, I was exhausted, and I needed a room. I also needed a good night's sleep. I'd be checking in at camp the next day.

I surprised myself by sleeping in until mid-morning. I took a shower, got my stuff together, checked out of the Holiday Inn, and headed for the complex. It was only about 15 minutes away. I drove straight to the team office, using that valuable map the team had sent. I went inside, got my ID card, my room assignment, and an itinerary for the first day of camp. The woman who checked me in said a new itinerary would be posted in the players' residence hall and in the clubhouse every morning, so I should always check that before I did anything else. Then she said, "Welcome to spring training, Brooks!"

You know those little moments that would otherwise seem like nothing? Yeah, that was one of those. To hear the words "Welcome to spring training" gave me goosebumps. I think I just giggled and said, "Thank you." Stoked doesn't come close to describing the feeling

I parked my car, then took my suitcase and duffel bag out of the trunk and backseat. I could hear the crack of the bat over in the stadium as the big leaguers took BP. I went in to find my room. My roomie hadn't checked in yet, so I put as much of my stuff away as I could and took the bed by the window, which I staked my claim to by putting my shaving kit and personal items on the bed.d. I wasn't sure who my roomie was going to be but I guessed his last name might start with a B. No easier way to arrange roommates than alphabetically, right? It turned out I was totally right. He showed up about 30 minutes later and his name was Travis Buckley, he was a pitcher and it just so happened that we had played together for a while in Gastonia, before he got promoted to Port Charlotte. We got along fine in Gastonia, but we never really hung out together or got to know each other all that well. This was his second spring training after being drafted out of a community college in Kansas City. It would be good to have him there to show me around. Good guy. Good midwestern downhome dude. And a good pitcher. I was stoked at my luck to land with such a good roomie strictly because our last names were similar.

We then grabbed our duffel bags and walked over to the minor league clubhouse. It was huge, because it had to hold full rosters for the entire minor league system. I walked in and was greeted by a guy who asked to see my ID, and then walked me to my locker. My name was already written on athletic tape at the top. A uniform was hanging on the bar inside it. Travis had a locker right next to mine.

We put our gear away, and decided to go for a jog around the complex just to shake the road trip off. We weren't sure we were allowed to do that, being a day early, but we asked one of the equipment guys and he said, "Yeah, guys. You got the run of the place. Have at it."

After the jog, we went back to our lockers and the big room was noticeably more crowded. It sure looked like a lot of guys were getting in a day early. And that doesn't even count a bunch of Triple-A and Double-A guys who were trying to make the team over at the stadium. Most of them would be coming back in the next couple weeks. It was exciting, a bit scary, and mind-boggling all at the same time. And it was still only about 1 in the afternoon. Travis said, "Hey, let me take you to the beach. We might only have this one time to enjoy it before camp gets rolling."

We went to Manasota Key, a tiny sliver of an island right on the Gulf of Mexico. I'd never dipped a toe in the Gulf, so that was my first mission. I could not believe how warm and calm the water was. Nothing like either ocean I'd ever been in. No jolt of cold as you step in. No waves at all unless you call a lazy four-inch break a wave. We just walked in the water, talking about our backgrounds and families, and sat in the sand for a while, soaking it in. He was like most people, in that he couldn't believe the stories about my parents, surfing, and the move to Minnesota. "Bizarre, man," he said. "I lived near Kansas City my whole life, and still live there. That's all I know."

We had our first dinner in the dining hall that night, pushing our trays through the buffet line. It wasn't anything to rave about but it was way better than fast food. We actually had a salad bar, and vegetables that may or may not have come out of a can.

After that, Travis and I went back to the dorm and hung out in the lounge on our floor, and I got to meet a bunch of guys. All the dudes in minor league camp were showing up and we'd all be living there for about a month. At least the guys who didn't get released would be. I wasn't worried about that. The Rangers had a lot of money invested in me, and I'd pitched well my rookie year. I just wanted to get acclimated and feel like I belonged there. By the time we went to our room to relax before going to sleep I felt like I'd been there forever. It's crazy how that works. Time is fluid. It doesn't always pass at the same rate, right?

In the morning, after breakfast, we headed over to the clubhouse around 7. You know me, I hate feeling rushed or worried that I might be late for something. That day

285

was the official reporting date, so no real workouts but a bunch of detailed stuff to take care of. The team started handing out some workout clothes, and that was cool. Blue shorts and matching blue T-shirts with the Rangers logo on the front. Travis and I put that stuff on and went out on the complex to do some running and play a little light catch. It was a long day, but nothing really happened other than the fact the clubhouse became totally packed. I shook hands a million times and tried to remember names, but failed a lot at that. The good news was we all had our last names at the top of our lockers, so that helped.

Seemed like we just hung out and met the coaches and managers all day. We did have meetings with the trainers, too, and they asked us if we had any issues or were getting over any injuries or strains. I had none of that, despite all the innings I'd thrown the year before. We finally changed back into our regular clothes and went back to the room to wait for dinner. I didn't think the next day would ever come. I didn't sleep nearly as well that night.

I know we were up at 6 the next morning, heading over for breakfast. We were at our lockers by 6:45 and had to be on the field at 8.

My uni fit great. We wore the same style the big club had worn the year before. Gray uniforms, with a block print "TEXAS" arched across the front. We had dark blue socks and belts. They looked nice. They looked big league. I checked the mirror. Yeah, I looked bitchin'.

I wandered around the clubhouse for a bit, and saw lists of all the minor league rosters stapled to a bulletin board. My buddy Dan Smith, from our time together in Butte, was on the Triple-A roster, which was Oklahoma City. He wasn't with us in the minor league camp though. He was over in the big league camp trying to make the team. If he didn't, he'd be going to Oklahoma City to play.

I also saw lists of all the leagues the Rangers' clubs would play in. Our Florida State League layout looked pretty crazy. We were in the West Division, but kind of sitting down there in Port Charlotte by ourselves. Clearwater, Sarasota, Dunedin, and St. Petersburg made up the rest of our division, but they were all bunched up near the Tampa Bay area.

The East Division had Vero Beach, Port St. Lucie, West Palm Beach, Miami, and Fort Lauderdale, so they were all on the other side of the state on the Atlantic Coast.

The Central Division was Lakeland, Osceola (which was really Kissimmee), Baseball City (I had no clue where that was or what it was) and Winter Haven. I knew where all those towns were, except for Baseball City, thanks to the fact I practically memorized the map of Florida before it was time to get to Port Charlotte. I wasn't sure, at all, how the schedule would work, but it was totally obvious that we'd be on the bus a lot for road games. Like, a *LOT!*

I asked Travis about Baseball City and he said, "That's where the Royals are. It's out in the middle of nowhere on I-4 between Lakeland and Orlando. They built it as an amusement park with a Spring Training and Florida State League stadium as part of it."

"What's that like?" I asked.

"It's ridiculous," he said. "The amusement park isn't very big; it's too close to Disney to draw anyone, and I-4 is always a mess. Basically it's a ghost town. And for our games, they don't draw flies. There's really no town there."

We finally hit the fields and all sat on the grass. The whole camp in one spot. Our manager, Bob Molinaro, and the Tulsa manager, Tommy Thompson, gave us a nice introduction talk. We'd be doing drills, the position players would be taking BP and practicing their fielding, and the pitchers would have a highly structured throwing program, increasing the number of pitches and the velocity every day. Tommy Thompson added, "And I sure hope you pitchers were following the program we sent you during the winter. If you didn't, you have to tell us. Don't lie about it and end up blowing out an elbow or shoulder trying to keep up. We'll slow you down to let you get in shape. Just let us know if that's you, otherwise we'll assume everyone followed the program and is ready to throw these bullpen sessions starting today."

We did about an hour of stretching, ran some lazy wind sprints, and then the coaches split us all up into our teams and we each went to different fields. Before our first bullpens, we did something we'd rarely done as Gophers and never did in Butte and Gastonia. I quickly learned from the grumbling that it was the least favorite drill in camp for about all the other pitchers. It's called Pitchers Fielding Practice, and everyone just called it PFP.

The pitchers line up next to the mound and take turns, pretending to throw a pitch without a ball. A coach then hits a soft ground ball right up the middle, and you field it and lob it to first, and then you go back to the end of the line. Then, it's the same thing but the coach hits it to a first-baseman. As soon as it's hit you're supposed to run to the base to take the throw. Some guys, like me, ran hard. Most jogged. The theory was you're supposed to work on getting to the base safely and be under control to take the throw from the first baseman. You don't run straight to the base, because if you did you'd cross the base into foul territory when you arrived, totally inviting a nasty collision with the runner. You instead had to run to a point on the foul line about 10 feet from the bag, where you would turn to follow the foul line to the base, running in the same direction as any runner would be. In real games, those runners would be right on your heels, wearing spikes, trying to beat you to the base at any cost. I thought it was valuable practice. Most guys were just bitching and moaning.

And the weather. It was freaking perfect, and I was beyond jazzed to be outside in 80-degree temps under a clear, deep-blue sky with a few puffy white clouds that looked like my mom had painted them, and with palm trees swaying in the breeze. Minnesota seemed like another planet. They did get on us a bit about not getting sunburned, so most of us put that white cream on our noses. Is that stuff called Zinc Oxide? That's what I remember. We were out there sweating and running and feeling like ballplayers. A year earlier, I was still working out indoors and shivering while getting to practice.

I asked Travis if it was always that nice and he said, "Usually, but if we do get some rain it tends to stick around for a few days. We lost something like four straight days of workouts last spring. All we could do was lift weights and stretch. It put everybody behind."

When it was time for my first bullpen session, I got paired up with a catcher I hadn't met yet so I told him what I threw and what I was trying to do in that first session. I wasn't going to air it out. I just wanted to work on my release point, my balance, and pitch location. Just like real estate, it would be all about location, location, location. It was the first time I'd thrown off a real mound, and real dirt, since September. It went great, with a couple of pitching coaches standing right behind me. Everybody was really nice after my 15 minutes were up. It felt awesome to be back on the mound. Stoked would summarize my feelings pretty well. That's putting it lightly.

After that first day, I finally got around to calling my parents. I'd warned them that I would probably wait until I was settled in before calling, collect again, so they shouldn't worry about me. There were some pay phones in the dorm, and I only had to wait in line for a few minutes to use one. I called my folks, and brought them up to speed. My dad said goodbye, saying, "Be careful down there, man. I can't even tell you how proud I am of you. We love you!"

Then, since no guys were behind me waiting for the phone, I called Eric. The first thing I did was apologize for calling collect and I promised that once the season started and I was in an apartment I'd get a phone and pick up the charges. I told him all about the trip, and the layout of the complex. He was totally interested in details like that, and our uniforms, and the clubhouse. He just kept asking questions, and that was very cool. Unlike his first camp, I never saw the big league guys, but I could hear them over there in the stadium. It sounded like he was having a good year at Binghamton, and that didn't surprise me. The dude was going to be a star.

Things fell into a real rhythm by the second day. It was like we'd all been there forever. Get up early, have breakfast, go to the clubhouse, get dressed, and be ready to stretch at 8. After a few days of just doing drills, they set up the first practice games where we'd play another one of the teams in camp. We played the Gastonia team first, and I got to pitch an inning. One, two, three, mostly mixing in the offspeed stuff.

I don't really remember how long we did that, but it seemed like just a few days later when we had a 1 o'clock game on the itinerary. After we ate lunch we went back out to the field and saw a bus pull up. Guys dressed in Phillies uniforms got off and came over to join us. We had real opponents that day! I didn't pitch in that game, and I really don't remember anything about it other than it was bitchin' to be playing a real game against guys in different uniforms. It was starting to feel a lot like baseball.

Over the next few weeks, when we'd have home games, we'd stretch in the morning, take some extended BP, then the guys would take infield practice. I pitched about every five days. If we were the road team, it was all different. We'd get dressed, jog a little, and then get on the bus by 9:30. All of the other teams in our division were pretty far away, and the bus driver couldn't count on smooth sailing in terms of traffic on I-75. We'd rather be early than late for a game. We'd get to wherever we were headed, have a boxed lunch if we wanted it, then do our stretching and loosening up. Believe me, by the third or fourth road game, the thrill of it was wearing off and it became pretty obvious that the bus rides were going to suck. But we were wearing Texas Rangers uniforms. We were pros. We just happened to have a home park that was a long way from the other teams in the division.

One day, word spread around that some reps from Wilson, Rawlings, Nike, Converse, Louisville Slugger, Adirondack and some other companies would be in camp during our lunch break. The staff told us, very bluntly, to leave them alone. They already had a list of players they wanted to talk to. I wasn't really thinking about it, and I was just minding my own business at my locker when I heard my name being spoken. I looked up and a guy put out his hand and said he was from Nike. He asked if I'd be interested in signing a shoe deal with them. I'd get three pairs of spikes per season, and they'd throw in a couple of pairs of sneakers as well. Can't be under contract to Nike and show up at the park wearing Pumas, right? And, if I got to the big leagues they'd control my rights for a year but we'd renegotiate the terms. I'd been wearing Nikes anyway, but I bought them at a sporting goods store. I shook his hand, signed my name, and said thank you. A few minutes later he came back with a pair of blue spikes in my size. That was, as I might say, totally rad. He also gave me his card and left a catalog so I could pick out some sneakers, and then he winked and said, "If you want some apparel, I have a budget for that, too. Get a few golf shirts, some shorts, whatever you want."

By the time the Nike guy left, another guy approached me. He was from Wilson, the company that made the totally legendary A2000 glove. I had pretty much always used Rawlings gloves, but the Rawlings guy walked right by me and the A2000 was very popular, from college all the way to the big leagues. The Wilson guy told me they really wanted me to use one for my whole career. It was pretty much the same deal as the shoes. Three gloves per season and then we'd do a better deal if I made it to the big leagues. He'd also throw in some big league baseball undershirts, the white shirts with colored sleeves (we basically just called them "sleeves" instead of shirts) in the correct color blue for the Rangers. After I signed the deal, he pulled a brand new A2000 and three undershirts out of his bag and handed them to me. The glove needed to be broken in before I could use it in a game but I promised I'd work on that as fast as I could, starting that afternoon. My head was spinning, but the one thing I'll never forget is the look on Travis' face, and on all the faces of the guys who had lockers near me. It was different. They were kind of wide-eyed. None of them had gotten anything. They didn't get approached at all. They'd be spending at least another year buying their own stuff. It hit me then that what just happened was totally unexpected but it was really a special deal. Travis just said, "Damn dude. You scored!" All I said was: "I guess so, right?"

A week or two before the end of camp, the clubhouse started to thin out. Guys were getting the message to see the manager, and they'd typically come out of that meeting all sweaty and red in the face. Dreams were dying right in front of me. I felt so bad for those dudes. All they wanted to do was play ball, just like me. It's what they wanted to do their entire lives, and they were told it wasn't going to happen. I hated it. It was a fact of life, and the club had to release 20 or 30 guys before the end of camp, but I still hated seeing it.

A couple of days before the end of camp the Cardinals' St. Pete club came down to play us. Our skipper told me I'd start, and he wanted me to throw at least 60 pitches. I'd started mixing in the fastball a lot by then, going with my regular strategy. I'd show them the heat, then buckle their knees with a curve or a change. I made it through five innings and struck out a bunch of Red Birds.

After the game, Skip told me, "I had this set up. You're going to pitch our opener when the real season starts. Get some side work in and do your running. You had a helluva spring, Brooksie. I'm not sure I've managed a guy who got through a full spring without allowing an earned run."

I did a double take, shook my head, and said, "I didn't give up an earned run? Are you sure?"

"Hell, yes I'm sure," he said. "We kicked a few balls around behind you, so those were unearned. You finished Spring Training with a 0.00 ERA, dude."

That, for sure, didn't seem real. I wasn't keeping my own stats, and I hadn't been focused on that. I was just trying to get ready for the season and get better every single outing. Crazy.

Finally, we had our last day and our last preseason game. Thankfully it was at home. After the game, our skipper called us all together and gave us the lowdown. Our season didn't start for three more days. The first thing we'd do is relocate all our stuff over to the stadium the next morning. That would be our home for the season. We'd get our real uniforms, and get acclimated to a big league facility. Then, we'd have the rest of the day off to cruise around town and hopefully find places to live. Travis and I decided we'd scour the newspaper to see how many "For Rent" properties we could see. If we found one that had enough room for another guy or two, we'd do that. If not, we'd just have to buck up and pay the rent ourselves.

It was also the final day of cuts. That sucked way worse than what had been going on for the last couple weeks. These guys had made it through the entire camp to the last day, and during our lunch break they got the axe. It's a wonderful game. I love it. I live for it. But it's a business, not a charity. They have to run it like a business and I assumed it would happen to me someday. Very few guys get the chance to end it on their own terms. Most have to be told to go home.

I could tell Travis was nervous. He shouldn't have been. I'd seen him pitch enough to know he was a damn good pitcher. When the final cuts were made, and no one came to tell him to see our skipper, he about melted into his locker. I patted him on the leg and said, "There was never a chance, dude. You're going to pitch for a long time." He just shook his head.

The next morning, we moved our stuff over to the stadium and most of us stood in the middle of the clubhouse just staring at it. It was Major League in every way. I mean, seriously, the big league guys had just left a few days earlier to start the season. It was built for them. Our names were on our lockers which, by the way, were huge. We had an actual equipment manager and he had all the uniforms stacked in the training room. We went through there one by one and picked out our home and away unis, our stirrup socks, BP jerseys, and hats. Most guys were flipping through the jerseys trying to find a number they liked but Gus, our equipment guy, stopped me and said, "We've got all your stuff ready. You're going to be wearing number 34, Brooksie."

Trust me, it was not lost on me that 34 was Nolan Ryan's number. All I could say was, "Bitchin'. That's awesome. Thanks, dude. I mean, Gus. Thanks."

After we got everything put away in our lockers, one of the front office people came in and handed us each a sheet of paper to fill out, so they could publish a game program. We listed our number, where we were from, where we were born, where we went to school, and any other fun stuff we could think up. I wrote a few sentences about being from SoCal and growing up surfing. We'd do headshot photos the next day, before our first workout.

After that, Travis and I got in my car and took off on an apartment hunting expedition. We stopped at a convenience store and bought a newspaper, then went straight to the want-ads. Guess what? We had a map. We'd need that because none of the street names in the ads meant a thing to us. We wanted to be near the ballpark, so we were looking on the west and northwest side of town. We circled a few that looked promising, especially the ones that came furnished, and went to the pay phone out front to make some calls to see what we could visit.

The first one was an upstairs apartment with two bedrooms. It was totally furnished and came with cable TV. The rent was $325 a month. We drove straight there, and the location was excellent. It was a two-story cinder block building with eight units. I think we were ready to sign a lease before we ever went inside. It was clean, bright, had a nice kitchen, and the furniture was outstanding. We weren't there 10 minutes when we both said to the landlord, "We'll take it."

We signed the lease, and I wrote him a check for the first month and the deposit. Travis had conveniently left his checkbook back in our room. We could move in the next day. Mission accomplished.

We then called the local phone company and put in an order for one desk phone. We'd put it in the living room.

With all that done, it was time to play baseball. Our opener was in two days, and number 34 would be starting on the mound.

The next day was going to be our last one without a game for a long time. We had a 132-game schedule and probably had no more than four days off the whole season. So, we had a bit of a different approach that day.

We had a morning round of BP in the stadium, and got some running in. Then, by about 10 they let us go. A lot of guys hadn't found places to live yet, so they'd have one last chance to do that. Travis and I would be using the time to get moved in at our new apartment.

Then, we all had to be back at the ballpark by 6 that night. We'd take another round of BP and a bunch of fielding practice under the lights. Every workout and every game we had played for the last month had been in the middle of the afternoon, so they wanted to let us acclimate to the lights a little before we opened the season under them the next day. I thought it was valuable. The stadium lights are great, but it's different. It would've been tough to do that for the first time the next night. I know a few outfielders I talked to said it was a really smart thing to do. It was totally different picking up the ball and tracking it. By the end of the workout, it all seemed a lot more normal.

The next day, Travis and I slept in a little. That had become my routine in Butte and Gastonia. In school, you usually didn't have that option. Lots of morning classes to leave my afternoons free.

We just relaxed, had a nice lunch at a deli we'd found not too far from the apartment, and then sat around the apartment for a couple of hours before heading to the park. I loved getting there early. Actually, if I wasn't the first one to the ballpark it made me nervous, for some reason. We were the first ones there.

I bet I took a good hour getting dressed, doing one particular part of the uniform at a time and then sitting around in my underwear for a while before moving on to the next piece of the puzzle. It all had to be perfect. It was a big part of the game I'd loved since I was a kid. It's a process. It's a totally rad process most people can't appreciate.

As the rest of the guys got there the clubhouse filled with energy. They all went out for BP and I finished getting dressed. It was time to "run some poles" like I'd been doing since high school.

After that, a little rub-down on my shoulder, bicep, and neck from one of the trainers. At around 6:15 I got my head into gear. I'd be pitching against the St. Petersburg Cardinals.

I kept to all my routines. I felt calm. When I got cranked up in the bullpen everything was working. I felt great.

My catcher was Barry Winford. He was a really good receiver, had a very good arm, and blocked pitches in the dirt like a man on a mission. That's a great thing for a pitcher. When you trust your catcher to save your butt if you spike a ball in the dirt, your confidence level goes way up. I was stoked he was behind the plate.

As we walked in from the bullpen he said, "I have an idea, but it's kind of backwards. These guys are going to be amped up to hit your heat. Let's start them off with some breaking stuff, then bring the fastball."

He was right. It was backwards. As a matter of fact, pitchers and pitching coaches call it exactly that. We call it "pitching backwards" because you usually set everything up with the fastball and then go with the off-speed stuff. They might be so wound up on Opening Night to hit the heat, and then watch some off-speed junk float right by them. I said, "Let's do it."

The team had already done the formal introductions, going out to the foul line one by one. Barry and I had still been out in the bullpen then, so I didn't get to do it. It's a cool thing, but if you're starting on the mound you're not part of it.

We stood for the anthem, and then I walked to the mound. My eight warm-up pitches felt great. I felt great. I felt totally confident. The lead-off hitter dug in, and I think Barry had been right. He looked amped up.

Barry put down his sign, wiggling all his fingers. That's pretty much the universal sign for a change-up. Bold call to start the game.

I let it go and knew I had the location right in terms of in or out. It was going to be right on the outside part of the plate. That was the good news. The bad news was I'd left it up in the zone, just above the belt. Still a tough pitch to hit, but you generally don't want to leave change-ups hanging around up there. The hitter spotted it, maybe he was smarter than we thought, and spanked it like a rocket into the right-center gap, one-hopping it off the wall. He creamed it. It was my first pitch of the season. Way to go idiot.

My first thought was, "OK, this really is a step up from the Pioneer League and Sally League."

My next thought was, "We're not doing that again. I hate getting hit hard with my third-best pitch."

Barry was with me. He asked for a fastball to start off the next hitter. Strike one. Two pitches later, a heater at the knees the guy just looked at. Two more strikeouts later, and I had struck out the side and left the lead-off guy stranded.

When we got to the dugout, Barry said, "Don't ever listen to me again. Shake me off if I'm stupid. That was stupid."

We scored a couple of runs early, and I started mowing them down. The fastball was on fire and the curve was snapping. I threw a few more changes, but only when I was way ahead in the count so I could try to throw it in the dirt, to see if I could get them to fish. That worked once. The guy was so amped up for the fastball he swung at a change that hit two feet in front of the plate. Barry smothered it and tagged the guy.

After five innings, we were up 3-0 and my night was done. One hit, no walks, 10 strikeouts. No runs.

After I cooled off on the bench, the skipper came down to see me and said, "Helluva job, Brooksie. But what the hell was that first pitch of the night?"

Before I could answer, Barry, who was sitting next to me, piped up. "That, sir, was a really bad idea. We won't do that again."

About an hour later, we were 1-0 on the season and so was I. Yes, I was stoked and yes, it felt freaking great.

By the next day, it might as well have been June. We were all wrapped up in the nonstop thing that is the minors, and for our second game we were repaying the favor for the Cardinals, busing our way to St. Pete to play them in their home opener. Travis pitched, and was really good. He got hit a little, but settled down and got a no-decision. We lost in the bottom of the ninth.

And then it was just this: the clubhouse, bus rides, ball games, and repeat. Over and over. You truly do lose track of time. When May actually did roll around, it felt like we'd been there forever. It definitely felt like we'd ridden the bus forever. That part never really got easy.

Life was good. Travis and I got along great and really motivated each other. We loved what we were doing. We were even getting paid. And we drew pretty decent crowds at home. More than 1,000 per game, on average. The first time we went to Dunedin to play the Blue Jays, I counted 125 people in the stands. St. Pete drew very well. The cool ballpark there is right on the bay and easy to get to for all the retirees. We played some games there in front of 2,500 or more.

We would play the teams in the other two divisions on two actual road trips, so we wouldn't have to commute back and forth. When we went to the Central Division we got to play the Tigers, Astros, Royals, and Red Sox. Two games each and we just stayed in a hotel in Lakeland. And yes, the Royals set-up in Baseball City was ridiculous. An empty amusement park anchored by a stadium that was also just about empty. I felt sorry for those guys.

By then, I had started nine games. I was 7-1 (the Phillies got me, up there at their place in Clearwater, in a 2-1 loss) with an ERA around 1.25 or close to that. I'd pitched about 60 innings and had racked up somewhere north of 75 strikeouts. I was also giving up way less than a hit per inning. It was all good. I was just staying focused.

We were getting ready to make our swing through the East Division over on the Atlantic coast, and I was actually leaving the park the night before the trip thinking about packing right away so I wouldn't have to in the morning. The bus was going to leave the stadium at 9 a.m.

Skip called me in his office, and said, "You can't go on the road trip."

I had no clue what he meant. "Why? Did I do something wrong?"

He said, "No, you did everything right. Go ahead and get packed tonight and take your gear with you. You're going to Tulsa tomorrow. Double-A. Sorry you'll miss the bus ride all the way to Miami."

My next line was, "This might sound stupid, but can I drive there or do I have to fly? If I fly, I don't know what to do with my car."

Skip said, "Let me find out. If you're not going to pitch for a couple of days, maybe you can drive. I'll call you when I know. Get your stuff together and dammit, Brooksie — you did great here. Really great."

And my biggest worry was about my Corolla. Funny how stuff like that is the first thing on my mind when I'd just been told I'd been promoted.

As it turned out, the Tulsa Drillers were finishing up a long road trip and wouldn't be home for two more days. I could get to Tulsa by then and meet them for the start of their next homestand. I was moving up. Another new challenge. Another new level. Stoked, dude! Totally stoked.

I packed all my gear and every guy in the room came by to wish me well. Travis was excited, but I could see some sadness too. We had become great roomies. I said, "Hey, we've already paid our June rent, so I'll give you a check for July too. That'll give you some time to find a new roomie and who knows, maybe I'll totally bomb in Tulsa and they'll send me back here in a few weeks."

He laughed and said, "You can write all the checks you want, but I won't cash them. They'll call someone up from Gastonia to replace you, and I'll have a new roommate. I'll forget your name. I'll have a new best friend. You'll be dead to me. And you will not be coming back here. Period. No way."

When we drove back to the apartment, Travis said, "I've been meaning to ask you this since the beginning of spring training. You're a pretty big bonus baby. Why are you still driving this Toyota Corolla?"

I said, "Because it was a gift from my dad's cousin, who pretty much saved us when we got to Minnesota from SoCal. He put me up at his place so Dad could be with my mom at Mayo, and he bought me this car so I'd have wheels. Damn cool guy. Plus, why do I need to waste my bonus money on a big flashy new car? I mean, I might move up to a Camry or a Celica or something, but I don't need any more than that."

I think he got it.

Before I could even call my parents, the phone rang and it was someone in the Tulsa Drillers front office with some details. They'd play two more games on the road and be home early in the morning after the second game. They had a hotel room reserved for me in Tulsa and the guy gave me some directions to the ballpark. I told him I'd be there by late afternoon the second day.

When I called Mom and Dad I played the same trick on them as the skipper had on me. I said, "We're supposed to leave on a road trip tomorrow, starting with a set of games in Miami, but our manager pulled me aside and said I couldn't go. I was shocked. I wondered what I'd done wrong."

Mom said, "Well what *DID* you do wrong?"

"Nothing," I said and laughed. "I can't go on the road trip because I've been promoted to Tulsa in Double-A. I'm leaving in the morning and have two days to get there. The Tulsa Drillers. Two steps from the Bigs. They're in the Texas League and everyone tells me it's a big jump up from the Florida State League. I'm stoked, I'm a little scared, but I'm really excited."

Dad said, "You can handle it. Just be yourself. You've handled everything you've faced so far. Congratulations, dude. Those days on the little dirt fields in SoCal seem like a million years ago, but I saw something in you then. Go get 'em. Let us know how to reach you once you get settled."

The next morning, I was loaded up and ready to go. Travis and I shared a hug and wished each other the best. My parting words were, "Don't be afraid to be aggressive. You should end up in Tulsa with me if you do that, dude."

I won't bore you with the details this time, but my trusty maps had it all planned out. It would take two 10-hour days to get there. Up through Tallahassee, then up to Montgomery and Birmingham. The next big destination was Memphis, if I could make it that far. The next day, all the way to Tulsa.

I actually got there around 3 on the second day, and went straight to the ballpark. The GM and the home clubhouse attendant, who was also the equipment manager, were there. The ballpark was classic, and it was nice. Totally impressive. I'd say the clubhouse was close to as nice as Port Charlotte, but just a little smaller.

The equipment guy was cool. In the low minors back then you were lucky to have a trainer, much less a clubhouse and equipment guy. In Double-A, this dude was in charge of everything from logistics, to doing the laundry, to putting out snacks and sandwiches. Then, after washing all the uniforms and cleaning and shining everyone's spikes, he'd have all your stuff back in your locker before you came to the park the next day. We always called the clubhouse guy "Clubbie," just like every trainer is "Doc" and every manager is "Skip." Clubbie took my duffel bag and showed me where my locker was. He said, "Leave it to me. Did you pack all this right after your last game or was it all washed?" I had to admit it all went in there sweaty and wet. He just said, "Pull out everything you want washed and I'll have it in your locker tomorrow. Your uniform is ready for you." The Tulsa uniforms weren't replicas of the Texas uni. They were specifically designed for the Drillers, from the hats to the jerseys, with a script "DRILLERS" across the chest. I saw my gray road uni hanging in the locker, too. It said "TULSA" in block print across the front. It all looked pretty cool. My number was 25. I do remember being absolutely jazzed to be there, and couldn't wait to meet my new teammates.

I pulled out my sweaty stuff and put it on the floor in front of my locker. Everything I owned had either Brooks or Bennett written on it in marker. I had a little extra chat with the GM and he was really nice. He said, "We're thrilled to have you here, Brooks. You're going to do just fine at this level, according to everything I've heard. Our manager is Bobby Jones, who is a great guy. You'll love him. He played a long time in the big leagues and has Rangers roots. Smart baseball man. Your pitching coach is Oscar Acosta. Another smart man.

"We just sent a pitcher up to Oklahoma City when one of their starters came down with a bad elbow. I'll try to find out who he was rooming with and maybe we can get you in with that guy, who's probably wondering right now how he's going to pay the rent without a roomie. We'll figure it out. Get a good night's sleep at the motel tonight, and plan on being here before 3 tomorrow."

"Oh, I'll be here way before then," I said. "I like being the first guy to the park."

The GM said, "Well, our guys just finished up a six-game trip to Wichita and Little Rock, so they'll be getting in late tonight. Bobby usually gives them some leeway to catch up on sleep before they come out here after a road trip, but you can feel free to come out anytime you want. And come to my office. You've got some paperwork waiting for you and a new contract to sign."

I got a raise. All the way up to something around $1,250 a month. I could easily live on that, and maybe even have a nice lunch or dinner a few times.

We were starting a three-game set with Wichita the next night. They were a San Diego Padres affiliate. The GM wasn't sure, but he said, "On the phone, it sounded like Bobby and Oscar had mentioned they wanted you pitching in this series. I don't get into their territory. They make those decisions. We'll learn more tomorrow. See you then."

I took a little walk around the park before I left. Drillers Stadium was big and pretty old-school. It had big steel beams that held up the roof over the main grandstand, so some fans would be sitting behind those like in the old Major League ballparks. But it was classic and they had it fixed up really nice. It felt like a ballpark, and the GM had already told me they drew pretty good crowds. They were third in the league in attendance, at about 2,000 a game. I couldn't wait. Just walking around I could smell the hot dogs and popcorn and hear the fans. It was going to be an awesome place to call home.

Before I left I went out to my car to get some more stuff that would stay in my locker. Fortunately, about a week before I got promoted a bunch of the things I was getting from Wilson and Nike showed up in Port Charlotte. Two more pairs of spikes still in the box from Nike, and two more A2000 gloves from Wilson. I also got my Nike apparel, but that would stay with me wherever I ended up living. Some nice golf shirts, shorts, workout clothes, a track suit, and two pairs of sneakers. I was living large, believe me. I took the spikes and gloves back into the clubhouse and put them in my locker.

I headed to the motel and tried to relax. I was pretty wound up mentally, but I was tired from the road and fell asleep as soon as I got serious about it. It seemed like it was morning in about 10 minutes. There was a diner next door, so I went over there for breakfast. I didn't unpack anything because I'd probably only be there one night. I was antsy as hell to get to the ballpark, so I headed out there very early in the afternoon. I was the first one there.

Man, I wish I could remember the Clubbie's name. I think it was Billy, but I'm not sure. Whatever it was, he was aces. I walked into the room and my locker looked like I'd been there all season. Everything neatly put away. My jersey with 25 on the back facing out, hanging on a hook on the front of the locker. My nameplate was actually a nameplate, not written in marker on athletic tape. And geez, the thing that stoked me the most was in the bottom of my space. He'd folded up my old generic duffel bag and stuffed it in the back. In front of it was a very nice, very impressive, Tulsa Drillers bag with the big square end-panels. Tulsa Drillers was printed on each end. There was a laminated name tag attached to it, with 25 on one side and Bennett on the other.

This was a huge step up. It was almost kind of an embarrassment of riches, in a way. It was rad, for sure, but I was going to be the new guy on this team and I didn't want to come off as flashy or "look at me!" in any way. I just wanted to be one of the boys.

Bobby Jones and Oscar Acosta showed up not long after I got there, and everything the GM said was true. Both great guys, and we sat in the office and talked for at least an hour. Bobby said, "It's my job to keep you healthy or the Rangers will shitcan me before you know it. So we're gonna be careful with your innings. Tonight we start a three-game series with Wichita. We want you to start the final game. You ready for that?"

I told him I was ready for anything, just put me in and let me go.

Oscar said, "I've heard everything about you from Butte to Port Charlotte. I'm not going to change a thing. If you get a little lost or lose the feel for something, then you come to me. All I've heard is how much you put into the little things, like balance, flow, your release point, and location. Most of these guys just think it's about going out there and throwing as hard as they can. I can't teach them much if they don't want to learn. I'm here for you, OK?"

Yes, very much OK. Like totally OK.

The guys started filtering in a few hours later. I tried to meet as many as possible as quickly as possible. We'd all been in spring training together, but I never really got to know any of these guys, although I recognized a few. And then a guy came over and introduced himself. He was a pitcher, a lefty, named Bryan Gore. We shook hands and he said, "The GM told me you'd be looking for a place to live. My roomie just got sent up to Okie City, so I'm looking for someone. It's a really nice apartment, not too far away. Two bedrooms with king beds, a good kitchen and a nice living area with a TV. Rent is $400, so $200 per guy. Interested?"

I said I sure was, and we agreed that I'd follow him there after the game. Another box checked.

I sat next to Oscar, the pitching coach, in the dugout that first night. I wanted to get a feel for the talent level and I wanted to pick his brain a bit. As for the talent level, these guys were good. Not necessarily flashy or anything like that, but confident and sound baseball players. It was definitely a different level.

I asked Oscar what the difference would be for me compared to the Florida State League, and he said, "Not a lot different, but the one thing you'll realize pretty quick is that these guys will take more pitches. They have a little bit better idea about what they're doing up there. They won't bite on stuff that's way out of the zone because they're a little smarter about not guessing." I could see that from the bench as I watched and mentally scouted the Wichita team.

After the game, I followed Bryan back to the apartment and he was right. It was really nice, and it would be a great place to live. I wrote him a check for the next month's rent right then, just to get ahead of it. It took me all of about 15 minutes to get unpacked and settled

Two nights later, I got my chance to see what Oscar had told me and experience it first hand. The Texas League. Double-A ball. Different level.

We had three really good catchers on the team, and until I got to the park and saw the lineup card I wasn't sure who I'd be pitching to. Chad Kreuter and Rick Wrona were veteran guys who had been around the block. Both had already been to the big leagues, and Kreuter would go on to play about 15 years up there. And then there was a 19-year kid who ended up being pretty good. His name was Ivan "Pudge" Rodriguez. Yeah, that Pudge Rodriguez. He was young, but he had mad skills and a smile that lit up the room. They all shared the catching about equally, and it was Kreuter who had me that first night. Like I said, in the first two games I watched I could tell Wrona was solid, and Pudge had "star" written all over him. Kreuter was an ace back there too. It was big-time catching.

We went with my strengths that night. Set the table with the fastball. Keep everything off the middle of the plate if possible. Be in balance. Be smooth. Let the ball do the work. It was a lot better start than the "pitching backwards" experiment in Port Charlotte. And Oscar was right. I threw some off-speed stuff either two inches outside or in the dirt, and I was used to seeing guys in A-Ball swing at that stuff. These guys mostly just looked at it. I realized I'd have to be more aggressive.

I gave up a few hits in the first two innings, and walked two guys. That was not typical for me. Oscar sat next to me and said, "You're being too cute. Be aggressive. Don't be afraid of these guys. Go right after them, OK?"

So that's what I did. Five more innings. Lots of fastballs, just moving it around in the zone. Only a few curves. I went with the change-up for most of my off-speed stuff. The hitters were human. I didn't give up a hit for those last five innings and sent a bunch of them trudging back to the dugout after a strikeout. It was cool. It was pitching. It was strategy. It was great to have a legit pitching coach there with me. Had Oscar not talked to me after those first two innings, I'm not sure I would have made any adjustments. Seven innings pitched. No runs. 10 strikeouts. Welcome to Double-A!

I made it my mission to not just relax during games when I wasn't pitching. I studied. I watched. I looked for tendencies. And I watched how our guys pitched.

I went on my first road trip with the team after that six-game homestand, and I drew a heck of a trip to start with. We went to Midland first, then to El Paso. In case you've never been there, I can tell you Texas is enormous. Just getting home from El Paso was an event. It was a solid 850 miles. At least 13 hours. We had to have a day off after the trip because there was no way to get back to Tulsa and play on the same day.

And our bus was at a different level, as well. It was pretty rad in a bunch of ways. The team owned it, so it was customized for long road trips and it was painted in Drillers colors with huge logos on each side. There was no mistaking who was on that bus. There were about eight rows of regular seats, but behind them there were at least eight sets of bunk beds, attached to the walls. Not the most luxurious beds ever, but it gave guys a chance to lie down and stretch out. They were tough to get in, and once you were in there you could barely turn over, but it was a treat to have them. They filled me in on how they rotated the bunks so that everyone got a chance to get some sleep. We also had a full bathroom, a mini-fridge and a cabinet full of snacks. Way better than a regular chartered bus with nothing more than seats that reclined all of about two inches.

I pitched against El Paso the first game and got knocked around a little. They had a very good team, and again Oscar had been right about the hitters being more disciplined. I managed to get through five or six innings and left in a 2-2 tie. We won the game, but I got a no-decision.

And that's how it went for the next two months. Massive road trips. Many overnights on the bus. Good lively crowds at home and often on the road. Infields so dusty they couldn't water them enough. Great teammates. Seriously, these were truly great dudes and I enjoyed being with them enormously. Once again, just like it had been since childhood, I had instant friends.

I kept in touch with my parents, and Dad really relished the stories about the Texas League. Looking back on it now, I relish them too. It's a unique league, in a very unique part of the country. It's a tough place to play, and a hot place to be as well, but the baseball was really good.

I stayed in touch with Eric, too. He was home after his year in Binghamton, and already working out like a fiend to be ready for his next training camp with the Rangers. He thought he had a legit chance to make the team and play in the NHL. I didn't need to hear that. I knew he did.

In the end, it went like this at Tulsa:

- 10 starts
- 6-2 record
- 65 innings pitched
- 72 strikeouts
- 11 walks (ack!)
- ERA of 2.33

Bobby Jones and Oscar Acosta were gems. Great dudes and really smart baseball guys. Bryan was a great roomie, and we were totally relaxed around each other. The bus was rad. The ballparks ranged from dust bowls to stadiums, but the experience was priceless. When the season ended, I was truly sad. What a year it had been.

And finally, I noticed one other thing about Double-A ball. The closer you got to the big leagues the more girls were around. There was some of that in Butte and Gastonia, but not a ton. There wasn't much of it all around in Port Charlotte, though. That's more of a retirement community. Then I got to Tulsa and it seemed like every guy on the team had a local girl waiting for him outside the clubhouse after the game. I couldn't tell if the girls were just in it for fun, like rock & roll groupies, or if they had other motives, which could even be noble, I think. In the end, almost all the guys I played with met their wives in the minor leagues, although not all of them met their future wives at the ballpark. Most of them seemed very happy. I had no interest. The deal with Donna had soured me on girls in general. There was a part of my brain that was telling me: "They just distract you and use you. Steer clear. Concentrate on baseball."

And I never got to stop at the Gateway Arch in St. Louis. Being in Tulsa, my maps informed me that I had to take a completely different route back home. It was a 10-hour drive and a straight shot all on one interstate.

As for the Corolla, on the drive home I decided it really was too small. If I went back to Tulsa the next year or got promoted to Oklahoma City, I'd want something just a little bigger with better seats. I'd take care of that during the offseason.

I was ready to get home. I couldn't wait to see my mom and dad. I wasn't sure where I was going to live and I wasn't sure what I was going to do for the winter, but I wanted to get home.

CHAPTER 32

Eric Olson

I had around $3,000 burning a hole in my pocket when I got home, and my No. 1 priority was buying a ring for Carol. But, I also knew I wanted to work on hockey and my training all summer so I couldn't spend all of it on a diamond. I figured a $1,500 ring was my limit. I'd need the rest to live on until the next season started.

It was wonderful to see my soulmate again, but I never spoke to Carol about my plans. I had a whole script written in my head.

The biggest new thing for us was that her career with the Target division was moving forward quickly and she was making good money. On top of that, her roommate had gotten engaged and had moved out, so she was in her apartment by herself. The funny thing is, I had no idea where I was going to live when I got back to the Twin Cities. I was homeless and nearly broke. I wanted to be there for Carol, and be close to her, but I had only been thinking of hockey for the last six months and hadn't exactly sorted that whole thing out. And then she asked me to move in with her.

"I can afford this place, and you don't need to blow whatever money you made in Binghamton on rent," she said. "Let's just live together." I was all for it. It sounded like a dream to me. I could work out all day while she was at her office, and then we could make dinner and watch TV together before going to bed. I never would've asked to do that, but when she brought it up I was all in.

A few days later, after I moved my single suitcase of stuff into her apartment, I went out shopping for a ring.

I found a three-quarter carat diamond in a beautiful setting, surrounded by other little diamond chips, and paid cash for it. I remember the exact amount because it was the most money I'd ever spent on anything. $1,498.99. I talked them down from $1,650. I still have the receipt.

That night, I paced around the apartment until she got home. It was my job to grill a couple of steaks for us, and cook some baked potatoes, maybe some green beans, but my brain was on something else. Carol had no idea, so when a project she was working on ran late, she stayed at her office for a couple hours. It was 7 o'clock before she walked in the door, apologizing.

I let her get settled, promised I'd get the potatoes in the oven, and fired up the little mini-grill she had on the balcony. Then I sat on the couch and said, "Hey, come over here. I have something I want to give you."

Her beautiful dark brown eyes got a little bigger, and she sat next to me.

I then pulled out a Binghamton Rangers puck, with my autograph on it, and said, "I want you to have this" in the most sincere voice I could work up.

I wish I knew how to accurately explain the look on her face. She was a mix of completely disappointed and totally caring all at once. I think she really believed I would make a big deal out of giving her a puck. I know I saw her shake her head at least once before she said, "Oh, wow. Thank you! I'll treasure it."

So then I said, "Oh, I have something else, too."

I pulled the little black box out of my pocket, and opened it up so she could see what was inside.

I said, "Can we make this official now?"

The tears flowed like a dam breaking. All she could do was nod. For one of the few times ever, I started crying like a baby, too. We just sat there hugging each other for what seemed like an hour. Then she said, "OK, official husband-to-be, cook dinner. I'm starved."

That's one of the things I loved about her most. She could be as emotional as anyone, and as caring, but she had a way to cut through that and get back to dealing in the language like a teammate.

Over dinner we decided not to pick a date yet. Although I thought I could make the Rangers that fall, I didn't know for sure and you never do. We'd see how that went, and if I was on the NHL roster for the full season a summer wedding seemed about right. We'd have to decide if we'd go up to Roseau or stay in the Twin Cities for that, but we'd put that decision off too. I think a part of that was my typical athlete's superstition about not jinxing it. First things first. Let's see if I can play in the NHL and the rest will fall into line.

We were both really comfortable as roomies, and I enjoyed cooking as much as I could. She was neck-deep in her new position with Target and on a lot of nights it would be pretty late by the time she got home, which made it tough to plan dinners in advance, but I understood it. She was determined to make her mark and rise through the organization, just like I was. We had to give each other the leeway to make that happen.

Early in the summer I heard from Paul Broten. He said that a bunch of Twin Cities guys who all played in the NHL for various teams were going to get together to skate and train at a rink down near Bloomington, at least four days a week. He asked me if I wanted to be part of the group and all I could do was laugh. Would I want to be part of a group of NHL players working out and skating together? Would I? Give me a break, Paulie. Just tell me when to be there.

The guys were great, and they even let the Binghamton guy slide on the rental fees.

It wasn't much money to rent the rink and they could all afford it. It would've tapped me out in a month or two to pitch in. Paul and both of his brothers, Neal and Aaron, were part of the group. There were at least six or seven North Stars involved, including Brian Bellows, Trent Klatt, and a very young Mike Modano, who was 21 but looked about 16. Man, he could skate and shoot like a veteran star, though. It was great to be on the ice with all those guys. They treated me great, and I learned a lot just working through drills and playing with them. I felt like one of the guys, and that was a big deal considering I'd be heading back to New York at the end of the summer to make my own place on an NHL roster. It was a huge confidence boost.

We had a gym at our disposal as well, and it was great to really get after it again during the summer. As far as I could remember, it was the first time in my life that I could skate and play with other guys all summer long. What a benefit that was. In Roseau, we waited all summer and most of the fall just to see the ice go back in at the Arena and North Rink. To drive down to the rink the guys had rented and lace them up four days a week was like a job, and I treated it that way. We did play, but none of the NHL guys were really looking for hard contact or big checks, so I just worked on my stick work and leaned on them a little in the corners. Still, it was fantastic to be out there skating with those guys and getting a feel for how they found open ice and each other. Their passes were things of beauty.

As the summer wound down, I started hearing from the Rangers more and getting updates and agendas in the mail. I'd be heading back to New York for training camp in early September. Meanwhile, knowing that a big season of hockey was ahead of me, I tried to also concentrate on Carol and be the best "roommate" and fiance I could be. I cooked, cleaned, straightened things up, and ran most of the errands, so all she had to worry about was her job. She was already a superstar in the Target division, and it occurred to me (once again) that she would almost certainly make more money than me that year, even if I made the NHL roster for the Rangers.

I got my new contract in late August. It was another two-way deal and the NHL portion of it was for $30,000. I had actually earned a raise above the minimum if I could make the roster. That was my plan for sure. And as I signed it the thought came to me that I should start making plans to hire an agent. It's one thing to sign as a rookie by yourself, but having an agent was important once you got to the NHL. It's not just that you want to milk every dollar out of the team. It's more that you just want to keep it from being personal. Let the agent haggle and argue. The player just gets updates and gets ready to play. I figured I'd ask around the locker room at training camp to get some recommendations. And, despite not having any representation, by signing that contract with the $30,000 NHL number, I thought, "Holy cow, I might actually make more money than Carol if I can stick with the team." Funny how important that seemed to me at the time, but it really was. I wanted to pull my weight after spending the summer with almost no money. I wanted us to be partners in this thing, and didn't want to be a freeloader. I wasn't raised that way.

As camp approached, I made a quick trip back up to Roseau to see my family and some friends before I'd be off on the road for so long. I just stayed one night, but it was great to be back there again. It will always be "home" for me.

I'd also been keeping in touch with Brooks, who put a heck of a year together for Texas. He started the season in Florida, with their Class-A team but by mid-summer had been promoted to Tulsa, which was Double-A. And he did great at both levels.

That was another big difference between hockey and baseball. He got a huge signing bonus but he had to work his way up through all those levels of the minors before he'd ever get a sniff of the Major Leagues. Everyone knew he was good. He was dominant. But the Rangers didn't rush him. He had to earn every step up that ladder. I got basically nothing to sign but went to the equivalent of "big league" camp my first season and then to Binghamton, the equivalent of Triple-A ball for Brooks. I'd already been there. He'd pitched as well as he could and hadn't gotten out of Double-A yet. It's weird, but that's the way it is. NHL teams don't have all those levels of minor league hockey. They don't keep hundreds of players on minor league contracts. You make it or you don't. I planned on making it.

Brooks and I got together exactly once after he got back in early September right before I had to leave for camp. He looked great, sounded great, and his stories from that season were awesome. We talked about which one of us was going to make it to "the show" (as baseball players call the Majors) first, and I looked him in the eye and said, "I'll be there this year. Maybe not out of camp, but I'll get there. And when I do, I'll be there for a while."

He said, "Yes, you will. You've earned every step of this trip. I think you'll stick with the Rangers and when you do I'll fly to New York to see you take the ice. Count on it. It's a promise."

I told him, "You'll get there soon, too. Probably next year. And when you get there, you won't be leaving. You're going to be an All-Star. That's my prediction." I meant that.

Just a day or two later I had my last night with Carol. I packed my stuff, and sat on the sofa. Most nights, I just wanted to go to bed and get a good night's sleep. This time, I just wanted to hold her hand and keep her close to me. I wanted the clock to slow down. It's such a jolt, as an athlete, to be home with the one you love one night, and gone for as long as seven or eight months the next morning. I had another one of those awful 6 a.m. flights the next day, back to Westchester County airport. Carol took me to the airport and then headed to work. Again, the hug on the curb was long and deep. I told her, "I'll be out of your hair now. Keep rocking at work. I'll call you when I get settled in out there."

She said, "You have never been in my hair for any moment that I've known you, except maybe sixth grade when you kept bugging me in class and then got *ME* in trouble for talking when I turned around and told you to shut up. You go make this damn team, my love. Make the team. Live your dream."

I had to laugh. Once again, this had never been my dream. I lived that when I made the Rams in Roseau. Here I was trying to make an NHL team. And not any NHL team. The New York Rangers. It didn't seem impossible, but it sure felt crazy.

The whole process, once I got there, was pretty much the same as the year before. Same hotel, same rink, same meetings and practices. I was getting a lot of ice time in the scrimmages and holding my own. The guys were great to me. No rookie hazing or anything like that, just a lot of support and stick-taps on my shins as I'd come off the ice. It felt different. These guys were solid pros. They wanted to win. If the new kid could help them do that, they'd be completely supportive. It felt great, and I really felt like a part of it. I tried not to think about it but I couldn't forget the words my coach in Binghamton said after the season, when he told me he didn't want to see me back there again and didn't think he would.

We started preseason games after a week or two and began with the Islanders again. I was on the second line! I almost couldn't believe it when that was posted on the chalkboard in the locker room. I played heavy minutes and took a bit of a beating, but nothing serious and no major mistakes. I can usually be my own worst critic, so of course I could see all sorts of things to improve on, but all I got was compliments after the game.

After another preseason game, a few guys got the word and started packing their stuff for Binghamton. A few older guys who were in camp to see if they could keep their careers going got their word, too, and for them it was time to pack up and either go home and call it a career, or see about playing in Europe. I just kept my head down and kept playing.

A few days later, Coach Neilson called a meeting. He said this:

"Look around the room, boys. This is your team. This is what we're going with and we're going to be good if we all just do our jobs. We have skill, we have speed, and we have two great goalies. We also have just one new rookie. Let's give it up for Eric Olson. Eric, welcome to the NHL."

I wasn't stunned, but I was kind of blown away by the thought of it. You might think that sort of news would happen in the coach's office, and I guess that's what I was expecting, so to have him do it in front of the whole team was incredible. They started an impromptu chant of "Oly, Oly, Oly" while tapping their sticks. I will never, ever, forget that moment. Needless to say, I called Carol, my folks, and finally Brooks, from the hotel room. I didn't care what the calls cost. My folks were clearly proud but of course they found a way to also give me some advice and rules. Carol cried and told me she loved me and was really proud of me. Brooks just said, "Whoa, dude! That is so awesome. I'm so stoked for you. You made the show, buddy. That is so rad. Now the real journey begins. Go get 'em, man!"

Since it was the end of camp and we were starting the season in just a couple days, I told him, "Look, man. No need for you to drop everything and spend a fortune to come to my first game. The cost of the flight will be ridiculous and so will the hotel room. Wait until we get to Minnesota, or maybe when we're closer, like Chicago or St. Louis." He didn't sound happy, but he agreed that it was the right call.

We opened the season on a two-game road trip. First stop was Boston and I was really glad to have gone there the year before, to get any intimidation out of my system.

It was just a hockey game in a really cool rink. We lost, and we didn't really play great, but I held my own and played regular shifts. Maybe one or two stupid passes but I played my role as the pest like I always had and it worked.

We were then going up to Montreal, a place I'd never been before but a place I'd always dreamed of in terms of playing this great game. When we got there, we heard some big news. Coach said, "We made a deal with another team, and we just upgraded our roster. He'll be here any second."

Like on cue in a movie, the one and only Mark Messier walked in the door right then. I hadn't been focused on what was going on with him and the Edmonton Oilers. He was their captain, and a league superstar. He was holding out on reporting, looking for a better deal, I guess, and the Oilers decided to move him and get some prospects in return. Only one of the three players the Rangers sent to Edmonton had actually made the team out of camp. That was Bernie Nicholls. The other two guys were in Binghamton. Basically, in terms of the Rangers, it was a one-for-one swap on the NHL roster and we got Mark Messier. I remember shaking my head and thinking, "That's flippin' Mark Messier. Right here. With us. We just got a lot better."

By game time the next night in Montreal at the Montreal Forum, yet another incredibly classic arena that had opened in the 1920s, we got to the rink and walked in the room and there was a blue Rangers jersey hanging in the best locker, with the name "MESSIER" on the back. I had goosebumps.

It was a fast and bruising game, and really tight. I clearly remember that. I just concentrated on doing my job and playing hard and fast shifts. We beat them in overtime and had a heck of a celebration after we scored. It was heaven.

After that road trip, it turned into a hockey season. An NHL hockey season. It seemed like we hardly had time to really practice, and rarely had more than one day off between games. We'd skate, have some light drills on the days off, and then skate again in the morning on a game day. Lots of planes, lots of hotel rooms, lots of cool arenas. I got to go to so many places I'd never been. And yes, sometime around mid-season, we went to the Twin Cities and played the Minnesota North Stars at the Met Center. I was scrounging tickets for weeks, because each player got two per game but usually only used them when they had family in town. My entire family came down from Roseau, Carol was there, and I left tickets for Brooks and one of his baseball buddies, too.

I'll never forget that game. To be playing at the Met Center against the North Stars with family, my fiance, and my friend in the stands was so much that for the first time in a long time I had to calm myself down after warmups. I was wired on pure adrenalin. We won, and it was a low-scoring physical game that ended 2-1, and guess what? I assisted on both goals.

It was all a blur really, once the season got going. I definitely wasn't used to things like having the PR guy grab me in the hall after a game and do a "live" interview for New York TV. It was kind of hard to focus, but the hockey itself was the real focus. NHL hockey.

You might be wondering what I did for a home in New York on my $30,000 salary.

As it turned out, four other guys had actually rented a house in Queens, and when one of them happened to be Bernie Nicholls, who we'd traded for Messier, they immediately asked me if I wanted to join them. The subway was only a block away, or we could drive to Manhattan because two of the guys had cars. I'd pitch in about $300 a month. I jumped at it.

We rode the subway a lot, which was another New York experience for me. I got good at it, but I had some solid guides to show me the ropes. None of us were big stars so nobody really bugged us, although I'd learn that's how the subway is most of the time anyway. Everybody minds their own business.

We cooked a lot of meals, we got to know the neighborhood and found a few cool delis and diners that had good stuff, and we fit right in. Queens is a cool place if you don't mind the planes landing at LaGuardia right over your head. I liked it. I liked it a lot. It really felt like the big time being in one of America's biggest cities and playing at Madison Square Garden. And I preferred the subway to riding in a car. The traffic, getting to the Garden, was always bad. Actually, horrible.

In the end, I had a few nicks and bruises that caused me to sit out a few games here and there, but I played in 74 games. I absolutely held my own. I ended up playing about 15 minutes a night, picked up 16 assists and scored four goals. The guys made sure to get the puck for me after the first one. I still have it. The equipment guys put some athletic tape around the edge and wrote on it: "Eric Olson - First NHL goal- Nov. 4, 1991 vs Calgary."

I got to play with Mark Messier. and I was really stunned by his skills. He was wearing the captain's "C" of course, and scored more that year. He was also a great guy and a fantastic motivator. I just followed his example when it came to being in shape, doing the work, and playing the game with the right intensity.

We had another big scorer on the team, too. Mike Gartner put about 40 in the net and was always solid. Paulie had a good year too, playing well and scoring 13 goals. That pretty much cemented his place in the NHL. And in the back, we had the best two-man goalie system in the league, in my opinion. Mike Richter and John Vanbiesbrouck were brick walls in front of the net. It was an honor to be back there with them and clear pucks that were loose in the area. To hear Richter yell "attaboy Oly" when I'd pick up a loose puck and get it out of there, never stopped being a very cool thing.

We ended up going 50-25-5 and won our division. We beat our nearby rivals, the New Jersey Devils, in a very tough seven-game first round playoff series. We moved on to play the Pittsburgh Penguins and gave them everything we had, but lost the series in six games. They had Mario Lemieux then, at the top of his game. What a deal it was to try to defend him. I figured every time we were on the ice together, if he didn't score I won.

Throughout the season I played against legends. Wayne Gretzky, who was with LA at the time, lit me up a few times by getting me all turned around, but I wasn't the only one he did that to. He was truly "The Great One." And here's the thing about Gretzky. He was like a shark out on the ice; always moving, swooping in big loops, searching for open spots, making himself available. He never stood still. He wasn't a big sniper, or a

307

boomer with a slapshot like a Bobby Hull. I think people use the analogy that we were mostly playing checkers and he was playing three-dimensional chess. You couldn't stay with him, and if you kept your defensive structure you couldn't cover all the ice. He'd always find a way to be open. If you never saw him play, do yourself a favor and find some highlights on YouTube. He wasn't a "mucker" right in front of the goalie, looking for rebounds to tap in. He was a magician. He really saw the game and the ice differently, as if he could see into the future. Like, "I need to be over there, because this pass will go that way, and the next one will go behind the goal, and then it will bounce over the defenseman's stick, and I'll be all alone with the puck." And I'm thinking, "The puck is over here, why is he over there?" He knew. And as much as he could embarrass me and the other defensemen, it was an honor to share the ice with him. He played with class, brains and skill. Amazing skill.

The St. Louis Blues had Brett Hull. Man could he play and it seemed like he could score at will. He had a lot of his dad's Hall of Fame traits and could shoot a puck through a brick wall.

Patrick Roy was playing goal for Montreal then, and I'd never seen anyone like him. If you scored on Roy, you ought to keep the puck. But, I'll say it again, with Richter and Beezer we had the best two-man tandem in the league. We could keep them both fresh and they never went into slumps.

Talk about a totally different level of hockey. It was the stratosphere. It was a challenge every night. For me, it wasn't just effort; it was also focus. I had to have a game plan for every opponent. I watched a lot of tape. I had to have an idea what I needed to do and I had to stick with it. In the NHL, you couldn't take a shift off and just hope it would all go OK if you coasted through it. It wouldn't go OK. It had to be max effort and max brain power.

And the Roseau contingent was all there at the same time, too. Neil Broten was playing for the North Stars, Aaron Broten was with the Winnipeg Jets, but his career was pretty much winding down by then. Paulie was with me in New York. Roseau Rams, all in the NHL.

The season was over, but every minute of it was beyond special. I played a full season in the NHL. I was coming home with some actual money in my pocket. I'd gotten to know guys I only knew from watching TV. I was part of a great organization in the Big Apple and was a regular in the lineup. And at the end of the year, I was a much better player than I was when the season started. I think it works like that in most sports. You improve the most when you're playing against very talented opponents. I was doing that every time we stepped on the ice.

After the final playoff game, before I packed my gear and my stuff, Coach called me into his office and said, "You did great, Oly. I'm really proud of you and never hesitated to put you out there. The best thing was, though, that you got better as the season went on. You learned the other teams, you got to know their moves and tendencies. By the last couple of months you were stonewalling some superstars. You've got a really bright future. We'll be in touch about next season. I want you here. I hope you enjoyed this."

Yeah, I enjoyed it. Man, did I enjoy it.

And before my flight even got me home, I knew I had one pressing detail to take care of. We had to settle on a date to get married. That was kind of important. But it wasn't as critical as you'd think. Carol and her mom had already been plotting it out, in terms of the date, the location, and the reception. They were just waiting on me to get home from my silly NHL hockey games to get on board. I sure as heck wasn't going to say no to anything they wanted to do.

CHAPTER 33

Brooks Bennett

As soon as I got home from Tulsa, I knew there was one important thing to address. Where was I going to live? I was going to stay with Mom and Dad until I figured that out.

I was done with school and basically all the guys I'd played with on the Gophers were gone. Plus, I wanted something more mature and having a place to myself seemed like a good idea. Dad and I went to see my financial advisor Jack to see what he thought. His immediate response was, "It sounds to me like you're going to play in the big leagues. Once you get there, you're going to need some tax deductions. You ought to think about buying a house or a condo."

That seemed rad and totally intimidating, but I understood the logic. Mortgage interest was tax deductible. Rent was just money out of your pocket, burned and never to be seen again. But where should I look? There were a lot of good reasons to think about Florida, where there was also no state income tax. If I was near Port Charlotte, I could work out there all winter at the Rangers complex. But, and this was totally important, if I did that I'd be a long way from my parents.

We went home and talked about it, and Dad summed it up pretty quickly.

"It might be the best thing for you to buy a condo down there," he said. "That will be an investment and it will help with your taxes, plus you really need a warm place and a good workout facility. We can come down to see you, and you can come up here any time you want. There will always be a room for you here. Think about it."

I did think about it. Basically, 24 hours later I told my dad, "Hey, I think the condo in Florida is the way to go. I'll get a big enough place so that you can both come down and spend time with me in the winter, and you can go there by yourselves during the summer if you want because I sure hope I won't be playing in Port Charlotte anymore. It will be a good investment and good for all of us."

He agreed, so we decided we would fly down and go on a house-hunting trip. My dad and I had never traveled anywhere before, other than in his Volkswagen bus from

310

SoCal to Minnesota, with Mom sleeping on a mattress in the back. It sounded like fun to me.

I also felt like I needed to start looking into having an agent to represent me in terms of contracts and endorsements. I was a little green about that, as well. Totally no idea on how to find the right guy, or the right agency, to represent me, but I was determined to at least get my first taste of the big leagues the next season so I knew it was important.

By the time I got home, Eric only had a few days left before he needed to be at the New York Rangers' training camp, so we got together for lunch and hashed over everything we could think of. So much was happening to both of us, and it was happening really fast.

I asked him about the agent deal, and he was in the same boat. He was interviewing with agencies and individuals who specialized in hockey, and his advice to me was "talk to teammates you trust who have gone through this."

He said there were some "mega agencies" sprouting up, but I should steer clear of them. He'd been pitched by one of them that a teammate had chosen, and just came away feeling like they worked harder at collecting clients than they did representing them. The teammate felt the same way and was considering finding someone else. Eric said they were really "high pressure" when they talked, like a car salesman trying to make his numbers but who wouldn't remember you the next time you came in.

He also told me that he and Carol were getting married the next summer. I was totally stoked to hear that, but I figured I might not have the chance to be there, and that bummed me out massively, but it's what was going to work best for them. Eric said, "I want you in the wedding, but unless you're hurt you're not going to be able to do that. I feel bad about it but summer is the only time that works for me. And I really hope you're not injured, so we'll have to do something special when we can." I got that.

He asked me about my love life and all I could say was, "I don't have one, but that's my choice. I want to get to the big leagues and get established. I don't need the drama and I don't need the distractions. You got lucky as hell with Carol, buddy. Take care of her and enjoy every minute of it."

It was beginning to sink in to me how different we were, but how close we'd become. His parents were 180-degrees different from mine. They provided, they made demands, and they raised their kids in a cool town up near Canada, although it could be really harsh in the winter. In their minds, the kindest show of love they could give to their kids was a warm home and food on the table. And you know, all of the Olson kids turned out to be really good people totally focused on doing well in life. My parents loved me, coddled me a little, and gave me direction mostly by example. I was surrounded by love, but I had a hard time drilling down to the focus I needed when it came to accomplishing what I wanted to do. Even during baseball games, I'd lose my focus if it was too easy.

Eric focused like a laser beam. By just about any measure, his dream of being a Roseau Ram should have been a hell of an accomplishment all by itself, and his organized hockey career should've ended there. He was too small, he wasn't fast, he wasn't a flashy skater or puck handler, and until he got to high school he wasn't

311

even that strong. He just focused and overcame it all. And there he was. Not a Ram anymore. Not in juniors. Not in college. And not in the minors. He was in the NHL. The National freaking Hockey League. The more I thought about it the more it all made sense to me. His parents weren't as open and giving as mine, but they gave him a great gift — the gift of hard work, dedication and never giving up. I wouldn't trade my parents for anyone, and that's not the point. My parents were incredible as I grew up. It was just a different approach and a different place. I began to not just like Eric more, but respect him 10 times more. What he had done was amazing, and it was just starting.

I couldn't (and wouldn't) go back and change anything in my life. But I knew, after all that deep thought once Eric and I had that long brother-to-brother talk over lunch, that there was more in me. If it was 1 percent more, there was still more. I could focus more. I could run the extra laps from pole to pole. I could work on my mechanics more. I could listen to the coaches and just be better. It was a rad concept. I'd never really gone there, mentally, before. I thought I was giving it 100 percent, but suddenly it was clear that maybe I wasn't. That I definitely wasn't. Man, I couldn't wait for spring training. I felt like I had turned a very important page. I was, as I like to say, totally stoked to move forward and show the world what I could do.

But first, my dad and I had a trip to make. We booked flights to Fort Myers and reserved a hotel room in Port Charlotte. When the day came, it felt really odd and really great at the same time. We'd never gotten on a plane together. My dad had only flown once or twice, I think, so I was kind of taking care of him and leading him around the airport to make it happen. It was just late September, so it wasn't super cold in the Twin Cities yet, but it still felt like a different world when we got off the plane in Fort Myers and smelled that Gulf of Mexico breeze. It wasn't warm; it was hot. And humid. It was Florida. Right then, I said to Dad, "This was a great decision. I'm going to get more done every week here than I did in a month back home. And you and Mom need to be down here as often as you can. Now let's go find a place to buy." We got a rental car, which he had to sign for because you had to be 25 in order to get one.

We checked into the hotel, bought a newspaper and picked up a few real estate magazines from a rack near the front desk, then went up to the room to look through it all. We spotted the agency that had the most ads and the most listings, and gave them a call. I told the receptionist the short version of the story, and what I was looking for, and she transferred me to an agent named Joe. We set up a meeting over dinner that night.

We found a cool seafood place near the Gulf and met Joe, who certainly looked and sounded the part. Handsome, nicely dressed and well spoken. We ticked off all the things I was looking for, including being close to the Rangers complex, and he said something like, "I'll work on this tonight, and I'll meet you in the lobby of your hotel at 9 tomorrow morning. We're going to have a great day and find what you're looking for."

I wasn't nervous at all. I was just jazzed to the max and ready to do it. I basically hadn't spent any of my bonus money at all. I mean, I'd bought some new clothes and shoes, and once we got back I was going to move up to a bigger car, but 99 percent of the bonus was still just sitting there in my savings account and Jack's investment account. It had actually grown a little, too. The Rangers paid me $80,000 to sign and I had about $90,000 by then, just from the investments and interest. So I felt it was absolutely the right thing to find a condo.

Joe had a stack of listings in his hands when we met in the lobby the next morning. My wish list included a nice view, probably a high-rise near the water or a smaller building if it was really near the complex and close to grocery stores and other retail, at least two bedrooms and two baths, and fully furnished. A pool and a gym wouldn't hurt either.

I don't remember how many places we saw, but I'd say half of them blew me away. Unfortunately, the ones right by the complex in Port Charlotte didn't do anything for me. It was the ones in Cape Coral, about 20 minutes south, that impressed the hell out of me and got me excited. They must have blown Dad away too, because we'd never lived in a place as nice as any of them. And at that point, the dollar figures started to scare me a little, but I remember thinking, "You can do this. Focus. You have the money and you're going to make more. It's a great investment in yourself, idiot. Just pick the right place, not the cheapest place."

Dad and I went out to dinner and brought all the brochures we'd put a check mark on. We talked about it all at length, over grouper sandwiches and over the meal and a couple of beers we came to two conclusions. The first was that the final small group of listings were all fantastic and we couldn't go wrong. The second was that neither one of us could remember a time we'd ever sat in a public restaurant and shared a couple of beers together. All sorts of firsts that day!

We ranked the top three and came up with offers we thought were fair. We'd start with No. 1 and go from there. If we didn't get it, we'd go to No. 2 and then No. 3.

We met with Joe the next day and told him our plan. He left us in his office to call the listing agent who represented the developer, with our offer on No. 1, and came back to say, "He didn't hang up on me. I think we're close." About 30 of the longest minutes later, Joe got the return call with a counter that was just $5,000 above what we'd proposed, which had been $15,000 below the listing. I didn't feel like messing around. I said, "I'll take it." A minute or two later, they faxed over some documents and I was signing everything. And I learned quite a bit right then and there about negotiating on something like a condo. It's not a loaf of bread. You don't just automatically fork over the price that's on it.

I'd already worked with Dad's cousin Don, setting up a pre-approved max for a mortgage, and this condo didn't come close to hitting the max. I wanted to put at least 20 percent down, too, so the payments would be easily manageable. I had a condo! Me! Stoked doesn't come close to describing it.

It was in a brand new 15-story building in Cape Coral, not overlooking the Gulf but on a more inland waterway with a marina. Still, it was a great view looking west, and it was in a really quiet and serene area. I thought that was important. The last thing I needed was to be in some congested city scene. I wanted to focus and be all about peace

313

and baseball. The fact it was new and I'd be the first owner of the condo made it more rad than anything I'd ever dreamed of.

It was beautifully decorated with great furniture. It even smelled new. My condo was on the top floor, about 1,200 square feet, and not far from the elevator. It was more than I ever thought I'd own. I got it for $190,000 and put 20 percent down. That was a good chunk of my bonus, like around $40,000, but the money wasn't doing me much good just sitting there. I wasn't blowing it on a boat or something dumb. It was an investment. Mortgage rates weren't all that good back then, I think about 8 percent or somewhere around there, so on a 30-year loan it was about $500 a month. The homeowners association fees were $170 a month, but that included utilities, cable, the workout room, and maintenance of the building and grounds. All I had to do myself was get a phone. I could swallow that HOA fee without a panic attack.

We couldn't close for a few weeks, so Dad and I flew home. Dad and I were super-amped the whole flight back up to Minneapolis, and Mom was crying when we walked in the door. Everyone was pretty emotional. Imagine that!

My new contract was also waiting for me there. It was for Oklahoma City, the Rangers' Triple-A affiliate, and it was for around $1,500 per month. Huge money!

Dad and Mom would both fly down with me when the closing was going to happen. Now all I had to do was make it to the Big Leagues. No pressure. Just focus. Be like Eric. Focus!

Three weeks later, all three of us got on a plane and flew back down. We stayed in a hotel the first night, all bunked in one room together like the old days. The next morning, I signed my name or scribbled my initials throughout a thick document in about 200 spots, and at the end of it I forked over a check and they handed me the keys. My mom was doing all she could to hold back the tears.

We went straight to the condo after the closing and I'll admit, putting the key in the lock and opening the door to MY HOME was solidly epic. The significance wasn't lost on me. I was flashing back to SoCal, to the tiny place in San Clemente, and the suburban home in Anaheim, which seemed like a mansion to me because I finally had my own room. This whole place was mine. Purchased with my own money. I was a homeowner. A totally 100 percent stoked homeowner.

And then Mom surprised us by putting down her backpack and pulling out a bottle of champagne. She had "run an errand" the night before, saying she was going out to find a drug store, and since the bottle had lost its chill we put it in the freezer for a bit. Sunset was about 30 minutes away, so when that was close we went ahead and popped the cork and went out on the balcony to toast the moment. It tasted great.

We all flew back home the next day. Mom and Dad wanted to get back and I needed to sort out my plans. I had a home now, full of nice furniture, but I didn't have any of my "life" there, including all my baseball gear. My plan was to go back home, buy a new car that was a little bigger with more comfortable seats, load it up, and head south in a week or two.

When we got home, the first call I made was to Don. He had bought the Corolla for me and I always felt like it was as much his as it was mine. I asked him, one more time, what I owed him for the car and he, one more time, said I owed him nothing. I should trade it or sell it if I wanted to. He wouldn't take "no" for an answer. Did I ever mention that he was a really cool dude and basically a lifesaver? Without Don, I don't know what would've happened to me. He saved me for sure, and he saved all of us because he saved me. If I'd have had no choice but to go live in Rochester with Dad, in his studio apartment, everything would've probably been different. Had I stayed in Bloomington with a strange family, I have no idea how that would've gone. Don stepped in and stepped up. He's a really great human being. The world needs more Dons.

I did admit to him that I knew nothing about buying cars. I asked him if he had any advice. He said, "My advice to you is to have me come with you. What are you doing Friday? I have the whole day clear."

On Friday, we headed to a Honda dealership first. Having Don there was like surfing with a pro from the Banzai Pipeline. He had the sales guy tied in knots in just a few minutes. Before long, the sales manager was in the room, and then the dealership general manager. And all Don kept saying was: "We can walk out of here with a new car, we just need the car to be something Brooks wants, the terms to be right, and the trade-in to be appropriate." He never backed off, even when they kept trying to steer him to some other distractions, like free undercoating or scheduled oil changes.

The only Honda that fit the bill was the Accord, and even it was on the borderline of still being too small. But the model that was finished-out the best had great seats, looked nice, had a fantastic stereo, and even I already knew that Hondas were pretty much bulletproof in terms of the engine. I was kinda speechless, but I finally told Don that I didn't think the Accord was quite what I wanted. Don left them his card and we walked out.

Next stop was the Toyota dealership where Don had bought the Corolla. The entire meeting lasted no more than an hour before I was signing the papers. I got a totally decked-out Camry, which seemed absolutely huge compared to the Corolla, and we got exactly what Don asked for on the trade. In the end, I put about half down and ended up with 36 payments of around $200 a month. And I had a new Camry, in a deep navy blue with a beige interior. It was amazing. I could NEVER have done that by myself. Once again, Don to the rescue.

I drove back to the house and showed it to Mom and Dad. They loved it. Then they said, "So what's your plan? When are you heading back down?"

I'd been putting that off. The whole thing seemed like the right thing from the moment we talked to Jack about what I should do, but staring it in the face was something I was totally unprepared for. It kinda seemed like jumping off a cliff.

I told Mom and Dad I wasn't sure. It was still only September. Maybe I'd wait until around Halloween before I left. I needed to talk to the Rangers about using the facilities all winter. I wanted to find out what other guys might be down there to work out with. I had to buy some new clothes. I needed to talk to Nike and Wilson about some new gear. I needed a new suitcase. I had to brush my teeth. I really needed to wash my hair. I had every excuse in the book, and then some.

Dad just looked at me and said, "Listen, man. This was a great idea. It's right for you. We're going to miss you every bit as much as you're going to miss us. You might be lonely for a while, until you get into the swing of things down there, but it's what you need to do. Look, we'll make plans to come down for Thanksgiving, and your mom will whip up a great meal in that cool new kitchen you have. Then we'll come back down for Christmas. And we'll come again when spring training starts. It will be baseball season before you know it, and then you'll be with your baseball family and everything will be cool. It's a huge step. You have to take it.

"Go buy a new suitcase. Get some Florida clothes. Buy a sports coat or a suit, too. You're going to end up in the big leagues by the end of the season and you'll need to dress the part. But call the Rangers tomorrow and get ready to go. It's a long drive, right? You need to take the step or the next thing we'll know is that it's the middle of February, you're still here, and you have an empty condo you're paying for but not using. Got it?"

I got it. Dad's advice was always priceless.

I called the Rangers and everything was fine with them. They were thrilled to hear about the condo down there. I'd have full access to everything, and as the assistant to the GM said, "There are always guys there. If we don't have any catchers, we'll get you one, but the gym is wide open for you and you can run and stretch anywhere you want in the complex. C'mon down. We love your commitment, Brooks."

I also needed to address the last gorilla in the room. I needed an agent. I couldn't talk to the Rangers about that since my new agent would be negotiating with them. I needed to talk to some of the guys. I called Dan Smith, who seemed kind of lukewarm about his agent, but he gave me contact info for a bunch of the big leaguers. I called Pudge Rodriguez first. We played together in Tulsa for a bit. He raved about his guy and gave me his info. I talked to a couple of pitchers, Jeff Russell and Bobby Witt, and by then I had a list to work with, whether it was their agents or ones they knew of. I think I had six or seven names scrawled on a notepad. I decided I'd start making calls when I got down to the condo. First, I needed to jump off the cliff.

With my new car, my new suitcase, some new clothes, and all my gear I hit the road around the first of October. Three days later I was in Cape Coral and unloading my stuff into the condo. The Camry had been awesome. I was cranking CDs the whole way, totally digging the fact it actually had a stereo and CD player. The next day I went over to the complex and found the guy who basically ran the place during the off-season. He set me up with a locker in the minor league building, and I put my stuff away. I was there. It was rad. I knew it was going to be a huge year for me. And heck, Mom and Dad would be showing up in just five or six weeks. I figured I better keep the condo clean and neat. Having them come down to live with me for a while was a huge motivator.

There were maybe a dozen other guys at the complex. Not all at the same time, and not every day, but it was a good mix. I wasn't going to start throwing for real until mid-December so I could play catch with anyone just to keep my arm loose. I ran a lot. I hit the gym pretty hard and the team did have a trainer there to work with us on what weights and machines we should use, and how best to use them, based on what position we played. I even took some regular BP in the cage, off a machine. I thought it was smart to do that. The Rangers were in the American League with the DH rule, but what if I ever got traded to a National League team? I'd have to hit. Swinging the bat came right back to me, and it was fun. One day I was hitting and an outfielder was waiting his turn. He said, "Wait, you're a pitcher right?" I said I was, but I thought it would be good to hit a little. He said, "Well, I was going to tell you to step out of there so a real hitter could get some hacks, but you hit better than I do. Son of a bitch." I fit right in.

After a few days, I took a morning to start making calls to my list of agents. Most of them were very interested and sounded like they'd be really happy to represent me. I made notes as I went, including things like commissions, how many people were on their staff, and the services they offered. One of them went really heavy on the super bonus of getting me equipment contracts, because most guys just out of Double-A didn't have those. I waited until he was done and said, "I signed last year with Nike and Wilson. I'm all set." The fact that news seemed to deflate him a little told me he wasn't the guy for me.

In the end, I chose a guy named Adam Fried. It's pronounced "Freed" and I learned that the hard way when I first said hello on the phone. It was just him and his brother at their agency. They only represented about a dozen baseball players, but they also worked for a few golfers and tennis players. Adam's line was: "We'd rather keep it manageable for the two of us and give you guys the best representation we can. The golfers and tennis players are easy. They get paid by the prize money they earn, and we just work on endorsements for them. The fun for us is negotiating for you guys in the baseball world.

"Oh, hang on for a sec. My brother Aaron just brought in your bio and stats from college and minor league ball. It's pretty clear you're going to the show if you stay healthy. So, if you want to work with us my mantra is always going to be: Stay healthy! You can make a lot of money in this game, Brooks. It doesn't happen all at once. You'll have to establish yourself at the big league level, but when you do you'll be a very rich young man. And we'll help get you there."

I told him I'd be honored. Two days later he flew down from New York and took me out for the nicest steak dinner I'd ever had. He had the contract with him, and I signed it. I had an agent. And he said, "You don't owe us a penny until the first time we represent you in terms of your contract. Sign what they send you this year." That was fair. I liked that.

For a guy who was so damn worried about heading to Florida on my own, the fall and winter ended up actually going by really fast. I spent at least four or five hours at the complex every day, I cooked most of my own meals. I did the mundane stuff like setting up bank accounts and paying my bills. Mom and Dad came down for Thanksgiving and stayed for a week. That was awesome, as was our turkey dinner. They came back for Christmas too, and I surprised them by having a tree all set up and decorated. OK, it was fake but it looked nice. I got them each a couple of presents, including some Texas Rangers gear for my dad, and we had another great time. They were already making plans to come back down once spring training officially started. Time was flying. And by then, I had a couple of catchers to work with at the complex (good guys who didn't mind the work) and I was starting to ramp it up. Baseball was close.

I didn't really do much in terms of socializing. For some reason, I couldn't stand going out to nice restaurants by myself and I'd just as soon have a cold brew at the condo rather than sit at a smelly bar somewhere. That stuff just felt awkward to me. I'd get take-out or make my own meals. I got really good at knowing where everything was at the Publix market just up the road and my cooking skills were improving rapidly. When in doubt, I'd call Mom. And she mailed me some great recipes for stuff I never would've tried to make. Meatloaf, stir fry, chicken parm, blackened chicken or pork chops, and pot roast were all in my regular rotation. And, I bought a crockpot and got all into that. Eating on the balcony at sunset wasn't too shabby either.

Finally, I moved my gear over to the big league side as a non-roster invitee, and the rest of the Major League club started showing up. I was technically assigned to the Triple-A Oklahoma City roster, but for at least three weeks I'd be working with the big leaguers and their coaches. It didn't suck.

The guys all treated me great. I was worried about that. Just a kid out of Double-A and a bit wide-eyed, so maybe they'd just ignore me, which would've been worse than having them pick on me. Instead, they were fantastic. I was relaxed and ready to go within the first 24 hours.

I knew Pudge, of course, and it was a treat to throw my bullpen sessions with him behind the plate. Geno Petralli was another catcher, and he was great to work with. Of course, the team brings in about every catcher from A-Ball on up for the first part of spring training, because so many pitchers need to get their work in, so I never knew who I'd be throwing to, but they were all stout and really good guys.

On the pitching staff, Kevin Brown threw darts and he was a cool dude. Bobby Witt was really supportive, and No. 34, Nolan Ryan, was there. I actually spoke to him early in camp, and that broke the ice, at least for me. Within a few days, the whole aura I'd placed around him kind of melted away. He was just a teammate. A surefire Hall of Fame teammate and one of the greatest pitchers of all time, but he was a teammate. He was a genuinely nice guy, but a man of few words. He did ask me about my life and career and was really great about making me feel welcome. He was also 45 years old, which was incredible. He worked as hard or harder than any other pitcher in camp. He was a physical specimen unlike anyone I'd ever been around, and his work ethic rubbed off on everyone. It definitely motivated me.

When the spring training exhibition schedule, with the pitching rotations, was posted in the clubhouse the hair on my arms stood straight up. Our second game of the spring, at the ballpark in Port Charlotte, would be against the Tigers. Bobby Witt would start and go one or two innings. Then Jeff Russell, followed by Dan Smith, Todd Burns, Steve Fireovid, and then there it was. My name. I didn't know how many innings I'd go. That kind of depended on how everyone before me pitched, but my name was there on the sheet. I called Mom and Dad. They had three days to get down there.

They arrived the day before the game, and we had a nice dinner together before heading back to the condo. Believe me, it was a thrill to fill out the "comp ticket request" form to leave them two tickets the next day.

Being a non-roster invitee to the big league camp, I didn't have my last name on the back of my jersey, and I had a typically huge number like most rookies. You don't walk into big league camp and get number 30 when you're not on the roster. I think my number was 67 or 68. Did I care? Hell, no. I was going to pitch in a Major League spring training game.

I wasn't nervous. I rarely am. The one thing I was kind of preoccupied with was when I'd spot Mom and Dad after they arrived. I knew where their seats were and, believe me, I kept looking for them. They'd rented their own car when they arrived and said they'd try to get to the ballpark at least an hour before the game. I was running a few poles on the warning track when I finally saw them. I jogged over to the railing and we all shared a group hug. This was kind of a big moment after all we'd been through as a family. Ya think?

When the game started I went to the bullpen and hung out down there. I could do some stretching and resistance training just to keep loose, but mostly I watched the game. Being the road team, the Tigers had only brought a few of their star players. I remember Mickey Tettleton was catching, and Bill Gullickson started on the mound, but no Lou Whitaker or Cecil Fielder. That was pretty typical back then. The veterans didn't have to make the bus ride if it was more than an hour. They could stay behind and just get some work in at their complex. In later years, MLB actually mandated a minimum number of starting players for all spring training games, because fans would follow their favorite teams even on the road and would be disappointed in seeing a bunch of guys wearing numbers in the 70s and 80s, who they had never heard of. I didn't care. Just like me, those were guys who were good enough to be in big league camp.

Bobby Witt went two innings for us, and the rest of the guys went one or two. It was cool to be sharing the bullpen with Dan Smith, and he pitched pretty well. In the seventh inning, they got the call down in the bullpen to get me started with my warm-up. I hadn't relieved in a long time. Hell, I'm not sure if I had relieved at all since maybe Little League. So that worried me. How fast do I get fired up? I can't run my poles to stick with my routines, so what do I do?

I just treated the seventh like it was pregame. By the time we were hitting in the bottom of the inning, I had a nice sweat going and felt ready. I walked into the dugout to be prepared to go in.

In the top of the eighth, I walked out to the mound like I'd done it with big leaguers a million times. It was an act, of course. I'd never done it. I took my eight warm-up pitches and took a deep breath. It helped, of course, that any veterans who'd made the bus ride were out of the game by then. But, like I said, these other guys were all good. I couldn't let down because they were rookies. They weren't letting down because I was one.

I honestly don't remember the score or who was on the field with me. I don't even remember who was catching. I just saw the signs and executed my pitches. To me, the

319

hitters were just the opposition. Nothing to be afraid of. I'd pitched in Double-A and most of these guys had just come from there, too.

In the eighth inning, it was three up and three down with two strikeouts. I walked to the dugout like I had expected to do that, and truthfully I kind of did feel that way.

I went back out for the top of the ninth and blew them away again. My fastball was hopping and I was hitting spots with it. My breaking ball was falling off the table. My change was great. For some reason, even that early in the spring, I just had a great feel for the ball and all three pitches. In my two innings I faced six batters and got six outs. Four of them were strikeouts. Mission accomplished. The whole freaking thing was just rad. When it was over, I saw my folks told them I'd meet them outside after I showered and changed. There was that look again, on my dad's face. Closed lips, misty eyes, and a slight nod. The "I'm so proud of you" look. My mom was beaming. I guess I might've been too. They headed back home the next day. I was so stoked they'd been there for me.

It was about as good as I could hope for. I'd gotten a ton of "Way to go, man" comments from my Ranger teammates, and the manager Bobby Valentine. It was all good.

I pitched in three more games over the next couple of weeks. I wasn't perfect. Maybe I was just super zoned-in for that first one, but I was OK. These were big leaguers. I pitched against the Cardinals in St. Pete and they had their regular lineup going. Since I was the second pitcher in that game, I went two innings and faced Ozzie Smith, Andres Galarraga, Todd Zeile, Ray Lankford and a couple of other guys I'd watched on TV. Gave up a couple of knocks but sent a few of them back to the dugout too, so we were even.

A few days later, I got the word I knew I'd be getting. The head of the farm system was in the room and he came over to see me. He said, "You're going to pitch in the big leagues, Brooks, and we think you're going to do it this year. But for now, we want you to get back into your starting routine and you'll do that at Oklahoma City. I think you'll do well there, and it's just a phone call from the show. I've never gotten through a season without having a pitcher or two called up, and I'm pretty sure you'll be the first one to go later this summer. Go on over to the complex, get your work in, get back to your routines, and just be yourself. Go get 'em. You did great here."

Like I said, it wasn't a shock or anything. I had a contract for Oklahoma City and I wasn't even on the Texas 40-man roster. I know a lot of casual fans don't understand the 40-man thing very much, so I'll try to simplify it. Every big league team can put 40 players on the big league roster. During my days, only 25 could actually be in the big leagues and play there (I think it's 26 now), but those who were on the 40-man were kind of interchangeable. I say "kind of" because there are some rules about it but we don't need to get into those details. I don't totally understand all of them. You could be promoted or demoted pretty easily.

If you weren't on the 40-man, it was a lot more complicated. The big club would have to remove someone from the 40-man to make room for you, and that meant exposing that guy to waivers. Any other team could claim him. 40-man spots are coveted by the players and closely guarded by the team. The reason guys like me generally weren't on the 40-man was the rule that the big league team had complete control over you for your first five years. After that, if you weren't "protected" with a spot on the 40-man, other teams could take you in what's called the Rule 5 draft. If a five-year minor league player is unprotected on the 40-man, he could be drafted by a different organization for $50,000. It's complicated, and I know this is really "deep-in-the-weeds" stuff, but as long as you're under five years in the organization and not yet ready for the big leagues, it would be really rare (or even dumb) for the team to put you on the 40-man. So that's how I knew I'd almost for sure be going to OK City.

Going from Butte to Gastonia and from Port Charlotte to Tulsa was a pretty big deal with a lot of planning and logistics involved. I mean, I had to get there! Going to the minor league camp to join the Oklahoma City 89ers meant packing my duffel bag and walking across the parking lot to the other side of the complex. No biggie.

Tommy Thompson was the manager for the 89ers. I met him in camp the year before. He played a long time in the minors but never made the big leagues, then he coached or managed for decades after that. A lot of guys think the best managers are guys who either never made it to the show or who struggled to stay there. Why? Because they had to work so hard to do it. Big league stars are gifted. They don't know the struggles. Tommy Thompson scratched and clawed for years just to keep his playing days going. I liked him immediately, and he said, "I know it's got to be a disappointment leaving the big league camp, but you're going to be our ace here. This is a tough league. Half these guys will play in the show and many have already been there. You're ready for this."

I just said, "Skip, I knew all along I was coming here. It was great to be over there but I'm ready to go and I'm ready to be everything you want me to be."

My pitching coach there was Oscar Acosta, who was my coach in Tulsa the year before, so there was some good continuity for me. I pitched in a couple of spring training games for OKC, and it seemed like time flew by before we were breaking camp and heading for Oklahoma. I locked up the condo, loaded my new Camry, and hit the road.

Speaking of the Camry, a number of guys were already asking me about it. With their bonus money or big league salaries, a lot of them were buying flashy cars and many of them wanted the biggest truck they could buy. They said: "Why are you driving that?" I guess they never saw the Corolla.

I told them it didn't mean a thing to me. I grew up with a dad who had an ancient VW surf bus and I loved it. My first car was a Corolla and I treasured it. I don't particularly like trucks and I don't need a car that's more than solid transportation. It's just not me. Some got it, some didn't. Maybe someday I'd step up to a BMW or an Audi or something like that. It just wasn't a priority for me yet.

Before we all left, we were kind of networking to see who might want to room together. Lance McCullers was a really good pitcher and on his way up through the organization, and we hit it off great. We wanted to find a third guy, though, to split the rent a little more. In the end, there were no pitchers still looking for a place. We were like the last kids to the Easter egg hunt and nothing was left. So we bit the bullet and decided we'd get a two-bedroom just for us. Lance and I both agreed that it was best to just room with other pitchers. Our routines and our needs were kind of the same, plus we could talk pitching when we were at home. We asked to be roomies on the road, as well. It was going to be good.

We found a nice apartment not far from the stadium, which was called All Sports Park and was basically part of the fairgrounds in OKC. Nice ballpark, and we'd soon discover it held the heat pretty well.

Lance actually got the start in our opener and he did well but we lost. I pitched the second game and remember thinking: "I just spent nearly a month with the big leaguers. I can get these guys out. Just focus and hit your spots. Don't be an idiot."

I was not an idiot. I think I pitched six innings and gave up exactly one hit. Struck out 10. Got the win. Rad to the max. Dealing my stuff at Triple-A. It was all kind of surreal.

I'd been keeping in touch with Eric all along, and after that first game, I called him. He was just home from his season and had done great again. He was what you'd call "established" by that point. I knew he had a long career ahead of him. I was stoked for him, and he was stoked for me. He had a ton of questions, like "What's Oklahoma City like?" and we had a great conversation.

By then, he and Carol were just a few months away from tying the knot around the fourth of July, and I was bummed I couldn't be part of that. I wouldn't say we were kindred souls yet, or anything like that, but Eric and I were really good friends of the highest order. He was really the only best friend I'd ever had. I couldn't imagine not being friends with him. He motivated me, he made me a better player, and the whole "focus" thing was something I worked on all spring and into the season. If I felt myself getting a little too complacent, I thought of Eric. It always worked.

In the American Association, we had Denver, Omaha, and Des Moines in our division. The East was made up of Buffalo, Indianapolis, Louisville, and Nashville. We'd play most of our games in our division, but I think we were scheduled to go to each team in the East twice. And here's a big step up from Double-A. Whenever we'd leave OKC, we'd fly. The only time we rode the bus was when back-to-back stops on the road were close enough. Like Omaha to Des Moines, or Indianapolis to Louisville.

Yeah, it was rad to fly that much, but it comes with its own set of issues. It was kind of like college. We flew on regular commercial flights, as a group, so there was a lot of waiting around at the ticket counter and at the gate. With a bus, as soon as the game's over you just get on and go. When flying, we'd have to spend the night in whatever town we were in and fly out in the morning, and that was often like a 6 o'clock flight to get us where we needed to be. We didn't have more than a couple of days off between the opener in April and the last game around September 1. We were constantly on the move. In some ways, the hum of the bus through the night was better, but it sure was hard to sleep on those trips.

We got into the routines quickly, and we had a bunch of guys who had been with OKC before, so there were plenty of guides to show us around each town or give us advice. For some reason, I liked Omaha the best. The ballpark there, Rosenblatt Stadium, was old-school but really cool. And it was the home of the College World Series, so there was a lot of history there. It was a nice town, and I'd usually go out and walk around downtown for a few hours before we left for the park. Maybe find a bookstore and thumb through a few paperbacks.

Basically all the towns in the league were nice, the ballparks were great, and just about everyone drew good crowds. With every step up in the minors, the crowds got bigger. It was common, in Triple-A, to play in front of 6,000 or more, and in Buffalo they drew huge crowds. Basically filling the place for every game, at around 12,000 fans. It was fun. It was feeling more real.

Over the course of April, May and the first few days of June, I was pretty consistent. It was a lot tougher than any other level I'd ever played at, but I just tried to keep my focus and forget about which hitters had played in the bigs. Just go after them. They haven't seen the likes of me, so I thought I had the upper hand. I got hit around every now and then, and lost a couple of games, but I struck out more than a hitter per inning, kept my ERA around 2.00, and I think I was something like 7-2 by the time June rolled around.

We had just finished up our first trip through the East division, and were getting on the early morning flight home to OKC from Indy. Skip came up to me in the gate area and said, "Come with me."

We took a stroll down the concourse and he said, "I have something to tell you. We're headed back to Oklahoma City and you'll come with us, but once we get there you need to pack your gear and your clothes. You're not staying."

I thought I knew what that meant, but I wasn't 100 percent sure. All I could say was, "Well, OK. Where am I going? Have I been traded?"

He said, "No. You haven't been traded and you're not getting sent down. Get the picture? You're going up to the big club. You'll have to be in Arlington tomorrow at the latest, but it's even better if you can get there today, if you can pull that off. Do you have a sports coat?"

I just looked at him blankly and then looked around the concourse. I had to make sure all the guys weren't hiding around a corner because it was all a big prank. I felt my heart absolutely racing. And I uttered the famous words, "That's totally rad, Skip. Are you serious?"

Then I said, "And yeah, I have a sports coat. I never put it in my closet. It hangs on the knob of the closet door so I can see it every day before I go to the park. It's my motivation to actually wear it because I'd only do that in the big leagues. What do I do? Where do I go? What's going to happen?"

He said, "Well, for right now we just fly back to Okie City. Then you can get your stuff together and bug out. We can fly you down to Dallas or you can drive. It's up to you. We'll have all the details when we get back to the ballpark. We'll work it all out.

"But here's a really big thing. I wanted you to know this so you can get your head wrapped around it. But, I need you to keep this to yourself until we get back. The big club has to make a couple of roster moves to make this happen. I don't want any word to slip out until they do that. Someone on the big club is going to get some bad news and they need to hear it from Bobby Valentine or Tom Grieve first. OK?"

I agreed. I didn't know how I'd do it, but I agreed. I didn't even call my parents, or Eric, or my agent. I just got on the plane and tried to act like I was sleeping. It was a 90-minute hop to OKC, but it seemed like a cross-country flight. I kept my eyes closed and faked it, but my brain was racing like it was on hyper-drive. Stoked? That was about 10 percent of how I truly felt. I'd never felt such a rush before in my life. Never. My skin was tingling. I couldn't believe it. I mean, I was confident I'd get my shot later in the year, maybe even in September when they could expand the active roster, but I never thought it would be in the second week of June. I still get goosebumps just remembering that flight and my conversation with our skipper.

By the time we landed I felt like I was going to burst. We took a bus from the airport to the ballpark, where all the guys had left their cars, and the first thing we did was go into the clubhouse to clear out all of our dirty clothes in our duffel bags. The clubhouse boys were going to have to hustle to have all that clean by late afternoon. I threw my uniform in the pile, but kept my underwear and undershirts in my bag. I was sure guys were staring at me, but that was probably just paranoia. I noticed that Skip had gone to his office.

A few minutes later, he came out and said to everyone, "Hey just stay put for a few minutes. We need to have a quick meeting. I'll be right with you."

Guys were looking around nervously. It's baseball instinct to assume that when something needs to be talked about, it would be about you.

Skip came back out and said something like, "OK, guys, just wanted to let you all know that the big club has made a couple of roster moves. They opened a spot on the 40-man by releasing a pitcher from Double-A, and they put a reliever on the 60-day Disabled List this morning. They've added Brooks Bennett to the 40-man and have called him up today. Congratulations, Brooks! Now come to my office for a bit. We've got details to work out." Everybody cheered and clapped.

We went in there and Skip called Texas. He got the traveling secretary on the line for me. He said, "Congratulations, Brooks. I hear you're driving down here, so when you get to Arlington we'll have you go straight to a hotel where we have a room for you. Then take a cab over to the ballpark. I'm faxing all this to the 89ers front office right now. It's about a four-hour drive. Can you get here before our game tonight?"

I figured I could. I had no idea what to do or where to go, but the fax would help and my road atlas would get me there.

When I came back out of his office there was a parade of guys coming by my locker. Lance was one of them and it hit me that he probably felt he should be going up, and now he didn't have a roomie. He'd be getting the call soon enough. I knew it. He was really good.

I got my fax and took a quick look. Then, we drove back to the apartment and I started packing. It didn't take long. I didn't have a lot of stuff, but the sports coat was the last thing I put in the car, hanging on the hook by the rear driver's-side door.

I had two choices about making phone calls. I could go back into the apartment and call everyone I wanted to tell, or I could wait until I got to the hotel in Arlington. I decided to go with Option B. I wanted to get there. I was afraid any one of those calls could last a while and wanted to make sure I got to the Dallas area as soon as I could. I said goodbye to Lance, and told him I'd see him soon. I was sure of that.

As I pulled out of the apartment parking area, it finally really hit me. I was going to the big leagues. I'd dreamed of this moment my whole life, since Dad was hobbling around those dirt fields in SoCal chasing the balls I'd hit. I dreamed of it in Little League. I dreamed of it in living color at Canyon High and then at Bloomington Kennedy. When I became a Gopher, the dream started to come into focus. By then, it wasn't as much a wild dream as it was a destination. When I got drafted by Texas and signed my first contract, my brain was telling me: "This is how you get there. The path is in front of you."

I never had any idea what it would be like or where and how it would happen. LIke, I hadn't even thought of learning about it in the concourse at the Indianapolis airport, then having to sit on a plane for 90 minutes pretending I was asleep so no one would bother me, but the whole thing was overwhelming. It was so freaking unbelievable. I kept shaking my head to make sure it wasn't a dream, and then I thought, "Hey, dude. Focus. Keep your eyes on the road and keep driving safely. It sure would be stupid to have a wreck driving to the big leagues."

So that's what I did. I focused. I kept my eyes straight ahead. I didn't speed. I didn't swerve. I just drove myself to the big leagues.

I got to the hotel, checked in and took my suitcase to the room, which was — well, unbelievable. This was the big leagues. This was the show. I'd never set foot in a room that nice. It was about 1 by then, so I had to hustle. At that point, I realized the big moment at the Indianapolis airport had happened the same day. It was that morning. It seemed like ancient history already.

I called home and Mom answered. She said, "Hey there. Are you still on the road? Where are you guys now?"

I said, "We flew back from Indianapolis this morning, but I'm not in Oklahoma City. I'm somewhere else."

"What? Where are you?"

I said, "Well, I'm in a hotel in Arlington, Texas, but I gotta get to the ballpark as soon as I can. The Rangers are playing the Mariners tonight. I'm in the big leagues, Mom. I'm in the freaking BIG LEAGUES! I can't believe it. They called me up."

She started crying, and I started crying, and then Dad got on the line and he started crying. It was total madness. We were all incapable of putting any words together other than "Wow."

I finally said, "Hey, I really gotta go. I just wanted you to know. We have games against Seattle tonight and tomorrow, and then we leave on a road trip to Oakland and Anaheim. How's that for fitting? I'll be in uniform and on the field at Anaheim Stadium. It's crazy. It's insane. But I love you both so much for getting me here. I'll call you tomorrow or later tonight. Wish me luck!"

325

Dad said, "You don't need luck. You need to be you. You earned this."

Then I called Eric but got an answering machine. I left him a short message and told him the basics, and that I'd try him again. He was home by then, after the season, but I didn't have any clue if he was on vacation or just on the golf course. Finally, I called my agent.

The funny thing was, he already knew. When you sign with an officially licensed agent, they contact the big club to register with them and let them know. The Rangers had called him, as a courtesy, about an hour earlier to let him know his new client was going to the big leagues.

"Congratulations, brother," Adam said. "This happened fast and you deserve it. So here's what's going to happen. You need to get to the ballpark and sign your new contract. I can guarantee you it will be for the Major League minimum, which is $109,000 this year. We have no leverage yet. You'll get paid every two weeks, so you'll make about 60% of that $109k by the end of the season. It'll seem like a lot of money the first time you see it in the bank, but it's nothing compared to what you're going to make. The average MLB salary right now is over a million for the first time ever. That's where you're going. Now focus on the baseball, my friend. That's what you need to focus on."

I went down to the desk and asked how to get a cab. They had the doorman handle that and one was pulling up in just a minute. I had put on khakis and had my navy blue sports coat on, over a golf shirt. Nike, of course. That was the best I could do. Buying some new clothes after the road trip would be a priority.

The driver took me directly to the players' entrance. I paid him and tipped him, and he wished me luck. I grabbed my duffel bag and walked into the most magnificent stadium I had ever seen.

It was rad beyond rad. It was gorgeous and huge. It was The Ballpark at Arlington. I followed the directions I'd been given and headed to the home clubhouse. I was nearly too afraid to open the door. When I did, I immediately saw a young guy wearing a credential around his neck, who said, "You must be Brooks!"

He was the assistant to the traveling secretary, and he immediately brought the head clubhouse attendant over. The clubbie would show me to my locker in the incredible clubhouse. As we walked through it, I saw jerseys with names like Palmeiro, Gonzales, Sierra and Rodriguez. It felt like a country club. I'd never even imagined anything like it. And then there it was. A huge wooden locker. Damn, it almost looked like mahogany. Hanging on a hook, on the front of the locker, was a jersey. It was number 49. The name on the back was Bennett. There was a printed Rangers name plate across the top of the locker, and it said Bennett, too. I swore I was going to pass out. I couldn't do that, though. I needed to act like I'd been there before. That was a lie, of course, but I had to act that way.

There were already a number of players in the room, starting to get ready for that night's game in a leisurely way. I knew most of them from spring training, and one by one they came by to shake my hand and welcome me. It was awesome.

Finally, another executive-looking guy, who was the senior traveling secretary, came by and said, "Can you come with me to the manager's office? We have some stuff for you to sign."

He introduced me to Bobby Valentine, and then the GM Tom Grieve came in. Tom was the guy who had called me to let me know the Rangers had drafted me, after my junior year at the U of M. It was all mind-boggling.

Tom said, "Brooks, we talked to Adam Fried and let him know. We've got a contract for you here. It's for a big league $109,000 salary, and you'll get paid the prorated amount every two weeks. If things go well, this will seem like meal money to you in a few years. If you look around this clubhouse, I think you can tell we take care of our ballplayers and we sign them to substantial contracts to keep them as Rangers. We're a tight family in here. We welcome you to the family."

I signed the contract, and some other stuff they put in front of me including IRS material. Then Bobby Valentine said, "Our pitching coach, Tom House, will be here in a second. I just wanted to welcome you to the team. We're going to use you. You're not here to watch."

I met Tom House and we talked about how they wanted to mix me into the group. I'd start out as a reliever. Their starting staff was good, with Kevin Brown, Jose Guzman, Bobby Witt, Roger Pavlik, and that guy named Nolan Ryan. They'd just put a reliever on the long-term DL and I'd be taking his place. I remember thinking it was really a good thing that they'd used me out of the 'pen in big league spring training. Doing that for the first time in the big leagues would be tough.

The traveling secretary came back in and dialed me in as to what was going to happen the next day. I needed to bring my suitcase to the park. We'd leave immediately after the game and take a charter flight to Oakland. When we got there, we'd take a bus to the hotel and all of our room keys would be in envelopes sitting on a table in the lobby. Just pick up your envelope and go. No roommates. Everyone had their own room. It seemed like a dream to me. It may have only been a four-hour drive from Oklahoma City, but the difference between Triple-A and Major League ball was about a million miles.

And speaking of the "meal money" Tom Grieve had referenced, that was another huge step up. In A-Ball I think we got $8 a day on the road. In Double-A I think it was $10. In Triple-A I remember it being $12. In the big leagues, at that time the meal money was around $60 a day on the road, although we'd always have food in the clubhouse. We got the meal money for the whole road trip, in cash, on the bus as we headed for the airport. How rad was that! For my first road trip, I'd be handed $360 in cash. Amazing.

He also let me know that the team was picking up my room in Arlington for one more night, when we got back from the road trip, and then I'd need to find a place to live. He said a lot of the young players lived in an apartment complex only about 20 minutes from the ballpark. He'd get me that information before we got back. I also had no clue what my paycheck would look like every two weeks. I tried doing the math in my head but everything was spinning so fast I couldn't, and I didn't have a calculator handy. Best I could come up with, thinking about it being at the same rate as $109,000 but only for the time I was there, and then having taxes withheld, it was maybe a little over $5,000 every two weeks. So maybe $10,000 a month. Somewhere in that range. It was a heck of a lot more than the $1,500 a month I was making the day before in Triple-A.

As soon as all that was over, it was time to focus. I wanted to feel at home. I wanted to feel like I belonged. By the time I got back to my locker, there was a clubhouse guy standing there with an official Rangers duffel bag. It had a laminated hang tag on it, with my name on one side and my number on the other. I'd be using that as long as I was a Ranger. He also said, "Don't ever carry your duffel bag. Just fill it up and leave it in front of your locker after the last game of every homestand. It will be waiting for you in the visitors clubhouse on the other end. Same with your suitcase. We take care of all of that. We'll have your suitcase waiting for you in your room."

Sheesh. I was blown away more by the minute. The fact I was going to be in uniform that night during a big league game seemed like the most manageable part of it. The baseball part I knew. All this other stuff was insane. And a bit overwhelming.

I finally took a deep breath and started to begin the routine of going from street clothes to my uniform. It's a slow process. It always has been, at least since early in high school. Back then, in Spanish class, our teacher showed us a movie about famous matadors in Mexico. I loved the fact they took at least an hour to get dressed for a bullfight. Everything in order. All a process. To me it was a vision of myself getting ready for a ballgame. If I was ever rushed to get ready, if I was ever late to get started, I panicked. It wasn't right. There's a process. Getting into that process in the Rangers' clubhouse grounded me.

Once I was ready, I headed out to the field. Walking through the tunnel and into the dugout was sort of like being born, I guess. You're all cozy and warm, then all of a sudden it's vivid colors, unimaginable surroundings, and completely different sounds and smells. I'll admit it, I was so stoked I stood on the top step of the dugout and just soaked it in for a minute. What an absolutely gorgeous ballpark. What a stunning green field. It was all perfectly manicured and every blade of grass was uniform and standing at attention. It was amazing.

I went out to run some poles and a few other pitchers were already out there. After three or four laps from pole to pole, we caught our breath and a couple of the guys told me more about Tom House, the pitching coach. They were all talking a mile a minute, saying that he was "way outside the box" but that they could feel the improvements they were making with him. One part of the training was having pitchers throw footballs to each other before games, and that was about to happen out in the outfield.

House came out with his bag of NFL footballs, and the guys all lined up, just like any ballplayers who are going to play catch, except they weren't going to throw baseballs. Tom came over to me and said, "Hey, I'm a little different, but we're learning so much about mechanics these days and all of these sports are connected. It's all about rotation and balance. Plus, throwing a football is fun."

I paired up with a guy and was as nervous as hell. I never played organized football.

I'd played some intramurals and tossed a ball around, but I was no quarterback and never thought I would be. Tom stayed right by me, showing me the proper rotational mechanics for throwing a spiral. It's legs, hips, torso, shoulder, and he even said, "Your non-throwing arm is all part of this. Otherwise it's just in the way." It was bizarre. But he was right. It was fun and I could feel the way all the muscle groups were working. All the guys seemed to have bought into it.

Oh, and by the way. When Hank Aaron hit his record-setting 715th home run in Atlanta, Tom House was on that Braves team and was in the bullpen, which was out beyond the left field fence. He caught it on the fly. Tom then ran it all the way to home plate and pushed his way through the crowd to hand it to Hank. For a long time, that's what he was famous for. By the time I got to Arlington, he was quickly becoming famous as a revolutionary pitching coach. He was breaking a lot of old-school "eyeball" rules and getting much more into the science of how the body works. Looking back on it now, he changed the sport. He moved the bar and got teams out of their old-school ways. Now THAT is rad.

After the football routine, Tom walked with me back to the dugout and said, "Just come on out to the bullpen for the game. You've had a long day and we don't plan to use you tonight. Soak it in. Watch how the guys go about their business, and then be ready for anything tomorrow. OK?"

Yeah, that was OK. And damn, he was right. It had been a long day. Just that very morning I was in the Indy airport learning I'd been called up. And now I was on the field at The Ballpark in Arlington. Crazy, rad, and bizarre. Insane, too.

I watched the game. I talked with a bunch of the guys. We basically got to know one another. Our starter (I'm thinking it was Bobby Witt) left after five and it was a procession of relievers, one after another, getting up, getting loose, and heading to the mound. I was in a different world. It was a close game, but my memory tells me we lost because the clubhouse was really quiet afterward. I took my shower, got dressed, and was ready to head back to the hotel. And then I realized my car was parked there. I'd taken a cab to get to the park. Tom House was right. What a helluva long day it had been. I asked around and found a ride back. I don't even remember who gave me the lift. I was pretty groggy by then. Slept like a brick when I got to my room.

The next night, it was my turn.

I checked out of the hotel and got to the park early, as I always do. This time I drove and parked in the players reserved lot. I felt a lot more like a Texas Ranger. When I got in the clubhouse, Tom House came up to me and said, "OK, now it's baseball for you. If we need you, we'll run you out there. You were able to soak it in yesterday. Now it's game time. So, be mentally prepared."

I talked a little more with the clubhouse attendants about what I was supposed to do with my duffel bag after the game. They just said, "Put anything extra you want in there, whether it's spikes or gloves. Then put your home uni on the floor. We'll take care of everything else." They took my rolling suitcase away as soon as I walked in. It was a pretty remarkable system.

I did my running. I played some catch and then we threw footballs. I shagged fly balls during BP. And then it was time for the national anthem. The funny thing was that I didn't really remember the national anthem from the night before! I must have been distracted or just zoned out. I remember every second of it from that second night.

Kevin Brown was the starter against the Mariners. I loved his delivery and his stuff, but it wasn't a style too many guys could do well. It's what suited him, and Tom House knew that. He drew his arm back like a normal overhand delivery, but then dropped his arm slot into a kind of hybrid three-quarter sidearm thing. Basically, he was nasty. He threw hard and everything moved. I made sure I was in the bullpen when he warmed up. I wanted to see it up close.

He pitched six solid innings, but had thrown a lot of pitches and even though we were winning, the call came down to the bullpen. I heard the words, "Brooks, you're up."

I loosened up, started throwing from in front of the mound, and then when I felt like I was ready I got on the rubber and motioned to the catcher that he should get in his catching position. I was throwing bullets within 10 pitches, and that almost worried me. Am I overthrowing? Am I too amped up? Maybe it's just the acoustics in the Rangers bullpen? I tried to put it all out of my mind.

And here's another "inside baseball" tidbit for you. In the game, the catcher signals the pitches in his crouch. You can shake him off if you want to, but he initiates it. He's calling the game. In the bullpen or when warming up for a new inning, it's the reverse. The pitcher signals the catcher and lets him know what's coming, and it's all done with the glove. Flick the backside of your glove up, and it's a fastball. Turn your glove over in a downward circle, and it's a curve. Flick it sideways and it's a slider. Open the glove up toward the catcher and push it forward, then pull it back, and it's a change. The only signal you'd give him with your throwing hand would be for a knuckleball. Those guys would typically bend their fingers like they were gripping the ball (or actually grip it) and wiggle it back and forth. I didn't have to worry about that one. I never threw a knuckleball. I didn't really have a useful slider either.

Anyway, Kevin gave up two pretty sharp hits back to back to open the seventh inning, and I saw Bobby Valentine head to the mound. Then I saw him point to the bullpen. I was going in.

The Rangers bullpen was elevated and behind the outfield wall. To get to the field, you walked down a small flight of stairs and went through a door. When I did that, I entered a new world.

We had almost a completely full house. I tried to focus on what I was about to do and not on the ballpark and the fans. I had to get to the mound and I wanted my blood flowing, so I jogged in there pretty fast. I was kind of surprised there was some applause going on but then I realized it wasn't for me. The fans were just acknowledging Kevin's effort as he walked to the dugout. I got to the mound and Bobby handed me the ball, saying, "Welcome to the big leagues, kid." Pudge said, "Let's just keep it simple. I know these hitters. If you hate the signal, shake me off. But stick with me if you can." I just nodded and said, "Let's do this."

I took my eight warm-up pitches and felt great. And this was the first time I could ever remember coming into a game in mid-inning. In spring training, I came in to start the innings as a reliever.

I had men on first and second with nobody out. Harold Reynolds was the hitter. These days he's famous for being an analyst and host on the MLB Network on TV. Back then he was known as a fine player and really tough out. He was also a switch-hitter, so he was batting left-handed against me. Pudge put down one finger and pointed it to his left thigh, which signified a fastball on the outside corner against Harold. He took it. Strike one. Next signal was for my change up. I was a little worried about being too amped for that, but I didn't argue. Harold saw it and was late recognizing it. He basically flipped the bat at the ball and hit a fairly slow roller into the hole by our shortstop, Dickie Thon. Dickie made a helluva play, backhanding the ball then leaping and throwing to Al Newman, our second baseman. They got the force out by inches. It struck me right then that I was in the big leagues. These guys could really play.

Now I had first and third and one out. The runner at third "belonged" to Kevin in terms of his stats, since he put him on base, and I really wanted to protect him and not let that guy score. The next hitter was just a guy named Edgar Martinez. One of the best hitters to ever play the game, and about impossible to strike out. We started him off with a fastball away and he was way more eager than I had imagined he'd be. He hit a two hopper to Dickie, who threw over to Al, and then to Rafael Palmeiro at first. Double play. Out of the inning.

I got to the dugout and a lot of guys were waiting on the top step, including the skipper and my pitching coach. Lots of handshakes and pats on the butt. Bobby said, "Way to go kid. You're done. That was a helluva way to make your debut against two good hitters. Well done."

I don't remember who pitched the eighth but Jeff Russell was our closer, and he came in to get three outs in the ninth. Game over. That was fun.

I took my shower and tried to do everything the clubbie had told me about my bag. It was all a bit of a fog though, so I was peeking around to see what the other guys were doing. Finally, it was time to get on the bus, which would actually drive right out onto the tarmac where the charter flight was parked, so there was no need for us to go through the huge DFW airport. There were a couple of security guards checking our bags and stuff, but nothing like we live with today.

When we got on the plane, I wasn't sure where to sit. The seats were configured two and two all the way back, and the last rows had seats that faced each other with tables in between. There were still way more seats than players, coaches, and staff but I figured the front of the plane, which was just like a normal First Class cabin, was for the skipper and his coaches, and the back of the plane would be where the guys who liked to play cards would sit. So I sat in a window seat right over the wing. No one looked at me cross-eyed or told me to move, so I guess I did it right.

The whole charter thing was just another amazing experience. A full flight crew with catered meals waited on us constantly. At first the guys were all pretty animated, but then

331

as we got into the flight more and more of them settled down and reclined their seats to relax. I had about zero chance of relaxing. I was staring out the window at the moon. I was reliving my inning. I was a kid again, just learning to pitch. I was at Dodger Stadium with my dad, watching Nolan Ryan, and the same Nolan Ryan was on the plane with me. It was rad beyond my wildest dreams.

We got to Oakland and sure enough, the lobby was quiet and the table was set up for us. I found my envelope and went up to my room. There was my suitcase, waiting for me. By then it was about 1:30 in the morning, Pacific time. I just lay on top of the bed and put my head on the pillow. I woke up around 4 in the morning, still on top of the bed, and had no idea where I was. I finally slept until 8 or 9.

The first thing I did was call Mom and Dad, collect, of course. I wasn't going to be the stupid bozo rookie who ran up a bunch of phone charges on his first road trip. I filled them in on everything. We talked for an hour. Then I called Eric. This time I got him, and the first words out of my mouth were, "OK, dude, now we're both officially in the big leagues! I pitched one inning last night against the Mariners. Got 'em out, too." He said, "Really? Are you kidding me?" He was neck deep in getting ready for their wedding in a couple weeks, but he wanted to know everything.

Looking back on this now, I'd forgotten we had a day off that first day out there. I'd also forgotten that we actually stayed in San Francisco. I guess there weren't any hotels in Oakland up to big league standards back then. Now, it's all coming back to me. I saw a couple of other relievers in the lobby, and they said they were going to walk around and maybe ride the cable cars. They invited me to come along and I was thrilled to do that. I'd never been to San Francisco and couldn't believe the place. It was like no American city I'd ever been to. I loved it. It was a beautiful day. The guys were talking about what their dinner plans were, and there were no shortage of fine places to eat in San Francisco. They asked me to come along, saying, "You better put your sports coat on. These places are nice."

I only worried about one thing. I'd been welcomed with open arms by the team, but I could imagine it might be a tradition to ask the rookie out to dinner and then leave him with the bill. My MasterCard limit had been raised to $1,500 by then, but a steak dinner in San Francisco could stretch what I had to spend. We went back to the hotel after our walk and the cable car rides, and met in the lobby a few hours later. I launched my preemptive attack on them. "Thanks for asking me out, guys. This is on me. You guys buy me dinner next time."

They looked a bit confused, and both started stammering "No way. No way. You haven't even been paid yet. This is San Francisco, not Oklahoma City." My reverse psychology worked like a charm! And dinner was incredible, right down on the bay at Scoma's at Fisherman's Wharf. I've been back there many times. We split the bill three ways.

The next day, we headed over to the Oakland Coliseum, and it blew my mind in some different ways. It was so spacious it was nuts. Our park in Arlington seemed to go straight up, and it towered over us. The Oakland park was laid way back, so it seemed a mile away. And there was so much foul territory next to the infield I think you could've played three games at once.

In that first game, Nolan Ryan was on the mound and you can imagine how much attention I paid to that. He didn't have his sharpest stuff but got through five or six, then Bobby went crazy with "match-up pitching," running different relievers out there to try to get the best match-ups against the hitters. As that happened, I realized that just about the entire bullpen had been used, which meant I had a pretty good chance of pitching again the next night.

I didn't though. Both of our starters went pretty deep in the next two games, but we lost both of them and I never got in. After the game, another getaway on the charter jet down to SoCal. We flew into John Wayne Airport in Santa Ana and stayed at a nice hotel right in Anaheim. I was home. I couldn't wait to get to the park the next day.

It was pretty magical. I'd been there many times but never by getting off a bus and walking into the private players' entrance. And I'd never been in the visitors clubhouse and seen my stuff, all cleaned and ready, hanging in my locker. And I'd never seen the park from the perspective of the playing field and bullpen. We lost that first one and I didn't pitch. I called Dad the next morning and told him how nostalgic it all was, but that I hadn't pitched again since that first inning in Texas. He just told me to hang in there and enjoy it.

I didn't pitch the next night either, but after the game Tom House put his arm around my shoulder in the dugout and said, "Don't worry, Brooksie. We'll get you in there. We need you."

The next night, the same deal. We lost again, but our starter went the distance. I got to watch from the bullpen. After the game, there was a long red-eye flight home. I don't think we got there before 4 in the morning. The team had gotten me a room again, because we had the next day off and that would be my chance to get out and find a place to live. I found a nice apartment in Arlington, in a complex with a pool and where at least six other young players lived, and signed my lease. It was for six months; the shortest lease they could offer. No matter what happened, whether I stayed on the team all season or got sent back down, I was going to lose my deposit when I broke that lease. That's life in baseball.

It all became the standard blur when we got back home and I had my first totally rad big league road trip under my belt. Homestands and road trips. Meetings before the game, with all the pitchers and catchers, to go over scouting reports and talk about how we wanted to attack the other team. Throwing footballs in the outfield, shagging fly balls, and being ready to go.

I pitched in Yankee Freaking Stadium. I think I saw the whole American League. Fenway Park. Incredible. The SkyDome in Toronto. Gigantic. Royals Stadium in Kansas City. Gorgeous. All of them. Some amazing, some just blah. All in the big leagues. Long road trips. Home stands that were broiling hot in Dallas. Plane rides that lasted forever and almost always got to the destination in the middle of the night. It was constant. Even when we did get a day off at home, most of the guys went to the ballpark anyway, just to work out or hit in the cage. They were such professionals. It was really bitchin' to watch how dedicated they were.

In September, we went to the Twin Cities to play the Twins in the Metrodome. My dad asked for the night off from vending so that he could watch the game and hopefully see his son pitch. I did. Three up and three down with two strikeouts, and one of them was Kirby Puckett. Unbelievable. My dad was as stoked as I'd ever seen him after the game. He wasn't giving me that "I'm so proud of you" look. He was smiling as wide as I'd ever seen him grin, and he just kept laughing. I think we were both equally proud of each other. I was sure as hell proud to be his son.

By the end of it, I wasn't intimidated at all. The guys I was trying to get out were phenomenal hitters who didn't often bite at bad pitches and often crushed the good ones, but the guys behind me made plays I'd never seen before and made them look easy. It was freaking amazing. If I never got back to the big leagues, I knew I would never forget any of it. And yes, Yankee Stadium was stout. Just another night when I walked out on the field and had my mind blown

As it turned out, I stayed with the team until the end of the year. I got in 20 games, all in relief.

- 20 games
- 29 innings pitched
- 18 hits
- 34 strikeouts
- 8 walks
- 2.10 ERA

And Bobby Valentine got fired in early August. I'd never been around anything like that. It was pretty gloomy in the clubhouse, but Toby Harrah was named the new manager and we all liked him. He was a coach on the staff, and a former Ranger himself.

It was the biggest adventure of my life up until that point and nothing is a close second.

I keep using the word "adventure" and I apologize if I'm using it too much. It's just the best way I can describe living that dream for four months of non-stop big league baseball. It's sure easy to get used to. I absolutely felt like a Major League baseball player. It felt really good, too.

And I was right about Lance McCullers. He joined us in early September. Heck of a pitcher and heck of a guy. His son, Lance McCullers Jr. is in the big leagues as I write this. He's a stud. Just like his dad.

CHAPTER 34

Eric Olson

As soon as I got home from New York, Carol and I shared the much-needed hugs and kisses then had a fantastic dinner at one of the great steakhouses in Minneapolis, which seemed kind of extravagant for us. During that dinner we talked about details for the wedding.

I probably don't need to say that she and her mom had already gotten well down the road on all of it, as they needed to do and as they both really wanted to do. Now that I was home, I could have some more input but I wasn't there to change anything. This was all about family. I was just the groom.

To me, the whole production of a wedding really is about family, as opposed to just the couple. That's the way it was growing up in Roseau. The grooms just kind of went along with the flow while the women planned it all out in deep detail. For one thing, there weren't that many venues available to hold much more than an average-sized ceremony and reception. And reservations had to be made well in advance. So, while I was flying around to Toronto, Montreal, St. Louis, Chicago and other NHL cities, they were getting it all lined up. My only real jobs were to select a tuxedo style and pick my groomsmen and ushers. I'd been thinking about that for most of the winter, but I needed Carol to tell me about the bridesmaids so I could match up the groomsmen, in terms of equal numbers. Carol didn't want to distract me while the season was going on, but when we'd talk on the phone she'd drop a few details on me, just to judge my reaction. At least I felt "in touch," although I couldn't be totally involved.

That summer, July 4th fell on a Saturday. That seemed like a great date for everything. I'd be sure to never forget our anniversary and we could always claim all the fireworks were for us!

So that was settled. Where to have the wedding was about 90 percent handled, but she wanted my "blessing," so to speak. Both of our families are Catholic, although my family was much less into the pomp and circumstance of actually going to church. My mom used to say, "God is aware of what you're doing. Just be a good person to everyone.

That means more than going to a building every Sunday to kneel down. You can pray wherever you want." That's how we were raised. We went to Sacred Heart Catholic Church on Easter and on Christmas, but that was about it. And we were all good people, heeding my mom's really important words.

Carol's family was quite a bit different, except for Carol. She and I had never gone to church together, but her parents were at Sacred Heart every Sunday, come rain, snow, or -25 temperatures. It was important to them. So Sacred Heart was the place for us. I was fine with that.

And here's a neat coincidence. Sacred Heart is basically right on the same parking lot as the Roseau Memorial Arena and the American Legion Hall. Back in mid-winter, Carol and her mom were already talking to the Legion about hosting the reception. They also talked to the people at Memorial Arena about it. That seemed like a really cool idea to me. There wouldn't be any ice, so the rink could be a dance floor, and the lobby could be set up for a buffet. Why not?

Well, the "why not?" ended up being how hard it was going to be to pull it off. We'd have to hire a caterer, all that would have to be brought in, a DJ setup would need to be brought in too, and the arena people really didn't want people wandering around the locker rooms, the Zamboni, and the ice plant. We'd also be 100 percent in charge of turning it from an ice arena into a reception hall, from tables and coverings to all the other decorations. We settled on the Legion. They had their own kitchen and a room we could rent. They also had a lot of experience setting it all up. We'd still need a DJ, but that was not a problem because they had connections. I think we were lucky as heck to get the church and the Legion on the 4th of July.

As for the guest list, we had to keep an eye on that because the Legion wasn't all that big, but Roseau is a small tight-knit community. We finally just came to the conclusion that if any other friends in town wanted to drop in, that would be fine. They were our extended Roseau family. We'd find a way.

In March, Carol told me who her bridesmaids would be. There would be a total of six, and one of them would be my sister Betsy, which I thought was really neat. So I needed six groomsmen and a couple of ushers. I asked Paul Broten, my three brothers, and two close friends I played with for all those years in Roseau, from childhood up through the varsity, Scott Vatnsdal and Sean Bucy. For my ushers, I picked Tracy "Bobcat" Ostby and David Drown. I asked my oldest brother, David Jr., to be my best man. He was always someone I looked up to.

The date was screaming up fast, and I hadn't settled on honeymoon plans yet. We both wanted to go somewhere exotic and a place we'd never been before, and Hawaii was the first choice. Once I saw the fares for flights, I was pretty shocked. I told Carol I didn't think we could afford it, but her response was, "We can afford it. We're only going to get to go on one honeymoon. Let's make it one we'll never forget." In the end, her parents and mine combined to give us a generous cash gift as one of our wedding presents, which we used to refill our bank accounts after I bought the tickets and booked a hotel in Honolulu.

Right after I got home from New York, Brooks called. He could always get a little more animated than me, but I'd never really heard him like he sounded on that call. He was almost hyperventilating. I think he said something like, "I'm calling you from a hotel room, but guess where it is." All I said was, "You tell me."

"I'm in Arlington, Texas, dude. They freaking called me up. I've got to get over to the ballpark right away but wanted to let you know. We've both done it, brother. We're both in the big show. How rad is that?!"

I had goosebumps and let out a big "Woo Hoo!" into the phone. Then I added, "I called this shot. I told you. I knew you could do this, and now you can prove that you deserve to be there. Get to the ballpark. Put on the uniform. Walk out onto the grass, man. Do it all. You only get one first day in the big leagues."

That was really fantastic. And it clinched the fact he couldn't make the wedding. But that was OK by me. My buddy was in the big leagues. We were both Rangers!

Within days, everything was finalized for the wedding. I picked out the tuxes, black and traditional. Carol and her mom settled on all the other plans and details, and all that was left to worry about was whether no one would come or everyone in Roseau would come. Carol and I didn't care. We'd make sure our families and the wedding party would be taken care of on the seating chart, and if more people came than we invited it would be something we'd always talk about later. Because the Legion room was actually a restaurant when it wasn't hosting events, they had a full kitchen and could keep up with the demand. A regular caterer would just run out of food and that would be it. We could settle up the bill afterward if we went over because they had to make more food. It's a small town. They knew where to find us. We'd also have a cash bar. We weren't going to buy beer for the entire town of Roseau. No one could afford that!

And, while all that was going on, one of my missions was to pick an agent. It might have been the off-season, but hockey was part of my daily life. After talking to a number of guys on the Rangers, I picked a small agency out of New York. I thought that would be good. As long as I was a Ranger I could at least go see those guys rather than just talk on the phone. They specialized in hockey, and had a great track record. I think three other guys on the team were signed with them and they all were very impressed. The owner was Robert Hamm and my personal rep would be a young guy named Peter Corbin. I liked them both, at least on the phone. I also told them about the wedding and the honeymoon, so I'd have to wait until all that was over before we could formalize it. I just said, "You have my word. I'm with you." They were fine with that. The name of the agency was Hamm Sports Agency. Gosh, there was a lot going on.

Carol was getting a little nervous. Her mom was basically a basket case by that point because she was really detail-oriented and a serious planner. Carol was, too, but she kept her composure and didn't let it get to her too much. My buddies and I were just along for the ride. On July 4 we'd put our monkey suits on and go do it.

On July 1 it finally really hit me. I was getting married. Roseau was home and always would be, but I had just spent about eight months living in Queens or in hotels, and Carol and I lived in the Twin Cities. There was a lot to figure out, down the road, including her career, where we'd live, and other "small stuff" like that, but we needed to focus on the wedding.

It's light outside until close to 10 p.m. that time of year in Roseau, so we decided to have the wedding start at 5. It would last about an hour, then we'd need to take all the pictures before we kicked off the reception. I had no idea of the deep level of planning that went into this sort of thing. I'd been to a few weddings, but never thought about it. The ceremony, the photos, the meal, and the dancing were all mapped out. We figured it might be 10 before it all wound down, and if that was the case we could all head over to watch fireworks in our formal clothes.

We had a rehearsal on Friday and that went well. Sort of like a scrimmage, I guess. We all had to learn our roles and know where to be. "You be here, and you fill in when he moves over there. When your bridesmaid starts coming up the aisle, you break and head straight for her. Stay tight. Stay together!"

July 4, our wedding day, is now a blur. Because all the guys were from Roseau, we all had our own places to stay and we could just get dressed at home and meet at the church. I was hoping I knew how to put on a tux the right way, and figured at least one guy would show up with something in the wrong place. I think we all did OK, though. Thank goodness for clip-on bow ties.

We got there at 4:15 and the photographer wanted some extra shots of just us guys, so we posed around the church for a bit. By 4:50, though, we had to be inside and in one of the back rooms behind the altar. Obviously, as is tradition, I wasn't allowed to see Carol until she walked down the aisle.

I really wasn't too nervous. I figured if I wasn't nervous playing the Canadiens, the Oilers, or the Flyers there was no reason to be nervous about a wedding. I didn't think any of the bridesmaids were going to plaster me into the boards, although I'd have to keep an eye on Betsy. She'd do something like that.

My guys and I walked out and were happy to see the place packed. One by one, the groomsmen went down the aisle and hooked arms with their assigned bridesmaids to walk them to the altar, and pretty soon I was the only guy left up there without a girl. Then the music started and everyone stood up. Carol came out, met up with her dad, and they began walking up the aisle to "Here Comes the Bride." For one of the few times in my life I thought I was going to cry happy tears. I basically never do that, but she was overwhelming me as her dad walked her toward me. I made my move, shook his hand, he kissed her, and Carol and I walked up onto the altar. She was gorgeous. My gosh, she looked like a princess and an angel all rolled into one. She had a white veil on, but those big, round, dark-brown eyes just pierced me, right into my soul.

As for the actual wedding, I don't remember much. I think my head was spinning too fast for any memories to lock in. It's like we walked up onto the altar and the next thing I knew we were saying, "I do."

I raised her veil and kissed her and all those years of being childhood friends, then getting a little interested in each other, then having to head our own ways after high school because we were both determined to follow our own paths, and then finally realizing there was no one on the planet better suited for us than each other, flooded through my mind all at once. And here we were with rings on, staring into each other's eyes. A couple of huge tears rolled down her cheek. I was the luckiest man in the world.

We walked the greeting line, got rice thrown on us, and then took a ton more pictures. Finally, we could walk over to the Legion and join everyone else. They all had a head start on us.

Again, I don't have a lot of firm memories of the reception. Some speeches, and David's was apparently great because people still talk about it, a lot of toasts, some champagne, some beer, a nice buffet, and then dancing. OK, dancing is not my forte but we had a riot. I got to pick the slow song we'd dance to as husband and wife, and I chose "Wonderful Tonight" by Eric Clapton. I really wanted "Thunderstruck" by AC/DC but was told it was impossible to slow dance to and it was not appropriate. I'm kidding. But seriously, I think "Wonderful Tonight" might lead the world in most wedding reception first dances, and it's a perfect song for a night like that. Carol was crying again, so it must have been a good choice.

To me, looking back on that night, it was like a dream where you're in a dark room and faces just keep swooshing by, almost like ghosts. You try to say hi and talk to everyone, and I really wanted to spend more time with my family, but my mom said, "You've spent your whole life with us. Now you're going to spend the rest of it with Carol. You stay by her side, young man. Forever." I gave her a hug and it felt like a real defining point in my life. Moving on to the next phase. What was then was then. What's now is now.

We did, indeed, find a place to watch fireworks. It was a great way to end the evening. And then Carol and I went to our little room in a roadside motel for our first night as a married couple. There weren't a lot of other options in Roseau. We also had a whole pile of cash from the "dollar dance" and the cards people left for us. Not gonna lie. That was fun.

Our flight to Honolulu left Minneapolis around noon Monday, so we were able to have breakfast with our parents and say goodbye to everyone on Sunday. We drove down to the apartment and finished the honeymoon packing we'd started before we went north for the ceremony.

What I remember most about the flight was that it was really long. Easily the longest flight I'd ever been on, but it was made a little easier by the fact we stopped in L.A. for fuel. Still, it was about 10 hours in the air before we touched down on Oahu. I was glued to the window as we approached. There'd been nothing to see for about five hours as we crossed a big hunk of the Pacific, and then there was a lush green island below us.

We were staying in Waikiki, right on the beach, so we took a cab there, checked in, put our stuff away, put on shorts and T-shirts, and went for a walk. The sight of Diamond Head looked exactly like all the photos we'd seen. Waikiki looked so exotic, with all the palm trees in the foreground and surfers riding small waves. I had my arm around Carol and we were both speechless. It was paradise.

For five days we swam, we walked and we ate like royalty. I had enough of a credit line by then, on my MasterCard, to handle most of that but I also brought a lot of cash along as well.

We went to Pearl Harbor and both of us really got our first understanding of the history of the place and December 7. I didn't know much about World War II but the Arizona Memorial was a place that grabbed me and shook me up. Then, we walked to the top of Diamond Head, which is a fun hike, and at the top there's more World War II stuff. There are old concrete gun emplacements still there.

We rented snorkel gear and swam around a small protected lagoon just off the foot of Diamond Head, looking small tropical fish in the eye as they swam by. We had Mai Tais, ate pineapple, and sat on our balcony overlooking the beach, every night, just soaking it all in. We were both sad to see it end. We loved every minute of it. And then there was the flight home. It's a red-eye that leaves Honolulu around 8 p.m. and gets into Minneapolis around 5 or 6 a.m. Pretty awful, but we were spent from all the excitement we'd been going through so it was easy to sleep. We even had one last Mai Tai on the plane, because as Carol said, "I don't think you can get these anywhere else, and we don't know when we'll have another one!" Sounded like good logic to me.

I felt like a bit of a slug when we got back. I knew I had to ramp up the workouts and get back in shape, so that's how I spent the rest of July and all of August. Then, it was back to Rye, New York, for training camp. I'd signed officially with Robert Hamm by then so he and Peter handled my new contract. Robert said, "You're a second-year player, but you're established pretty well already. We're not taking their first offer. We'll see what we can do."

The first offer, it turned out, was for $34,000, which was a $4,000 raise. Robert and Peter came back at $40,000, which really scared me. Peter said, "Don't worry. They get it. It's a negotiation. It's a dance. But you deserve to get every penny they can afford to give you." We ended up at $38,000. I was happy, and relieved.

I had to leave Carol to play hockey, and that stunk. Her job was way too important, and I needed to be fully focused on playing and surviving in the NHL, so we both knew it was coming. She was already scouring the schedule to see when we'd be playing the North Stars in Minnesota, but she also noted when we'd be in St. Louis and Chicago, because both of those cities are easy to get to from Minneapolis. On top of that, she really wanted to come to New York and experience the city. I figured we might be able to see each other four or five times during the season. We'd make it work.

With my nice raise, I teamed up with just one other guy as a roomie. He was Doug Weight, who was only 22 and looking for a place. We found a nice two-bedroom in Queens, right near the subway again. It was a better arrangement than sharing an apartment with three other guys. Doug was a center, so that would be different but I thought it would be valuable. I wanted to hear what he expected from his defensemen, and what made his offense click the most. Plus, he was a really good guy.

I remember we opened on the road in DC against the Capitals, and then it was the endless series of rinks, buses, planes and hotels. I do remember the first time we played the North Stars at the Met Center, because I got to see Carol and my family, but the team plane left right after the game to head back to New York to play a few nights later. We had two days off before that game back at Madison Square Garden, and a couple days before we played Detroit, so Carol flew in for that whole homestand. Hockey life is busy, but we made time to ride the subway, visit Central Park, walk up and down Broadway, and even went to see a play one night. I have no memory of what it was, other than it was a musical and I had no clue what was going on. Carol loved it. That's all that mattered.

She also fell for New York, and said "I could see living here. So much buzz. So much hustle and bustle. It's electric." I told her I'd have to play a few more years and finally land a really big contract if she wanted to live in Manhattan. I also had no doubt she could land a marketing job with just about any firm in the city.

Carol went home, I put my head down and just kept trying to do the work. I was playing as well as I had the year before, but I wasn't sure I had gotten any better. Maybe the wedding and honeymoon had an effect on me, or maybe it was just a hockey hangover after my first year in the league. It takes its toll on a guy, especially a defenseman. You really need the rest after all those collisions and checks.

I had seen no indication in training camp that we weren't basically the same first-place team from the year before. Nothing at all showed itself to me. Basically the same guys with some new young talent. I just figured we'd be good. We did get off to a bit of a slow start, but I think all of us assumed we'd find our stride and get going. We just never did.

After 20 games, which is almost a quarter of the season, we were mucking along at 10-8-2. After 40 games, we were 19-17-4. That hot streak we all expected seemed to show up here and there, but it never stuck around. We finished the season with a seven-game losing streak and our final record was 34-39-11, for 79 points. We finished last in the division and missed the playoffs. What a stunner that was, but I think once we sensed we were out of the playoff hunt, there at the end, the wheels just came off. It was a hard thing to accept.

It was also hard to accept that our head coach Roger Neilson was fired midway through the season. Ron Smith came in to take his place, but nothing really changed.

I felt like I did OK, and I got better as the year went on, but as a D-man it's hard to do your job when the wingers and centers just don't have it going. The passes don't click. The plays don't work. You go through stretches when just getting the puck out of your own zone seems impossible. I hadn't gone through anything like it since Des Moines. It's hard to stay motivated.

I did score six goals and dish out 12 assists. I rarely got beat to any loose puck, and I kept my poise even when giant guys with a head of steam were barreling toward me. At the end of it, I was tired. Dead tired. Losing makes the bumps and bruises feel just a little bit worse.

So there we were. Heading home to play golf when so many other teams were gearing up for the Stanley Cup playoffs. It didn't seem right. I missed my new wife desperately, but I would've accepted being apart if it meant we could go deep in the playoffs. Good or bad, it had been quite a year. I got married, we had a spectacular honeymoon in paradise, I played another full season in the NHL, but we weren't very good. The highs and the lows, right there in living color.

It had surely been one wild roller-coaster of a year, and a season. And now it was about to be summer again. I couldn't wait to see Brooks on the mound in a Texas Rangers uniform. Maybe I'd sneak down to the front row at The Dome during batting practice and yell, "Hey, mister, can I have your autograph?"

CHAPTER 35

Brooks Bennett

I hadn't yet turned 24 and I'd spent nearly half a season in the show. I learned the routines. I even knew how to pack my duffel bag but never carry it. I left my suitcase in the clubhouse and it was magically in my room when we got to the next city. I threw my uniform on the clubhouse floor and another miracle happened when I found it washed and in my locker the next day. And my Nike shoes were shined up and the spikes were clean of any dirt from the day before. It was, in every possible way, a totally different and very rad world. I'd never experienced anything like it, and I could quickly tell how much I started taking it for granted. I went from commercial flights and buses to charter flights and world-class hotels in the blink of an eye. It's a very pampered lifestyle, and even back then it was kind of over-the-top crazy. We were big leaguers. I wasn't in Oklahoma City anymore. Or Tulsa, Port Charlotte, or Gastonia, and definitely not Butte, as much as I loved playing in all those places.

I'd also noticed something else during those months in the big leagues with the Rangers. Everywhere we went, it seemed like there were pretty girls. I was totally focused on making sure I would stay in the big leagues so I never did anything to act on the fact they were there, and I didn't even talk to any of them, but I absolutely noticed it all around me. I hadn't been on a date since I discovered Donna was cheating on me and I really didn't miss it because, I suspect, I was pretty soured on dating and relationships, but I did notice. For sure. Late in the season, while we were in Toronto staying in another totally rad 5-star hotel, one of my teammates (who shall remain nameless) and I were in the hotel restaurant and he said, "That blonde at the bar has been staring at you for 15 minutes. Why don't you have our waiter get a drink for her?"

I looked at him like he was speaking Greek, and said, "Why on Earth would I do that?"

"Dude, you're in the big leagues," he said. "These ladies are here for the same reason groupies are at concerts. Understand? If you don't do it, I'm all over this."

When I didn't move, he just shook his head and said, "You might be hopeless." In

343

terms of that sort of stuff, I probably was hopeless. At least up until that point in time. He sent her a drink and within an hour they were leaving together.

But over the next few days, a thought ran through my head. It was "Hey, dude — maybe this is the way to go. No fuss, no muss, no cheating, no heartbreak." I didn't act on it, but I thought about it. For a while. That thought was on my left shoulder, battling the one on my right shoulder that said "That's not you. Find a girl you can trust. A girl you really like. And then you date for a while, then you get married and have a family." I just wasn't sure about the first part. A girl you can trust? Donna had left a scar on me deeper than a knife wound. I had been so naive it never crossed my mind that she wasn't "the one" but in the end she wasn't. The more I got to know Eric, I saw how the whole thing worked out for him and how he and Carol were meant for each other and totally trusted each other. They were best friends. Carol never saw Eric as a hockey player. Definitely not as a hockey player in the NHL. She saw him as a good person and a man she could trust. They were so honest and so in love. How was I ever going to find that now? I was in the big leagues. Anybody I met would know what I did for a living and see me as a target or a sugar daddy. How could I trust anyone? Maybe I'd just ignore that whole part of my life until I was retired. I had no clue what to do, especially in terms of romance or even simply dating. I was totally lost. So I did what I do. I compartmentalized it and shoved it away in the deepest part of my brain. I'd worry about it later. I had baseballs to throw. I needed some time off and I needed my family.

After I got back to the condo in Cape Coral, I got it straightened up and in good shape (things somehow get dusty when you aren't there!) and got all my stuff put away. Then I called Mom and Dad and let them know I was buying them tickets to come down and see me for a week. We'd mentioned it before, so they were expecting to hear that, I think. They hit me right in the sweet spot when they both said, "How soon do you want us? We're ready to get down there right now."

About a week later I picked them up at the Fort Myers airport. That first night, they insisted we go out to dinner and that they would pick up the tab. I fought them on that, for style points only, and in the end I eased up and let them win that debate. It was something they really wanted to do. And it was fantastic. Mom looked great and Dad had those James Taylor eyes glistening. We were all smiles. Mom filled me in on all the artwork she was doing and it was like seeing her 10 years younger. Dad was beaming with every word she spoke. Man, we had come a long way from the dark days.

It was a great week. We hit the beach, we did some shopping for a few things I still wanted for the condo, we ate out a lot but also cooked in my kitchen, and we had some wine on my balcony each night. The wine thing was something new. I was never really a crazy beer drinker. I drank beer because that's what guys do when we go out, but a few of my Ranger teammates were kind of smart about wine and they introduced me to the various types. I wasn't yet totally an "educated" wine drinker, but I knew what I liked. On a hot day, I loved a good cold glass of Chardonnay. Over a big heavy dinner, I'd go with Cabernet or Merlot. I was interested and it seemed like something a "successful" guy would know more about. I kind of dove in and started testing other types and other regions. To me, beer was beer. It was OK, but back then the local craft beer craze hadn't started yet, so it all just tasted like Bud Light to me. Wine was different. There were so many subtle differences. It was a fun education to dig into it. I also never really got a taste for hard liquor, other than a margarita every now and then, and that's maybe a good thing.

Mom and Dad got into what I was doing with the wine thing, and every night while they were there we'd have something different, or two bottles that were different, so we could talk about what we tasted and how it hit the tongue. I still thank those teammates for taking me out to dinner and for bringing me into the world of wine.

When the week was up, I was truly sad to see Mom and Dad go. I missed them. I loved them. I may not have had any luck with girls, but I was lucky as hell when it came to the two best parents in the world. I made sure they understood there was always a room for them whenever they wanted to come down, especially during the winter.

I was staying in touch with Eric, too, and he was already in New York for the start of preseason training and exhibition games. While I was stoked just to have spent half a season in the big leagues, he was still way ahead of me. He was established as a solid NHL player. Whether it's baseball or hockey, it's hard to make it to the top, but it's even harder to stay there. Getting there is a gigantic accomplishment. Staying there for multiple years, or a full career, is a whole different level. It makes you one of very few people on the planet who can do that. Fans remember the stars, whether it's Nolan Ryan or Wayne Gretzky. They typically don't remember the hundreds of other guys who get there for a bit, then can't find a way to make it last. Making the big time in sports has got to be one of the hardest things to do in life.

I looked at the New York Rangers schedule for the upcoming season to find a few games I could get to over the winter. There was a new expansion team in Tampa called the Lightning, and the Rangers would be coming down to play them in early December for two games. Those were two dates I'd totally be circling on my calendar. But I also had an urge to get to some Canadian cities I hadn't been to. Like Ottawa and Montreal. Maybe Quebec City, too. I was plotting it all out.

After my folks were gone for a week or two, I realized I kinda liked living solo. It was peaceful, I could do what I wanted when I wanted to do it, and I could work out at the Rangers complex every day. It was good. Maybe that means I'm a loner or it just means I was comfortable in my own skin, but either way it felt like a good thing. Some people can't stand being alone. I loved it.

At that time, my agent Adam was already working on a new contract with Texas. He made it pretty clear we still didn't have a lot of leverage. What he said was, "We'll try to get you a nice bump from last year's minimum salary. The key is how this next season goes. If you kill it, and we think you will, we can go for a long-term deal. With arbitration and free agency, teams are more willing to sign young players to five- or six-year deals. Can you make more by holding out? Maybe. But at this stage if we can get you six years you'll be set. Let's just see how this season goes."

In the end, Adam got me a nice "bump" as he called it. I went from the $109,000 minimum to $185,000. More money than I ever dreamed of, and I knew it would give me a lot more flexibility when it came to the off-season and traveling. I wouldn't have to watch every dollar like a hawk anymore. Adam added, "Just like I told you, Tom Grieve already brought up a multi-year extension if everything goes well this year. They don't want to lose you. Put it this way, Brooks: You're already their No. 1 pitching prospect. Dan Smith was their first-round pick, but you're well ahead of him on the depth chart. We can give you a lifetime of financial security if this works out. I don't see you as a guy who is much into spending cash on bling or foolish investments. There's no need to change that now. Let's get the money and let's get that new contract a year from now." Sounded good to me!

And then there was Susie. Yeah, totally different subject but oh boy, let me tell you about Susie. She was a server at the one restaurant I didn't mind going to by myself. They always gave me a nice private table and everyone there got to know me pretty quickly. By "nice private table" I actually mean the worst booth in the restaurant. It was tucked behind the reception desk and right by the swinging door to the kitchen. But, I loved it. I got to where I could say, "Do you have my single-guy booth available?" and the hostess wouldn't even flinch. She'd just laugh and take me right to it.

It wasn't that I was worried about being recognized. Nobody would know me there at that early point in my career, but I hated sitting by myself in the middle of the room. I always felt so self-conscious and paranoid doing that, like other customers were looking at me and talking about me. It felt like everyone in the room was staring and trying to figure out my entire life by the fact I was by myself. In the "single guy booth" I could just eat and watch the servers go in and out of the kitchen.

Susie was really cute, and physically a lot like Donna, with short blonde hair, blue eyes, a killer body, plus a Florida girl's beach tan, and on top of all of that she was funny. I just kept adding in a few lines each time she waited on me, getting to know her a little more, and the thought of maybe taking her out sneaked into my loner's mind. By that time, I was seeing her there a lot and asking for her to be my server, and our initial "How are you tonight?" conversations had grown into talking about where we were from and what we were into.

I was eager to maybe have lunch with her or something, but once baseball was brought into the conversation and she knew I played for the Rangers, all those alarm bells went off in my head again. Let's just say she sure got a lot more interested in me once she knew I was in the big leagues. Still, she was adorable and she made me laugh. I asked her if she wanted to have lunch the next day. I was about 50/50 torn between being wary of her intentions and flattered by the attention, but man, she sure was cute. Totally adorable. I'm pretty sure she must have dotted the "i" in Susie with a heart.

When we met for lunch, she got there a few minutes before me and when I pulled up she looked at my Camry. When I got out of the car, she said, "I thought you guys made a lot of money." I'm 100 percent serious. That's what she said. I'm not kidding.

"It's the big leagues," I said. "We do pretty well. It's the top of my profession. Like being a doctor in the best hospital or a lawyer at the best firm. We do get paid well, but I'm still basically a rookie."

She just shook her head and said, "Well, why this car then? Why not a Mercedes or a BMW or something? If I made the kind of money I think you make, I'd be cruising around in style in my dream car."

If the alarm bells had been going off earlier, they were screaming at me right then. All I could say was: "I'm not into expensive cars. It's never been important to me. I love the game. The money isn't why I do it."

We ate lunch, talking more about baseball than what she did, while my brain was spinning about the whole car and big-leagues thing, and then I did something I'd never done before. I imitated what I'd heard a bunch of my teammates do over the years, and just blurted out, "Do you want to come over to my place for a glass of wine?" I was 99 percent sure she'd say, "Maybe some other time."

She said yes. We went back there. We had some wine on the balcony and then it progressed from there, quickly and without any questions or conversation. Yes, she was cute as hell. Yes, we had a good time. No, I had no interest in her as a girlfriend, companion, or even as a friend. We just did what we did. She was more than willing. I was willing. She was actually pretty aggressive. It was fun in the moment, but that's all it was. It was a first for me. I'd never done anything like that. It was also the last time I ever saw Susie. I stopped going to the restaurant because I didn't know how to handle it or what to say. I felt really sad about it actually. It was just supposed to be fun, but it felt hollow and wrong. I was dealing with a total guilt thing. I sure wasn't proud of myself. It was so unlike me. I think I was just trying to be like some of my teammates, but it all felt wrong. I wasn't them. I was just me.

I went back into my loner shell, found a new restaurant, and started my workouts at the complex. I think that lesson with cute Susie got me focused again, if only because I realized how careless I had been with her. My parents came down again for Thanksgiving and Christmas, but I never even mentioned Susie or what I had done. I was a grown man by then. They didn't need to know. No one needed to know. I never talked to anyone about her or that afternoon at my place.

On a more positive note, I saw Eric when the Rangers came down to play the new Tampa team, and since they were playing two games against the Lightning they had a couple of days off in between. It was great. It felt like our friendship was at a new level. It was honest. We were getting to be more open with each other. Let's put it this way: We TRUSTED each other. There was no pretense or effort involved. We just liked each other and we respected each other. He's a truly good dude. We're very different in a lot of ways, especially our upbringings, but we're more alike than we're different. We love what we do and we focus on it.

Over a glass of wine on one of their off nights up in Tampa, I told him my true feelings about the lack of a relationship in my life. I said, "You know, I'm really stoked for you and Carol. You two are totally made for each other. I've never had anything like that. I thought Donna was a good catch, but you know how that went. So now I don't trust any cute girl I meet. Maybe I ought to tell them I'm an appliance repair guy, or a cable TV installer, or something like that. Once they know I play baseball, I lose all interest because I think they look at me and see a bank account.

"And you know what, dude? You're the best friend I've ever had. Growing up as an only child I didn't have many good friends. My parents were my best friends. I've always had teammates I liked a lot, and had fun with, but you and I clicked as soon as we met. I'm honored. You're a good man, dude, and I'm proud of what you've done so far and what you'll do. I hope I can live up to that on my end."

For the first time ever, Eric looked a little emotional. All he said was, "I feel the same way. We trust each other, we like each other, and we care. That's all good. You're a good dude too." He put a little added emphasis and actually did "air quotes" on the word "dude" just to let me know he was making fun of me. Just a bit. I appreciated it.

Later in the winter, I booked a ticket to Montreal to see Eric play against the Canadiens. It was a bold thing for me. They speak French there, and the only French I know is "Oui." But it's a bucket list city. I got a room at the same hotel the Rangers were staying in and it was nothing short of fabulous. Loved it. Loved everything about it. It was a phenomenal adventure. Way outside my comfort zone, but those are totally the best trips. And man, do those Montreal fans love their hockey team. It's not just interest; it's passion. It was an amazing experience. The whole thing had me hyped up, amped up, and wide-eyed. North Stars games at the Met Center were nothing like that game at the Montreal Forum.

When spring training started, my new contract was signed, I was in top shape and I was totally stoked to get going. I'd been throwing off a mound for a month. I'd been running like a mad man at the complex. I'd even adopted a few new yoga and stretching routines our trainer had learned about. It was all based on what European soccer players were doing to stay healthy.

He said, "I did some research and it was crazy how few soft tissue injuries the top soccer players have. Things like hamstrings, quads, calf muscles, rib muscles, and that. And then I watched a tape on their training techniques and it was about 180 degrees out from the way we do it. When we go out on the field and stretch, it's all about really pushing the muscles to get loose. To the point of pain. They take it really easy, just to get the blood flowing. Just light jogging and some bending over. Nothing excessive or painful. And it works. The body does marvelous things. We don't have to push it like crazy." I was never more ready for a season.

Spring training went great. By "great" I mean I pitched in 12 games and didn't give up a run. It was typical spring stuff, just throwing an inning or two at a time, but we ramped it up a little as we got closer to the season. Every time they sent me to the mound, I shut the other team down. I mean, you can't do better than zero runs.

We also had a new manager, Kevin Kennedy, and a new pitching coach, Claude Osteen, but to me that was all good. From the first day, both of them told me their plan was for me to be a starter, not a reliever. I'd be in good company. We still had Nolan, who announced that it was his last season and he'd retire at the end of it, along with Kenny Rogers, Charlie Leibrandt, Kevin Brown and Craig Lefferts. Our bullpen was strong, our hitting looked great, and basically I thought we were stacked. Just to be in that rotation, on that team, seemed like the biggest leap I'd ever made.

The one thing I was working on was a slider. I figured if I was going to start, and the other team's batters were going to see me multiple times in a game, I needed one more bullet in my arsenal. Claude was working with me on that, and throughout the spring it got better. We never really used the term "cutter" back then but that's basically what it was, now that I look back on it. I spun it enough to get it to run down and in on a left-handed hitter or start it in tight on a right-hander and get it to dive down and away. We worked on it a lot in Port Charlotte during spring training to see if I could master it without losing the bite on my other pitches. By the time we broke camp to start the season, I felt really good about it. I had four pitches and still had great zip and life on my fastball.

I was the Rangers' "fifth starter" that year because the veteran guys all went ahead of me in the rotation and I pitched the fifth game of the season. After that, it's a rotation just like the batting order is. When it's your turn, you go in there and try to do your job. In my first start, I did my job. We were at Fenway and I shut down the Red Sox. Five innings. No runs. Two hits. Six strikeouts. Not bad for the fifth starter.

I just kept grinding away at it, mixing in the new "cutter" or slider or whatever you want to call it. I got a lot of strikeouts with it, actually. Once I established the fastball and they had to look for that, I could bury that cutter down in the zone and they'd almost always get fooled by it. By the beginning of June I was 6-0 and had beaten some really good teams. Hell, they were all big-league teams. They're all good. If you get a "W" against anyone in the show you should be proud of it.

Right about then, at the beginning of June, we went to Minnesota to play the Twins at the Metrodome. My folks were there, Eric and Carol were there, even Don was there, and more than a few other former Gopher teammates showed up. Luckily, my spot in the rotation came up during the series, so all of them were in the Dome that night to see me pitch. We only scored one run, but I didn't give up any and we won the game 1-0. It was huge. To that point in my life, if it wasn't the biggest game I ever won it was sure close. A complete game shutout. Only gave up a handful of hits and struck out a bunch. OK, I just looked it up: I gave up four hits and struck out 12.

It was great to see everyone after the game but a little weird to then have to say goodbye and get on the bus back to the hotel with my teammates. Some of the veteran guys had no problem taking a cab or not riding the bus, but I felt like I had to follow the agenda. I was still basically just a rookie. I followed the rules. So I got on the bus and everyone went home. Eric and I did commit to having lunch together the next day in downtown Minneapolis.

We had a great meal at a pub, and talked about what it was like for both of us. He was already into his preseason workouts, even though it was still something like four months before he'd even go to New York for training camp. He was an absolute animal when it came to outworking everyone. It's what got him to the NHL, and what would keep him there.

More than just talking hockey and baseball, I wanted to pick his brain about being married. I was a million miles from being married, but what he had with Carol seemed incredible to me. I told him that and he said, "You know, I'm just lucky. When you grow up in Roseau you know everyone, and we went through school together from kindergarten to high school graduation, so there wasn't anything like trying to learn each other's likes and dislikes in college or as adults. I'm sure that's really hard, at that point in your life. We knew all of that stuff before high school.

"But you're in a tough spot now," he said. "We talked about this right after we both signed our first contracts. You have to be careful. People will try to take advantage of you, whether they're agents or marketing reps, or women who aren't really honest about what they think of you as a person. Just be careful." That was more priceless advice. It echoed what I already thought, but it was totally great as an affirmation of what I'd assumed.

Around that same time, I heard the words "All-Star Game" more and more. Whether it was from teammates or the media, the whole concept of it kept coming up in conversations. I guarantee I didn't feel worthy, and I thought the mentions of it were nonsense. Basically, I was clueless and didn't even want to think about it. Would it be totally rad to make the All-Star team? Of course! But I couldn't let that be my only goal. I was in the big leagues to win and make a long career out of it. If I ever made an All-Star team that would be awesome, but all I could focus on was being the best pitcher I could be. Start by start, inning by inning, batter by batter. One pitch at a time.

As we neared the end of June, I was 9-1 with an ERA of 1.63, and with 88 strikeouts in 72 innings. When the All-Star lineups were announced, I got the call from my skipper, Kevin Kennedy. We were on the road in Detroit, and he called me in my hotel room.

"OK, dude, are you ready for this? Are you sitting down? You're an All-Star. You earned it. You earned every bit of it. Enjoy the hell out of it, and don't let yourself get too hyped up. It's a huge stage and I've seen a lot of great pitchers completely lose their stuff just being too overhyped. It's not just another game, but it actually is just another game. And it's the best All-Star game in all of sports, because everyone goes all out. If anything, some guys go all out a bit too much. Just be yourself. Congratulations, Brooksie."

He let me know that Pudge Rodriguez and Juan Gonzales would be going with me. The Rangers would charter a private jet for us, and we'd be headed to Baltimore in mid-July. You're kidding me, right? As much as I'd played it off and tried not to think about it, when I got the word it absolutely blew me away. I had figured I'd probably play pro ball since my freshman year at Canyon High in SoCal. I truly believed it. I sensed it. I figured if I could be successful in the minors I might have a chance to play in the big leagues. I never even contemplated being named to the All-Star team. Those guys were all superstars. I was just the son of a surfer and an artist. Just a beach kid from SoCal. I was just me. They were legends.

I called Mom and Dad first. Yes, there were tears shed. Dad could only spit out,

"Oh my God, Brooks. Oh my God. This is amazing." After that, it was just a lot of blubbering from all three of us.

I called Eric, too, although I waited until later in the day so he'd be home from his workouts. This was not the sort of news I'd want to leave on his answering machine.

I told him, "Dude, this is you next year. You'll be an NHL All-Star. I know you will. And we can always look back on that first day in the dorm when we plowed into each other and met. Look where we are now, dude. It's freaking unbelievable."

When I got a copy of *USA Today* the next morning, I stared at the rosters. It was like *"one of these things is not like the others"* when I saw the list. Randy Johnson, Cal Ripken, Kirby Puckett, Wade Boggs, Mike Mussina, Frank Thomas and all those other superstars. And there was my freaking name, right along with them. It was an absolutely insane moment, just to see it in print. It was for real.

When it got to be a day or two away from the All-Star break, the traveling secretary was in constant contact with me, Pudge and Gonzo. What to pack. Where to go. Where the plane will be. How to get to the hotel in Baltimore. There's a lot more to the All-Star game than just the actual game itself. My itinerary must have been five pages long.

With Baltimore being the host city, the American League would be the home team. That's kind of important to know. We had to take our home uniforms with us. More than a few guys mentioned a player who got to the All-Star game with his duffle bag, but he'd forgotten to pack his jersey. He had to buy a replica souvenir jersey at a concession stand. True story. It was the great Lou Whitaker of the Detroit Tigers. I would've died if I did that.

When we got there — and yes, it was my first time on a private jet — a limo was waiting and it took us to the American League hotel. Just walking into the lobby was off the charts. Baseball greatness everywhere, past and present. One second I was staring at Randy Johnson and then Reggie Jackson walked by. He was long retired by then, but Reggie was clearly in his element. He had an aura around him you could almost see. I felt invisible. I'd literally been in the big leagues all of about one calendar year. I was surrounded by players who had played 10 or 15 years at the highest level. It was totally surreal. Like being on the set of a movie and seeing every Hollywood star you ever admired. It was just crazy. Until then, I guess I really just thought of it as another ballgame. I had no idea how many idols and legends would be milling around with a nobody like me.

We had banquets, workouts, media schedules and meetings. Cito Gaston, from the Blue Jays, was our manager. Basically what he said was, "This is a baseball game. We are here to win. But it will be really easy to overdo it and try to do too much. Just take a deep breath and play your game. We'll try to get all of you in it, but I can't guarantee that. Just be ready."

We did our normal routines on game day. Stretching, running, throwing. We had the incredible All-Star player introductions with all of us lining up on the foul line and each guy getting announced and waving to the crowd and the TV camera. I'd seen that on television many times, and it always gave me goosebumps. To be out there myself, with that camera in my face, hearing my name on the PA system, well, it was damn near impossible not to cry, knowing Mom and Dad were watching, but I held it together.

I went out to the bullpen not knowing if I'd pitch or not. I remember telling myself I probably wouldn't, just to prepare myself for that. I was there. I was an All-Star. That was enough. I was the little puppy in the middle of a huge gaggle of alpha-male dogs.

In the sixth inning the phone rang in the bullpen. The coach yelled, "Bennett. You've got the seventh. Get loose." My heart rate must have jumped 50 beats. I remember having to take a deep breath before I tossed my first warm-up pitch.

By that time in the game, most of the starting position players were already out, but the guys on the bench were still All-Stars. They were all great.

I walked in from the 'pen and tried to act like I knew what I was doing. I faced Tony Gwynn, Mike Piazza and Jay Bell. I did not strike out the great Tony Gwynn. Hardly anybody ever struck out Tony Gwynn. But, I got him to pop up. I then struck out Piazza and Bell, and calmly walked off the mound. Before I got to the dugout the thought flashed in my head, "I can't wait to call Mom and Dad," although I knew they'd seen it on TV.

It was just incredible. It was overwhelming. Right up until that night I really figured I was just a nobody who Texas Rangers fans didn't even really know. The other All Stars were amazing to me. They treated me like an equal. They were kind, complimentary, and supportive. Was it the highlight of my career to that point? Yes. I was floating until the game was over. And we won, 9-3. Cito was really proud of us. We put on a great show and made the effort to win that game. I called Mom and Dad from the clubhouse. Man, we sure are an emotional family. I know lots of guys who look at me funny when I tell them my dad and I cried, or my mom and I cried. They're like, "Really? You cried?" Yeah. Really.

When I got back to Arlington the Tigers were there waiting to play us. And immediately, it was like the All-Star Game had never happened. We were back in the groove and ready to play every day, against great teams. Games that counted in the standings.

I started 16 more games. I went 6-2 in the second half of the season, with a string of no-decisions when our bats went cold. I finished the year like this:

- Record: 15-3
- Innings: 156
- Hits: 129
- Strikeouts: 171
- Walks: 33
- ERA: 2.95

I finished second in the "Rookie of the Year" voting, and that stunned me. Tim Salmon, from the Angels, won it and I always thought position players had the rightful advantage for stuff like that. They play every day, and that makes a much bigger impact on their team. I pitched in one-fifth of our games. I was just honored as hell to finish second behind a superstar. As for the team, we had a good year, finishing second in the division with a record of 86-76.

I was really proud of that season. It was one of the first times in my baseball career when I stopped and thought about it after the season ended. Being proud is not what I'm usually like, but I was. I had established myself as a big league starter and I'd made the All-Star team. It was a dream come true.

But that's not the end of the story.

In late September we were playing the White Sox in Chicago. It was cold and felt like it might even snow. I remember feeling like I couldn't get loose when I was warming up. I did all my normal routines, but I just felt tight all over. I remember walking out to the mound in the bottom of the first thinking, "Man, I hope I don't pull a hamstring or something. That would suck."

I didn't pull a hamstring. Instead, in the second inning I went back out there and felt something odd in my right elbow. Not serious pain, but just a sensation that was new and different. Like a vibration. Like I'd hit my funny bone. It burned a little on the back of my elbow, and it felt like getting a small electrical shock. I sucked it up and got three outs and knew what I needed to do. I talked to Kevin and our trainer. All I said was: "I don't know what it is, but I felt something in my elbow. Not really a pop or anything horrible, but I've never felt anything like that in my elbow. It's weird. Like I hit my funny bone. I can still feel it."

Kevin said, "That's it. You're done. It's a crappy day and I'm not going to put you back out there. Doc will take a look and we'll see what we do from there."

In the training room, it didn't hurt and the vibration thing was gone. The trainers pushed me this way and that way and it was all good. But they said, "When we get back home tomorrow, we'll do an MRI. There's only a week left in the season. There's no reason to push this."

We flew home that night and the next morning I was sitting as still as I could while the MRI machine scanned my elbow. The doctor thought it was just some inflammation, or at the worst a pinched nerve. There was nothing structurally wrong. Nothing too serious, but my season was over. Just rest, and don't pick up a ball for at least a month.

After an amazing year, that was not what I wanted to hear.

CHAPTER 36

Eric Olson

Summer was going too slowly for me. I know that sounds idiotic for a Minnesotan, but missing the playoffs was a huge letdown, and I know most of the guys felt the same way. We were a good team. We had grit, talent and dedication on our side. I still don't understand how we missed the playoffs.

I did get to see Brooks that spring and summer, once when we went down to Tampa to play the new expansion team, the Lightning, and again when the Texas Rangers came to the Dome and he started a game. He was lights-out. It was amazing to see. The Twins couldn't touch him. I don't think he threw one ball down the middle of the plate. Everything was on the corners and fooled the hitters. He wasn't just a big-league pitcher — he was a phenomenal pitcher. It was great to see.

We didn't have much time to talk after the game, so we planned to have lunch the next day in Minneapolis. We met at a pub, had some good food and talked nonstop. He was insistent about steering the conversation to relationships. I could tell he was still pretty dinged up by what Donna had done to him, and he really wanted to know what magic Carol and I had. I told him it wasn't magic. It was great luck. We'd known each other since we started school. We'd been friends for years and then took it to the next level. And then we had to slow it down when we went different directions after high school. But the trust and friendship we had won out. It was like winning a playoff series after being down three games to one. We figured it out and got our act together.

I told him I didn't think he had a chance to do that at that point in his life. That wasn't what he wanted to hear but it was reality. He was a big-league ballplayer and the thing that worried him the most was having anyone take advantage of him. I don't blame him for that. It worried me too, for his sake.

I was beginning to sense that Brooks was a bit naïve. Maybe more than a bit. He had a very interesting upbringing, and he loved his parents enormously. He wasn't pampered in terms of material things, but he was definitely sheltered in terms of how his parents treated him as he grew up. By adulthood, in the big leagues, it was kind of "all or nothing" for him. He was either going to find the perfect companion or avoid romance completely, and even if he did find the perfect bride he might not believe it. He was just negative about the whole thing. I didn't have any great answers for him other than to tell him to be careful. There are some great people out in the world. There are also some really bad ones. It's a common tale, sadly. You can get used without even knowing it's going on. It happens all the time. As athletes at the top of our professions, we weren't a lot different than rock stars or Wall Street millionaires. The bad side of people is hard to understand but it's out there.

During the summer, we also learned we had another new head coach in New York. The team let Roger Neilson go after our less-than-stellar showing the year before, and put Ron Smith in the head coach position. Looking back on it, I don't think they intended to keep Ron long-term and, sure enough, they brought in Mike Keenan. Mike was well-known as a strict guy — a hard-ass coach, as we'd say. He didn't ask for the best out of a player; he demanded it. He could be abrasive, and he already had a reputation for having a difficult time with upper management and ownership, but he won games. I thought he was a great choice. We needed a coach like that.

As for me, my agent, Robert, and his agency delivered. I'd thought he was risking a lot the year before, demanding $40,000 and then settling on $38,000. But he was right when he told me to relax and understand the fact the Rangers knew it was a dance and a negotiation. It wasn't personal.

This time around, he pinned them into a corner and told them that if they wanted me long-term, I absolutely deserved a multi-year contract at an amount that was fair for one of the top young defensemen in the league. After that, they could lock me up forever and pay me what the stars made. I stayed completely out of it. I just got regular phone calls with updates, but I never asked for anything.

In the end, before training camp, I signed a four-year contract that totaled just a bit over a half-million dollars. The first year would be $120,000, and it would go up incrementally each of the other three years. There were teammates on the Rangers making way more than that, but I was still a new guy and the security of the contract was what got me to be all-in. It was all guaranteed. They couldn't release me and stop paying. If they sent me back to the minors, they'd still have to pay me my NHL salary. If I got hurt, same thing. They could trade me, but the team on the other end would be on the hook for the whole thing. For the first time in my life, I knew I was making a good living and would be for four years. That's a long way from just hoping I could someday be a Roseau Ram.

The next big life hurdle for me wasn't about hockey. It was about Carol and what we would do. She was still a star in the Target organization, but neither one of us really wanted to be apart again for a whole hockey season. Plus, she loved Manhattan. She made a really gutsy call to leave Target. I wasn't sure it was the right call, but it's what she wanted to do. She'd be coming with me. If she wanted to work in New York, I was sure she could land a top job without any worries.

We decided to visit a month before camp started, and the Rangers hooked me up with a real estate agent who had helped a lot of the guys. He found us a really nice second floor rental just a few blocks from Central Park on the Upper West Side. We could walk to restaurants, jump on the subway, and walk through the park with ease. It was small but incredibly cool. And I could be at Madison Square Garden in minutes. It was ridiculously expensive, especially with Carol quitting her job, but I was done with rooming with teammates in Queens. Carol and I would have to pinch our pennies but it was what we wanted.

The apartment was furnished and the stuff was nice enough, but I told Carol to do anything she wanted with it. If we bought new furniture she loved we could put it in storage after the season. She's a really practical person, though, so we didn't buy anything more than a few new pots and pans.

Once training camp was over and the season started, we were all moved in and loving it. We were discovering new restaurants and taking long walks in Central Park when I was home from the rink. It was such a different experience, but she loved it so much it was impossible for me not to love it too.

On the ice, I thought we were better but I was remembering how good I thought we were the year before, when we didn't make the playoffs. We still had Mark Messier as our captain, and now we had Sergei Zubov, a 23-year-old defenseman who opened my eyes the first day of camp. Let's just say he was not shy about jumping in to join the play in the offensive zone, but he was amazing at getting back on defense — basically, a totally different approach than mine. I just figured if we were on the ice together I'd have to be the stay-at-home defender I'd always been, but even more than usual, because he was likely to be across the offensive blue line. And we still had Mike Richter in goal. Coach Keenan had a reputation for pulling goalies really quick if they let in a soft goal, but with Richter there would be hardly any of that. He was one of the best in the league.

Once we got settled into the apartment, Carol told me that she absolutely wanted to find a job and get back to work. She said, "Going to the games at night will be awesome, but I need something to do each day and want to help with our income."

She updated her resume and started the search. Within a week, she had interviews set up with Macy's and Bergdorf-Goodman for jobs in marketing and promotions.

She slayed them both. Both offered her jobs and got into a bit of a bidding war. Macy's won out, hiring her in the marketing and promotions department at around $60,000 per year.

After she joined the company and got to work she was instantly handed more and more responsibilities. I had worried that she was jumping out of the Target job where she was a rising star and she might get shuffled to less meaningful jobs at a big New York company, but she shined.

She clearly remembers the day her boss came into her office during lunch and, over sub sandwiches, they began to talk about what it was like for her to move from Minnesota to New York. She let him know that she had loved Manhattan since the first time she visited, and she left Minnesota to be with me. It was for my job, and she didn't want to stay behind another year. He asked what I did.

"Well, he plays for the Rangers, so I moved here with him," she said.

She said his entire demeanor changed. He'd been really professional and full of praise for her work, but when he learned what I did it was a whole new level. Like a super-fan level. That just goes to show you how men, no matter their age or status in life, are all boys at heart. He was a little starstruck to have the wife of a Ranger on his marketing team. He was also a season-ticket holder.

"Wait, what's your husband's name?" he asked. When she told him who I was she said he just started giggling like a school boy.

"You never told us you were married to Eric Olson! My gosh, he's awesome. He gets the job done every night. That is so cool. Why didn't you tell us?"

She said, "You never asked and I didn't think it mattered who I was married to. I wanted this job because I'm great at it and I can help all of us move forward. But yeah, he's pretty special. We're both from the same little town in northern Minnesota, called Roseau, and we've known each other since we were little kids. He's my soulmate, and I'm his."

He quickly said something she never expected from a New York executive. "You mean the same Roseau, Minnesota, where Neal Broten and his brothers are from?"

She laughed and said, "Well that's not the first time I've heard that question. I used to get it a lot in Minnesota, but I never expected to hear it in New York. Yep, same Roseau. It's a great town. I mean, I'm from there so it must be great, right?"

That's my girl. She's never wanted a shortcut to success. She is just the actual definition of success, wherever she goes.

As for my job, on the rink we got off to a pretty decent start and then caught fire. After 20 games we were 13-5 with two ties. We were playing well, and Coach Keenan was pushing all the right buttons. It was so much better than the year before. Everyone was putting in the max effort every day in practice and every night during games. It's neat how much it changes the team when you feel everyone around you is bearing down, never quitting, and doing all they can. It makes a player like me a lot more productive. I can do my job at the back end, I can concentrate on defense and I instinctively know where my teammates are going to be. We all clicked.

As the calendar tripped over into 1994, we were all aware that the NHL All-Star Game would be at Madison Square Garden that year. I thought that was neat, and was pretty sure I could get tickets for Carol and me to attend. And then I got word from Coach Keenan that I shouldn't worry about tickets. He said, "If you don't get named to the team I'll go ballistic. You're one of the best defensemen in the league. We'll know here in the next day or two."

Sure enough, I got a call from the league office just a day later, letting me know I was on the team. I couldn't believe it, despite the hints Coach was giving me. I still couldn't believe I was even in the NHL, but the All-Star team? That was beyond what I could even imagine. Seriously, never in my life had I even had a thought of being on an NHL All-Star team. Not once. I rushed back to the apartment as soon as I could get out of the rink to tell Carol. I wanted her to hear it directly from me. I stopped at a liquor store near our place and bought a bottle of bubbly stuff.

357

She got home about an hour later and the first thing she saw was something out of the ordinary. It was the champagne on ice right in the middle of our dining table. We didn't have a dining room in the small apartment, but we had a small table just off the kitchen. It sat two. We wouldn't be having anyone over for dinner in that place.

She said, "What's this about?"

"Well, I have some news," I said. "We're going to the NHL All-Star Game on January 22, at the Garden. Think you can be free to go to that?"

"Cool. I'm sure I can meet you there if I go straight from work. Did we get the tickets for free?"

"Yeah, they're free," I said. "But I won't be needing one. You'll have to sit by yourself with the other wives."

I could see a look of confusion in her big brown eyes.

She said, "What the hell? Where are you going to sit?"

I said, "Well, on the bench for a lot of it, when I'm not on the ice. I was named to the Eastern Conference All-Star team today. I actually made the team!"

She literally ran to me and jumped into my arms. I'm sure the neighbors could hear us both yelling and screaming. Then I reminded her that when my agent negotiated my contract, he managed to get an All-Star bonus squeezed into the wording. If I made the team (and I doubt either side in those negotiations figured I would), the team would pay me a $25,000 bonus. Life just got a lot better.

I'd have Brian Leetch, Mark Messier and Mike Richter on the team with me. Four of us, playing in our home arena, for the All-Star game. I was hardly able to even talk about it with Carol. I don't get overcome by much. I rarely get emotional. This was different.

The next day, after word got out, just about all the guys and staff members came over to shake my hand and congratulate me at the morning skate before our game. Messier was the first to have a seat next to me and let me know what I was going to be in for.

"It's an amazing honor, so be proud of that," he said. "It's a whirlwind and there's a lot going on for a couple days. Just try to soak it all in and make sure you keep your eyes open for the team photo! If you blink, you'll hear about it for years.

"But here's the thing about the game. It's going to be different than anything you've probably ever experienced. It's an exhibition. It's a skill show. There's not much hitting but there's a lot of skating and passing and a lot of goals scored. It's almost not fair to the defensemen and the goalies because everyone on the other team will be coming at you full speed, making passes you've never seen before. You can't let that get you down. I've seen Hall of Fame goalies just get plastered and shellacked, but two days later the good ones bounce right back for the next regular season game. It's a game full of the most talented guys in the world, and it's wide open. And if you crunch someone into the boards like you do in our regular season games, they will remember and you'll pay for it at a later date. We're just there to put on a show. It gets a lot more competitive if the score is close in the third period, but up until then it's a bit like the Ice Capades. Be ready for that."

I laughed and said, "I'm not sure I know how to lace up my skates and not go 100 percent, but I'll remember that. I'll get a feel for it. Thanks for the advice, Moose."

I called Brooks the next day. It was a cold and snowy day in New York so I played it off as a weather call. I said, "So how's the weather in Cape Coral? It's 18 degrees and snowing here."

"It's pretty cold here, too," he said. "I don't think it's going to get above 60 today."

I then said, "Well, you and I are back even again. In a couple weeks I'll be playing at Madison Square Garden but the jersey will say Eastern Conference All-Stars."

He let out a huge yell and said, "I told you, I told you, I told you. I knew it. Damn, dude. How cool is that? You're phenomenal and this is a gigantic honor. I'm so stoked for you."

I said I was "stoked" too.

The All-Star break came up fast. We had a full itinerary of banquets and special events, and then we were on the ice for the NHL Skills Competition the night before the actual game. It was wild. The greatest gathering of hockey talent in the world and every guy was trying to outdo each other in various skills. I wasn't a part of any of it; I just watched with my mouth wide open. Goalies stopping shots, forwards racing around the ice to be the fastest skater, snipers breaking plastic plates with shots on all four corners of the goal, and the fastest shot contest. Guys were going flat out. Al Iafrate won the fastest shot with a 102-mph slapshot blast. It was great. It was surreal.

The game was the next night and I was buzzing around the apartment just waiting to go. We did have a short morning skate, just to talk about strategy and get to know each other. Most of the strategy was "Don't get hurt."

And before the game I got a huge surprise. Brooks called me at the apartment and said, "When and where can I see you tonight?"

I said, "On TV, I guess."

He said, "Dude, do you think I would miss this? I've got a ticket. The Yankees helped me out through one of their sponsors. But I know it's a big night for you so I don't want to bug you. Can we meet after the game?"

I was sure we could. I promised to get with one of the Rangers' staff members to make sure Brooks could meet me as soon as I was showered and dressed. Carol was there, too, so the three of us planned to go out for a couple of drinks. It's a good thing New York is the city that never sleeps. There were plenty of options. And Brooks said he'd buy the wine for us. But first we had an All-Star Game to play.

It was unbelievable to be a part of it. The player introductions gave me goosebumps, and with me being a Ranger I got a big ovation. I never even considered that anyone in the Garden that night would know me. Just a kid from Roseau, really. That's all I was. That's all I'll ever be.

Messier had been right. There wasn't much hitting at all, and what there was was kind of polite. But man, could those guys put on a show on a night when they weren't being mauled by the other team. It was at hyper-speed. I was on the fourth line but it was still insane to be out there watching all those guys do stuff I'd only seen at a few practices, when guys would make stuff up to try to outdo each other.

And in the end, we won. It did, indeed, get a lot more competitive in the third period. It was tied going into the last few minutes and Alexei Yashin from the Ottawa Senators scored to give us the lead, 9-8. That's how it ended. And guess who was the MVP. My teammate Mike Richter! A goalie winning the MVP in the All-Star game was kind of unheard of. Those guys are usually shell-shocked by the time it's over. He was fantastic. 100 percent effort. There's nowhere to hide out there when you're the goalie. Pride kicks in. Mike had a lot of pride, and a ton of talent. He was just nails.

I got about 12 minutes worth of ice time that night, and loved it most when I wasn't intimidated or afraid of doing something wrong. It was beyond fun. Even in the locker room after the game, it felt like a huge win. Everybody was celebrating.

I met Brooks at the appointed spot as soon as I could and Carol was there with him. He was beaming, and so was I. Carol looked like she wanted to cry.

We found a nice wine bar and spent at least an hour there. We sipped on three different styles of wine and Brooks gave us a brief explanation of all of it. I had never been much of a wine drinker, but it was fascinating to hear him talk about the Cabernet, the Chardonnay, and the Pinot. We learned a lot and loved the wine. We were all a bit toasty after that, but it was all good. It was a night I'll never forget.

We all went outside, and Brooks hailed a cab so he could go back to his hotel. I knew it might be a while before I'd see him again. He'd be ramping up his training within days and then spring training would begin. Depending on whether or not we'd make the playoffs, and how far we might get if we did, I wasn't sure if I'd see him before June or July. We shared a hug, and Carol gave him a huge one. She was really getting to appreciate the guy he was. When he got in a cab, she said, "I wish I had a girlfriend I could introduce him to. He deserves it. He's a great guy." I agreed. He is a great guy, and at that point in his life and career what he really needed was an introduction from a trusted friend. Unfortunately, all of our lives were relocated and kind of in motion. He just needed to be careful.

The season picked up after all the All-Star hoopla and we stayed hot. Really hot, actually. Yes, Coach Keenan wasn't afraid to raise his voice or bench guys when he thought they were only playing at 95 percent, but he got results. Personally, I loved playing for him. I know he had a history of wearing out his welcome, but he got results. I'm results-oriented. He didn't need to baby me or any of the other guys. We just needed to win.

In the end, we finished the regular season 52-24-8. We won our division and had the best record in our conference. On top of that, we won the President's Trophy, which is awarded to the team with the best overall record and most points in the entire league. We had won our way to 112 points. I had never been on a team that good. We weren't perfect, but we found a way to win consistently and not get into any long losing ruts. At home or on the road, we could beat anyone.

For the regular season, I played in every game and did my usual stuff. With Zubov next to me a lot, and his desire to press up into the offensive zone, I paid a little more attention to being a lock-down defender who stayed at home. But Sergei was great at getting back when the play got behind him. I'd never played with a defenseman with his type of all-around skills. He actually ended up leading the team in scoring, although he only scored 12 goals. Where he excelled was on the assist side of the ledger. He could spot an open man and thread a pass in there like no one I'd ever seen. He finished the regular season with an amazing 77 assists. I finished the season with 13 goals, more than he had, but concentrated more on the back end so my assist total was a "normal" total of 22.

When we went into the playoffs, we held a team meeting to talk about capitalizing on the opportunity. Messier was the ringleader, and he spoke about responsibility, to ourselves and to the fans. We were good enough to win the whole thing and it would (and should) be a huge disappointment to everyone if we went out early. We were all on the same page. Not "rah-rah" fired up, but damn serious about giving it every ounce of energy we had.

We played the Islanders in the first round. We swept them in four games.

We played the Washington Capitals in the second round. They got one win.

Then we played the New Jersey Devils in the conference finals. The winner of that series would go on to the Stanley Cup Finals. The big show. They were tough and it was a hard-fought series. They won three games, but we won four. We were going to the Stanley Cup Finals.

What I remember most about that seventh-game victory was our reaction to it. Yes, there was a lot of back-slapping and "Way to go, boys!" shouts, but once we were in the locker room it was all business. No big celebration. Just business.

Messier, our captain, stood up in the middle of the room and shouted something like, "We aren't done boys. We are NOT DONE! Trust me, nothing will have been accomplished if we don't win the Cup. No one will remember who lost in the Finals. We have a lot of work to do. We are NOT DONE!"

That got an ovation. We were all focused on one mission.

When I got home that night, Carol and I were on the sofa in the living room and I was sipping a glass of red wine (thank you for the introduction and appreciation, Brooks). I said, "We've come so far. We've done so much. But you should've heard Messier's message in the room after the game. This means nothing. We have a chance to claim a spot in history. We have to win.

"And baby, I can't believe I'm about to play in a Stanley Cup Final. I can't believe it. I don't know how to even put it. I've been playing hockey since I could lace up skates, and here I am. I never dreamed of this in any real way. I mean, every kid envisions himself playing for the Cup when you're playing street hockey, but I never really thought of it as something that would happen. We're in the Finals. I'm still shaking my head."

I talked to my family. I talked to Brooks. I talked to my agent. It was all pretty calm. My folks weren't going to come to any of the games. My dad said, "You have a job to do. You concentrate on that. We have jobs too, so we'll watch you on TV. We don't want to mess with what's been working. Just keep your head up, do your job, and do the best you can. We'll be watching."

Brooks was already deep into his season, so he couldn't come either, but he said the same sort of things: "Do your job. Help your teammates. Be the best defender out there.

Good things will happen. And you better freaking believe I'll be paying attention. I'm taping every game on my VCR, so I'll watch them all after I get home. Go win a Cup, dude. Your name will be on that sucker for everyone to see. I'm so stoked for you."

We played the Vancouver Canucks in the Finals. They were an extremely talented offensive team, with Pavel Bure being the superstar who powered them. They had a great goalie in Kirk McLean. Once they got going in any given game, they could steamroll right over you. That's how they got to the Finals. They didn't win their conference and didn't even win their division. The Calgary Flames were the best team in the west, but the Canucks found a way to get by them in the first round and that got them going.

We hosted the Canucks for the first game at the Garden. It was as tough and aggressive as I thought it would be. There's nothing like playoff hockey, but even saying that I can now tell you there's nothing like the Stanley Cup Finals. It's so intense you have to calm yourself down. Every second you're on the ice is like the most important thing you've ever done. Guys who don't usually finish their checks that hard are going full speed. I'm surprised the boards and glass can take all the hits, much less the players who are also absorbing that contact.

It was tied 2-2 after three periods. We lost in a heartbreaking way. There was less than a minute to play in the first overtime period when Greg Adams put one in the net. Maybe we were a little lax thinking the clock would run out and we'd go to a second overtime. I don't know. It just crushed me.

In Game 2, we were back at the Garden two nights later. It was another nail-biter, but we held a 2-1 lead late in the third and then Brian Leetch buried one to make it 3-1. I think we all felt like we could get back to being ourselves after we won that game, but we were headed to Vancouver.

So we flew across the continent to play them at their place. Pavel Bure worked his magic and scored first, but we came storming back. It didn't hurt that Bure hit one of our guys in the face with his stick and got thrown out of the game. He was their most skilled player. We pounded them after that. We won 5-1.

I'm sure the Canucks felt like they had a huge upper hand in the series when they won the first game at the Garden. We felt that way after winning the first game out west. We had a lot of confidence, but we were still focused. You had to be focused with Mark Messier in the room and Mike Keenan behind the bench.

In the fourth game, they jumped out to a 2-0 lead early, and they were buzzing. We kept our heads on straight and came back. Brian Leetch carried us offensively and Mike Richter was like a brick wall in goal. We won 4-2.

In Game 5, back at the Garden, we were up three games to one and just one game from hoisting the Cup. They blitzed us again. We lost 6-3 and gave them life. Was it deflating? Yes, but we knew it wasn't going to be easy. We had work to do.

Game 6 was in Vancouver. We still just needed one win to lock up the Cup. The Canucks had a different view of it. They had to win just this one game to get to a seventh game. They beat us 4-1. We'd all be flying back to New York to settle the series in the final game.

We were quiet on the long red-eye flight. We'd let it get away for two games in a row. It would be easy to let that get you down for game seven. Maybe the Canucks were destined to win. We didn't think so. We thought we were better than them. We knew we were.

Yes, I've heard the stories about how the city of New York had already worked out a date for a Stanley Cup parade when we were up three games to one and home for Game 5. I don't know if that's true, but it wouldn't surprise me if it was. New Yorkers are used to winning and are a pretty confident group. When we lost that game, they had to cancel their plans. I can tell you that it had no impact on us. We knew it was going to be a long, tough series and it was.

Before the final game, it was all business in the locker room. But there was also some apprehension. We'd come so far. We were the best team in the league. We should win this. I didn't read the New York papers at all because they loved to stir up stuff in the sports section. But, Carol peeked every now and then and she saw what they were writing. We'd blown it. We were toast. We were going to let everyone down.

It kind of felt that way in the building when we took the ice. Sure, lots of cheering but also not as electric as the first few games at home. Maybe it was just me, but I sure sensed there were some folks in the sold-out crowd who might have been buying the media coverage.

Once the game got going and we were playing tough, the crowd came to life. They were screaming so loud we could barely hear each other on the ice. It was scoreless and very tight until about 15 minutes into the first period. Then, within a few minutes of each other, Brian Leetch and Adam Graves gave us a 2-0 lead.

Let me tell you about any Game 7 in the Cup Finals. It's so intense the hardest thing for a player to do is loosen up and just play. Every move, every pass, every hit can cost you the Stanley Cup. There are no more games to play. This is it, and with every minute clicking off the clock you don't know how it's going to end. It's stressful, but as professionals we did manage to settle down and just play hockey. We didn't know what the final result would be, but we weren't going to leave the building that night thinking we'd left anything on the table.

The Canucks came back with a shorthanded goal in the second. Those really take the air out of you. You're on the power play and have one more guy on the ice than they do, and then some fluke of a play costs you a goal. We had to regroup.

When Messier scored late in the second, I had a fleeting thought that we'd done it. We just had to hold on. That's not how it works. The other team is playing for the Cup too, and they were trying to break our hearts. They scored early in the third and it was 3-2.

There were so many chances and so many close calls from there to the end. Great saves, great chances, and hard hits. I was on the ice when the referee blew the whistle with just over one second left to play. All we had to do was win the face-off. We did, and we went absolutely nuts.

It was madness. I'd never experienced anything even close to it. It was pure emotion

363

all trying to get out of your body as fast as it could. We were hugging, screaming and losing our minds. So were the fans. It was deafening in there.

We did the handshake line with the Canucks, which I think is the single neatest thing in all of sports. We'd just battled our butts off for seven games, hitting each other as hard as we could, and in the end we all shook hands. It's one of the great things about hockey. We try to kill each other, and we may not even like each other, but we respect each other.

NHL commissioner Gary Bettman came out with that beautiful silver trophy. When they wheeled it out, it was the first time I'd ever seen it in person. It was like the Holy Grail or something even more mystical than that. I was trying to find Carol in the stands but my head was spinning so much I couldn't even figure out what section the wives were in.

Messier went out to center ice and the commissioner made a speech, then said, "It's your Stanley Cup, Mark. Share it with your team and your fans."

The place erupted once again, and Mark looked like a little kid who had just gotten the toy of his dreams on Christmas morning. It was the most emotional I'd ever seen him. The guy who shouted "We are NOT DONE" was holding the Cup above his head and carrying it around the ice, and I swear he had tears in his eyes.

After that, it became a blur. From watching the Finals on TV, I knew the protocol. Mark would pick the next player to carry it (Brian Leetch) and from there on each guy would hand it to someone else. About halfway through the team, Sergei Zubov was handed the heavy Cup, and after his trip around the ice, he spotted me and handed it over. He yelled, "You had my back all year, this is for you now!"

I wasn't really sure what to do. I just circled around and listened to the crowd. And oddly enough, I don't have any memory of who I handed it to. We were all just going nuts.

We stayed out on the ice forever. Usually, the game ends, you give your goalie a congrats, and you head to the locker room. Instead, the staff was putting carpet runners down on the ice, while someone else was bringing our wives and families down to the bench. While they were arranging that, we all flopped on center ice with the Cup and had photos taken. I love those team photos. They're not staged or pre-arranged. Not everyone is even looking at the camera. We all had smiles as big as the Grand Canyon and everyone was holding up one finger. We truly were No. 1!

After the photos, we all went over to find our wives. Carol held it together until she saw me. I'd seen her first and could tell how excited she was, but when she saw me her face completely changed and she just started bawling. I held her as tightly as I could.

I just kept saying, "We did it! We did it! We did it!" She just nodded and said, "I'm so proud of you. I love you, Eric."

I was proud, too. I'd worked so hard, from childhood all the way to the Stanley Cup. It was all worth it. Every bit of it was worth it. Doing sprints pulling that big tire around was worth it. Running the stairs at school was worth it. A ton of work got me to that moment.

There was a lot of booze being sprayed around and consumed in the locker room, and a lot of other nonsense, but it all just felt so emotional and uplifting. I swear, the Stanley Cup is the hardest trophy to win in all of sports. I know some people disagree with that, but I've lived through it. It's more intense than anything I've ever gone through. And I was just a small cog in the whole machine. The machine that won the Stanley Cup.

We did have that parade. It was crazy, too. A hundred thousand people or so lining the streets screaming at us, people throwing shredded paper from office windows and making a racket. My gosh, it was loud.

When that was over, Carol and I finally had a chance to just go back to the apartment and flop on the sofa. We were both exhausted. But we couldn't stop smiling at each other, shaking our heads.

We did it. The New York Rangers did it. I did it. Carol and I did it. Everyone I ever played with who pushed me did it. We all did it. Roseau did it, too.

CHAPTER 37

Brooks Bennett

Not long after the season was over, when I was back at the condo abiding by the strict rule that I was not allowed to pick up a baseball for at least a month, I got a notice in the mail from the Rangers. It was a receipt for a deposit into my bank account for something like $38,000. I had no idea what that was about.

So I called my agent, Adam, and asked him what I should do with it.

"Leave it in the bank," he said.

I asked, "What's it for?"

He said, "You might not remember, but on top of your salary we built some incentives into the contract too. $50,000 if you made the All-Star team was one of them. We had another $50,000 if you were named Rookie of the Year, but we just barely missed that. Heck, if you would've been the MVP of the American League that would've been $100,000. You went one-for-three and that's awesome. The $38k is $50 grand minus taxes and our commission."

I had no clue. I must have been daydreaming or otherwise distracted when he told me about those incentives, and I sure as hell hadn't read the fine print in the contract before I signed it as fast as I could. It's not like I could have tried harder to win the other two, but it was a total surprise to get that payment.

And another funny thing about that was the fact I almost didn't want it. I was actually kind of mentally struggling with the amount of money I was being paid just to play baseball. I knew I had trust issues, after Donna and Susie, and it seemed like my income was the source of all that. I knew I was being stupid, and that I had totally earned that money, but it just confused me. I was financially set, as far as I could tell. I had all the money I needed. Compared to my life before pro ball, I had way more money than I needed. And, I owned a condo in Florida. I didn't want any of that to define who I was. I was still just me. I grew up with two loving parents and basically nothing else. To me, and my mom and dad, money was just what you needed to pay the rent and keep food on the table. There was never any dream about making millions.

At the same time, Adam was already talking to the ballclub about a new long-term deal. I just let him do his thing. What did I know about that sort of stuff? Almost nothing. To me, I was still playing the same game I played on dirt infields with my dad, or at Canyon, Kennedy, or the U of M. I just wanted to play baseball. If a Major League team was willing to pay me crazy money to do it, I had to learn to accept that. Sounds nuts, I know, but it's just how I felt and I was having to figure out how to deal with it and accept it as a fact.

Adam called a few weeks later and said: "The Rangers want to lock you up. Right now they're at four years and I'm asking for six. They know you can be the ace they need to replace Nolan and some other guys who are at the end of the road. I'll keep you posted."

During the early part of the winter, he got the deal done and we ended up at five years, fully guaranteed, for $10 million. That was insane. I didn't even know how to absorb that. This time I paid attention to the incentive bonuses and they were all in there too. All-Star game, MVP, Cy Young Award, stuff like that. But honestly, at that point I didn't care. I was going to make $10 million over the next five years. Give me a break! How do you even imagine that?

When I heard what the deal was, I called my dad and told him:"This is the big one. I want to buy you guys a house. Let me get the first season of this new deal under my belt, and I'll be able to get you anything you want for cash. You have to let me do this."

He fought me on it. He said, "The place we rent is great. We love it here and we love the neighborhood. You take care of yourself."

I cut him off and said, "No, a year from now we're going house-hunting and I'll pick out your new place if you won't do it. I have to do this. It's in my heart, Dad. This is what I have to do. I can't repay you for all you've done for me since I was born, but I can do this and I wouldn't be able to do it if you hadn't been out there with me when I was growing up. You got me here."

My elbow felt fine. No pain, no tingling, no "funny bone" buzzing sensation. I was seeing the trainers at the complex three or four days a week, doing some stretching and resistance training, but no real heavy lifting. I was totally anxious to get back into that. It felt like the winter was slipping away from me and I wouldn't be ready. I like to be ready way far in advance, not just the day spring training started.

As for Eric, he was in the midst of something really special. His New York Rangers were outstanding. They were very talented and very consistent. I kept tabs on him and his Rangers all winter. It looked to me that they should not just make the playoffs but go deep into them.

As my spring training started, I could see that they were clearly the best team in the NHL. I couldn't fathom what that would feel like. My team, also called the Rangers, was good. We won our share of games and had some studs, but I don't think our name was ever in the sentence "the best in Major League Baseball." Eric's guys were the best in the National Hockey League, and that meant they were likely the best hockey team in the world.

I'd been throwing easily for a good month before we opened camp, and didn't have any issues. The elbow felt good, the ball was coming out of my hand nice and easy, and I had good command of all four pitches. I was ready to rock when the spring training schedule started.

Here's the thing about spring training. In the old days, guys like Babe Ruth showed up totally out of shape. Most guys did. They didn't have the training facilities or options we had. Most of them worked winter jobs, as crazy as that sounds. They might not have swung a bat or thrown a ball for five months! That's hard to even comprehend now.

For us, we got there pretty much ready to go. As pitchers we just needed to stretch it out to where we could go multiple innings and the hitters had to see "live" pitching they hadn't seen yet. Personally, I think you could accomplish that in two weeks. Maybe three at the most. But spring training was two months long and we played close to 30 games. It just seemed to totally drag on and on. I thought it was ridiculous. OK, for rookies that was probably a good thing. It gave them a chance to show their stuff just like it had for me. For starting pitchers and veteran players, it seemed to never end. And then we'd finally break camp and go north and might be playing in the snow if we opened in Cleveland, Detroit or Chicago. It was "too much and too long" followed by "too cold."

I did fine in camp. I threw my innings, I hit my spots and I stretched it out to two innings, then three, and finally four. With the Rangers, the feeling was if you could leave Florida throwing four innings, you could throw five during the first week of the season, if all went well. Within a month, you might be throwing 100 pitches and going seven. I didn't go scoreless like I did the year before, but that's because I was working on stuff and being careful with my arm. No need to impress anyone in Port Charlotte. I wasn't trying to just make the team. They knew me, and I knew me. I was stoked to get going.

I thought we looked pretty loaded, despite the loss of Nolan, who did indeed retire. We still had Kevin Brown and Kenny Rogers in the rotation, and I was the third starter. After me, though, it was kind of a "mix and match" series of guys. John Dettmer was probably our most steady starter after me, but I don't think he won a game.

In the lineup, we still had Pudge and we had Will Clark, Jose Canseco, Dean Palmer and some other solid guys. Looked like a stout big league club to me.

The schedule did us absolutely no favors. Like I wrote earlier, you're down on the Gulf Coast of Florida forever, getting sunburned and sweating like crazy. Then you open the season up north and freeze your butt off. We started the season with two games at Yankee Stadium and three in Baltimore. It was brutal.

Once we got back to Arlington I stayed in a hotel for a few days, then went back over to the apartment complex I'd been in the year before and signed a lease there. It wasn't luxury, but I didn't need that. It was close to the park, there were some other Rangers living there, and I was fine with it.

We did not get off to a good start, though. We were in a real rut through most of April. We'd either score some runs but give up too many, or not score much at all. We were losing way more than we won. In that first month, I was the winner in game three over the Orioles, thanks to seven runs backing me up, but in the cold I really didn't have a feel for much of what I was doing. Pitching is all about feel. If you're cold the ball feels like a round popsicle. I think I went 2-2 for the month. I never really got rocked or anything, but I was also never totally dominant. It just still felt like I was searching a little.

At the same time, I was following Eric and his Rangers. We'd talk on the phone whenever we could, trying to match up hockey and baseball schedules, and they swept the Islanders in the first round of the NHL playoffs. My idea that they could really go far seemed realistic. After the Islanders series we talked and I told him that, but all he'd say was: "One period at a time. One game at a time. We still have miles to go, but we're pretty good and we have a great goalie. In the playoffs the goalie can carry you, but we're scoring well too."

In May, I went 3-3 and again, I never really got rocked but we weren't stacking too many good games together. Some nights we'd hit, some nights we'd pitch, and some nights we wouldn't do either. It was confusing to me. What had happened to us? Was this all because Nolan retired? I didn't think so. He was still great in '93 but not the totally ridiculously dominant Nolan Ryan of the past. I think our veteran guys were just showing their age a little, on the mound, at the plate, and in the field. Will Clark was raking as he usually did, but beyond him it was really hit and miss, and that description fit me and the rest of the pitching staff too.

Also in May, Eric and his boys waltzed through the Washington Capitals to win the second round, and then had a really tough one against the New Jersey Devils. Somehow we were finding ways to talk almost every night. The New Jersey series took a lot out of them, and he sounded exhausted after the games, but they got out of it in the seventh game with an unbelievable 2-1 win in double overtime. As soon as I'd get back to the apartment or hotel room each night, I'd tune in to ESPN to see the highlights, and then figure out the time difference to give him a call. It was cool as hell to see Eric out there battling. They were going to the Stanley Cup Finals to play the Vancouver Canucks. Damn, I wish I could've been there.

By June 5th, they were up two games to one over the Canucks. We were playing in Boston. I got the win but never felt right. My fastball was flat. No snap on the slider. Basically I was throwing BP. I was trying to get outs with magic, and I actually did. I didn't have much velocity or bite, but I still had location and I just made it up as I went along.

In the sixth inning, it all exploded. I threw a slider and felt the pop. BANG! Right in the elbow. It was impossible to miss. I figured all of the fans in Fenway Park could hear it, but I think it was only me. I just dropped my glove on the mound and grabbed my right elbow to make sure my arm was still attached. And I walked off the field. Kevin Kennedy and our trainers met me before I got to the foul line. It was not good.

The trainers took me to the clubhouse, and started prodding around and asking me how everything felt. All I could say was, "It's basically numb right now. But I felt it pop and I even heard it pop. I think it's bad."

We were headed home that night after the game, so the trainers wrapped my arm in

369

ice after I gingerly changed clothes. They set up an MRI for the next day, and gave me one pain pill for the flight.

I'd never had a bad arm. I'd never felt a sensation like that when something in my arm just broke, or tore, or did whatever it did. And this wasn't my knee or ankle. It was my elbow. My pitching elbow. I had no idea what to do, or how to do it, or what was going to happen. Before the game ended, I called home and told my dad about it. Somehow he already knew. All he said was, "You're going to be OK. They'll take care of you. You're going to be OK. We love you!"

Once the game was finally over, all the guys came in to see me in the training room. One by one, they came by and asked how I was. The whole damn team. All I could say was: "I don't know. We'll find out tomorrow. I felt something let go in my elbow, so we'll see. I'm freaked out and pissed off. I know that much."

The flight home was forever. I didn't sleep a wink. They had iced my arm so much it was pretty numb, and to keep me from moving it, they put me in a tight sling wrapped around my chest with an ACE bandage. I just couldn't possibly get comfortable on the plane, physically or mentally.

Once we did get back to Dallas, I didn't think it was too wise for me to drive, so I asked one of the younger guys who lived in the same complex if he'd drive me back home. Other guys pitched in. Another teammate drove his car, he drove mine, and we got back there some time in the middle of the night. One of the guys got my suitcase to my apartment. They all made sure I was OK. I went to bed and just laid there. I was mentally lost. I kept thinking I'd wake up from this dream, except it wasn't a dream. It reminded me so much of the knee and ankle injuries back in high school. Like, "Is this really happening to me? Is this for real?" I was still awake when the sun came up, and I had a 10 o'clock appointment for an MRI. Talk about miserable.

Eric called me right before I had to leave for the MRI appointment. I had called a cab, because not having a mobile right arm is not good for driving.

"I heard last night but knew you guys were flying home," Eric said. "How are you? How bad is it? What do they know?"

I said, "I don't know how I am, other than crazy. I'm heading to an MRI in about 10 minutes. We'll just have to see. Something popped. I felt it and I even heard it inside my head. If I need surgery, they're doing great things with this stuff now. But I don't think I'll be lifting any weights or doing any bullpen sessions for a while. It's bad, dude. I just know it is. I'm usually optimistic, but I just know it's bad. It sucks."

I did know Eric and his Rangers had a chance to go up three games to one that night, in the freaking Stanley Cup Finals. I just told him: "Screw me, I can't help you. Go out and win tonight. That's all you need to think about. Win the first period. Win every battle. Win the second, and then win the game. I'll be OK." He was so close to being part of a Stanley Cup winner, and I was so far from being a pitcher again.

The cab got me there, the nurses set up the MRI, and I just tried to take a deep breath and relax. It takes a while, it's noisy, and it's uncomfortable as all hell.

A doctor came in to see me after the MRI and said, "I got a glimpse of it, but I want to look at it in more detail today. Head back to your place and I will call you when I feel I have a complete handle on it."

A few hours later, I got the news I was dreading. Completely torn ulnar collateral ligament. Gone. Busted. Finished. They can't just fix those. You need a new one. We all call it Tommy John surgery. These days, most young players have no clue who Tommy John was. Maybe they think he's the surgeon that invented the operation. He was a pitcher. He had the first reconstructive surgery to replace the ligament. It's been called Tommy John ever since. He came back and pitched in the big leagues again, but he had to kind of reinvent how he pitched. Still, without him going through it there would have been hundreds of pitchers whose careers would've been done. And in reality, many were done anyway, despite the surgery.

I had to absorb the news. It wasn't sinking in.

I got a call from our head trainer and my skipper, Kevin. Skip said, "We should do this as soon as possible. You're going to be on the shelf for a few months and in rehab for close to a year. Are you up for this?"

I said, "Of course I'm up for it. And I'll work like a freaking maniac to get back."

The team had a preferred surgeon for the procedure, and I was booked to be in Los Angeles just three days later. The Rangers sent me out there on a private jet.

I met Dr. Abrahmson right after we landed. He was up front with me.

"So, you already know that your ulnar collateral ligament is completely torn. It's what basically holds your elbow together. We need to replace it, not just repair it. A repair wouldn't hold if you ever want to throw a baseball again."

I just nodded.

"So what we have to do is find a new ligament and put that in your elbow. We can get a donor ligament from a cadaver, but I very much prefer to take one from a different part of your body. That lessens the chance of your body rejecting it. It's already yours. You're right-handed, so taking one out of your left forearm would be the best option. You won't miss it. You'll never know it's not there. We'll take it from a very low-stress place."

I nodded again.

"It's a tricky surgery," the doctor said, "but we're all getting better at it every year. We know what works, we know the pitfalls, and we know how to make you a pitcher again."

Then he showed me a cutaway model of an elbow, which he had right there on the shelf, and pointed out the ligament, plus what they would do with the new one. He said, "If the ulnar collateral ligament looks really small to you in this model, that's because it is. It was designed to hold your elbow together for chopping wood, holding a fork, raking the leaves, and maybe shooting some baskets in your driveway. It was never designed to throw a baseball as hard as you can, with an overhand delivery. It's not big enough. It's not strong enough. That's why so many pitchers over the decades have had to quit the game with what they only knew to call a bad elbow. So, we'll fix you up and in a year you should be as good as new."

One more time, I just nodded. I was kind of speechless.

371

Surgery was scheduled for the next day. Wow.

I called my dad as soon as I got to the hotel the team had set up for me. Again, he was just as calm as he could be.

"They're going to fix you up," he said. "You'll have a lot of work to do, but you've done that before. It's going to be a tough year, but you've gone through that before, too. You'll be good. After the surgery, just head back to Cape Coral and your mom and I will come down to spend some time with you. Are you OK, my man?"

I said I was OK. Pretty worried, but OK. Thinking of them coming down to be with me in Florida was just like a pain pill. It made a lot of the worry go away.

My dad's demeanor was a direct connection to when my mom was so sick. He kept it real. He just always kept saying, "Now that we know what's wrong, these doctors will make her better." It was kind of strange to be on the receiving end of it this time. My career could be over, but he made me feel invincible. What a dude. You could not possibly have a better dad. He got me through those first traumatic days, when I went from pitching at Fenway Park, to feeling it pop, to flying home and getting the MRI, and then flying to L.A. to meet the surgeon. He got me through it. Like it was totally nothing. Just part of life.

And hey, huge props to the Texas Rangers for how they handled all of this. They did all the legwork and totally took care of me. I just went where I was supposed to be, flew on a private jet, and got the surgery. I can't imagine how much work that all entailed. They were epic. First-class all the way.

The next morning I was at the surgery center in the hospital. The doctor walked me through all the procedures, although I'm not sure I was absorbing what he was saying. Things like, "We'll drill some holes in the bones around your elbow" and "then we'll do a figure-eight with the new ligament." Of course you will. Sure. Whatever you say, Doc.

I'd be put under, of course, and the first thing they had to do after I was out was "harvest" the ligament from my left forearm. That's about the strangest wording ever. They prepped me, put me on a gurney and wheeled me into the operating room. Five seconds later I was out cold. Being put under is really weird.

The next thing I knew I was waking up and shivering. I was so cold I was shaking uncontrollably. And I wasn't all there, if you know what I mean. I was still groggy, but Dr. Abrahmson was next to me and I do recall him saying, "It went great. We got the ligament out of your left arm and it went right into your elbow like it was meant to be there. It's a strong ligament, so you really should be good to go once the rehab is done and the strength is back."

I had two sets of stitches. One set in my left forearm and the other one, which was scary looking, on the side of my right elbow. I had some healing to do before I'd even be released. They put my right arm in a brace that locked it in about a 90-degree position, and put it in a sling. They wheeled me away and put me in a private room. I didn't have any pain at the time, because I was still doped up, so I basically just fell asleep. And then the nurses did what they do. They come in and wake you up every hour to see how you're doing.

It was late afternoon when I started getting emotional. I was there alone. I had no wife, no girlfriend and no family there with me. It was just me with my arm in a brace and a sling, in a hospital room out in L.A. I felt about one million miles from home. I did get a call from the Rangers, who let me know they were flying one of the trainers out to be with me, just to oversee what the doctors were doing. He wouldn't be there until the next morning, but just knowing I had support coming made a lot of the stress go away.

I remember that first night. I'd be sound asleep and they'd come in again to look in on me and check my vitals. It was like ghosts coming into my room. It was dark; they were quiet. It was really freaky. They were also checking the stitches and wounds. Even in a hospital, infection can happen. That would be a totally bad thing.

I had an I.V. needle stuck into the back of my left hand, and I'm pretty sure they were putting some magic juice in that line. When they'd leave me alone, I slept like a brick.

The assistant trainer from the Rangers showed up that next morning. His name was Terry, and he was a good guy. He looked me over and just said, "It's going to be OK. We'll start some rehab this afternoon and get some walking in, up and down the hallway. We have to give the elbow at least a couple of weeks before we do anything there. We have a full rehab plan in place for you, but let's just get through these first few days and then get you back to Dallas. We have a rehab specialist at the complex in Port Charlotte too, so you can head home when you're ready to do that, or you can stay in Arlington and be with the team." I hadn't even gotten that far with my plans. I just wanted to safely get out of the hospital with no drama.

That afternoon, Terry and I took a long walk up and down the hallway. I felt good, but my right arm felt like it weighed about 50 pounds. When we got back to the room he pulled a foam ball, about the size of a baseball, out of his bag and we officially started rehab. I squeezed that ball about 20 times. We couldn't do anything with my elbow, and with the sutures in my left arm we couldn't do anything there either. It was walking and squeezing that ball. That's all we had.

I was there one more day, and the Rangers sent the jet back to pick Terry and me up. It was great to get back to Arlington and the park, and it was even better to be surrounded by teammates, coaches, and friends.

I decided to stay there in Arlington for the first few weeks. Those were going to be critical in setting me up for the long haul the whole next year would be. If all that went well, I'd go back to Cape Coral and do rehab at the complex. I called my dad and told him my plans.

After I got back to Arlington, it went something like this: After a couple weeks they put a hinged brace on my arm, so I could start moving the elbow but with some support. Each day, we'd slowly and carefully try to extend my arm a little more, and then back up to 90 degrees again. The absolute worst thing you can do after Tommy John surgery is to try to be a hero. If you don't follow the rules, you can tear the whole thing apart and then you're screwed. It was great to be working and moving, but it was hard to hold it back.

I wanted to pick up a baseball so badly. I think it was about the third day after the new brace was put on when I was handed a ball. A real baseball. It felt great in my hand, and I was allowed to clench it and relax over and over. For some reason, doing the careful arm extensions with the hinged brace on felt a lot more productive when there was a baseball in my hand. It was like a reminder to tell me why I was doing all this.

By the end of that first month, I flew back to Fort Myers and went to the condo. My parents came down the next day. Life was getting back to something like normal as the surreal terror of the whole process began to seem like ancient history. At that point, I just needed to get better. Mom and Dad stayed for a week and babied me. That felt good, but it also made me feel guilty. My mom had gone through much worse than this. My deal was just an injury. She nearly died. We supported her through that, so maybe it was her way to give that back to me. She made breakfast, lunch and dinner every day. We all shared a bottle of wine on the balcony every night.

As for Eric, I had been out of the hospital and back at my Arlington apartment, when they got to Game 7 of the Stanley Cup Finals. They were in New York, on their home ice. I got to watch it on TV at the apartment. I can't even find the words to tell you how cool it was to see them win that game and carry the Cup around the rink at Madison Square Garden. I also can't tell you how hard it was to sit there as still as possible while they did that.

We talked a few days later, after the celebrations and the parade, and his first words were: "How are you doing? How's it feel? I'm worried about you."

I said, "I'm good. But dude, you won the freaking Stanley Cup! Let's talk about that instead."

He told me about all of it. The tension, the travel back and forth, and that last game. He said he'd never felt anything like that before, once the final horn blew and they knew they had won. He swore he'd never forget a minute of it, although he also admitted he never remembered who he handed the Cup to after he got to skate with it. I thought that was hilarious, and figured I'd be the same way. I hadn't even remembered that I had an All-Star bonus in my contract. He promised to come down and see me later that summer. That sounded awesome to me.

I think it was early August when I got to take the brace off. Once we did that, the rehab ramped up quite a bit. Lots of range-of-motion exercises on various machines, work on the stationary bike, and walking. At first, they didn't want me running because of the jolts each step can create, but pretty quickly I was able to jog. The trainers had already let me know that throwing a baseball was still a solid six months away. That sounded like an eternity. And I knew that "throwing" would start with soft toss and take weeks to progress to actually throwing something that resembled a pitch.

Eric did come down, as he promised, and he was there the day I was allowed to go without the brace for the first time. The dude had memory flashbacks to his knee injury as a Gopher when he saw me take it off. "Oh my gosh, the brace," he said with a grimace. "I thought I'd never get that off. This is a big day for you. I'm glad I'm here."

At the same time, there were loud grumblings about a work stoppage of some sort in

Major League Baseball. The owners had insisted on a salary cap, claiming teams would start going out of business if they couldn't put a lid on salaries. The players' association was completely against that. I should have been more dialed in with that stuff, but just as it was coming to a standoff was about the time I got hurt. I wasn't thinking about a lockout or a players' strike. I was just thinking about myself and getting better. Maybe I was being selfish, but I had to look out for myself. My arm wasn't going to magically get better by itself.

The players finally took a vote and on August 12 they walked out on strike. It was a power move because it hit the owners the hardest just when they were making their biggest money of the season. There were pennant races heating up, people were flocking to games and buying tons of tickets. They had a stout TV deal in place that paid the teams a lot of money. When you have fans and TV, corporate sponsors line up, too, with their checkbooks open. And there I was. In rehab and kind of watching like an outsider when we went on strike. I wasn't sure what that meant for me. I didn't really feel a part of it. I was a spectator too.

At the time, the Rangers were 10 games under .500, at 52-62, but the club was somehow in first place in the division. I was in Florida doing my rehab.

I finally got to talk with some of the front office people in Arlington after the strike began. Everyone seemed to think that it wouldn't be long before both sides would come to some common ground and we'd get back to playing. Until that time, though, I couldn't even consider coming back to Arlington. I would've been crossing a picket line, and I couldn't do that to my teammates. Fortunately, the Port Charlotte complex wasn't part of the Major League operation that time of year, so I could still go there for my therapy and rehab. I even got the players' association to approve that, just to be on the safe side.

As you might remember, the strike would last for the rest of the season. No more pennant races, no playoffs, and no World Series. Meanwhile, I was down in Florida going to rehab every day. It was freaking bizarre. I felt cut off from all of it. I don't know for sure but maybe for me it was better. I didn't feel like I was missing anything, but I figured everyone would come to their senses pretty soon and it would all start up again. It didn't feel like I was on strike, but for the first time in my life I was.

I just focused on recovery. I started throwing again, to a minor leaguer, in early September. It was just playing catch, nothing more than that. We had a detailed plan in place, literally spelled out day by day and week by week. The trainers thought I could get back on a mound by December. They wanted me to have the outline in case the organization shut the complex down. I was hooked up with a minor league catcher who also lived in the area, so if we had to we could find a local field and work out there. The thing that worried me the most was losing out on the rehab facilities and the instruction from the trainers. They were guiding me. I was just following orders.

As it turned out, they kept the complex open because the minor leaguers weren't on strike. So, I could go there as long as I didn't actually play any baseball games. The Rangers weren't going to option me back to the minors, so all I could do was play catch on the side, start to pitch again, and use the facilities.

A bunch of the guys called me during that stretch in the fall. They all said the same thing. "Get your work in. You're not breaking any rules and not crossing the line against the strike. We'll work this out, but your arm and your health are important to all of us. Just stick to your program."

That felt good to hear. I was worried about how my teammates might react to what I was doing. All those guys just walked off the job and stayed away. I was still going to the complex and had started throwing.

I kept to the program and also joined a health club. I was afraid they might shut the complex down and I wanted a place to go where I could lift weights. By then, we were just doing normal machines, nothing specialized, so a good health club would have everything I needed. I was feeling pretty good and making good progress, so I stopped going to the complex. It was my act of solidarity with the guys.

I was on target, we all felt sure the 1995 season would start on time, and I'd still need another six months to even think about pitching in a game, so it seemed like I had everything in place. At the earliest, it would be June before I could pitch in a game, and if that was the case the Rangers would probably send me to one of their minor league clubs to get some innings in before they brought me back. I was all for that.

I was meeting my catcher at a local high school, and we started ramping it up. It felt great. I was only throwing at about 50 percent when we started with me actually on the mound, but there was no pain. There was also no progress on the strike.

At the same time, there was also no progress on avoiding a work stoppage in the NHL. Eric had been telling me about it, but he wasn't sure anyone had the guts to stop playing. As it turned out, those guys didn't go on strike. They got locked out by the owners. The lockout started on October 1 and it cost the NHL its All-Star Game and competitive hockey all the way until January 11. So Eric and I were both out of work. Their deal was mostly about a salary cap, too. No baseball and no hockey for months. I'm sure Eric was going nuts, but I just kept focusing on my rehab. I wouldn't have been playing anyway. But still, it's absurd to think the super-rich owners in both leagues would shut it all down to try to squash the players' organizations. Absolute insanity.

The NHL went back to work on January 11, but the month came and went for all of us baseball players. I was throwing a bit harder and still hitting the weights as much as I could. February arrived and still no progress on the strike. Things were at a standstill. It sucked.

Then the owners announced that if the players didn't settle the strike, they'd play the 1995 season with replacement players! That was insane, and the fans knew it. The owners knew it pretty quickly as well. The Blue Jays announced they wouldn't participate because of strict labor laws in Ontario. One by one, some other teams backed off. But there were still teams willing to bring in the replacements and play. The strike continued. It was terrible. It really felt like the owners were doing all they could to break the union. It was really bitter. I didn't see any light at the end of any tunnel, but I kept working out.

Finally, it all went to court and the ruling was against the owners. They had to settle and there would be no salary cap. We'd just automatically revert to the latest working agreement that had expired. The strike ended in early April. Once that happened, I decided to get back to the complex again. A short spring training would be happening, and my Major League teammates would be back in Port Charlotte. The season would only be 144 games, instead of 162.

Once the actual season started, I wanted to be back in Arlington with my guys. I wouldn't travel with the team, but I'd be with them for all home games.

And boy, did the fans hate all of us. They hated the owners, they hated the players, they hated the commissioner, and they hated the head of the union. Most of the ones who did show up came just to boo us. No one came out of that thing on top. I just kept my head down and did my work.

Finally, I was throwing again at close to 100 percent of what I had in me. It just didn't feel anything like the 100 percent I had before. By that time, the Rangers were being really careful with me, and let me know that in early June I'd be going to the minors to get some innings in. They weren't sure which level or which team, but to me it was a target. I needed a target.

It had been a year since I heard the pop. A very long year. It sucked. I was lonely, alone and still wondering why it happened, but I couldn't wait to put on a full uniform and get back on the mound. The mound has always been my safe place. I belonged there.

CHAPTER 38

Eric Olson

Life sure moved fast after we won the Stanley Cup. All sorts of endorsements came our way, and I landed a few of them. I did a couple of TV commercials for a Volvo dealership in Westchester County with my script being something like, "Hi, I'm Eric Olson with the New York Rangers. As a defenseman, it's my job to protect my team. With a Volvo, you'll be protected too. They're the safest cars on the road." I won't say I was good at it. I was probably really bad, actually. They wanted to pay me by giving me the free use of a new car per year, as long as we kept doing the ads, but living where we did we wouldn't have a place to park it for less than $200 a month, so it wasn't worth it. Instead, they gave me $500 per commercial. Not bad for about an hour's work.

I headed down to Florida to see Brooks, after he tore the ligament in his throwing elbow. He had a long road ahead of him, and it was important for me to get down there and see him, maybe give him some motivation. I could tell he was very worried about it, but he was fired up to do the work and give it his best shot. He probably wouldn't pitch until mid-summer of '95, at the earliest. I didn't know a lot about Tommy John surgery, but I knew it was serious and not a sure thing.

On the hockey front, I mentioned in my last chapter how coach Mike Keenan had a tendency to do great work but not stick around for long. That's how it was with us. He lasted one season, and it was a season when we won the Stanley Cup. He landed a job immediately with the St. Louis Blues. Our new coach was Colin Campbell, a former player we all knew. He'd even coached the Binghamton team in the minors! The first team I played on as a pro, although he wasn't there when I played in Binghamton.

Carol and I decided to stop paying New York rent and instead find and buy a small condo on the Upper West Side. We knew the area and liked it a lot. We found a place that was no more than 750 square feet (picture Jerry Seinfeld's apartment from the TV show) but it was nice, it was pretty new, the building had a doorman, and there was an elevator. We were on the 15th floor and from our living room, if you plastered your cheek to the window and looked to the right, you could see a little bit of the Hudson River.

It was ridiculously expensive, but we wanted the investment way more than we wanted to keep paying the equally expensive rent. There were no houses in Roseau as expensive as that condo, and probably very few that small, if any. That's the price of living in Manhattan.

As the short summer wore on (if you win the Cup, you have the shortest offseason of any team), we got our workouts in and kept in shape. Carol and I also managed to do a weekend getaway to Roseau, although that's not easy to do. The best option is to fly from New York to Minneapols and then get a rental car and drive up to Roseau. That's about a six-hour drive. You could also connect in Minneapolis and take a puddle-jumper up to Grand Forks, which is only about a two hour drive to Roseau, but then you have to factor in the connection (and possibly missing it when flying out of LaGuardia) and how much time that costs you. Or, you can hire a private jet but we weren't quite at that financial level. We weren't anywhere close to that level. We decided to fly to Minneapolis and drive.

It was a very important trip. Each player gets a few days with the Cup to take it wherever he wants. I was taking it to Roseau. I couldn't wait.

The high school put on a big pep rally and I got to walk into the rink carrying it. The roar was enormous. I was blown away. Carol was, too. She was wiping away tears just standing there listening to the crowd. After that, we went over to my parents' house and just sat with the Cup on the front porch. My sister and all my brothers were there, and Carol's parents came over too. Any neighbor who wanted to come by to hang out with us and see the Cup was welcome. Yes, there was some beer and wine consumed. I think it's a fantastic tradition to let each player take the Cup somewhere, and to experience it myself was truly a huge moment for me.

We couldn't stick around though. We hustled back to New York the next day because there was so much going on. In case you're wondering, no, you don't have to carry the Cup on the plane. The guy known as "Keeper of the Cup" handled all of the logistics for the NHL. There's no way they'd ever put it in checked baggage. You may have seen that guy on TV. Perfectly styled blond hair and he's always wearing white gloves. He's the caretaker, and he tries to keep it in one piece and not too dented up. It does get tossed around and dropped every now and then. I remember just a few years back seeing photos of the Cup in Mario Lemeuix's pool, after the Pittsburgh Penguins won it. It was at the bottom of the pool, in the deep end! That must have been a hell of a party. I've seen photos of it on boats, at private homes, in Europe, on mountain tops, in Moscow's Red Square, and all sorts of places. It's a great tradition that I hope never ends.

Right around that time, the baseball players went on strike. I think the owners wanted to institute a salary cap and the players gave them a firm "No" on that. So they walked out, right in the middle of the season. I wasn't sure what that meant for Brooks in terms of his recovery and rehab, so I called him to find out. He said he couldn't go to the Rangers ballpark, but he could use the complex they had in Port Charlotte because it hosted minor leaguers during the summer, and the minor league guys weren't on strike. He said both sides were completely entrenched and not budging. The whole thing sounded bad.

It was bad. Both sides were dug in, and it was up to the players to stay strong and not give up some of the financial benefits they had earned over the years. Most of the MLB guys made hundreds of thousands of dollars a year. A good many of them made millions. A few made huge millions. It sure seemed to me, looking at it as a professional athlete, that the owners were trying to break the union. I don't know if that's ever been admitted, but it also seemed to me they were going to break the game itself by trying to get there.

For baseball, it stretched on for months, into the playoffs and wiping those out. There was no World Series. Nothing. It was crazy. Then it stretched on until the spring and some teams threatened to play with replacement players. Give me a break! It was awful.

And here's what made me really mad. The owners were pressing for a salary cap to save them from themselves. Nobody put a gun to their heads to make them pay what the superstars deserved as a fair share of the enormous revenues pouring in. They made the decision to do it. They couldn't trust themselves to keep a lid on anything. Or maybe they just didn't trust one another. Baseball had always had a problem with the haves and the have-nots and the have-nots struggled to be competitive because they couldn't afford top-level players.

And guess what? We had the same issue, but it was right before the season started. The hockey owners wanted a salary cap and we said no. We didn't go on strike, but they locked us out. We couldn't work out in any team facilities, and we missed about two months' worth of games, including the All-Star game. We didn't play our first game until mid-January. What in the world was going on in sports? Two leagues pulling this crud in the same year? Did anyone in management or ownership even realize what they were doing to the fans? It sure didn't seem like it. And from a personal standpoint, I was sitting on an expensive new mortgage and not getting paid. We could handle it, as long as the lockout didn't stretch on forever, but it seemed like complete nonsense.

Brooks and I talked about it every week. It was insane. It's the fans who keep our sports alive, and they locked them out, too. To me, I got the impression the owners thought they owned the sport. They didn't. They only owned their individual teams. Without the fans, there would be no sport and no teams.

Fortunately, the NHL came to its senses a lot sooner than the baseball owners. At least we got back to the rink by January and played 48 games. That's about half a normal season, but we were all happy to be lacing up the skates and playing again.

The shortened season was pretty condensed, and we wouldn't have to play anyone out west. That was a good thing, but the short season left you no room to have a slow start or any long losing streaks. We busted our butts from the first day.

The only problem was, all the other teams we played felt the same way about it. It was like starting the season with the playoffs. Everybody was extra amped up, just flying around the ice. We ended up 22-23-3, which was a disappointment, but we somehow made the playoffs.

In the first round, we beat the Quebec Nordiques four games to two. We moved on to play Philadelphia in the second round. It was a brutal series, in terms of the hitting and the animosity. Their rivalry with us, the Islanders, and the Devils was personal on the Philly end. They saw us as part of a huge city that blocked out the light in their town. We got crunched a number of times, and I actually got my "bell rung" once on a rough hit into the boards. I don't remember if the guy got two minutes for cross-checking, but he should have. It was a dirty hit.

We didn't know as much about concussions then. I probably had one, but I went back to the bench and waited for my eyes to clear. Then I was back out there. We lost in four straight games, and I've always felt I had something to do with that. I definitely wasn't as sharp as I normally was after the big hit. I know I didn't play well.

We gave up five goals in two of the games (and lost the first two games in overtime) and four goals in the other two. When you give up 18 goals in four games to a team like the Flyers, it's going to be hard to win. We couldn't overcome that.

As the off-season started, I still wasn't feeling 100 percent. I knew I'd been dinged pretty well, and had a lot of headaches. I tried to get as much rest as I could for a couple weeks, and then got back to work. It took me a while to overcome it, but I felt normal by about the third week of my workouts.

Right about that time, Brooks was starting to throw on the mound, and he sounded funny about it. He said there was no pain, and he felt like he was pitching well, but it wasn't all there. His velocity was down and the other pitches weren't as sharp. I did not like the sound of that. I hoped it would just take some time and it would all come back.

That summer, the talks picked back up between the NHL players and the owners to finally settle things that were left hanging after the owners ended the lockout. I kept track of how it was going by listening to the team veterans who were attending the meetings or getting full transcripts. Mark Messier was our best conduit.

One day, one of the veterans said something like, "I think the baseball thing scared the owners to death. They see how much damage can be done if we do any more lockouts, so they're actually bargaining. One of the things we're pushing for is unrestricted free agency. I don't know if we'll get it but if we do, anyone who has played out his contract can declare he's a free agent and bargain with every team in the league. It would be huge for all of us."

My agent was tuned into it as well. I still had three more years left on my contract, so it wasn't a pressing issue for me, but he said, "Just keep this in the back of your head. Once your deal is up, if the Rangers don't step up to pay you what you're worth, we might have the option to go free agent and look around. It doesn't mean you can't sign back with the Rangers, you can do that. But you'll have a lot more leverage. Let's just see how the negotiations go. If we get free agency, the hockey world will change. And for the players, it will change for the better."

My initial response was: "This is three years away for me. I can't get distracted by it."

Robert then said, "Look, I'll get the door open if we get free agency. If they know you're planning to file for it, they may want to either extend your current deal at much better pay, or they might want to trade you to get something back. But let's just wait and see how it goes."

By late summer, just before training camp started, we got the word. It spread like a wildfire in a field of dry grass. We had a new collective bargaining agreement with the owners, and with it we got the unrestricted free agency thing we'd been hearing about. I'd still have to play out the three years that were on my contract, but at the end of that I could make some decisions.

Robert told me his plan. He was going to start laying the foundation regarding what I could do when the contract was up. He was trying to gain us the leverage we'd need to get me what the stars of the team made, in terms of salary.

I put it out of my mind and got to work. I wouldn't have much leverage if I played bad.

Just like the roller coaster we'd been on since I was with the Rangers, we managed to bounce back in '95-'96 and have a heck of a year. I played well. Very well. The best hockey of my life.

We finished 41-27-14. We were second in our division. That 14 represents ties and that's a lot of ties. Back then, we didn't have the goofy rules they have now, playing three on three for a few minutes and then going into a shootout if nobody won. To older guys like me (that's what I am now) settling a long and hard-fought game with a shootout is ridiculous. It's a gimmick. We'd play the game and if the score was tied that's what it was. Both teams got one point.

We beat Montreal in the first round, four games to two. We played the Penguins in round two and they took it to us pretty well, winning four games to our one. For that series, we were overmatched. Looking around, I thought we still had a ton of talent but there was no getting around the fact that we were getting older. Some of our best players were getting older. As analysts like to say, "If you're going to win in this league, your best players need to actually play like your best players."

Heck, I turned 30 that summer. Me, the little squirt from Roseau, was 30. A lot of guys don't make it much longer than that, but I was playing my best hockey.

By then, Carol and I were solid New Yorkers. We loved it, and loved it even more in the summer. We'd make trips to Roseau, or Florida, and even to Texas to see Brooks, but we felt totally at home where we lived. We didn't own a car, but we knew every way to get around and we could walk to whatever we needed.

As for Brooks, I could tell he was frustrated when we spoke. He'd gotten back to the Rangers in late 1995, a little behind schedule. As he put it, "I had nothing."

No pain, but no sharpness and nothing overpowering. I think he was babying it more than a little bit. That's common for most pro athletes. This is your living. This is what you do. You've been through a traumatic injury and no matter how it feels, the biggest hurdle to get over is to just completely go flat out. If you hold back even a tiny bit, it changes your game and that can cascade into other problems. In hockey, you're a step slow if you're coming back from a knee, and most of that is in your head. I'd seen plenty of hockey players sprain or injure a knee and then come back to blow out a hamstring, a groin muscle or even an Achilles tendon. They changed the way they skated and that caused new problems. In baseball, as a pitcher, you're hittable after being dominant. It's hard to deal with, both mentally and physically. He had an army of trainers looking after him, and I was a hockey player. I just listened with sympathy and kept telling him to hang in there. It will get better. I didn't know if that was true, but that's what I told him.

Meanwhile, as the summer wore on, Robert called me with an alert. He'd talked to Neil Smith, the GM, and told him that I had every intention of looking into free agency when my contract was up after the '97-'98 season. He told me Neil didn't sound surprised, but he did groan.

He relayed that Neil had said, "Well, we want to work this out. He's a great player and a great teammate. He's got a lot of years left. Where do you want to start?"

Robert just asked for a proposal. Whether it was a contract extension at a higher rate or a binding outline for a new contract after this one was up.

It's interesting that in the first year of free agency, not too many big names took advantage of it because most of them were locked into long-term deals. The real free agent floodgates wouldn't open until those guys were free to bargain. Same with me.

Right before training camp, Robert called me again and said, "They're worried about losing you. I know all the code words. They're all the opposite of what they really feel. If they say you're just an average player and they can survive without you, they want you very badly."

Robert also said that the Rangers had brought up trading me. That way, they could at least get a player or two in return before I was gone. Of course, Roger threatened, "We'd have to find a team willing to take on his big contract."

Robert said he replied, "His big contract? You got him for a steal. I'm still not sure how he and his wife can live in Manhattan on that money. Go ahead and look into that, if you want to. We'd be open to that."

Great, now I had that to distract and worry me. I've always been pretty good at putting that worrisome stuff aside, but this was pretty huge. I did realize, however, that getting the sort of contract I could dream of depended on me playing as well as I can play. I just told myself I'd make that happen.

The trading deadline, which was the date teams couldn't make any more trades after it came and went, was March 20, so the Rangers didn't have to do anything until then.

Robert said, "If they're going to do it, I bet they'll do it before the season. They can't risk any major injuries that would kill any deal and leave them on the hook for the last two years of your contract and ruin your trade value."

Sure enough, Robert was right. Just before training camp he sprung the news on me. Our world was going to change in a huge way.

"OK, are you ready for this? They are trying to work a trade. They have two or three teams that are interested and could really use you. I didn't ask who they were because we don't have any clause in the contract that allows you to block a trade. I'll keep you posted."

For the next few days, Carol and I were as lost as we've ever been. We loved New York. She loved her job at Macy's. We really did not want to leave. For me, there was the fear they'd trade me to a team that wasn't very good. I'd be leaving a Stanley Cup winner to join a team that hadn't made the playoffs. And, I had no say in it. But, I had a great agent who knew what was best for me and knew exactly what the market dictated I should make. If I represented myself, I'd still be playing for $38,000 a year.

Finally, Robert called with the news.

The Rangers had agreed to a trade with the Tampa Bay Lightning. They'd be picking up the last two years of my contract, and the Rangers were receiving one defenseman and one forward for me.

At first I was mostly speechless. I finally just said, "Well, can I call you back in an hour? I know there's nothing I can do about it, but I need to digest it and I need to let Carol know. I assume I'll need to be there right away, correct?"

He said, "Oh, yeah. They open camp in two days. If you can get there by then, you should. If not, try not to be more than one or two days late."

We hung up, and my head was absolutely spinning. "What do we do with the condo? What do we do about Carol's job? How do we move our stuff? Who is even on that team?"

I actually thought they were a team on the rise. We'd play them a few times a year and they always played us tough. As for other questions in my head, I didn't have any answers. They'd had a very rough start as an NHL franchise, with there even being accusations of fraud or money laundering or other illegal things going on with their ownership. They'd come very close to going out of business in the first couple years. But by 1996, I thought they were stable and getting better.

I called Carol at work, and said, "Well, Robert was right. We've been traded. To the Tampa Bay Lightning. They want me there fast, so when you get home tonight we'll have to talk about it and see how we handle it. I'll tell you up front it's not going to be easy on you. I really don't want you to stay here for the whole season, but you'll have to be in charge of selling the condo. Anyway, let's talk it all out. It's going to be bizarre spending a hockey season playing in Tampa."

She actually got home a little early that night, clearly looking worried. I just gave her a big hug and we went to our little sofa and sat down.

I said, "I'm trying to see the bright side of this. OK? They're a team that's getting better. They beat us a couple of times last season. They have a brand new arena in downtown Tampa that will open this month. They obviously wanted me, and gave up two good players to make it happen. I can't take any of it personally. It's a business. The Rangers got two good players instead of not getting anything if I left after next season. And I'm going to a team that wants me. Plus, it might be nice to play a hockey season down there. No more sleet storms and blizzards!"

I was trying to keep it light and positive, but I could tell she was really worried.

I was supposed to call Robert back in an hour, and I knew I had to do that. I told her I had to make that call and we'd continue to figure it all out after that.

Robert said, "It's a done deal. The GM of the Lightning is going to call you, and they'll take care of everything logistically. Flight, hotel, all of that. You should hear from him tomorrow. He said he understood if you were a day or two late getting down there."

I also mentioned putting the condo on the market and Robert said, "Either of those two guys the Rangers are getting from Tampa might want to rent it, so hold on. If you do want to sell, it will go the first day. That's the market here. You'll probably get a bidding war going."

Carol and I got back to business and here's how it laid out: She wouldn't put her two weeks' notice in until the condo sold. She'd stay in New York and handle that. Some of the furniture was ours but some of it came with the unit, so we figured it might be better to see if we could sell it "as is" with all the furniture.

There were so many unanswered questions, but we agreed we had no choice but to dive in and just let it work itself out. This stuff happens to athletes all the time, and by association it happens to their spouses too. I told Carol that if she wanted to wait until winter before selling the condo, I could deal with that. We didn't need to bite off too much right now. I could tell she appreciated that. It took a lot of the pressure off.

So the plan was for her to keep working at Macy's and stay in Manhattan until around December 1. Then get the condo on the market and plan to quit her job and relocate. The bonus to that was that it would be getting to be serious winter time in New York, and she'd get the benefit of getting on a plane and landing in Tampa. It would be pretty palatable that way.

When I got there, I'd have to figure out where to stay and I could start looking at condos or even homes. Once we sold the condo in Manhattan, we could step up big time for what that money would do for us in Tampa. There was a ton to do, but like I said, this happens to athletes all the time. I was lucky I had such a great agent. I'd heard stories from guys who said they learned they'd been traded on the radio. No one even called them.

I did hear from the GM at Tampa. I'll be honest. I knew hockey legend Tony Esposito was involved with the franchise and helped get it launched, but I had no clue he was also the GM. He just talked in generalities and welcomed me to the organization. Then he said, "Our traveling secretary will call you in a minute or two. He'll get everything arranged and will help you out any way he can. Welcome to the Lightning, Eric. You're going to love it here."

The traveling secretary did call within minutes, and his first question was: "Is your wife coming with you?"

I told him the story and he said, "Well that makes it easier. When can you leave New York?" I told him it would be a couple of days. We still had a lot of details to iron out. He said that was fine, and he'd book a flight for me. He'd also have a car and driver waiting for me at the airport, and a nice hotel room booked for a week.

The two days flew by, and then I was at LaGuardia waiting for my flight to leave. It was a pretty nice late-summer day in New York. When I got off at the other end, it was basically stifling hot and very humid, but I could smell the salt water on the jet bridge and sure enough there was a guy in a black suit holding a sign that said "E. Olson" at the bottom of the escalator. We waited for my bags, one full of clothes that may or may not have been suitable for that time of year in Tampa, and one with all my gear. Off we went.

The hotel was a Hyatt and it was great. They got me a suite on the top floor. I'd already been told to just relax, talk to Carol and take a cab to the new arena at around 8 a.m. the next day.

When I got Carol on the line, she asked me how it all was. I said, "Well, I won't see the arena until tomorrow, but I've heard it's amazing. I'll tell you this though. It's stinking hot and incredibly humid here. Seems like a really odd place for a boy from Roseau to play hockey, but we're going to make the best of it. I promise you that."

And hey, during the winters Brooks and I would only be about two hours apart. So we had that going for us!

This big new adventure was just getting started.

CHAPTER 39

Brooks Bennett

I can sum up my recollections of late 1995 and most of 1996 with one statement: Everything sucked. I had no pain in my elbow, but my brain hurt, like I was getting an error code that said "Unable to Process," and I started to feel other things go wrong that had never been a problem before.

Through rehab, when they let me start throwing, I was doing all I could but there was just no zip or bite on anything. I'd spent my whole life as a pitcher just throwing it up there and watching it dart, move and pop. After the surgery, the fastball was just straight and must have lost at least five miles an hour. The curve didn't bite; it just kind of spun up there and said, "Hit me!" The change-up was OK but it's hard to make a living on a change-up alone. I decided to ditch the slider. That was the evil pitch I threw when the tendon broke. I knew I wouldn't be able to throw it with conviction that soon. Maybe ever.

We had a new pitching coach, Dick Bosman, and he was very patient with me. We also had a new manager, Johnny Oates, and he was the same way, although for a while all we could do was talk on the phone until the strike ended in April. Nobody wanted to rush me, and that was a good idea. If they rushed me they would be getting an expensive guy who threw nice BP. To the other team. In games.

My arm just felt dead, and that's an actual baseball term. Guys will say, "I've got a dead arm, there's just no life there."

I was throwing bullpen sessions once the season finally started, and I was on the 40-man roster but I wasn't activated. There's no sense in activating a guy who doesn't look like he can contribute when all you have is a 25-man big league roster. Spots on the 25 are beyond precious. There will be nights when all of your position players and half (or more) of your bullpen will be used. You can't have one "dead arm" on the 25-man.

In May, they asked me to head to Port Charlotte to be with the Class-A team there. They wanted to see me actually pitch instead of throw. I was all for it. I mean, I

387

could throw to hitters, try to fool them, and see how it felt, in real games. Plus, I had a home there. So, let's go!

I decided to drive, so I'd have my car when I got there. I figured if I somehow looked great and they called me back up I could fly and find wheels in Arlington when I got there. I knew the team had sponsorships with a few local dealerships. I figured we could work something out, but my first job was to actually pitch.

It was great to be back in a lively clubhouse as part of the team and not just a guy who worked out and threw in the bullpen. I didn't really know any of the guys on that team, but I never in my life had any problem treating every teammate as an equal. We'd all made it to pro ball together, and anyone who was in the Florida State League could play the game. It was a tough league filled with serious prospects. They were good.

The Rangers could've sent me a level lower, but I'm thinking that would have been a waste of time. These guys in Florida were all really talented. It would be a test. The low A-Ball team might be too much of an easy path and end up being misleading, in terms of results. Plus, in Port Charlotte we had the complex, with all of its benefits. If I'd gone down lower I just would've had a locker in a cramped locker room. Picture "Bull Durham."

I met with the manager, Butch Wynegar, a former star catcher for the Minnesota Twins, and the pitching coach, John Tudor, who was a longtime star pitcher with teams like the Boston Red Sox and St. Louis Cardinals. So, yeah — they were coaches in Class A, but they were stars in their big league days. There was a ton of knowledge and experience there.

They were great. They told me the plan was to pitch at least one more bullpen session then bring me in as a reliever as soon as possible after that, if I was OK with it. I was totally OK with it.

I threw my bullpen that night before the game, and sat in the dugout getting to know the guys a little bit. Jeff Russell, from the big club, was down there too for a rehab assignment just like me, but we didn't just sit in a corner by ourselves. We both wanted to feel like part of the team, so we mingled, we talked, we introduced ourselves as if we were just new guys, we asked questions, and gave advice whenever we were asked for it. I was so stoked to be there.

To be completely straight, it was heaven. It felt so rad to be back in uniform and with a team.

Two nights later, our starter got rocked a bit and I was told to get loose. We were playing Fort Myers, the Twins' affiliate in the league. At the time, I didn't know how totally stocked they were. Looking back on it, there was practically an entire big league team on their roster, just moving up through the organization as a group. Torii Hunter, Jacque Jones, Corey Koskie, Doug Mientkiewicz and others.

I came in for the third inning and was sweating bullets. Yeah, it was hot in Port Charlotte, but I was sweating the existential kind of perspiration too. I was nervous. I was also pretty fired up, though. I hoped that would help me ramp it up a bit.

I can't tell you who I faced because I didn't know any of those guys would be big league stars. They were just guys in uniforms to me. I'm pretty sure I faced Torii Hunter, though.

I felt good. I felt free and easy. But those future stars didn't care about how I felt. They knocked me around, and if the guy I think was Torii was actually him, he took me deep on a fastball I left right out over the plate at probably no more than 89 mph. It was a rocket.

After one inning, I'd given up four hits, three runs, and I had one strikeout. I was throwing BP. It was what I feared the most. They took me out.

After I came out, John Tudor and I talked at length. He said an interesting thing, after I said I felt like I was throwing BP.

"You actually looked like you were throwing BP," he said. "You weren't letting it fly. You looked like you were being super careful. You need to work on finding that fluid but strong delivery you used to have. Hey, I know how tough this is. You may think that what you had tonight is all you have, but there's more. There's lots more. The surgery gave you your arm back. You just have to unlock it. OK?"

I nodded and agreed. There had to be more. I'd been through two check-ups to get the elbow looked at and scanned, and the doctors all said the same thing. "It looks perfect. There's no reason you shouldn't be back to 100 percent. And some guys come back stronger after Tommy John, so you need to have that mindset."

That was easy for them to say. I didn't feel scared. I honestly didn't feel like I was babying it. I felt like I always did, but it wasn't there. Was it me? Was it all in my head? I wasn't sure.

I'd been talking to my dad at least three or four days a week, and I laid that all out for him.

"Is it me? Am I fooling myself? I'm I too scared to let it go?"

He always said, "Who cares? Just realize this. You've already achieved your dreams. And your dreams could easily take you to levels you never considered, if you just let it go. If it blows up again, you've already done it. Just do what they say and stop worrying."

He meant well. But again, easy for him to say. Just stop worrying? OK. You got it, Dad. I'll stop worrying.

I could tell I was getting really frustrated and kind of mentally lost. I had never once second-guessed my dad. He had never irritated me. And now I thought he was talking bullshit to me. There was definitely something wrong in my head. I just wasn't sure if there was anything wrong in my elbow.

I pitched again a few nights later, and did a little better. Didn't give up a bomb, so that was a step up. A small step, but a step. I guess.

I went out there with the mindset that I was going to fool them. I'd be "pitching backwards" again, starting off with the off-speed stuff and then trying to sneak my now pedestrian fastball by them, or I'd rely on my change-up, which had actually gotten better since I came back from the injury.

I pitched two innings and struck out three, all on change-ups they missed by a foot. No runs allowed, but two sharp hits. It still felt good to walk off the mound without being terrorized or embarrassed. Lots of high-fives and pats on the butt from the guys in the dugout. I'm sure they were thinking: "He's back. He's got it." To me, it was all a charade. I wasn't back. I was a different pitcher. I didn't have my mid-90s heat, and I had put the slider/cutter on the shelf. I felt like I was an imposter.

Tudor asked me if I wanted to start a game. He said the Rangers had brought it up but they deferred to him. If he didn't think it was a good idea, they could just keep running me out of the 'pen.

I said I'd like to try it.

I wasn't me that day. I wasn't the confident guy just going through his routines knowing that he had a great chance to shut the other team down. I was nervous as hell. Running my foul poles helped, but even as I was running I was thinking: "What if I suck? What if it explodes again? What if I don't even get out of the first inning?"

And I couldn't help asking the big-picture question: What the hell was wrong with me?

Well, I didn't suck but I wasn't all that good. We were playing the St. Petersburg Cardinals and just by pitching to them I didn't think there were any legit prospects on that team. I got by pitching backwards again. They knew my reputation. They knew I threw hard. So I fooled them with the slow stuff and some of it was really hittable. They just didn't square too many of them up or we made great plays.

Four innings. Two runs. Five hits. Two strikeouts. No walks.

I felt like a fraud.

I talked to Dad after the game and told him about how I felt mentally. He was quick with a response.

"Maybe you should go see a psychologist. Explain to them all you're going through and how you can't get out of your own head. They might be able to help. Do you want to try that?"

I had to think about it, but I did say yes. I wanted to talk to the Rangers first, to see what they thought. By that time, I was just searching for answers.

And then I woke up the next morning and my right shoulder hurt. At first I thought I must have slept on my right arm wrong, but it didn't go away. It wasn't a horrible stabbing pain, but it was nagging and deep in the shoulder. You've gotta be kidding me, right? My shoulder had really never bothered me. Before calling a shrink, I needed to go see our trainer. And maybe a witch doctor.

All during this time, I hadn't been much of a friend for Eric. He was calling me a lot, and I'd always take the time to tell him how I felt, but it was still his off-season and I honestly didn't want to talk to anyone and just chat. I hate that word, by the way. Who came up with a word like chat? I didn't chat. I talked. I had real conversations. What the hell is chat?

The trainers didn't seem to think the shoulder thing was a problem, but they shut me down for at least a week.

"It's probably just tendonitis, but if you want we can have it scanned to make sure there's no structural damage," the head trainer said.

I was getting used to that sort of thing, so I didn't see any reason to put it off. I went in the next day and had MRI images taken of it. When we got the results, the consensus was no damage, but that meant almost certain tendonitis. The trainers advised a cortisone shot and a week's rest. We went for it. And for the record, cortisone shots hurt. They are deep with very long needles.

It felt better immediately, but that's just the cortisone masking it. I still needed a week of rest. Great. Just as I was getting in the groove a little, I was back on the shelf.

After the week was over, I was out on the field at Port Charlotte, although the team was on the road. I was allowed to play catch and just ease into it. It felt good. The elbow felt good too. The next day, they let me get on the mound and throw to a catcher. Again, it all felt good. I still didn't have much stuff, but at least there was no pain. Over the next three days, my catcher and I stepped it up and I felt like I was throwing free and easy.

If I was going to pitch in another game, though, it would have to be done soon. The minor league season ends around September 1. We were nearing the end of August. I was just trying to be ready. I figured if anything went crazy or haywire, I'd have the whole winter to get over it. If there was nothing structural, a lot of it was just rehab and physical therapy. And the guts to get through it.

The team was back, I felt I was ready, and they slotted me into the bullpen to be ready whenever needed. I was needed that night. I entered into a mess the starter had left me, and needed to get two outs with the bases loaded. Even as I walked in from the bullpen, my brain was already tormenting me. "Go right at them, or pitch backwards again?" kept rattling around in my head. I threw my warmup pitches and it all felt fine.

We went right after the first guy. He took a fastball right down the middle for a strike. Now I was in the driver's seat. Two change-ups later I had a strikeout on three pitches.

I started the next guy with a change and he hit a dribbler back to me. Flip to first and out of the inning. It almost felt like the old days. Almost. The fastball was still 89 to 90 and hittable. I got lucky when the first guy just looked at my first pitch. And on the way to the dugout I noticed I was unconsciously rotating my right wrist. When I got into the dugout, one of the trainers asked me if anything was wrong.

I said, "I don't know. I didn't realize I was doing that until I got back in here. I guess I was just trying to loosen things up and stretch it out."

He prodded my forearm and kept asking "Does this hurt?" or "Anything odd there?"

Finally, I had to admit it. "Yeah, there's some pain in my forearm right where your fingers are. It's been there since I started throwing again but it wasn't bad so I just ignored it. I figured I just had to get back into the groove and it would all smooth out."

He said he was 99 percent sure it was tendonitis and not structural. If it was structural I wouldn't be able to even grip the ball. Fantastic. More tendonitis. My old friend.

This time, with only five days left in the Florida State League season, it was official. I was done for the year and I wouldn't be making a return to the Rangers.

I did go back to Arlington to meet with the trainers and staff, and they brought in the team doctor. Everyone was hemming and hawing and mumbling. It was like none of them wanted to say anything too negative. Finally, the head trainer said, "Brooks, this is proof you've altered your mechanics, maybe subconsciously, to protect your elbow. That put some strain on the shoulder first and then the forearm. We're going to have to find a way to fix that. We've got to get you back to the same form you had when you got here. It's really a tiny little change, but any change at all can do this. Let's just let you rest and we'll figure out a plan in a week or two."

So that's where I was. Still in that in-between world of being a Texas Ranger while also not a Texas Ranger. I was making a ton of money, but I sure as hell wasn't earning it. That wasn't cool with me.

That same day, after I got back to the apartment (I'd kept the lease going in the hope I'd need it for my return), I got a call from Eric. I figured it was just another nice call from him to check on me, and he did that first. I filled him in. Then he stunned me.

"I've been traded. To the Tampa Bay Lightning."

"What? Are you kidding me? What the hell?"

He told me about the free agency thing, and how his agent convinced the team that he'd be gone if they didn't extend him at a fair rate of pay, and they decided to trade him to at least get some bodies back in return. He told me what he and Carol had planned, and that he had to leave the next day. I was stunned. Could there possibly be more turmoil going on?

"Are you OK with this?" I asked.

"Well, I have to be. Someday you'll have to be too, I imagine. This is a business. In the end, we're just assets on a spreadsheet. It'll be good. They're an up-and-coming team and you and I will only be an hour or so apart. It'll be great to see you a lot this winter, and I'll admit I won't miss the New York winter weather."

I was so impressed by how he kept emotion out of it. He was so damn practical. So grounded.

I made plans to head back to Cape Coral as soon as the Rangers' season was over. Until then, I'd be in shorts and T-shirts just working out with the trainers after they gave me a strict order to not screw with my arm for a week. The forearm felt fine, but I wasn't throwing baseballs so it was impossible to know if it was fixed. Once again, I'd need to be patient.

I also had to fly from Dallas to Fort Myers because my car was in Cape Coral. Bad planning, all around, I guess. What a hell of a two-year stretch it had been. I was so ready for it to be over. So ready to be back to normal, whatever the new normal would be. I was just over it.

First thing, I found a sports psychologist in Fort Myers. I heard some other players had hired her too, so when I met her I was ready to dig into my brain and figure it out.

Why was I so worried?

Why was I protecting an elbow that, by all measures, was fine?

Why couldn't I even find that perfect old delivery?

I needed to dive into it and figure it out. She wasn't a pitching coach, so she couldn't help me there, but she could hopefully open up my mind and get the negative stuff out of there.

At our first meeting, I just filled her in on my history and she nodded a lot while she took notes. She pushed me back further, asking about how I grew up and what my family was like. We worked our way up through school, through my mom's illness, through all of that. We talked about my knee injury in high school and how I got through that. Then through college and pro ball. The recurring question was: "And you didn't have any problems or doubts then?" I didn't. The word "doubts" set off an alarm in my head though, and I told her that. It was doubt, wasn't it? All she'd say was: "We'll figure it out, but it sure sounds like something like that. Let's meet again next week."

And I thought I'd spend an hour with her and come out completely healed. Wrong.

I had some easy exercises to do for my forearm and shoulder, but I wasn't supposed to touch a ball again until January. I was totally getting tired of hearing "Don't touch a ball again until …" So I concentrated on the exercises and I saw my psychologist every week. I'm not sure I was making headway with the arm stuff, but I knew I was making headway with my doctor. We talked about my upbringing, and how loving it was. We talked about Mom's illness, and how dire that was. We talked it all out. I didn't know if she had a plan for this or if we were just talking.

Then, by about mid-December, I think she had formulated it all in her head. We didn't really have a discussion at that meeting. Mostly she talked.

I'd been sheltered.

I'd never had to deal with doubt.

I knew my parents would be there for me.

I was scared by my mom's problems, but she pulled through and that erased any doubts I had.

All the way through high school, college and pro ball, I never had a doubt. Not one.

Now I had doubts but I had no experience dealing with them.

She finished with this:

"Everyone has doubts. It's natural. You've been spared that until now. You knew how stable and safe you were, and you knew how good you were as a baseball player. Now we have to deal with doubt.

"Doubt isn't a tangible thing. It's not a tumor. It's not a disease. It's an issue. We can deal with issues. I'll give you some meditation exercises and I'll be able to tell you how to confront doubt and defeat it. It won't come easy, Brooks. You're going to have to totally give in to it. Are you ready for that?"

Hell, yeah, I was ready for that.

I did have one other thing to say.

"I have to tell you I do have tons of doubts about relationships. Especially once I signed my contract. I doubt any woman would love me for being me, and not just be interested in my money. So I've just walked away from that part of my life. I'll deal with it later."

She said, "Well, I can understand that. You've had a really calm and sheltered

393

life. I'd be worried about it too. I wouldn't call that doubt. I'd call it skepticism and you're probably in a good place with that. Someday, maybe after your career, you'll find someone who doesn't know what you did, or how much money you made. My advice would be to keep it that way until you know you both respect each other and love each other for what you are as people. You'll be OK."

CHAPTER 40

Eric Olson

Once I got settled at the hotel in Tampa, I had a few things on my mind. There was the fact the team was putting me up in that gorgeous hotel, but only for a week. So, I needed a place to live once that luxury ran out. On top of that, there were just the typical little details that come with picking up and moving your life from New York to Florida on about two days' notice.

I called the Lightning office and told them who I was. I asked who might be able to help me with some logistical stuff. They put me through to Debbie, who was an expert at helping players sort out relocation details. She was a miracle worker.

It was still only around noon, so I told her that I'd lived in New York for about five years and never needed a car. But now that I was in Tampa, I couldn't just jump on the subway to get to the arena. Or to get anywhere, for that matter. I needed a car.

She gave me a number for an Audi dealership that worked with a lot of the guys to get them loaners during the season. They were a sponsor of the team. She also gave me the name of the best guy to work with, and I'll never forget it because it stuck with me from the beginning. He was D.J. Davenport. He sounded as slick as a wet sidewalk on the phone, but within 30 minutes he had me hooked up. They were bringing a 1996 Audi A4 over to the hotel within the hour. Wow.

I still had to get insurance for it, but it had dealer tags and it was just going to be a long-term loaner, so I wouldn't have to register it. Debbie gave me the number for a State Farm agent who was also a team sponsor, and we took care of that. I'd just have to call the guy back with the VIN and a few other details after the car was delivered. I gave him my credit card number to make sure the policy was in place as soon as we did that.

D.J. the Audi guy asked me to put as few miles on it as I could and I figured that wouldn't be hard. Basically, all I'd be doing during the season was driving it back and forth to the arena, and maybe to the grocery store. After a year, they'd be happy to swap it out for a new loaner.

My payback to them was that I agreed to do four "meet & greet" deals before games with the VIPs and customers they brought to the games. I was happy to do that. Heck, I'd have done more than that if they'd asked.

And then there was the problem of finding a place to live. Debbie helped out there, as well. For the immediate future, there was an apartment complex with really nice townhomes that would do short-term leases for the Lightning players. I think they got a free ad in the team's yearbook or something. She got them on the phone and hooked me up with a furnished townhome and a lease that ran until January 1, although I could extend it month by month if I needed to, even if I wanted to stay all season. The fact it was only $900 a month was just added icing on an already nice cake. I figured once Carol got down there, we'd look for a place to buy. I was taking the townhome (and the car) sight unseen.

It turned out that the car was magnificent, easily the nicest vehicle I'd ever driven, and the next day when I went to see the townhome it was also fantastic. It was in a gated community over in Clearwater, which is about 30 miles from the arena, but it's a heck of a gorgeous drive over a long causeway. I was all for it. I could sign the lease, put down my deposit and first-month's rent, and pick up my keys the next day after practice. Driving to the rink and back over such a beautiful expanse of turquoise water with big pelicans flying right next to me off the shore, was not a bad way to go.

There were a lot of other things to sort out, too. Back then, it wasn't that easy to keep your bank account in one city and live in another. They just weren't networked that well. So, once the car was delivered I went to a bank Debbie recommended, and opened both a checking and savings account. Then I gave her all the account info, and my checks would be direct-deposited. Seamless. I left the New York account active, with $5,000 or so in it, because you never know what might come up, and Carol would still be depositing her checks into that account, so she'd have all she would need. The rest of the money I moved to the new Florida account.

I also needed a phone. No cell phones yet, or at least not any cellphones people would even recognize today, and very few people had them. So I needed a landline and Debbie got me hooked up with that.

I was thinking I should show up at the arena with some sort of "thank you" gift, for when I met Debbie the first time. I couldn't have done much of that without her. Certainly not in six hours. The Lightning sure knew how to treat their players. The Rangers had always had a few pieces of advice, offered here and there by various people in the front office, but there was no one on the staff who was like Debbie. She even faxed over to the hotel a map of the arena area with drawings of how to get there and where to park in the players lot.

I think most fans think life revolves around us, as professional athletes. We are, indeed, pampered with charter flights and luxury hotels, but they don't know how much of this stuff we have to take care of when we get traded. It's a bit stressful, but it's exactly why the team told me to relax and take care of any personal business before I went to the arena the next day.

You're uprooted, thrown in a new environment, and told to play hockey with guys you might have just played against, who you hit as hard as you could, but now you're teammates. It will make your head spin a little. Or a lot.

And as for those pampered charter flights and luxury hotels, I think most fans would be surprised at what we have to do for six months. Many flights (it seems like most) are overnight red-eyes, because we typically leave right after a game to either get home or to the next away game. And the hotels are indeed very nice, but you often get there at 4 in the morning. There were a few road trips where we'd stay in a hotel for two days, so that second day was a fine reward and a lot of us would relax together in the lobby or by the pool, depending on whether we were in Calgary or Los Angeles, but you sure pay a price on the other trips. Especially when you're flying cross-country like we did for New York and like I'd be doing again for Tampa Bay. We're paid well, but it's not as easy as you'd think. And that's not even factoring in the wear and tear on your body playing NHL hockey more than 80 times in basically six months. There were usually a lot of bandages, unseen bruises, ice packs, and even fresh stitches on the guys when we would board the charter at midnight.

The next morning, I followed Debbie's directions and they took me right to a reserved lot at the Ice Palace, which was what the new arena was called. In later years, it would go through a variety of corporate titles, but in the beginning it was just the Ice Palace.

It was a beautiful arena. It's hard to compare anything to Madison Square Garden, but the Ice Palace was incredible to me. The Garden had history, while the Ice Palace had every modern convenience. Everything was thought out and well planned. The Garden had quirks, because it's so old and had gone through a few major renovations. The Ice Palace had everything in the right place, and the sightlines for the fans were fantastic. It was going to be great to play there.

In the front office, I sat down with head coach Terry Crisp and the GM Phil Esposito, and we just talked about me. I can't say I got to know them much that morning, but they got to know me, they got to know about Roseau, and they got to hear about my career.

Crisp said, "You know, we wouldn't have traded two starting players for you if we didn't think you could make this team better just by being part of it. You just play your game the way you play it, and I'll be thrilled. Don't try to be anything other than what you are. You're one of the best defensemen in the NHL. We firmly believe that, and we're thrilled to have you here."

Esposito then pulled out a contract from his top drawer. It was for exactly the same money as I was scheduled to make with the Rangers, and I expected that because all they'd done was take over that existing contract. It was for two years, because that's what I had left on the deal.

He said, "We hope to keep you beyond this contract. If everything goes like we think it will, we'll make it a big step up. The Rangers got a hell of a deal with this one, but for a guy like you it gave you some security. That's valuable. Let's see how it goes. Welcome to Tampa, Oly. I don't know if that's what everyone calls you, but it's what I'm going to call you."

I laughed and said, "You can call me anything you want. But yeah, that's a pretty standard nickname for me. I'll just call you Mr. Esposito, if that's OK."

I had dropped my gear bag off at the locker room when I first got there, and by the time the contract was signed and we all shook hands, all my stuff was taken away and moved over to the practice facility. A lot of teams, probably most actually, did not practice every day in their home arenas, just because of schedule conflicts with basketball teams, concerts, or tractor pulls. That's still pretty much the way it is. The facility was about 10 miles away. I was told it had everything we needed and a good sheet of ice.

I hadn't really called anyone since I flew down. I made a one-minute call to Carol from the hotel room, keeping it short so the team wouldn't cringe when they paid the bill, and the same with my folks. I figured I'd call Brooks as soon as I was settled in the apartment and had a phone there.

I knew a little about the team, but it was good to stare at the roster in the locker room. There were some good players on the Lightning. Some really young, some really old, and quite a few in the middle. Chris Gratton, just 21, was probably their best young player. Ancient old Dino Ciccarelli was the most senior guy, at 120 years old. OK, he was "only" 36 but he could still play at a very high level. I'd seen him a bunch when he played for the North Stars in Minnesota so it was going to be an honor to finally play with him.

In the back there was Roman Hamrik, Bill Houlder, Drew Bannister, and some other solid players. I'd played against them. They were tough and they were good.

Rick Tabaracci was the No. 1 goalie. He was solid and dependable. I was spoiled playing in front of Mike Richter, but Tabs was a solid NHL goalie.

I thought we had the makings of a good team. Maybe not a great team, but you don't know that until you play the games. With the Rangers, every time I thought we had a great team, we didn't play very well. Every time I thought we had a good team, we played well above that.

I needed to get over to the practice facility for my first official workout with the boys, but first I really wanted to meet Debbie. I stopped in the office and asked for her, and she popped out of her office (or cube, I don't know because I didn't go invade her space) and she was all smiles. So was I. I told her how great it had been to have her help and how settled I felt, even though I hadn't even moved into the townhome yet. And then she said, "I was hoping you would come in to say hi. Here's a detailed map on how to get to the practice rink." She was amazing.

When I got there, I went to the locker room and my stuff was all put away in a locker, along with Lightning practice gear. And it was a nice locker. Right in the middle of the room. That's a veteran's perk. Geez, was I already a veteran? That didn't seem possible, but I had just been traded to a team who gave up two very good players to get me. I guess I had some respect in the room before I ever got there. That's a great thing.

I started to get dressed for practice, even though I was very early, and as I did that the guys started walking in one by one. They all came over to greet me. I think it was a great thing that I had played some tough games against them, but it was all clean and legal. There wasn't anyone in the room I had to pull aside and apologize to, or bury the hatchet with, but there was a lot of respect for the way I had played against them.

We went out and had a great practice. These guys were not only fine hockey players; they were totally dedicated to it. It's easy to go through the motions at practice. It takes all your effort to put the pedal to the floor and treat practice like you play in a game. I was impressed. By the end of the session, I felt like I knew most of them. The transition was happening.

After practice, I went over to Clearwater and signed my lease and handed over a check. I had a place to live. To give the team a break, I went back and checked out of the hotel right then. All I had for "stuff" was in one bag, so I took that to the townhome and carefully put my clothes and shaving gear away. The phone was set to come the next afternoon.

We spent about two weeks just practicing, and working on alignments and responsibilities. We had a few guys who could really skate, and Dino might have been the "old guy" but he was all business. He practiced like a kid trying to make the team. We were going to be OK, I figured.

We opened the preseason against the Florida Panthers, who played in Miami, and then they came up to our place a few days later. That's when it sunk in just how remote our two markets were. The next nearest franchise was Dallas, as far as I could figure. The Carolina Hurricanes didn't exist yet, and the Atlanta Flames had long since moved to Calgary.

We were going to be flying a lot. And that takes its toll. When I played in New York, we had Boston, Hartford, New Jersey, the Islanders, Washington, Buffalo, Montreal, Toronto, and Philadelphia all within our region and they're short trips. We rode a bus to play the Devils and Islanders, and we often took the train to play the Flyers. You get a lot more sleep playing those guys. From Tampa, unless we were playing the Panthers, it was going to be a legit trip. Oddly enough, I wouldn't be learning a lot of new opponents. The way the NHL had it set up, we were in the Atlantic Division, with the Devils, Flyers, Rangers, Capitals and Islanders, along with the Panthers. Same type of schedule, but a lot farther to get to the games. Suck it up. This is the NHL.

My landline phone was in at the condo by then, and I was talking to Brooks a lot. He sounded really down. They'd shut him down for the year. His elbow seemed fine, but his shoulder and his forearm were nagging him and the mental part of it was clearly wearing on him. He was also back in Cape Coral by then, so I told him to come up for our home opener. We started the season on a road trip, to Pittsburgh, Washington, Toronto and Buffalo, but then we came home to the first official game at the Ice Palace. And who were we playing? The New York Rangers, of course!

We also had a bunch of days off before the regular-season opener, so we could spend quite a bit of time together. Even better was the fact my new townhome was a two-bedroom, so he could stay with me if he wanted to. I figured he'd decline the offer, for sure, but he instantly said, "That would be awesome. That will give us a lot of quality time together, whether we're watching TV or sipping wine on the balcony. We've never really been able to do that." I was really looking forward to it. I wanted to get a sense of where he was mentally, because I knew it had to be tough.

We played well on that opening trip. We got creamed in Washington by the Caps, but we beat the Penguins, Maple Leafs and Sabres. Was it big to go 3-1 on a trip like that? Sure. That's a great way to start.

Brooks drove up two days before the opener against the Rangers. He loved the townhome, and got settled in his room. After that, we headed to dinner on Clearwater Beach. Over some wine and some grouper, we talked about all he had been through, but he really wasn't giving out a lot of information. He kept switching it back to me. "What's it like to get traded? How did it all work? When is Carol coming down? How did you find this place? How do you like the Audi?" It was funny. I think he was just protecting himself from thinking about negative things, so I backed off. We'd have three days together. It would all come out. We were temporary roomies and it was really great. He's an easy guy to share your home with. Caring, funny and very considerate. Every morning when I got up, he was already up and his bed was perfectly made. With a laugh, I asked him, "Did you actually sleep in that bed?" And he said, "My life is a jumble right now. It's good to have a feeling of order where you're able to have it. I've always made my bed, but it seems more important now."

It was really a great couple of days, and I could see us doing this a lot more. We'd talk late into the night, over some red wine, and he slowly began to open up more. He told me about his sports psychologist, and their discussions. He told me what the trainers were telling him. And he told me how he felt physically and mentally. Maybe the wine was the key. It opened him up.

When I'd go to the facility for practice, he would either walk around the area or head to the beach. He's got the beach in his blood. Clearwater Beach is pretty amazing, so I know he found some benefit there.

We were both pretty wired on the day of the opener. I had a 10 o'clock skate so I'd be gone for a couple hours. He went to the beach with a book. We met up again after my practice and I began my pre-game routines. He was really interested in that.

"I have a ton of them, and I'm totally lost if things get out of whack and I don't get to do it all," Brooks said. "You're lucky you don't have rain delays. Those drive me insane. I don't think I've ever pitched at my best after a rain delay. You just sit around for minutes or hours and then they say, 'OK, let's go. We have a window in the weather so we have to get going'."

My routines included a nap after the morning skate. Then a big lunch, and then I'd start to ramp up the adrenaline. I'd hit the coffee pretty hard once I got to the rink, but mostly in the afternoon it was soda. Just to get my blood really moving. The rest of my routines were at the rink. How I got dressed. What I did first. How I took the ice for the pregame warmup. Stuff like that. One more time, I realized we were quite different, but very much the same. For me, it was amping up. For Brooks, it was all about slowing down. But we both very much needed our routines.

I asked him if he wanted a seat for the game or if he wanted to be up in a suite. He said, "It's your first game in this arena. Every seat will be sold out. If you can find me a suite I can hang out in, that would be great. I don't even need a seat. Just get me in the door."

I actually got him in with Phil Esposito and his guests. I had warned Brooks that Phil would probably be very focused and all business during the game, but he needed to introduce himself as soon as he got there.

For me, it was completely focused. During pregame, when we were just skating around in big circles, I shared a few stick taps with some of my old teammates. But by the time the puck dropped to start the game, they were just opponents. Guys trying to steal the dinner right off my plate. It was business.

In the second period, we really controlled the puck in the Rangers' end, almost as if we were on a power play, but we weren't. We were even strength but we had managed to get them bottled up in their end. I got up there and joined in. Our guys were rifling the puck around with precision passes. The Rangers were scrambling. I felt it. I knew we had them on their heels and on the ropes. The puck came out to me at the left point, and I didn't see anyone wide open. I sure didn't want to throw the puck in there and give it away. So I wound up and fired. I figured a shot on goal was the best option. Hopefully somebody would be in position to tap in a rebound. Our guys had the goalie screened pretty well, and he never saw it. Upper right corner. Goal.

Final score was 5-2 in our favor.

Did it feel good? Of course. Every win feels good. Any win where I score is even better. But there was no revenge or anything like that. OK, I'll admit it was special. It was special to do that for my new team and just as special to do it against the Rangers, and to do it with Brooks up in the suite with Mr. Esposito.

The next day, Brooks headed back south to his condo. We shared a big hug and stared at each other for a good long while. It felt completely different. Just spending a few days together changed the friendship. I felt I knew him better, or I was at least getting there. It was so comfortable. He could be my roomie anytime he wanted. I'd probably have to defer to Carol on that, but you know what I mean.

After that, my analysis of how tough the travel would be came true. My gosh, it was nonstop. It was a grind. Like I said before, the planes were nice and the hotels were amazing, but the hardest thing to figure out was when you were going to get enough sleep. Hockey players are hyper, but we need rest. Everyone needs rest. We were constantly back and forth across all four corners of North America and all through the middle. It was just constant. I'm not great at sleeping on planes, so that didn't help me much.

Carol and I had been strategizing, and the call was made. She'd get the condo on the market, and as soon as it sold she'd put in her notice at Macy's. Our Realtor scheduled an Open House and after it was over and Carol got home from work, she said there were 36 names on the sign-in sheet. By that evening, we had six offers. By the next morning we had six more.

We took the best bid, and netted a profit of about 35 percent over what we'd paid for it. That's real estate in New York, in a nutshell. And we did sell it "as-is" so everything went.

She put in her notice, and there was a lot of pushback from the executives. They were asking, "Just tell us what it would take to keep you here" and stuff like that but they knew about my job and knew there was nothing they could do. She was sad to leave, but eager to get on with this new part of our life.

Two weeks or so later, I was picking her up at the Tampa airport. No hug in my lifetime ever felt better. It had been nearly four months apart for us. And both of us had been going at it flat-out the whole time. We really needed each other.

She loved the townhome, and one of the first things we realized was that she was going to need a car. If I was practicing or at the arena early for a game, she'd be stuck. We went over to the Audi dealership that had taken care of me with the loaner car, and strolled around their used-car lot. Carol could not have cared any less about what she drove, as long as it was safe and reliable. She saw an Audi that was a few years old with 55,000 miles on it, and the price looked right. My guy D.J. then worked his magic. He showed me the invoice and said, "Don't look at the sticker. This is what we've got in it, from a trade in. You can have it for this exact number." Done deal. I don't even remember what model it was, but it was silver, it was a four-door, and it was in great shape.

I told D.J.: "When you and your family want to come to a game, just let me know. I'll get you the best seats possible."

Within a few days Carol and I were deep into discussing what we'd do next. Do we stay and rent this place? Do we buy a condo? Do we buy a house? I really believed the Lightning wanted to keep me and extend my contract, and the thought of what we could get in the Tampa/Clearwater area with the money we just made selling the Manhattan condo was pretty exciting. We could buy a mansion if we wanted to (we didn't) and still have money left over for furniture and other things. It was like free money. The Manhattan condo had served us well, but it had also been what we hoped it would be: A great investment.

We decided house-hunting would be Carol's job. She'd work with an agent and see as much as she could. Whenever she'd see something she really liked, I'd go with her if I was in town. Otherwise, I trusted her and her taste 100 percent. If she saw something perfect, and I was on a five-game road trip, she should pull the trigger. I knew she'd been worried about having nothing to do, after resigning from her position at Macy's, and this obviously gave her something to focus on. She was excited about it. I was too. I actually kind of hoped I'd be gone when she found a place she felt she had to have. It would be neat for her to quarterback the whole thing, start to finish.

I was in Dallas when she called me at the hotel.

"I really think I've found the perfect place. It's a three-bed, three-bath home in a beautiful neighborhood in Clearwater. Palm trees everywhere. A huge screened-in pool. It's a gated community, and it's a brick ranch style, so all one level. Everything in it is perfect or brand new. The kitchen alone is bigger than our Manhattan condo. The house is only two years old. We can afford it with air to spare. What do you think?"

402

I said, "What does the agent think? Does she believe there's a lot of interest in it already?"

Carol said, "Yes, there are already two offers. If we want it, we can't wait. We should go in at the top."

"Do you really want it, sweetie?"

"I really do, babe. I want it. It's us. It's not over the top, and it's not more house than we need but we'll still have room if we ever have family or guests come see us. It's so private and so nice, and you'll be about the same distance from the rink as you are in the townhome."

"OK. Put the offer in. Let's get it."

Today, I'd instantly be on my phone or laptop looking at it. Back then, I trusted Carol to be the expert. She wasn't a showy person. She didn't need a huge house just to say she had one. If she loved it, I was sure I would too.

They accepted our offer the next day. We were owners of an actual house!

As soon as I got home, Carol arranged for the agent to open the house for us so I could see it. It was everything she said it was. Absolutely perfect for us. I loved it. And I loved Carol too. She'd been amazing throughout the whole process, and she took on the home-buying responsibility like a real job. She was proud of what she'd done, and she should have been. I was proud of her, too. She's pretty phenomenal.

We had a huge homestand coming up, right after the offer was accepted, so we pushed to have the closing during that 10-day run of home games. Generally, as I learned with the condo in Manhattan, the title company and the sellers feel like they get to dictate everything about the closing, as if there's no leeway. Take it or leave it. Be here on this day, at this time, and block two hours of time.

When they said they could accommodate us, but it had to be on a particular February day at 10 in the morning, I had to pull the NHL card.

I told the guy, "Listen, I play for the Tampa Bay Lightning. We have a morning skate on every game day, right at that time. That's a game day. We're playing the New Jersey Devils. It's going to be hard enough to do this on a game day but impossible to do it when I have to be at the morning skate. This is not negotiable. We can't ask our boss for time off. We have to be there."

Yeah, I was probably a bit snippy but it's another example of life as a professional athlete. We don't have much free time, and we have almost zero chance of missing any practice or games because of life. Unless it's the birth of a baby. They will generally let you miss one day for that.

He said, "Umm. OK. Uhhh. Would 2 o'clock that afternoon work?"

It did. We got the closing done, and took the keys. I had to be at the arena in about an hour. We also had no furniture, so we'd be staying in the townhome for a while.

That became Carol's next job. She'd be in charge of furnishing the house. We had three bedrooms, a huge living room, a dining room and a den to furnish. And we figured the den would be a home office. She might need that. Everything from beds to sofas and a dining room table with chairs. Oh, and a TV. We sat down one night and drew up a budget. She loved doing stuff like that. I was more "just keep it in line," but she wanted it all detailed out.

Over the next two weeks, she was swamped but loving it. Each night, she'd fill me on what she'd bought or what she wanted. I was fine with all of it. Give me a nice bed to sleep in, a table to eat at, and a sofa to flop on and I'm happy. I don't need china cabinets, exotic mahogany chairs, an antique buffet, extra fancy stuff everywhere, or anything like that. We'd need pots and pans and plates too, but that was easy.

It was crazy to see how much she got done in just a couple weeks. The delivery trucks were nonstop, she said. I was only there for a few of those moments. Each time I'd have the chance to get back over to the house, there would be more stuff. And then it was fully move-in ready. All we needed was our clothes.

I closed the townhome and ended the lease, thanking the manager profusely for being so flexible and being a Tampa Bay Lightning sponsor, and off we went. The new place looked like a million dollars. Not a New York million. A Tampa Bay million. And everything came in under budget. We had a home. And it felt like we were home.

In terms of the Lightning, in January we went through a really tough spell. We lost four in a row at one point then did that again in February, although we did finish that month with a four-game winning streak. We were really hot-and-cold, and the travel might have had something to do with that. It's easy to get completely worn out.

We had another huge 10-day homestand in March. We were playing the Calgary Flames right in the middle of that set, and the game was tight. It was 1-1 in the third, and as we say in hockey, "it was getting chippy." There'd been some hard hits, a few retaliation penalties, and at least two legit fights. We didn't like each other.

A puck went into the corner, and I went after it. A Calgary player was right behind me, but I didn't know that at the time. I had my head down trying to get to the puck along the boards as soon as I could. Then I vaguely recall seeing all white as I went head first into those boards. The Calgary guy had viciously cross-checked me with his stick, right across the middle of my back, just when I was about two feet from the wall.

The next thing I knew, everything was blurry and I was on my back on the ice, with a bunch of people standing over me while the trainer held my head and neck still. I had been knocked out completely, for about 30 seconds. Yeah, it was scary as hell.

The trainer asked me, "Where are you?"

"Ummm. Tampa!" I spit out.

"Can you feel all your fingers and toes? Can you move them for me?"

I could and I did.

"OK, let's get you up."

They helped me to my feet and two teammates held my arms as we slowly skated to the bench and then walked straight to the locker room.

I don't really remember much about it. The part about saying I was in Tampa and moving my hands and feet is just stuff I've heard and seen on video. I don't even remember going to the locker room.

Carol was not at the game. She was working on the house with some last details in the area of home decor. Curtains, pillows, vases, things like that. Looking back on it, I'm glad she wasn't there. She would've panicked.

Back in the training room, my head started to clear slowly, but it was coming into focus.

"What the hell happened?" I asked one of the trainers.

"That jackass cross-checked you into the boards. You went in head first. You were out cold when we got out there. But the jerk got a game misconduct and I'm sure a nice suspension will be coming his way. You OK, Oly?"

"I'll be OK, but I hurt all over and I'm still a bit foggy. I don't remember any of that."

"So, have you ever had a concussion? I don't see any records of that on your file."

I had to figure that one out in a hurry. I'm sure I had a concussion a couple of years earlier, but I never reported it and never told the trainers about it. I just went back to the bench. I got over it. So I just said, "Not that I know of, but man we get beat up out there all the time. It's pretty vicious."

I was afraid if it was my second concussion they'd sit me down for a long time. Not telling them about that other problem was maybe not the smartest strategy, but at the time I was just thinking of hockey and how long I could play.

They didn't want me to drive home, so I called Carol and said, "Hey, I'm OK but I got hurt a little and they don't want me driving. Can you come get me or should I just take a cab home?"

She said, "Oh, my God, what happened? I'll come get you. Just wait for me. What happened?"

"I got checked into the boards and went in head first. They said I was out cold for a while after they got to me. I feel better now, but I'm sure it's a concussion."

Carol got me home, and all I wanted to do was lie on the couch. She got me a cold towel to put on my forehead and that actually felt great. A lot of things were still spinning.

I was out of the lineup for 10 straight games. I just wasn't getting over it very quickly. They were doing eye tests, reflex tests, bright-light stuff. Back then, concussions were still a mystery, for the most part. At least the Lightning staff wanted to err on the side of caution. In football, I think a guy would say, "I'm good. I'll just rub some dirt on it and get back out there coach," and they'd let him do that. The Tampa trainers were pretty forward thinkers.

When I felt like I was getting back to normal, I called Brooks. He was at spring training, and was staying in his condo during camp. The thing about concussions is that when you think you're mostly over it, you're not. People tell you later about how spacey and confused you were, and you think you were just fine.

I told him about the hit and he said, "Who was this jerk?"

I told him, but you may have noticed I haven't mentioned his name here. He was notorious for dirty hits, and I'm not going to give him the joy of seeing his name in this book. Guys like him actually like being the bad guy. They get joy from it. Screw him.

Later on, Brooks would tell me that I almost sounded drunk. Kind of slurring my words and talking slowly. Again, I thought I was fine.

While I was on the mend, the team went on a trip to Edmonton, Calgary and Vancouver. I was watching on TV from our new house. I was glued to the screen for all three games, but especially the Calgary visit. The guy who cross-checked me had gotten a four-game suspension and by then he was back in the lineup. The first time he stepped on the ice, the puck came his way and three of my teammates just absolutely jumped him. The toughest of the three dropped the gloves and the fight was on. He pummeled that poor bastard. I don't think he'll mess with us again, and I was so appreciative of my boys stepping in to make it right.

While the team was on that trip, I was cleared to skate on my own. It felt good. It reminded me of how I had to take my time coming back from the knee at U of M. A lot of lonely days on the ice alone, skating cones and down-and-backs. I just wanted to get in the best possible shape for when they let me play again.

And to this day, my NHL health records still show that as my first concussion.

In the end, I got back in there and did my best to block it out of my mind. I think I played OK, and I was clear-headed and sleeping well, so that was good. In hockey, you really can't be careful trying to avoid concussions. They find you. If you play your best and give it everything you've got, they might still find you.

We finished 32-40-10. Not great, but just missed the playoffs. We had a good core, and it was something for the organization to build on. I had one year left on my contract. I also had a beautiful house and a smart, loving wife. And a great friend who was still struggling to find himself on the mound.

CHAPTER 41

Brodes Bennett

I got a phone call from Eric around the beginning of October, and we caught up on things. His season was starting in just a few days with a long road trip. But then he said, "Hey man, I'm renting this really nice townhome in Clearwater, and it's got two bedrooms and two baths. When we get back from the opening trip, we have four days off at home before we play the Rangers, of all teams! Want to come up and hang with me? You'll have your own room and won't have to get a hotel room. Bring some wine and teach me more about all of that. Want to?"

I didn't hesitate. It sounded like exactly what I needed. He had me at "Want to come up?" and didn't even need the incentive of sharing some wine with each other. I was all in.

I don't really know how to say all this. In some ways it might have been one of the more important three nights of my life, at least without my family being involved. It changed me. We totally bonded. I think we both knew we were good friends since our freshman year as Gophers, but we'd never lived together and we always had things going in opposite seasons. The chance to just hang out with him, have some great meals, watch a little mindless TV like boys do, and just talk without there being a hurried time limit between classes, or between games, or whatever, was magic. It cemented our friendship.

It also opened my eyes some more. What Eric had done with his life to that point was just incredible. And by those days, we could see it all through the big lens. A scrawny kid from Roseau who just willed himself to be a hockey player.

And here he was in the NHL with a new team, and they'd given up two solid players to get him. His contract would be up soon, and he'd either go free agent or the Lightning would re-sign him to a big new contract. He'd earned it.

But what sunk into my brain was how he never wavered and never gave 99 percent. Even when he was coming back from his knee, he never babied it or found any way to work other than all the way. The dude was absolutely stout.

So I kept thinking, "Why can't I do this? What am I doing wrong?"

We talked about it and he said, "Everyone is different, man. I know guys who play the regular season fully fit and don't give 90 percent. Is it will? Is it laziness? You know what I think? I think it's fear. They're afraid of a major injury, so they spend a lot of time on the ice avoiding contact instead of initiating it.

"I know football players who talk about this, but what they say is that as soon as you cruise a little to try to avoid an injury, it immediately finds you. That's why they're all honored to make the Pro Bowl, but none of them want to play in it. The fear of getting hurt in a meaningless exhibition game haunts them."

I said, "I don't feel afraid. But maybe I am. I've never been in this position and it is scary. Will it blow up again tomorrow? I mean, they're still figuring out this kind of surgery. Maybe it won't last. If you were me, what would you do?"

He didn't hesitate, "Well, I'm NOT you, but you asked so here's my answer. I'd concentrate on throwing the damn ball as hard as I possibly could. Air it out. Stretch it out. Dominate it. If the elbow holds, you're golden for many more years. If it doesn't, you've already accomplished more than 99 percent of the guys who ever dreamed of playing baseball at a high level. You're an All-Star! You're an ace. But you need to tell that arm who's boss. It's your body. Those muscles work for you!"

I laughed a little, and I knew he was right. This was exactly what I needed to do. But yes, I was already thinking: "Yeah, but not right out of the box. You don't walk out onto a mound and just fire bullets without even warming up. I've got to follow the program, but once they give me the green light to go all out, I'm all over it."

The wine was good, too.

At the game against his former team, I got to sit in a VIP suite with the Lightning general manager. I had no clue the GM was Phil Esposito, one of the most famous players and Hall-of-Famers in hockey history. He played way before my time, and I was just a passive hockey fan until I met Eric, but I knew who Phil Esposito was. What an honor. I introduced myself and told him I was one of Eric Olson's friends, and he cut me off.

"I know exactly who you are, Brooks. You pitch for the Texas Rangers. You've been hurt, though, right?"

I could barely answer. I was baffled that he knew that. Maybe someone gave him a cheat sheet, or something.

I stayed out of his way during the game. After all, that was his team down there and he was laser-focused on them. At the end, when the Lightning had won, we spoke again briefly and he wished me well. He said, "Listen, injuries are hard things to get over. Give yourself time, but work your ass off."

Words well spoken.

And Eric even scored a goal in the Lightning's 5-2 win. I was jumping up and down with my hands in the air, up there in the suite, and Phil Esposito came down from his perch at the top of the suite to double high-five me. Does it get any better than that? It was rad. It was surreal. And I wanted to pick up a baseball right then and fire it 100 mph.

We shared a 12-year-old bottle of Silver Oak on Eric's balcony late that night, talking in hushed tones to not disturb any neighbors.

I said, "Listen, dude, I really appreciate this. You having me up here did something. I think it grounded me. I felt like I'd been spinning out of control, like some rogue planet in a science fiction movie. This really brought me back into my orbit, I guess you could say."

"It's been my pleasure, man," Eric said. "I could tell you were a little lost and a little depressed. I wasn't far from it, either. We loved New York, I was part of one of the greatest NHL teams in history, playing at Madison Square Garden, and all of a sudden I'm in Tampa and Carol is still back in Manhattan. It all just happened so fast. This was good for both of us. I'm glad you took me up on it."

When I threw my bag in my car and got ready to leave in the morning, we shared a hug. We'd hugged before. Like, you know, man-hugs. One arm and a pat on the back. This was a hug, like I typically share with my dad. Neither one of us got emotional, but we looked at each other and I think we were both thinking the same thing and I clearly remember nodding and patting him on the cheek.

We were both thinking, "Thanks for being here for me."

When I got back to my condo, I remember being kind of agitated. I wanted to run through a brick wall and throw a ball through a two-inch piece of steel, but the trainers wanted me to rest my arm and not throw until January. That was killing me!

I talked to the head trainer and begged him to at least let me start in December. I had a plan, I had a good frame of mind going, and I wanted to be ready for spring training. He reluctantly agreed, but he put his foot down a little by ending with, "Brooks, this is a long process. We're dealing with a lot here. You can start throwing in December, but it's going to be outlined, regimented and all planned out. I don't want you doing anything close to flat-out mound work before February. You're young. We have the time. We want you to be healthy. Are you with me on this?"

As much as I hated to say it, I did. "Yeah, I hear ya. I'm with you."

October and November officially took forever. I flew my folks down for Thanksgiving in November, just when the north winds start reminding Minnesotans about what was coming soon. We talked for hours each night. I'm not sure how totally dialed in they were to all I'd been going through mentally. They knew about it, but probably not the depth of it.

I told them about my three days up in Clearwater with Eric, and even I could tell my voice was elevated and I sounded happier just talking about it. They were smiling and nodding.

"Sounds like you both gave each other some good support, man. That's a great friendship," my dad said.

When December finally came around, it was more important to me than Christmas. I could start throwing. Or tossing, which would be the better term. There was no pain.

At the same time, Adam called and said he'd been talking to the Rangers. There was some consensus on an extension, beyond the end of my current contract, but obviously they were still worried about my shoulder, my elbow and who knows what else. My brain? Their feeling was if I could get healthy, I could still be their ace. My contract was running out after the next season. I was still on the 40-man roster, but while I was hurt I was on the injured list, so I wasn't on the 25-man.

They were pitching Adam on something like this: "We want to extend Brooks two years, but with so many question marks we can't keep paying the current rate. He could be great again, and we hope he is. We really need him. We have no real stopper in the rotation right now. We'd like to go one more year at $1 million, and then have a team option to pick up if he's healthy. The option would get him back to $2 million. It's security for both of us. No matter how his arm is in '99, he's going to make a million dollars. If it's all good, he goes back to $2 million."

Adam ran it by me and honestly I was all for it. I'd gone through a lot already, and often felt guilty about all the money they were spending on a guy who couldn't pitch. And hell, I had no idea how healthy I'd be. I was doing all the right things, but it was a long road. That 1993 All-Star Game seemed like a lifetime ago. It sure seemed like a different me. I was fearless then. I was super confident. I had everything I ever wanted in baseball. I wasn't that same guy.

So I said, "You're probably not going to like this, but let's do it. Just see how many incentives you can cram in there. If I'm really healthy, I can do a lot of things. Make sure "Comeback Player of the Year" is in there, for sure."

He just said, "I'm glad to hear that. I was going to advise you to say yes. The Rangers are making a million-dollar bet. I'll get the contract done. Congrats. Now let's get you back to the form you were in."

I still couldn't fathom getting paid a million bucks to play baseball, with or without a bad arm. But it was a 50 percent pay cut for one year, so I felt like I was doing my part to help the team. I might've been the only guy in the game who felt that way. I signed the extension one or two days later. I knew I had at least two more years and possibly a third. That felt good.

I also started thinking more about what I was doing with that money. Jack, my financial guy, was really "by the numbers" and I liked that. I wasn't going to hit the jackpot when times were good, but I also wasn't going to lose my home and the shirt off my back if things went in the tank.

I talked to Jack after signing the extension, and I said, "Anything we should be doing differently?"

He said, "Look, you can point me in any direction you want, because this is your money. I work for you. We're diversified in a lot of different funds. Some push hard, others stay pretty neutral. It's a good mix and it's done us well. I really don't see any reason to change anything, except we may want to put some of your money in more of a cash situation. If the game ends quickly for you, and I sure hope it doesn't, a lot of these funds are locked in for a while and you'd pay huge taxes and fees for getting out of them. Savings accounts are paying basically nothing right now. Under 2 percent. But I can find some similar deals that are making 4 or 5 percent, and you can take your money whenever you want it. Do you want to do that, just to be safe?"

I said, "Sure, sounds like a good idea. How much would we move?"

"That's up to you, Brooks, but if we put a half million over there, it would be safe and liquid, and it would earn a little money."

I then went in a different direction. "OK, now here's another thing I'm thinking about. Would you be pissed if I kept a little pile of money to play with on the stock market? I'm kind of intrigued by it, and I want to learn more. But I want to do it myself."

"Doesn't bother me a bit, Brooks, and I'd be happy to give you some advice and guidance if you want it. No charge. Just let me know. Maybe next winter you can come up to see your folks and you and I can spend some time together. I'll show you how it works."

This seemed like the first time I had a positive plan in forever. I wasn't going to dive in until after Jack and I talked, but it was a fun thing to think about. I mean, I'm good with numbers. I ought to be able to figure out which stocks to buy. Right?

Back in the real world, the outline the trainers had prepared had me adding throws and effort, just a tiny bit each day, and all on flat ground for the month. I wanted to be on a mound so bad, but it wasn't in the script.

And I actually really wanted to go up to Minnesota to spend Christmas with Mom and Dad, but that would mean missing workouts. So I arranged to have them come down and spend the holiday with me.

I threw on the appointed days, but I also had a full circuit of machines I worked on and did stationary bike and treadmill work every day of the week. I was in good shape. To me, it was all about the arm. It was all hard work, and I really couldn't see the finish line yet.

By mid-January I could throw from an indoor mound, the full 60-feet 6-inches to a catcher behind the plate. I was still on a strict program and couldn't let it loose, but that was the first big graduation to a new level.

By February I was allowed to ramp it up. I threw every other day, and each day I was on the mound I'd let it loose just a little bit more. It felt great. No pain, no fear. I had no idea if my velocity would come all the way back, or if the off-speed stuff would be effective again, but I knew one thing: I was in a much better mental space. I had just wrapped things up with my psychologist, too, although we left it open-ended so I could come back to see her anytime I wanted. She said, "I think you have a handle on this now. It's time to go out there and prove it to yourself."

Our first official day of camp was around February 15. I wanted to be fully ready to go by that date. Stoked doesn't come close to describing how I felt.

A lot of guys had been in camp since mid-January, but there's something special about the official reporting date for pitchers and catchers. It's like the first day of school, if school is the thing you love most in the world.

I huddled with the Dick Bosman and Johnny Oates and we mapped it out. I had thrown three out of the last five days, so they slotted me into the second day of camp. That first day we had a lot of meetings, got a lot of running in and had our first day of everyone's favorite activity. Yes, pitchers fielding practice. It may be boring and it may seem overly simple, but during the season if you ever see a pitcher cover first and he takes

411

the wrong angle, or his footwork is off, he probably wasn't taking PFP very seriously that spring.

On the second day, I threw my first session. It felt really free and easy. My curve had much better spin and bite and my change-up was just fine. It was the fastball that had me giddy.

I had purposefully decided against having any radar guns around when I was throwing before camp started. I didn't want to know, and I wasn't throwing flat-out anyway. It wasn't my choice to make in camp. The Rangers had someone holding a gun behind every catcher in the spring training bullpen. It looked like a firing squad.

After my session, my catcher (a minor leaguer I barely knew who had never caught me before) said, "That was great. Pinpoint with a lot of life. Great job, man."

As I toweled off and walked out of the 'pen, Dick Bosman came up to me with a smile..

"Great first session, Brooks. Of all these guys, you're the one in the lead in terms of where you're at with your program. The off-speed stuff was great and your fastball had a lot of life. And you were hitting your spots like it was June."

So I said, "OK, I'll bite. What did the gun say?" I'll admit I was nervous to hear what came next.

"Brooks, you were solidly 93-94. On the first day of camp! That's fantastic."

Yes it was. It was fantastic. It was beyond fantastic. The cutter could stay on the shelf. Everything else was back. My arm and my mind were both back. I had no fear and no doubt. I was just pitching. The hardest thing to do was play it cool and not go nuts when I heard those numbers.

I got into a nice routine for the next week or so and had no setbacks. All the guys were there by then, and the next big moment was going to be game action. We opened spring training at home, although I don't remember who we faced. We played the Twins and Red Sox a lot because they were both in Fort Myers, so it was probably one of them. I was on the lineup card as the third pitcher in that game. That would probably be the third inning, unless one of the other two guys got three outs on less than 10 pitches. That was the one thing that worried me about spring training. It's all set, but it all has to be fluid. It's really hard to know, for sure, when you need to get going and when you're going in.

I recall that it went according to plan. I started stretching when the second inning started. I started throwing when there was one out. When we came to bat, in the bottom of the inning, I was popping the mitt with my best stuff. I was ready.

When it was time to go, I took a big swig of water and walked to the mound.

My eight warm-up pitchers were fine. No nerves at all. It felt so NORMAL! I knew going out there that the "pitching backwards" philosophy was out the window. That was for scared wimps.

I started the first guy with a fastball on the inside corner. He kind of jumped back from it. Then a change-up. He missed it by a foot. Then I purposefully spiked a curve in the dirt right in front of the plate. Nobody on and nobody out, so why not? Sometimes you can get guys to chase that because they have no clue what's coming. Like that time. Swing and a miss and a nice block by my catcher.

The second guy hit two balls, but both foul on pitches he was late on. If he'd been paying attention in the on-deck circle, he'd realize what I threw 0-2 to the first guy. So I threw him a nasty change, instead. Strike three.

OK, the third guy made somewhat solid contact on a change, but he hit it right to the first baseman. I bounced off the mound, got my angle and footwork right, and took the throw just as I crossed first base. See? That PFP pays off.

Three up, three down. No fuss, no muss. And no pain. My gosh it was glorious. It felt like those two dark years had never happened.

I kept my dad and Eric both up to speed. Even though Eric was just up the road in Tampa, and they had some days off, there was no way for him to come to a game. They practiced and worked out every day. But both he and my dad were really positive and supportive.

Throughout spring training, I think I only gave up two or three runs. And none of them were tattooed. A bloop here, a stolen base, another bloop and a sac fly. And there's a run scored without hitting the ball hard.

As the spring season was winding down, the hitters were finally getting up to speed. It seemed to me that the pitchers were always ahead of the hitters in Florida. We could throw and be ready. They could take a lot of BP and get their swings in, but the pitching machines just threw whatever was dialed in on the knob. They weren't robots. They couldn't think about what to spin up there. Let's hope it stays that way. One thing the world does not need is pitching machines that can think and reason. Really. Might make a bitchin' movie, though.

We opened at home against Milwaukee, and that took a big load off my mind. I really didn't like opening on the road in a cold-weather city. In '97, our schedule had us playing the first five games in Arlington. But even that didn't work out. The schedule almost always has you opening and then getting the next day off before playing that same team again. That was a built-in fallback in case the opener got postponed for any reason. There was no day off, though, after that second game and it was rained out. That was the one I was scheduled for. The Brewers had to head back home so we'd have to play a double-header against them at some point later in the season.

Ken Hill, a really fine pitcher, had gotten the assignment for the opener. He pitched well and we won. I got to the ballpark nice and early and got into all my routines for the second game. I had never expected to pitch the opener, and they were still being careful with me, so I figured, or at least hoped, that I'd get the second game. I did my pregame stuff, I ran my poles and noticed some dark clouds moving in. Just as I was about to head to the bullpen to start warming up, the skies opened up with a typical Texas thunderstorm. We all retreated to the dugout to see if it would pass over quickly, but it didn't. It rained for hours and there were more storms lined up and headed our way. They pulled the plug on it pretty early.

It was a disappointment to not play (I hate rainouts), but I was actually thrilled I hadn't thrown any pitches in the 'pen. I'd be totally fresh the next day.

413

The next day was sunny and not too hot. Perfect weather actually. I got back into my routines and was amped up and ready to go when we went out there for the top of the first. We were playing Baltimore. I remember we had a great crowd that day, and they were loud!

The plan was for me to go four innings, if I could. The most I'd done in camp was two in a game.

It felt so damn good to be on the mound. It felt so damn good to be wearing the Rangers uniform and hearing the cheers.

I got them out 1-2-3 in the first on only nine pitches. One strikeout, one pop-up behind the plate, and a two-hopper back to me.

Same thing in the second, except it was two strikeouts and a pop up. My pitch total was 15.

I walked a guy in the third, but got a ground ball from the next hitter and my big league infielders gobbled it up and turned two. A strikeout ended the inning. PItch total 25.

In my fourth, and supposedly last, inning I got a little more fired up. All these guys were seeing me for the second time in the game. Time to change tactics. I started off the first guy with a change-up. He just stared at it. Then a curve, strike two. Pudge put down one finger for a fastball, but then he curled his fingers a couple of times to signify he wanted it up. This is what we call "climbing the ladder" to change a guy's eye slot. I'd thrown him two off-speed pitches down. Now we went up. Strike three swinging. A weak ground ball and a routine fly later, and I figured I was done. But I'd only thrown 35 pitches. I think our target was four innings or 45 pitches. I was thinking they might leave me in.

When I got to the dugout, I could tell I was done. When you're zoned in and ready to pitch again, they pretty much leave you alone. When everyone comes over to congratulate you, you're coming out of the game.

And that was OK. That was what we had talked about. The fact I was really efficient in the four I threw was just good news. Dick Bosman sat down next to me on the bench and said something like, "That was terrific. One helluva first start. Let's not screw around on your first time out. You did everything well, but we just want to be safe. There's 160 games left on the schedule. We're going to need you."

When I got up the next morning, my right shoulder was just a little sore. But so was my right hamstring, and my left quad. I was just kind of sore all over, and that's not unexpected after throwing four innings in a Major League game. I went to the park and had the trainers do their stuff. Ice at first, then a little massage on the sore areas, a little Ultrasound, and finally heat packs spread out all over me.

When we were done, I felt pretty good again. I wasn't worried about it.

My next start was in Baltimore. It was just about what you'd expect the weather to be like in Baltimore in early April. Misty, raw, and windy. Just perfect. Not.

Everything actually went OK once I shook off the cold and got into it. I think I pitched five innings and gave up a run. That was the first ball really hit hard off me in the two starts. A gapper to the deepest part of Camden Yards that scored a runner all the way from first. My pitch count got up a little, with too many 3-2 counts, and after four they lifted me with 56 pitches. We were tied, I think. The Orioles pulled away late against our relievers, and they won the game.

I felt pretty good. I really don't like pitching in those cold and damp conditions, though. They remind me too much of the day I hurt my knee and ankle in high school.

The next day, we were still in Baltimore and I woke up sore again. Not so bad in the hamstring and quad (I think I was building that strength with every inning), but the shoulder was nagging me again.

The trainers looked it over and asked me to rate the pain on a 1-10 scale, with 10 being excruciating. I said it was a 2. I could pitch with it. We flew home after the game (another loss) and we had a homestand against the White Sox. Then we'd go play the Royals. I had the second game against KC. This time, I felt it warming up. I didn't say anything. I just tried to pitch through it.

I don't know if I can explain this very well. When a pitcher thinks he can "pitch through" any pain in his arm, whether it's the elbow, shoulder, forearm, or even a finger, he's wrong. Oh, you can pitch. And you might even get guys out, but you're not pitching through it. You're not making it better. You're not even keeping it the same. If it hurts and you keep pitching, you're making it worse. I had already learned that lesson. I was ignoring what I'd learned, because I so desperately wanted to be out there, but I had learned it.

I went five and shut them out. Six strikeouts, one walk, two hits, that was it. I just stayed away from the curve and concentrated on the fastball and change. Those two pitches didn't seem to hurt at all. If I really needed a curve, I could dial one up and I felt it. But yeah, looking back I know I was making the mistake of trying to be a bulldog and pitch through it. The relievers kept the door closed and we won 2-0.

I put ice on everything related to my right arm, like I did after every game, and then we got on the plane and flew home. The next morning, the shoulder actually woke me up.

It wasn't a stabbing pain. It wasn't too deep. It was just there. I felt it. I knew it was there. I had to tell the trainers and coaches. It was my responsibility to the team and to myself.

The consensus was more tendonitis. I got a cortisone shot, and I was told I'd be going on the injured list for 10 days. The statement Johnny Oates made on TV that night was something along the lines of, "This is preventative. Brooks hasn't thrown much the last two years and he's had some brilliant outings so far this season. We want to let the tendonitis settle down and get him back out there. We don't see it as anything long-term or worrisome."

After my stint on the injured list, I came back and threw a bullpen session. It was a lot better, but it was still there. And I had to have that conversation with myself. "Be a bulldog and pitch through it, or do you wuss out and tell them you need more rest?"

The problem with the rest was, the longer you don't pitch the more you have to get back into shape to be able to pitch in a game. If you sit out for 20 days, which was what I'd be up against, you would need a week to be ready again. I just wanted to pitch.

This would repeat itself for weeks. I'd say I was fine and go back out there, but the next day it was back and painful. Or I could go on the injured list and get another cortisone shot, then think it was all better. But it wasn't.

The funny thing was, with it being in my shoulder I never worried about the elbow again. That was ancient history. I'd had such a hard time getting over my fear of the elbow, but I felt like I could manage the shoulder and just tell it to shut up.

Somewhere around the first week of June, I got knocked around pretty hard in a game. I was using the curve only when I had to, and the advance scouts had clearly noticed that. The other teams knew they didn't have to worry about it.

And then after that game, a reporter asked me, "Are you worried that your velocity has dropped off so much the last couple weeks?"

I said, "I didn't know it had."

I went into Skip's office and asked him about it. He said: "Our guys with the guns said you were 88-90 tonight. That's all I know. Are you OK?"

Not after hearing that I wasn't. I went back to my hotel room and just sat on the bed, staring into the distance. It was like, "Now what? Now what do I have to deal with?"

Four nights later, we were back home. I don't even remember who we were playing. I started. In the first inning, I knew this wasn't just a sore shoulder. My arm was completely dead. I could try to throw as hard as I wanted, but it just hurt worse and it was wobbling to the plate like a high school pitch. A bad high school pitch.

And then the knife sliced right through me. I think it was the second inning. I can't believe they let me go back out there, actually. I wasn't even throwing good BP. I threw a fastball to start a guy off and a searing, hot, horrible pain started in my shoulder and went straight to my brain. I grabbed my arm, and for the second time in my short career I just started walking to the dugout.

"It's my shoulder," I said as I passed Johnny, Dick and the trainer. I went straight to the training room. I got on a table, laid back and closed my eyes. Man, it hurt. Something bad had happened.

We'd had the shoulder looked at twice earlier that summer. The MRI showed nothing major, so at the time it was diagnosed as a slight strain of the rotator cuff area. You can't throw without a rotator cuff. It's the mass of muscles in the cap of your shoulder that holds it all together and gives you strength.

The next day I went back to have it looked at again. I was really getting tired of the MRI machine. By the time I got to the ballpark, the word was in. Skip came to see me and took me to his office. My rotator cuff was torn. Not completely severed or anything, but a major tear. I'd need surgery.

It's not like Tommy John surgery. I don't think anyone has yet figured out a way to replace a torn rotator cuff. There are two many things going on there and a lot of the muscles and tendons are anchored onto bone. The only fix was to stitch it back together.

I'm sure I turned white. I felt like I was gonna pass out. I knew it was bad, but not that bad.

"When do we do it, and what's the rehab?" I asked.

"There's some swelling in there now, so we need to get that down," said the trainer. "So maybe a week from now for the surgery. As for rehab, it's a tough one. You're completely rebuilding a torn up part of your anatomy. For people who work on assembly lines doing repetitive things, it's a long and tough rehab. For a Major League pitcher, it's worse. You have so much ground to cover, so much to heal, and then you have to strengthen it back up. It'll be a long haul, and it won't feel good. I don't know, Brooks, maybe four months if we're really ahead of schedule. I don't think there's any doubt that you're done for the season."

Oh, my. I wanted to scream and I wanted to cry. How could this be happening? I'd be doing everything right. It was all back. I was striking guys out at will. And now this.

I called Dad and told him. He was really quiet on the phone. To the point where I had to say, "Are you there?"

He muttered, "At least we know. This is going to be hard on you, man. It's going to be a huge challenge, but I know you can do it. Guys have come back from this. You can too. Give me a call before you go into surgery and just try to zone this out. There's nothing we can do about it now. You just rest. You're going to need some help when you get home. Can we come down?"

That sounded wonderful. The answer was, "Yes. Please!"

I called Eric. He answered the phone by saying, "OK, what's wrong? I know something's up just from your last few outings and your stints on the injured list. What is it?"

"It's my shoulder," I said. "Rotator cuff, and it's torn. I'm done for the season. It sucks so bad, dude. I can't believe it. And I'm not all that optimistic, either. The Tommy John deal was hard, but more and more guys are bouncing back from that and some are even stronger when they do. This is different. A lot of guys never even get close to all the way back from this. And I'm going to be in rehab for months again. Holy crap. I'm still in denial. I can't believe this."

"Well, we gotta take this one day at a time, my friend," he said. "It's a long road. There are no shortcuts. But you can do it. You've still got plenty of a career left. Do you mind if I talk to our trainers to see what they think? We don't get a lot of rotator cuffs in hockey, but maybe they'll have some insights. Extra opinions, right?"

I had no problem with that, and really appreciated it. But I was still in denial.

I really didn't know what the road ahead of me was going to be like, but I knew it was going to be long, bumpy and painful.

Here we go again ...

CHAPTER 42

Eric Olson

Missing the playoffs might have been a blessing for me. I got more rest, I had more of a chance to get over the concussion after-effects, and Carol and I got settled. It would've been great to get into the playoffs and feel that incredible energy again, but there was that silver lining to a bad situation for me.

And I recall the day, maybe about a week after the season ended, when Carol and I were sitting on the sofa and she said, "You know what? This is really nice. I loved New York, and embraced it, but this is pretty incredible. This is a good life, babe."

I told her I'd come to the same conclusion. At first, I was shocked I was going to play hockey in Florida. We were both so into Manhattan. But even at the rental townhome, it began to soak in how relaxing and beautiful it was.

We were from Roseau. We lived in the Twin Cities. We became New Yorkers. And now we were Floridians. I'd done the Queens thing, taking the subway to the Garden every day. We'd done the rental thing. And finally, we'd bought a west end condo about the size of a really nice master bedroom suite. When you're there, if you just look at the positives, you adapt and embrace it. Now, in Clearwater and playing for Tampa Bay, it didn't take much to adapt. It was a really easy way to live.

At the same time, my agent Robert was on the phone a lot.

"Listen, Eric. With you going into your last year on this deal it's time to see if the Lightning are serious about keeping you. Talking about it was one thing. Making it happen will be another. I'm going to initiate those conversations. Let's get a new extension done before next season starts. Get it out of the way. Otherwise you're going to be playing with free agency hanging over your head and they're going to have to hope you don't leave. You good with that plan?"

I said what I always said to him.

"Sure. Whatever you think is best. We'd love to stay here. This team can be really good. The Gulf Coast is fantastic. It's a good life. See what you can do."

I didn't want to ramp up workouts until the playoffs were over. I used that as my timeline. Until then, walks on the beach, bicycling, hanging by the pool, and lots of warm Florida life. I was feeling 100 percent.

Once the playoffs were over (Detroit swept Philadelphia in four straight), I got back into the gym only a little worried. Other than walking and biking, and a few rounds of golf, I hadn't done much since our season ended. What if the headaches came back when I started running and lifting weights?

Fortunately, nothing bad happened. It fired me up to know I was completely over it. It was still going to be a long four months before training camp started, but I was ready.

Right about that same time, though, in early summer, we got some really bad news. I got a call from Brooks and he sounded pretty bad.

"I can't believe this crap, dude," he said.

"What? What's up?"

"My shoulder has been a little sore, and we've been treating it. Everyone was pretty sure it was just some tendonitis we could work through. Two nights ago I was pitching against the Giants and it felt like I got stabbed. Completely torn rotator cuff. I'm going in for surgery in a week or two and I'm out for the year. The rehab can be eight months to a year. I just can't believe it."

I didn't know what to say. Usually, I'm the calm voice of reason, just like his dad always is. I was just silent for what seemed to be forever.

I finally said something like, "Oh, I'm so damn sorry buddy. Geez, you can't catch a break right now. This sucks."

I said all the things I meant. Stuff like "You can do this. Guys come back from it. It's going to be tough but you can do it." I wasn't trying to cheer him up. I was trying to build him up. After all he'd been through, this was a really tough blow. It would be easy for him to just feel sorry for himself and feel like quitting.

I added, "I'll do anything I can for you. Do you need me to come down after the surgery to help you out?"

He said his parents were coming down, so he'd be fine. I said, "Well, if you don't mind, I'd like to at least drive down a few times just to see how it's going and be there. It would be great to see your folks too."

I could hear that made him happy. "Awesome, man. Yeah, that would be great. I'm stoked. Let me get through the surgery and the first week after, or so, and then you're welcome here anytime. Just don't let the visits screw with your workouts. Promise?"

I promised. If I could get my workouts done in the morning, I could be in Cape Coral by early afternoon whenever I went to see him. And then I could be back home for dinner with Carol. She said she'd even like to go with me a time or two.

And speaking of Carol, the next topic on her mind was one I was waiting for. Now that we were all settled in the new house, she was itching for the next big thing. She wanted to go back to work.

My only request was that she wait until the summer was over. We'd have all that time together before my season was firing up again. I thought it might even be the longest stretch of uninterrupted time we'd ever spent together. She agreed with that, although she said she wanted to at least start looking by August. She wasn't sure what was out there in Tampa. That sounded good to me.

With it being the off-season, with me trying to relax and tune everything out, my contract had to be tuned in. Robert had daily updates, and even that surprised me. I still saw myself as Eric Olson from Roseau. I knew I was doing a good job on defense for the Lightning, just like I had in New York, but it still seemed odd to me that the Lightning would even have enough interest for there to be daily updates.

Finally, there was something to ponder. As Robert said, "I'm asking for four years starting at $2.9 million going up to $3.5 in the final year. They seem pretty stuck on two years, but have already tossed out numbers like $3.2 and $3.5, fully guaranteed. I don't know if I can get a full no-trade clause but I'll try. By listening to them, kind of between the lines, I think they're a little worried about concussions. They don't want to invest in four years because of that. If you get hurt a couple more times, they're throwing pretty big money into the wind. And the way they want to do it is to tear up your contract for this coming year, and start the new one immediately. What do you think? That's a give and take for both sides. You lose a year off this contract, but gain a lot of money on the new one. They save a year, but have to pony up the big bucks. Basically, it nets out to a one-year extension, but at much bigger money."

I said, "I'll defer to you." Then I told him that honestly, two years at that kind of money was astonishing to me. I'd be set for life, and I just wanted my life to be full and pain-free. Maybe that was the way to go. If, after the two years, I felt great and had no issues, we could work on another one. I just really wanted to stay in Tampa.

Meanwhile, Brooks had his surgery and had his dad call me. Everything went well, and the doctors firmly believed he could be back to 100 percent in a year, maybe less. I told his dad to pass along my good karma (I knew that would go over well with the Bennetts) and that I'd be down to see them all in a week or so.

I called him five or six days later and we talked about it. He seemed like himself. Not groggy or anything, and more accepting of the fact this whole shoulder thing had happened. I said I wanted to get down there that weekend, just for a visit. He said, "OK, so get your ass down here."

It was a Saturday, and I took the Audi on its first road trip. It was fantastic to see his mom and dad and they both gave me huge hugs. Brooks often talked about when his dad gave him "the look" that meant he was proud of him. Mouth tightly closed, eyes locked on him, and a few nods. He gave that to me. I was honored.

Brooks was really only a week into rehab, and still had lots of pain from the surgery. The program was a slow one.

"Dude, they had me exercise a little on the second day after surgery," he said. "You know what the exercise was? They took my arm gently out of the sling and said, 'Can you lift your arm an inch?' Seriously, could I lift my arm an inch? I could, but holy crap did that hurt. Every day we add in a little tiny bit more, but I'm roughly two million miles from throwing a baseball, and a light year away from pitching. Talk about needing patience! They said I might be able to hold my arm up at shoulder height in two months. Damn, I'm not made for this."

We talked about it, and my only message was, "Life's throwing you some hurdles lately. You have to adapt. You have to be made for this. You can do it."

When he asked me what was going on in my life, I told him about my agent and the goal to get an extension at big-time pay. When he heard the numbers he just said "Whoa" and then he asked, "Do you have a financial advisor? You're going to need one now, dude! I've got one I trust. He's not crazy, and he doesn't put my money in anything too risky. I've made quite a bit of investment income off what he's done."

I did not have a financial advisor. I figured if this contract came through, I should really think about that. I'd saved a ton of money to that point in my pro career, and we made some nice gains on the sale of the condo, but most of it was earning just a bit over zero interest in a savings account and the rest was in an IRA I set up. Like any sport, hockey can go away any second. I wanted to make sure I had some retirement money sitting out there, out of my reach.

I told him I'd look into it and asked for his guy's number. I also said I wanted to talk to some of the other Lightning players to see what they were doing. It's always best to have options. Just like when you're bringing the puck out from behind the net, it's good to have options!

Just days later, Robert called with the news.

"Here's the deal, if you want it. They were firm on the two years, fully guaranteed, but I got them up to $3.5 and $3.7, with a team option for a third year at $4 million. If they pick up the option, you would be bound to it. If not, you could become a free agent. And I got a "limited no-trade" clause, which allows you to submit a list of 15 teams you would not agree to go to. What do you want to do?"

I hesitated just for a second, and then said, "When can we sign it?"

I heard him chuckle a little. He said, "I'm not bullshitting you. You're the best client I've ever had. No ego, no expectations of things that are unrealistic, no bull. And you've earned this. You're a helluva hockey player, Eric. We let the Rangers off for damn near free just to get you some security when you weren't making a hill of beans. We turned that into this, with the Lightning. And there's more out there if things go well. Just keep working hard, and I'll do the same. I'll talk to the team and see when they can have it all ready. I plan on being there with you to read any fine print. I'll let you know."

I thanked him profusely and hung up the phone. Carol was in the living room. She knew we were talking about an extension, and I'd said it would be a nice raise, but I hadn't told her the dollar amounts. I didn't want to jinx it.

I walked out there, trying to maintain some calm, and surprised the hell out of myself by how bad I was at that.

"I was just talking to Robert, and he got the extension done."

"Wow, that's phenomenal. I'm so proud of you! Tell me about it. Did you get a raise?"

When a big tear rolled down my cheek, she knew something was up. I never cry over bad news. It had to be good news. I could barely hold it together enough to speak.

"It's for two years, but it starts right now so my final year on the old contract is gone.

421

It's for 3.5 this year, and 3.7 the next, plus the team holds the option to pick it up for a third year at 4."

"She looked a little confused, and cocked her head a little to one side. She said, "Wait, 3.5 and 3.7? I'm not sure I get it. 3.5 and 3.7 what? What do you mean? Is that hundreds of thousands? That would be way more than you're making now. Wow."

I said, "No, sweetie. It's millions. 3.5 million dollars." I didn't have just one tear rolling down my cheek by then.

She just stood still and stared at me. I think she was shaking a little. And then she crashed. She grabbed me as hard as any hockey player ever did in the corner, and started bawling. It took us both a good 10 minutes to collect ourselves.

"I can't believe it, but I want you to know I don't care about the money," she said. "I care about you, and I'm so proud of you. You deserve this. We've been living like royalty with what you've been earning. Even that was beyond my wildest dreams. This is surreal. Are you 100 percent being straight with me? I can't believe this."

I said, "I'm 100 percent being straight with you. Robert is setting up the meeting with the Lightning and he's coming down for the signing. I know it's crazy, but I have no desire to do anything insane now that we've gotten this far. I need to find a financial advisor, and I'm going to start looking into that tomorrow. Brooks has a guy he trusts. Says he's really conservative and doesn't do anything risky. But I want to talk to some of the guys on the team and find out what they do and who they work with."

All we could do at that point was flop on the sofa and stare at the ceiling. It was hard to believe it was anything close to real.

The first call I made was to my parents. My mom got on the extension phone so I could talk to both of them at the same time and Dad said, "Is this good news or bad news?"

"Oh, I sure hope you think it's good news," I said. "I just agreed to a contract extension with the Lightning. Remember, this coming season was going to be the last one on my current contract. They tore that up and I'll start the new one immediately. It's a pretty big raise."

"Like how pretty big?" my mom asked.

"Guys, it's for 3.5 million the first year, 3.7 the second year, and the team controls an option on me for another year, at 4 million."

There was silence on the line. I finally heard my dad say, "Wow."

I filled them in. They just basically said "Uh huh" and "OK" a lot.

Now keep this in mind, a lot of players from Roseau and Warroad had made a lot of money playing pro hockey, although at that time I don't know if any of them had made more than $3 million a year. So my family wasn't oblivious to the fact you could make incredible money in the NHL.

The little runt who drove everyone crazy just did that. I was going to make a lot of money. Even if it was just for two years. It would be a lot more money if I could make the third year happen, but first things first.

I asked them to tell my sister and my brothers, and that Carol and I hoped to get up there as soon as we could to celebrate with them.

After that, I called Brooks.

"What's up dude?" he said.

"Well, dude, I agreed to that new contract, effective immediately, and it's pretty incredible."

"Why, isn't it enough? And for how many years? What's the deal? And don't make me go too nuts, OK, because it will really hurt."

"It's two years with a team option for a third. Best we could do with the concussion still fresh in everyone's mind. And if you're asking if it's what I deserve, that could be answered two ways. Part of me says yes, but a part of me says no. The side that says no doesn't think anyone should make this kind of money to play a game. It's for 3.5, then 3.7, and if they pick up the option for the last year it's 4 million."

He just said, "Hold on, dude. I gotta let that sink in. I'm still on some pain pills and I want to make sure I heard what I heard. Holy crap. I mean, dude, holy crap. Now let me say this, you absolutely should make that kind of money. You hold the damn team together. You always have. No team would pay you that if they didn't think you were worth it. It's not a charity. It's a business. You make business sense for them. I'm just so happy for you. I'll be off the pain meds in a few days, so a few more days after that, if you've signed it by then, get your ass down here for a bottle of Dom Perignon and a classic Silver Oak. We have to toast to this in person.

"And I know I'm not whooping and screaming, but it's only because I can't do that. I'm supposed to stay calm and get my work in. Plus, my folks are taking a nap! But dude, I'm stoked times 10 right now. I am so proud of you. You're my hero, bro!"

When things calmed down a little, I decided to see if I could make Carol cry again. I'm kidding, but I knew the conversation would probably result in that.

We had finished dinner and were still at the table when I said, "So with this contract, you absolutely don't have to work. I know you love purpose and you love being busy, though, so I was wondering if you'd take on an added responsibility around here."

She looked at me like she thought I was going to say she'd have to take the trash out from that point forward. "What exactly are you talking about?"

I said, "Well it's a full-time job and the contract can last forever. How'd you like to be a mom?"

Bingo!

"Oh my gosh I would love that so much. Are you serious? Can we do it? Is this the right time? I have more questions than answers."

I said, "Let's just decide that we want to start a family. We'll figure out the details soon. I think having a baby in the summer is the best time, in terms of hockey. I'll be home to share the load. Can we do it? No future parents know if they can do it, but most figure it out. We have the resources, more than we ever dreamed of, to give a kid or two a wonderful life. And hopefully a hockey life. Who knows. Down the road, maybe we'll sell this house or maybe we'll keep it as our warm-weather place. And if we do that, maybe we'll move back to Roseau or to the Twin Cities. We turned out pretty good coming from Minnesota. There's lots to think about, but let's just start knowing we're going to be parents someday. Maybe next year, maybe the year after that. But we are. Deal?"

"Deal," she said. When we had to be, both of us could be pretty down-to-earth and practical. One step at a time.

So, I got into my workouts, Carol kept tinkering with interior design at the house (which she had looking absolutely incredible), and at the end of each work day we hung out at the pool. It was all good. In the summer heat, we were both developing a real taste for a nice cold glass of Chardonnay. White wine was a whole new world Brooks had steered me toward.

I went down to see Brooks two more times that summer, and each time he was a little further along with the rehab. We'd both heard what a slow process that shoulder surgery demands, and apparently his tear was as bad as they get. Almost a rupture. Usually, rotator cuffs let you know they're injured over time. It just gets more and more sore until you can't function. Obviously, his was hinting at that for a long time, when they thought it was just tendonitis, but then it just blew. He was in good moods, generally, and doing his work exactly as he was told. The last time I went to see him, just before my training camp opened, he could raise his arm up parallel to the ground, and hold it there for 15 to 20 seconds, then raise it up as far as the shoulder would let him go, before putting it back down slowly. That's a long way from raising his arm an inch.

It was time for me to get ready for camp.

But first, Robert called with the info on signing the contract. The Lightning wanted to make a big deal out of it, so they'd had their PR department setting this up with a press conference, and a series of one-on-one interviews with me. That caused a bit of a delay in getting it scheduled, but we were on for the next Monday at noon. Robert would come in the night before, and we'd all have a nice dinner together.

The actual signing would be in private, in the front office. The press conference would follow immediately.

When Robert got into town, he took Carol and me out for an incredible meal. And the wine was flowing, too. I didn't know he was a big wine guy until then, and he picked out what we drank. It wasn't cheap, but he was about to make a boatload of money off my new contract. So was I.

I put on a suit the next morning, but no tie. I didn't want to look too formal. A nice white shirt with a dark suit, jacket unbuttoned. Everything went great. Mr. Esposito went first at the press conference and said a lot of really nice things, including: "When you're building a winner, you need to have a foundation. To do that in hockey, you need to keep your best and most important players. Eric Olson is one of the top defensemen in the league. We need to invest in him and we have."

I answered a bunch of questions the best I could, as the reporters raised their hands. I just kept to a couple of key points when possible. The first was, "I firmly believe we're building a winner here, and we're close." And the other was "My wife, Carol, and I absolutely love it here. I'm a Minnesota boy, so when I got traded I wasn't sure what to make of playing hockey in Florida. It didn't take long for me to understand how lucky

I am to be here with the Lightning. Tampa is a great city. The Ice Palace is one of the nicest buildings in the league. And the fans are great. This is a wonderful situation and I'm honored to have signed this new contract. I aim to live up to it, and then exceed expectations." I had only practiced those two points about 50 times.

After the press conference, the local TV and radio stations were set up around the room and our PR person escorted me from spot to spot. When you do that, you end up getting asked mostly the same questions, but it gives the station a chance to get their own clip for the news that night. It was all good. It actually played into my two talking points. I could use them, in some variation, over and over. It was a big day, to say the least.

When camp opened at the practice facility, I thought we looked pretty good. We had a bunch of new guys, and in practice I could see a few were natural scorers. Over the course of a couple weeks, I began to think we had one or two real snipers, then maybe a group of about 10 guys who would support them and score a dozen or more goals each. The only big fear I had was that we'd have a really good first line, and then it would drop off pretty sharply after that. Paul Ysebaert looked like the best pure scorer on the team. After him I wasn't sure. So I put my head down and did my work. At least, if I could help the goalies keep the other teams from scoring, we'd have a chance. In goal for the '97-'98 season, we had Mark Fitzpatrick and Daren Puppa. They were solid fundamental goalies. Not flamboyant or Hall of Fame material, but they could make the plays that had to be made and not give up big juicy rebounds. I honestly figured we'd be about a .500 team, if everything went well.

Nothing went well. We were basically terrible. After just 11 games, they let Terry Crisp go as our head coach. We had won two, lost seven and tied two. A lot of them weren't close.

I hate to even mention this, but there was also something big happening at home. I began to get my first paychecks under the new salary. I don't recall exactly how much they were for, but to me it was astronomical. After taxes and commissions to my agent, I think each one was around $225,000 every two weeks. I had gross annual salaries close to that big with the Rangers, but this time it was every paycheck. And I still hadn't hired a financial person to handle it for me, and I knew I needed to get on that. I was naturally skeptical of the whole thing, but I didn't know enough about finances to do it myself. And I didn't want the distraction.

I talked to a few of the veteran guys and the same name came up over and over. I did talk to Brooks' guy, too, and he seemed great, but something about sharing a finance guy with a good friend was a little weird. I had no idea why.

The guy everyone was talking about was Phil Loeffler, and even though he was based in New York, the guys all said he was very attentive and easy to reach at any time. He always deferred to the player, and never once lectured them or tried to persuade them to do anything they didn't want to do. Plus, he specialized in hockey. So I gave him a call.

We talked for about an hour and he said, "Just think about it, but don't take forever. You're two checks in now and it's all sitting in a savings account. It could be making more money and still be safe. But you have to pick a person you're comfortable with. When do you guys come up to play the Rangers, Islanders or Devils?"

425

As it turned out, we wouldn't play any of the New York area teams until mid-December. I couldn't wait that long, but I looked at the schedule and saw we'd be in Philadelphia on November 20. We'd get in on the day before.

Phil said, "If you want to have dinner I'll take the train down there and we can get together. You'll be about four checks in by then, but just keep doing what you're doing now and let me know if you've signed with anyone else. And this will just be between you and me. I love all your teammates I'm working with, but this is all about you. I don't want guys milling around the table interrupting us."

I liked that. No pressure. Flexibility. He seemed honest and the other guys really liked what he was doing for them. I told him I'd love to do that. We'd talk about a week before the trip, once I knew the hotel in Philly.

When we got to Philly, I took a cab to a restaurant Phil had picked out. It was just far enough away from the hotel, and more of a locals' kind of place, so he felt we'd be able to talk in private.

We just had a glass of wine to get started, and talked in real general terms about my upbringing and things like that. He knew about Roseau and Warroad, and said, "What's in the water up there? Two little towns like that, and they're both hockey factories."

I said, "All I can say is that hockey is everything in Roseau, and in Warroad. Every kid plays, whether it's in the street or in uniform. By the time you're high school age, it's pretty clear who's going to the next level, and a lot of guys do. In some ways, I'd say the toughest team I ever had to make, in terms of pure skill and competition, was the Roseau Rams. There are always twice as many very good players as there are roster spots, trying to make the team every year. Half of them have no chance at it."

We ate a great dinner, and then ordered another glass of wine to wind down and finish the conversation.

Phil said, "Just knowing you're from Roseau, I think I know what you want. You need trust, stability, and the knowledge that I'm not going to break the news to you someday that I invested in a disco roller rink and lost a lot of the money you entrusted me with. Am I on target?"

"Yes, you are on target. Roseau is a town where everybody knows everybody. Where people don't lock their doors. Where you can walk anywhere, and everybody is a friend. That's what I'm looking for. I never dreamed I'd make even a percentage of this kind of money, and it scares me a little. Once I left Roseau and was surrounded by strangers, I didn't like that feeling. I need that trust. I really don't care how much more money you can make with my money. I can't spend all of this anyway. Just keep it safe, keep an eye on it, don't do anything very risky, and let's stay out of the stock market. Can you do that?"

"Of course I can," he said. "Every client I have gets a custom-designed plan to their liking. If we're good to go, I'll get that to you by the end of the week. And then we can sign the documents so that I can make it all happen."

"We're good to go."

Sure enough, an overnight envelope arrived a few days later at the house, and in it

426

was Phil's detailed plan. He'd invest in some very conservative mutual funds. Nothing too risky. He'd open a new IRA for me, just to keep putting a pile of money away every month. It would be a pretty liquid IRA after just a couple of years. Since I'd already paid income taxes on the money, it wouldn't hurt much to pull that out if I needed it. I couldn't see how I'd need it, but if we were going to have a kid or two I figured there would be plenty of things to pass along and pay for, all the way up through college. We were good to go. I transferred about a half million to him and he got it all started. I'd get detailed reports every month, and informal updates two or three times a month.

With the team, Rick Paterson took over on an interim basis and we went 0-6-0 for him. As far as I know, that's his final career record as a head coach in the NHL. Yes, I feel bad about that. It would've been nice to win at least one for him. He did the best he could with what he had to work with.

Then the Lightning brought in Jacques Demers. He was a veteran coach with a good history of success. He'd coached St. Louis, Detroit and Montreal over the course of 10 full seasons. He went to the playoffs every year except his last year in Detroit and his last full season in Montreal. Talk about a cruel sport. You get your team to the playoffs six years in a row and then you come up short once, and you're gone. I thought Jacques could turn us around. There was still a lot of time left.

Well, we won 15 games for Jacques, and tied eight. The only problem was we lost 42. We finished the year 17-55-10. I hadn't been on a team with a record that bad since Des Moines.

Yes, it was frustrating. Yes, it was demoralizing. I played my regular game, but it always seemed I was the only one back and here would come another two-on-one or even a three-on-one. I bet it wasn't much fun for Jacques either. Definitely not fun for the goalies.

The good news was I stayed healthy. No concussions, no big strains, and the only time I missed two games was when I came down with a pretty lousy flu bug that we were all passing around the locker room.

Throughout the season, Carol came to most of the games. She got to know the other players' wives very well and liked them. They even formed a charity group for Christmas, raising money and collecting toys for Tampa kids who otherwise might not have had a Christmas. She basically took charge of that. That's her. She needed a purpose, and that was a great purpose. I even had a few teammates say stuff to me like, "My wife adores your wife and says she's incredible. They all thought they were putting some fun little charity together and your wife turned it into a real thing, doing really good work for the community. That's really cool, Oly."

After Christmas, she got together with a few other wives and debated what to do next. The consensus was to use the charity to introduce ice skating to Tampa kids who had never so much as stepped on a rink. They had a great time, and a lot of us guys would go to the rink every time they had enough kids signed up to put on an event. It was great. I loved it.

Brooks was hanging in there. All through the winter he was making progress, but he told me, "I gotta be honest, dude. I'm still not even to the point of wanting to throw a baseball. I can't even envision it. It's so far over the horizon I can't see it. This is really going to take a while." I went down to see him at least once a month, on off days when all we'd have was a morning practice. His parents had gone back to Minnesota, and although he was doing a lot of his rehab at the Rangers' complex and had friends there, it had to be tough to live by himself and have to worry about everything that could go wrong. It sure seemed like his career was hanging in the balance.

After missing the playoffs, we had a long summer ahead of us. Carol and I were talking about having a baby just about every day. If we could make it happen, the best time to have the little one would be June the next year. Our target for getting pregnant was September. We spent most of the summer reading up on what to do when trying to get pregnant and then what to do if we were successful. Hockey players usually love summer. I was going a bit nuts. I wanted September to hurry up.

Another small thing, but I think a key thing that happened that summer, was that we bought our first computer. It was an Apple iMac. More and more people were starting to discover and inhabit the internet at the time, but it was pretty basic back then. It was all dial-up, it was awfully slow, and there wasn't much to see or read. Everyone I knew with a computer had signed up with AOL, so we did too. At least that meant we'd have email, and that was getting to be a necessity. The team was corresponding with us more and more that way and I needed to be in the loop. Brooks did the same thing, following my lead, and we could stay in contact that way too. Back then, though, you had to be careful about how long you were on AOL or any other service. You had a limited number of minutes before you started getting billed for being over. Seems like the dark ages, now.

After all the big excitement, the summer moved along. I played a bunch more golf and got a little better. I was never a great golfer but, for the most part, hockey players play a lot of golf in the summer, so I wanted to at least be respectable. When I shot my first legit 89 the guys I was playing with bought me a drink. The next time we all got together and teed it up, we were on a par 3 that was about 175 yards. I hit my shot flush, just sweet as heck. It landed about five feet past the hole and I'd gotten enough spin on it to make it back up, just like a pro. It rolled to within an inch of the pin. All four of us back on the tee thought it was going in. When it stopped rolling just short, there was a huge collective groan from all of us. I heard one of the guys say, "Almost had it, Oly. So close! You're going to get one. You've got enough game." You must be getting better if you're disappointed you didn't get a hole-in-one.

I was still thinking about when September would finally arrive, and when it did we'd see if we could be successful in bringing a new little Olson into the world, nine months later. And I'm not going to lie, I was hoping our team would be a lot better, too. The past season had really been tough.

CHAPTER 43

Brooks Bennett

So after the operation, I just kept at it in terms of rehab and physical therapy. It was such slow going. I'm a guy who says, "I want to do this," and I expect to immediately be able to do it. This deal didn't work that way.

I felt like an outsider at camp. I didn't like that feeling at all. The guys were all great and always looking out for me, but I wasn't part of it. That was really hard. The mound, the clubhouse and the ballpark had always been my "safe place" where I was immersed in what I loved to do. Now I was an outsider? It was crushing. It was dark. And yeah, it was very depressing. But, I had to try to compartmentalize all that. I needed to do the work and try to get better. It was going to be a long slog.

When the team went north, I stayed behind. That made sense. In Arlington, the trainers would have a full clubhouse of big league players they needed to look after and work on, even in terms of just daily maintenance. In Port Charlotte, there might be one or two other injured guys. I'd get much more immediate attention.

Finally, the head trainer from Texas called and said, "I've been talking to the guys treating you, and I know it's going slow, Brooks. We have to be careful, though. If we get in a hurry and screw this up, your career would most likely be over. We can't risk that. So we're putting you on the 60-day injured list. It's the best thing for you and for us."

I understood that. I still hadn't done that much soft toss and when I did that there was always a trainer right behind me, watching what I was doing. On the 60-day list, that pretty much meant June before I could get back out there, and that's only if everything went great. It was totally frustrating.

I did have a lot of free time on my hands, though, and sitting around the condo wasn't the answer. I was getting the itch to start getting into the stock market and mutual funds, and just seeing what I could do. So I called Jack.

I asked for some basic advice.

"I don't know when I'll actually start trading but I want to start to figure it out. Like, I don't even know how to see what stocks are doing well and which ones are tanking.

429

And it would be great to be able to read some analysis by experts in each field. Where do I start?"

Jack said, "OK, how about this? I'll move $100,000 into your checking account, but not until you give me the green light. Right now that money would be making more money in a savings account, but it won't earn a penny in checking. So, if you're OK with it, I'll put it in savings and when you're fully ready to go I'll transfer it for you. But here are some keys to think about. If you're getting into day trades, thinking you'll swap stocks every time there's a profit to be made, the hundred grand will be gone in a flash. You need to find some stocks that are established and on the way up. Then hold them. You have to be patient.

"The next thing is, don't touch any tech stocks. Not even with a 10-foot pole. This whole dot-com boom is an illusion. Some people who got in really early have cashed out big, but there's no sustainable reason why these start-ups have any chance. Tech stocks like IBM and Dell will be fine, but again you have to be willing to hold onto them and wait. All these new dot-coms have such a limited audience that could be long-term investors. Many of them don't even make a product that mainstream consumers need, or even want. It's going to burst. Stay out of it. Also, I'll send you some valuable websites that cover all corners of the market. Their analysts often do a really great job of seeing what's got potential. And finally, get signed up with a brokerage. Have you done that yet?"

I told him I hadn't but I'd settled on Fidelity. They were a little more expensive, in terms of fees, but they consistently ranked number one in customer service.

"OK," Jack said. "Just let me know when you want to pull the trigger and jump in. Just stay out of those start-up tech stocks. You'll thank me for that."

I appreciated his insight, and looked forward to digging into those websites. I wanted to be totally comfortable before I dipped a toe in the water.

Back at the complex, April turned to May and May to June. I was throwing from a mound by June, but probably only at about 80 percent. And even after a session like that, I still had to ice the shoulder and it still bothered me. Not big pain. It was just there, reminding me what it had gone through. Other than building strength back up, I really didn't think I was making much headway. They finally gave me the green light to go all out, just to see what was there. It turned out there wasn't much there.

My fastball was 85 to 86, with basically no movement. That's great velocity in the big leagues if you want to create a disaster. I was throwing as hard as I could, and I wasn't holding back at all, but there wasn't much to be happy about. I couldn't get high school hitters out with that stuff. I didn't know what to do.

The head trainer said, "We've got a few options. You can rest for another week, because you've been on a pretty regular throwing schedule, or we can have another MRI done to see if the surgery wasn't perfect. Finally, we can bite the bullet and have you pitch for Port Charlotte. What do you think?"

Well, I really didn't want to rest again. I'd been "resting again" for more than a year. And I didn't want to get shellacked at Port Charlotte either. Let's go back to our old friend, the loud and claustrophobic MRI tube.

We got it scheduled for just a few days later. Once the doctor had a chance to go over it, he gave me a call.

"I don't see any major dysfunction, Brooks. The wound itself is healed and perfectly fine. But this is not totally uncommon. You've thrown a lot of baseballs in your life, and never had a problem. But then the rotator cuff blows up and when that happens and we operate, it's almost impossible to do that without tightening everything up. It all needs to be stretched into place so the sutures can reach and get a good grip to bring all the torn parts back together and let them regenerate. That's probably what we have here. Your shoulder is now much tighter. When you're going at 100 percent, you don't have the whip and flexibility you had."

"So what can we do about it?" I asked.

"About the best thing we can do is to try to stretch it out and loosen it up. That won't be easy. When did you start pitching? As a kid, I'm guessing."

I said, "Oh, probably around six or seven years old."

"Well, imagine trying to duplicate what all that pitching did to give you such a fluid and loose arm action. It's not going to be easy to duplicate that in a year. I'm sorry to tell you that, but it's going to be hard and might not be possible. The good news is you have a functioning right arm. When your rotator cuff was torn, you would've basically been living in constant pain while semi-disabled if you hadn't gotten the surgery. But there's still a chance to get you back to the big leagues. You're just going to have to work your butt off, and it may hurt and scare you, but it's your only chance."

You gotta be kidding. More bad news. Awful news. Exactly the kind of news no baseball player ever wants to hear. Without a miracle, my baseball career could be over. I'd been in some dark places over the prior two years, but there was always the vision of getting it all back and being myself again. We did that after the Tommy John. It came back and I was nails again. And then the shoulder. I was not in a good place. I was, in fact, in a terrible place. I wasn't even motivated to do the work. It seemed fruitless. And worse, I'd kind of shut down in terms of talking to people. I was only calling my dad about once a week and I don't think I ever sounded normal to him. I know he's all about motivation, but I think even he knew I didn't need that right then. So he just said, "It's going to be OK, bud. Maybe not the same OK as before, but you'll overcome it."

Man, I wanted to slink into a cave and hibernate. It was really bad.

I'll admit, I did start to think about reinventing myself as a junkballer. Breaking balls, change- ups, and maybe sneak a not very fast fastball by someone. I even thought about throwing a knuckleball. I had never been able to master that when I was healthy, but who knows. Or maybe I could switch to a sidearm or submarine delivery. You don't have to throw harder than 86 to do that, as long as you get a lot of sink.

All these thoughts were swirling in my head. Calling me a bit lost would be understating it. I didn't know what was going to happen to me. Could I get back to pitching? Could I handle it if that never happened again? I had no clue. I was spinning out of control, more than a little bit.

I finally made the rounds on the phone, filling everyone in, and they were all saying the same thing. "Give it everything you've got." I didn't want to say it, but I'd already been giving it everything that I had.

We did give it another week's rest, although I was the one who was against that. If we're trying to loosen it up and stretch it out, rest didn't seem right to me. But, I went along with it. I'm not the trainer or physical therapist. I'm just the pitcher who wants to pitch.

During that week, the trainers put together a whole new regimen of drills. Since the day I could pick up a ball again, we'd been trying to strengthen it. That was probably working against us. These new exercises were designed to stretch it out, and they were pretty brutal. A lot (a TON) of resistance training. Lifting light weights with my arm straight out from my side. A bunch of different resistance moves where we tried to increase my range of motion. Even stuff as simple as tying a rubber tube to the fence and then I'd make a throwing motion holding the other end of it. Anything we could come up with to stretch it out. It was exhausting but I was doing all I could. We even threw a weighted ball, which a lot of teams do now. Just stretch it out. Loosen it up. I had no idea if any of it was working, but my range of motion was getting better

After a full month of that, we were getting into mid-summer and playing baseball seemed like a distant memory. We decided to try another bullpen session. I warmed up and It felt pretty good. Not perfect like back in the old days, but pretty good.

My catcher got down in position and we started off with 10 fastballs. Then 10 curves. Then 10 change-ups. It looked OK to me, and the pain was gone. When we were done, and soaking wet with sweat, I got the word from the coach who'd been holding the radar gun

"You picked up a little," he said. "Mostly 87-88 on your fastball. The curve was kind of sloppy, and the change was great. I think we just need to keep working. It's having an impact, but it's a slow process."

We repeated the whole thing the next couple weeks, just busting it as hard as I could on the exercises and machines. That next time, I was still 87-88, but I did hit 90 once. The curve was still basically slop.

I needed to think long and hard about this. I'd always felt like I was in control on the mound. I felt totally out of control at that point. I wasn't sure what to do.

I called the Rangers and asked if manager Johnny Oates could call me back.

I think my voice was shaking a little when I told him I didn't think this regimen was working. I honestly felt like I wanted to cry. I talked him through everything we were doing and just said, "It's a little better, but I can't see ever being back to the way I was when I went to the All-Star game. There's just no life and no velocity."

"OK, what do you want to do?"

"I think I've got one valid option and a couple that are long shots. I could try to reinvent myself as more of a junkballer, but right now my curve is pretty helpless too. One longshot is maybe changing my arm slot to sidearm, or even submarine. And another long shot is to learn how to throw a knuckleball."

"Have you ever thrown a knuckleball?" he asked.

"Not for real. Like most guys, I've messed around with it on the side. I'd have a long way to go, but Skip, I think the fastball is gone. I'm more than just a little desperate."

He said, "OK, let us talk about it here for a day or two. You're going to need some intense coaching to make any transition like that. We might have to bring in a new coach or a consultant. But let us talk about it. I'll call you back in a day or so. What's the best time of day?"

I said, "Well, I work out at the complex between 8 and noon. I get back to my condo around 1 each day. Anytime after 1, Florida time."

"You got it. We'll get our heads together and I'll call you with Dick on the phone with me"

At least we had a plan. Of some sort.

Johnny and Dick called me a couple days later. Here's what they both had to say, taking turns.

"If it's not coming back, we need to do something. You're a hell of an athlete, so we wouldn't rule anything out. This is going to sound a little backwards to you, but we think we ought to try the knuckleball first. If you just can't get a feel for it, we'll rule it out, but there are two possible good sides to the knuckler. If you really get it and it's jumping around, you'd make a great relief pitcher and maybe ever a starter.

"Charlie Hough was one of the best ever, and he pitched for us for 10 years. We could try to get him over here for a week or two, if he's interested, and let him show you what he knows. It would be worth trying that. And if it doesn't work, we've got plenty of other coaches you can work with on a split-finger fastball, a two seamer, or a second change-up. It's all worth looking into. You want to do that?"

I said, "Sure, absolutely. It would be an honor to work with Charlie Hough. He was amazing."

They said to just keep doing my work, and they'd get back to me when they had details.

That didn't take long. About four days later they called me and said, "We talked him into coming over to work with you. Charlie is originally from Hawaii and he lives there. To make it an easier trip for him, we're flying him into DFW and think you should come here to meet with him. We'll fly you in, too, and put both of you in a nearby hotel. Can you be here next Monday?"

Of course I could. This was going to be a huge adventure, listening to and trying to learn from one of the best of all time. The darkness was beginning to lift. We had a chance.

I let Mom and Dad know and called Eric too. They were all supportive and Eric just said, "Be a sponge. Absorb everything he says. Good luck, buddy. You can do this." I think I was maybe withdrawing a little bit, because I didn't want to drag anyone else through what I felt was happening to me. I just didn't want to hear any more "Hang in there" comments. I was already hanging in there. My arm had just deserted me.

When I met Charlie, he was as gracious and kind as he could be. He said, "I've been keeping track of you, and these injuries are tough. Now you want to see if you can throw

433

a knuckler? I'm in, but let me tell you this. Most guys can't throw it. It's such a finesse pitch and the grip is unlike anything you've ever done. Let's start with that.

"You need short and really strong finger nails, because they hold the ball and let it go. The knuckles have nothing to do with it. They just stick up in the air for the delivery. You need to hold the ball with your first finger, your index finger and your ring finger, although some guys will only use two fingers. Whatever works best. Put your fingernails just in front of the laces, and grip the ball with your thumb which should be under the ball. Just let your pinkie hang off the ball.

"You throw it easy and it's not a real throwing motion. You should feel like you're pushing the ball to the plate. Nice and easy. When it's good, they can't hit it and oftentimes the catcher can't catch it. Geno Petralli was my catcher one day, and he was a heck of a catcher. I put him in the record books with four passed balls in one inning. He just couldn't catch it. So that's about it for the oral instructions. Let's go out to the bullpen and try to throw a few."

We went out to the 'pen. It was around 9:30 in the morning, so it was just hot, not broiling yet. And we basically had the place to ourselves. We wouldn't need a catcher for a few days, and even that was based on seeing something positive with the experiment.

We stood out there and practiced the grip. I just tried to completely copy what Charlie was doing.

I'd never caught a knuckleball and never hit against one. Charlie just lobbed the first one to me and I was absolutely mesmerized by the fact it hardly rotated at all. It wobbled a little, but it didn't make one full rotation on its way from him to me. And by the time it was halfway to me, I wondered if I could catch it. It floated in and about a foot in front of me the bottom fell out. It actually hit me in the foot. I couldn't get my glove down quick enough to catch it. It went from about belt high to my foot in just the last couple feet.

Charlie kind of laughed and said, "I'm sorry, but that's what it does. That's the beauty of it. Even the pitcher doesn't know what it's going to do."

Then I put my imitation Charlie Hough grip on it and tried to throw one. I did my best to "push it" instead of throw it, but that was asking my body to do something it had never done after about 22 years of pitching. It left my hand OK, but it didn't do much of anything. It spun too much and it went straight.

Charlie was very patient. He'd have to be if we were going to make this work. I guess I threw maybe 20 pitches and of those maybe one or two had the right look to them. They still didn't move or wobble too much, and they sure as hell didn't dive into the dirt like his had.

We did this for five straight days. I never really got any better. Hello darkness, my old friend. One of my favorite Simon & Garfunkel songs, but it was one I wished had never come into my mind.

Charlie was really honest with me.

"I don't know, Brooks. It's such a specialty pitch and all the guys who have thrown one were a bit nuts to even try it. I think you have to be a bit nuts, because you can't analyze it. You just toss it up there and hope for the best. When it's going good, you make big league hitters look like fools. When it doesn't knuckle, some lucky kid in the second deck above left field will go home with a souvenir."

"So you don't think I can do it?" I said.

"I didn't say that, but you're, what, 30 now? It's asking a lot. Like me, most of the guys who made a living on this pitch had been throwing it since they were kids, and then they still spent many years trying to perfect it. I was one of the lucky ones. It just came natural to me. My biggest challenge was finding catchers who could catch it. I guess I have to be straight and tell you I don't see it happening. I love your determination, and I love how much you love the game, but I just don't see it. I'm sorry."

I got it. I thanked him profusely and told him it had been a huge honor to work with him. Charlie Hough will always be a gem in my book. He's a marvelous man.

So it was back to square one, or back to the drawing board, or whatever other cliche you want to use. I talked to Dick Bosman and filled him in on it.

My first question was, "Can we try a new arm slot?" I'd known of a few pitchers who had hurt their shoulders who then went to a sidearm delivery and jump-started a whole new part of their careers.

Dick said, "Sure. I want you to be comfortable though, with as little pressure as possible, so you ought to head back to Port Charlotte. We'll dig up a catcher for you. We have a couple of kids at the complex who weren't ready for A-Ball, so we put them in the extended spring training program. Basically they just work out every day. Are you up for that?"

I said, "Hell, yes. It's my last shot, I think. I've thrown to a few of those guys. They can catch the ball. Are there any pitching coaches who can watch what I'm doing to give me some tips? I don't even know how to adjust my windup to get to a sidearm release point."

He said they'd hire one, if they didn't have one available.

I got my stuff together and headed back to Florida. Charlie got to go back home to paradise a week earlier than planned.

So it was down to this. My career hung in the balance. Absolutely for real. It would've been easy to fall back into the malaise, but I was able to put it all aside and just focus on what had to be done. The knuckleball was the longest of long shots, but it was a good idea to try it first. If we did it the other way, we'd end up with the knuckler being the last resort. That would not have been a resort you'd want to depend on.

The good news was this: After nearly a week with Charlie, my shoulder didn't hurt at all. It might be different with this next stage, because you do need some velocity to get guys out from the side. You get a ton more sink on your fastball, but if it's 85 mph it's going to get crushed.

The day after I got back, I went up to the complex and a young guy, who looked about 12 to me, introduced himself.

"Hi Brooks, I'm Jay Holder. I'm in camp here, and they want me to catch you. I'd be honored."

435

I said, "OK, Jay. It's me and you, dude. We gotta make this work or pretty soon you'll be telling your teammates 'Remember Brooks Bennett? I caught him when he was trying to make his comeback.' I hope you never have any reason to say that."

That first day, we just went out and played catch on the outfield grass. No mound. I'd never thrown sidearm seriously, I'd only played around with it and back when I did, I remember my dad saying, "Don't do that too much. You have a perfect delivery and you don't want to mess that up."

He was probably right. But now it was all I had left. And I was running out of time. My contract ran out at the end of the season, and if I didn't show some real promise with the sidearm stuff I couldn't see any reason they'd pick up my option. No pressure. No pressure at all. It was nothing less than pure survival in the game.

It felt pretty natural, to be honest. The ball came out of my hand nice and easy. I was only throwing at about 50 percent, but it was encouraging.

The next day, the pitching coach from extended spring training came over and introduced himself. I feel bad about this, but I don't remember his name. He'd been playing pro ball in the minors until the end of the prior season. When he was released, the Rangers hired him as a coach.

He said, "Tell me what we're trying to do. What's our goal?"

I replied, "Well, our goal is to get me back to the show, but to do that I'm going to have to learn how to pitch a new way. My shoulder is a mess, so we're thinking about going sidearm and see if I can do that. It's a lot less strain on the shoulder. I'm starting from scratch, though. I've never worked on a windup or a sidearm delivery. I don't even know what grips to use to get movement from the side."

He said, "OK, let's start at the beginning. We'll get on a mound and Jay will catch you. Let's do it."

I jogged a little to get loose. Then Jay and I started playing catch, nice and easy. It felt pretty good.

When Jay put on his mask and got ready to catch me, I got up on the mound and threw a few pitches. The windup felt awkward as hell. It was my regular windup, but all of a sudden I had to drop down and throw from the side. It was a tough transition.

The coach stopped me and said, "That's not going to work, I don't think. We need to get your setup and delivery into this new position. And you know what? A lot of sidearm guys never use a windup. They just throw every pitch from the stretch. You eliminate a lot of moving parts by doing that."

So we did that, and it felt a lot better. More consistent and under control.

The coach had some great input on getting some torque by rotating my body to the right a little to get my arm into the right slot. We talked about grips. If I threw a standard four-seam fastball, it would sink a little but not a lot. He showed me how to hold a two-seamer. There are lots of ways to hold the two-seamer, it's just a matter of what feels comfortable and getting the ball to fly with only two seams cutting through the air. The third grip he showed me felt right. It was with the tips of my two fingers placed right over the top of the first of the two seams, where they come together the closest on the ball.

436

That first day was pretty eye-opening. This could possibly work.

As that week went on we ramped up the effort. With the no-windup approach, I felt way more under control. With two different grips to choose from, a pitch from the exact same arm slot at the same velocity could do two completely different things.

I think I got to max effort around the fifth or sixth day. I liked it. The ball was diving and sliding naturally. I didn't have to put any spin on it. That was good. Now we had to work on a breaking ball. Man, this really was having to learn how to pitch all over again.

The trouble with a curve from the side is that if you just spin it like an overhand curve, it would just kind of flatten out and float up there like a frisbee. That's not a good thing. So the coach worked with me on a way to get to the same release point but just as I was letting the ball go, I'd yank down on it. The curve came to life. That was the good news.

I don't know if it was because I was really having a lot of self doubt then, but the first time I threw one that way, I said to the coach, "That's bitchin', and it really is a great counterpoint to the fastball, and it might work in the minors, but big leaguers are going to see that downward yank and know it's coming. We have to work on that." I wasn't seeing the glass half empty, I was seeing with maybe one sip left in it.

His reply was really interesting, and I bought it. He said, "The key is the same release location. The same arm slot and the same point of release off your hand. If you get that right, the hitter may consciously see the yank but it will probably be too late. And if you're nailing the outside edge with it, they'd have a tough time doing anything with it anyway. Remember, don't telegraph it by changing your slot. Trust yourself to get enough tight spin on it from the same location."

Finally, after two weeks, with the end of the big league season approaching fast, the Rangers asked me to come back to Arlington so that they could assess me. I was there the next day.

Dick Bosman and I went out to the 'pen in the morning. He was pretty impressed with what he had heard about the all-new me. I had the delivery and approach of a real sidearmer. Nice twist and torque, good arm slot and everything was moving and diving. He asked me how it made my shoulder feel.

"It feels fine. It felt fine before, when we gave up on my old delivery because there wasn't enough velocity."

"Well, let's see what we got," he said.

Dick pulled out a radar gun and stood behind a screen, right in back of the catcher. I threw five or six sinking fastballs, then spun a few curves up there. We hadn't really worked on a change yet.

When he said, "OK, that's good." I grabbed a towel to dry off. Dick said, "Let's have a seat," as he pointed to the bullpen bench.

"You've done a remarkable job changing everything you ever knew about pitching," he said. "I'm really impressed with that. You look like you've been throwing sidearm your whole life. That's the good news."

A chill ran down my spine. If that's the good news, I didn't want to hear the bad news.

"The breaking ball is good, but that jerk downward to get it to move down in the zone will get eaten up by big leaguers if you're not perfect with your arm slot. One time through the order and they'll be looking for it. And finally, you topped out at 85. For a sidearmer that's close. I mean, if you can get to 88 throwing from there, you will at least give right-handed hitters fits."

"Holy crap," I said. "It sure felt harder than that. That sucks. Damn it."

Dick said, "And it might improve, Brooks. You're learning how to pitch in a whole new way. You could pick up three or four miles per hour over time. The question is whether that's enough. We only have 10 games left in the season, and five are on the road. We could bring a minor league catcher up while we're on the road, because their season is over now. What do you want to do?"

I told him I thought I could do more back at the complex. That was probably not a smart decision, but I really didn't want to be around the team when I was trying all these new experiments. I'd get back to work with the coach in Port Charlotte.

Dick said they'd be watching and getting daily reports. He wished me all the best. For some reason, and maybe it was mentally self-inflicted, I felt like I was saying goodbye to him and the Rangers. I was really sad as I sat on that plane flying back to Fort Myers. The Rangers were the first team to talk to me, back at Canyon High. They followed me through Kennedy and the U of M. And then they drafted me in the second round and gave me a shot. I just knew it was over. A couple of times I had to look out the window so no one would see the tears rolling down my cheek. I knew it. I knew it was over.

I did go back to the complex, and my boy Jay even stayed behind in Port Charlotte after extended spring training was over. He said, "Hey man, I'm invested in this. I want to be known as the guy who caught you when you made your comeback." I could only hope, but I didn't feel like my reserve tanks holding the hope were that full.

About five days later, I got a call from Doug Melvin, who had taken over as the GM of the Rangers. He got right to the point, which is the way it should be. Don't dance around. Don't try to make the player feel better. Just get to the point.

"Hi Brooks, I'm calling to let you know we're not going to pick up your option. There's just too much ground to cover, and since it's already written in the contract that you'd make $2 million this year if we picked it up, it just doesn't make sense for us. All of us thank you for all you did for the Texas Rangers baseball club. You were a great asset and a great teammate. You'll be missed. I urge you to keep trying. It would be great to see you get another chance somewhere, but we have to move on. We wish you all the best."

All I could say was, "Thank you, Doug. I appreciate your honesty. I wish you guys all the best, as well. I think I'll always be a Ranger." And we hung up.

I just sat there in my living room staring blankly at the ceiling. I knew it had been coming, but you're never prepared to hear "We wish you all the best" for real.

Before I called home or called Eric, I called my agent Adam.

He didn't even say hello. He answered the phone and said, "I just heard. This sucks. But you don't have to be done. If you want me to, I should be able to get you a minor league contract, or at least a non-roster invite to some team's spring training. You want me to do that?"

I wasn't exactly jumping up and down at those words. I'd already thought about it, but I wasn't sure I wanted to go through it all again. The hope. The work. And, eventually, the disappointment. It had worn me out.

I looked at it this way, and was surprisingly coming to grips with it. How many guys ever played college ball at a Big 10 university? How many signed pro contracts? How many shot up the minor league ladder in two years? How many made the big club and stuck? And how many pitched in the All-Star game? I was so damn lucky to have done all of that. I had a lot to be proud of. I had to come to grips with that.

I told Adam to go ahead and look around, but if any offer came in that didn't include an invite to spring training, I was done. I'd give it one more shot, but that was it.

Only four or five days later, he called me back. The St. Louis Cardinals had instantly agreed to bring me to spring training as a non-roster guy. I'd sign a new contract at the Major League minimum, just so they'd have me locked up and I couldn't just walk out of camp to sign with someone else. In effect, it was a try-out. If they let me go at the end of camp, they wouldn't have paid me a thing. Players don't get paid during spring training. I wasn't sure what I thought about it, but I had to put pride aside and give it one last full-effort shot.

With that in my hand, I finally called my parents. I gave it to them straight. The Rangers had let me go. I could hear they were crushed, not for themselves, but for me. And I told him about the invite from the Cardinals. I said it was my last shot. If it didn't work out, I was good with that. I didn't just want to hang on, or go to Japan to play, or any of that stuff. I had a lot left to do in my life. I was OK with it.

I gave Eric a call next. They were just starting their season. I knew I didn't need to sugarcoat anything with him. He was living the same lifestyle. When I told him about the Cardinals, it was like he was reading my mind.

He said, "Well, buddy, you've got one more shot. It may work out or it won't. Just do me and yourself one favor. Don't end any day with them thinking you left something out there on the field. Burn it all. Spend it all. Empty the tank. I know you'll do that. I'm sorry about all of this, my friend. You didn't deserve it. It was all out of your control and you busted your butt to come back from two horrible operations. Now let's see where you can take it." Eric knew he didn't have to sugarcoat anything for me, either.

A few days later I got a call from Walt Jocketty, the GM of the Cardinals.

He said, "Brooks, I've always been a big fan. We know what you've been through, and I've gotten word that you're reworking your delivery into a sidearm approach. The Cardinals are willing to help with your workouts, and give you all the support you need. I don't have room on the 40-man right now, so all we can offer is a non-roster slot in the big-league camp. We'll give you every opportunity to succeed. Can we count on you to be there?"

I said, "Mr Jocketty, I'd be honored, and I'd really appreciate it if you could help me set up some regular workouts. Structurally, the elbow and shoulder are fine. No pain whatsoever. I just lost a little too much velocity after the rotator cuff. So I've been working on the sidearm stuff and it's coming along. I wouldn't want to show up in big-league camp without keeping the workouts going."

He said, "We can do that. We just have to figure out the details."

He asked me where I lived, if I was there full time, and could I come over to Jupiter, Florida, where they trained and had their complex. Again, we'd work out the details, but I was willing to do whatever it took. Jupiter was over on the Atlantic side, just north of West Palm Beach. Basically straight across Florida from Fort Myers. Too far to drive every day, so that was the first hurdle we'd have to get over.

I couldn't say I was going to be a Cardinal. I couldn't even say I thought I'd be a Cardinal. But I was willing to give it a shot

It struck me then. You need hope.

CHAPTER 44

Eric Olson

September finally arrived and Carol had seen an obstetrician, getting all the best advice as to when, during her cycle, would be the best time. Turned out it was later in the month.

We did our best and hoped like crazy, but the window came and went without success. We decided we'd give it one more year of trying to pick the time, and after that we'd just keep trying. If she got pregnant and then delivered the baby during a road trip, we'd have to figure it out. I knew the team would give me a day or two off if that was the case. We also both got tested to make sure we "had what we needed" to make it work, and the doctor said we were both good to go. We'd just been unlucky.

Things had really been going bad for Brooks, and I felt truly sorry for him. He's usually such a joyful, optimistic and outgoing guy, but after the shoulder surgery he became pretty withdrawn. It had to be tough to go through Tommy John surgery and work so hard to get back from it, and then tear his rotator cuff. I couldn't imagine. I wanted to help, but I also didn't want to just make it worse by getting in his way or pestering him with questions. And trying to be all bright and cheery wasn't going to do him any good either. I'd go so far as to say he was pretty testy on the phone some of the time. He was clearly depressed.

His recovery and rehab was so slow it was even driving me crazy, and I wasn't the one who got hurt. I sure wasn't going to say it to him, but I was really worried he wouldn't bounce back from this and his career would be over. What would he do then? Go into coaching or scouting? We never talked about it, so I didn't know. It's pretty common for athletes who have their careers cut short like that to walk away. They can't stand to be around it but unable to play. After a while, a lot of them come back just to be part of the game again. I just hoped we would have a chance to talk about it soon in person. There was so much he could do outside of baseball. He was incredibly smart and insightful. I thought he'd make a great agent, but almost all of those guys have law degrees. I didn't see him dropping everything to go to law school. I figured he

441

could also make a seamless move into the broadcast booth as a color analyst. However it went, I'd be there for him.

When camp opened, we were faced with meeting with and playing for another new head coach. He was Steve Ludzik. It was his first coaching job at the NHL level. He'd done a great job in the minors, and we were all hyped to play for him. In camp, he was way more of a tactician than motivator, cheerleader or screamer. To me, that was going to be kind of refreshing. We'd all been together awhile, so maybe just give us some new schemes and let us play.

We had one new kid who opened everyone's eyes from the first day of scrimmages. He was 19 years old and his name was Vincent Lecavalier, and he could just flat light it up. Huge speed, great hands, and a sniper shot whenever he got near the goal. It would be easy for anyone who was on that team to say "Oh, yeah — the first day I saw Vinnie I knew he'd be a star," but I actually felt that way. If all went well for him and he stayed healthy, he could be a superstar in the league, and the kind of guy they could build the franchise around. We just needed a couple more pieces to make it all work. Vinnie was the real deal. And I was anxious to get on the ice with him. He was the kind of guy who could inflate assist stats all up and down the lineup. Get the puck to Vinnie and let him score.

We opened against the Islanders at home, and everyone was fired up and ready to go. We won 4-2 and it felt like we were supposed to win that game. We were the better team all night, in all zones. But then we didn't do so well. We weren't terrible during the early part of the season, but we sure found ways to lose. We'd be right in a game, maybe even ahead, and just give it away or run out of gas. Maybe we weren't in good enough shape yet, I don't know. There's no excuse for not being in shape. That one was hard to accept for me, but the proof was right there in the scores. We had a tendency to play strong early on then lose late in games

In the locker room, some coaches like to divide up the season into four 20-game segments, and Ludzik was definitely one of those guys. Doing that, the sense of urgency gets real. Of course, that only adds up to 80 games and we played 82, but it was a nice, neat way to break it up. If you're going to make the playoffs, and especially if you're going to go deep in the playoffs, you need to consistently have a winning record in all four parts of the year. We were 8-10-2. I remember beating some really good teams, so the skill was there, but we'd then lose three in a row where it seemed like we were just going through the motions.

Just a few weeks into my season, the Texas Rangers didn't pick up Brooks' option. He knew it was coming. As he said on the phone, "If I were them, would I pick up my option for two million bucks? Hell, no!" Still, he was standing on the edge of a cliff he never saw coming. When the Cardinals offered him an invite to spring training, for a look at least, it gave him some hope. The guy needed that.

At home, Carol at least put on a brave face and didn't let our 0-for-1 on pregnancy get her down. The problem was, being pregnant and being a mom was supposed to be her job. She was so task-oriented and needed a purpose. I really didn't want to see her go back to work in the classic sense, so I asked her to look into working for a charity. She still had the Lightning wives thing going, but that was hard to do because our team was really transient. We had so many guys coming and going, it was almost impossible to keep the charity alive.

And in terms of splitting the season up into four 20-game segments, just to keep it manageable in our heads, we were just plain awful in the second 20. I think we were 2-13-5, with one stellar 0-10 losing streak right at the end of it. That will ruin your season. If the 20-game segment concept was supposed to give us a sense of urgency, we weren't doing our part to cause that. It was giving us a sense of failure. By then, the mood in the locker room was pretty bad. Vinnie Lecavalier was brilliant, and I did land a few extra assists just getting the puck to him with long passes as he flew up the ice. The kid was a gem. I'm sure he'd never been on a team that lost as many games as we were.

I had a hard time putting my finger on what was wrong with us. I know it seemed like I was always the only one back, handling my responsibilities. The other guys weren't greedy, and they weren't lazy. Maybe they just didn't quite have the quickness and toughness to be good defensemen. They seemed to be caught flat-footed a lot, and in the corners they scrapped for pucks, but it just wasn't quite right. It was like they knew they had to do it but they weren't totally all in on the effort. It's a really tough gig down there, up against the boards. I knew that. I felt it every night.

It was getting to be very frustrating. You can be the best D-man in the world, but if you're left back there on your own you're going to be facing a lot of 2-on-1 rushes. And some 3-on-1 landslides. It's frustrating as hell to be the last line between all of them and your goalie. And your goalie doesn't like it much either.

Early in January, we were on a three-game swing to play the western Canadian teams, Vancouver, Edmonton and Calgary. On that trip, during that time of year, I could instantly tell how Floridian I'd become. It was weather pretty much like we had every winter in Roseau. But my gosh, I was shivering and frozen to the core. I was liking Florida more and more. And the only moral victory in that swing was a tie with the Canucks. Edmonton drilled us (pun intended, and yes more of those 2-on-1 nightmares coming at me) then Calgary edged us by a goal. It was a long and unhappy flight home. When we got back to the Ice Palace we played the Islanders, and we beat them. But that wasn't the biggest thing that night.

I was in the corner battling for a puck and in all that mayhem I think I stepped on someone's stick. Either that or I got tripped. I don't remember because I don't remember much of the play. Right when I lost my balance an Islander gave me a shove and I went down hard, then the back of my head hit the ice with a smack. Yes, I wore a helmet, they had been mandatory for a long time by then, so there was no physical skull injury. But, when I tried to get up, the whole rink was spinning. I went back down to my knees and closed my eyes, just to try to make it go away. By the time the trainer got out there, it had pretty much cleared up, but I knew what had happened. It was another concussion. A slight one, for sure, but a real one. I skated back to the bench and took a seat. The trainer was right in my ear, from behind the bench.

"Where are you?"

"I'm in the Ice Palace in Tampa playing the Islanders. C'mon man, I just took a knock. I'm OK."

He went and talked to our head coach then came back to say, "Coach says you're done for this period, at least. We'll take a look at the intermission. Don't you dare jump over these boards. If you do, we'll have too many men on the ice."

I had to sit there for 10 solid minutes watching our guys gut it out. It had to be one of our hardest-working games in months, just like I love to be involved in, and all I could do was watch.

At the intermission, Coach came over to see me and asked how it was.

"I'm fine. It was just a little knock on the back of the head when I went down. Did they call tripping on that play?"

He said they hadn't.

"Well then, I guess I stepped on somebody's stick and when I lost my balance I hit my head. That's about all I can figure. I'm OK. I want to be out there." Coach said he'd give me a shift early in the third and he'd keep an eye on me. If I wasn't playing like myself, I'd be back on the bench for the rest of the game. Fair enough.

I felt OK, and had my fair share of hits and skirmishes. I blocked at least one shot and assisted on Vinnie's empty net goal with 10 seconds left. I felt fine. I also knew it was my third concussion, but I still only had one on my record. Two had gone unreported.

I remember having a bit of a headache the next morning, but even that was not uncommon. You tend to hurt all over the next morning anyway.

We plowed through the rest of that third 20-game segment and not much had changed. We finished 5-14-1, throwing in a seven-game losing streak and then another seven games without a win. We scraped out a tie after the fifth loss in that second streak. It was brutal.

I didn't let it get me down. I definitely didn't take it home with me, or at least I sure tried not to. Carol was my shining light, my port in the storm. Even after another blown lead and a late loss, by the time I got home all was good. I was playing in the NHL, living in Florida in a beautiful home, making enough money to take care of my incredible wife, and hopefully our family, for good. Losing sucks, but it's not your life. All you can do is your best. If you give it 100 percent and empty the tank every night, there's nothing to be ashamed of. There's nothing to regret. You can't play every position at once, and you have to support your teammates. They were going through hell too.

I tried to be optimistic around the guys. I was constantly saying, "Give me your best shift right here" as guys would hop over the boards, or "Give me everything you've got. Empty the tank!"

About that time, spring training opened for Brooks. I wished him luck and told him just to do his best. Keep working on that sidearm stuff. Keep battling. I knew he would.

On the ice, we put our heads down and tried to finish the strong, but it just wasn't there. I think a lot of the guys had really run out of gas, whether it was physical, mental, or both. Every now and then a teammate would talk to me in the locker room about it. The conversations were always just about the same.

"How do you do it, Oly? How do you keep going? It's getting to the point where I don't want to come to the rink and be embarrassed again. And practice? That's easy when you're winning. Hell, you want to go to practice when you're winning. What's the point of putting all that effort into it when all we do is lose?"

I'd just tell them one key thing. "This is your career. People are watching. It's a matter of pride. It's a matter of your immediate future and your legacy. Don't quit. You'll never forgive yourself. And if we all had that attitude, we'd be a lot better team. All I can do is what I'm doing. I'm playing at 100 percent and I don't look at the scoreboard. It's as simple as that."

During the rest of the year, unfortunately, I think a lot of guys checked out. Maybe they didn't realize it, but I could see they were a step slow and they started making passes that looked more like they wanted to get away from the puck more than make the connection. It takes massive effort to skate as fast as you can at the end of a shift, when you're totally gassed, just to try to poke the puck off a guy's stick. You may think you're going flat out, but it's not there.

We finished that last 20-game segment 4-16-1. And that of course left those last two games (to get us to 82) yet to be played. We lost them both, to the Maple Leafs and the Senators. It wasn't close. We played those two on the road. The flight home to Tampa was like a funeral. We'd all have to own this season. We were all a part of it.

We won a grand total of 19 games out of the 82 we played. Not good.

I talked to Brooks a few times during spring training. It wasn't easy to connect. To make it worse, we had some long road trips in those last couple months, so it was hard to reach each other at all. Early on I told him, "Hey, it's going to be hard to talk, and you need to focus on playing. Hell, we both do. If anything big happens, call me immediately. Just focus."

For me, it was time to recharge, play some more golf, then get back in the gym. And each day, I had a beautiful home and a gorgeous wife to come home to. And she made me proud once again. She went to work as an outreach executive for the largest charity in the Tampa area that worked to provide food and shelter for homeless families, and she donated her salary back to the charity. I was all for that and so impressed. It wasn't work for her. It was purpose and passion.

I'd lived through a few brutal seasons since coming down from New York. But I never had to doubt that I'd been a pure winner on the marriage front. I was one very lucky boy from Roseau. And the next season would be better. It had to be.

Plus, that option for a third year was hanging out there.

CHAPTER 45

Brooks Bennett

The Cardinals were great. They were dealing with a possibly washed-up pitcher who was trying to reinvent himself, but they treated me like gold.

They had a deal with a condo management firm about a two-minute drive from the Jupiter complex, and had exclusive rights to a six-unit building. All the condos were furnished, and they came with free golf on the course where they were located. All the condos were three bedrooms, and they asked me if that would be a problem. I said no, it would not be a problem. We'd be three non-roster guys all trying to make it together. I kind of looked forward to that. Going through all the rehab by myself was getting pretty old. Like totally old.

We agreed that I'd come down right after the first of the year. By the fifth or sixth they'd have a catcher for me, and a roving coach who would give me as much time as he had. I was truly excited. It seemed like a fresh start after a couple of years of doom and gloom. I wanted to get there right away, but January wasn't that far off.

I kept everyone informed, and got to a couple of Lightning games to see Eric play. We hadn't been talking that much with all that was going on, and it was great to see him after those games. The only bad part was the fact his team wasn't very good. They were losing at a pretty stout clip. I was impressed by how he could get over another bad game so easily. He'd say, "Once that buzzer goes off, the game is history. You can't go back and change any of it. As soon as I'm out of that locker room I'm thinking about the next game. You can't stew on it. You have to erase it and start clean."

I had my folks down again for Christmas, and as soon as that was over I was really itching to get down to Jupiter. From the day the Rangers let me go until that moment was as long as I had gone without throwing since I was a little kid. I was a little worried about being rusty, but I was stoked to get there and work on it.

They had told me I could come down "after the first of the year" but I wanted clarification. I called the Cardinals' office and asked, "Can I literally get there January 1? I don't want to waste a single day."

The woman on the line laughed and said, "We have problems getting some guys to camp by the official reporting date. It's refreshing to hear a star like you being so eager to get there. Sure, go on down there and get checked in. You'll get a key to your condo, you can put your stuff away and check out the complex. It might be a day or two before the other early arrivals get there, but you can run and work out all you want. If there's anyone else there, I'm sure you can talk them into playing some catch."

By New Year's Eve I was packed and ready to go. No celebration for me that night. I got up early and was on the road by 9. I'd done my due diligence in terms of maps and routes, and had it all figured out. It felt almost exactly like my first trip south to spring training. Geeking out on maps, studying the towns and landmarks along the way, and ready to hit the road. If I could get out of Cape Coral without too much traffic on New Year's Day, I'd be in Jupiter in three hours.

Of course, that didn't happen. A couple of fender benders blocking a lane or two and a few police cars that had pulled over people still partying from the night before gunked everything up. It took nearly an hour to get out of town. I didn't have a deadline, but I was eager to get there and start this new chapter. I hadn't felt so amped up and confident in a long time.

I drove across the state and marveled at the rural countryside that's in the middle. Most of south Florida's population is on the coasts. There's a lot of empty space and ranches in the middle. And Lake Okeechobee, not to mention the Everglades farther south.

I got to Jupiter around 1, and used my dead reckoning to find the ballpark and complex. Any baseball guy knows that trick, and it's especially easy to use in such flat surroundings. You just look for the light towers!

I found the office, got checked in and got my key and my ID card. The woman at the desk was all smiles. So was I.

I was the first guy at our condo, so I picked a room with a view of the pool and unloaded my stuff. Then I went over to the complex and decided to go for a stroll, just to check everything out. I found the Cardinals clubhouse and went inside. One of the guys there must have been a clubbie, because he was folding towels and organizing equipment. He looked really young, and had a weathered old Cardinal cap on, with the brim bent down the middle like an A-frame, and a small dip of Skoal or something bulging inside his lower lip. The requisite empty Coke can was nearby, for spitting. I said, "Hey, I'm Brooks Bennett, and I came down a few weeks early. Just wanted to say hi and look around."

"Cool," he said. "I heard they invited you to camp. How's it going? How's your arm? I'm sorry, never mind. That's none of my business."

I said, "Don't worry about it, dude. Seems to me it's everybody's business these days, and I don't mind the questions. I have a million of them too. It's all good, I think. The arm is good, and we're working on a new delivery that should be better for me. I came down to keep my workouts going. I want to be ahead of the game, not behind it, when camp starts."

447

He was kind enough to show me around. The clubhouse was big, but as he described it, "The first three weeks are basically total mayhem in here. We don't have enough lockers when all the non-roster guys are here, so some have to double up. That's no offense to you. You've been a star. An All-Star, actually. Seems to me some of the guys they invite are just here as fodder for the machine. All it costs St. Louis to bring in a few pitchers and catchers who have no chance, just so they can throw and catch BP, is basically the travel money and the price of a uniform. You're definitely not one of those guys, but I'm not in charge of lockers so I can't tell you how that's going to work out. I'll give the head clubhouse manager a few gentle nudges if I can."

I thanked him for that but told him not to worry. It had been a long time since I'd shared space with other guys, and it would be fine for spring camp. I was looking forward to it.

He showed me the weight room, the hot and cold tubs, and the training room. Then he said, "One of us is generally here from 6 in the morning until at least 7 at night. Once we get into the spring training schedule, we can end up here until midnight. I've slept in here more than a few times. You're welcome here any time, doing whatever you want. And until the masses start to arrive around the first of February, you can dress at any locker you like. I'll get you some workout shorts and shirts by tomorrow, if you wanna come in."

"Awesome, I plan to be here every day. And what's your name, dude?"

"My name is Trevor. Trevor McDaniel. It's a pleasure to meet you," he said, as he stuck out his hand.

It was classic. It was also heartwarming. What a good kid, trying to make it his own way in the sport. Someday, when he's retiring at 68 after decades of working his way up through the Cardinal organization, folding towels, washing uniforms, shining shoes and taking care of his players, maybe he'd look back and remember the day we met. If I could succeed with the Cardinals, he just might. And I'm pretty sure I'd remember him.

Trevor said, "If you don't know much about the complex, go look around. It's pretty amazing. We share it with the Expos, alternating days in the stadium when we play spring training games, but there are two completely different complexes. Each team has their own fields, batting cages and everything they need. It's cool."

I did that, and he was right. I'd never seen anything like it. They were two identical complexes joined at the hip by the stadium. Bizarre, really, but rad. Seemed like a good idea, too. By far, the most expensive piece of any spring complex is the stadium. By sharing that, both teams could have the same facilities and then just swap the ballpark back and forth, whoever built the place (I'm assuming the city of Jupiter) got two for the price of one.

I did my best to relax that day. Sat by the pool, swam a little, found a deli and had a nice late lunch, then headed back to the condo. There was a phone, but it wasn't connected. I figured I'd wait until my new roomies showed up before doing anything with that. We were all non-roster guys and there was no telling how long we'd be there. A couple weeks? The whole camp? A few hours? It just didn't seem right to get it hooked up but we could all take a vote. Right around that time, cell phones were starting to take off, so I thought I'd just go that way.

No one joined me in the condo that night, so I watched some TV (which was actually connected to a decent set of cable channels) after I'd found a wine store in town. It was going to be time to sip on a Cabernet out on the balcony as the sun went down.

It was remarkable how different I felt. I felt like a young rookie, excited and nervous. It was like a trip back in time. For the last few years, I'd felt lost, depressed and frustrated. Also in a lot of pain. To feel that adrenaline again, that love for the game, had me all fired up. I sure didn't feel like a "star" though people kept saying that to me. I was once a star, for a fleeting couple of summers. I was now just a guy trying to become a different player. And if you think moving to first base and trying to hit again never popped into my head, you'd be wrong. I dismissed that completely. I needed to get the pitching right or give it up, but hitting sounded kind of fun. I just hadn't had an official at-bat in, oh, 18 years or so. I had no time for nonsense like that.

I had my glass of wine, maybe two, and headed in. The place was really nicely furnished, and I had flopped on the bed once just to see how it was. It was firm and supportive. The place was all good. Considering the accommodations I'd been experiencing in the big leagues you might think it would've felt like a big step down, but it didn't. It felt like a huge step up, because it was a rebirth. It was a rad feeling, and I didn't really understand it, but those luxury hotels and charter flights didn't mean much to me. When you get to the top, the camaraderie pretty much only exists in the clubhouse and dugout. In camp, with two roomies on their way, it felt like baseball. It was pretty sublime, actually. My heart was racing a bit.

I got up early and headed over to the clubhouse with my duffel bag. Good old Trevor was there, and he said, "I put a few pairs of red shorts in that locker over there, along with an assortment of T-shirts and a few Cardinal hats for you. If the hats don't fit, let me know."

I felt right at home.

I donned my new red Cardinal stuff, put my turf shoes on (OK, they were blue, so I had to get with my Nike guy on that, and the next day I had a pair of red spikes and a pair of red turf shoes) and my hats fit perfectly — 7 ⅜.

I did some slow poles out on one of the fields, just to shake the rust off. Then 20 sprints or so, from the foul line to about center field. Some stretching, a couple more poles, and then into the workout room. I was working up a good sweat. It was nice and warm there, but the advantage Jupiter had over Arlington came in two ways. It was hot, but not suffocating. And you could smell the ocean. I used that as motivation. When I was done working out, I was heading over there to the beach. The ocean loved me. I loved the ocean. It made for a great workout in the weight room.

When I was done, Trevor handed me a marker and asked me to put my name inside the waistbands of all the shorts, under the bill of my caps and at the bottom hem of my shirts. Then, like a good big league clubbie, he said, "Just put it all in the bin over there. It'll be clean and back with your other stuff in the morning." You're a good man, Trevor.

I showered, got dressed and headed back to the condo. To my great relief, one of the other guys had just gotten there. I had at least one roomie, with one more expected. The "new guy" was a pitcher named Danny Hoff. He had been in the Royals organization for five years, coming out of Vanderbilt, and had been called up in September a couple of times. I think he said he'd made three appearances total. When the Royals let him go after the end of the last season, his agent got him a non-roster spot just like my agent had done for me. I dug that.

"Hey, man, we're in the same boat," I said. "To me, we won't be competing with each other. I'll help you any way I can. I'm not here to cost anyone a job. I'm just here to try to get one for myself. Let's work together, right?"

"You're the man," he said. "I'm with you. I still love the game and I know I can still pitch. I can't walk away yet. If the St. Louis Cardinals saw enough in me to even extend this look, I'm giving it everything I've got. If they sign me and want me in Triple-A, I'll make it impossible for them to leave me there. Let's do this, roomie!"

I told him I was going to the beach, just to be there and be one with it. I asked if he wanted to come along. I wasn't surprised when he said, "I think I'll just go over to the clubhouse and get a lay of the land, maybe get some running and weights in. Next time you go, I'm with you. I'm from southern Illinois. I don't get to many beaches."

I said, "I'm originally from southern California. I surfed until we moved to Minnesota when I was 16. I was raised at the beach. I need the vibe. I'll see you when I get back and we'll go to dinner. It's on me. Decide what kind of food you want."

Danny was going to be a good roomie. I liked him immediately. He was to the point, honest, and I could tell he was dedicated. He knew who I was, but never once used the word "star" or mentioned my All-Star appearance. I loved that. We were just roomies. It was totally awesome. And he looked a little like Ron Guidry. Same thin but strong body, same angular face. He even had the mustache going. Good guy. I can tell the good guys in just a few minutes, and I can tell the bad guys even faster. It's the guys in the middle that take me a while to figure out, especially if they don't talk much.

I drove straight to the beach, with my board shorts and flip-flops on. As my feet hit the soft sand I felt a jolt of something shoot through me. I swear it was the beach welcoming me back. It was the other side of the country, but all these coastal beaches, on every continent, are born from the same mother. The waters of Earth. It's really just one big ocean. They may tag parts of it with different names. Pacific, Atlantic, Indian, Arctic. But they are all connected and one. We just live on the big islands that share the planet with the water, and the whales. It was a buzz that went through me so fast I almost came to tears. OK, I might actually have come to tears. I put my big towel down, pulled off my T-shirt, and laid down on my back. Totally still. I reached off both sides of the towel and dug my fingers down into the sand. I was saying hello back to the beach. It was totally Zen.

I was in a different place. It was a very good place. I was home. At the beach and at the ballpark. Home.

I swam little, and even body surfed a few feet at a time on the small waves. To me they were small, but compared to the Gulf they were just fine. It was like being back in the womb.

When I got back to the condo after that mental health break, I got more good news. Our third roomie was there. He was also a pitcher (I'm assuming they put us together for that reason) named D'Andre Sparks. He was a righthander and I knew about him. He threw serious heat. He'd had some control problems in the White Sox organization, and that had kept him from spending more than a couple of months in the show over the last six years. Like Danny and me, the Cardinals were willing to take a chance on him. Maybe that's why the Cardinals were known as one of the best organizations in baseball. They never stood still. They were always developing players and checking out new ones. We were three of those new ones they wanted to check out.

D'Andre was from Tampa, and had been drafted by the White Sox out of high school. "I didn't go until the 21st round," he said, as the three of us sat in the living room telling our stories. "I had scholarship offers from South Florida, Ole Miss and Vanderbilt. My dad told me not to sign. I said, 'Dad, this is my dream. I can't say no to my dream. I may be passing up a much bigger bonus after I go through college, but I could also get hurt and end up with no money, and no dream. I feel like I need to sign this contract, and I need you to sign it with me, 'cause I'm only 18.' So I did, and he signed it too.

"Started in rookie ball, then low-A, and all the way up the ladder in just two years. In Triple-A, I found some control and was striking out every dude who came up. Got my first call-up. Nervous as hell. Walked the first two guys I saw on eight pitches, and all that confidence kind of drained away. After that, four years of up and down. Great games and others where I was hitting the backstop on the fly. It ain't been pretty, but it's still my dream."

I told him what Danny and I had talked about. How we weren't there to compete with each other. We were there to earn jobs. I had his back and Danny's. We were a team. We should bond. Do our workouts and running together, and never be afraid to point things out if we see anything another guy could do better. Not instruction or criticism, just helpful pointers.

We were all in. The Three Musketeers of Jupiter!

D'Andre needed to get over to the clubhouse and grab a locker and meet Trevor. "Tell him you want to be right next to me and Danny. When camp starts, all this will be out of our control. Let's control it while we can. Then get back over here and I'm taking you two guys to dinner. Danny, did you pick what you want?"

"Mexican. I want Mexican," Danny said. I loved Mexican, but I was a little spoiled by SoCal and there hadn't been any Mexican worth eating in Minnesota. D'Andre said, "I'm in." For me, that was great. It was going to be a cheap date. At least Danny didn't say "Ruth's Chris."

While D'Andre was over at the complex, Danny and I faced the issue of how to find the best Mexican food in Jupiter. No Google then! Danny had a flip-phone, so I called the Cardinals camp office and kind of sheepishly said, "Hey, this is Brooks Bennett. I'm taking my two new roomies to dinner, and we want Mexican. Do you ever hear any guys talking about the best Mexican food over by the beach?"

The woman who had answered the phone laughed and said, "Yes, I do Brooks. But I don't need their advice, I know the best Mexican food in Jupiter. It's a little hole-in-the-wall called El Serape. It's just off Highway 1 next to a Publix, down by Jupiter Beach. It doesn't look like much from the outside, or even on the inside, but it's awesome food. Everything on the menu. And the margaritas are pretty good too."

That's the sort of advice that makes the world a better place.

When D'Andre got back we headed out to my car. When Danny saw it he said, "The rental company gave you this?" I cracked up for about the hundredth time when people would ask about my little Toyota.

"It's mine. I know, it seems ridiculous, but it's a good car and it gets me where I need to be. Of all the things I can spend my money on, cars come way down the list. I'll probably step my game up here soon. I have a buddy who is a hockey player for the Tampa Bay Lightning, and the team worked out a loaner program for him with an Audi dealer. They gave him an A4. I'll admit, it's a damn nice car and not too flashy. I absolutely never see myself driving around in a Porsche or a Mercedes, or anything that shouts 'Look at me!' I can see stepping up in terms of space and a little bit of luxury, but for now the Camry does the job."

Once we were in the car, D'Andre said, "So you know a guy on the Lightning? Who is he? I've probably seen the dude play."

I said, "I don't just know him, I'd say we're best friends. He's Eric Olson, a defenseman. We met our freshman year at the University of Minnesota and have always stayed in touch, and over the years we've gotten to be really close. When I had my Tommy John surgery, there was nobody who called or came to see me as much as Eric. Same with the rotator cuff deal. He's a really good dude. We play at opposite times of the year, so it's hard to get together, but I have a condo in Cape Coral now so we can see each other a lot easier than when I was in Oklahoma City or Arlington and he was in New York. Good dude, I hope you get to meet him someday."

We found the place, after a couple of wrong turns, and went inside. It was literally in a shopping center wedged in between a manicure place and a dry cleaner. We were lucky to get a table.

I rarely drink hard liquor, but you just have to have a margarita, right? I think it's a law. All three of us got the "top shelf" version and man, oh man. I'd never tasted anything like that. I can feel the sensation on my tongue right now, just writing about it.

And the woman at the camp front desk was right. It was fabulous Mexican food, and that's hard for a SoCal boy to admit. Nothing over the top. Nothing with supposedly innovative ingredients that really just get in the way, or worse yet, ruin it. Just good solid enchiladas, tacos, burritos, red sauce, green sauce, beans and guac. Even the chips and salsa were perfect. D'Andre went with the carne asada and said it was the best he'd ever tasted.

We had great conversations, focusing on how we all grew up, what life was like, stuff

452

like that. We were all single, but Danny had a longtime girlfriend and D'Andre had been divorced for a couple of years. Danny said, "We're gonna get married, but I need to see how this camp works out before we plan anything." I got that.

I asked D'Andre about the divorce, if he wanted to talk about it.

"We went to high school together, and were dating when I signed. I don't think she completely understood how pro baseball works. I mean, I was a star in high school and a big man on campus. I think she really figured I'd just go straight to the big leagues and we'd move to Chicago. Instead it was the Sally League, the Carolina League, the Midwest League and the Southern League; she was getting frustrated. I was moving around so much we hardly saw each other. When I finally had my first call-up, she got excited. I didn't know what to think about that. She was acting like she got called up. I was a baseball player but I was also a person, ya know? I was the same man in Nashville as I'd be in Chicago. We play where they tell us to go. You have to work at it to make it a life, ya know? It ain't glamorous, sweetie.

"But she persuaded me to get hitched. I don't know how, but she did. We got married over the winter, and all I could afford for a honeymoon was a few days in the Bahamas. When I went back to the minors out of camp the next year, she was already busting on me pretty hard. Laying the guilt on me like, 'Why are you going back to the minors? What did you do wrong? Why didn't you pitch better?' She just didn't understand and I couldn't get her to understand. I was supposed to be a star, making big bucks. She felt like I'd let her down. Hell with that, I'd let me down more than her."

He said he caught her cheating on him a few weeks later, and he divorced her right away.

He had touched on so many of the things that had gotten in my way, and still were, for real or just mentally. All I could say was, "I feel it, dude. I understand it. Trust me, I understand it."

All in all, a great meal and conversation. By the time we got back to the condo, it felt like we'd known each other for months. We'd only known each other for about six or seven hours. Baseball, man. Instant friends and all kinds of different guys. I love the damn game so much. Baseball and family have been two core elements of my life. There's nothing like it.

We plotted out our plan for the next morning, watched some mindless SportsCenter, and one by one headed to our rooms. I had one last half-glass of Cab sitting on the balcony. For a few years my life had been really really bad. On that balcony, on that night, life was good. Life was really good.

We established our routine the next morning. There was a cafeteria in the main complex building, so we'd head there at 7 and get some protein in us. Then over to the clubhouse to start the process. It's not like putting on the uniform. Not nearly as involved as that, but you take your time and enjoy the actual activity. Compression shorts, then the red basketball-style shorts with the STL logo embroidered at the bottom of one leg. Short white socks. A Cardinal Baseball T-shirt. And your hat. Done deal. And don't forget the sunscreen!

453

We'd run our poles. Then our sprints. Then some more stretching. Finally we'd put our gloves on and just play catch. With there being three of us, we'd rotate each day with regard to who was the single dude who threw to the other two. Baseball players just do that naturally. You want to play catch but everyone is all paired up? Just walk up and stand next to a guy, and the dude he's playing catch with will alternate his throws to the two of you. You want to rotate that, because the guys who are next to each other only get half the throws.

It felt good. It felt great. It was heaven. And whether it was just loosening up or heating it up a little playing catch, I never threw overhand. Every throw was sidearm. And as we increased the velocity a little, my stuff started moving. Both guys made comments when a two-seamer would run in and dive. "Nice!" was a common thing for all of us to say to each other.

The Three Musketeers of Jupiter!

Right about then, a couple of non-roster catchers showed up, and one of them was either really intuitive or he had been clued in by the Cardinals to seek me out. He said, "Before camp opens, I'd love to do some bullpens with you. Are you up for that?"

I said, "Damn right I am. We just finished our stuff here. Let's go get some water and get to work." His name was Darren. He'd just finished his first year at Double-A.

We went out to a mound and chatted for a bit. I brought him up to speed on the arm slot and what I was trying to do with it. Also mentioned the curve and the challenge of not tipping it off. He said, "OK, I got it. Let's get to work."

We just tossed for a second, and then I just yelled, "OK" to let him know I was ready. He put his mask on and got down in his crouch. I toed the rubber in the stretch position. I flipped the back of my glove straight forward to let him know a fastball was coming. I let it fly.

"Nice man, that is a heavy ball. The sink goes two ways. Cool!"

I threw about 20 fastballs, ramping up the velocity with each one. Then I signaled with my glove that we were switching to the curve. He nodded.

I didn't go full bore on the first one. It spun OK but it wasn't much to admire. I threw the next one with more conviction. It bit. Darren had to reach for it. I started it in the middle of the plate and he caught it well outside the strike zone.

I said, "OK, I want you to keep an eye on these. Do you see me yanking my hand down at the point of delivery?"

I threw the next one and it was sharp as well. Darren took off his mask and said: "I think you're worried about nothing. I mean, I'm just trying to catch the thing. I don't have time to watch your hand after the ball comes out of it. I'm locked on the ball. Hitting is way harder than catching. I don't know how anyone could see that motion if they had any plans of hitting the ball. I say just keep going for it. It's nasty."

I had never thought of that. But I had also never gotten to this point with it.

Finally, I said, "I'm working on a new change. It's a circle change, and I'm going to turn it over a little at the release point. Just a little. That's all it will need.

The key to this was arm speed. I should use the same arm action and speed as

454

the fastball. The loose grip, with my first finger and thumb making an "OK" circle on the side of the ball, would slow the pitch down. If I turned my hand just a little counterclockwise on release, it should really dive down and in.

It was magic. Darren actually missed the first one.

"What the hell," he said. "Man, I have never seen anything like that, and I'm pretty sure I could never hit it. Let's throw a few more."

It was great. I wasn't even close to my full velocity, but after the session Darren said, "It'll be even better when it picks up some speed, but I'm telling you right now, on this day, you'd strike a lot of guys out in Double-A. I could not possibly hit this. If we pick up five miles an hour before camp starts, you're going to be lights-out against everybody."

That was really nice to hear, and I told him that. To get it in perspective, though, I locked on the words "in Double-A" and filed them away. I wasn't here in Jupiter to get guys out in Double-A.

We had a great couple of weeks together, doing that. Morning work with my roomies, a quick break, and three days a week I'd throw to Darren. It was bitchin' to be out there like we were, working so hard. We weren't even supposed to be there yet, and we were weeks into it. And by then the clubhouse was filling in with other early arrivals, including a lot of big-leaguers. I had never played the Cardinals, so I didn't really know too many of them. But man, there were some serious studs on that big league team. Mark McGwire, Fernando Vina, Edgar Renteria, Jim Edmonds, J.D. Drew, Ray Lankford, and the one guy I had actually played with before, Will Clark. On the mound they had guys like Darryle Kile, Rick Ankiel, Andy Benes and Pat Hentgen.

They were very good, but I was really interested in seeing how they looked during actual workouts and spring training games. I'd heard a few friends from the Rangers tell me, "This is a good spot for you. Their lineup is stacked, but their pitching staff is just good, not great. You can make that team if you're at your best. They have some weakness in the bullpen."

The next week or so it was still all the unofficial stuff, but with that many guys there it had to be organized. There were a few coaches in camp, and we had four full fields to use, so they divided that up. They'd hit grounders to infielders on one field, hold batting practice with pitching machines on two others, which meant guys like us could shag fly balls for hours, and they'd let guys freelance and run around on the fourth. Over there, you weren't going to get beaned by any errant throws or batted balls. The pitchers and young catchers could go out to the practice bullpen and throw as many as they wanted. It was pretty amazing to watch, and everyone knew what to do, without being told.

I was getting sharper by the day out in the bullpen. It felt great and seemed to have a lot of life. Man, it did feel good. It had been so long since I could say that.

Finally, the official first day of camp. It felt like I'd been there forever. It had been about six weeks.

The day before, the clubhouse was set up and lockers were assigned. I wasn't expecting a locker to myself. I figured I'd have to share. But, I actually did get one. It was tucked in a corner and hard to get to if the two guys next to me were both there, but it was mine. Danny and D'Andre shared a locker.

Lots of guys came over to shake my hand and say hello. They were great. I met a young lefty pitcher, I think he was only about 20 years old, and he was already one of those mythical legends all around baseball. He was Rick Ankiel, and he had the most beautiful mechanics you could ever see. With those sound mechanics, he threw absolute bullets. He was a phenom. He was also a really nice kid, and a little shy. I told him I looked forward to seeing him pitch, and he said, "Thank you. I look forward to seeing you pitch, as well." I was not 100 percent sure he knew who I was.

Speaking of mechanics, the change to sidearm obviously completely changed mine. Since I was a kid my dad would talk about big-league pitchers, and which ones were kind of violent versus the guys who were smooth. His favorite term for the smoothest of the smooth was "elegant" and I always wanted to be elegant. No wasted motion, no hesitation, just a beautiful flow and total balance. In other words, Jim Palmer.

I had already realized that sidearmers can't be elegant. It's a funky delivery that causes you to spin a little, torque your upper body and fire it from a totally different spot. The follow-through is what's most different. When an overhand righty throws a pitch, his follow-through is going to pull him to the left. Sometimes all the way to the left, so he's not even facing home plate anymore. When you throw from the side, your release point still has you a bit sideways, and the follow-through will often just straighten you up. You end up in a perfect fielding position, facing the hitter straight on. A lot of sidearmers and submarine pitchers put together really quirky and herky-jerky deliveries. They figure it's a goofy delivery to begin with, so why not make it even goofier? Anything to deceive or distract the hitters. A lot of them will throw the pitch and then hop straight up and land on both feet at the same time. I hadn't gotten that far yet.

We did all the normal spring training stuff those first few days. PFP of course, while the position players took BP or ran the bases. The Cardinals were very methodical about all of this. They didn't have catchers throwing to second like they were throwing out a runner any earlier than they'd let their pitchers go all out. It was a good plan.

On the third day, they posted the pitching rotations for the practice bullpen. I was on mound two and the second guy to throw there. I don't remember who was the first guy, but I stood right behind him stretching and loosening things up. When three or four guys are pitching all at once, the sound is amazing. It's like rifle shots going off when those balls hit the catchers' mitts. It almost seems dangerous, because we're all so close together, but it's very controlled and we were surrounded by high chain link fences covered with mesh green curtains. It's alway a jarring experience, though, on the first day.

Darren wasn't my catcher that first session, which disappointed me but I was not in control of that. It was another minor league catcher, and all I did was tell him the deal, where the release point was, and what three pitches I'd be throwing.

As I made my way to the mound, it was impossible to miss the gaggle of coaches, staff members, and other men with radar guns and notepads. I was, literally, being scouted by the Cardinals, who had a great amount of interest in whether or not this sidearm experiment was going to work.

I'd picked up quite a bit of velocity since Darren and I had started. It was good to hear my catcher's mitt pop like one of those rifle shots. I was afraid the other pitchers would get those pops and my pitches would just kind of go "poof."

The big-league pitching coach, Dave Duncan, was standing right behind me. After about eight fastballs he said, "Brooks, are you married to this delivery, or can I offer some tweaks?"

I said, "Dave, I'm not married to anything or anyone. If you see something, tell me."

He said, "I just think you're keeping the ball in your glove a little too long. Your arm is having to catch up a little and then you're not getting full extension. Try bringing the ball out and reaching back with it right when you start your delivery. Just see how that feels. If you don't like it, we won't do it."

I knew what he wanted. I did my best to do it. Starting from the stretch like that, I'd be standing in front of the rubber with my pitching hand and the ball in my glove, right around my belt. I'd been leaving it like that for maybe another half second after I lifted my left leg. That was a carryover from my old delivery. This time, as soon as I made my first move I pulled my hand out and brought my arm way back, as far as it would go. Damn. It felt awesome. The whip action my arm had was eye-opening. The pop was a little louder. The catcher pointed at me before throwing the ball back. Totally stoked. That solved one of the mysteries, which was "how can I get more whip and velocity and still stay balanced?"

Duncan said, "Was that OK? Because that was actually pretty nasty."

We finished the session and Duncan said, "Really good stuff, Brooks. It's great to have you here, and even though we still have a long way to go down here, you've got a real chance. Let's just keep working on it. This is going to be fun."

I thought so too.

About a week later, after I'd thrown three more bullpens with Dunc watching over me (I felt comfortable calling him Dunc, by then), we started playing games. The Grapefruit League season didn't start for another few days, but a lot of teams scheduled games against colleges, and we also had the Triple-A Memphis team in camp, so we played them a couple of times.

The first game was against the University of Missouri. I was scheduled to throw the third inning.

It went well. Not perfect, but well. I actually lost command for a little bit, which is really rare for me. I just got a little wild low and the Mizzou hitters were disciplined. I got an easy ground out from the first hitter. Then walked the next guy on four pitches. I wasn't used to that. It was weird. Got the next guy on a foul pop up, and then walked another on four. What the hell?

I ran the count to 3-1 on the next guy, stepped off and took a deep breath, telling myself to relax and just let it go. Sinking fastball for strike two. I thought, what's the last thing this kid is going to be looking for right now? I shook off my catcher twice, to get to the change-up. I mean, why not? I'd be throwing it for all of two or three weeks.

It dove down and in on him. He swung and missed. I jogged off the mound.

And that was another thing that was different. No more calmly walking to the mound and back to the dugout, like most pitchers do and I had always done. I was going to run, maybe even hop over the foul line like it was some superstition. Because sidearm relievers are goofy. It felt good too.

No one really said much to me in the dugout or after the game. Under any circumstances, you can't be too high on yourself if you walk two guys. Then factor in they were college kids, and I'd barely call it a good outing. No runs, but no style points.

Danny, D'Andre, and I had our routines well in place by then. I'd say we were cooking our meals and eating at the condo at least four nights a week. We'd watch TV for a bit, talk about our day, and head to bed. We were getting up at 6 each morning, and we needed the rest.

D'Andre was throwing rockets but still struggling with his command. One night, at the condo, he said, "I don't get it. In the pen I throw nothing but strikes. I get out on the mound and for five or six pitches, I've lost it. I won't make any team pitching like this."

I said, "I only see one thing that you might want to think about. You throw hard. Very hard. But if you'd slow the whole delivery down so you can stay balanced, you're still going to be throwing hard. When I watch you in games, you look like you're in a huge rush, and no two deliveries are exactly alike. If you throw a bullpen soon, see what that feels like. Just calm it down, stay the same, and stay balanced." He said he would.

The Grapefruit League plodded along. It's a slow process that you wish could go faster. It's like, "Can we get to the end of this movie to see how it turns out?"

I did pretty well, I think, for a guy learning a new way to pitch. But here's the thing: There are no freebies for the guy learning something. All that matters is the scoreboard. That's it. I needed to get a little better. I needed to get from hitting one side of the plate to hitting corners. If I could refine it to that, I might have something.

By the time we got to the last week, I was still there. D'Andre had been sent to the minor league camp. Danny had been released. I was the only Musketeer left. And with just a few days to go, it was getting stressful.

On the day before the final game, Tony LaRussa, our manager who hadn't said much more to me than "attaboy" a few times, brought me into his office. It was "the talk" and my stomach sank.

"Hey Brooks, have a seat," he said. "I don't want you to be disappointed. You did really well. All this stuff you're trying to perfect is getting better. The only hangup is the fact that we have our 25-man roster, and we don't have any open slots on the 40-man. It's a numbers game. In a perfect world, we'd option you to Memphis and let you keep working on this down there. If a guy like you can get those hitters out, you'll be fine in the big leagues. It'll be a new start."

"But to do that, we have to list you as 'Designated for Assignment' and let all of baseball know. That means you'll have to get through waivers to stay in our organization. For my sake,

I hope that will happen. But, my guess is someone will claim you. I'd hate to see that, but we have no control. We can either release you, which we're not going to do, or put you on waivers. If you clear, and want to go to Memphis, the club will work out a deal for you. You deserve it. You've earned it. I guess we'll just have to wait and see. Sorry, Brooks."

I said, "Tony, it's been a totally rad honor to wear the Cardinal uniform. No matter what happens, this will be something I'll never forget. Before I signed my first contract, it never crossed my mind that there are teams, and then there are what I'd call the legacy teams. The legendary teams. And the Cardinals are absolutely one of those. I appreciate the patience, and all you and Dunc have done for me. When will the word go out about the waivers?"

"Pretty quickly, I'd say. Maybe even later today. You hang in there, Brooks. The way I see it, the whole thing is in your hands. We're releasing guys right and left. It's over for them and it's devastating. If you get claimed on waivers, you get to make the decision. You can still pitch, but you need to have a life and a real direction too. It's going to be up to you."

I thanked him again, and walked back to my corner locker. Most of the guys were looking down, or facing the other way. The guy in the locker next to me was pitcher Mike Matthews. He was just getting started in the big leagues and still on pins and needles wondering if he'd get called into Tony's office next. He said, "Are you OK, man?" I smiled and said, "Yeah, I'll be OK. I'm going on waivers. What happens after that is up to me. I can keep trying this sidearm experiment, or be thankful for all I've done and move on. I'm at peace with it. I'm good."

I went on waivers that evening. Until someone claimed me, I was still the property of the Cardinals so I went to the clubhouse in the morning. I just did some running to clear my head. When I was done, Tony waved at me from his office.

"Bad news for us, Brooks. I mean that. We were excited to have you here. You were claimed by the Montreal Expos. They'll be in touch, I'm sure. The administrative staff will get with you on all the exit details. I wish you the best. Take it easy on us when we play the Expos."

I cleaned out my locker, and hauled my bag back to the condo. I had a huge decision to make. I also had no phone, so I wasn't sure how the Expos would reach me. For some reason, that seemed fine to me.

I had no clue what to think. The Expos were a certified mess by then. They had been a "super team" up until the work stoppage in 1994. Their owner stripped the club of its high-priced stars after that, and the fans deserted them. They played in Olympic Stadium, which just about everyone complained about. Terrible turf, oddball field (it was built as a track and field stadium for the Montreal Olympics) and zero vibe. I heard one guy say, "It was like playing inside a gigantic nuclear power plant cooling tower. That's how bad it was." Nobody liked it, including the fans. After dumping a ton of superstars and their salaries after the work stoppage, they were bare bones. By 2000, though, one of their prospects paid off huge. It was Vladimir Guerrero. He was a megastar, but he was pretty much all they had.

I went back to the condo and had a glass of wine.

As I took the last sip, there was a knock on the door. That startled me. I answered it and it was one of the administrative women from the front office.

"Hi Brooks. I'm so sorry to hear we lost you. The Expos are trying to reach you from Montreal, but they didn't know how to do it. They asked me if I could round you up so that you could call them back from the office. Do you want to do that?"

I said, "Well, I think I have to do it. Should we go now?"

She gave me a phone in an empty office and closed the door. I dialed the number and a woman answered it with a noticeable French accent. That was kind of cool, actually. She put me through to the assistant GM, who had a noticeable Alabama accent.

My head was spinning a bit, but I did my best to listen closely. He told me they'd claimed me, that they were excited to have me join the club, and they had every intention of keeping me in the big leagues. They needed pitching help right now.

Then he got to the nuts and bolts. "Listen," he said. "I'm not going to BS you. We have the smallest budget in MLB, and this year it's twice as big as last year. We have a new owner, but our entire budget is about $30 million. We'd be able to pay you $550,000. You'd be in the top third of our salary rankings. What do you think? We'd love to have you. And you'll love Montreal."

I was in no position to say yes or no. I really needed to think about it. I asked him if he could give me 24 hours. He said yes.

I hung up and went back to the administrative woman's desk. Her name plate said "Carolyn Lee" and I felt bad. I never knew her name until right then. Bad on me. I said to Carolyn, "Thank you. I have nothing packed, and I really don't want to drive back over to the Gulf side in the dark. Would it be OK if I checked out of the condo first thing in the morning?" She smiled so sweetly, and said, "Of course you can. Don't you worry about it. I wish you all the best, Brooks. You've been a joy to have here. Good luck with everything."

Whew. Just another crazy whirlwind circling through the world of one Brooks Bennett. I had a ton of thinking to do that night and basically had to make the decision before noon at the latest. The Expos were right there at the complex with us. I could drive my car to the other side of the ballpark if I decided to play for them. And there were a lot of people to talk to. Basically everybody to talk to. In the end, I set a deadline of midmorning the next day. I needed to make the decision and let the Expos know. Then I'd either drive to their side of the complex or drive to the other side of the state. Just as important, I needed to call my parents, my agent, and Eric. If I only had a phone.

There were no more Musketeers in Jupiter. And this former Musketeer wasn't sure what he wanted to do.

I didn't sleep much that night. Actually, I don't think I slept at all. I mostly just lay on my back and stared at the ceiling. I kept going mentally back and forth on the pros and cons. Like, any time I'd think of the money, and what a step down that was, the other side of my brain would scream out: "Dude, just a few years ago that would've seemed like a fortune. Get over it. So your pride is hurt? Get the hell over it."

If I thought about the Expos and their situation, and began to think how bad it was, I'd hear the counterpoint saying, "They are a BIG LEAGUE team. They play in the National League. They will not go 0-162 this year. They will beat other big league teams. And you can help. Get over it."

The thought that kept circling back the most was this one: This new delivery was difficult, and I had absolutely not totally figured it out yet. It had to be absolutely precise. There was no room for even the slightest error, like having a sinker only drop two inches instead of four for no apparent reason. That would turn a swing and a miss into a rocket. It was going to be high stress all the time. No more reaching back and just blowing it by hitters. Those days were over.

At some point, there in the dark, my brain just settled down. I knew.

I was going to turn down the contract. My playing career was over.

I needed to get away from the game and the injuries. Maybe I'd take Mom and Dad on a vacation. Maybe a cruise, or something. Maybe island hopping in Hawaii. I wasn't sure about that, but I knew I was done and I needed some space from the game I'd loved since early childhood.

Breakups suck. This one made me cry. Big tears, but no remorse. Just sadness. I had to deal with the fact and understand the reasons. I was trying to do something my body wasn't meant to do. Like, totally trying to create a new me and a new experience. The problem was, I was still me. Plus, I was burned out, wasted by the whole thing.

It was over.

CHAPTER 46

Eric Olson

I had caught up with Brooks a few times during spring training, and then got a call from him right when spring training was over and the teams were all heading out to play another 162-game schedule. He'd sounded pretty upbeat throughout camp, so I was hoping the call was good news. That he'd made the Cardinals roster. Even being sent to Triple-A would be positive. He could easily earn a promotion within weeks. The call was not good news.

As he explained it, he got caught in a numbers game with St. Louis. They wanted to keep him, and they did want him to go to Triple-A to keep developing his pitches. The only problem was, they didn't have any room on their 40-man roster. They couldn't just assign him to Memphis without releasing him first or "DFA'ing" him. They'd have to file a form that said they had designated him for assignment. I think they could have released him and then re-signed him to Triple-A, but they didn't want to do that because once they released him he would be a free agent and able to contact every MLB team to find a better fit. The whole thing sounded kind of convoluted, and I wasn't sure what it meant. Hockey seemed a lot less complex.

As Brooks explained it, they said they'd have to put him on waivers and if no other team claimed him, they could send him to Memphis. The Cardinals were honest about it, and said they didn't see any way he'd go unclaimed. And they had no way of protecting him and no way of knowing which team might claim him. All the teams in MLB would have their chances in reverse order of the prior season's standings, the way I understood it.

The next day he learned that the Montreal Expos had claimed him. They told him they would put him right on the big league team, but their salary budget was so low all they could offer was $550,000. And, this was important, the Expos were a total mess, about to go bankrupt, and really bad. He said he wasn't sure what to do.

Late the next afternoon I got another call from him. I said, "Where are you?"

He said, "I'm at my condo in Cape Coral. That should tell you something."

"Well, it kinda does, but tell me straight. What happened?"

"I just couldn't do it. The money meant nothing, although I had to tell my pride to take a hike on that one. What mattered was me. I was awake all night. I went through every possible scenario. I felt the stress and I felt a lot of anxiety about signing with Montreal. That was my first clue that the whole thing was wrong for me. I've never felt a moment of anxiety signing a contract. I've never felt any anxiety in baseball, period. Going all the way back.

"I just realized I was fooling myself. I'd pitched pretty well, but it wasn't good enough and I wasn't sure it ever would be. Why go find out the hard way with a last-place team? I'm done."

I asked him how OK he was with that.

"It's gonna take some time, for sure, but I'm good. I'm smart enough to know this is right. I'm gonna decompress for a few weeks at least. Probably have my folks come down. I just need to get away from all of this. I'd love to go surfing, especially out in SoCal, but we'll see.

"And you know, in a couple of years I might finally be ready to get back in as a coach or even a scout. The scouting thing intrigues me a little because you wear normal clothes and you sit in the stands. Like, right now, if I put a uniform on my brain would melt. Same thing if I sat in the dugout wearing sweats while the guys were playing. A couple years from now? Maybe I'll finally be over it. But it's a done deal. I thanked the Montreal people and let them know. But how are you doing?"

I filled him in on the last month or so, and how bad we were. I had told him about the most recent concussion back when it happened in January. This time I added a little more.

"I really can feel what you're saying, man. I'm at a point where I'm a little afraid of what could happen. I'm making huge money, everything is good, and Carol and I are focused on starting a family as soon as we can. I'm not even worried anymore about trying to time it for the off-season. Having a baby is more important than that. And if having a baby is that important, my health is the most critical thing to worry about. Not paychecks, not fame, not screaming fans and great buddies in the locker room. I have to stay healthy if we're gonna have kids."

Brooks said, "So what's your plan?"

"Well, my first two years of the extension are done, so it depends on whether or not they pick up the option or I become a free agent. We're working on that. At this point I'm just going to hope I don't get another concussion anytime soon. Because the next concussion will be the last one. One more and I'm done. I don't care if we're fighting for a spot in the playoffs. One more and I'm done."

I paused and then, for me, got about as philosophical as possible.

"It's kind of crazy, isn't it? How all this has happened and we've gone through so many things in common. You know, if I was five steps slower or faster getting down the hallway in Pioneer Hall, and because of that all we did was pass and nod at each other, all of this stuff between us wouldn't have happened. We might have ended up friends, but nothing like this. It's just nuts.

"We played for the Gophers at the same time. We signed our first pro contracts at the same time. We went on our minor league journeys and both made it to the top, and we both played for teams called the Rangers. And now we're one concussion away from both being done with our careers. It's been a wild trip, dude. Mine's not over yet, but the ending scares me. Not because I won't be a hockey player anymore, but because it's going to hurt and that will be my last memory of playing hockey. That is, if I remember it. Stuff like that, not having any memory of injuries, will scare the living crap out of you."

And then I added, "Hey, let's make the most of this. It's the first time we will have ever had a chance to hang out during the summer! Want to play some golf?"

He said he didn't really play but wanted to. My guess was that he would be a natural. We made a pact to hit the driving range as soon as we were both settled in.

Carol was really liking her gig with the charity, and they loved her there. They also couldn't believe she was donating her whole salary back to the charity. She told me the CEO/Executive Director had told her, "You don't have to do that. All of our salaries are at the bottom end of our peers in this corner of the charity world. Our budget is designed to send the vast majority of our funds directly to the shelters, the day care centers, and the other outreach programs we work with. We have a budget for salaries. We don't expect anyone on our executive team to work for free."

She told them it wasn't negotiable.

She was happy. And I knew I had to have the talk with her I'd had with Brooks.

I told her where I was mentally. I told her where I was physically. And I made it clear that the next one was the last one. And that wasn't negotiable either.

She said, through a few tears, "Well, I hope we don't have to cross that bridge. Seeing you with these concussions breaks my heart. Are you good with this? Are you OK?"

I said, "I wouldn't have told you this if I hadn't come to grips with it. I'm good. And to take it one step further, it doesn't really even need to be another concussion. If I'm playing and I feel any odd effects, or any carryover from the first three, that's a reason to walk away, too."

I was loving just being home, but the first few weeks after the end of the season have always been hard for me. It's just a gigantic disconnect that happens all at once. One minute you're in a game with 10 seconds left. When the buzzer goes off everything changes. No more skating, no more workouts, no more games, until the fall. You'll be having a peaceful morning and a nice breakfast, some day in July, and you'll panic. "I'm gonna be late for the morning skate!'

Same thing around 4 in the afternoon. "Oh my gosh, it's time to get to the rink."

It's weird, but it mostly fades over time. OK, it only fades a little. That stuff is totally wired into your brain. It's hard to delete.

About a month later, I was talking to Brooks and he said, "OK, let's go hit some golf balls. Are ya in, coach?"

I was in, and excited about it.

Then he added, "OK, here's my plan. I need clubs and all the other stuff. Take me to a good golf store and let's get me decked out. Nothing outrageous, but good solid clubs for sure. Knowing myself as I do, if I enjoy it even a little bit, I'll dive all-in, so I don't want to buy cheap stuff now and then have to upgrade. When can we go?"

Since we were just going to hit at a range, we could go anytime we wanted. I knew of a range that was usually wide open, so we decided to go shopping in the morning and hit the range that afternoon.

We went to my favorite golf store, and got him fully outfitted. Some really nice TaylorMade clubs, with a decent bag, and all the other stuff he'd need. A lot of the apparel had Nike swooshes on it.

We went back to my house and got the clubs all unwrapped and in the new bag. He took extra care to make sure all the tags and stickers were off everything. He was kind of meticulous. Then I grabbed a bag of plastic practice balls I had and we went out to my backyard. I didn't know where I'd have to start.

I threw one plastic ball on the grass and said, "Now, just pull out your 8-iron and grip it like you're going to hit that ball. And get in a stance that feels comfortable to you."

He looked about perfect. I told him to go ahead and take a nice easy swing and hit the ball. He hit the grass a little behind the ball but just about everyone will do that. I put another one down and said, "Rules of the road. Head still. Eyes on the ball. Come through the contact zone going straight ahead. Remember, don't sway back when you pull the club back. Keep that head still. And don't look up until after you've hit it."

He put a beautiful swing on it. If that had been a real golf ball, we'd be talking 120 yards, sky high, right at the pin. I knew he'd be like that.

I asked him how many rounds of golf he'd played in his life.

"None before I was 18. Maybe five or six since then. That's it."

We hit enough plastic balls for me to make the call.

"OK, next stop is the range. And then play nine holes. If you're free, let's do it tomorrow."

He said, "I'll have to check my calendar. I'm pretty busy, you know."

I got us an 11 a.m. tee time at a course I knew would be kind to both of us. The fairways are wide and only a couple of water hazards, but some fun par-5 holes with some bunkers to avoid. We'd meet there at 10 the next morning.

When we said goodbye, he said, "Don't be fooled. I have no idea what I'm doing."

I told him, "That's good. Golf will drive you crazy. There are plenty of times I wish I had no idea what I was doing. That means you're playing naturally, and for you that's pretty damn good. I think you just need to play. Repetitions are the key to consistency."

I pulled into the golf course parking lot the next morning and there was the Camry. And there was Brooks, decked out in his new Nike clothes and Nike shoes.

I said, "Well, you look the part. Couldn't you have gotten the shoes and some more shirts from your Nike guy?"

"I'm pretty sure I could have, but that's not me. I'm of no benefit to them now. I'd feel like I was cheating or taking advantage. I'm a shoe free agent now, but I'm still loyal."

We hit a bucket of balls apiece, although most of the time I was watching him as he

465

went through his bag to see how far, and how cleanly, he hit each club. It all looked really good. Stupidly good. It was ridiculous.

So I asked him to pull out his driver. I asked him to tee one up and take a nice easy swing.

"Don't crush it. Just get the club head to it and try to hit it cleanly."

Right down the middle, 225 yards. I was shaking my head.

We got him up to 290 yards within five swings. I told him to do whatever he wanted for a few minutes; I needed to hit some.

He actually stood there and stared at every part of my swing. I was hitting them pretty sweet, and I could see the wheels spinning in his head. He was analyzing every nuance. I was beginning to wonder if he was normal, or even human. I had worked for at least 10 years to hit the ball as solidly and as straight as he had on the range. On his first day with his new clubs. Maybe innocence is golden. He had no bad habits. The key was to keep it that way.

We loaded our clubs on a cart and went to the first tee. I went first, and hit it to the middle of the fairway, maybe 220 yards.

Brooks teed his ball up. He took one practice swing. Gripped the club. Took a deep breath (just like he was about to throw a fastball) and let 'er rip. Bam! Right down the pipe and he outdrove me by 20 yards. I gave him his first high five of the day.

It really was amazing. He was a complete natural at the game. The one place he lacked natural skill was on the green, and the area around it. Everyone seems to struggle with the short game, and he just had no practice at it. He was about 10 yards short of that first green, after his second shot, and tried to chip it on. But he skulled it and hit a screaming line drive all the way across the green and off the back side.

We then had to tackle putting. Again, a totally different deal with its own necessary changes. Putting is hard, mostly because not too many weekend players practice it much. A typical round of golf for most guys will include more bad putts than bad fairway shots. Far more, actually.

Brooks had the time of his life. We had a riot together, and for the first time we were actually cracking each other up with baseball and hockey stories. It was fantastic.

When we finished, we added up our scores. We had played it straight. No kicking the ball back into the fairway or leaving a putt three feet short and just picking it up. I shot 43. He shot 47. That's incredible. Maybe impossible.

"You did great, man," I said. "More than great. You're good at this. Let's play all summer. I have a few Lightning teammates who live here, and we get together a lot. You'll fit right in."

He said, "OK, I'm all for it. I think I'm hooked. Hope I don't live to regret this new addiction."

I laughed and said, "You'll regret it every time you play a round, but then you'll play one hole perfectly and you won't be able to stay away. It always pulls you back in."

Then he added, "I don't think I ever told you this, but my dad was a hell of an athlete before he tore up his knee. The first time his buddies kidnapped him and took

466

him out to play golf was the first time he'd ever swung a club. He shot in the high 80s. Seriously."

That made perfect sense to me.

Everything was great at home. Carol was really happy that Brooks was around a lot, and he even mentioned selling his condo and buying one in Clearwater. He loved the area around our home, and loved Clearwater Beach. I told him that would be awesome. It's a great place, and he had no need to be down by Port Charlotte anymore.

Carol and I were still paying attention to when it would be the best time of the month to get pregnant, but it just wasn't happening. She got us an appointment at a fertility clinic for the end of July. Apparently we weren't the only ones not getting pregnant. The appointment was almost two months away.

My typical day, by June, was a quick jog in the morning, before it got too hot and humid. Then a dip in the pool to cool off. I'd have a small breakfast, eat a protein bar, have a big glass of juice, and then head to the practice facility to hit the weights and do some "dry land" drills. That would include resistance running, working on bursts in the first few steps, and sliding side to side in my socks on a small plastic replica of the rink. The one set of muscles that will weaken the quickest are the groin muscles. As normal humans, we just don't use them as much as hamstrings and quads. Doing those back-and-forth slides will keep those groin muscles toned. We also had a couple of shooting cages, where you could hit the puck toward a tarp that had a goalie printed on it. He was at the ready in front of a goal and there were small holes cut in the corners and between his skates. Blasting at that thing is a good way to keep the feel for the puck and the shot.

We usually had four or five guys there on any given day. I'd say half the team, at least, went back to their hometowns for the summer, including home towns in Scandinavia and Russia. Others would go on vacation, or rest injuries. But you could always count on there being a few teammates there. That made it a lot more fun and motivating than doing it alone. There was also one flight of stairs at the facility, which led to another workout area for the public. Go ahead and guess what I did with those stairs. Yep, move it, move it, move it. Quicker, quicker, quicker. Get those knees up. Whenever I'd head to the stairs, at least one or two guys would come with me. It's great to cheer each other on and see the work pay off. It's always better to have company.

Brooks and I played golf twice a week, on average, although I remember him taking a few trips where he'd be gone for a week. If some of the Lightning guys set up a round and it was an odd number, I'd get on the horn to Brooks right away. They all knew who he was and all really liked him. He fit right in, and he wasn't far behind in terms of golf skills.

In late July, Carol and I went to see the fertility specialists. We listened to everything they advised us to do. We talked at length about how we were trying and they had a few pieces of advice. Mostly, though, they said it would just take time. Any month now. And, after they analyzed the samples, they'd give us a call.

The next day we went in to see the doctor, and he said, "You're both in the average range, so we can't blame this on that. It's just going to take that one lucky month. I don't see any reason to go in-vitro yet. That field is advancing rapidly, so let's just try to follow the schedules and keep trying. We'll score a goal here soon." He winked at me when he said that. I didn't think it was really appropriate, but apparently the doctor was a big Lightning fan and he knew who I was. I'll tell you who I was. I was Mr. Embarrassed.

I told Carol, in the car, that the doctor had made me very uncomfortable with that comment. She said she felt the same way. Kind of violated, because you want to believe you're anonymous when you're doing this pregnancy stuff. We both reluctantly agreed we'd come too far to start over with a different practice. There were two other doctors in that particular office, though, so Carol said she would call and see about having them switch us to another specialist. She didn't want to throw anyone under a bus, but she thought if she just said "I think we need a new look and new opinions" that should do it.

She waited a week to make that call. She was afraid they would be too curious about why we were calling if she did it the next day. And they happily switched us over to a new doctor, who was female. We'd met her there early on, and she seemed really professional.

In terms of my contract, Robert called before camp started and said, "We're talking about the option. They are leaning toward doing it, but they want a complete physical and a neurological exam before offering it. Are you willing to do that?"

I said I was. If I passed, I passed. If not, I'd become a free agent. I wanted to play.

I saw the doctors just a few days later. In terms of the regular physical, I passed with flying colors. Then we went down the hall to see the neurologist. The first thing they did was a CT scan, which doesn't hurt at all and is much easier than an MRI. The worst part is drinking four huge cups of some liquid they give you to add contrast to the images. It's not terrible, but it's a lot to drink in just a few minutes. Then we went into a strange little room with all sorts of Star Trek consoles arranged around the walls. We did bright lights, they spun me around in a chair, and I sat at one board that had about 20 little buttons on it. They would light up one by one, and I'd have to press the correct button to turn it off. As it went, the lights flashed quicker. I think I did pretty well.

When we were done, the doctors told me the physical was great. They would need 24 hours to evaluate the second part of the exam, but the consensus was I'd done well.

The next day, they called and gave me the green light. The specialist said, "There's evidence of concussion, but I'd call it a Grade One on a 10-point scale. Are there options out there for you, in terms of a helmet? I know they're mandatory, but I've seen hockey helmets and they don't protect your head very well at all."

There were some options. They looked bulky as hell, and I'd never worn one of those, so I promised to look into it. The lead doctor said he'd call the team right away, with the results.

Two days later, I was signing the option forms for the extra year. Now it was time to get ready.

And then September rolled around. I often told Brooks about how September was my least favorite month when I was young. The weather was still generally nice up in Roseau, but school had started and the ice wouldn't be in the arena for about another month. And, I said to Brooks, "By the end of September, you guys down in the Twin

Cities still had 60s and 70s, and the nights were just a little chilly. In Roseau, we were getting down into the low 40s, and even the 30s were pretty normal. It was just a hint about what was coming. And that wasn't all bad. We all dealt with the cold, and we'd have hockey when it got there. The part that bummed me the most about winter was how short the days were. It's like you never saw the sun."

We started training camp. We got into the grind, and man I was hoping we'd be better. I was also hoping the concussions would stay away. And I was very much hoping I'd hear the words "We're pregnant" one day soon.

There sure was a lot going on.

CHAPTER 47

Brooks Bennett

When I called everyone after I had made my decision, they all took it well and were very supportive. To be honest, I think my mom and dad were relieved. They'd been going through all the great moments and all the turmoil with me. They let me know how proud they were, and I felt the love.

I think Adam, my agent, knew it was coming. He said, "I could hear it in your voice when you were in the Cardinals camp. The fire wasn't there. It was almost as if being 'pretty good' with all the new pitches was worse than being bad. Because you knew it wasn't enough. When I heard that the Expos had claimed you, I had a pang of fear that you might sign with them. You don't need it. You don't need the stress. You've had a great ride, and a very tough few years to wrap it up. You need to walk away. Thank you for letting me be part of it, Brooks."

I talked to Eric at length, and before long we were hanging out together, mostly up at his place. Every time I visited, I liked Clearwater more and more. It just had more of what I like than Cape Coral ever did. Cape Coral was safe and quiet, which was good, but it didn't have much in terms of a variety of restaurants and even though it was technically on the Gulf coast, it wasn't a beach town. It was mostly a retirement community and it was close to the Rangers complex in Port Charlotte. Although I was now "retired" I still didn't fit the profile, and I had no need to be close to the complex.

I let my financial guy Jack know what had happened, as well, and his first words were, "Brooks, I'm not sure I've ever said this to any other client, but that was a hell of a run you were on and as long as you and I aren't foolish, you're more than set for life. The only worrisome thing for me is that you're still so young. Next time you're up here, let's sit down and map it out." I thought that was a good idea, and I had some homesick feelings anyway. I wanted to get up there.

Jack added, "And the really good news is that if in a couple years you feel like being back in the game, whether it's coaching, or in the front office, or whatever, any salary they would pay you will almost certainly cover your annual expenses. You live a frugal life, and I've always appreciated that. It makes my job easier. I know last time we talked you mentioned trading some stocks. I really want you to be careful with that. Rather than even use the word 'trading' we should just say 'accumulating some stocks' instead. You need to see this as an investment, to build a stock portfolio for yourself. That's really important, Brooks. I've seen too many people who were set for retirement blow it all on stocks. It's tragic, and I don't want to see it happen to you."

I agreed. His words from the months before, about holding blue-chip stocks over long periods of time, had stuck with me. I had a little bit of an itch to someday be a stock advisor and broker for other people. If I did that, and they wanted me to take some risks for a big payback, I'd be using their money. For my money, I'd be very careful. It had to last a long time. I was about to turn 31.

I plotted out a plan to drive up to the Twin Cities to see Mom and Dad and have a sit-down with Jack. I wanted to see it all with my own eyes. Mom and Dad were thrilled. I packed a bag and a bunch of snacks. It was time to hit the road, and I knew the drive itself would be good for my soul. I love long drives. I needed one. And I needed the warmth of home.

I took off very early the next morning, and planned to make it a two-day trip. My target for the first night was Nashville. I made it before dark, found a Holiday Inn by the highway and got a great night's sleep.

The next day, I was out of there at the crack of dawn. I had toyed with the idea of taking the more westerly route, through St. Louis and up through Iowa but there's always a chance of delays when you go right through a major city, so I kept to the more boring program of heading straight up through Illinois, and then avoiding Chicago altogether to get to Wisconsin. I was pulling into my parents' driveway around 6 o'clock.

And guess what. For the first time ever I was on the road with a cell phone. About a week earlier I finally pulled the trigger and joined the future. It was a Nokia flip phone, because those were kind of everywhere, and I signed on with AT&T for service. As I crossed the Wisconsin border just south of Janesville, I gave Mom and Dad a call. My first ever cell phone call from a car. Times were changing!

Mom and Dad rushed out to the car when I finally got there. The hugs were medicine.

They looked radiant. I swear they were glowing.

The house looked great too. I never got to live there much, but it felt like home because it was their home. My dad had never let me help him buy a new house, because they absolutely loved that place, even though they had to write a check for the rent every month. They never wanted to leave. I had some thoughts about that, but they could wait.

They hadn't been sure when I'd get there, so Mom had made a big salad and had a plate full of various cheeses and crackers. That was far more than just "good enough" for me. It tasted incredible. And they even had a dozen bottles of wine in a small rack on the counter! We sipped a chilled Chardonnay after the salad, and kept nibbling on the cheese. It was so damn peaceful and secure.

471

We sat around the table and just talked our way through what I'd been through. They'd been down to Florida a number of times, and had seen me at my worst, so it was good to put a period on the long story and move on.

They are both so psychologically perceptive it borders on magic. As Mom said, "We could tell you were in the darkest place you'd ever been, after the shoulder surgery. The elbow was bad enough, but it was your first major surgery and you attacked the rehab like we knew you would. The shoulder was different. It was very different, and I know it was difficult for you.

"We weren't going to play amateur shrinks and tell you what to do. We just wanted to make sure you knew where the love was coming from, and that it was unconditional. We always loved that you played baseball, and that you got so much joy from the game. We would've been just as happy if you had surfed for no money and just lived the life we knew, maybe bartending or working in a board shop like your dad did. We know you'll miss baseball, but now you get to immerse yourself in all kinds of other things. Baseball took up so much of your time, year-round. Now you get to have a life, without throwing a ball."

I thought that was a great message. It hit home. Only looking back could I see how consumed I was by baseball. When you're doing it, you don't see it. You love it, you crave it and you just let it ride. Pretty soon you're 30, and hurt, and baseball has taken at least 80 percent of your attention since you signed your first contract. It was time to live.

We went out into their neat and tidy little backyard, with a bottle of something red, and just kept talking. The Rangers, the Cardinals, and then the Expos courting me.

Dad said, "This must have been the toughest decision of your life, right?"

I surprised him by saying "Not even close, dude. The toughest decision of my life was to come up here to live with Don, while you and Mom were down at Mayo. I was young. I was naive. I was a little nervous and a lot scared. I was in a very strange state, living with a guy I didn't know. Mix in going to a new school and having no friends there, and it was totally rough. All I wanted was to be with you. My sensible side won out, though, and it was the right thing to do. I shouldn't have been scared. I should've known I could do it, and make friends, and make it all work. But that was the toughest call I ever had to make. This one was hard, for sure, but it came to me as soon as I heard that the Expos had claimed me."

Even that word bothered me. They "claimed" me. How does that make you feel? We toss around terms like "I belong to the Rangers" or "I'm the Rangers' property" and then in the end another team claimed me. It's bizarre. The teams really dictate your life. Where to go, what to wear, when to be here, when to be there. It's a great life, and it sure as hell pays well, but it's totally consuming. From showing up in Butte to walking away in Jupiter, it's about all you have time to know.

I told Dad, "It wasn't a hard decision. I wasn't the same. The game wasn't going to be the same. I just couldn't do it. I had this magnetic pull to walk away and just live life. I'm very fortunate. I made a lot of money. I didn't make many friends in baseball, because we were all transients, or more like mercenaries, and I haven't had any good dating relationships in my personal life. I knew it was time to walk away. It wasn't that hard of a decision."

I had been looking at Dad the whole time I was talking. Until I stopped, I hadn't noticed that Mom was crying. Really crying. She got up and came over to my chair. I stood up and we nearly hugged the life out of each other. We're all emotional, to the point of being basket cases sometimes, but that one was off the charts.

Once the mosquitoes got bad, we went back inside. That's when my mom went to the fridge and pulled something out. It was a bottle of Dom Perignon. For them, it cost a fortune. But the thought, to commemorate this new beginning, was priceless. We did a toast, with Dad saying "I've been proud of you since the day you were born. I'll always be proud of you. I can't possibly be any prouder than I am now."

Mom followed with, "You're a man now. But to me you'll always be the kid in the cage out in the studio. The little boy who rode with his daddy on the surfboard. The sensible one who hung out with crazy surfer buddies who were anything but sensible. I never worried about you, ever, until the shoulder thing. That worried me. I'd never seen you like that. Now it feels like a rebirth. Cheers!"

I thought I was making the road trip just for the long drive, just to think while pointing the car north. It turned out the drive was just a means to get home.

I had a meeting with Jack the next morning. He was prepared for me. I was still uncertain as to where all my money was sitting and what it was earning, so he boiled it down with a lot of charts and graphs. Seeing it that way, it was totally easy to understand with one glance. It was like looking at a map. And you know me and maps.

I had a lot of money. It's all relative, right? When I signed my first contract and got an $80,000 bonus, I thought I was filthy rich. It was more money than I could conceive of. And there I was with Jack staring at the subtotals on each page and then seeing the grand total at the bottom of the final page. Over the years, Jack had nearly doubled the money I'd put in from my salary. There were some dips, and he wasn't afraid to point them out, but for the most part the guy was really on top of it. We were holding long-term, and after the dips came the rebounds. He was really smart. I was lucky to have him.

My most pressing questions were these: What do you think about me finally getting out of the old Camry and buying a new car? What do you think about me helping my parents out so they don't have to pay rent anymore? And, what do you think about me starting that stock accumulation? I think I'm ready, and I see how you've made this work for me.

He laughed about the car. He said, "As long as it's not a Lamborghini or a Rolls Royce, get whatever you want. If anyone out there is offering zero percent financing, go ahead and take it. It's free money. Literally, they are loaning you money and all you have to do is pay it off month by month. But do what you want."

He was all for helping my folks, and he had a great feel for it. "Listen," he said. "Your folks are very proud people. They've accomplished so much and have spent nearly all their lives living a very basic way. Your dad once said, 'We have everything we need.

We don't worry about material things we might want.' I really don't think they would want you to buy them a house and hand it to them like it was charity. Let's find a way to make it work."

I said, "I've already been thinking about that. They love that rental house. I want to talk to Dad and see if he'll have a conversation with the owner about selling it to them. If the owner will, they get to stay in the place they love and not just throw money at it. And they won't have to move. They'll just wake up the next morning in a house they own instead of rent. I'll offer to put down the deposit and pay off half the purchase. I bet the market price for that house can't be more than $175,000. Once the mortgage is in place, their payment shouldn't be more than $500 a month. Maybe less."

Jack thought that was a great plan if the owner of the house would go along with it. We'd have to find out.

As for the stocks, he said, "OK, let's give it a whirl. I think you should open up another checking account for the funds you're going to start with, just to keep it all neatly separated. I think we talked about $100,000 to get you going. Are you signed up with Fidelity yet?"

I was, and I thought the checking account was a good idea. I'd open up a second savings account too. Way easier to keep the records straight if all this didn't mingle with my living expenses.

Jack strongly advised me to avoid certain stocks. Airlines and plane manufacturers. One plane goes down and the whole business craters. Oil companies. Even more volatile than the airplanes. And, of course, start-up tech stocks in the dot-com boom we were living in. He called them money traps. "They'll seduce you and break your heart. It isn't going to last." He also said, "Do you have a plan for what you're going to buy and how long you'll hold it?"

I said I did. "I'm thinking of IBM and Microsoft for sure. Maybe $20,000 in each to start, and hold for as long as 10 years. Just let it ride. And I'm thinking about finding a company that manufactures a product that we all need. Not a luxury. Not just for the rich. A staple in life. Any ideas?"

"Let me look into that," Jack said. "That's a good idea. I'll see what's buzzing out there for long-term investment. As for how long you hold the IBM and Microsoft stock, my rule of thumb is this: If you get to where you've doubled your money, it's time to at least analyze it. What are the projections by the analysts? Is this the top, or is there more out there? Don't just knee-jerk and sell. Two years later it might have doubled again. You got your money, but you left a bunch on the table. You're going to have to learn how to read the tea leaves and understand the analysts. OK?"

Absolutely.

And then I hit him with my last idea. I wanted to sell my Cape Coral condo and move to Clearwater.

"Cape Coral was the right place because it was close to Port Charlotte and the Rangers complex," I said. "But there's not much there other than a bunch of snowbirds and retirees. I really like Clearwater, and it has a real beach. I need that. And my best friend, Eric Olson, lives there. Plus, I need a bigger place. I'm going to need a dedicated office for this new stock venture. I own the Cape Coral condo free and clear. Sell that, hope to make a profit, and plow it all back into a condo in Clearwater. What do you think?"

He said, "I think it's the right thing for you. We are, after all, not just talking about numbers in boxes here. We're talking about your happiness. If Clearwater makes you happy, and if the numbers in those boxes work, it's a no-brainer. First things first. Talk to an agent and get a feel for what your condo might sell for. If that sounds right, start looking around in Clearwater. When you're selling and buying, the timing is always tricky and it sometimes doesn't work out. You know what I mean? You sell your condo at the first open house, and then can't find what you want up in Clearwater, or miss out on some units that go fast, and then you can be out of a home for weeks. Same the other way. You find what you want to buy, but your condo doesn't sell. My advice is to find the new place you want and put an offer on it. When that's accepted, put your old condo on the market at once. Worst-case scenario is you might own two places for a few weeks or a month. That's better than being homeless."

So there you have it. The new Brooks Bennett. A very conservative stock accumulator. How rad is that? About to buy a new car. Also rad. And about to start the process of moving to Clearwater. Super rad.

I stayed one more day and got to see Don for an hour or so. That man got me through a lot. He was a saint and a savior for all of us. He's a great guy, and a wonderful person. He looked after me and took care of me. I love the man.

Over dinner that night, I ran the house idea by Mom and Dad. I had it all worked out in my head.

"I know you love the rental house, and that it's home. So what I want to do is have you talk to the owner. See if he would have any interest in selling the house to you." My dad began to open his mouth but I cut him off.

"We can make this work, if he'll sell. I'll cover the deposit and I'll cover half the purchase price. You'll need to get a mortgage, but that's a good thing. You'll be investing in your own home instead of just paying money to live in it. And you'll probably get a tax deduction. It's a win all around. And, listen, I would not have this money if it wasn't for you. You made me what I am. Dad, you made me a ballplayer. Now it's my turn. I want to help you. Your landlord might be the greatest guy ever, but if his expenses go up, or if the economy slips, your rent is going up. Once you get the mortgage, that's the monthly payment. It never changes. Let's do this. OK?"

They both looked at each other and started to cry. We Bennetts must have massive tear ducts. You'd think we'd run out of capacity at some point.

They nodded and said, "Brooks, we would love to work with you on buying this house. I'll call the owner tomorrow. I hope he's willing to sell."

I said, "Every landlord is willing to sell. It's not a matter of yes or no; it's a matter of how much. I did a little research before I came up here, and this house should be worth about $175,000 at the top end, looking at the comps in the neighborhood. It should be an easy transaction, but you know how that goes. Dad, when you call him, if he says he's willing to sell for the right number, throw $160,000 out there. And we'll pay the closing costs."

When it was time to head out the next morning, we shared our hugs and kisses. Dad was going to call me after he spoke to the owner of the house. I was on my way back to Florida.

I decided to do the Iowa-St. Louis-Nashville route. Ever since I'd gotten a glimpse of the Gateway Arch on my first trip to spring training, I'd promised myself I would go see that someday, and if I had the nerve I'd go up to the top.

With an early start, I got to St. Louis around 2. I found my way to the Gateway Arch parking area and strolled over to the monument. It was awe-inspiring. When I was right underneath it I was practically dizzy. The triangular shape of the legs makes it seem to twist and turn as it goes up. From the highway, it seems almost delicate and I had wondered how it stays up. When you're standing under it, right next to one of the legs, it's massive. What a totally rad place.

I went down to the underground museum and ticket area, and went for it. I got a ticket and only had to wait about 15 minutes for a tram.

With a crowd of strangers all around me, I waited in a boarding area way below ground, staring at a series of small elevator doors. When the tram came down to unload, the doors opened and the people kind of unfolded themselves to get out. Behind each set of doors was a single little pod-shaped car. The thing was TINY! I wasn't sure I'd fit. I did, but barely. There were five small seats in there, so you'd better be ready to rub knees with a stranger. It was crazy. When we went up, the little pods had automatic levelers, which scared the hell out of me when the first one went off. They don't rock like Ferris wheel cars; they are firmly attached to the mechanism, so they go through a series of mechanical leveling activations. Whew.

At the top, we squeezed out and found ourselves on some stairs that seemed to go straight up. We were maybe 30 feet from the viewing deck, which is right at the top, 630 feet above the ground. It was all really nuts. But, once I was up there next to the windows, it was just beautiful. You could lean against the wall and look out at downtown, with Busch Stadium being the dominant structure in the view. It was a place I would never play, despite how close I came. That stadium is now long gone, but to me it was the most beautiful of all the 1960s "cookie cutter" circular multi-sport stadiums. With a cantilevered small roof over a bit of the upper deck, the design was a nod to the Arch just a few blocks away. It was all made of perfect arches. From the observation deck 630 feet above the ground, you could see forever. Man, that was an experience.

I had a bit of an urge to walk over to Busch just to see if I could say hello to Dave Duncan, but I wasn't ready for that yet. And, I needed to get to Nashville, or even Chattanooga if I could make it that far. Maybe next time. Or maybe, someday, I'd be willing to go see the Cardinals on the road. This stuff had to happen at its own pace. I didn't want to force any of it.

Somewhere in southern Illinois, my fabulous flip phone rang. The range of people who could be calling me was very small. It was Dad.

"Hey, man. I talked to the owner. He said he'd think about it but he was pretty sure he'd sell for the right price. He asked me what I was thinking, and I said I figured the house might be worth $165,000 tops and that I'd be willing to offer $160,000 plus all the closing costs right now. He just kind of went 'Hmmm' and I couldn't tell if that was positive or negative. He said he'll call me tomorrow."

"OK, Dad. That's cool. Everything you just said adds up to him being willing to sell. That was the big question we didn't know the answer to. It's going to come down to the numbers now."

He said, "If he calls back any earlier, I'll let you know. Where are you?"

"I'm in the bottom part of Illinois, headed for at least Nashville. Dad, I stopped in St. Louis and went to the Gateway Arch. I have to get you there someday. It was one of the raddest things I've ever done, to go up to the top. It's crazy but it's so worth it. I think we need to go on a road trip some time. Right, dude?"

He said, "Right, dude. That would be bitchin'."

I got through Nashville and made it to Chattanooga just before dark. I slept like a rock, which is a good thing because I had a 6 o'clock wake-up call and a long day ahead of me. The miles ticked away. The towns flew by. Mom had made me enough sandwiches to last a year and feed 12 guys, so all I had to stop for was gas and bathroom breaks.

As I got near Tampa, I clearly remember thinking I'd almost be home if I lived in Clearwater. I still had 90 minutes to go to get to Cape Coral.

Dad called right about then. When I said "Hello" he just said "HEY!" and I could tell he was excited.

"He said yes. He took the $160,000 offer. Neither one of us has a real estate agent, but he's owned and sold enough investment properties through the years to navigate selling it by himself. He knows the title people and he can guide us through it. There are some fees for all of that stuff, so I offered to split those with him. He seemed really pleased with that. I think we're going to own this place, dude. You're amazing. We get to stay here forever!"

I let out a big "Woo-hoo!" and congratulated him on it. The amount of details we'd be dealing with, not having a real estate agent, would end up being mind-numbing, I was sure of that. But the concept worked. I got them their house, and they could be proud of having a very small mortgage on it. I had only told Mom and Dad that I'd cover half the purchase price and I'd make the deposit. I hadn't told them what I planned to do for that deposit. They would've balked at the whole thing if I would've said it was going to be way more than 20 percent. I was going to put $60,000 down. We'd each owe $50,000 to close the deal, and they needed to get approved for a mortgage. I told Dad he needed to get that done as soon as possible. And if there were any hangups, I'd co-sign. We were gonna get it done. Period.

I finally got home to Cape Coral and headed inside. It was a smothering hot and humid day, even at 7 o'clock. And I'd forgotten to close the drapes that faced the setting sun. My bad. It was really hot in there. I cranked the AC down to subzero and hoped for the best. It only took an hour to cool off in there.

477

I just relaxed and watched some TV. I did not plan on falling asleep on the sofa, but at 3 in the morning I woke up and wondered where I was. I went to bed and fell right back asleep. Long road trips are hard work.

The next day I called Eric and asked him for some contact info so that I could get in touch with the real estate agent he had worked with in Clearwater. With that in hand, I made the first call to Sandy, a self-proclaimed Clearwater expert. We talked about what I needed, what I wanted and what I could dream about. We talked about price and I gave her a pretty wide range. After all, I wasn't totally sure what my limit was going to be until I sold the Cape Coral joint. I gave her enough leeway though, to put together a good day's worth of showings.

I met her at her office the next morning. She was pretty much everything I thought of when I conjured up a Clearwater real estate agent. Probably in her mid to late 40s, platinum blonde hair, high heels, bright red lipstick, and a sweet accent I couldn't put my finger on. Definitely Southern, but nothing specific.

We sat in her office and went through listings. There were about 20, and she knew I'd probably rule out at least five. I think I said "That's a no" to maybe seven of them. There were even a few single-family homes in the pile, and I didn't get that. She said, "Honey, I just thought this was a steal and wanted you to see it." I had to make it clear to her that I wanted a condo. Preferably in some sort of high-rise and with Gulf views. The must-haves were three bedrooms, a nice large kitchen, a reserved parking spot, and it had to be furnished.

We headed out with our pile of listings in hand.

We saw a few high-rise units that were all really nice in their own ways, but none of them checked all the boxes.

In the car I asked her about the market. She said, "It's good, but not great. We've gone through cycles where we sell condos and houses without even listing them. We'd have people calling us saying, 'Just call me when what I want comes on the market.' This is more a standard market. We'll get multiple offers if it's a nice place, but right now we don't see bidding wars. If you see the one you want, though, we ought to pounce. Just to keep from being heartbroken. You don't want to be heartbroken, do you, honey?"

She asked me if I was pre-approved for a mortgage and how big that could be. I said, "I'm verbally pre-approved and can make it happen in an hour."

The next one we saw actually made me involuntarily say "Wow" when we walked in. It was on the beach, with a 25th-floor view of the Gulf. It had the three bedrooms I wanted, it had two and a half baths, a reserved parking space, a huge balcony overlooking the water, a full laundry and two living rooms. There was even a gorgeous wet bar in one of the living spaces. It was absolutely set up for entertaining. And it was very modern and updated.

I kept walking around staring. I didn't say much. I guess I was trying to keep my cards hidden. I remember regretting saying "Wow" when we walked in. I don't know why. She was on my side.

The price was near the top of my range, but it was within the range and the building blew me away. It had a gorgeous lobby, a full gym and three pools, including an indoor one for those "cold" Florida winter days, when it gets all the way down to 55 (above zero.) It was listed right around $600,000.

She asked, "Do you want to put in an offer?"

I did, but I wasn't sure how it all went down. So I asked her, "What do I do first? Do I need to get a copy of the mortgage approval before we make the offer?"

She said that would be preferable. We could do it on the fly, but if there were any hang-ups with the approval we'd probably lose it. I knew there would be no hang-ups, but I wanted to get it done. I asked her if I could use one of the rooms to make a call.

I called my banker, James, in Minnesota. He had set me up with their mortgage broker. That guy's name was Kevin. I'd talked to him once before and he was definitely a guy who always covered his butt and made sure there were numbers in every box. Correct numbers too, not just any numbers. He was not the guy you'd want when you're in a hurry. A couple of times he asked for information and I'd say, "Kevin, I already bank there. You have access to all of this. I don't have time right now to gather all that. I'm literally standing in the condo I want to make an offer on. James said this would be automatic and just take minutes. If it can't be done that way, would you please transfer me back to James?"

He put me on hold and came back in a minute. "Mr. Bennett, you're approved for $750,000. I'll email you a copy at the AOL address we have for you. Will that work?"

Yes, that would work. Sometimes you just have to bring my boy James into the mix to get things done. He'd been my personal banker since the day my dad deposited my signing bonus. I'd even gotten tickets for him a couple times when we came in to play the Twins. He was a good guy. He knew me. He knew about my investments and my IRA. For him, it was a slam dunk but it wasn't his job at the bank. For Kevin, it was numbers in boxes for a guy he'd never met and didn't know. Bottom line: We got it done. One more rad step.

I went back out to the living room and told Sandy, "OK, I'm approved for $100,000 more than they're asking for this place. I know you have more to show me, but unless you can say, without any doubt, that at least one of them is even better than this, I want to put in the offer right now."

She said, "Honey, I don't know. What I think is better might not be for you. If you're in love with this place and know it's the right one, let's put the offer in. OK?"

I agreed and asked what she thought we should put on the table.

"Normally I'd say go for the asking price, but this place has been on the market for five days. That's surprising to me, but it's a unique place that actually appeals to a guy like you. It's kind of cool and young looking, not old and frumpy, and it happens to check all your boxes. I can go in at $575,000 and hold my breath. If they hang up on me, we'll probably lose it."

I said, "Let's just go in at $590,000. And come right back at the asking price if they say no. If they try to push us higher than asking, on a place that hasn't sold yet, we walk."

"Good plan, honey. Let me make the call."

About 20 minutes later, after I'd walked around the living area 32 times, she came out smiling.

"They tried to get me all the way to five thousand above asking. I said to the agent,'If you want five grand more than you asked for, why didn't you just list it that way?' I knew the reason. It would've put the condo over the next big dollar threshold. To get it in the most searches, they listed it at $599,500. But I think they blew it. And I sense they think so too. Anyway, honey, it looks like you got yourself one beautiful home, right here on Clearwater Beach. Congratulations, Brooks!"

I know I was smiling as broadly as I could. I just shook her hand and said, "Thank you, Sandy."

It was a dream home. The furnishings were nice, but over time I figured I could swap some stuff out, piece by piece, to make it more like me. That kind of stuff never bothered me. I could be patient.

In the car on the way back to her office, she said, "Can I ask you something, Brooks? You're so young, but it's clear you've got a lot of assets. I haven't seen your application because we didn't do it at the office. We should have done that before we left, but we were a little late and I could tell you were antsy. There's a section in there about employment. What are you going to write in that box? I'm intrigued."

I laughed a little and said, "Well, 'Retired,' I guess, but not by choice. Up until a few months ago, I was a Major League pitcher for the Texas Rangers. But my arm blew up and I went through two big-time surgeries. So I quit the game. I'll go back to work someday, probably in baseball, but for now I'm working on investments and protecting the money I've made. I think this condo is a great investment. That's a million-dollar view. Those don't lose value."

She said, "Well, I'll be. My husband is a big baseball fan. He's originally from Philadelphia and that's why he chose to move to Clearwater. The Phillies have spring training here, and he goes to just about every game. I'll have to ask him if he remembers you."

"Please do, and if we close on this deal maybe you two can meet me for dinner somewhere."

I made the drive back down to Cape Coral and knew two things: I'd have to call Eric and my folks, and I needed an agent to help me list my condo as soon as possible. I still had the card for the guy who helped my dad and me when I found this place. It was late in the day and I didn't know if I could reach him, but he picked up on the first ring. He remembered me, and I told him the deal.

I said I'd just put in an offer on a condo in Clearwater, and I needed to sell the Cape Coral place ASAP. I was hoping he'd represent me and get the place sold. He said, "Sure. There's a reason you bought the place after seeing it once. It's great, and it's in a wonderful location. Can I come over to see you tomorrow and get it all written up?" We settled on 10 in the morning. I was still a little bent out of shape from the trip up north and back. I didn't see myself being coherent at 8.

Jim showed up right on time. We sat at my dining table and the first thing he showed me was a list of comps in the nearby marina area. Everything that was close to my condo, in terms of views, amenities, bedrooms, all that stuff, was at least $100,000 higher than what I'd paid for mine. That, as we say, was good news.

We settled on that as the asking price. $495,500. That wouldn't net me $100,000 because there were fees and commissions to pay, but it gave me a jump start on the new place. The investment had paid off. This home buying stuff is complicated, but I found it invigorating, too.

Jim got it all in order and had the condo on the market the next day. He'd told me, "I think we'll have a lot of showings, so that's going to be a hassle for you. I'll call you every evening with what I have scheduled for the next day, and you'll need to go for a walk or a drive for a while. I'll then call you when each showing is done. Just keep the place clean and we'll sell it fast." I always kept the place clean. That was the easy part.

That night, he called me around dinner time. "You want the good news?" he asked. I said sure.

"I have requests for 10 showings tomorrow. I don't think we can do that many, and it would run you out of your house for basically the whole day. What do you think?"

"I think I'll be out of my house all day. As soon as I make the bed, I'm gone. You have my cell number, so just let me know when I can come back."

First thing in the morning, I got out of there and called Eric. I asked him what he was up to and he said, "I'm going to work out now. I'll be back around 11. Why? What do you have in mind?"

I told him the deal, about buying and selling and all the showings. He said, "Get your butt up here. We'll figure something out."

I had some time to kill before he got home from his workout, so I remember heading to Clearwater Beach first, right by the place I'd just bought. I hadn't really looked around much at the outside and the landscaping but was relieved to see it was really nice. It looked first-class. I kicked off my flip-flops and took a walk on the beach, turning around to count the floors until I got to 25. I could so totally see living there. It was so much more than I ever dreamed of, and I could afford it.

Eric and I got together and had some iced tea by his pool. We talked about everything, and finally got around to the subject of golf. He'd asked me to play before, but I really didn't play golf then. Just a few rounds in my whole life and that was mostly before college. I knew hockey players were good golfers, so the intimidation factor was very real, too. He said, "Nah, it'll just be me and you. We'll get you all set up with clubs and all the gear, and we'll go to a driving range first. We'll let you just stick a toe in to see what you think. You're a great athlete. I think you'll be fine. C'mon man, just me and you. Let's do it."

We didn't waste any time. He took me to a nice golf store, and I picked out a set of cool TaylorMade clubs that felt good in my hands. Not too expensive, but not cheap, and obviously they were good clubs. I got Nike shoes and a bunch of Nike gear, from shirts, to shorts, to socks. I might not be any good, but I was gonna look bitchin' out there.

We went back to his house and took some plastic practice balls out to his backyard.

481

I had no idea what I was doing, but when I hit my first one it went straight and high, right to where I was trying to hit it. Eric just started laughing. Convulsively laughing. I'd never seen him laugh like that. I actually said, "Was it that bad?"

"No, it wasn't bad. It was freaking perfect. Somehow I knew it. That's just ridiculous."

It was getting later in the day and I was expecting the call from Jim, so we couldn't head to a range then. Eric said he'd get us a tee time the next day at a wide-open and very forgiving course he liked, and we'd meet there an hour early to hit a bucket of balls. My new adult golfing experience was going to happen. I was equal parts excited and scared, but the whole day had been rad as hell. I only called him because I had all day to kill. And there I was, fully decked out with clubs and everything else. And the next day we were actually going to play. Or something like that. I had no clue how it was going to go, but my goal was to have fun. I'd had enough stress in my life the last few years. Golf wasn't going to stress me out.

Turns out, I played way better than I thought. I couldn't chip or putt to save my life but I could get from the tee to the green pretty well. And we had a great time. We laughed the whole 18 holes. It was awesome. I was so stoked he'd pushed all those buttons to get me to do that.

We ended up playing a lot that summer, and I joined in with a bunch of different Lightning teammates. They could all crush it, man. They were great golfers. Maybe because they make a living using a long stick to hit a puck that's down at their feet, usually going fast, so hitting a stationary golf ball on the ground, also with a stick, just wasn't that hard. Who knows? They were damn good and I learned a lot. I'd never again be intimidated to play golf with someone. It was a way cool sport I'd ignored for too long. I was addicted,

Back to the condo adventure. We had six offers the first day. Two were above asking. Jim worked his magic with the other agents and finally got an offer that was $20,000 above asking. We took it. As it turned out, closing would be two days before I closed on the new place. The profits from the Cape Coral joint would go straight to the Clearwater home. Like clockwork, right?

Moving out meant throwing all my clothes in the car. Moving in was the same thing in reverse. I was going to stay in a hotel for the two nights, but Eric refused to let that happen. I stayed at his place with him and Carol. We had some great conversations. He was really interested in my stock market plans.

Before the night ended, I asked Eric about his Audi and what he thought of it. He loved that car. He was like me, not pretentious or looking for people to stare and drool over his car. It's just a car, but that doesn't mean it can't be really good, really solid, and really safe. I told him I thought I wanted to buy one and he left the room for a few seconds. He came back with a business card for a guy named D.J. at the Audi dealership. All he said was: "Call D.J. That's it, just call him. He'll get you the best possible deal, and he'll take the Camry off your hands for what it's really worth." I couldn't do any of that right away, but as soon as things were settled that was my next big goal.

A few days later, right before his preseason camp started, we played a round of golf and were having a beer at the club's bar. Eric said something that really got my attention.

"You know, I've been thinking about something," he said. "Someday soon, when my career is over, we ought to find something we can do together. You're so damn smart in so many ways I'm not. There ought to be a way to work together. What do you think?"

I said, "That's a rad idea. I'd be all for it. We just have to figure out what it is. I can tell you this, it won't be a restaurant. Under no circumstances are we buying, opening or even putting our names on a restaurant. And that goes for bars too. Those are sure ways to lose a lot of money. Chefs should own restaurants. Period. So no restaurants and no bars, right?"

Eric said, "Oh I'll agree to that. I don't want you emptying the wine inventory. But I get ya. Let's just keep it in the backs of our minds for a while. I have a season to get ready for. But seriously, I think we should and I think we will."

All I said was, "Me too, dude. Me too."

CHAPTER 48

Eric Olson

Training camp was going fine. I'd been through enough of these things to know how they went, what needed to be worked on, and how it all came together for the season opener. At least it's supposed to all come together then. I'd also seen enough wheels come off to spot the dawn of another bad season from a mile away.

We did our drills, we scrimmaged and we did more drills. We hit the weight room hard, and everyone seemed intent on getting out to a quick start. It felt like our chemistry was really good.

The biggest revelation in camp was a rookie. I clearly remember when Vinnie Lecavalier took the ice for the first time a couple years earlier, and we all knew he was special. What he lacked during those early years was a go-to linemate. A sidekick. Someone he could play off of and who could play off of him. We had that guy show up in the fall of 2000.

His name was Martin St. Louis. He was from Quebec, so his name was pronounced "Mar-TAN San Loo-EE." He played college hockey at the University of Vermont, and then bounced around the minor leagues for a couple of years. What was holding him back from an NHL career was his size. Take it from me, NHL coaches and GMs are fixated on size. If you don't have it, you have to overcome it.

After moving around to a number of teams in the International Hockey League and the American Hockey League, he finally lit up the scoreboard enough to get a look from the Calgary Flames. He played, but he just couldn't break through. You needed some sharp hockey vision to know what was there. You might also need a center named Lecavalier next to him on the ice.

The Flames thought so little of Martin they left him exposed in the NHL expansion draft. No one took him. So they bought out his contract and let him go. They just let him walk. When I learned all this history I was stunned. A few teams made him offers, but he said he chose Tampa Bay because we needed the help and he thought he'd get more playing time.

Marty was listed at 5-foot-9. I knew for a fact I was 5-9. He was shorter than me. Maybe an inch shorter.

The first time Marty was on the ice with Vinnie, playing right wing while Vinnie was at center, they looked like Mutt and Jeff. Vinnie was 6-foot-4. Marty looked like his kid brother out there. But they didn't play that way. They had chemistry from the drop of the first puck. And a ton of talent.

Maybe being so small helped him as a winger. Vinnie was a marked man. He was getting double-teamed all the time and pushed around with cross-checks and slashes. I'm sure the word around the league was: "To beat Tampa, just clamp down on Lecavalier." Marty could dodge around and swoop through traffic, kind of disappearing in the big trees, and most important he could get himself open. They made a really dynamic line with whoever was on the left wing. I didn't know how long it would take, but I felt I could see the future of the Tampa Bay Lightning. It was right there in front of us.

When the opener came around, Coach Ludzik was back at the white board drawing up our hopes, goals and ambitions. Once again, he broke the season up into four 20-game blocks. "This is what I need from you," he said. Loudly. "Right now, I need 20 games of your life. Twenty games where you give it everything you've got. Leave it on the ice. If you're not totally exhausted when we come back to the room after the final buzzer, you left something out there. I need 20 games right now, gentlemen. And tonight, I need one game. It's up to you. How good do you want to be?"

Well, we didn't lose. We tied the Islanders 3-3. At least we got one point. That was better than losing.

In that first block of 20 we went 8-10-2. Compared to the last couple years, that wasn't all that bad. We just needed to keep improving as we went. Vinnie and Marty were getting smoother by the game. Kevin Weekes was going to be our main goalie. We'd have to ride him because the back-ups weren't as good as Weeksie. Dan Cloutier was the first backup and he'd come up to the NHL with the Rangers, not long after I left. There really wasn't much to call up from the minors, so those two were going to have to suck it up. Weeksie was a solid fundamental goalie. You could have confidence in him doing his job and not making mistakes. But again, I seemed to find myself staring at breakaways way too often. You can't lay that on the goalies. They were doing the best they could.

The second 20 was our downfall. Maybe the pregame speech didn't sink in as well. Maybe the guys had tuned Coach Ludzik out. Maybe they just gave up after it all went to hell on us. We got beat. We got creamed. We got embarrassed. It was deja vu, and it wasn't any fun. When you're giving up five, six, seven, or even eight goals a game, it's brutal. I felt I was playing my game, but I was overwhelmed. We went 4-14-3 in that second 20. We obviously didn't give Coach 20 games of our lives. On too many nights, a lot of guys just mailed it in.

I remember our 39th game, because that's when it all came to a head. Coach kept a big chart of the current 20-game segment on the bulletin board. With a win, someone would color the corresponding box green. With a loss, it would get colored red. A tie was blue. The damn chart looked like it was on fire, there was so much red on it. Thankfully

485

it didn't go on the road with us. It was too vivid of a reminder about how bad we were playing. After an 8-3 loss to Ottawa, Coach Ludzik got the word. He had been let go. The team brought in John Tortorella as the new head coach. Only a few of us had ever heard of him.

Torts had played college hockey and minor league hockey. He'd coached in the AHL and earned a spot behind the bench in the NHL as an assistant coach for Buffalo, Phoenix and the Rangers. The Lightning job was his first NHL head coaching gig. His first game as head coach was the 20th game of Ludzik's second segment. We lost in Chicago 7-4.

When we got back home to Tampa, we all noticed something as soon as we walked in the room, but we only whispered about it to each other. The 20-game poster, full of red ink, was gone. It was torn up and in bits, right there in the trash can below the bulletin board. None of us knew who had done it, but the consensus was it was our new head coach.

Did we rebound and play our butts off for Tortorella? I wish I could say we did. We didn't. We just mucked along like the Tampa Bay Lightning we'd become. Were we happy? Absolutely not. We were satisfied? Also no. We were used to it? I'm afraid we were.

We were tightening up a little bit, defensively. Coach Torts had some schemes that forced all the defensemen to make it a priority to be back, be sound, and not make stupid passes that turned into turnovers right in front of Weeksie. It was a work in progress, and I could still see the foundation of a very good team. We could score, and Marty and Vinnie could bring any crowd to its feet when they got going, but we had so far to go. And poor Weeksie needed a break. Cloutier got regular starts the last couple months of the season.

In early March, we were playing the San Jose Sharks at home. Brooks and Carol were at the game, sitting next to each other. That's basically what I remember. In the first period, a big veteran winger for the Sharks went after a loose puck in the corner. I got there first. And then the lights went out.

Like I said, I don't remember any of this. I was out cold on the ice. This time, it took so long for me to come around they brought a stretcher out. I was being carried off into the Zamboni tunnel so that they could put me in an ambulance and take me to the hospital. According to Carol, she and Brooks managed to get there just as I was getting shoved in. My eyes were open, but I couldn't talk and I really wasn't aware of where I was or what was happening.

Carol managed to find out where they were taking me, and she and Brooks sprinted to her car to drive over there.

When they arrived, the people at the desk went into their "We don't know anything about this" routine. If a person who is even slightly famous gets brought in, the hospital staff's job turns into being gatekeepers. They finally called in the supervisor and Carol said it took her 15 minutes of pleading to get through to the guy who was at the desk pretending she didn't exist. She finally realized she had proof hanging around her neck.

It was her Lightning "Full Access" credential with her photo on it and her name, That got his attention.

The guy said, "You can go up to the third floor. Wait in the hallway. They'll let you know when you can go in. Now, who's he?" He was pointing at Brooks. Carol said, "He's family. He's with me." Later on, Brooks said, "She wasn't messing around. I think the dude was scared of her."

By the time they let them in my room, I was coming back to my senses, but still groggy. It had been a bad one. The worst ever. Carol gave me a kiss. I thought Brooks was going to do the same thing for a second, but he gave me whatever hug he could with me flat on my back. With the hug came some cheek-to-cheek contact. Later on, he'd tell me he planned to do that and said, "That's like a man kiss. Same thing, but no lips. I had to draw the line somewhere."

The doctors had checked me over, given me a scan, and had done all sorts of tests. They finally released me just after midnight. By then, the Lightning's PR guy was there to get statements and facts for a press release. All I wanted to do was go home. I had a headache that wouldn't stop and felt like it was going to blow the top of my head off.

Carol told Brooks to go home. She had this. I learned later that Brooks had to remind Carol that she'd driven them both to the arena, so his car was at my house. I have zero memory of the ride home or the fact Brooks was in the back seat.

They wheeled me out to her car, and all I had on was one of those thin hospital gowns that are open in the back. They had gotten me out of my uniform, destroying my jersey in the process by cutting it off, and the PR guy did what he was told and took all my gear back to the rink. I was so happy I was going home and we had an attached garage. I was thinking clearly enough to mutter, "Good thing we're not on the road. I can't see walking through a hotel lobby like this."

I went straight to bed, I remember that, but sleep wasn't going to happen for a while. I felt dizzy every time I closed my eyes, and there was so much pressure in my head. It honestly felt like my brain was trying to bust out of my skull. The doctors had said, "Take a few aspirin, but nothing else. Absolutely no narcotic pain pills. You're going to have to ride this out." I took three aspirin with a big glass of water and felt like throwing it back up immediately. Somehow, I didn't, but Carol saw the close call and went and got a trash bin for the side of the bed.

Carol wanted to know if I wanted her in bed with me, or if she should leave me alone. Talking made my head hurt, but I managed to say, "I'm sorry, sweetie. I just need to be alone. I just want to turn all the lights off and lie still. But please come check on me when you can. I'm so sorry this happened. I never saw him coming."

She gently rubbed my head and said, "I'm so sorry for you, babe. You don't deserve this. It's not your fault. Get some rest. I'll look in on you every hour."

I guess I did fall asleep, because what I remember most is waking up. The pressure in my head was just enormous. I'd never felt anything like it. I was still getting dizzy spells, too, and basically I just felt disconnected from reality. Carol told me later that Coach Tortorella called to check in, as did a bunch of players. She told them I was OK but it was a bad one and I just wanted to lie as still as possible in a dark room. She told Coach to call anytime he wanted for updates.

It was just awful, and it didn't seem to be letting up at all. I'm a hockey player. Pain and injuries are things I know far too well. We're all like that. You play 82 games in a regular NHL season and I bet you have some minor injury, or multiple ones, in at least half those games. You just try to play through it. I could barely stand this. This was a whole new level of awful.

By the third day, it was finally easing up but I wanted nothing to do with getting up and moving around. I could tell the depression was setting in. It's a giant heavy blanket weighing you down. You literally feel like you can't move, or if you did your head would explode.

Brooks called and Carol told him to come on over. When he came into the room he looked really worried.

"Do I look that bad?" I asked.

"No, you look like Miss America. But this must be a bad one if you're still in bed."

"Yeah, it is," I said. "It's got me beaten down and I don't even want to get up. Hopefully by tomorrow I'll be able to get out of bed and move around a little. I think it's getting better."

Carol came in then, so all three of us were wondering what to do or what to say. I went first.

"I told you both about this. The next one and I'm done. Well, the concussion gods obviously wanted to go out with a bang. This last one is my worst one. It's still killing me, and I'm still in a fog. But that's it. I'm done. I'm never going to play another game in the NHL, no matter what."

Carol was nodding and crying a little. Brooks was just looking down and shaking his head. He finally said, "I'm so sorry, buddy. This should never have happened. It was a cheap shot you never saw coming."

I said, "We all get hit by those every night. Usually you hop right back up and just snipe at the guy, calling him every name in the book as you chase him back down the ice. This time, for me, there was no getting up. I don't remember any of it other than chasing that puck into the corner at full speed."

It took a few more days before I was fully lucid, but the fog was still there and my head hurt massively if I made any quick movements with it. But day by day it was getting better. I was even eating, but only because I had to. I had zero appetite.

I was at the table eating a slice of cinnamon toast, when Carol sat down next to me. She said, "Tell me how you are. Tell me honestly."

I said, "It's getting better, and the depression is getting better, but it's still got me. On a 1 to 10, I'm a 5."

She said, "OK, now tell me how your heart feels. What's all this feeling like to you? Are you even able to process it?"

I remember taking a deep breath and thinking about what I wanted to say. It went something like this:

"When I told you and Brooks that I'd be done after the next one, that was me starting the process. I was getting prepared, because I knew there'd be a next one. In one way, I'm glad it's a severe one, because that leaves me no way out. If it was a mild one I got over by the end of the game, I might have tried to rationalize it as 'OK, that one doesn't count' and that would've been untrue to me and very unfair to you. By the time I woke up in the ambulance and figured out where I was, I knew it. I was done.

"Babe, I've gotten so much out of this game. In a lot of ways, it completely defined me for most of my life. Only in the last couple of years have I been able to see what else is out there. We're going to start a family, and I need to be fully present and fully functional for that. I guess we don't have to worry about missing a game for the baby's birth.

"I think I'm coming to grips with it pretty well, and I hardly feel any sadness. When the last game hurts this bad, you just want it to stop. I don't want to go through it again. I don't want to lose anymore. I don't want to put all that effort into it and have some jackass end my career, but if it wasn't him it would've been someone else. I'm almost there, and I will get there. This is the right thing and it feels like a relief. I mean that. And I love you."

She said, "Can I hug you?"

"I wish you would. But gently."

I stood up, a little wobbly, and she put her arms around me. I had to say, "You're making me cry and it hurts my head. I love you, Carol. I don't know what I'd do without you. And now you're married to some bum who's about to be jobless."

She asked me, "Have you thought about how all this is going to go down? Like, when are you going to tell the team?"

"No, I haven't really thought about that yet. I want to get better first. Right now, any big decisions I make might be the wrong ones. I'll get it sorted out. I do know this, right off hand, I'm not telling them anything until I'm back to 100 percent. If I have any setbacks, my team insurance will cover everything. The day I walk away, we'll have no insurance. That's just the way it's gotta be."

She nodded, and said, "I'm with you. I'm always with you."

A few days later, I felt a lot more like myself again. I was still battling some dizziness at night, but the pain was mostly gone. I was running out of time if my plan was not to tell the team until I had to.

Carol had talked to my parents, and kept them up to date. She said my mom's response was, "This is the way it should be. He played his heart out and was great at it. He made enough money for you two to be set and your family will want for nothing. I'm relieved he's going to be OK. I thought he was playing with fire coming back from the last one. And he was. He made the right decision. I'm relieved."

I talked to my financial guy, Phil, and told him all about it.

"Hey, Eric, I'm really sorry to hear that and I hope you're feeling better every day. You're all set on this end. Everything is in place. You don't have to earn another nickel if you want to go that route. So don't worry about anything. Just let me know when you pull the trigger on retirement and I'll keep getting you the monthly updates."

489

I also talked to my agent, Robert.

He listened and said something like, "Once I got word that they had taken you out on a stretcher, my first thought was: 'He's done. He won't come back from this.' And I felt a sort of sense of relief for you. You're so damn dedicated to the game, I was worried you had blinders on. The last concussion was a mild one, and you never hesitated to get right back to work. I'll admit that worried me.

"It's been one of the great pleasures of my career to work with you. You're a role model, a leader, and a very sensible and honest man. Don't lose touch. If there is ever anything I can do for you, just let me know. And that's not one of those hollow 'I'm getting off the phone now' cliches. I mean it 100 percent. If you want advice, or a good word put out somewhere, I'm here. You take care of yourself. Be a good husband. And hopefully soon, a fantastic dad. I'll be thinking about you."

About a week after the concussion, I felt good enough to head to the rink to meet with Coach Torts and the trainers. I wanted their evaluation. It would be good to see the guys in the room again. It felt like a year since I'd been with them.

They were playing Columbus that night, so I went in around 3 and went straight to the training room. Coach came in to join us.

The trainers talked to me for a long time, just getting a feel for how I was speaking and stringing words together, I imagine. They acted like it was just conversation, but I knew it had a purpose. Then they started some tests. Balance, hearing, and bright lights were the parts I remember most. The one where they had me look straight up and spin around was a failure. I got really dizzy and had to sit down. And I hated having a bright flashlight shined in my eyes. I don't think I would've liked that no matter what kind of shape I was in.

At the end, the trainers and Torts said, "We'll be right back, just hang tight here."

A few minutes later they walked back in and Coach said, "Oly, you've still got symptoms, and some of them are pretty serious. We can't put you back out on the ice. It wouldn't be safe. We're going to put you on the injured list and it will be for the rest of the season. I'm really sorry to have to tell you that."

I said, "Coach, this one was bad. I came here for you guys to take a look, and I admitted to myself that it might be bad news. I could also tell I wasn't anywhere near ready to skate again, much less hit guys or get hit. So I'm good with it. I just want to get better. Do we have any other plans? Should I come in every day?"

The head trainer said, "Take another week at home. Relax. Stay in calm situations. Rest all you can. We'll revisit in a week, and if we think you're ready for some stationary bike work, and maybe a few weights, we'll cross that bridge. But right now, I think you have a feel for what helps you and what sets you back. Go back home and follow your instincts. There aren't any pills for this. It just has to heal. Right now, I wouldn't even want you at home games up in the press box. It's loud here, and that can trigger all sorts of reactions. Sorry."

I asked if it was OK if I could stop in the room and see some of the guys. They said that was fine, but don't go nuts.

It must've been around 4, so just a few guys were filtering in. Everybody seemed glad to see me, and most comments were, "Man, you were out cold. We were all really worried about you. We've been getting updates but it's better to see you here in person." It was good. The hardest part about all of this post-concussion stuff was not seeing the guys and not being part of it. It was my new world.

I drove home and Carol got home from work right after me. We went out to the pool and I eased myself into the water. It felt great. I had hardly been out of bed or out of my sweats for a week.

I got out and toweled off, then sat next to Carol. I filled her in on the meeting and the exam, and told her what they were doing with me. I was out for the rest of the year.

"They were worried I was going to argue with them, or be crushed by the news. I told them I knew I wasn't close to ready, and I agreed this plan was the best. It was funny, we came at it from totally different directions. I felt like I had to at least act a little bummed out, but it was good news to me. I come first now. My health is my priority. Hockey is a million miles away.

"And the really good news is that I have two paychecks left this season. You know, if they had pushed me to get back and been really aggressive about it, I would've retired right there on the spot. I went in ready to do that if it took a turn like that. Had I done that, no more salary because I would've initiated it. I'll go back in a week and they'll look at me again. Sounds like the most aggressive things they might consider are a stationary bike and some very light weights. I'll do that. It's the best thing. We'll put together a plan to pick a day to tell them I'm retiring once the season is over. I'm sure they'll want to do a press conference."

She asked me how I felt about getting paid. I said, "There's a part of me feeling a little guilty knowing what I know. Knowing I was going to quit anyway. But babe, I earned this the hard way. The whole time I've been with the Lightning I've earned it all. It's in my contract, and the contract runs until the season is over."

Rick Dudley was the GM then. He'd taken over after Jacques Demers was let go. Jacques had convinced the team to name him head coach and GM, and that rarely works. I guess some guys think they can do it all, but at the NHL level it's about impossible. Rick was a good guy and had everyone's respect. He communicated well and talked to all of us regularly. Right before game time that night, when Carol and I were eating dinner, he called.

"Eric, I just wanted to touch base and hear your voice, young man. I know you met with Torts and the trainers today, and now you're out for the season. That was a wicked blow you took. I was trapped up in the press box and couldn't get down there, but from what I've heard you wouldn't have known I was there anyway. I was really seriously concerned. I'm glad you're beginning to feel better.

"And listen, the other reason I called is to let you know I'll carve out some time as soon as you feel up to having a meeting. You've been all we could have hoped for when we made the trade for you. You worked harder than anyone. You were a leader. It hasn't been good, but I'm telling you right now I can't even fathom how bad it would've been if we didn't have you, and your steadying influence, on this team. If you're interested, we can talk about some options we might have when your career is over. I've been around. I know enough to realize you're right on a razor's edge right now. We should have that talk soon. I want to have it, if you do."

I told him I'd be very interested, and that I just wanted to take the next few weeks to see what kind of progress I could make. We'd see where we stood at that point. I thanked him profusely and told him I'd see him soon. I absolutely did not see that coming. I never factored a conversation like that into my plans.

When I hung up, I looked at Carol and slightly shook my head. She asked me what was up.

"That was Rick Dudley, our GM. He was checking on me, but then he shifted gears. He asked if I'd be interested in having a meeting to talk about what other things I could do for the Lightning whenever my career was over. I think he's pretty smart. He knows I won't ever play again. He also knows my only option to play would be to go the free agent route. He wants me to be part of the organization. I never even thought of that. I'm honored. It will be an interesting conversation to have."

"So what does that mean? What kind of role? A coach?"

"No, I think if they wanted me behind the bench it would be Torts making that overture, and maybe he will once I actually retire, but who knows. I'm guessing some sort of assistant in the front office. He knows I know the game. He knows I know players. Maybe he's got an idea. We'll see. As soon as I officially retire, we'll have that meeting. It's gonna be interesting, for sure."

Over the next few days, my other new future project began to take shape in my head. I called Brooks and had him come over from his new condo on the beach, which was drop-dead gorgeous, by the way. An incredible place.

We got together and I laid it out for him.

"Here's what I'm thinking of doing, and this could be the thing we do together. I'll form an LLC first. An LLC is kind of a new thing. It's like a half step between private business and a corporation. It stands for Limited Liability Company, and it protects the principals from personal liabilities, including losses. And, it allows you to earn income that goes to the LLC. If you want to pay yourself from the proceeds, you can do that. There are no taxes on the profits at the LLC level. They get passed through to the members who draw salaries from the LLC.

"I see it this way. I'll be the CEO and you will be the president. We'll be the only two officers and the only two employees. I'll seed it with about a half-million dollars. We'll both be authorized to access that. My thinking is that you'll do the legwork. I want to invest in some stocks and mutual funds, to build a solid portfolio, and you'll do that for me. If, way down the road, anyone wants us to provide that service for them, we can talk about that. We might not even want to. For now, I see this as our chance for you to use your smarts and your knowledge to benefit both of us. I don't think we need the overhead of a real office for the near future. We both have offices at home. Throw in a FAX machine and email, and we're up and running. What do you think?"

He smiled and said, "Well that's a helluva concept. I'm learning more every day about accumulating stocks, and I'm digging into things like mutual funds. There's a lot to learn, but I'm a pretty good sponge.

"I can tell you this, just to be straight and upfront, I don't see the stock market as a game. I'm into accumulating blue chip stocks that have long-term track records. No 'stock of the week' startups for me. I'm into IBM, Microsoft, and a few other legacy companies. Some of those stocks can be pricey, so I don't dive in all at once. I accumulate over months. I don't bite off too much at a time, but it won't be long before I have a pretty good interest in those firms. How's that fit with what you're thinking?"

I said, "It sounds like exactly what I would want to do. I don't like risk. I don't like wild chances that can hit big or bite you in the butt. That's why I want to work with you. You'll be free to handle your own stuff just like now. The LLC will be my stuff, and you'll be authorized to run the business. I think we'll make a great team. Sounds like we both need a new team now anyway, right?"

We agreed with a handshake.

The short-term plan was for me to set up the LLC with the state of Florida. These days, that takes about 10 minutes online. Back then it was a stack of forms that had to be mailed in. It could easily take two months. Once I was approved, I'd open a new business bank account for the LLC and Brooks and I would go sign the forms for that. When everything was in place, I'd put in the seed money. My plan, which I'd tell Phil about, was to use those last two paychecks to get things rolling. That would be nearly $600,000. I didn't want Phil to invest those paychecks into something long-term. I wanted them to come straight to me. I'd hold them in my savings account until we were ready to launch

The two of us were off on a new adventure.

Back in the hockey world, I went back in for my follow-up with the trainers. They still thought I should avoid any kind of strenuous physical activity. I asked about swimming, since I had a pool at home, and they were all for it as long as I wasn't trying to lower the Olympic record for the 100-meter freestyle. Just nice easy laps.

Just a few days after that, the season came to another abrupt end for the Lightning. Coach Torts had gotten a little more out of them but I could tell on TV that I was missed. The back end was a mess. Guys out of position, guys just poking their sticks in rather than hitting anybody. Guys making blind passes from behind the goal that always seemed to be intercepted and then in the net. I was pretty sad. They finished with a record of 24-47-6. Not good.

I gave it about a week and called Torts. I said I wanted to come in and meet with him and Rick Dudley, if he could set that up. Torts called me back and said, "How 'bout tomorrow at 10 o'clock?"

I said I'd be there.

I was right on time and so were they. We sat in Rick's office and I jumped right in.

"Guys, this was a bad one. It's still around. I still have dizziness and a fog around me a lot of the time, but it's slowly getting better. I just can't envision playing again. I can't risk it. Carol and I are trying to start a family. I want to be the world's best father and husband, and I can't do that if I'm out there risking my brain by playing. I'm pretty sure you weren't going to offer me a new playing contract anyway, so this probably doesn't come as horrible news for you. I've decided I'm going to retire. I'm settled on that. I wanted you two to hear it first."

They were both nodding. Torts said, "I saw this coming when you came in the first time. From what I've heard you've had a few others since you came into the league, some you just played through. You didn't play through this one. You really shouldn't play again. I'll be sad to lose you. I was just getting to know you. You need to take care of yourself, your wife and hopefully a new baby soon. You're making the right call."

Rick said, "Eric, I'll speak for myself and I totally support this. I saw it coming when they wheeled you out on a stretcher. I knew what that meant. It broke my heart. You were such a key cog in the machine here; you'll be impossible to replace. But I mentioned to you before that there could be some interesting things for you to do here, and you could really help me. I'd like to take a week to confer with some of the other department heads and the player development staff. I want to find the perfect fit, and if you think it's something you'd like to do, we'd love to have you here long-term. I hope you still want to be part of the Lightning organization. Can I call you soon and set up the next meeting? And in the meantime, I suspect the PR department will want to do a press conference with you, to let you announce your retirement. I hope you'll do that, too. Those guys will set it up."

I said, "Rick, I'm looking forward to that next meeting. I'm retiring from playing hockey, but I'd love to keep working in the sport. And I'm good with the press conference. Good gosh, we better put my wife in the back of the room. She'll be crying from the moment the mic is turned on."

I heard from the PR department later that day. They asked if they could set up the press conference two days later. I said that would be fine. It felt like I'd just done the last one, which was to announce my extension.

Just about everyone has seen the typical retirement press conference on TV. They are usually very emotional, and the biggest toughest guys in the world have a hard time getting through it. I did too. I made it, but not without a few Kleenex as I went. When it was over, that was really a feeling of finality. The book was closed. It wasn't probably over. It wasn't that it might be over. It was over.

So there we were. New pages turned. New pages yet to turn. It was hard to digest how fast this all happened for both Brooks and me. More reason to understand why you should appreciate every day you get to be a professional athlete. It can all be gone in a blink.

Time to set up that LLC.

CHAPTER 49

Brooks Bennett

I sold the Cape Coral condo, got the funds and closed on the new Clearwater place. I'd have a mortgage, but it wasn't bad. I saw this place as two distinctly different things. It was really cool and it made me happy. And, it was a helluva Florida Gulf Coast investment. It was going to be market-proof, I figured. There's a thing about the Gulf Coast housing market. When the U.S. economy goes south, properties on the Gulf become very attractive to Europeans. The dollar becomes cheap and they can swoop in and get dream homes at extraordinary prices. I'd done a lot of research on housing prices, and in times when other regions were tanking and people were foreclosing, the Gulf Coast stayed consistent, sometimes even setting record highs. This was a great investment, and it was spectacular.

It was so beyond anything I'd ever dreamed. I could sit on the massive balcony for hours, especially around sunset, and just go all Zen out there. In the mornings, I'd get up, make a cup of tea and walk out into the main living area to be mesmerized. The view never ceased to blow me away.

I hadn't been there more than a week or so when I decided to pull the trigger on the last big purchase I was going to make. I called Eric's buddy D.J. and gave him the plan. He said, "Be here at 3:30 and we'll make this happen."

When I got there, he had three Audi A4 sedans lined up in front of the showroom. One was dark blue, another silver, and the last one white. Basically they were all the same. Totally loaded with options and six-cylinder engines. I was just picking the color. I drove the dark blue one and loved it. What an amazing car. I told D.J., "It would be totally like me to take the white or silver one, but I love this blue color. Let's figure out how to make it mine."

We went to his office and he pulled out the invoice. He said, "OK, here's our starting point. We have a few promotions going, including a $2,000 discount for new buyers. That's supposed to be off the sticker price, of course. It won't be. I know how to make this happen."

Within 30 minutes he'd found a couple of other promotional discounts, he'd had my Camry appraised and then told the appraiser, "This isn't going to work. This guy was meticulous with this car. It's in perfect condition. I need more to make this go." He was acting like I was a tyrant customer who was beating him up.

It also happened to be the last week of their sales quarter, which I hadn't known but that's probably why D.J. was so eager to get me in there right away. Boom. There went another $2,000 off the number, thanks to the end of the quarter. I don't totally understand how all this works, but the dealers get a better discount from the factory based on units sold. At the end of the quarter the dealers are ready to deal if one or two cars will put them over a threshold. In the end, I put $12,000 down, they maxed out what they could do on the Camry, and I took out a loan for about $9,000. I drove it home. It had been a helluva rad time for the surfer boy. New condo, new car, and about to start a new business at some point. Whenever Eric was ready.

Eric's season was winding down. The team was once again pretty terrible. I don't know how he put up with that. I'm just a casual fan, so I had zero clue why his fellow defensemen were always getting caught up ice, or turning the wrong way, or even doing the matador's "Ole" move when they let a forward from the other team come right at them. Meanwhile, Eric was busting his butt trying to do his job and cover for their mistakes. On a lot of nights, it looked like amateur hour out there. Five goals, six, seven, even eight. An 8-1 loss in the NHL is about like a 20-1 loss in MLB. Which is something I could relate to.

Carol and I went to a home game with about a month left in the season, just to support him. That was the worst atmosphere I'd ever experienced at the Ice Palace. It was a bad team, after multiple years of being a bad team. There was no life in the crowd, and about half the seats were empty. You could take a nap in there.

I don't remember who they were playing, but I will never forget the hit Eric took in the corner. It was cheap as hell. A guy six inches taller and 40 pounds heavier took a run at him from behind as Eric tried to freeze the puck up against the boards. It was a sickening sound. It was a crunch, followed by a bang, followed by silence. Eric was crumpled on the ice, on his right side at first, but then inertia caused him to fall mostly face down. The scary part was that he never moved his head or his arms. He was totally limp.

Carol and I were speechless at first. We were kind of frozen. She finally said, "We have to get down there." I just followed. Fortunately, she had a permanent credential that got her basically everywhere, and on any night when I'd be going with her to the game, Eric made sure to have a one-game credential that allowed all the same stuff for me. We ran right past the security guy and were in the Zamboni tunnel, where an ambulance was backing in, lights flashing.

They brought Eric through on a gurney and I could see his eyes were open but they were still kind of rolling around. As they slid him into the ambulance, Carol was pleading with everyone nearby to find out where they were taking him.

"I'm Eric's wife! I need to get to the hospital! WHERE ARE YOU TAKING HIM?"

She was shouting and demanding answers, but everyone was ignoring her. Finally after he was fully loaded, and a trainer had gotten in the back with him, one of the EMTs looked at her and mouthed, "Tampa General."

Carol said, "We gotta go. Let's get there."

She knew her way out the back door of the arena, which is where the players and their wives parked. We were in the car and rolling as the ambulance took off. The hospital wasn't too far away, but the last thing Carol wanted was to get lit up by a squad car if we ran any red lights following the ambulance. As worked up as she was, a traffic stop could take 30 minutes and could end really badly if the stress of the moment got away from her. She was smart enough to be aware of that. We hit every red light, of course. By the time we got to the hospital, she parked in a small lot right by the emergency room entrance.

We went inside and there was no sign of Eric. We went to the desk and she asked where they had taken him.

"I'm sorry, ma'am. I have no record of that. It can take up to an hour for our system to update after the floor personnel enter the information. You can just wait over there," she said, pointing to a jam-packed room full of trauma patients. Carol was having none of that.

"No, actually you're going to tell me where they took my husband. He plays for the Tampa Bay Lightning. He got hurt and they brought him here. You are going to tell me what floor he is on and how I get there. That is what is going to happen. Do you hear me?"

"I'm sorry, ma'am, it's not our policy to divulge any of that."

"He's my husband and he was out cold when they put him in the ambulance. If he was your husband would you take no for an answer?"

The woman just stared at her, clearly taken aback by the question. She buzzed her supervisor instead.

A burly guy in scrubs came out, and we had to go through the whole spiel all over again. "He's my husband. I know he's here. I was standing next to him when they put him in the ambulance. He plays for the Lightning. He got hurt very badly. Did you hear me? HE'S MY HUSBAND!"

The guy tried to calm her down, which wasn't going to happen, and he finally said something like: "How do I know you're his wife?"

Carol looked down, saw her laminated credential still around her neck, then held it in her hand and put it in front of his face.

"This is me. That's how you know."

He pulled us aside and said, softly, "Take that elevator to floor three. Go to the desk and tell them who you are. I promise you, they will not let you into the room until they check him out and get a read on what's happened to him. Let them know you're there and sit as close as you can to the nurse's station. Make eye contact if you can."

"Thank you. We're going up there," she said.

"OK, but who is this guy?" he asked, pointing at me.

"He's family. He's coming with me."

We headed to the elevator.

We checked in at the desk, and Carol was ahead of the game this time. She held up her credential and said, "I'm Eric Olson's wife. I know he's here and no one will tell me a thing about him. He was out cold when they put him in the ambulance, and I need to see him or hear from a doctor. LIke right now."

The nurse said, "I understand completely. I know how this is. Right now the team is in the room with him and they are checking all his vitals and his condition. If you'll have a seat right over there, I'll call you when you can go in."

We sat against the wall and it seemed to take forever. It was probably 15 minutes. A couple of doctors and nurses came out of a room, and one of the doctors stopped to talk to the nurse behind the desk. At one point, he looked over at us and nodded his head. He came our way.

"Are you Eric's wife?"

"Yes, I'm Carol. How is he?"

"He's going to be OK, but he's banged up. He also had a small laceration between his eyebrows, so we stitched that up. That was no big deal. Has he had a concussion before?"

She told him the history, and he just nodded. All he said was, "I see."

Then, after a moment, he said, "You'll be able to go in and see him very soon. I'll have a nurse come get you."

Right about then, one of the Lightning PR guys showed up. I don't know his name. And I don't know how he managed to get through the defensive shield, but he did. He had a credential, too, so I'm sure that helped.

They finally said we could go in and see him, and Carol went first. She gave him a kiss and rubbed his hair a little. He looked a little groggy, but his eyes were focused and he seemed sharp.

"Oh, man, so happy to see you," he said. "Was it hard to get up here?"

Carol said, "You have no idea, but we're here. Brooks is here, too." I was standing right behind her, but he'd only been looking at Carol.

"Oh, hey man. I'm glad you're here. I might need your help getting into the car. Sorry about this. I don't remember anything. I remember skating toward the corner, and then I started to wake up in the ambulance. I thought I was dreaming or something. It was really weird."

I gave him a hug and said, "I'm just glad I'm talking to you right now. That was bad."

"I guess it was. But this was it. That was my last shift in a hockey game. I can't have any more of these. I'm done. It's over. And man, it hurts like hell. I hurt all over but my head is killing me."

The PR guy came in around then, and Eric said, "Hey, Justin, what are you doing here?"

"Well, I'm trying to get some info on your injuries, but no one will tell me anything. And I have to gather up your gear and get it back to the rink. Look at this."

He held up Eric's jersey from that night and it was in about five pieces. There was no way to remove it without cutting it off him. How they got his skates and all the pads off, I will never know. All he had on was one of the light blue surgical gown things. I doubt he had anything on underneath it. After the PR guy hauled his stuff away, a nurse came in and discharged Eric. She had a list of things he should and shouldn't do, and she warned him, "This is probably going to get worse before it gets better. There's not much you can take for it. It's a brain injury. Stay still, stay in a dark and quiet environment, and try to get some rest. Tomorrow, you can take some aspirin."

The nurse helped him into a wheelchair and Carol stayed right with him. I took the keys and went to move the car to the emergency room doorway.

When Eric got up and slid into the car, the theory that he had next to nothing else on under that robe was proven correct. It was a full moon rising. All he had on was his jock strap and a pair of hospital socks. The young PR guy had taken everything else back to the arena, not realizing that Eric wouldn't have even a sweaty T-shirt to put back on. I don't think Eric cared.

We got him back to their place, where my car was, and Carol said, "Go on home Brooks. I got this. We'll be fine."

I tried to debate the point, but she'd have none of it. And, I reminded myself to never be on the wrong side of Carol when she was hell-bent on getting what she wanted. It had really been something to watch. Any family member of another patient might have had to sit there in the waiting room, with people holding bloody rags to their heads, until they brought their loved one down. Carol took complete control. She was not to be denied.

I could tell that Eric was in for a really awful week. I'd never seen anyone so miserable and I don't care to again. The pain had to be terrible, because I'd never seen him like that before. This guy was tough. He played hockey! On any given night those guys get the hell beaten out of them and they never miss a beat. Nobody is tougher than a hockey player.

Most times, he could barely speak above a whisper. He just said the pressure in his head was so bad his brain felt like it was trying to bust out of his skull.

I went and saw him every day after things stabilized, and it seemed to take forever for him to make any progress. He's never said this to me, but I could see some fear in his eyes after that first week. He just wasn't getting much better, and I could tell he was worried about it.

Finally, after maybe 10 days, the pressure and head pain started to ease up. He felt like he'd turned a corner. He told me he still had bouts of dizziness, especially in the dark, and his balance was pretty screwed up, but he was feeling better.

By the middle of the next week, I felt like he was back. He was lucid, engaged, and not in nearly as much pain. One day, when Carol and I were both there, we sat around their dining table and he laid it all out.

"I think I might have said this in the hospital, but that's all kind of hazy to me now. I made a promise to myself, and to you guys. The next one would be the last one. That's the way it is. I'm getting better, and I'm never going through this again. They want me in the trainer's room tomorrow, and the staff will look me over and get their take on it. I don't want to retire until the season is over, but that's just a few weeks from now. It's gonna happen though. I will retire. It's over."

He turned toward me and said, "Brooks, when you were recovering from the shoulder surgery, I felt so hopeless, because I couldn't help you. It was such a slow process for you, but you got through it and you came back one more time. It was so damn impressive I'll never forget it. You knew when to walk away, and I'll always respect that. Now it's time for me to do it, too. All these things we've done in unison, whether we planned to or not, and now this. We're both done with our pro sports careers, but we're not done with our lives. Once all this is settled and I officially retire, we'll get to work on the LLC and have some fun with that. Right?"

"Damn right, dude."

Things worked out pretty well in the retirement world for Eric. The team put him on the long-term injured list and at the end of the year they declined to pick up his option. Yet another thing we had in common. When teams had the option to keep us, they passed on both of us. We'd sure been through a lot together. Not all of it good, either.

There was some good news though. When the team put him on the injured list for the rest of the season, he continued to get paid. To this day, I believe the Lightning knew he wanted to quit on the spot, and that's why they put him on the list. That way, he'd get two more paychecks. I think they truly believed he'd earned that. Maybe I'm too naive or I saw more than what was there, but I still believe they did that as a thank-you for the hard work he'd put in. It was a class move.

I'd say about a month and a half after the injury, he was fully back to normal. The season was ending, the Lightning got to go play golf rather than be bothered by those pesky playoffs, and the team was setting up his retirement press conference. When the day came, Carol sat up front and I stood in the back. I had never had the chance to do one of those deals, and I never really thought I would. I was just the shell of the pitcher I had been and I walked away. I kind of slinked off into the night. I figured I would always be part of the question, "Do you remember Brooks Bennett? Whatever happened to him?"

Eric was still in the prime of his career. Still at his best. And a terrible injury ended it all in one split second. He deserved to have a press conference to say goodbye. I knew it was going to be emotional. I was hoping Carol had plenty of tissues.

It was really great. The team people had nothing but raves to say about him. Marty Lecavalier spoke and said something like "I only got to play with Eric a few years, but I probably owe him at least one-third of my goals. He could find me anywhere on the ice and put the puck right on my tape. He was one of the most special players I ever played with. One of a kind. I'll miss you, buddy. You made me better."

Finally it was Eric's turn. He adjusted the mic, coughed once or twice and took a deep breath. I don't remember any of the exact words, mostly because everyone in the room seemed to be crying, even a few reporters. I remember him thanking the New York

Rangers for giving him a chance. The little runt from Roseau. He thanked the Lightning profusely for seeing something in him and making a big trade to get him down there. He thanked the coaches and his teammates, and then came the tough part.

He got out, "And my wife, Carol …" and things got tough from that point forward. Through the tears he let the world know how much he loved her, and how he knew he couldn't have gotten through all the bad stuff, and wouldn't have enjoyed the good stuff as much, without her. I was in the back of the room, but even from there I could tell how emotional Carol was.

He talked about their plans to have a family, and how that came first. He knew he needed to be there, and be fully mentally there, when they started having kids. The one line I'll never forget was the last one he said.

"I love hockey. Hockey has given me so much I never dreamed of. But health and family have to come first. Love is more important than hockey. Thank you."

That was amazing. He did such a great job. I was glad I never did one of those deals. I would've been a basket case from the moment I adjusted the microphone. I couldn't have done it. He was so honest and brave.

I gotta admit, I was glad when it was over. It was heartbreaking, heartfelt, and the room was full of love for him. He'd had a spectacular career, he'd won a Stanley Cup, and most important he had the respect of his peers. All of them. The entire NHL. It's just that the ending was so damn sad.

I gave both Eric and Carol a hug after it was over. All I said was, "You were spectacular. I'm blown away. Now I'm going to go home to process all of this. You two should go be by yourselves, and do the same. Call me when you want to get together. I love you guys."

A few days later, Eric called and said, "OK, I've got all the forms for the LLC. It needs a name, so I chose EO Holdings LLC. That shouldn't be hard to remember. I've got them all filled out and there doesn't seem to be a place for you to sign. There's a box where I list officers, and I've listed you as president.

"If I did this right, we should be official in a couple weeks. Once that happens, and we have the paperwork, we'll go to the bank together to set up the new business account, and I'm sure we'll both have to sign for that. Sound good?"

It did. The only real unknown was how long it was going to take the state to process the application and get us our official documents.

It took nearly a month. It was the end of July, or maybe early August? Hell, it might have been mid-August. I don't really remember. I was playing with my own research and my stocks. I was accumulating IBM and Microsoft once a week. Just small buys, but over the course of a year they'd add up. The more you own, the more you might make, right? If you own a thousand shares of something and it goes up 5 percent, that's what you make. Own 10,000 shares, and you make 10 times as much.

I was also thinking about things that are kind of recession-proof. Like cereal. I love cereal in the morning. Even when times are tough, people eat cereal. Seemed like General Mills would be a good bet, but my research was luke-warm. Why? Because cereal manufacturers didn't often see big fluctuations. It's not like they introduced amazing new products that rocked the cereal world all the time. They don't make software or microchips, and they won't be bringing out a new prescription pill that will save lives. They just make Cheerios. I still bought a bit and figured I'd accumulate that as well. Maybe I should buy some Chiquita stock. I always put a sliced banana on my Cheerios.

I don't remember the date, but it was late in August when we went to Eric's bank and got the account started. It was a pretty simple process, and we both signed as officers who could access and move money. Eric had them transfer $500,000 he'd put in savings just for this. Within a week, we'd have a business account with EO Holdings LLC checks. That would make us official.

It was maybe just a few days later when I was out for a jog early in the morning. I got home all sweaty and was ready to get in the shower. Eric and I had a strategy meeting scheduled for noon at his place. Right then, Eric called.

"Did you hear? Did you see it on TV?"

"I just got in from a jog, what's up?

"A passenger jet just crashed into the World Trade Center and it's on fire. OH HOLY HELL. WOW. Another one just hit the other tower. Holy crap. This is awful. Just hunker down man. Who knows what's going on. This is insane."

I watched TV for the rest of the day, horrified. It was surreal. I watched people jump to their deaths rather than burn alive. I watched the towers fall. I couldn't believe what I was seeing. It didn't seem real.

I tried calling Mom and Dad but couldn't get a connection with my cell. I finally got through on the landline. We all just checked in and told each other to be safe. It was a day I'll never forget.

In Clearwater, we weren't on the final approach for Tampa International Airport, but when the wind was from the north the jets would fly south right by my condo windows, out over the Gulf a mile or so away. On a clear day you could see them make the big left turn to line up with the runways with a northbound approach. Air traffic seemed typically heavy for about an hour, then nothing. No planes approaching and none up in the sky. It was eerie. It was scary too. I felt kind of lost. I think every American felt the same way.

That night I went over to Eric and Carol's house and we hardly spoke. We just wanted to be together.

As you may remember, the New York Stock Exchange didn't open that day. The planes hit just before the markets were due to get started. They were afraid of a huge panic sell-off and a total market meltdown, so they shut it down and emptied the building. It wouldn't open again for about two weeks. The hope was that it would give sellers a chance to calm down and see that we were going to be OK. There was still a huge sell-off when they reopened, and I had my first chance to see if my conservative blue-chip accumulation strategy worked.

It was pretty scary for a week or so. Huge losses in some segments, especially the airline and insurance businesses. But when things were down 14 percent, I was only down around 7 percent. It worked. It wasn't glamorous or sexy, but it protected me.

About a week into it, Eric said, "Should we just sit on the bench before we get going with this? It seems like a mess."

I said, "Let me watch for a couple more days. The market should reopen soon, and there will be big losses right out of the gate. EO Holdings doesn't own anything yet, so it can't hurt us in that regard. But the American stock market is incredibly resilient. A lot of people are going to see things to buy at very low prices in the near future. We need to be ready to pounce. Are you with me on that?"

He said, "This is why I wanted to form this partnership. I trust you. Do what you think is right."

I buried my head in the research and tried to formulate a plan. The risk level went up for everyone at that time. No one had lived through anything like 9/11, so you could only speculate about what was going to happen. No one knew where the bottom was, but I wanted to be ready the second the turnaround began. In my gut, I just knew it was going to happen. We would bounce back. Business would get going again.

Was it speculation? Hell, yes, it was. I just wanted to speculate and be right. I could make Eric a lot of money if I hit the timing and stocks on the sweet spot.

CHAPTER 50

Eric Olson

Retirement itself wasn't that hard. I'd made peace with it after the third concussion. I knew that was it, and I was actually looking forward to getting it all behind me. Concussions are no fun and the last one was brutal. I had zero desire to ever go through that again.

What was hard, though, was the press conference. I'd gotten a lot better dealing with the media during my pro career. At first, I couldn't understand why anyone with a recorder or a notepad would want to talk with me. I wasn't important. I was just a defenseman doing his job. When the Lightning signed me to my extension, and we did that press conference, it finally sunk in that people really care, especially the fans. Without them, we wouldn't have jobs.

The front office understands that (at least they should) and they know the fans crave information all the time. Back then, it was pretty hard to come by other than in the morning paper, pre-game shows or the 6 o'clock news. Now, they can soak themselves in it on social media. But way back then, press conferences were really important. It was the way to get on the news for stuff other than highlights or lowlights of that night's game.

It was a phenomenal honor to be there. The short speeches made by the front office people, Coach Torts, and my teammate Vinnie Lecavalier were really great. I actually allowed myself to understand that they were being very honest. They meant those words, and that hit me right in the heart.

When it was my turn to take the mic, I wasn't sure what was going to happen. I had an index card with me, with about five bullet points on it. That's all I needed. I could glance at each bullet point and ad lib the words. It was easy, because it was honest. There's nothing easier than being honest.

When I got to the last bullet point, which was simply CAROL, I was blindsided. I had kept my composure pretty well. I was channeling my inner Roseau demeanor. But when I said, "And about my wife, Carol…" all the emotion didn't just bubble to the surface, it erupted like Mount St. Helens. I had to take a deep breath and wipe my eyes. I knew I had my hands full with all the feelings, but I had to go on. I was a blubbering fool through most of it, but I got the words out. The biggest problem was seeing her, right there in front of me, going through tissues so fast I couldn't help but lose it in response.

Somehow we all lived through it. I will go on record saying it's a good thing I will only retire once.

I was feeling really good by then. Totally back to normal, and even out on the golf course a lot. Brooks got out there with us, and it was great just to be feeling like myself, even if my game wasn't that sharp. Brooks was Brooks. All pure natural talent, but he still needed to work on his short game.

I was also putting the pieces in place for our new joint venture. When I got the thick stack of forms to fill out, to register the LLC, one of the first items I had to address was the official name it needed. I thought "Two Retired Guys LLC" for a few minutes, but I knew we needed something more professional. I went with my initials. We would officially be known as EO Holdings LLC. I had talked with my former agent about it, asking his advice, and he said, "The title needs to be all about you. It's your LLC. Brooks is going to work for you. Make that clear in the name."

I sent all the forms in, and the wait was unbearable. It's the state that licenses the LLC, and the Florida government seemed to move at the same pace Floridians do when it's 95 degrees with 85 percent humidity. Everything is in slow motion. It took nearly two months to get all the forms back and make us official.

Brooks and I opened a bank account for the LLC, and we were both listed on it. That would need to happen because I wanted Brooks to make the calls and buy the stocks or funds. He'd be the brains. And I trusted him to do that because he was already making money in the market by himself. He was never afraid of doing research, and back then it wasn't that easy to do. He dug in and took it very seriously.

That's something I loved about the guy. He was the son of two hippies. He was a surfer dude from Southern California. He was as much of a free spirit as anyone I had ever known. It's what made him so likeable, so cool, and so much fun. But when it was time to get serious, whether it was school, or his baseball career, or the stock market, he was laser focused. He could shut everything else out and just get after it.

I spent a number of days with him at his condo, just to kind of see him in action. It was bizarre. There was this whole different guy sitting next to me, and he looked and talked just like Brooks but the words were a different language. He'd show me websites or reams of information he'd printed, and rattle off terms I had no clue about. He was trying to show me what he knew, but it was like meeting a guy from NASA and having him try to teach me about launching a rocket. It was so far over my head.

Brooks was always a numbers guy. That came easy to him. He used to say, "Numbers are like words to me. They tell a story. You just have to master the lingo." It might as well have been Chinese or Russian to me. I could barely understand anything beyond the price per share.

By late August or early September, we had the bank account set up, and we had even had a few strategy meetings to discuss how it was all going to work. We'd both work from home, so we needed to have policies in place to make it efficient. It felt really good to me. We were two hard working guys who were serious about it, and we had a track record of success in just about everything we'd done. I felt like I had the best LLC president I could find, and he'd been my closest friend for more than 10 years.

The goal wasn't to get rich. We were both already rich. The goal was to invest a lot of my money in safe places that would also earn new money to keep the train running forever. Carol and I were still trying to get pregnant, and we were determined to do all we could to make that happen and have a family. This money wasn't for me. I was doing this for Carol and our future children, and grandchildren down the road. Hockey made me rich, in many ways, and I wasn't going to blow it. I knew a lot of guys who had. That wasn't going to be me.

And then September 11 happened. Carol was sipping a cup of coffee when she got a call from her mom, who said: "Are you watching TV? It looks like the World Trade Center in New York is on fire."

We turned the set on and there it was. Flames and smoke pouring out of the upper floors of one of the twin towers. The news people were still gathering information, and not all of it was correct. First, we heard a private plane had crashed into the building. Then we heard a military jet had hit the building. They were all frantic to get it right, but also just plain frantic.

Finally, a reporter on the ground called in and said, "It was a passenger jet. A large one, and it flew directly into the building. Everything exploded on impact. I'm sorry it took me so long to get to you, but it's mayhem down here. No one knows what to do."

The news was horrifying, but what hit me the most was the tone of the reporter's voice. This was not a small deal. This was not a fire they could put out. He was terrified.

I called Brooks. He had just gotten in from a run in the morning heat and didn't know what had happened.

Then Carol and I saw the second plane hit the other tower and I think I screamed into the phone. After that, I just said, "Watch TV, buddy. Just watch. It's awful." Carol and I could barely speak. We both just held our breath.

We stayed glued to the TV and terrified for the rest of the day and into the night. I had former teammates who still lived in Manhattan. I had no idea how they were or what it was like. I didn't have a cell phone when I played for the Rangers, so I didn't have any of their numbers. I tried calling the front office but the phone just rang and rang.

A few days later, I called Brooks and asked him what we should do. The stock exchange had closed before the opening bell, right after the planes had hit. It was still closed and no one knew when it would open again. I figured we'd just put all our plans on hold. Maybe for a long time. Nobody knew.

Brooks said no to that. He was sure the market would tank as soon as it reopened, but it would rebound. He figured that would be partly due to patriotism and mostly to do with some fine blue chip stocks trading at very low prices. He believed there were going to be opportunities out there, once everything leveled off.

I told him I trusted him to do the right thing. I knew he would.

And I was right to do that. The market was closed for about two weeks, and it did take a plunge the first couple days. But it leveled off after that steep drop, and Brooks was in action. Stocks he held, like IBM and Microsoft, were trading at their lowest levels in years. It was time to get in, and that's what he did as his first moves for EO Holdings LLC. We bought more IBM and Microsoft than we ever would've purchased before 9/11.

Then he called me and said, "I'm going to take a personal position with Apple. Steve Jobs is back in charge and I just have a gut feeling he's going to take the company to the moon. They have the technology but they also have the sexiness that consumers love. The iMac is still selling, and the word in Apple circles is that they have some wild new stuff to introduce soon. I'm doing it for my portfolio, but this time I wanted to ask you what you thought about EO Holdings. It's not a sure thing. Apple has almost tanked a number of times when Jobs was sent packing. I just have a hunch, and I'm not comfortable spending your money on a hunch. You tell me."

I told him I was all for it. Whatever he was buying for himself, he should buy the same for me. Apple was still dirt cheap then, about $5 a share, and 9/11 dropped it even further. He bought 10,000 shares for himself and another 10,000 for the LLC. If it started to increase in value, we could add more, but as Brooks said, "This is as close as you can get to being in on the ground floor with a company that's already established and has a great reputation. I'm banking on Steve Jobs."

At 10,000 shares, we each now held about $50,000 worth of Apple. At the time I thought, "Maybe this is gonna be a good deal. Maybe not. But we can't get hurt too bad."

We settled into a nice pace, and it was really great to see Brooks dive in and get smarter as he went. He got me into a few really conservative mutual funds. He kept accumulating the blue chips, and at the end of every week he'd send me a full report on what my positions were, how much they'd appreciated, and what the overall value was.

"I almost don't like doing this," he said. "It's easy to see where we started from and what value we hold now, but I want you to stay focused on the long run. This is for you, Carol, and your family. This will be the trust fund you need for college, the money you need for a second home somewhere, and anything else you want. You have all the money you need already, for having kids and living life the way you want to. This is the reserve. Hold it until you're actually old enough to retire."

Around that same time, Rick Dudley called me. He asked if I was ready to come over and meet with him at his office in the arena. We set it up for a couple days later, and we'd meet for lunch first and then head to his office to talk about stuff in more detail.

When we met, at a really nice Cuban-themed restaurant, it was pleasantly surreal. That's the only way I can describe it. I've sat across tables from a lot of hockey executives, but I've never felt as comfortable as I did with Rick. He wasn't that much older than me. I think he was in his 40s, but he seemed much younger than that.

As we ate, we talked. He started it off.

"Eric, I'd like to have you on my staff. You know the game, you know what to look for and you know how hard it is to apply max effort. Some guys can do it, some can't. You never did anything but that.

"What I see, and what I want you to think about, is an executive assistant to the GM type of role. I don't envision it as anything set in stone. You won't be a scout, you won't be a player-personnel guy and you won't be a coach at practice. You'll be none of those things, because you'll be all of them. I want to be able to utilize you in any way, and I know you can do a great job at anything I throw at you. Let's finish lunch, and then we'll head over to the office to flesh it out a little more. OK?"

Sure. It sounded interesting, and I was ready for it. I'd paid the price for playing the game, and this offer was a way the game and the Lightning could get more out of me. I was ready to hear the details.

When we got to his office, it instantly became clear that he was prepared for both parts of the meeting. At lunch, he spoke in general terms, just laying the groundwork for the serious stuff. In his office, he pulled out a few pieces of paper and slid them across his desk to me. He was clearly ready. I was anything but prepared, but I knew I wanted to be back in the game.

It was an outline of the job responsibilities. Basically, I'd be his right hand. Need to see a kid who's lighting it up in Finland? I'd go there. Need an extra set of eyes and opinions to sit in the war room for the NHL draft, and decide who we were going to select each round? I'd be there. Get on the ice during practice and work on the defensive schemes the team so desperately needed? That's me. And lots more. It sounded great.

Then he slid another piece of paper my way. It said "Compensation" at the top. Below that title was the number $250,000 per year, payable in installments every two weeks for each calendar year. It was a three-year contract offer.

"You don't have to make your decision right now. Go home and think about it, and definitely talk to your wife. Eric, it won't be an exhausting job, because you love this stuff. It will keep you in the game and it will help us keep improving. We still have a long way to go, but you'll be an important part of getting us there. Give me a call when you're ready to talk again."

We shook hands and I headed home kind of giddy. I missed the game. I didn't miss the bruises and injuries, and I sure as heck didn't miss the concussions, but I missed the camaraderie and the game itself. I knew I wanted to do it. And the fact was, $250k was more than enough for Carol and me to live on, and then some. I wouldn't have to touch any of the money I'd made playing, and I could add to that nest egg every month. It was a no-brainer for me, but I had to talk to Carol.

When she got home, I told her how it had gone. I got right to the point. I'd basically be Rick's right-hand guy, doing anything he needed me to do, and it would pay $250,000 a year, all year 'round. There would be no off-season for me, but that would be OK. I'd be in the game making it happen for the Tampa Bay Lightning.

She said, "This is wonderful, sweetie. They appreciate you and respect you. Rick knows what you can bring to the team, and he wants you. This would be a great hire for them and a great thing for you. I'm all for it. But you'll need a few new suits."

I called Rick the next day and said yes. The season had just started, so to keep the focus on the players, they didn't schedule a press conference. I was fine with that. Instead, the PR department did set up a bunch of one-on-one interviews with the local TV stations and radio outlets.

My first day at work was a lot like the first day of school. A lot of people I hardly knew, a new place to sit, lots of meetings, and I wore new clothes. At least for the first week. After that, I kind of just blended in with the rest of the office. I'd wear a sports coat to work but take it off when I got there. It was all about the work.

Before long, I was poring over scouting reports and flying off to various cities to see those guys with my own eyes. Some were underperforming and I found it really rewarding to try to see beyond the numbers. I looked for effort as much as skill. Was the guy saddled with bad linemates? Was he set into a structure that didn't utilize what he could do? Or was this the real guy? Was this all he had to give? Rick really liked my reports. It helped him make deals and say no to a few.

I thought the team was better. Torts was still coaching, and he had their attention. At least once a week I'd lace up the skates and get out there with them at practice, working with the defensive unit. My gosh, it felt great. Like I'd been out there just the day before. I hadn't been on skates for so long I did wonder what it would feel like. It felt perfect. I felt like I could put the uniform on and play that night. Thankfully, I knew better and the team would never allow me to do it. I'd played my last game, but I still had a lot I could contribute.

Every morning, I couldn't wait to get to work. I rarely knew what was going to be on my plate and that was part of the fun of it. On any day I might hear Rick say something like, "Hey Eric, St. Louis has a defenseman they're down on. They don't think he plays hard enough, and they're willing to move him for a draft pick. I want you in Miami to see the Blues play the Panthers tomorrow night. Tell me what you think." Or it might be, "Get out there for tomorrow's practice and get through to these guys. A few of them are soft and don't like contact. They might need to find a new line of work." It could be anything.

Meanwhile, Brooks was doing his thing. We were seeing growth and increased values. It wasn't profit at the time, because we weren't selling. We were accumulating and holding. I had never heard or used the word "accumulate" before in my life. I seemed to be saying it 15 times a day when I spoke with Brooks.

One day, he was over at our place for dinner and Carol said, "I know you've been burned at least once, but would you consider meeting a friend of mine? We work together at the charity and she's gorgeous, smart, and totally normal. Just think about it. It can be low-key. Like maybe we'll have a small dinner party with some hockey people and I'll invite her and introduce you to her. If you don't want to, I understand, but I know you well enough not to steer you wrong."

Brooks said, "You know, if anyone else had said that it would be a hard no before they got to the second sentence. But it's you, and that's all that matters. If you want to set up a small party, that would be a great way to meet her. No one-on-one pressure. Go for it!"

Carol got to work on it. Her friend's name was Diane. She had a master's degree in something. She was a top executive at the charity and smart as could be. Carol figured if she just said "We're having a small party at our house, and I'd love for you to be there," that would be slightly dishonest and likely to elicit an "Oh, thanks. But I can't make it" response.

So she spilled the beans a little. She told her about the party and then said, "And there's a guy I really want you to meet. You've both been burned and bummed out about relationships, but I can vouch for him 100 percent. Plus, he's really good-looking, hilariously funny and a genius. If there's no interest then no harm and no foul. But it's worth meeting him, I think."

Diane said yes and Carol sprang into action.

The party would be 10 days later on a weekend when the hockey team was home and had the night off. We had about eight Lightning couples coming, and a few other friends from the neighborhood. And Brooks.

My incredible wife nailed it. Just fancy enough to be a real party, but casual enough to make it relaxing and easy. We had it catered by our local grocery store, and the wings, brats, veggie tray, salads and sides were all perfect. The bar was open, and everyone was chilled out and mingling. When Diane arrived, a little fashionably late, Carol brought her into the room and introduced her to me first. She was exactly how my perceptive wife had described her. Serious but smiling. Able to laugh freely but honestly. She asked questions and they all were sincere. Clearly very smart.

After Carol took her around the room, she spotted Brooks out by the pool and took her out there. I was in the living room, so I couldn't hear anything, but they both smiled, shook hands and started talking. After a bit, Brooks brought her into the kitchen and they loaded plates, then headed back out to a poolside table. Brooks got back up and headed to the bar to pour them each a glass of Cabernet. I managed to strategically pass by him and say, "She's really pretty. Is she as smart as I think she is?" All he said was, "I think so. One small step at a time, bro. I just want to get to know her and let her get to know this Napa Valley Cab. I'm close friends with this Cabernet. I wouldn't steer it wrong. Well, maybe she'll get to know me, too."

It looked to me like Carol had lit the flame and it didn't go out, but Brooks was a unique guy. Let's just say if he was the Starship Enterprise, his shields were always up at maximum defensive power. Time would tell.

Time would tell for all of us. My new job. The Lightning, and my shared hope with Carol that she could get pregnant sooner than later.

In that order, the job was great. The Lightning were getting better. And I had no clue why we weren't already expecting a baby. We just kept hoping.

CHAPTER 51

Brooks Bennett

In terms of the new LLC, I think we did pretty well coming out of the national state of shock after 9/11. There was a part of me, deep in my surfer's soul, that felt extremely conflicted by it. A tragedy, a horrible terrorist attack, had killed thousands of Americans and emotionally scarred nearly all of us. The emotional side of me was devastated by it. At the same time, the analytical side of me saw a chance to do my job for Eric and serve his interests in the best possible way.

There were more than a few evenings when I flopped on my sofa and watched the sun set over the Gulf, wondering if what I was doing was right or wrong. The best I could come up with was the theory that I'd been entrusted with a mission, and my best friend was the one who brought me into this because he knew I could do a good job. I had to compartmentalize again. I'd been doing that for much of my life.

I had a job to do. Most Americans had jobs to do. We were collectively shaken by what we had seen, but I had a job to do. Just like an assembly line worker, an accountant, or a teacher, we all had responsibilities. My job was to benefit my boss and friend.

I did that. We bought low, accumulated and built our portfolio. At one point, I had decided that Apple was a rich opportunity, and I bought 10,000 shares back when it was still scraping the bottom at about five bucks. I'd mentioned that to Eric, and told him my rationale basically centered on Steve Jobs, who had come back to run the company after the regime that forced him out had all but ruined a once shining star. With Jobs back at the helm, I had a serious hunch that Apple might be positioned to take off like a rocket. I typically don't play hunches. Basically, I never played hunches. But this was different and it was so cheap you really couldn't get hurt all that bad. Eric was in, too. We were either going to make some serious money or later talk about "That year we thought Apple was going to succeed and got in cheap. Remember that? What a misread that was." I wasn't so much investing in Apple. I was investing in Steve Jobs.

Right about then, Eric surprised me when he accepted a job. He went to work in the Lightning's front office, working with the general manager. I guess retired life didn't suit him all that well. Honestly, I was really happy for him. And maybe a little bit jealous. I could see myself in a front office some day, although I was still loving the investment stuff as my job. The Lightning clearly appreciated not only everything he'd done for them, but they understood what he could do moving forward. He wouldn't get to play as much golf, but he had a reason to attack every day like it meant something. Because it did. He could help mold that team into what it could be. I was stoked for him, and I knew he'd be great at it.

Also around that time, Carol wrangled me into a small dinner party because she wanted to introduce me to someone. She actually went to all the trouble of setting up an actual dinner party at their house, inviting friends, having it catered, and being the host, just so she could introduce me to someone. That's hard to believe, looking back on it, but that's Carol. She'd move mountains for someone she cared about.

At the get-together, I was sipping a glass of wine out by their pool and talking with a few of the Lightning guys I had played golf with. At that point, I had basically forgotten the plot of this play. When Carol came out from the house with a very attractive woman by her side, I'll admit I was more than a little interested. Diane was very pretty, and at least my age if not a year or two older. She had beautiful blonde hair in natural waves that seemed to reflect the sunset light. Shimmering eyes that were green or blue — I couldn't tell — and radiant skin. Maybe 6 feet tall. I'd guess you'd call her statuesque. If she reminded me of anyone, it was Lauren Bacall, the movie star from the 1940s and '50s. She was that striking.

We said hello, and Carol got the conversation going by saying, "Diane, this is Brooks Bennett. He's Eric's closest friend, and basically his advisor. They work together now. Brooks used to be a Major League baseball player, but now he's a stock analyst and investor. Brooks, this is Diane Shaeffer, and she's one of my best friends. She's in charge of growing our corporate donor and sponsor base at work. I just wanted you two to meet. Can I get you anything?"

The part about me having played baseball made me cringe. That was history. That wasn't who I was anymore. I wish she hadn't said that, but it was out there.

Diane never mentioned it. She just said, "I've heard a lot about you, and it's a pleasure to finally meet you. Carol thinks a lot of you, and I respect her opinions on just about anything. Well, not movies. She has really odd taste when it comes to movies, but I don't hold that against her."

It was so easy to talk with her. Never a hesitation or an awkward pause. She was really smart, articulate, and she listened as intensely as she spoke. It was kind of a revelation for me.

I'd been burned by one girl who was still just finding her way and very immature. I'd had a fling with a girl who was more interested in my money and my car than me. Those were bad experiences that stayed with me. They were still young, immature and still playing the field. We were all younger then. Diane was an accomplished woman, and when I found out she was divorced and it had been ugly, I felt a kind of kinship or connection with her. We'd both been wronged. She was fascinating. I remember, vividly,

512

feeling right there at the time that I might not be interesting enough for her. Maybe I'm not worthy!

We had a few glasses of wine and before long we launched into the tell-me-about-yourself phase. Her reactions to my stories about childhood, my parents, surfing, and all that ancient stuff made her say "Wow!" more than a few times. I didn't skip the baseball stuff. I couldn't. I told her about my baseball past but it was mostly just "I played college ball, got signed, bounced up the ladder in the minors, and ended up in the big leagues with the Texas Rangers. It was a great experience. I got hurt though, and that ended it. I still love the game, but those days are gone." No more detail than that. The way I figured it, if she had any real interest in it, she'd ask over time. I was happy she didn't ask right then. I think it intrigued her, just like the surfing part did, but it wasn't that important.

We chatted for most of the night, and exchanged phone numbers. I definitely wanted to see her again, but even that night I knew I had a plan. I just wanted to get to know her. I wanted us to be friends first. No rush to romance. I'd take it as slow as I could, and we'd get to know each other. There was no working toward a goal of any sort. We'd see if we were compatible, if we made each other laugh, and if it felt easy or forced. When I left, I told Carol, "Thanks for the introduction. She's an amazing woman. We'll see each other again, I'm sure."

Eric got into his job and I continued mine. He was loving it. He kept saying that Rick Dudley was a really good man. He was never afraid to delegate, he trusted those around him and he chose them with care. He was one of those rare executives who didn't want the credit. He surrounded himself with smart and dedicated people and gave them the freedom to steer him in the right direction. As Eric said, "Rick always says he wants to concentrate on the 30,000-foot view from above. It's our job to do the footwork on the ground. He never micromanages."

I'd say the team was better, but they still weren't all that good. At least they didn't finish last in their division, but they missed the playoffs again.

During the winter, I did get together with Diane a number of times. I was going about it just like I wanted to, one small step at a time, to the point where I started worrying that she might wonder if I was interested at all.

I remember our first "date" because we had a chaperone. It was just a couple weeks after we met at the party, and the Lightning had a Saturday night home game against the Chicago Blackhawks. I know this because I kept the ticket stub. Carol called me and said, "Have you taken Diane out yet? She hasn't mentioned anything at work." I told her I hadn't but we'd talked on the phone quite a bit. Carol then said, "Well call her again, and ask her to come with me and you to the hockey game Saturday night. Do it!"

I did, she said yes, and the three of us went to the game. I remember sitting on Diane's left, and Carol was on her right. The second we sat down that way I recall thinking: "This could be bad. What if they talk shop the whole time and I'm just the fifth wheel?"

It wasn't totally like that. They did talk to each other a lot, but Diane was really skilled at working both sides. She asked me a lot of hockey questions, because she hadn't been to many games and really didn't know the rules. I did the best I could. Finally, she said, "So about that baseball you played. What was that like as a lifestyle?"

I spent as much time talking about the minors as I did the big leagues. I told her that when I think about "lifestyle" the minor leagues are what come to mind for me. That's where you learn to be a man, look out for yourself, be responsible, and find your physical limits. The minors, to me, are what define the game and the young men playing it. Many can't handle it, whether it's the grind or the freedom. I flourished there, and I knew why. It was my parents. They gave me the maturity and self-reliance I needed. I always felt at home in the minors, no matter what level I was at. Diane cocked her head to the side a little and said, "That's really an interesting take on it. I had no idea about minor league baseball. It sounds like as much a mental test as it is physical."

I told her she was exactly right. Then I said, "I think the minors make you what you are. The big leagues are the goal, and when you get there you have to maintain that version of what you are and not get sucked into the big league life. It's a fantasy world. Big money, charter jets, five-star hotels, and a totally pampered and unrealistic way to live. It was harder to stay true to myself there than it was in Butte, Montana."

I asked her my big question during one of the intermissions when Carol went up to the suite "to see Eric," or basically, to give us some time alone.

"Do you talk about your divorce, or should we just skip that?"

"Oh no, I'll talk about it. I should because it's a lesson I have to keep in mind every day. It was a marriage that happened for all the wrong impetuous reasons. I just went along with it. He was handsome and very serious, and for some ridiculous reason I thought I was in love with him.

"He was nothing like me and didn't like the concept of me getting my masters or working as an executive. He wanted dinner every night when he got home from work, no matter what time it was. I got pretty good at making meals that could sit for hours and then be reheated. He was a sales guy, and he hopped around from job to job as better opportunities came to him. Sporting goods, hardware, medical supplies and finally pharmaceuticals. Lots of time on the road, and not much time for me."

She paused for a second, took a deep breath, looked me right in the eyes, and said, "And then I was doing his laundry one day, after he came home from a trip, and a pair of women's underwear fell out of the pile. I confronted him with them dangling from my finger tip. He just stammered and said, "It's not what it looks like." I said, "You have to do better than that crap, Mr. Salesman. I'm not buying it."

She said he finally admitted it but wouldn't say if it had been the only transgression. She filed for divorce and never saw him again. She'd been single for eight years.

"I like being single, although it can get lonely from time to time. Luckily, my parents live in Sarasota and I have an older brother and younger sister who live in Tampa. At least holidays are good. Being single would suck if I had no family around. Now tell me about you."

I filled her in on the details with Donna, and gave a slightly whitewashed version of Susie. She seemed a little confused by the whole story.

514

"You only seriously dated one girl and she cheated on you, so since then you've basically had no relationships? How do you do that?"

I said, "In baseball, there were always plenty of women around but I'm just not like that. My parents are my role models. That's the kind of relationship I want. I just didn't want to go through what Donna had done to me again, so I shut it all off. It wasn't that hard. Baseball was my mistress."

"Do you see that changing any time soon?" she asked.

"Yes, I do. I've matured a lot, I see the world differently, and I definitely have a better idea of what a good, solid relationship should be. My eyes are open. I just don't want to push it or force anything to happen. I'm glad I met you. Very glad, actually. I want to get to know you better. I hope we can continue to see each other. I'd be stoked if we could do that."

"You'd be stoked," she said with a little laugh. "I'm guessing that's the surfer dude in you. I'll take it as a compliment."

I assured her it was a compliment of the highest order.

Then Carol came back with beers for all of us. We'd have to pick the deep conversation up on another night. I looked forward to it, but remember thinking: "I hope I didn't get too far out over my skis there. I need to keep the brakes on a little. I don't want her to think I'm chasing her."

We saw each other quite a bit after that. At least once a week, whether it was out to dinner or at a movie. I had not forgotten the hilarious comment about Carol's taste in movies. I always asked Diane to pick what we would watch. We kept learning more, and I was enjoying finding my way around her many layers of personality. She was brilliant. She could be anything from a little humorous to absolutely hilarious. She made me laugh. And she challenged me to be the best me. Plus, she was gorgeous. Not cute like a college girl. Gorgeous. She was every bit of the woman I had hoped I'd find someday.

One night after we'd had some wine on my balcony, she said, "Well, I better be going now. This was another fun night, Brooks. Thank you."

As we got to the door, she stood in front of me with those Lauren Bacall eyes burning holes in me like laser beams, and she said, "I'm going to kiss you now. Be ready." It was a kiss I'll never forget. I saw stars. When it was over, all I could say was, "Wow. You're amazing and that was amazing."

She winked and said, "There's more where that came from. Don't be shy, baseball guy."

I laughed and said, "Ex-baseball guy. Now I'm just a dullsville stock market geek. Hope you can handle all that excitement."

"Oh, I'm sure I can," she whispered. Then she winked again and headed for her car. I swear I expected to turn around and see Humphrey Bogart behind me, saying, "Ya did good, kid. Keep it up and you might have something going here."

I was smitten. I hadn't told my parents about her at that point, but I fixed that the next day. They were really supportive. Mom said, "Trust yourself first, Brooks. If you trust yourself and your judgment, it will work out for you."

That's what I thought, too.

On the LLC front, I was feeling good about what we'd done after 9/11, and feeling even better about America and her resilience. Within just a few months the market was back up to about where it had been on September 10, the day before the attack when we were all blissfully ignorant. I'd bought some great long-term stocks at two- or three-year lows. I bought Apple when no one was paying attention to it, and it was starting to rise.

Apple is famous for being secretive about new products and, for the most part, analysts and researchers could only sense that "something" was coming down the pipe. Less than a month after I bought our two positions at 10,000 shares each, they introduced the iPod. That was luck. I knew something was coming, but I never would've guessed it was an MP3 music player.

The market hardly reacted to it. Apple was a computer company. This was a thing no one knew they needed. It was cool as hell, but what was it? Most stock traders and analysts are older guys. It didn't resonate with them. The stock creeped up a point or two.

It took about six months but suddenly everyone needed an iPod, and Apple kept updating it with more features and more capacity. With iTunes, you had a place to go in order to fill that bad boy up with any music you wanted. The ad campaign was brilliant, aimed at teens and twenty-somethings. It all worked. The stock began its rise.

It took a while for people to see it, but it changed Apple. We were onto something. Time to let it ride and let Steve Jobs work his magic. That magic changed a lot of lives, including mine and Eric's. My "hunch" about Jobs and Apple paid off. We made a fortune when we finally sold.

I really enjoyed putting my weekly updates together for Eric. I knew there would be weeks, or months, when those things would not be fun, but I knew I was doing a good job for him and I was proud to show him the results. We were up across the board, and had a total value in terms of the whole portfolio about 60 percent higher than when we started. And things were just getting "back to normal." There was still plenty of room to grow. More importantly, I felt there was still room for me to grow. I was getting better at it. I was learning how to dig through the tall grass to find the meaningful messages companies would share. It's in a sort of code, a lot of the time. The more confusing it is, the more you need to step back a little. If an official announcement had a confident and assertive tone, I got interested. Sometimes, when a company actually did way better during a quarter than everyone expected, you'd get another sort of pushback. They'd downplay it to lower the expectations for the next quarter. You gotta know the language!

Eric had also mentioned a new idea to me, although I initially couldn't tell how serious he was about it. He wanted to maintain some roots in Roseau. I got that but I just wasn't sure what he had in mind or if I'd be involved. It sounded to me like he was toying with the idea of buying a house there. He missed his hometown. He missed his family and his friends from school. Clearwater was going to be his home, but he wanted to have a place to get away to and decompress. Roseau was that place. I'd be happy to help, if I could.

It seemed to me that he was really flourishing in the front office. I was going to have dinner at their place one night, after the season had ended, and Eric was late getting home. So Carol and I hung out in the living room and I said, "Man, he sure seems to love what he's doing. Right?"

She said, "He absolutely loves it, and Rick treats him so well. They're already talking about a new position for him, more clearly defined. It's been great. He's totally himself again. That last concussion changed him for a long time. I wasn't completely sure he was still in there, but he's back now and he's out of bed early and eager to get to work every day."

We played a bunch of golf that summer, and it was great. It was definitely the old Eric. And he even convinced me to work on my putting and chipping. I still wasn't very good at it, but I got better. When I shot a legit 86 in the early summer, he went about nuts. He shot in the 90s that day. The next afternoon, he came over to my place with a little plastic golf trophy. It went right on my desk.

Diane and I were getting pretty serious. I think, by that time, we were falling in love. I mean, all I could come up with was that we were. I'd never actually been in that deep before, so it sure felt like love to me. Plus, I actually picked out a few movies and didn't get any grief about it. That was a definite win.

Was I still afraid of a new relationship? Yeah, I was. But I'd never met a woman like Diane in my life. I was really looking forward to having her join mom and dad and me for Thanksgiving.

Eric and I even bought some season tickets to the Tampa Bay Buccaneers football games. We both liked football but between the two of us, I think we'd been to maybe five NFL games. It was going to be fun. Maybe even do some tailgating before the games like serious fans. No face paint, though. We drew the line at that.

As for local baseball, the Tampa Bay Rays had come to St. Petersburg a few years before (they were the Devil Rays when they first got there) but I just couldn't do it. They played in a horrible stadium that was a lot of things, but it wasn't a ballpark. It was good that it had a roof, because late-day thunderstorms are kind of common around Florida. But whoever designed the joint must not have known much about baseball. It was terrible, and they drew lousy crowds usually made up of people rooting for the visiting team.

I went to one game, with Eric, the first year they were there and saw one of the Yankees' hitters absolutely obliterate a fastball right down the middle. It had 500 feet written all over it. But it hit a catwalk attached to the low point of the roof and fell to the artificial turf between the left fielder and the center fielder. They both ran for it and that confused me. Why would they run after a ball that's not in play? They did that because it was in play. That catwalk was considered "inside the park" and any ball that hit it could even be caught for an out. That wasn't baseball. I didn't know what it was, but I never went back. I remember saying to Eric, "I can't believe the Yankees even play there. It's not baseball. It's just awful."

Other than that, Eric was good. Carol was good. My parents were good and already had their plane tickets to come down for Turkey Day. The world was a good place. And I still lived in the coolest condo in the world. I tried to never miss a sunset out on the balcony. Wine included.

And then I got a phone call from a former Rangers teammate of mine. We'd stayed in touch and he knew what I was doing in the market. He called quite often asking for advice and he was a good guy, so I was happy to help. He'd blown out a knee and that ended his career. He recovered enough to have a normal life but he was 37 by then and baseball was over.

When I heard my cell phone ring, I opened it up. I said, "Hello."

CHAPTER 52

Eric Olson

Things were going smoothly at work with the Lightning, and once again I looked at the team and thought we had a real chance to get better. Maybe I was just an optimist. Or maybe I wasn't that good a judge of talent. That would be a bad thing, because Rick Dudley was counting on me to have serious input on trades and draft picks.

I still saw a team on the rise, but I'd been seeing that for a few years. Somehow, we weren't getting over the hump and into the promised land. There's no doubting the fact we had talent, especially on the offensive side of the lineup. We were absolutely capable of scoring a lot of goals. Young center Brad Richards was opening eyes all around the league. He was just 21 but he played like he was 31. He had vision on the ice well beyond his years. Vinny Prospal was our third center, and he could be a No. 1 center on a lot of teams. Dave Andreychuk was a 38-year-old veteran, but still a solid winger who led by example. And then there were Vinnie and Marty. They hadn't reached their full potential, but I still saw them as a pair of guys who could carry the franchise.

Was the defense still really that bad? I took that personally. I was out there on the ice with those guys at least once a week. I felt like they were engaged and trying hard, but the mistakes just kept biting us. I so wanted to put on the uniform and get out there to help, but there's a river you cross when you retire and as hard as it is to accept that, you can't go back. You're on the other side. We'd just had to keep working.

Rick called me into his office about a month into the season, and said, "Let's get right to the point. We're still not there. I think it's time to name you assistant general manager and make it official. Up until now, you've just been a jack of all trades. Being called a special assistant to the general manager makes it sound like you get me coffee. I want you to work on our scouting, overseeing the full staff in that department. I want you to work on the defensive end of our roster. That may mean moving some people in trades or even letting them go, and that's never fun. And I want you more involved in contract negotiations. That will be something you'll need if you land a GM job.

"Here's the honest truth: GMs get fired, especially when good teams don't perform.

When a new GM comes in, they often clean house to bring in their own people. You and I both have to be ready for that. I'm just laying that out there for you. It's a business. The owners are in charge. We just work here."

Then he paused and took a deep breath.

"If you're up for it, let's make the announcement. Hell, if anything the fans need to know we take this seriously and their favorite ex-defenseman is on the case. Are you good with that?"

I was good with it. We still had a lot of ground to cover and some of it wouldn't be pretty. I had played with a lot of these guys. I knew them very well. When I took the job, I never really thought about the bad side of letting guys go or trading them. I had a lot to learn, but I was on board.

It was going to take a full team effort to get this club where it needed to be.

There were a couple of other things on my personal agenda around that time. Brooks had brought up the idea of buying a couple of season tickets to the Tampa Bay Buccaneers, and he didn't have to work very hard at convincing me. I thought it sounded neat and every other Sunday it would be a good diversion for both of us. Just a way to be sports fans without having any vested interest in it. We'd let off some steam.

We'd been to our first few games and really enjoyed it, but damn — I couldn't help seeing things from a scouting and player personnel viewpoint. The Bucs were pretty good, but what they really excelled at was defense. They had a shut-down core on that side of the ball and it made them a very strong team. On offense, they weren't quite there. I saw them as the polar opposite of my Lightning. We could score, but we couldn't stop anybody. Still, it was a fun thing to do with a buddy, and our seats were great, in a sort of VIP section that had its own concession stands and restrooms. I'd gotten some help on that by reaching out to some people I knew over there. It's good to know people. I actually could have gotten us season tickets in a suite, but I didn't want to do that. I wanted to at least be out in the open with other fans.

I also was thinking of Roseau a lot. I missed home. I really hadn't been back that much since I made it to the NHL, and things were changing with my family. My mom and dad were getting older, but still doing the same things and keeping the hardware store going. Mom had quit working at Polaris and just focused on the store with my dad. My oldest brother had moved to St. Cloud, but my twin brothers were still there. Jon helped my dad at the store, and Brent worked at Polaris. Those two still rented a house together just a block or two from the family home, and from what I heard from my sister, they both had serious girlfriends.

Betsy was the one kind of caught in-between. She had a good job at Polaris, working in the office, but she still lived at home and had never found the right guy. I wouldn't say she was struggling, but whenever I talked to her on the phone she just sounded kind of flat. She'd always been a really positive person, and the life of the family party. I sensed she was kind of losing her motivation.

I wanted to buy a house up there. Nothing new or modern. Just a standard Roseau house like the one I grew up in. Was it nostalgia kicking in? I'm sure it was. Carol and I had made a great life for ourselves in Tampa and Clearwater. We loved it there. But we hardly ever saw our families. They were too busy tackling life in Roseau, and we never seemed to have the time. I wanted that anchor and connection to home. And Betsy could live in the house full time. Whenever we'd come up, the master bedroom would be waiting for us. We'd be reverse snowbirds, escaping to the cooler temperatures when Tampa got to be a sauna in the summer.

There was no way I could take the time to make that happen, so I asked Brooks if he could do it. I said, "Consider it a real estate investment for EO Holdings. I'd like you to go up there and see some homes with Betsy. She knows what I like and what I would want. Nothing flashy, but nothing that needs to be gutted and rebuilt either. Just a solid and comfortable Roseau home close to our families."

He was eager for the assignment, and I got Betsy to set up a real estate agent for us.

I also had another task for Brooks. The few times I'd gone back home I always wrestled with how to get there. You could connect in Minneapolis to fly up to International Falls or Grand Forks and cut the drive down to a little over two hours, instead of the six it takes to drive there from the Twin Cities, but the risks with those flights were things people from Roseau knew all about. They were small, prop-driven airplanes, and there weren't many flights each day. You could easily miss the connection or, even worse, the connecting flights would often be delayed by mechanical problems. It wasn't that easy.

So I told Brooks, "Let's book your flight to Winnipeg. You'll have to connect somewhere, probably Minneapolis, but there are plenty of flights every day and they're regular jets. Winnipeg is a full-sized airport. And it's only a couple of hours to drive back south to Roseau. I want to know how you feel about it once the trip is over. While you're there, find me a house! Betsy will help."

Brooks flew up a few days later. He called me both days he was there. The inventory in Roseau was never too large. There's just not a lot of turnover in town. But, they saw four or five that Betsy liked, and one in particular that she loved.

It was a 1920s wood-frame house, with a big front porch. Inside, it had been renovated a couple of times, and was really nice. It even had all new Marvin Windows throughout, shipped all the way from the Marvin factory in Warroad. Three bedrooms, three baths, a big living room, a separate dining room, and a den. It had a nice yard, with mature trees, and was two blocks from my folks. They wanted $135,000 for it. I had Brooks offer $120,000 and they took it. In a month, when we closed, I'd have a house in Roseau. I'd be the last one to see it, but there was no one I trusted to get it right more than Betsy.

Brooks also said the Winnipeg route was seamless. Lots of rental cars available, a simple drive, and no worries. I knew the only potential problem could be the border station, but he said it just took a minute. You only needed ID to get into and out of Canada then, no need for a passport, but Carol and I both thought it would be better to have our passports with us any time we went north. That would speed up the process at the Winnipeg airport, arriving and departing.

A month later, while my Lightning were still mucking along with yet another losing

521

record, playing in front of more disappointing crowds, Carol and I flew up to see the place and close on the purchase. I was going to put $100,000 down and finance a $20,000 mortgage.

It was fantastic! It had the down-home charm of Roseau. The porch was perfect and had been recently rebuilt and stained. Inside, typical Roseau with small windows and fairly small rooms. Back in the '20s, people must not have had much in the way of clothes. The closets were miniscule, but we weren't moving there permanently. The kitchen was totally redone, and perfect. Having three bathrooms was a real rarity for a house that old, too. The home had a new roof, new furnace and water heater, and fresh paint. All the floors were hardwood. Betsy came with us and I asked her if she'd picked out a room yet. She said, "Well, you get the master for whenever you want to come up and bug me. I'm taking the room next to it. I have to believe they turned a sitting room or another bedroom into that master bath. It's gotta be the biggest bathroom in Roseau."

When all the papers were signed and the keys exchanged, we went over to christen the place with some champagne. It was like a dream come true for me. As much as we loved Tampa Bay and Clearwater, Roseau would always be home for Carol and me. It was great to reestablish those roots. We clinked our glasses and Betsy said, "Here's to roots, and family, and Roseau!" Then we took a look around. Carol and I both loved it. And Bets was right. The master bath was so big it almost looked out of place in that house, but it was really nice.

Mom made a huge buffet dinner at their place, and we all got together with Carol's folks. It was great to all be celebrating our new home together, and I know Carol was really happy to see her mom and dad again. Neither one of us had been home enough. That was obvious.

Dad even did the inconceivable by putting one of his younger workers in charge of the last few hours at the store.

Everyone was really interested in everything that had been going on, and I did my best to fill them in on the new job, our house, and what Brooks and I were doing. Carol told them about her charity and the work she was doing there.

It was all very Olson matter-of-fact without a lot of emotion, but dad actually said, "I'm really proud of you, son. We're all proud of you. You overcame a lot just to get to the NHL, and now all of Roseau looks at you like another great example of what our town can do. You're doing great, and I'm glad you're not playing anymore. You did enough. Your health comes first."

There was a round of "Yeahs!" It felt good.

The house wasn't furnished, so I had provided Betsy with the money to take care of that over time. She had to work a full-time job too, but she was excited to fill the place and make it a home. I specifically told her, "Don't try to furnish it for me, with modern guy stuff. I want it to feel like family and feel like home."

We went back over to the place and sat on the floor, just looking around and soaking it in. That gave me a chance to talk with my sister and see how she was doing.

"So how's life, big sis?" I asked. "Everything good?"

522

"Yeah, it's OK. I go to work and go back home. Mom and Dad are getting older, but they haven't really changed much. I have some friends, but they're all married with kids now so it's not like I have anyone to get together with. It's just OK. I don't know.

"What you're doing with this house is unbelievable, little brother. It's great for you to keep yourself grounded here, and it's wonderful for me. I think the independence will make life better. When I go home after work I feel like I'm still 16 and Mom is going to tell me to do my homework and wash the dishes. It's like life is kind of suspended. I'm stuck. This is really going to make a difference Eric. You're an amazing little brother."

I didn't want to ask, but it came out before I could stop myself.

"Any guys in your life? Anyone you're seeing?"

"No. To be honest, none of these guys interest me in the least. You know this town. It's a wonderful place to live, but I don't fit in with most of the guys here. The ones I might be interested in are already married to my friends from school.

"And, there's this," she said, and then she took a really deep breath. "Are you ready for this? I'm not sure I am, but here we go. I've been waiting so long to have this conversation. I just didn't know when it would happen. I mean, really, I've been waiting years to tell someone this and it's been weighing on me so much I just can't live with the secret anymore. I've felt different since grade school. I didn't know why, but I felt different. You're the first people I've talked to about this, and I was hoping we could have this talk while you two were here. For now, I want to keep it between us. I don't think I could ever tell Mom and Dad, and if I told Jon or Brent they'd have it all over town in an hour. I've known this for so long, but I've kept it sealed up inside of me. I always have excuses for not going on dates, or dumb reasons why I'm not interested in this guy or that guy. I just think it's there. It's me. I'm a gay woman."

Carol and I both smiled and I said, "You're Betsy to us. That's all that matters. You have to be true to yourself. When you're ready to face it and maybe be open about it with the family and your friends, I'll be here. I love you and always have. You're my big sister, and you were always my protector and my best friend. I love you and I want you to be happy. It's that simple. Do you understand? You have to be true to yourself. That's the only way you can be happy.

"I could tell by high school that you were unique. I wasn't worldly enough to really put it all together, but you weren't like most of the girls in school. They were just being teenage girls. You had a different outlook on life and a totally different way about you, and I saw it. So I guess I kinda knew. Look at me now! I'm the brother to one of the best women Roseau ever produced, and I'm married to the other one. I scored!"

One tear rolled down her cheek, and that opened the floodgates. Sitting there on the old wooden floor in the house I'd bought, she broke down. The facade couldn't hold out any longer. She scooted over and hugged me, crying on my shoulder. Carol came over and we all hugged for what seemed like forever.

I said, "This is your life, Bets. These are your decisions. You need to do what's best for you no matter what that is. I'll always have your back. You can call me anytime. Which, by the way, is another thing. You don't call me enough. I probably don't call you enough, either. Let's fix that. After all, I trust you to furnish this house, but you better ask me about it if you're hopelessly in love with a lime green couch."

She smiled, wiped away the last few tears, and said, "I promise. I'm not big into lime green. Maybe bright yellow, though. The couch would look like a big banana." We all had a laugh.

It was getting late. Carol and I had a hotel room up at the Winnipeg airport for an early flight the next morning, and needed to get there. We all shared a group hug and we each said, "I love you" a dozen times.

On the drive up to Winnipeg, Carol and I hardly talked about the house. It was perfect. It was exactly what I envisioned. It was my anchor to my heritage. I loved it.

What we talked about was Betsy.

I said, "I think, looking back on it, I was too naive to know exactly what I was thinking as a kid, but I knew she was very special. She was way more like a big brother than a big sister, and compared to my real big brothers she was much more caring and protective. The boys wanted to beat the hell out of me to make me tough. Betsy wanted to make sure I was OK.

"When we were little, she never did that dress-up thing she said her friends were always doing, where they'd wear their mom's dresses, put on lipstick, and clomp around in oversized shoes. When high school came around, she was never into makeup at all. She was so pretty I didn't think she needed it, but looking back on that, I just don't think she had any interest. She never had any drama with high school boyfriends. All her friends were getting new boyfriends and then breaking up twice a month. To me, Betsy seemed above that. She was just her own person, but she took such an interest in me. I would not be where I am in life right now without her. And I'll never forget when you and I were getting serious and she told me I'd scored, because you were the best catch in our whole class. She was right."

Carol said, "I always felt that way about her. I looked up to her, and admired her. To me, she was like Amelia Earhart, or some other female hero I'd read about in history class. She was just different and I felt something like you were feeling too. I wasn't wise enough to know what it was, but she seemed so above all the boy/girl pettiness of high school. She was friends with everyone. I hope she can be strong about this. I don't know your parents well enough to even guess how they would handle it."

"I think they'll be fine," I said. "They're stoic and not very emotional, but they love their kids and have done all they can for us. All she has to do is be honest with them. That will take care of it. They love her. I think she's always been my dad's favorite, actually. He's always adored her, and he actually shows it from time to time. It will be OK. I know it seems like a mountain to climb for Bets, but it will all be OK."

I sure wanted it to be OK. She deserved to live the life she was meant to live. The only comparison I could make was silly, but it brought it home for me. I said to Carol, "What if I never really liked hockey, and didn't really want to play, but I went along with it because that's what we do here. I'd end up being good but I would get no joy out of it. It would all be hollow. That's no way to live. I know that's dumb, but I can understand it that way. I can't even imagine what she's going through."

We flew home and got back to work. I thanked Brooks one more time for finding that place with Betsy. He said, "It's not a lot different than places like Huntington Beach or San Clemente. Old established neighborhoods that have spanned multiple generations. It's just the architecture that's different. I loved the place when we walked in. And your sister is amazing. I think she's the best. So easy to talk to. I enjoyed the whole trip."

Back at the rink, things were still going sour. And then, that last big talk Rick and I had shared came to life. In mid-February, with the team and our attendance going nowhere, they let Rick Dudley go. He came to see me and filled me in.

All he said was, "They're promoting Jay Feaster. You've worked closely with him here, and you know he's a good man. He'll do well. I hope he keeps you, and he should. If he cleans house, you'll get offers. Don't worry about that. It will be up to you to decide which way you're going to go. Take care. Eric. Stay in touch."

I was dumbfounded. He had tried to prepare me for something he knew might happen, but I never saw it coming. Rick had been so good to me. He'd mentored me and thrown project after project at me to see what I could handle. I owed him everything.

Jay had been in the front office since I was playing. He was the top guy when it came to structuring contracts and handling a lot of legal stuff for the team.

Jay and I had a meeting the next day, and he was right to the point.

"I want you here, Oly. You're a valuable asset in the front office and out on the ice with these guys at practice. We have some tough decisions to make. I think more than a few of our defensemen have had enough time to get better, and they've had you out there trying to get through to them. We need to find better players. I'm going to count on you to be right there with me on this. We can score. Now we have to find a way to keep the other team from burying us. Will you stay?"

I said I'd be thrilled to do that.

We got to work right away. Jay was easy to work with and meticulous. He gave me an outline of my duties and said, "Get after all of this. Go find us some new defensemen. We've got a team to build and a franchise to save."

Before it could even compute in my brain, another bad season was over and it was summer. I think we finished around 27-44-11 and didn't get a sniff of the playoffs. A couple months later, I was hopping from one small arena to another to see a bunch of summer rookie camps. It was good to get a read on what players other teams were looking at. Those guys could be trade material if the right deals could be made. In the office, it seemed like I was always on the phone with agents who represented guys without contracts. That's a tough way to build a team, because those are players who didn't get contract extensions that seemed good enough to them. We had at least six of those free agents ourselves, and wouldn't be crying if we lost them all. I thought we were getting better, but man it was a slow process.

I didn't get up to Roseau but once or twice. Betsy was still in the process of furnishing the house, and with a new boss I was running pretty nonstop. Even just to drop in for a day or two, it was good to be there and a great break from the oven Florida always became that time of year.

It was home.

CHAPTER 53

Brooks Bennett

When my phone rang that day, and I saw the number, I knew it was my former teammate from the Rangers, who was dabbling in the stock market. I answered and said hello.

"Hey, dude. It's me," said my ex-teammate. "Is this a good time?"

I said it was and he kept going.

"Well, listen. Thanks to you, I've made some money and I'm going to make some more. I'm buying and selling a little, but mostly I'm accumulating, just like you advised. So now I want to pay you back.

"There's a pharmaceutical company that is about to introduce a new AIDS drug. It's been approved and it shows incredible promise. Buy some of their stock. Like today. That's all I can say. You won't be sorry."

I asked him how he knew about it.

"It's going to sound crazy but this is how it is. My older brother, who also played pro ball, played college ball with a guy whose brother is in the pharma business. He's the one who heard about it, from a friend who used to work for the company that has the AIDS drug. That guy's retired now. I trust my brother to know what's right and what's wrong."

I was naturally skeptical. There obviously was a chance to make some money if it was true, but when you get three layers deep from the truth, who knows. I'd gotten a lot of good advice from people over the prior year or so. I'd played one hunch, with Apple, and that was doing way more than OK. The only difference with this was, I didn't know anyone but my former teammate. I didn't know his brother, or the guy his brother played college ball with, and definitely didn't know the guy who used to work at the pharmaceutical company. I just said thanks and hung up.

I tried to call Eric just to run it by him, but he was on a scouting trip to about four cities in five days and he wasn't answering.

I did the best research I could on the company, and as in most situations like this there was nothing public about the new drug. They were trading at about $20 per share. I decided to buy 5,000 shares for myself, and another 5,000 for EO Holdings. If it didn't pan out, we'd still have a position in a well-respected pharma company that had been around for a long time. It would be a good stock to hold. I didn't think we could get hurt with it. At the worst, it would hold its value and if it ever went up five or six percent we could get out. It seemed worth the risk.

I pulled the trigger a few hours before the market closed and both purchases were finalized.

I got up the next morning and checked my favorite market websites. The company hadn't made any announcement. I can't say I was surprised. Maybe just another rumor or unfounded piece of advice.

I had dinner with Diane, and we just talked like we always did. I didn't mention it to her because I never talk about stocks or funds. It's all speculation and I don't like jinxes. If I bought a new stock and said anything about it to anyone other than Eric, I felt like it was talking about a no-hitter right in front of the pitcher in the dugout. You just don't do it

But, just after the market opened the next day, the press release hit. It was indeed a new AIDS drug that medical professionals felt was groundbreaking. It could save a lot of lives in poor and developing countries.

After the announcement, the stock skyrocketed. While I watched, the volume of trading went from big to huge. The price passed $30, and then $40, finally leveling off around $52 per share. You could sense there was some profit-taking there, as it actually started to dip. I went against all my better judgement and all the advice I'd ever heard or had ever given out. I put in sell orders for both myself and the LLC. We each netted around $150,000 in one day. It was my biggest day ever in the market. It was my only day like that in the market.

When I did finally talk to Eric, I told him I'd bought the stock and it was a bit of a risk, but it paid off. When I told him I'd sold it by the end of the next day and we netted $150,000 on it, he said, "Holy crap, good work, man. I hope you bought some for yourself while you were at it." I said I had.

I also promised myself that I'd never do that again. If I didn't know the actual person who had the initial advice, I'd steer clear. I was nervous as hell that whole day, and it wasn't like me to sell so fast but I thought we'd made the most we could make.

I had dinner with Diane again that night and, again, never brought it up. It was a fantastic meal at one of our favorite restaurants, with starched white table cloths, attentive waiters, a phenomenal wine list, and fresh fish right out of the Gulf, purchased at the dock that day. She had come from a charity function and was dressed to the nines. In the flickering candlelight, she was stunning. I felt my heart melt. I was over the edge and it felt really good.

We went back to my place and it didn't take long for things to progress. For the first time, we went to my bedroom. She left the next morning. You can fill in the blanks. It was an evening this surfer boy would never forget and had never experienced before.

Diane was so sensual and slow about it all. I just followed her lead. It was a helluva lead to follow. In love? More like madly.

Eric was back a few days later, on a Friday, so I had my weekly report to deliver to him. We'd accumulated a bunch of great stock. Our overall value with the portfolio was at least 50 percent higher than it was when we started. And the big stock win pushed our cash on hand back to where we were when we only had the first purchases of IBM and Microsoft. It was all good. He was all smiles.

He said, "OK, what do we do next?"

It was getting to be summer then, although that's hard to tell in Florida. I told him to take his first vacation since he'd joined the Lightning and go to Europe or on a cruise. He'd earned it.

He nodded and said, "Well, I was talking about what you and I do next, but I'd actually love to do that, too. I think a cruise sounds fun. I'll talk to Carol. Neither one of us has ever been on one. Great idea, man.

"But seriously, what do you and I do next? What's our next investment? Let's think outside the box. What businesses are appreciating the most right now?"

I said, "Off the top of my head, I'd say you're not going to believe this, but it's pro sports franchises. We don't have anywhere close to the kind of money you need to be a primary owner, but a lot of teams have limited partners. You don't make any cash flow from a sports franchise, you make it when you sell your stake. The value of MLB, NBA, NFL and NHL franchises is going through the roof. Every time one sells, the lid gets raised a little more. But that might be a conflict for you, since you work for a team."

He said, "I never would have thought of that, but I read the sports pages too and now that you mention it every time I read about a team being sold it's for silly money. I'm not sure where anyone gets that kind of cash."

"Most of them don't," I said. "They get tax breaks and funding from the cities to improve the venue, which will improve revenue, or they take out huge loans they can ride until they sell. The TV rights are astronomical and that gets split up. TV is a cash cow. And there's revenue sharing in some form or another, depending on the league, to help the small market teams survive. There are still a few legacy ownership families left in major sports, but it's nothing like it was before our time. Back then, one grumpy old man with a cigar might own a team for 20 or 30 years, and make a decent living off the ticket sales and concessions. Now, most teams are owned by investors who might not even care about the product on the field. It's totally nuts, dude. You look at owners today, and the list looks like a Wall Street board of directors."

I said again that it might be a conflict for him, so we'd have to look into that. Maybe we could just invest in the Lightning and not worry about it. That could be the way to do it. We already lived there, he already worked for them and he was a well-known and highly regarded former player. I think I was fairly well-known, but nothing like Eric was in Tampa. We decided to move slowly and study it for a while. At least for a few months. He rarely spoke with the Lightning owners, but he could do that at some point to see if it was even feasible.

I also told him I thought the next big market was going to be cell phones. I had no doubt that the little flip phones we were using were going to be antiques in just a few years. It was hard to see who was going to lead the charge, and most people were still on Nokia flips or Blackberries. The RAZR phone didn't do much more than the Blackberry did, but it was sexy looking and people liked that. The Blackberry user base was the most loyal. As soon as I felt like I could sense the new horses at the front of the pack, we could pounce. But not until then.

Eric ended up booking a suite on a Holland America ship, to tour the Caribbean and the northern ports in South America before going through the Panama Canal and up the coast to San Diego, stopping in Costa Rica, El Salvador, Guatemala and a few ports on the coast of Mexico. It sounded idyllic.

I just kept my eyes on our nest egg and found a few places to put some of the income we'd gotten off that one big trade, keeping it liquid while still making a few percentage points each month.

It was all going great. Diane and I were seeing each other four nights a week, at least. We were even thinking about some sort of vacation together. London and Paris sounded like an option, but so did Hawaii. We chose Hawaii. Our plans were to go in late August or September.

One day about the second week of August I was home alone, had a glass of wine on the balcony to watch the sun set, and went to bed early. It had been a great day. Diane and I were going to a concert the next night.

Around 5 in the morning, there was a loud knock on the door. I was afraid there might be a fire so I pulled some clothes on and ran out there. I opened the door and there were two very serious looking guys in dark suits, holding badges in their hands. I was beyond confused. I figured they had the wrong condo. They didn't.

One of them said, "Are you Brooks Bennett?"

I said I was.

He said, "We're from the enforcement division of the Securities and Exchange Commission, the SEC. We'd like to talk to you. May we come in?"

I said, "Of course you can. And I sure hope the first thing you do is tell me what this is about." They just nodded. We sat down at my dining room table. The first guy read me my rights. That blew my mind. It was just like on TV, but it was very real and I was the guy getting his rights read to him.

The other guy said, "We've been investigating some stock purchases. Shares of a pharmaceutical company that developed a new drug. Did you have any involvement in that?"

I said the name of the company and added, "If that's the one, yes, I bought some stock and it did really well. Did I do anything wrong? I thought it was a risky buy in terms of return, but it panned out great. What's the deal?"

They went on to explain that many millions of dollars had been earned in the first 48 hours after the company disclosed the new drug. They felt there had to be some insider trading for that to happen. They were following all the leads they could find by studying the purchases they could see. Anything purchased above 2,500 shares in the last few days before the announcement represented a red flag for them.

I really didn't know what I'd done wrong, and told them that. I wasn't being evasive or combative, I was just calmly telling them that I didn't know I'd done anything wrong. Damn, I've never been so nervous in all my life.

Guy No. 1 said, "Mr. Bennett, the company in question has very rigorous security procedures in place to keep confidential information from leaking. Clearly, there were some leaks in this case. We'd like to know your involvement."

I told them, "Well, I'm a former professional baseball player. My career is over now, but I accumulate blue chip stocks as long-term investments. A day or two before the new drug went public, I got a call from a former teammate who knew about the drug. I'd given him lots of advice since he began to invest in things, and I thought he was just giving me advice. He'd heard about it, and he told me about it.

"It's absolutely not my style to react to stuff like that, and I'd never done it before. But the company is well-known and well-regarded, so I figured even if the drug wasn't a success, it would be a good stock to own. I bought 5,000 shares for myself and another 5,000 for the LLC I manage."

Guy No. 2 said, "Mr. Bennett, you could be in a lot of trouble here. You might face some serious fines, you might lose your right to trade on the stock market, and potentially you could face jail time."

"You're kidding me," I said. "How can that be? A guy just gave me a tip. Like 'buy low, sell high.' It was just a piece of advice.

"Guys, I'll cooperate, I'll tell you everything I know. I'm not a big wheeler-dealer like I'm sure you investigate all the time. I'm an open book for you guys. Just tell me what we do now."

One of them said, "We came here to arrest you and take you downtown. I think we can avoid doing that if our conversation goes well. Let's talk, and yes, you're being recorded." He pressed a button on a small recorder.

We talked about my stock market activity. They asked about the LLC and I told them I was hired to invest money for the guy who owned it. I was the LLC president and had power of attorney to do that. Of course they asked who that was. I suspect they already knew all of this before they got there. They were probably just trying to trip me up or see if I wasn't being totally honest.

I was adamant when I told them Eric didn't know anything about the purchase when I made it, and he didn't know how I got the tip to buy it. He had nothing to do with it.

We talked about what other investments we had, as well as the ones I had personally. I listed them all, and made it clear we were accumulating, not trading. This was for the long haul. Both of us had been forced to retire from our sports at a young age, due to injuries. The stocks we owned were a nest egg for us and our families. My decision to buy shares in the pharma company was out of character, and I knew that at the time, but I sure didn't know it was even the slightest bit wrong.

They asked who told me about it. I gave them my former teammate's name.

They asked how he got the information, and I said, "He told me his older brother had told him. His brother was a former college teammate of a guy who was in the pharmaceutical business and that's who told him about it, and that guy knew someone else associated with the pharmaceutical company."

"Did he mention how the friend of his college teammate knew anything?"

I said, "As I recall, yes. I think he said the guy was somehow associated with the company, but I really don't remember exactly what was said. After the call, the way I saw it from the top down was that some person associated with the company had told another guy in the pharmaceutical business and that got passed on to my former teammate's brother. Or something like that. It was all kind of blurry to me, but I think that's accurate. Again, guys, if I had any idea this was illegal, I wouldn't have touched it with a 20-foot pole. That doesn't make it right, but that's how it was."

The first guy said, "Mr. Bennett. Can I call you Brooks?"

"Of course you can."

"Brooks, you're at the bottom of this ladder. We want to get all the way to the top. We're not going to haul you in. We knew most of this already and just wanted to hear what you had to say. I'm convinced you're telling the truth and you didn't know what was wrong with your stock purchase.

"We have to be careful and follow procedures, however. We're going to put you under house arrest for the time being, until we dig into this further. We'll put this ankle bracelet on you, and we'll keep an eye on you. We also need your computer so that we can copy everything and go through it. We have to talk to your partner who owns the LLC, as well. He'll have his chance to corroborate what you said or give us his own version. We'll get your computer back to you as soon as possible, but I can't say when that will be. I'll call you tomorrow with any other news. It's likely we'll put a suspension on your stock trading until this is all sorted out. And, finally, I'd advise you not to talk to any of the people you've mentioned in this conversation. Protect yourself. You've been honest and forthcoming, so don't screw that up. It will make things very bad for you. Understood?"

"Yes, but can I at least talk to Eric and just let him know you'll be talking to him? I'm the one who screwed up here. He wasn't even in touch with me when I did it."

"We'd advise you not to do that. We'll call him as soon as we get back to our office. Can you give us his phone number?"

I gave them his cell, his home, and his office, and added, "Knowing Eric, he'd greatly prefer to talk to you on his cell. He's as honest as any man can be. He'll be that way with you. I just think it would be a shame to have his wife hear the conversation, or his boss."

They said they understood. I didn't know if I believed them, but I sure wanted to. Guy No. 1 gave me his card and said, "If you remember anything else, or if you have any questions, call me. Thank you for being honest with us."

It had been one of the worst mornings of my life. I couldn't grasp how shattered everything was. I knew it was life changing, but I couldn't get a grip on it. I was sitting in the same chair at the dining room table, shaking uncontrollably. And then the tears came. I couldn't stop shaking and I couldn't stop crying. I just kept saying: "Why? Why did I let this happen? How stupid am I? There were warning signs from the time I said hello on that phone call. I'm not this dumb. Maybe I am this dumb. Do I deserve this? I guess I do, because here I am with no computer, a bracelet on my ankle, and I'm pretty close to having no friends. I came damn close to being hauled out of here with my hands behind my back, in cuffs."

The sun came up. It didn't look all that beautiful.

The next two hours were the longest I'd ever lived through. Then Eric finally called.

"What in holy hell? What the hell happened? How bad is this? This is terrible, Brooks. I'm stupefied. I don't know what to say. I just don't know what to say."

All I could say was, "For now, Eric, we're not supposed to talk. I hope this is over soon, and I'm so sorry I can't even put it into words. It was an honest mistake. As soon as the SEC guys give me a green light, we can talk."

That afternoon, my former Rangers teammate called. I didn't answer the phone.

I did call Diane. I was sweating bullets.

"Babe, I have some news and it's not necessarily very good. I got caught up in something I was unaware of, on a stock purchase, and I guess I did something I shouldn't have done. I had no idea it was bad. I thought it was just another stock purchase. Now a bunch of people are going to be in trouble, legal trouble, and even though it doesn't look like I'll be one of them, that's not out of the question yet. This is one of the worst days of my life."

I filled her in, and she asked if she could come over. I told her I didn't think that was wise, at least for a few days. I really didn't know how deep the SEC guys got in this sort of thing. Heck, they could be listening to me on the phone right then.

What a royal mess I'd made. Holy shit.

CHAPTER 54

Eric Olson

My cell phone rang at about 8 o'clock one late summer morning, and I almost didn't answer it. I finally did and a very serious guy was on the other end. Never in my life had I expected to get a phone call from the SEC. There was an investigation that somehow involved me and my LLC. I was stunned. I was damn near speechless. Talk about a blow you never saw coming. That was it. It was a haymaker to the chin.

The agent began to ask questions. I never considered telling them anything but the truth. If Brooks had distorted his story, that was on him and he'd pay the price. I was honest and straightforward, and the conversation didn't last very long. I didn't know about the tip. I didn't even know about the purchase until after it had happened and Brooks had already sold it all for a big profit. I thought it was all perfectly normal and by the book. Maybe I should've been more skeptical or suspicious, but I trusted Brooks and he had never done anything to betray that trust. I thought he'd done a great job, just like he'd been doing with our whole portfolio.

The investigator said, "Thank you for your time, Mr. Olson. That's really all I need for now. I want to thank you for your honesty and the background you provided. If we need any more information down the road, I might give you another call, and I would expect we're going to need a sworn deposition soon, so be aware of that. I appreciate your candor. I'll call Mr. Bennett and let him know you two are free to talk now. Your independent accounts of what happened match up 100 percent. Mr. Olson, you don't have much to worry about. We're not specifically investigating you or your LLC."

I asked, "Is Brooks in big trouble? He's never been anything but an honest guy with me. I've always trusted him. This is just so unlike him."

He said, "We'll have to see. All I do is investigate and turn over the information to our prosecutors. I can recommend certain things, but that's not my pay grade. Again, thank you for your time."

I hung up and just sat there. I didn't know what to do and I didn't know what to think. I couldn't even imagine telling Carol, but I had to. Would this be in the paper?

Would word get out any other way? I had no idea. It's not like I went through this all the time.

I just desperately wanted this to all be a nightmare and go away. The thought of all the people I'd have to talk to and explain this to was too much to handle. And I knew it would be bad for Brooks. People would say, "Wow, I never saw that coming. I'm glad you're OK, Eric. But wow — it's too bad for Brooks."

I didn't feel like I'd thrown him under the bus. I mean, I still had no idea what Brooks had told them, other than our stories matched "100 percent," as the agent put it. Hell, I still had little idea what Brooks had actually done. He had a lot of explaining to do.

The longer I sat there, the more the shock wore off and the disappointment built. I was mad, for sure. But more so, I was hurt. We'd been friends for a long time. We were business partners now. He'd never been anything but a wonderful and sincere person. He'd always been there for me, and I cherished his friendship. He was my best friend. Now I wasn't sure what was going to happen. I knew it had all changed because of one stupid decision, but the future was like a wall of fog. I couldn't see through it to the other side.

My first phone call was to Brooks. I should've waited, but I couldn't. I was pretty hot and didn't let him get too many words in. As I recall, he still thought he wasn't supposed to talk with me, and he was eager to get off the line. I just ranted. It didn't make me feel any better.

My second phone call was to Jay Feaster at the office. "Hey, Jay — a personal matter has come up today and I need to address it and see what I can do about it. Unless there's something big going on you need me for, I'll see you tomorrow."

He said that was fine.

Brooks called just a few minutes later. Clearly, the agent had called him and given him the OK.

"Hey, man. Can you come over? We need to talk face to face. I need to explain this to you."

I told him I'd be right there.

When I rang the doorbell he answered it quickly, and saw a face I'd never seen before. He was always bright, effusive and happy. On that day, he looked like he'd been hit by a car, gored by a bull, and berated by every person he'd ever met. He looked completely shattered. He could barely look me in the eye, and mostly just hung his head and looked at his feet.

We went and sat down in his living room. He was wearing shorts and sandals. Above his left sandal was a plastic bracelet.

"See this?" he asked. "They know where I am all the time. I'm under house arrest and I don't know for how long. I can't leave here. It's hell. And at some point I'm going to run out of food, but they don't know how long it will be like this. They don't have many answers, but they sure have a lot of questions."

I cut to the point and asked him what he'd done, and why he did it.

"Dude, I have a hard time explaining it to myself. I hold myself responsible for not knowing all the SEC rules better. I should have done that on Day 1 before I got into the market. I thought the rules were in place for Wall Street multi-millionaires who used insider information to make billions. It wasn't something I ever envisioned and didn't really understand.

"I got a call from a former teammate I had advised a lot, helping him get started in the market. He had a piece of advice about a pharma company. This is where I screwed up and should have run away. He called me because his older brother knew a guy, who knew a guy, who knew a guy. Gimme a freakin' break. Why did every alarm in my head not go off? I have no clue. It seemed like no big deal to me at the time. Maybe we'd make a few thousand, and if we didn't it was still a highly respected company with a history of innovations, so it would be a good stock to own long-term. That's how I saw it. I was an idiot."

I said, "Well, I'll agree with you on that one. I just don't understand it."

He said, "Look, I can't be more sorry for dragging you into this. I told them everything and told it totally honestly. I made it clear that you had zero to do with this and weren't even aware of the stock purchase because you were on the road and I couldn't reach you. I was adamant about it. This was all on me.

"I'm so sorry, Eric. I know having your name even associated with this changes your life and it definitely changes mine. I think I'm going to be OK in terms of having to go to jail or shit like that, but I can't be sure. My life is trashed right now, to a great degree. All because I was an idiot for 24 hours. I can't get my head wrapped around it at all. I don't expect you to forgive me; I just want you to know how sorry I am. I wish I could go back in time and make it all go away."

I said, "I wish you could do that, too, but you can't. It's what happened, and we both did the right thing by being totally honest about it. For now, though, I'll say that I still love you and appreciate all you've done for me, but we can't work together. I have to let you go as the president of the LLC. I'll just let the stocks ride for as long as it seems right. I appreciate you setting all that up. It's a phenomenal nest egg for the future."

He nodded and said, "I figured that had to be the case, and I understand. You shouldn't be associated with me in any official way right now. It's sad, and I caused it. You need to do that. I hope at some point we can at least still be some kind of friends."

All I could say was, "Time will tell." I got up and left. I didn't even shake his hand. That felt awful. I should not have walked away without shaking his hand.

Later that day, Carol came home and I had to tell her. I explained it as best I could, including my own special conversation with an SEC investigator. She sat there with her face in her hands, not moving, not speaking.

When I was done, she finally looked up. She looked broken. She said, "This is terrible, sweetie. In so many ways. Brooks is a good person. He's been a great friend. He's always been there for you, and he screwed up royally for one day of his life. That's really bad for him, but it affects so many other people. You, me, your family. This is just awful.

"I feel crushed, and I'm so sorry you had to go through this," Carol continued. "But to be honest, I feel terribly sorry for Brooks, too. In a lot of ways he's still very naive about a lot of things. I mean, he's about to turn 33 and he's just started a relationship with his first real girlfriend! He was brought up to be trusting and honest, and he's always had his parents to fall back on. Socially, he's kind of stuck in a state of arrested development. I think Diane has been great for him, and I'd hate to see that crumble. He made a mistake he never should've made, but the punishment seems way worse than the mistake warrants. Good people making bad mistakes are not criminals. They might be idiots, but they're not hardened con men or crooks. He's responsible for what happened. But it's a shame. It's just too bad."

I was enlightened by what she had just said. "You know, it's been a helluva long day and I've gone through every emotion I know and a few I didn't know were in me. But you're right. He's not a criminal. He didn't know what he was doing. I hope he comes out of it OK. He's a good man."

We hardly spoke for the rest of the evening. The TV never went on. We just sat there most of the time. I just wanted it to go away.

Over the next few days, the shock wore off. It still followed me around like a low black cloud over my head, but it eased up a bit. I made all the phone calls I thought I needed to make. My parents were as expected. Basically the message was "Look out for yourself. You don't owe him anything." Betsy was way more emotional.

"Eric, he adores you. He admires you. He's such a good guy. He screwed up, and it sounds like he still doesn't know how it's going to turn out. I feel so bad for both of you guys. He's a very good person, Eric. He just screwed up. I hope someday, you'll forgive him."

Carol talked to Diane the next day at work. She said Diane was shattered by it, and still very confused. Brooks hadn't really told her much, but he promised he would soon. All she could say was: "Give it some time, Diane. He got wrapped up in something he didn't understand. He's being honest about it and needs to find his life again."

Meanwhile, I still had a job to do. All I told Jay was that a very close friend of mine had made a stupid mistake and he was dealing with it. It was a shame.

During camp and preseason I could tell we were a better hockey team. When the season started, that core group of scorers got off to a fast start and it was a wonderful thing to see. Prospal, Lecavalier, Richards and St. Louis were lighting it up. Other teams had a hard time matching up with them. We could roll our first line and when they came off the opposing team didn't have the horses to stay with our second line. In effect, we had two first lines. And we had firmly planted Nikolai Khabibulin in goal, where he was rock solid. Our defense even got better. We added a few pieces, subtracted a few lost causes, and I worked their butts off.

By the end of the season we were 36-30-16. We were 13th in the league in the "Goals For" category, and I'm proud to say we were 12th in "Goals Against." We finished first in our division, with 93 points. And the fans started coming back. By the end of the regular season, we were packing the place and it was loud.

We beat Washington in the first round of the playoffs, but lost to New Jersey in the second round. Disappointing at the time, for sure, but a huge step forward. We were getting there.

And we had a local lesson in "getting there" as well. The Tampa Bay Buccaneers won the Super Bowl. Carol and I went to the first playoff game but they were on the road after that in the postseason so, like everyone else in the entire Tampa/St. Pete region, we watched on TV in amazement. Their offense was good enough. Their defense was smothering.

I don't take anything away from any team that wins the Super Bowl. It's a very physically and mentally taxing ordeal, and they never even had a close game. But, in the end they won three games to do it. We won three games in our two playoff rounds and went home only halfway to the Stanley Cup Finals. I know it's apples to oranges, but it gave me hope.

If the Bucs could win the Super Bowl, we could win the Stanley Cup. I saw that as a direct connection.

I think Brooks was getting there too, but we rarely talked. They took off his ankle bracelet so he could actually leave his place. He just didn't want to very often, and when he did I assume he just went to the beach. That was always his sanctuary. As for him and Diane, I got most of that from Carol. They hadn't broken up, but Diane said he just wasn't the same. He was scarred by it and it was taking a long time for him to come around. She was afraid he never would. She was finally wrestling with whether or not to move on, but she felt like Brooks might sink even further if she did. The SEC thing was a big investigation, and it was grinding on very slowly. It was weighing him down.

My former business partner and longtime friend was truly lost. And it didn't seem like anyone knew what to do for him.

CHAPTER 55

Brooks Bennett

Telling my parents about it was something I dreaded. Not that I thought they'd be mad at me, or anything like that. It was just that I knew it would disappoint them. I couldn't bear that. I finally built up the courage and called them that night. Mom answered the phone and it took all my self control to say, "Mom, can you get dad on the other phone. I need to talk to both of you."

I hardly took a breath for the next 15 minutes, as I walked them through the whole thing. I actually didn't want to hear what they might say, so I dominated the conversation. When I finally ran out of things to tell them, there was a pause.

"Brooks, we love you," Mom said. "This isn't you. I think you were in a little over your head with all this stock stuff. You got hooked into something you weren't ready for. It was just a mistake you couldn't have seen coming. We'll all get over it. It doesn't change you. It doesn't define you.

"We're proud of everything you've done. I've never once been disappointed in you, and that absolutely includes this. There's a huge difference between a crime of commission and a crime of omission. You're not a criminal. You didn't know. You had no intent to do anything wrong. You're going to be fine and when this is all over we're going to come down and see you. We need to do that."

Dad added, "Listen, man, this happened. You're going to be OK. We taught you to be honest and sincere, and that's what you've done. Just keep doing that, every day of your life. You never have to wonder what to say if it's always the truth. It's gonna be OK. We love you, son.

"Now here's your next step. You're going to need a lawyer. Somehow you need to find an experienced defense lawyer to help you from this point forward. Can you do that?"

I said, "I don't have a clue, Dad. But I'll get on it right now. I've seen enough detective shows on TV to know I could have asked for one as soon as they walked in, but I'm pretty sure they would've said 'That's fine" and slapped the cuffs on me. I just wanted to get the truth out there and I'm glad I did, but from here on out I'm gonna need an expert."

"OK, son. Get an attorney and be careful. I don't have much experience with lawyers, but I know how they work. It's all billable hours, and if they so much as look at their phone and think of calling you, that's an hour. Get all that straight up front. We love you and will do anything we can for you."

I needed that. The first brick in the rebuilding of my foundation.

The next day, I took a shot and called the law firm I'd seen advertising the most on Tampa TV. They were Fick, Johnson, and Steinberg. I called them. They advertised a free one-hour consultation, and I asked for that.

A guy got on the line and he sounded very young. Maybe the young clerks or interns got these plum assignments, I thought. After about 15 minutes, he said, "Let me get my boss on the line. This sounds like more than I'm used to."

I spoke with one of the junior partners, a guy named Gary Blum, and he listened well. When I was done he said, "We'll be happy to represent you. You haven't done anything purposefully wrong. And I'll say this: Had you asked for a lawyer when they walked in, this would be playing out differently. In your case, you did the right thing. Had you lawyered up, you would have spent at least one night in jail and you'd be talking to a public defender."

We talked about the billable hours thing, and we agreed that they'd spend a couple of hours, at $125 per, doing the diligence to get fully up to speed. From there, I wasn't really going to need them again until the next time the prosecutors wanted a statement or they announced sentencing. They'd be on alert. I paid them $750 up front and we'd go from there. I wasn't sure how I felt about it. Something about having a lawyer made me feel guilty. Couldn't the truth work just as well? I knew I was naive. I had to get over it.

About the fourth or fifth day into my house arrest, Diane called. She asked if she could come over and have dinner with me.

I said, "I'm about out of food, so I can't make anything and I can't leave the condo to shop. I'm sorry."

"Don't be sorry, Brooks. I'm bringing Chinese for us. And before I pick that up I'm going to do a quick run to the grocery store and get you some provisions. You're going through enough. You don't have to starve."

It was my second glimmer of hope and happiness since the knock on the door. It was nothing more than a tiny feeling, but it helped.

She came over in the late afternoon. With two bags of groceries, I'd be able to eat for a week. With two entrees from our favorite Chinese restaurant, we'd dine like kings. At least that's what it felt like to me.

We really didn't talk when we were unloading groceries and putting them away. And we just looked at each other as we were eating. It was tense. I didn't know what to say.

Finally, after we cleaned up she opened the bottle of Prosecco she had brought with her and we went out to the balcony for the sunset.

"I haven't even been out here since they put the ankle bracelet on me," I said. "I've been so paranoid. I feel like I'm being watched and listened to. I was afraid to open the sliding door, thinking they'd bust down the front door and come rushing in. I need this. I mean, technically I'm still in my condo, right? I think I am, anyway. I guess I'll find out if this is against the rules."

She smiled and said, "I think this is OK. It's part of your condo. Can I talk to you now? We've been pretty quiet since I got here."

In a blink I transitioned to being 99 percent sure she was about to break up with me. I'd made the mistake of hoping we'd be OK as we ate dinner. Since the moment the investigators left my condo, I had totally believed this moment was coming. I was hoping I was ready for it, because if I wasn't I didn't know what I'd do. Sink even lower? I didn't see how that was possible.

She looked me in the eye and reached over to hold my hand.

"Brooks, I haven't said this to you before, but this is the time. I love you. I love you very much. You're a good man, Brooks. What happened to you isn't what you're about. You might have made a mistake, but it was so buried in all you were doing I can see how it happened. You didn't know how much you didn't know. You had no idea what was going on, legally. And it tripped you up.

"I'm with you. I love you. I want to help you recover from this. I'm not one of those women who's always looking to fix broken or flawed men only to find out they can't do the impossible. You're not broken. You're nearly perfect and I hate to see you beating yourself up like this. I'll be by your side. We're going to get through this together."

I couldn't hold back the tears. We stood up and she hugged me so tightly I could hardly breathe. There was light. It was dim, it was hazy, but it was light. I had thought I'd lost her. Truth was, I'd lost myself and she saw the good in me.

We poured Prosecco and watched the sunset. I was struck by how different this sunset felt compared to the sunrise I watched after the SEC guys left my condo and my life was spiraling out of control. I'm not going to say I felt grounded or healed, but it was progress. It seemed surmountable. I had my parents and the love of my life in my corner. I had their strength. I could find mine again.

We moved into the living room and sat on the sofa. She put her head on my shoulder and reached over to hold my hand.

She said, "We don't need to talk. We just need to be. I'm here. You're here. We're together. Let's not move for days. This is where we're supposed to be."

All I could do was nod. My brain and my heart had been shattered like broken glass for days. I was a captive, internally and externally. I couldn't flee and I couldn't fight. All I'd been able to do was wallow in my own self pity and fear of the unknown. I never want to disappoint anyone and now I was facing the reality that I had done something that would disappoint everyone. It was overwhelming.

I had to look down at her hand holding mine. I looked at her head on my shoulder. I needed to convince myself this was real and I deserved it.

Diane spent the night. For hours, all we did was hold each other on the sofa in the darkness. Then we went into my room and laid on the bed. That was it. Nothing more. Just comfort. Just security. Just love. It was the most important night of my life. I knew it. I'm not sure I slept at all. I just kept my arms around her and felt her breathing. She was breathing life right into me.

In the morning, we woke up staring at each other across a mutual pillow.

I had only one thing to say. "I love you, Diane. With all my heart. I've never felt anything like this. Is it a dream?"

She smiled and said, "Maybe. But if it is, we're in the same dream together."

The only thing that broke the mood was that she had to get to work. It wasn't sad. It was the happiest goodbye I'd ever been part of.

A few hours later, my phone rang and it was one of the SEC guys.

"Brooks, we've got your computer and we'd like to bring it back to you. You don't use it much, do you?"

I said, "I really only used it to research stocks and keep spreadsheets of what I've bought."

He said, "It's all good. We'll be there in about 30 minutes."

When the knock came on the door, it was almost delicate compared to the pounding I'd heard when they arrived the first time.

I let them in. They handed me my bright blue gumdrop-shaped iMac and I put it on my desk. We sat down at the table.

"Brooks, we don't see you as any kind of flight risk. We're going to take the ankle bracelet off. You're free to live your life normally. The only thing we'd advise is that you stay in the country. To follow our procedures, we're going to flag your passport number. If you try to leave the country, the immigration officers should be alerted, but if they aren't we'll get word where you went. So feel free to go wherever you want in the United States, but don't leave until this case is settled."

That sounded fine to me. Just to be able to go to the beach or out to dinner felt like freedom. Normalcy was getting so close.

I asked if they had any idea how long it would take for the case to be decided.

One of them said, "Not really. All these are different. Some take a month, some take a year. We're digging into the characters who made the leak and passed on the information, and I'd say we're getting close. Call us anytime you want. As a matter of fact, we'd like you to check in regularly, especially if you leave town. The one loose end we have is that the prosecutors may want a deposition from you, given under oath. You shouldn't have anything to worry about with that. Just be honest, like you were with us.

"We'll let you know when things are getting close to wrapping up. When the case is settled, there will be a sentencing hearing and you'll need to be there for that. We'll let you know. I can tell you that we've put in writing that we believe the prosecutors and the judge should consider maximum leniency for you."

I told them I'd secured a lawyer, but added that I didn't see needing him until we got to the deposition and sentencing. It just seemed like I shouldn't go through that by myself. I wasn't smart enough to know where the pitfalls could be. The first guy said,

"That's fine. You should do that. This stuff can get complicated. Just keep telling the truth."

I still had no closure, and didn't know what was going to happen to me, but I was in a better place. I felt I could survive. There were days when that didn't seem possible, so I knew I was on the right path. I was beginning to feel like myself again.

One thing I noticed right away was that I didn't feel any overwhelming desire to be out and about. Even before all this, my normal activities centered on going to see Eric and Carol, doing some shopping, eating out, and going to the beach. I didn't feel any need to do more than that, and the part about seeing Eric and Carol seemed pretty improbable. Maybe impossible. Maybe forever.

Eric had been understandably cold, angry, and distant the last time we saw each other. He didn't even shake my hand when he left. He just got up and walked out. I didn't blame him for that. I deserved it.

I decided to just let that go for a while. I didn't want to put any pressure on him and I didn't want to intrude in his life.

I knew I had to call him at some point. I needed to finish up some paperwork so that he could be the sole person who controlled all the LLC and the stock portfolio. I figured once I got that done, it would be a good reason to call him. And I'd be strong about it. No more apologies. No more pity party. I'd be me.

It took about a month, but I got the papers and filled them out. I needed to get them to Eric so he could sign them as well.

In the meantime, right around then the Buccaneers won the Super Bowl. That was crazy. And it was really bittersweet for me. I enjoyed watching the games on TV, but it brought back all the memories of Eric and me going to the stadium, just being friends, having a beer and cheering for the Bucs. Having your team win the Super Bowl should be momentous, and I was happy for the team and for all Bucs fans. But I knew I'd never go to another game.

Finally, I finished the paperwork and went to his house. I was sad Carol wasn't there. It would have warmed my heart to see her.

Eric wasn't nearly as cold this time. We never talked about the ordeal, but he looked me in the eye and asked how I was doing. I gave him the papers and the address to return them to, and got up to leave.

"Do you have to go?" he asked.

"Yeah, I've got some other things I need to take care of. You take care, Eric. And please give your wife a hug for me. I think about both of you all the time."

He looked a little sad, but I really couldn't think of anything else to say. I put my hand out and he shook it.

"I'll talk to you later," I said. "Call me if there's ever anything I can do for you."

Eric nodded, and said, "You too, Brooks. Please stay in touch and take care of yourself. You look good."

The SEC had temporarily suspended my trading rights, so even though I finally had my computer back I wasn't able to do anything more than look at my portfolio to see how it was doing. It was all moving nicely in the right direction. I still had the proceeds from the stock sale in a cash account with my brokerage, and I had plenty of money in the bank or with my financial guy, Jack.

In my darkest days, I didn't have the courage to call Jack, but Dad did and he said Jack was pretty pissed off. Not at me, but at the SEC. He said people like me make these mistakes literally every day of the year, but the SEC typically understands the circumstances, and most of the time they just send a nasty letter or make a phone call. It's not even a slap on the wrist. He wasn't sure why they came down on me so hard. Because I was a former baseball player they wanted to make an example out of? Maybe. But they must also have had a good idea who they were after at the top of the ladder, so they kicked off the investigation with me in order to start climbing.

My dad said Jack told him, "You tell Brooks to be strong and stick to his morals and convictions. There is no precedent for them to come down hard on him. He needs to keep cooperating, but that's all he has to do."

Months went by. I kept tabs on the Lightning but didn't go to any games. That still cut too close to the bone. A few times, I thought about going to the arena and buying a seat in the rafters, but I didn't even want to do that. Why stir up all those memories? I could just watch them on TV.

They had a good team, for the first time since Eric had been traded to them. That seemed like a lifetime ago. We were both young, healthy and unaware of the challenges ahead of us. Life was simple. We were successful. We made a ton of money to do something we loved. It would last forever, right?

Another couple of months went by, and there were actually days I forgot about it and just lived life. The best way to do that was at the beach. The water was warm, the sand was soft, and the salt air always seemed to cleanse me.

One day, I'd just returned from the beach when the SEC guys called again.

"OK, Brooks, here's the one last thing we need. We'd like you to come downtown and give that sworn deposition we talked about earlier. It won't take long. Once we add that to the evidence, there should be a ruling."

I went down there that afternoon, and Gary Blum met me. The billable hours clock was ticking, but I knew I had to do that. We sat in a small room with a classic old reel-to-reel tape recorder running. I solemnly swore to tell the truth.

It was basically a rehash of what we'd gone through that first morning, but this time I was under oath. That wouldn't change a thing for me. I was honest the first time.

It took about 30 minutes and I was free to go. It felt good to get it done.

Two weeks later, they called again, and told me to be at a specific courtroom at the city courts building by 2:30 the next day. I was there by 2.

There were some procedural things to go through, and it was basically a couple of SEC prosecutors, one of the investigators I had been working with, my attorney Gary Blum, and me. It was not a jury trial.

When the judge said my name I stood up.

"Mr. Bennett, I find you guilty of the insider trading charges as filed by the

543

Securities Exchange Commission, but I also am aware of your honesty and cooperation, and will sentence you as follows. Five days in jail. Five days of your house arrest will be applied. One year of probation, which can be reduced to six months with good behavior. Six months of stock market suspension. The six months you've already spent will be applied. And, a fine of $148,458 payable in full within 10 days. Failure to pay can result in new sentencing guidelines. Upon completion of all matters in this case, your record will be expunged. Do you understand these charges as written and placed into the record?"

I said I did. It was not lost on me that any potential jail sentence was history, my suspension from the stock market was also over, and my probation would end up being only six months. There was no way I would screw that up. What was also clear was the specific amount of the fine. That's exactly the amount of money I had netted in the stock sale. I had no idea if they had fined or punished Eric at all.

It was over. It wasn't even going to be on my permanent legal record. I shook Gary's hand and that was it. Magically, they sent me a bill with a zero balance and an invoice for exactly the $750 I had paid up front.

I called Diane as soon as I got home, not realizing she would still be at work. I left a message and asked her to call me as soon as she could. When she got home my phone rang. She was nervous.

"What happened? How did it go? Are you OK?"

I told her all about it. She asked if she could come over. I said, "Well, I guess. I mean I'm pretty busy, but sure. Come on over if you want."

She laughed a little and said, "I know you're feeling like yourself now. That's the first funny thing you've said in months. You were being funny, right?"

"I was trying."

Then I called Eric. I told him about it, and he sounded genuinely happy.

"People like to say that we get what we deserve in trying times, and in this case that's true. You didn't deserve any legal punishment. I'm really happy for you, Brooks. Thanks for letting me know."

I asked him, "Did they ever do anything with you? Were you fined or anything.?"

He said, "I had to give a deposition under oath, which was easy. They said they had a legal right to file a claim for restitution with EO Holdings LLC, since the stock was purchased by the LLC. I was ready for that. I'd put that money aside the day I found out about this. I sent them a check immediately. I didn't want it anyway. I'm glad it's over. For both of us. Take care of yourself, Brooks. You're a good man. Stay in touch."

The darkest days of my life were behind me. In a few months, there'd be no record of the entire thing. Other guys up the ladder were going to jail. I was going out to dinner with Diane.

The one wound that hadn't healed was my relationship with Eric. I vowed to work on that — slowly, as if we were back at The U and starting over.

Without the collision in the hallway, of course.

CHAPTER 56

Eric Olson

Considering how much a part of my life Brooks had been since that momentous day when we plowed into each other at Pioneer Hall, it came as no surprise how much of a hole he left in my life. I was still disappointed, and maybe still a little angry. His poor judgment — or maybe I should call it his poor judgment based on lack of preparation — had hurt us both. He had to deal with all of that. I just had to deal with the fact he'd blindsided me with something I knew nothing about. Honestly, though, had he been able to talk to me before he bought the stock I'm not sure I would've blocked it. I didn't know much either. At that point, we both felt like experienced men of the world. Bulletproof and secure in our jobs. We learned we weren't, the hard way.

I paid the net profits back, and that was the end of it for me. It was dirty money to begin with, and the same day Brooks and I talked about the whole SEC thing I put it away and never touched it. I figured they'd want it, at some point. I also knew I didn't want it. It wasn't mine to keep.

The jarring part was that we had rarely gone more than a couple of days without speaking or seeing each other. We were now going weeks, and seeing each other was usually just a matter of a quick meeting to sign some paperwork.

In late December of '02, Carol and I had gone to the Buccaneers first playoff game in Tampa. They won, and it was fun, but it was also a bit hollow. I have to admit that some of the most fun Brooks and I ever had together was at those games. We left our jobs at the gate and just cheered and clapped. And no one ever recognized either one of us. It was awesome.

The Bucs won their next two playoff games and somehow, some way, they were going to the Super Bowl. It was in San Diego, and they played the Raiders at the end of January. Money would've been no object, and I really wanted to go, but I had this hockey team that signed my paychecks. Jay probably would have said, "Sure, it's a big deal. Take a couple of days and go," but I couldn't. It would be a bad look if I took a couple of days off to have fun while my guys were busting their butts to keep winning. I watched the Super Bowl on TV like everyone else.

It was just Carol and me, watching the game. It seemed like the empty swivel chair in our living room needed someone in it. When the Bucs won, we celebrated. I couldn't imagine what it would've been like to have Brooks there.

And that's the thing. A big part of me felt he'd wronged me. I felt let down and embarrassed by what he'd done. I couldn't just whitewash that. It was real and it was there. But the truth was it never really intruded on my public life. Word got out a little about Brooks, and there was a 300-word story in the Tampa paper, but it never really changed anything for me. If anything, people who understood what had happened felt sorry for me. I'd been concerned that it would be a huge scandal and it might ruin my career. It didn't. And I did miss the guy. He'd been a great friend, but I wasn't there yet. I didn't know if there was enough time to get over it. I'd never been through anything like it before.

I was having dreams. One I had all the time was about grade school. It was the end of my eighth-grade year and I'd be moving on to Roseau High. We had term papers to turn in, and I did mine, but I never noticed another student take it off my desk when we were heading to lunch one day. He'd stayed behind, and apparently he made copies right in the principal's office (that took nerve) and used it to write his own paper. He didn't copy it, but he used all the same themes. All of this, of course, was part of a dream and it jumped around like crazy, but the recurring thing was that term paper. It ended with the teacher bringing me and the other guy to the front of the class, saying, "Can you two explain this?" I was shocked. I didn't know anything about it. I couldn't breathe. I was stammering and couldn't really speak.

Right about then, I'd usually wake up soaking wet. And I couldn't avoid having the dream. It was a constant reminder.

It's not that Brooks and I never talked. There were still some minor LLC issues to work out and papers to sign, but to his credit it was always Brooks who brought those things up. I'd hired him so I could focus on hockey. I didn't know a lot of details. He'd see something that still had his name on it and he'd immediately call to tell me, then we'd sort it out. We had found a decent place to be with each other, but it was different. I was pretty sure it always would be.

Carol kept me up to speed on him and Diane. She had forgiven him, or as Carol put it, "She never blamed him. She just wanted to help him put his life together again. She loves him, and it's going well for both of them."

That fall, at the rink, the real season began and we were playing very well. I allowed myself to believe that this was the best Lightning team I'd ever been a part of. As we got into the grind of it, that core group of five scorers took off. Stillman, Richards, Lecavalier, St. Louis and Modin could strike at any moment, and carry us for multiple games at a time. The big thing was the next five guys. There was no huge drop-off when those players were on the ice. They were game managers and worked hard to hold leads or score themselves. We were 10-deep in front-line NHL players.

At the back end, Khabibulin had probably his best season in the league. He wasn't overly flashy, but he had great vision, he stopped the puck and he rarely gave up rebounds. I finally felt like we had the horses and the desire to be a good defensive unit. We were firing on all cylinders.

As we entered the last phase of the regular season, it was pretty clear we'd make the playoffs. We rested a few guys and that gave us a chance to let some of the third and fourth line guys get more playing time. You never know in the playoffs. If someone goes down, you need a capable body to step up.

We finished the regular season 46-30-6. We were first in our division.

The stat I looked at most proudly, though, was the one that showed we'd finally flipped the numbers in the "Goals For" versus "Goals Against" columns. We scored 245 goals. We gave up 192. All that hard work was paying off.

We handled the Islanders easily in the first round, 4 games to 1.

We torched the Canadiens in round two, 4 games to 0.

Our hands were full against the Flyers in the Conference Finals, but we pulled away to win in seven games. It was a hard-fought and physical series. They'd been dubbed the "Broad Street Bullies" as early as the mid-'70s, and the nickname had stuck. No matter who put on the Flyers uniforms, and no matter what the year was, they always played as if they had to live up to that nickname. It was a major accomplishment to beat them.

We were going to the Stanley Cup Finals. The Tampa Bay Lightning. I was still convinced there were thousands of NHL fans who thought they knew everything but didn't know we even existed.

We played the Calgary Flames. That is never easy.

We opened at home, and Calgary caught us flat-footed, I guess. We played well on defense, only allowing about 15 shots, but they had a bunch of breakaways and by the end of the second period the Flames were up 3-0. We lost 4-1.

In game two, we didn't just bounce back. We returned the favor. We scored the first four goals and they finally got one in the last few minutes of the game. We won 4-1 and we were headed for Calgary.

With their home crowd going nuts, they shut us down completely, 3-0. We fired a lot of shots, but none of them got through. Yes, it was only the third game of what could be a seven-game series, but you could just tell it was going to continue like that. Back and forth, supreme efforts on both sides. Every little detail could count in a huge way.

In game four, if they won we'd have a hell of a time digging out of a 3-1 hole to come back and win the Cup. Brad Richards scored for us just a minute or two into the game, and that took the crowd out of it a little. Somehow, our defense clamped down and Khabibulin was stellar. We won 1-0 in a very tense game. We were still very much alive.

But, of course, in game five the back-and-forth theme had to continue. They went up 1-0. We tied it 1-1. They went up 2-1, but we came back to tie it. Then, late in the game, Jarome Iginla scored to give them the 3-2 lead and that's how it ended. It was a heartbreaker.

The sixth game was back in Calgary, and it was another classic. The Flames, I'm sure, could taste the champagne they'd be drinking out of the Cup if they won the game. We were fighting for our playoff lives.

It stayed true to form. We scored first, they tied it, and then we scored again. They tied it with about two minutes left in regulation. You could feel the deflation. I was in the press box but I could see some heads down on the bench. We needed to put it behind us and get after it again.

In the playoffs, there are no overtime gimmicks. You just line up with your regular lines and the clock gets set to 20 minutes. The first team to score wins the game. No one scored in the first overtime. I think that gave us life. We'd weathered that storm and were still standing. They pressed and pressed, but hadn't won the Cup.

Just 33 seconds into the second overtime, Marty St. Louis scored and we were still alive. The guys went nuts mobbing him. We were going back to Tampa for the final game. Winner takes all. BYOC. Bring your own champagne.

It was tight out there in Game 7. It usually is. Both teams know they have to score (you can't win if you don't score) but no one wants to blow a coverage and give one up. That's the beauty of Game 7. Any bit of luck might make you a hero. Any slight miscue could cause your team to lose the Cup. It's the last game of a long and hard season, and only one team can win.

Ruslan Fedotenko had been a solid winger for us all year. Not spectacular, but really good, night after night. He would probably be the last guy you'd think would step up at a moment like that.

Fedsy scored in the first, then again in the second. About halfway into the third, they scored to make it 2-1. Now the clamps had to come down and lock it up. All that work with this defensive group had to pay off. All the repetitions had to be automatic. You don't have time to think about it. The clock was moving in slow motion. They had a chance to tie it with just a few seconds left, but we stopped them.

When that buzzer went off, our fans went wild and our guys absolutely went bananas. It was a celebration for the ages. Pure joy. Pure elation. Pure primal happiness. I had been biting my nails up in the press box, trying to will my guys to do whatever it took to hold on and win that game. And they did it. I was so proud of them. I was proud of all of us. I remember having a flashback to winning the Cup with the Rangers. That was amazing, but it was different. They were the New York Rangers, one of the most historic and prestigious franchises in the sport. To see a headline that said "RANGERS WIN THE CUP" wouldn't be the sort of thing people would do a double-take after seeing. This was different. This was Cinderella. It was David beating Goliath. It was unbelievable. What an honor it was to be a small part of it.

I found Carol, and we went down to the bench. I watched the commissioner hand the trophy to our captain Dave Andreychuk, and saw him skate around with it to a roar from our fans I'd never heard before. One by one, all the guys got to carry it, and then came the coaches. I stayed back and let the bench coaches go first. Finally, it got carried over to me. All I could do was hold it high and shake it above my head. The Tampa Bay Lightning were Stanley Cup champions. Us. This group. I still give Coach Torts a ton of credit. He believed in those guys even during the worst days. He had a plan, and he stuck to it. And he took us all to the promised land.

I'm not a big party guy, but how can you not be on a night like that? Carol had agreed to drive us home. We could come back to get my car the next day.

I was pretty toasty when we got home. I collapsed onto the couch and said, "Can you believe we did that? What a series. What a game. We won the Stanley Cup! WE WON THE FREAKING STANLEY CUP! I can hardly believe it."

Carol said, "You need to take some credit sweetie. You rebuilt that defense. You pounded them mentally and physically, and they responded. I saw them all when you were holding the Cup. It was nothing but pride and joy on their faces. They were as happy for you as you were for them."

We never spoke of Brooks.

The next day, through the fog of a hangover, I went ahead and said it.

"I wish Brooks could have been there. He would've lost his mind. This just illustrates how one little mistake can knock down enough dominoes to keep changing things, month after month and year after year. I feel really bad about that."

It had been a year we'd never be able to forget. The worst days of our lives, and one of the single greatest days of our lives. We still weren't pregnant, but were still trying. We'd canceled our cruise when the SEC stuff came up, but it seemed like a really good time to reschedule it. And I knew where I'd be taking the Cup if they gave me a chance to have it for a day.

I'd take it home. To Roseau.

CHAPTER 57

Brooks Bennett

It had been a time of great reflection. I leaned on my parents a lot, basically any time I felt doubt or pity. My strength of character was rebuilding, but it wasn't fully autonomous yet. It couldn't run on its own 24/7. If left to its own devices, it could fail at a moment's notice. I had to keep working at it.

Diane was spectacular. We were in love and inseparable. I asked her if she wanted to move out of her small condo and move in with me. Her face lit up a bit, and she said, "Wow. Are you sure of that? Are we there yet?"

I told her I didn't know. I still had good days and bad days, but I felt my life was mine again and she was the single biggest reason for that. I said, "Just think about it. I'd love to wake up with you every day."

I was still searching for the last bit of closure, though, and I had an idea for that. It would take some skill and some help to make it happen, but I wanted to do it.

It started with Diane talking to Carol about the Olsons' plans for the summer. Carol said they intended to head back to Roseau in late summer for maybe as long as a month. It would be a good way to escape the Florida furnace and they'd both love to spend some time there in the house they'd bought. Carol had said, "Betsy just about has it fully furnished now, and we can't wait to see it. The only loose end is when Eric will get the Stanley Cup for a couple days. We'd like to time it so it happens in Roseau. Somehow, we'll get the plans all figured out."

I couldn't push it. I had to play it low-key and use Diane as my conduit. But I had a two-pronged plan.

Once Carol mentioned their travel plans were set and I knew when the Cup would be there, I could put the wheels in motion. I actually didn't want to intrude on the Cup being at Eric's house. But I wanted to be there before or after.

The second step of the plan came next.

I bought Diane a stunning diamond ring, and had to plot out my method of giving it to her. You know me, I'm always looking for an angle and a surprise. I hid it carefully.

550

A few weeks later, I suggested Chinese takeout. I'll never forget the night she came over and I was sure she was breaking up with me. We had Chinese and all my fears washed away when she told me she loved me.

This time, I waited for Diane to get to my place and then I went out and picked up another Chinese dinner I'd ordered. We ate out on the balcony and we did talk about that other night with Chinese on paper plates. There were a few tears.

The plan was working seamlessly.

I said I needed to go to the bathroom but I swung through my bedroom to pick up my surprise. I stopped in the bathroom to keep the ruse going. When I got back to the table I said, "I feel great sweetie. I feel like I ought to thank you for that every day. There are some loose ends I feel I need to tie up, and then everything should be just like we want it to be. Like, for instance, have you thought more about moving in? I'd love for that to happen."

That was a big risk. What if she said it wasn't a good idea?

She said, "I have. You hadn't brought it up for a while, so I was waiting. Is the offer still on the table?"

I said it was, while I stared into her eyes so that she wouldn't look down to see me fishing around in one of my pockets.

"I would love to have you here, and if we're doing that we might as well have a reason for it, right?"

I pulled out the velvet box, opened it, and said, "Like, we should totally get married. I mean, I think so. Will you marry me?"

She shivered a little. She shook her head a bit and stared at the ring. Then she stared at me and the first tear welled up in her eye.

"Oh, my. Oh, my. You are the love of my life. Wearing this ring and being your wife would be an enormous honor. Yes. YES! Of course I will marry you."

We hugged, kissed and cried. The joy that flooded out of me, the pure emotion and happiness of that moment, was like a tsunami. I could tell she felt the same way.

I put the engagement ring on her finger. It sparkled in the sunset.

"It's gorgeous, Brooks. Absolutely beautiful."

I managed to say, "I think that's appropriate. You are absolutely beautiful too, and the most gorgeous part of you is what's in your heart. You're the strongest and most amazing person I've ever met."

She said, "So what do we do now?"

I said I had a plan, if she was up for it. And it would probably entail taking the ring back off for a bit while the plan unfolded. I think she knew what I had in mind.

A few days later, I called Eric's sister Betsy and swore her to secrecy. That wasn't hard. She had wanted Eric and me to finally put it all behind us as much as anyone did.

I told her the rough idea. Travel dates and arrival times. I wanted to make sure the Cup had either not gotten to Roseau or had already left. Once we got that all settled, I'd need her help some more.

Over the next couple weeks, we worked it all out.

551

Diane and I would fly to Winnipeg and drive down. Betsy would be in charge of having Eric and Carol out on the porch, enjoying a nice glass of Chardonnay. All we needed was good weather.

It played right into our hands that Betsy had just learned that she was in line for a new promotion at Polaris. Nothing huge, but nice recognition. She hadn't told the family yet, and she wasn't even sure she would. It was just a small step up the ladder. But, it gave her the ammo to force Eric and Carol to be out on the porch at the right time to share a toast.

On the appointed day, we flew up and drove a rental car south. We didn't want to drive by their Roseau home, despite the anonymous rental car, so we parked around the corner. I texted Betsy and said, "We're go for liftoff."

She wrote back, "Roger that. The Eagle is in place."

Diane and I got out of the car, turned to the corner on the sidewalk, and walked toward the house. We could see the three of them on the porch. Eric actually had his back to us (Betsy and I hadn't gotten down to that level of detail) but when we were maybe 20 yards away, I could see Carol put her hands to her mouth and I could hear her gasp. Eric turned around and saw us coming toward them.

"Oh, my gosh! I don't believe it," he said. "I don't know what to say. I'm really glad both of you are here. What, were you just in the neighborhood?"

We walked up onto the porch and Diane had her clutch in her left hand, with her fingers wrapped around the bottom of it.

Eric said, "No, seriously. What are you two doing here? Did you have this all planned out? I can't believe it."

"Well," I said. "There's something we wanted to tell you, and we wanted to do it in person."

Diane brought out her hand and showed them the ring just as I said, "We're getting married."

Eric just yelled, "Oh, my God!"

Carol said, "I could not possibly be happier for any two people! You are made for each other. I love you both. Congratulations! Oh, my gosh, this is wonderful."

I said, "Well, I also have a question to ask, if you don't mind."

I turned to look at Eric and said, "Eric, we've been through a lot. We've survived it. Nothing would make me happier than to have you stand up with me as my best man. Would you be willing to do that?"

Before he said a word, he hugged me. "Of course I will. What a huge honor. I'm really touched by all of this. The fact you came up here to surprise us like this makes it even better. I'm speechless."

Then Diane said, "Carol, will you be my maid of honor? You changed my life."

They hugged and actually jumped up and down a little.

It all felt so right. It felt like the true beginning of closure.

And then it went to a whole new level.

Eric said, "Betsy doesn't even know this. No one does. We just found out today that we're pregnant. This is a big day all around!"

We all went nuts. And Betsy was crying when she said to Carol, "So that's why you haven't touched your Chardonnay! I thought you didn't like what I picked out. You're pregnant! Wow. I'm gonna have a niece or nephew to spoil. What a crazy day this is. Holy moly, this is amazing."

When it all calmed down, Eric softly said, "Brooks, I have to apologize. I shut you out and shut you off for a long time. You handled it so graciously, and I didn't deserve that. You did just enough to keep us connected. I'm sorry all of this happened, and I should have supported you more when it all went down. I just didn't know how. But damn, I'm glad you're here and I'm thrilled to be a part of it."

Diane and I got married a couple of months later, on the beach in Clearwater, of course. Mom, Dad and Don came down and were beaming. Diane's Florida family was all there. It was magic. Diane had moved in as soon as we got back from Roseau. For our honeymoon, we finally got to Hawaii. It was paradise.

And yes, I finally decided it was time to call the Texas Rangers to see if they had an opening for a scout here in Florida. They did. I took the job and now, eight years later, I'm still watching baseball games for a living. I love the game. I love my wife. Life is good.

What a crazy trip this has been. Thanks for coming along.

AUTHOR'S EPILOGUE

Bob Wilber

When my first book, my autobiography "Bats, Balls, & Burnouts," was published in the spring of 2017 after almost a year and a half of writing, proofing, editing and formatting, it was time to begin a second season with that book. It was time to promote it. I'd been promoting sponsors, race teams and race car drivers for more than 20 years. It was finally incumbent upon me to promote myself, and that was way out of my comfort zone.

I did a book signing tour at about half the 2017 NHRA races, I did too many interviews and podcasts to count, and I took every opportunity to promote it on social media. At the races, NHRA public address announcer Alan Reinhart was incredible. We had an informal understanding that kicked into action any time there was a sizable "down time" due to a clean-up on the track. He'd send me a text and it would say "Get up here." I'd dash to the announcer's booth in the tower and he'd interview me "live" on the PA. I'd head back to Tim Wilkerson's pit area and the line would start to form. And I can't even mention that memory without thanking Tim and Del Worsham, who both put a decal of my book cover on the back window section of their Funny Cars.

After all those years of being a PR rep, where my job was to get that priceless publicity for my driver and sponsor, it was a stark role reversal. I did hire a publicity pro, Elon Werner, who is one of the best in the business and had been John Force's PR rep for a long time. He was in charge of lining me up with all the high-profile shows and publications and he did so masterfully, but I also needed to dig in on my own and understand that it was not just OK to promote myself and my work, it was necessary. It kept the book alive. It was uncomfortable at first, but I got the hang of it and got over the trepidation. I'm fully comfortable with that side of things now. It's fun. Writing and editing is hard. Talking about it is fun.

For my second act, I had a few ideas but nothing really gained traction with me. The concepts sounded OK, but that was it. I needed to find the right challenge. Something totally different.

At the same time, I began to hear the recurring questions, over and over, from family, friends, blog readers, and social media contacts.

"What are your plans? What's next? Are you going to write another book?"

I still didn't know, but it sure seemed like the thing I had to do. I just needed to figure out what it would be. I only knew that I wanted to do something completely out of my natural writing style.

I don't recall the specific moment regarding the mental "slap my forehead and realize this is it" when this concept came to me, but for some mysterious reason I was thinking about a favorite book of mine entitled "War Day." It was co-written by Whitley Strieber and James Kunetka and was about a very brief but totally devastating World War III, which was completely nuclear-based. It was a horrifying yet gripping book to read and Strieber and Kunetka alternated chapters, writing in the voices of two fictional characters who ventured out of New York City to see what was left of the country. I couldn't put it down. I felt like I knew the two characters and understood the horror of what they were seeing.

When I was thinking about "War Day" I do recall telling my wife, Barbara, "I'd like to do something like that. I wonder if I can find a compatible co-writer to do it with me." I had the outline of it in my head within minutes.

The next day I said to Barbara, "That was the wrong question. I should be asking if I can do this myself. I know I can. I'll write it as two different characters but it won't be about nuclear wars. It will be about two very different guys who are athletes. There would be a million reasons why they should never have met. But through one chance encounter, they did. And their lives then become forever intertwined. I'll alternate chapters and find their voices. I'll write it as them. I know I can do this."

She raised an eyebrow and said, "Are you really sure?"

I said I was. There it was again. That "plow forward" mentality that was a central theme in "Bats, Balls, & Burnouts." Don't overthink. Don't let doubt or common sense creep in. Just go for it.

How did I know I could do it? I didn't. I had no idea about what it would take to create this. I was the classic "blissfully ignorant" fool jumping into the deep end, feet first and holding my nose. I just had a feeling I could do it, and I wanted to try. I would do it all myself.

This book is as far from an autobiography as I felt I could get at this point in my career as an author. The genre is "historical fiction" so my two characters were obviously totally made up, but a lot of what you just read about and much of everything and everyone around them is real. There are, of course, other fictional characters throughout (can't have fictional guys without fictional families and fake friends!) but there are also many real people in real places.

There are also hidden references to other unmentioned real people from front to back. Like Easter eggs, they're hard to find and almost impossible to sort out if the referenced person isn't you, or someone you know. I know who they are. They know who they are. I hope the references are enjoyed and certainly hope they are appreciated.

There are also plenty of additional fictional characters in this book who are based on people I've known, and many of the fictional friends and family characters were combinations of various people I've known.

As for Eric and Brooks, they were not based on any specific individuals from my personal experience. They are each, instead, a compilation of numerous people. People I have befriended, admired, and followed. I allowed the two guys to show those tendencies and personality traits as we went. They, literally, became their own men. Now, I don't see those specific characteristics from the original outline. I just see Eric and Brooks. I know them. They're friends of mine.

To be completely truthful, though, I will divulge that I could visually see them before I wrote a word. There are no photos in this book because Eric and Brooks do not exist, but in my mind I saw them physically, based on real people. That helped me when I started, because I could envision them in various situations. In my imagination, Brooks is a dead ringer for former MLB pitcher C.J. Wilson (who, coincidentally pitched for the Texas Rangers and the Anaheim Angels) and Eric is a physical clone of NHL hockey player Jared Spurgeon (who plays for the Minnesota Wild). Google them if you'd like to see how my vision of them as Brooks and Eric differs from how you saw them. That ought to be a jarring comparison.

For my research, I filled two file folders absolutely to the breaking point with printed stuff I found on the internet, so that I could pore over professional baseball and hockey stats, rosters, standings, and schedules as well as stock trading, legal ramifications, real estate prices, and more through all the applicable years. I got terrific help from the people of Roseau, a place I visited twice to get a real feel for that remarkable town. On my first trip the superintendent of schools, Larry Guggisberg, had meetings set up for me every two hours for three days to speak with local legends, some of whom were former Roseau Rams. Many of them had returned after college or pro careers to live in their hometown. I met everyone from the guy who maintains the ice at the arena to the mayor of Roseau. They are real people. It's a real town. The guy who maintains the ice at the arena was David Drown, a class of '84 Roseau Ram who actually did go to Des Moines to play junior hockey with his fictitious roommate Eric. Tracy "Bobcat" Ostby, Larry Guggisberg and Paul Broten offered tremendous assistance, as did many other former Rams. And, I capped off my initial trip by having a lengthy chat with Newell and Carol Broten on their front porch. Their boys Neal, Aaron and Paul are true Roseau legends. I was enamored with the town and the people. When writing about Eric's town, his home, and his family I didn't have to make that up. I'd already seen it. I'd been there.

And how did I decide Eric would be part of the class of 1984? Pure luck. I was in my high school class of 1974, so I figured it would be easy to have Eric be 10 years younger. I'd always know what age he was in each grade of school. It was the easy way out. I had zero idea the '84 Roseau Rams team is legitimately considered one of the best of all time, despite the fact they did not win the Minnesota state championship.

I also did a "scouting" trip to Southern California, driving the streets of Huntington Beach, San Clemente and Anaheim to soak all that in, to better understand what it looked like and felt like. A former drag racing colleague, Jeff Morton from "National

DRAGSTER" magazine, took the time to compile stacks of printed information about high school and college baseball in the area. We met for lunch and he filled my head with vivid stories. When I arrived at Canyon High in my rental car, I said, "This is the place. Brooks started high school here." I knew it. I got out of the car and walked around. I could see him out on that field. I could see the Brady Bunch neighborhood Brooks lived in, walking distance from the school. It's all real.

When I was doing the research for where Brooks would've gone to middle school after they moved to Anaheim, it was clear that Cerro Villa would've been his school. I had no idea that both daughters of my friend and former boss Del Worsham had actually gone there. Small world, once again.

And Del Worsham… The dude who surfed long before he ever drove a 300 mph race car, was much of my inspiration for the lifestyle, the look, and a great deal of the language. Growing up as a surfer and BMX bike racer, he knew the rules and the respect one had to show when starting out at a new beach or track. I was fortunate to spend 12 great years with Del on the NHRA tour, absorbing all those tales by osmosis.

I live in the Twin Cities now, and was already familiar with much of that part of the book. I knew the schools, the suburbs, the Gophers, and I got to know Brian Raabe, that former Gopher baseball player (and later a professional infielder who made it to the big leagues with the Twins, Mariners, and Rockies) who was happy to be part of the "cast" in this book as Brooks Bennett's first roomie at the U of M. One of the first things Brian told me about was the peculiar dorm room they called "the bowling alley." He was actually there playing ball for the Gophers when Brooks would have also been there, and he lived in that dorm room at Pioneer Hall. Brian offered key insights on the tiniest colorful details, and graciously allowed me to bug him with additional questions for months. He always answered my emails within minutes. The details were ultra-valuable. To me, the beauty is in the details. And as of this moment, when I'm writing this epilogue, I've never met Brian Raabe face-to-face. Just a great guy who jumped in to help whether it was on the phone or via email.

I had a vague deadline, but it was so far out in the future I will admit I could sometimes go a couple of weeks without writing anything substantial. I needed more urgency and yet I wanted to take my time to get it right.

As the characters, Brooks and Eric, quickly developed I began to hear their voices and the pace picked up. It was like they were telling me, "Let's get moving here. We have a story to tell." By the time I was a quarter of the way done I felt like they were writing the book. I was just typing; transcribing what they said. It was an incredible experience. Life altering, actually.

So much of this book was subconscious. I tried to have a basic outline to work from, but time after time Brooks or Eric would do something or say something that altered the course, and that was always the right way to go. I just followed them. It became very organic. Very spontaneous. And I felt them growing as people and as autobiographical writers. That would've happened in real life. Their writing styles would have improved. They would sound like themselves, but slightly different, as they matured into real writers. It was wonderful to feel that happen but I never planned it. There was no bullet point in any outline that said "They get better as writers." It just happened naturally and I knew it was right.

Beyond the subconscious was my adherence to the mantra that I had to get it right. Their years as kids. Their families. Where they grew up. The teams they played for. It had to be right, from taping a stick to getting the baseball uniform to look bitchin', and I utilized every expert I could find. While Paul Broten (who lives here in Woodbury, the same St. Paul suburb Barbara and I call home) brought Roseau to life for me, it was a minor league hockey player named CJ Eick who spent a few valuable hours with me after one of his Kansas City Mavericks games in KC, calmly but vividly telling me about junior hockey with the Green Bay Gamblers and college hockey at Michigan Tech, followed by the grind of minor league hockey in the ECHL with the Mavericks. Those were places and teams I was not totally familiar with, and he brought all of it to life for me while being so gracious to do it. Plus, I had a few chilled craft beers for him in the suite. Huge thanks to CJ and his wonderful wife Alexa, who just happens to be my former next-door neighbor. It's not always what you know, but it's almost always who you know. Real people tell real stories. The stories are the beautiful part, just like the details.

There were also an astounding number of totally unforeseen coincidences in the book. I'd be writing and following what my two fictional guys were doing and as I did my morning research I'd discover things I never knew or anticipated. Things that made for amazing plot enhancements. They often were about real people I actually knew, but I hadn't yet connected the dots to see how they would be part of my characters' lives. For instance, when our fictitious Brooks was drafted in the second round by the Texas Rangers, their first-round pick that year was actually the pitcher from Creighton named Dan Smith. The U of M Gophers' catcher, who would have been behind the plate when Brooks was on the mound for The U, was Dan Wilson. He was drafted in the first round by the Cincinnati Reds that year. True life. Not made up. Both great ballplayers, hence their high placement in that year's draft, and real guys. You can Google them.

In the late '80s I was playing for a very good semi-pro baseball team called the Sauget Wizards, and we played the USA National Team at their home stadium near Memphis. We beat them. I drove in the first run of the game with a single off Dan Smith, and then later hit a three-run homer to dead center field. The USA catcher in that game was Dan Wilson. Those same real guys. You can't make that stuff up.

My editor and mentor, Greg Halling, had been the glue that held the first book together, and he was excited to dive in with me again. He never intervened and never made demands, but he constantly cleaned up my overly wordy messes and he'd ask a lot of questions as he was going through each new chapter. His positive reinforcement was motivating, uplifting, and priceless. His contribution to this project was amazing. I learned so much from him during the first book, but I learned even more during this one. After all, I was writing as two fictional people. I had twice as much to learn!

It became a mutual passion of ours. Near the end of the process, as we were finally getting close to the finish line, I began to write two chapters a day. For a year, I'd been writing one or two chapters a week and that felt like a lot. By the last few weeks, I was on fire with the characters and the story. It was the writer's version of "I couldn't put it down." I just couldn't stop. I lost my appetite, I didn't sleep well or at all, I developed back, neck, wrist and abdominal problems that very much challenged me and kept me in pain, but I kept writing. There were many days when I didn't feel like I could do it, but I kept writing. I finished the initial manuscript at 3 p.m. on July 4, 2021.

Greg said, "I've been living this with you for two years, and until I read the last chapter I didn't know how it would end. Well done!"

I said, "I didn't know either. It was up to Brooks and Eric."

Yes, July 4 should be an easy date to remember. What will also be easy to recall is the fact I spent five days in the hospital not long after the raw manuscript was completed. Those maladies I was suffering from weren't psychosomatic fiction. They were very real, pretty serious, and no doubt stress-related. Fortunately I had a phenomenal team of doctors and nurses looking out for me in St. Paul. Just like I never really knew how much of a challenge the book would be, I don't think I had much of a clue just how sick I was until after I got better. Funny how that works. The body and mind can handle a lot and find mysterious ways to defer the pain in order to get to the finish line.

To round this book into its final shape I enlisted the help of my former NHRA colleague, the uber-artistic Todd Myers, to do the cover. I gave Todd the freedom to create what he wanted, but we did share thoughts about where we thought it should to go. I trusted him completely, and he delivered.

As for the words, I asked my friend Terry Blake to proofread my entire manuscript for grammar, spacing and punctuation. There are times when I'm really good at writing. There are zero times when I'm good at proofreading. I am grateful to Terry for volunteering to make sure my text was ready for the show.

And I can't wrap this up without saying this: You would not be holding this book in your hands if I hadn't had the fully committed support of my wife, Barbara Doyle. She pushed me, she supported everything I was doing, and she kept me going when I felt I was stuck. She fell in love with the process and the characters just as much as I did. She also had valuable input when it came to things that a corporate finance and investor relations executive would know. She was my rock. She will always be my inspiration. And when I completed the manuscript and then ended up in the hospital, she was there every day.

To put it in plain language: Barbara Doyle is the smartest person I know, and she cares deeply about people she loves. Those are very important traits in my opinion.

I'm proud of this book. I hope you liked it.

I wonder what's next…?

Stay tuned.